I0817888

BY EZEKIEL EVERSAND

Kingfall - Book One

Spellblade - Book Two

Greyfire - Book Three

Goldfyre - Book Four (coming soon)

Ashenwave - Book Five (coming soon)

The Neverborne Series will be a work of ten novels.

SPELLBLADE

The Neverborne Series

Book Two

EZEKIEL EVERSAND

Spellblade is a work of fiction. Names, characters, places, and incidents either are the product of the author's imagination or are used fictitiously. Any resemblance to actual persons, living or dead, events, or locales is entirely coincidental.

First published in 2022.

Library of Congress Control Number: 2022908030

ISBN 978-1-7342737-5-5

Book Cover Art by Soós Gerg @deviantart.com/random223
Book Cover Design by Lance Buckley @lancebuckley.com
Map Illustration by Cornelia Yoder @corneliayoder.com

Printed in the United States of America

2026 Content Revision Edition, Hardcover

CONTENT DISCLOSURE

Let this serve as a notice to the story's intended audience. The reader should understand that this work is a novel of mature content that would be considered rated R, with certain topics mentioned that may be found offensive. Reader discretion is advised, as this book may be inappropriate and unsuitable for younger audiences.

IN MEMORY OF

HERO

May 1st, 2012 – May 7th, 2022

(2 weeks before publishing *Spellblade*)

Life is unfair, timing is unpredictable, and the irony we endure in-between is often cruel. You were the one soul that was there for me from the very beginning, from the first words to the last to this day. And not just the words of the first chapter and first book … But the world of Penthara itself, the origin of the characters, the histories, cultures, concepts, and all else. You were the one by my side throughout the evolution of the Neverborne Series, and throughout the maturity of my own life, through so many experiences and adventures. You were my road buddy, my wingman, my constant closest friend who loved me above all else unconditionally. You were my son, and you always will be. Thank you for saving me when I needed it the most. I will never forget you my baby boy … You are forever my Hero.

INTRODUCTION

Spellblade is the second novel in *The Neverborne Series*. It is not the sequential volume to the first novel, *Kingfall*, but rather a parallel story occurring simultaneously to the events in *Kingfall*. While *Kingfall* follows POV characters located in the northern region, *Spellblade* will follow different POV characters located in southern locations. Prepare for developed plotlines from both sets of characters to collide or impact one another as the story progresses.

There are several annotations and maps available in this novel to help with references when needed. It is encouraged to visit the maps when geographical points are mentioned to better come to know the world of Penthara. The Pentharam System, the Racial Descendancies, the Geographical Demographics, the Powers and Organizations, and a Word Glossary are included in either the front or the back of the book to browse at your leisure.

Penthara is a world of two main races: the humans and the elven. Among the two, they have many subcultures, all differentiated by their elemental descendancies — tairan, fire, sky, shadow, water, or mixed lineages. Elven have impowers which enhance them with special abilities granted from their elemental lineages. There are also evolved versions of the races such as the umbran, quasi, and animayan for the elven, and qindrid, mages, and hyperi for humans. There are even halfkinders and more to be discovered.

Each of the five elements of the realm correlate with one of the five seasons. The Dawning is to Spring, which is to tairan (earth). The Sunder is to Summer, which is to fire. The Reaping is to Autumn, which is to sky. The Umbra is to Winter, which is to shadow. The Torrent is a unique season to Penthara, which is to water. Each novel in a whole is intended to cover an entire season, which is five months long.

Italicized phrases are inner monologue from the point-of-view characters. "*Italicized phrases in quotations*" indicate translations of dialogue spoken outside the Civil universal language.

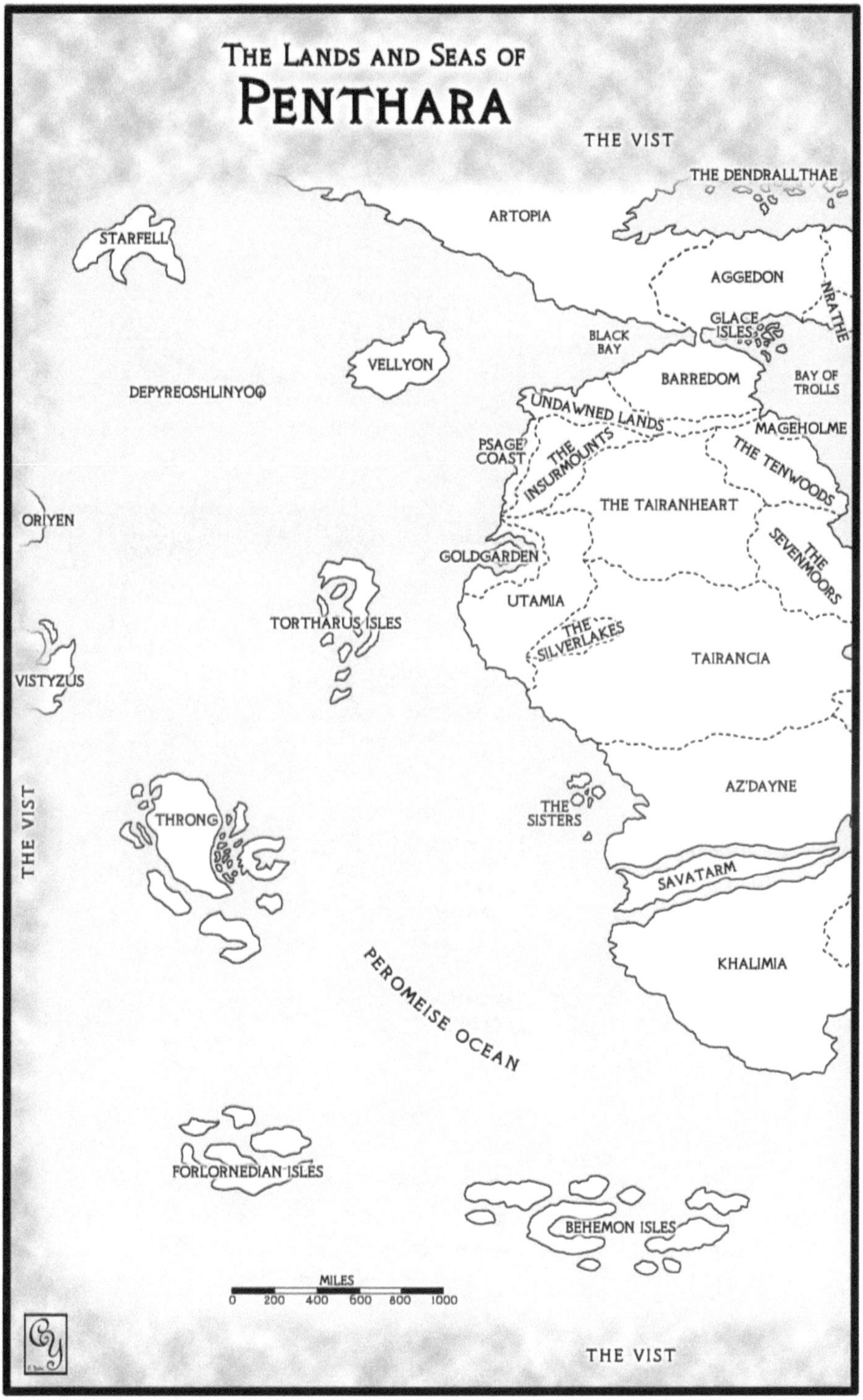

The Lands and Seas of PENTHARA

THE VIST
THE DENDRALLTHAE
ARTOPIA
STARFELL
AGGEDON
NRATHE
GLACE ISLES
BLACK BAY
VELLYON
BARREDOM
BAY OF TROLLS
DEPYREOSHLINYOO
UNDAWNED LANDS
MAGEHOLME
PSAGE COAST
THE INSURMOUNTS
THE TENWOODS
THE TAIRANHEART
ORIYEN
GOLDGARDEN
THE SEVENMOORS
UTAMIA
TORTHARUS ISLES
THE SILVERLAKES
TAIRANCIA
VISTYZUS
AZ'DAYNE
THE VIST
THE SISTERS
THRONG
SAVATARM
KHALIMIA
PEROMEISE OCEAN
FORLORNEDIAN ISLES
BEHEMON ISLES
MILES
0 200 400 600 800 1000
THE VIST

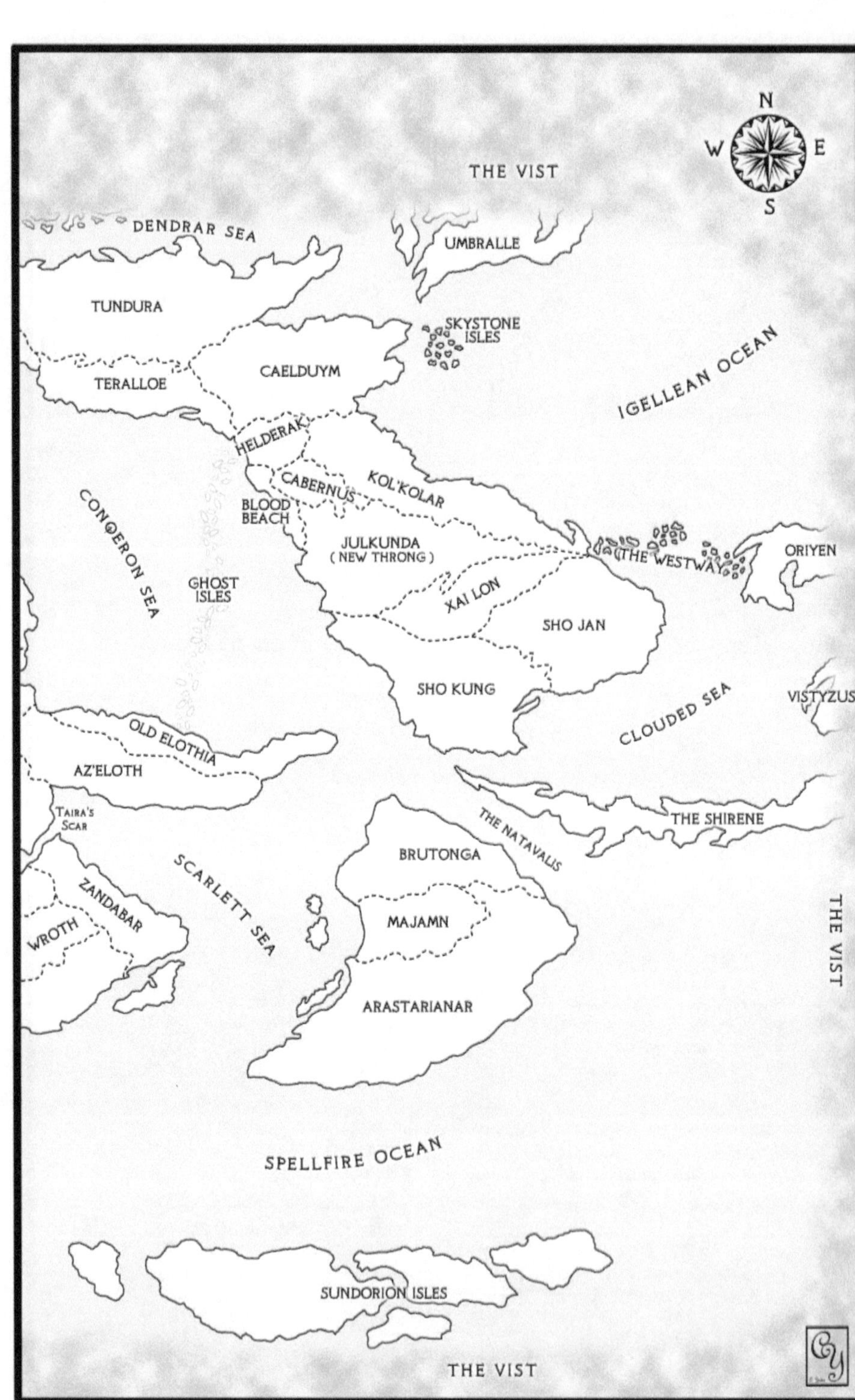
N
W
E
S
THE VIST
DENDRAR SEA
UMBRALLE
TUNDURA
SKYSTONE ISLES
CAELDUYM
TERALLOE
IGELLEAN OCEAN
HELDERAK
CABERNUS
KOL'KOLAR
BLOOD BEACH
CONGERON SEA
JULKUNDA
(NEW THRONG)
THE WESTWAY
ORIYEN
GHOST ISLES
XAI LON
SHO JAN
SHO KUNG
VISTYZUS
CLOUDED SEA
OLD ELOTHIA
AZ'ELOTH
TAIRA'S SCAR
THE NATAVALIS
THE SHIRENE
BRUTONGA
SCARLETT SEA
ZANDABAR
WROTH
MAJAMN
THE VIST
ARASTARIANAR
SPELLFIRE OCEAN
SUNDORION ISLES
THE VIST

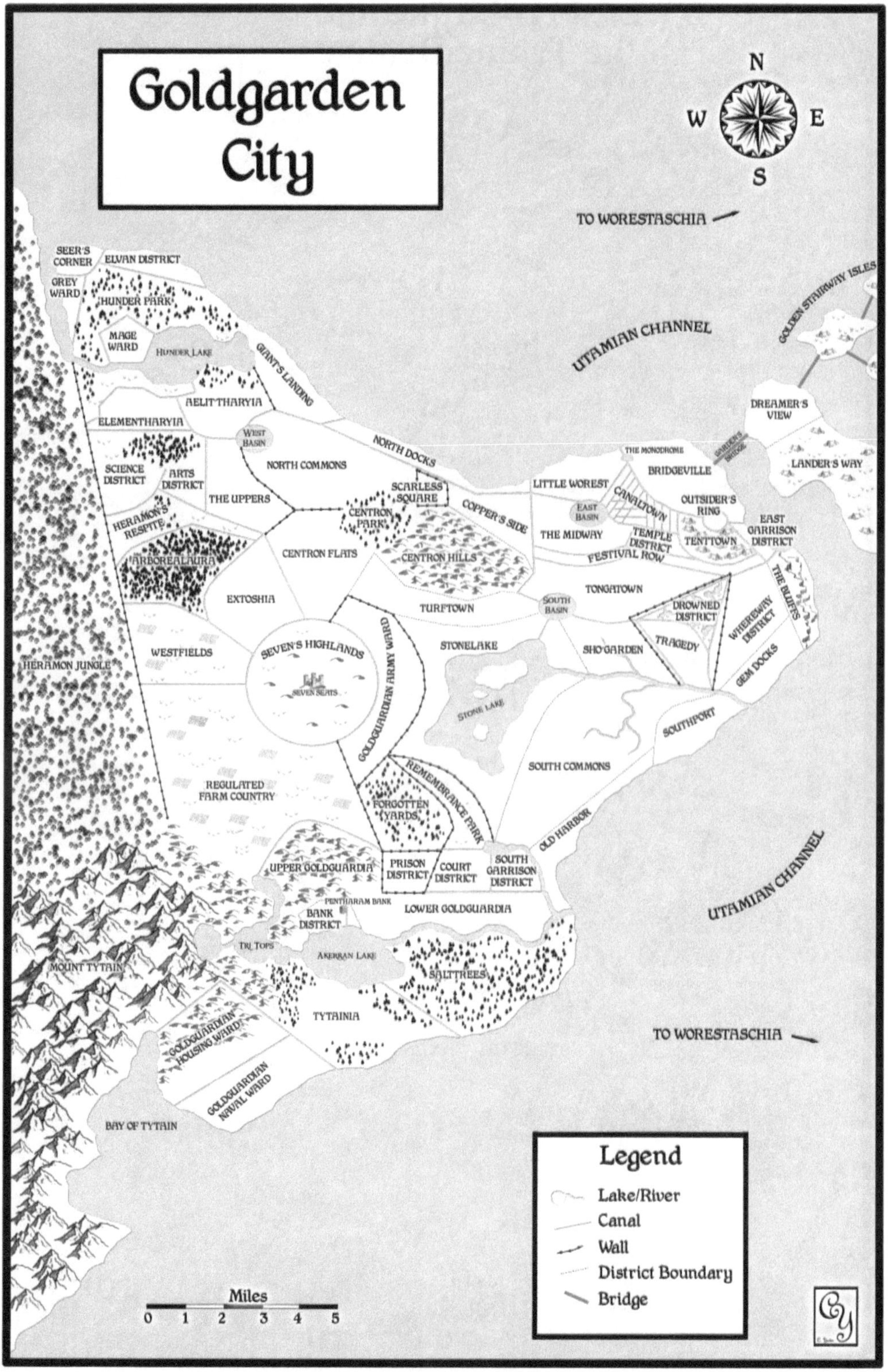

Goldgarden City

TO WORESTASCHIA

SEER'S CORNER
ELVAN DISTRICT
GREY WARD
HUNDER PARK
MAGE WARD
HUNDER LAKE
GIANT'S LANDING
AELITTHARYIA
ELEMENTHARYIA
WEST BASIN
NORTH COMMONS
NORTH DOCKS
SCIENCE DISTRICT
ARTS DISTRICT
THE UPPERS
SCARLESS SQUARE
CENTRON PARK
HERAMON'S RESPITE
ARBOREALAURA
CENTRON FLATS
CENTRON HILLS
COPPER'S SIDE
EXTOSHIA
TURFTOWN
WESTFIELDS
SEVEN'S HIGHLANDS
SEVEN SEATS
GOLDGUARDIAN ARMY WARD
STONELAKE
STONE LAKE
HERAMON JUNGLE
REGULATED FARM COUNTRY
FORGOTTEN YARDS
REMEMBRANCE PARK
SOUTH COMMONS
UPPER GOLDGUARDIA
PRISON DISTRICT
COURT DISTRICT
SOUTH GARRISON DISTRICT
OLD HARBOR
PENTHARAM BANK
BANK DISTRICT
LOWER GOLDGUARDIA
TRI TOPS
AKERRAN LAKE
MOUNT TYTAIN
SALTTREES
TYTAINIA
GOLDGUARDIAN HOUSING WARD
GOLDGUARDIAN NAVAL WARD
BAY OF TYTAIN

UTAMIAN CHANNEL
GOLDEN STAIRWAY ISLES
DREAMER'S VIEW
THE MONODROME
GARDEN'S BRIDGE
LANDER'S WAY
BRIDGEVILLE
LITTLE WOREST
CANALTOWN
OUTSIDER'S RING
EAST BASIN
THE MIDWAY
TEMPLE DISTRICT
TENTTOWN
EAST GARRISON DISTRICT
FESTIVAL ROW
TONGATOWN
SOUTH BASIN
DROWNED DISTRICT
TRAGEDY
SHO'GARDEN
WHEREWAY DISTRICT
THE BLUFFS
GEM DOCKS
SOUTHPORT
UTAMIAN CHANNEL
TO WORESTASCHIA

Miles
0 1 2 3 4 5

Legend

Lake/River
Canal
Wall
District Boundary
Bridge

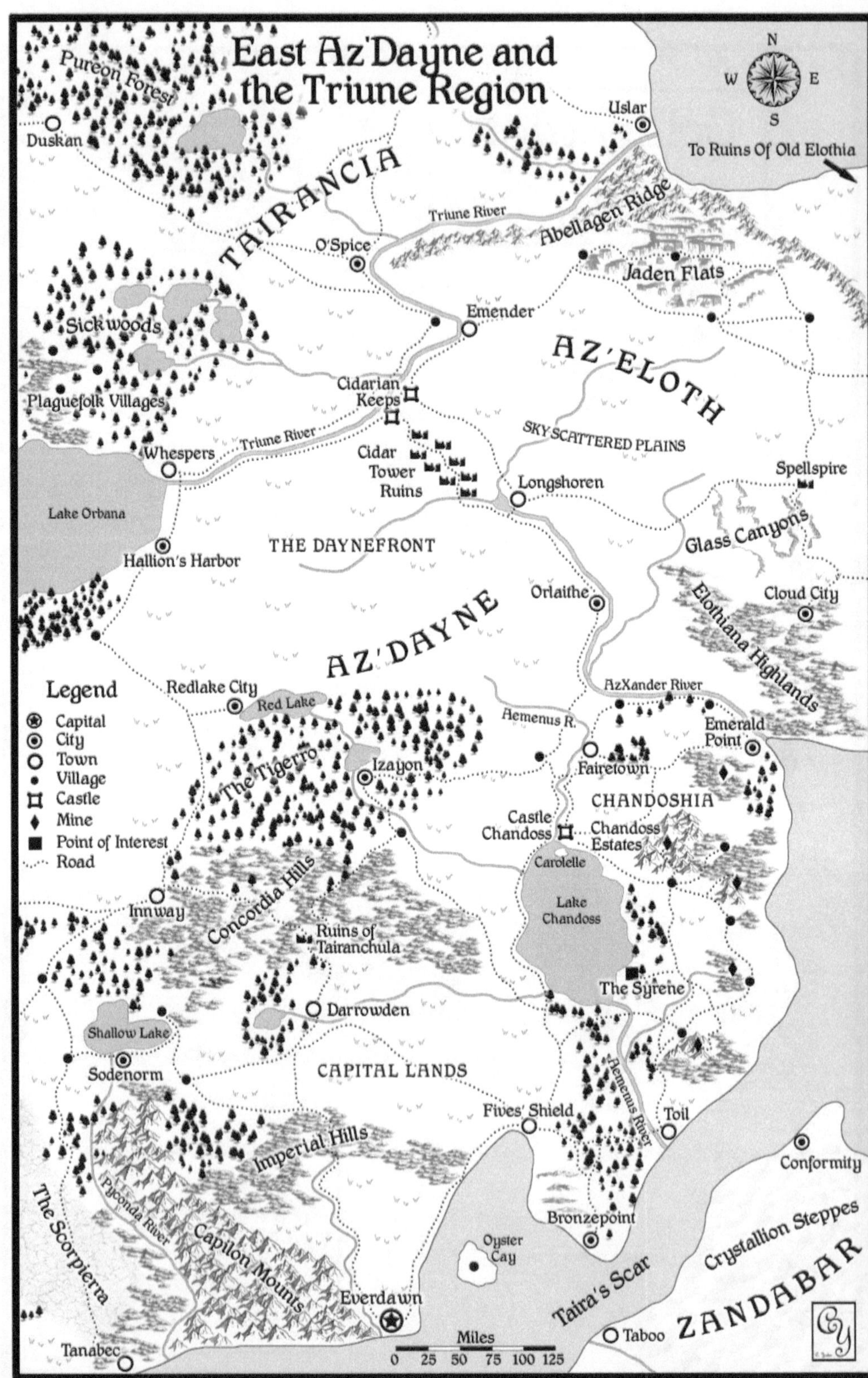
East Az'Dayne and the Triune Region
N
W
E
S
To Ruins Of Old Elothia
Pureon Forest
Duskan
TAIRANCIA
Uslar
Triune River
Abellagen Ridge
O'Spice
Jaden Flats
Sickwoods
Emender
AZ'ELOTH
Plaguefolk Villages
Cidarian Keeps
Triune River
SKY SCATTERED PLAINS
Whespers
Cidar Tower Ruins
Longshoren
Spellspire
Lake Orbana
THE DAYNEFRONT
Glass Canyons
Hallion's Harbor
Orlaithe
Cloud City
AZ'DAYNE
Elothiana Highlands
Legend
Capital
City
Town
Village
Castle
Mine
Point of Interest
Road
Redlake City
Red Lake
AzXander River
Aemenus R.
Emerald Point
The Tigerro
Izayon
Fairetown
CHANDOSHIA
Castle Chandoss
Chandoss Estates
Carolelle
Innway
Concordia Hills
Lake Chandoss
Ruins of Tairanchula
The Syrene
Darrowden
Shallow Lake
Sodenorm
CAPITAL LANDS
Aemenus River
Fives' Shield
Toil
Imperial Hills
Conformity
The Scorpierra
Pyconda River
Capilon Mounts
Bronzepoint
Crystallion Steppes
Oyster Cay
ZANDABAR
Taira's Scar
Everdawn
Miles
0 25 50 75 100 125
Taboo
Tanabec

PRONUNCIATIONS

CHARACTERS

Xalo: ZAY-LO
Zahnastaazjah: ZON-AH-STAYZ-SHUH
Symbelle: SIM-BEL
Fyheir: FYE-AIR
Athaniel: ATH-AN-YEL
Adyssaira: AD-ISS-AIR-AH
Odysserae: OH-DISS-ER-AYE
Valaythea: VAL-AY-THEE-AH
Sundorion: SUN-DOR-I-ON
Uubakrath: YOU-BAH-KRATH
Khomo'Jhuvonus: KO-MO-JSHEW-VON-US
Drevlijhun: DREV-LIH-JUNE
Kavajin: KOV-AH-JIN
Jhukamwi: JSHEW-KOM-WEE
Ethiass: EE-THY-ASS
Taizsha: TAYZ-SHAH
Timmurian: TIM-YUR-EE-AN
Sashka: SOSH-KAH
Sheyelle: SHAY-EL
Carolelle: CARE-OH-LEL
Djediheth: JSHED-I-HETH
Desdjlandar: DEZD-SHLAN-DAR
Thoravus: THOR-AV-US
Zsa'vauge: ZUH-VOGSH
Ise'andahr: ICE-AN-DAR
Zsinsinyrahn: ZIN-SIN-EER-ON
Mesdarro: MEZ-DAR-OH
Haelyn: HAY-LIN

PRONUNCIATIONS

PLACES & THINGS

Elothia: EE-LOW-THEE-AH
Khalimia: CALL-EEM-EE-AH
Tairancia: TAIR-AN-SEE-AH
Tairanchula: TAIR-AN-CHEW-LA
Barredom: BARE-UH-DUM
Aggedon: AG-ED-ON
Teralloe: TAIR-AL-LOW
Depyreoshlinyoq: DE-PIRE-OSH-LIN-YOK
Chandoshia: CHAND-OH-SHEE-AH
Syrene: SYE-REEN

Wyldenar: WIELD-EN-AR
Terollar: TEAR-OH-LAR
Shiniryn: SHIN-EAR-EN
Ibyssai: IB-ISS-EYE
Zandaryn: ZAND-AR-IN
Lunaril: LUNE-AR-IL
Khalimishe: CALL-EEM-ISH
Psage: SAGE
Qindrid: KIN-DRID
Quasi: QUOSS-EE

Glazjhendun: GLAZ-JSHEN-DUN
Pentagogue: PENT-A-GOG
Oathemic: OATH-EM-IK

Animayan: AN-EM-EYE-AN
Crystalyte: CRIS-TAL-ITE
Hyperi: HYPE-EER-EE
Ejahra: E-JAH-RAH
Solesce: SOLE-ESK
Wyrkenido: WEER-KEN-EE-DOE

CHARACTER GUIDE

CHANDOSS FAMILY HUMANS
(by what is known to the reader at the beginning of the novel)

Athaniel Chandoss: *older brother to Valaythea, Adyssaira, Odysserae, and Sashka … an assassin of the Oathemic Cabal*
Valaythea Chandoss: *triplet sister of Adyssaira and Odysserae, sister to Athaniel and Sashka*
Adyssaira Chandoss: *triplet sister of Adyssaira and Odysserae, sister to Athaniel and Sashka … born hunder-touched*
Odysserae Chandoss: *triplet sister of Adyssaira and Odysserae, sister to Athaniel and Sashka … born deaf*
Emberalda Chandoss: *cousin to Athaniel and the Chandoss sisters*
Ethiass Chandoss: *father of Athaniel, Valaythea, Adyssaira, Odysserae, and Sashka, husband of Taizsha, brother to Nikayle … Ambassador of Chandoshia*
Nikayle Chandoss: *uncle to Athaniel, Valaythea, Adyssaira, Odysserae, and Sashka, father to Barturon and Emberalda, brother to Ethiass*
Barturon Chandoss: *cousin to the Chandoss sisters, brother to Emberalda, son of Nikayle … fugitive spellblade*
Valdean Chandoss: *the Count of Chandoshia, great-granduncle to the Chandoss girls and Athaniel*

HALFKINDER (Z'SHUN)
Sashka: *half-elvan, half-human, half sister to Athaniel, Valaythea, Adyssaira, and Odysserae, daughter of Ethiass and Taizsha*

ELVEN
Zahnastaazjah: *alias "Scarless", the Crime Queen, the youngest daughter of Khomo'Jhuvonus, and guildmother of the Stormtrees*
Uubakrath: *a renown Terollar marksman, bloodguard of Scarless assigned by Khomo'Jhuvonus*
Sundorion: *a Zandaryn elvan explorer*
Timmurian: *a quasi-Zandaryn elvan, bound to Emberalda Chandoss as his lifemate*
Taizsha: *a quasi-Zandaryn elvan, bound to Ethiass Chandoss as her lifemate, mother to Sashka*
Ise'andahr: *a rogue-Neveril elvan, son of Zsa'vauge*
Zsinsinyrahn: *the Neveril emperor*

OTHER HUMANS

Xalo: *an Elothian spellblade, companion of Scarless in the Stormtrees*
Atrick: *overman of the Copper Jacks gang under the employ of the Stormtrees*
Usurp: *overman of several gangs under the employ of the Stormtrees*
Devonduer: *chamberlain of the Stormtrees*
Dockjaw: *overman of the Salt Lords under the employ of the Stormtrees*
Pyphan: *foster brother to Symbelle, assassin for the Oathemic Cabal*
Symbelle: *a volatile hyperi raised by the Oathemic Cabal, daughter of Endrith Goldfyre "Coldborn"*
Endrith Goldfyre: *founder of the Oathemic Cabal, Az'Dayne's assassins' guild, and the only Umbra archmage on Penthara*
Daerlem Black: *an assassin of the Hive Order in the Oathemic Cabal who regularly works with Athaniel Chandoss*
Izayus Az'Ampion: *Prince of the Az'Dayne Dominadom*
No-Name: *the hyperi son of two recently deceased archmage parents: Brigatha Emmonost, the Torrent archmage, and Imaniko Palestorm, the Reaping archmage*
Thoravus: *the Thrench bloodguard assigned to No-Name*
Djediheth Emmonost: *the Thrench emperor, Lord of the Ashenwave*
Oldan Boldandgold: *founder of the Boarneck Company*
Terrib Ango: *Maestro of the Monodrome*
Claydius Orlaithe: *Director of the Oathemic Cabal*
Omen: *a Psage seer in Chandoshia*
Thederick Tyme: *secret Seat of the Black in Goldgarden*
Baldric Whereway: *secret Seat of the Blue in Goldgarden*
Arro Gemenis: *secret Seat of the Gold in Goldgarden*
Amethyst: *secret Seat of the Red in Goldgarden*
Serafinelan: *secret Seat of the White in Goldgarden*
Shypriss Sol-War: *secret Seat of the Green in Goldgarden, and the only Sunder archmage on Penthara*
Mesdarro: *a master hyperi, Magistrate of Spellspire*

UMBRAN

Zsa'vauge: *the Orchestrator of Chandoshia*

THE DAWNING SEASON

PROLOGUE

The fetid trudge through the combined sewers of the largest metropolis on all of Penthara led through undeniably the most putrid zone in the realm. Goldgarden, the City of a Thousand Canals, the Untouchable All-Touching, the Capital of Commerce, the Isle of Innovation—the list of its world-renowned titles went on and on. And yet the last place a person would want to be was in its foul-smelling and often dangerous bowels, known as the Flush, beneath the overpopulated streets. But this was not an unfamiliar place. This was all familiar territory for Xalo the pit gladiator in the underworld of illegal slave trade.

His wrists had been tethered tight behind his back, bound by a thick rope, while his ankles were shackled and chained together. Disarmed but unharmed, he stood surrounded by his eager ushers, each nervous but ready to discard his company for good.

He glanced over the decem men in the escort party. All were dirty creatures of the poorest crime syndicate in the entire cityscape—a gang of miscreants known as the Copper Jacks, who controlled all of Copper's Side. They dressed in mismatched leather scraps with random tears in the fabric patched over with cloth rags of browns or yellows. Their hair and beards looked like they had never discovered the mysterious arts of the somehow elusive abundance of city barbers. Each of them carried their crude weaponry in hand, including butchers' blades, fishing knives, makeshift spears, and spiked clubs. And these were the alleged elite of their clique, vicious killers proven in their crafts of murder and mayhem.

Their underboss, Atrick, stood several paces from Xalo, in front of the lot. His blond beard was trimmed, and his hair was cropped short, spiked up. His studded black leather vestments were an obvious testament to quality and price. And he was the only one in the group wielding an actual sword—in fact, two swords. The one sheathed at his right hip was none other than Xalo's famed spellblade.

The word *spellblade* had a twofold definition. Both the magically sentient sword and its chosen wielder bound to it were termed spellblade.

Every spellblade sword ever made had been forged at the same time and devised of the same shape, all crafted by the same smiths in Elothia long ago.

The ambiguous components used in forging such relics were said to be taken straight from the Vist and fabricated in Spellspire, the ancient capital of Elothia. With a single-edged, slightly curved blade, it was expressly designed for swift slashing precision. The magic swords were known for their enchanted glass blades, unnaturally sharper than any metal and more indestructible than diamond. The guard was oval-shaped and gold-coated. The most sinister piece on the weapon, however, was its hilt, made from an elvan's spine. A spellblade's pommel was capped with a signature brilliant emerald of the most flawless cut, which, of all the gems on Penthara, had been proven to have certain arcane capacities.

The swords had originally been made for the purpose of hunting down and exterminating mages. The final requisite in the making of a spellblade sword was its infusion with the essence of some rare entity beyond Xalo's knowledge. But he was aware that it was this special binding that enchanted the weapon to sense nearby humans born with the faculty to become mages. Weaker, untrained spellblade wielders were often caught in a form of possession by the sentient blade they were bound to, and they could easily lose control and attack a mage potential not of their own accord. Xalo, though, was not a weak or untrained spellblade.

Furthermore, if a spellblade killed a mage by the sword, they could absorb the mage's signature spell, which would be inscribed as a glyph on the glass blade, representing the spell's correspondent season, from which it pulled power. The wielder of the sword could then invoke these particular spells, and the power to cast the same spell again was replenished quite quickly if the sentient sword felt a sense of trusting synergy with its wielder.

All Xalo had to do was touch the glyph on the sword and whisper the name of the mage from whom he had stripped the spell. The glyph, along with the edge of the glass blade, would then glow a bright green—the color of raw magic—the same as the halo around his right eye, which would shine when revealing the blade from its bone scabbard.

A spellblade also imbued the wielder with martial weapon mastery, honed by each of its former chosen wielders. It kept a fraction of their essences inside the emerald pommel, which acted as a form of phylactery. The current wielder from the lineage could engage in combat with an identical form to those before. The sentient swords only bound themselves to those in the same lineage who were eligible to wield it. The blade might not always choose one in the next generation—sometimes the one following, or even further down the line. The rationale for why the swords picked whom they did, when they did, had become a fruitless debate.

Xalo had the embedded swordmastery of four of his ancestors locked within him through the power of the spellblade, along with seven spells he had acquired from the seven mages who had met their untimely ends at the edge of his sentient weapon. Each of their names was now a part of him: the two Dawning mages Qandor and Bellarae, the two Sunder mages Lichael and Yhondar, and the three Reaping mages Jezzerac, Herovocus, and Anasian.

He had come a long way since his upbringing in the Jaden Flats, a plateau territory against the Abellagen Ridge, which divided the country of Az'Eloth from Tairancia along the Triune River. His nomadic tribe had suffered the calamity of the Daynish forces encroaching on his now-crumbled former nation. He counted himself as one of the lucky ones to have made it out alive as a child from the massacre. Being a slave in Az'Dayne and eventually in Goldgarden, after being sold by one master after another, was the only life Xalo had ever known.

As an adult, he had earned a reputation as the deadliest pit gladiator throughout all of Goldgarden. The difference between a pit gladiator and a free gladiator was all in the name. Free gladiators were just that: free. They were popular citizens in organized public duels, fighting for prize and prestige for themselves. Death matches were always prohibited. But the inglorious life of a pit gladiator was never free—perhaps just more privileged than an average slave. Their masters might reward them with fine meals and whores after a win, and they held their own quarters within the estates, but they had no liberty to leave or roam the city without chaperone from an assigned custodian. And their illegal secret matches were often to the death.

Xalo had been forced to duel hard criminals, mage fugitives, elvan vagabonds, and even trained beasts. Oftentimes the pit masters would attempt to cheat the odds of his wagered fate by experimenting with more than one opponent against him, but such finagling thus far had found them failing at every attempt.

Slavery was indeed strongly prohibited in the region, but this was also a city called Goldgarden, where coin could buy turned eyes and hushed lips. It was a metropolitan hub of the most modernized entrepreneurs and upstarts from any social class in the realm, a place of opportunity where the poorest thug could become a street king by night and where the influential might transition day by day. Goldgarden was a city-nation, a world of its own, away from the outside political matters and wars across Penthara and even its own country of Utamia. As a paradise for urbanites, the city stood as a land of opportunity for the cunning, the strong, and those with the gift of the golden gab. The great city was a haven for new beginnings, so long as one had the stomach for it.

It was also a place known for utilizing its nation's elemental descendancy for novel inventions rather than religious reverence. With the Utamians being of the tairan and water cross-descendancy, the citizens of the metropolis were generally a conglomeration of the most innovative minds in building complex aqueducts and the most massive sewer system on Penthara. They furthermore utilized Torrent mages during their season to purify badwater, as they called it—contaminated, of the sea, and of the sewage flow—into fairwater, able to be consumed or used for bathing.

The urgent push through the underground channels rushed Xalo and his ushers to their destination point, where the group of thugs impatiently waited for their buyers to rendezvous with them. It had been several hours, after passing a labyrinth of corners and bridge planks, before the elaborate network of brick tunnels had delivered them to their intended terminus at a crossway.

The water from the storm drains and inventive sanitation system, along with the flow of liquidized waste, had been shut off at this point by sluice gates. All the walkways around could be accessed. It was the driest area Xalo had seen on the trek.

On a concrete corner ledge, a man higher than where he and the

Copper Jacks were filtering in from, was a ladder attached to the wall, which led back to the streets. Next to the ladder was a symbol painted in yellow over the brick for engineers to better navigate the Flush. Xalo knew what each of the symbols meant. This one marked their location in Goldgarden, directly below the end of the East Basin, in the Midway.

On the elevated area stood five armed mercenaries. Each bore a signature necklace with two punctured wild boar tusks as its ornament. They were each clothed in boiled leathers, and four handled longspears with broad heads. The fifth, their obvious leader, with a boar's head engraved on the spaulder over his right shoulder, held a two-handed scimitar and was marred by burn scars across his bald head.

Xalo couldn't refrain from unleashing his dry wit to antagonize. "My fellows, you truly shouldn't have." He feigned admiration, devoid of expression on his face. "I say, your hospitality is the topic of legends. I did not expect to walk the golden carpets themselves."

Xalo never smiled or smirked, or sneered or frowned. He always had the same plain look with his narrow brown eyes, heavy with a lifetime of distributing death. He kept a clean-shaven face that contoured his angular jawline and gaunt cheeks. His blond hair was worn in Elothian warrior fashion, slicked back and tied up in a topknot but razored to the skin around the sides of his head. There was no denying his ethnicity in a single glance, having a similar easterner look to the Sho'Lonese and Oriyans.

His armor tattoo, which covered his entire right arm and the same side of his chest, was a trophy earned for being deemed an elite Goldgarden gladiator, with over fifty victories. There were but few others that shared the same brand of prestige in the city's underworld. But the symbolic mark was currently covered in an oversized shirt fit for a prisoner, rather than his preferred garb, suited to agility.

As anticipated, Atrick seemed to get irritated and piped up. "Always got somethin' to say. Like a starvin' jester with bad jokes. The only fuckin' clown I know that doesn't smile." Atrick didn't even turn around or motion with his fingers.

But Xalo knew his worth to his buyers. And he knew each of these men he was in the custody of, as he had spent the last few years in their despicable company. "It pains me to learn that my time has to expire with the generous Copper King. Serving in such a prestigious outfit has been an honor fit for royals."

A couple of the men spat. A few more cursed him. Atrick just continued with attempted professionalism. He was the most experienced combatant in the group, and definitely the hardest. But Xalo knew he had a weakness in his temper if tested.

"Took long enough," the burn-scarred mercenary simply said.

Atrick answered for his gang as his henchmen and Xalo filed in from the sewer walkway to organize themselves in the dry cistern beneath. "Xalo, your employer is now Oldan Boldandgold, boss of the Boarneck Company. Meet your new custodian, Gastion."

"Thus far I've only been introduced to cutthroats and slave-driving docklords," Xalo replied cynically, hoping to get a rise. "Remind me to thank you also, Atrick, for being such a merciful custodian yourself these past few years."

And that did it. Atrick swung around and neared as close as he dared, which was still a throw away. "Xalo, you're weak. Ya always have been. Ya never won't be. Ya can't even lift a cheese knife without gettin' sick from betrayin' that bond between ya an' that blade you're cursed to. You're just a skinny fuckin' cornered cow that we all keep milkin' in the dens. An' that's your life, ya see? Till your employers decide you're worth more to be butchered than milked."

Xalo's facial expression still didn't change. It never did. "Never been the cow, Atrick." *I am the caged bull.* "I've never been the cornered cow …"

"Gastion, apologies an' greetings." Atrick swiftly shifted back to business. "Got orders for a change of plan on his account. Had to send a separate crew to get those papers delivered to your guild, as requested."

"Yeah, yeah, we heard the deal," Gastion retorted. "All o' youse are just more o' a shamfucked lot is all, but we ain't here to size our cocks today."

"'Kay then," Atrick replied, obviously annoyed, seemingly ready to break as always. "We ain't here to bump on horse fuckers and pig stickers either. Down to blood and gold." As he walked behind Xalo, Atrick condescended to release his frustration by shoving him forward. "As promised, Xalo the Zero, Champion of the Underover, Blood of the First Spellblade, Copper's Killer, Magebane, the Ear Collector, the Eloth—"

"The Elothian Element. Yes, we know all his aliases. Needless grandiosity. The sale is already—" Xalo's new employer's custodian attempted to shun the upsell but was cut off by Xalo himself.

"That's Elothian Elephant. Not Element."

"What in the Fives," was all that Gastion could counter with, clearly dumbfounded by a slave backtalking.

"Elephants. They are from Elothia, my homeland. The strongest beasts in the realm, known for utilizing one extra-strong limb."

Xalo saw that he was getting no response and only wide-eyed looks, so he continued to explain. "Like a spellblade?"

Still no response came from either group.

"Hunted and endangered now, like the elephants?"

Only more stares were shot due to the insolence of his audacity.

"You still don't get the reference," Xalo said, nodding to Atrick and Gastion. "Okay, continue."

Atrick shook his head in seeming embarrassment for representing him. "Let's get this over with."

Gastion simply snarled, "Let's."

"Here's his blade," Atrick proclaimed, walking up the steps to release the dangerous weapon into the new caretaker's possession. "Don't let him get near it, or ya all know the end. We'll take the other half of the coin now for the deal. The reins are yours, horse lords."

"Ear Collector?" Xalo interrupted, and all stopped to take full notice of him again. "Never actually collected an ear as a trophy. That is just manipulative flair to declare I've slain many elven. Wise for street hype, I agree, though all of those kills were forced. I actually prefer their lot over ours."

And just then another voice chimed in, feminine and foreign. "Pleased to hear Xalo holds no bad blood with the elvan race, as the chattering urchins like to whisper otherwise."

She came into the light, entering from the tunnel opposite the one used by the Copper Jacks. "Scarless" was hissed in fear by the mouths of each thug near Xalo, referencing the most popular nickname by which she was revered.

"But what if there is a higher bid than the Boarnecks can offer?" Scarless teased, with her own three menacing companions striding in beside her.

Scarless was a Terollar elvan, one of a race commonly slandered by being vulgarly referred to as trolls. If one lived in Goldgarden, one would undoubtedly have heard of her. Rumored to be the youngest daughter, or progeny in elvan terms, of the king of the Glace Isles, she was a rare find in the metropolis realm of humankind, even though the city was known to harbor almost all the races of Penthara.

She was taller than an average man, probably just over six feet, built strong and muscular, but still feminine. Her skin was fair and without a single blemish or scar, as all Terollar were known to regenerate from any injury quite rapidly. Her piercing light-green eyes were the distinctive trait of all her ilk. Her blond hair was most eccentric, Xalo thought, shaved short, almost to the scalp, around the sides of her head, with precise lines razored to the skin and the top grown out excessively long in a mane of thick-braided tails that almost touched the backs of her knees. She had the youthful looks of a woman in her midtwenties, but Xalo and everyone else knew this to be an elvan facade, since most could attest to her having been around for nearly a century by recorded accounts—such were the blessings of the slow-aging race. Her stern but beautiful face was savagely painted, as were her companions'. They each had a different way to depict a particular dead white tree upon a black background.

Scarless wasn't dressed in much for her disruption of the trade meet, fitted in leather pants dyed to a dark green, tucked into cheap, mundane black boots that matched her gloves. A thin white shirt with ruffled cuffs and loose laces down her bosom adorned her torso, as if she had no care in the world for protection from an impending fight.

She was armed with a spear like none Xalo had ever seen. It was altogether alien to look upon. The Terollar weapon was entirely made up of the same otherworldly material, from its haft to its guard to its blade point. The singular substance appeared to consist of small, metallicized frost shards layered over one another. A red veinlike network was incorporated throughout the white spear, pulsating underneath, between, and over the material of the weapon's construction in no set pattern. Xalo thought spellblades to be the most exotically beautiful weapons that had ever existed in the realm, but he had never seen one of these before. Yet one couldn't necessarily classify it as beautiful. It was instead terrifyingly outlandish and mesmerizing. He judged a person's choice of weapons before he even analyzed the shape of their body or took note of their face. It was the gladiator ingrained in him.

None had thus far come to learn the full story of why Scarless was here, so far from home. But once she had arrived in Goldgarden, she had swiftly climbed the ranks of the underworld, risen to become the most feared crime overlord in the vast city. Few to no gangs would ever dare oppose her as of late. Almost none, that was, but for the Boarneck Company, which was still establishing itself on the island metropolis.

"Why're ya getting involved in this, Scarless?" Atrick demanded. "Ya had your chances to bid, and yet ya always avoid the buys. The deal's done with Oldan of the Boarneck Company. Ya can't compete with him."

Scarless made her purpose for the intrusion simple for them. "Not here to make a deal with the Boarnecks. Nor with the Copper King. My bid is for Xalo alone."

Gastion snorted at her effrontery, agape in amused awe. "You are about to make a powerful enemy, troll. You know the sway we hold here on these streets now, and far 'yond the gates o' Goldgarden."

"Xalo. Never forget this." Scarless commanded his heed. "I do not like being called a troll. You will kill him first." She indicated Gastion of the Boarnecks as she set her own condemning gaze on Atrick.

Everyone erupted into a sudden frenzy of fighting stances and murmured echoes of profanities.

"Is this troll bitch serious?" Gastion refused to credit the gall of this stranger to Atrick. "Challenging the Boarnecks?"

"Plain new to this isle, Gastion? Clear as Behemon water. If ya get a visit from Scarless, what she says is heavier than blood an' gold," Atrick affirmed with his shortsword visibly shaking in his grasp at the threat.

"The only deal is this," Scarless resumed, unwavering before Gastion's failure at intimidation. "Xalo, you are no longer a slave of Goldgarden. Not to the Copper King, not to the Boarneck Company, and definitely never to me. All the profit from your winnings, right here."

Scarless motioned for the men beside her to slide in a large chest of loot for all to see.

"It has been intercepted and is yours in full."

The lid of the wheeled trunk was lifted by her henchmen to reveal the spoils: coins, gems, trinkets, and other valuables Xalo had never had the liberty of owning.

"My one request is that you follow me in my pursuit, and in return," Scarless promised, "I will ensure you a life of freedom, due compensation, and you will never again fight against your own free will."

Atrick was clearly pleading now. "Scarless, you're about to start another gang war. Ya prepared for this? We can make a deal!"

"This she-troll's got fuckin' four, and we got fifteen seasoned between our lot," Gastion shouted, discernibly astounded by the timidity of the Copper Jacks. "What's the damn faintness about?"

"That's not just four. She's the daughter of some legendary troll warlord—worst of his kind! Got his killer blood in her veins!" Atrick warned the antsy lot around him. "And she's the guildmother of the Stormtrees—the one gang ya don't sidefuck in this city."

Usually Xalo was quip-ready, but he held restraint to let Atrick's extolment of the imminent threat continue. Even Scarless's and Gastion's gangs allowed the spiel to go on, possibly out of sheer interest.

"Ya got Usurp, Dockjaw, an' Sundown 'side her too," he elaborated, with only their infamous aliases. "If ya live in the northside, ya know about 'em. Period."

"You workin' propaganda for her or what, Copper? Why you boostin' her?" Gastion demanded to clarify the antics of the suddenly frantic veteran thug.

"We are not just four," Scarless calmly clarified, as she and her three henchmen slowly advanced toward Atrick. "We are five. Xalo is mine now."

Every man moved with purpose now. The Boarnecks jumped down from the ledge, weapons readied to initiate the inevitable bloodbath. The Copper Jacks flanked Xalo, prepared to guard their property with their lives. However, Atrick was the first to act.

"Ya ain't got just five neither. Xalo, remember this an' forgive me when it's over." Atrick quaked and rushed up behind him with his sword, swiftly severing the rope tied around Xalo's wrists. "Ya got six!"

And just like that, Xalo found his precious magic sword back in his grasp from his former custodian. Before Xalo could unsheathe his weapon, he caught a glimpse of the Copper Jack underboss already shoving his small sword through one of his own unsuspecting men. The fight was on.

Xalo's glass sword left its scabbard, and his left eye flashed with a glowing green rim around the iris. He instantly touched the Reaping glyph of Jezzerac, and the formerly white glyph on the glass blade lit up with the same green glow, and an unnatural fog suddenly enveloped the entire sewer chamber. The Boarneck men charging toward the Stormtrees and the Copper Jacks all became blind in the thick of the cloud.

But not Scarless and her three Stormtrees, as Xalo touched the second Reaping glyph, and it lit up next, calling the spell of Herovocus, which enhanced the vision of those he chose to see through the fog as clearly as he.

He saw one of the Copper Jack thugs flailing wildly with his club, which was about to bat the brain matter right out of an unsuspecting Atrick, blind as the rest of them.

The glyph from Anasian radiated green as Xalo's fingers pressed it in turn, using his final Reaping mage spell to control the air to snatch the club from the man's grip and send it directly into Atrick's temple, tactfully knocking him out as a favor for a favor to save him from becoming a casualty.

Scarless's men seemed hesitant to advance on the mired enemy, still confused by the magical fog, even with their unhindered senses. Scarless herself, on the other hand, stood her ground in front of Xalo with her exotic spear braced to defend him at all costs. But Xalo the Zero, Champion of the Underover, Blood of the First Spellblade, Copper's Killer, Magebane, the Ear Collector, the Elothian Elephant, needed no protection. He was the most dangerous man alive and knew it.

He stood in front of Scarless and strummed Lichael the Sunder mage's glyph and watched it flare up green. He slashed his sword in a wide horizontal arc as if meaning to cleave several men in front of him. But the edge of the weapon only hit air while the fire spell inside threw a blazing wave the size of the sword blade toward the impending hostiles. Two of the Boarnecks caught fire and burst into a dying fit.

Xalo charged toward Gastion, summoning the fifth glyph, Qandor's, to light up as the others. The experienced combatant obviously sensed the presence of his enemy and attempted to hack through Xalo from neck to waist with his scimitar. But the Dawning mage's spell trapped inside was there, and so was Xalo's blade. Iron against glass clashed, and Gastion's sword magically shattered on impact.

The mercenary then prompted a headbutt that exploded Xalo's entire nose, leaving him washed in dizziness, ready to faint. The spellblade took over in semipossession, with the self-survival initiative to activate the sixth glyph. *BELLARAE.* Xalo heard the whisper in his mind from the sentient sword. The Dawning mage's spell to heal wounds triggered, and instantly his nose was fixed anew and his vertigo gone.

The other two Boarnecks tried to assail him with wild, estimated swings in the obscurity of the fog but failed and fell quickly to Xalo's augmented proficiency.

Gastion was relentless, however, now weaponless, trying to grapple and tackle Xalo with a dominating bear hug from behind.

YHONDAR. Xalo allowed the spellblade possession once again to conjure the seventh and final spell in his arsenal, to ignite his skin to scorching hot, inflaming anything that touched him. The Boarneck mercenary screeched back in wailing agony as his body was set ablaze to die.

Xalo didn't offer the stranger mercy and left his fate to the fire. He instead began making his way over to the cluelessly blind remaining Copper Jacks.

Scarless and her Stormtrees were standing back now, safely watching in the opaque gloom of the conjured fog, as if interviewing him for worthiness to enter their guild. They never attacked a single one in their vicinity.

Xalo looked at the daunting elvan and thought of her as the loveliest creature he had ever laid eyes on. She was his savior. And he would indefinitely owe her his life for all his days.

As the magic of the fog began to dissipate, Xalo casually presented his presence as blatantly as possible before each of his former handlers. He used no spells this time, even though half of them had been replenished for use again by now. Invoking the spellblade's powers too soon concurrent to the same one just casted could render him sore or even entirely debilitated for a following period.

Instead, he stood in the middle of them all and gauged the fear on each of their faces. They all knew it in that moment. Cycles of prejudice in hiding, years of mistreatment. And they felt it with swift, efficient, martial punishment within a matter of seconds.

Scarless looked at him with her perfect green eyes when it was finally nothing but calm and blood, and she drew her palm across the tip of her outlandish spear, offering the weapon point to Xalo to do the same. As he returned the gesture of respect, she clasped her bleeding hand in his and pulled him closer, speaking softly. "Welcome home, Xalo. You are free."

SCARLESS (I)

THE STORMTREES

Zahnastaazjah sat up in bed with her naked back against her headboard. Her voluptuous breasts were as exposed as the rest of her body. Her right leg lay over her lover's adjacent thigh as she ran her light fingertips nonchalantly over his skin, tracing his complex armor tattoo, which enveloped the right side of his upper body. She used her free hand to slowly stroke herself from stomach to nipple to neck, back and forth.

Her light-green eyes watched him dreaming next to her. He always slept after they made love, and he always had the same few dreams, or so he had told her. She decided not to interrupt his rest, even though she was still in the mood for him.

She got out of bed to adorn herself in her choice of garments for the day. She slipped into a black corset that matched her bracers, going with her fitted brown leather pants and expensive boots.

She did not need to fix her hair. Her blond locks were thickly braided to rest down her back, hanging long in typical Terollar style, down to her calves.

When she finished getting dressed, she turned around to find her lover awake and staring at her with lust in his hard brown eyes. "Another boring dream?"

"The most boring dream ever," Xalo lied, playing their little game.

On the cue of his sarcasm, she knew it was the recurring memory he had of the time she had helped to free him from his life as a gladiator slave, three years ago. They had quickly become sexual partners just days after, with a growing affection fueled by something far deeper, mostly on his end, ever since.

"You are quite perfect, my Zahna."

She squinted in distaste. "I've told you not to do that. Over and over. We elven do not do pet names. If you say my name, say it the way I was born into it. Or you can call me by my street name."

But Xalo never called her Scarless, like all the rest. That was the alias she was renowned for. He knew she hated the shortened version of her actual name, but if there was any flaw the spellblade owned and proudly wore, it was that he fancied his own dry wit. And he never smiled, which often made it difficult to gauge his seriousness. He was a constant irritation but someone she had been unable to go a day without since they had met. She had saved him from an undesirable fate the day she had first met him, and she had done so many times since.

She had a new recruit to meet that had been highly sought after—a member that would elevate her already indomitable reputation. "Get dressed. We meet the new one today. I need you to behave when you see him."

"Yeah, yeah, our first mage." Xalo leaped naked out of bed and snatched up his spellblade, then swung around to face her innocently with his weapon in hand. "What harm could I do?"

Zahnastaazjah huffed and ignored his perpetually satirical remarks. Attempting to argue with the quip master was futile and entirely frustrating. And with that, the two unlikely partners left her private abode to start the morning's busy agenda.

Zahnastaazjah would turn ninety years of age this year, though being elvan, and Terollar at that, with their regenerative impowers, she still held the youthful appearance of a woman in her twenties.

She had been around the human civilizations for so long, she hardly ever referred to her own age in cycles, as the elvan culture did, adhering to years for time measurement instead.

She was the youngest daughter of Khomo'Jhuvonus, the most notorious Terollar warlord the north had ever known. The fact that she even referred to herself as a *daughter* instead of a *progeny* was further testament to her conviction that she hadn't belonged to anything remotely elvan in decades, as her race did not use such terms. Sons and daughters were progeny and parents were progenitors, called patriarchs or matriarchs down the line of ancestry.

After a long story of hard life turned sideways in every which way since she had been spawned from her cocoon into the world, she had been exposed to betrayal from her Terollar people and her very family. Her mother, her siblings, and even her very own lifemate, Drevlijhun, had all turned from the core principles of the elvan Balance and what it meant to be Terollar.

Drevlijhun was the worst of them all, a nostalgia of wasted possibilities she was now vexed into. Once an elvan conjoined with a lifemate officially, they could never again do so with another. They could only produce offspring with their original lifemate. Such was the curse of the elven. Humans could procreate as much as they wanted, for as long as their body could handle, with as many different partners as they so desired. The elvan culture's population was under much more stringent control due to their mating constraints. It took much longer between the birthing—or *spawning*, as elven called it—for an elvan to even be able to breed with their lifemate again, five seasonal cycles to be exact.

The only good thing to come of Drevlijhun was the cocooning of her son, Sorovronus. But he had been taken by her father at a young age to become instituted into some clandestine political scheme she was not privy to of Khomo'Jhuvonus's own ambitions.

But these were stories she forced to be part of her past. Just as Xalo felt reborn through her freeing of him, she had undergone a similar changeover to liberation when she arrived in Goldgarden thirty-seven years ago. She had left the Glace Isles by boat to Mageholme and hired a crew of mages for a safe escort across human lands to the famous, racially tolerant city.

With no purpose in life and years of suffering disappointment in her own race and the direction of the Terollar culture, she wanted nothing to do with them. Goldgarden was a place where any, from all walks of life and of all hues of skin or shapes of ear, could begin anew.

Being a progeny of Khomo'Jhuvonus had ensured she was rigorously trained in Terollar combat styles during her upbringing. This had proven vitally useful in her initial attempts at work within the metropolis of boundless opportunity. She had been able to easily attest her worth in martial prowess and gained employment as hired muscle for her first gang, the Blue Blades, who had practically controlled the northeast wards of the city.

Zahnastaazjah had acquired her nickname of Scarless immediately, seeing as she was Terollar, with the impressive impower to near instantly regenerate any wound with a resultant lack of scarring, no matter how many injuries she received throughout her life.

Within the Blue Blades and other opposing gangs she had encountered, it had become common that none even cared to know her real name, and she had embraced the alias of Scarless.

She became the most feared asset of the Blue Blades as a reputable killer in the city underworld, eventually rising to become the leader of the gang. Over the years, she outlived and outlasted all her rival gang leaders, converting most of the elite members into her own. The old name of the Blue Blades was dissolved, and the structure of the gang became more like that of an organized crime guild. The new name she dubbed it was the Stormtrees. The old members of the absorbed Blue Blades still carried their blue-ribboned knives as an honorary token of prestige for those who had been part of the original gang.

Ultimately, Zahnastaazjah became the figurehead overlord for all gangs in Goldgarden. She acted as the peacekeeper among their discrepancies and turf feuds, and they all paid homage of monthly tribute to her for protection and afforded favors.

Nine years ago, she had been elected to the highest position merited in the secret council of Goldgarden: the Seven Seats.

What had once been only five seats of designated officials who presided over specific operations to maintain order in the massive metropolis had evolved into seven seats at the time of her invitation to elevation. Her station was ranked the Seat of the Grey as the lead liaison in charge of criminal-activity control and reimbursements, along with underground knowledge from outer-nation spy networks. The only stipulations bestowed upon her illicit operations were that she and her bracketed gangs must refrain from what the Seven referred to as "petty or vile crime": pickpocketing, burglary, open theft, unjustified murder, public rape, or death-dueling. All else was fair game and permitted to her.

In recent years, her focus had been entirely committed to one foe in her way. The Boarneck Company, which she had only first encountered with Xalo some three years back, had evolved into a truly tangible threat to the city she had come to call home. It was a multiplying organization of unscrupulous mercenaries with seemingly bottomless riches, capable of buying out anything and everything they swarmed through. Oldan Boldandgold and his especially malicious son, Tristostopher, maintained a cunning reputation not to be trifled with, conquering the entry zones of eastern

Goldgarden Isle through means of property buyouts and shop shakedowns, hushing the Goldguardian Watch and influential politicians with a surplus of coin to pass around. The sellswords had proven to be resistant to outside greed and had taken the lives of far too many of her Stormtrees, though she knew it was because of her intensified meddling in their spreading affairs.

She had plans in motion to turn the tide of the street war. And it would all begin with the recruitment of the mage she was set to meet today.

Zahnastaazjah and Xalo, armed with their notorious weapons, as always, strolled through her guild district, formerly labeled the North Garrison, now rightfully known as Scarless Square. The walled ward in the city had originally been constructed with a dual purpose, serving as a defense against would-be hostiles and as a base to house hundreds of trained fighters. And to those ends, it still did exactly that.

Nods, bows, salutes, and honorary hails of "Guildmother" addressed her as she trekked down her familiar zone. She took in every man and woman and nodded back. She knew each by name and story and had handpicked only the best of the best, personally involving herself in the meticulous recruitment process of each one earning the privilege of joining her movement. They were not a mob of lowly thugs. They were a guild of professionals, just over five hundred strong, each trained in specialized skill sets, and some couple of hundred more in commissioned informants. These were the Stormtrees.

The sound of steel on steel rang to her left in the training bailey as two score of her men practiced their martial efficiency on each other as required in morning sessions. She made eye contact with their instructor, Usurp the Vellyan, and he paused to nod in respect.

The balding giant man, just at seven feet tall, was considerably fat but undeniably dangerous and surprisingly nimble for his size. His black beard hung in a disheveled bush down to his chest. Usurp's incessantly hoarse voice rasped out orders across the Yard, clearly bellowing more harshly in the presence of his superior.

Usurp was one of her five major underlords and the first to have been promoted by her in the Stormtrees to such rank. He was the only one of them who had originated from the Blue Blades, recruited from Giant's Landing, and she had worked beside him on many heists. He was especially reputed to be her prime henchman, utilized in subjugating smaller upstart gangs for the guild's growth. He was also the only underlord on her roster who controlled more than one still-standing turf gang. He was a bully and a habitual tyrant, but he was known and feared by the entirety of the underworld and trusted by Zahnastaazjah. The cruel killer was perfect for exercising acts of needed coercion in his designated districts of operation.

The savory redolence of smoked bacon and sausage filled Zahnastaazjah's nose as she passed her butcher's shack, with an excess of cooks madly trying to prepare breakfast for the abundance of hungry affiliates. Amaris, the newest up-and-comer of the promising guild talent, stood there chewing down a brief breakfast.

Amaris was a thick and capable street-bred Daynish woman in her thirties with a penchant for scrupulous connections with the locals in several city districts. She carried a lot of valued information about the Boarneck Company specifically and had recently been promoted to overseeing the Stormtrees' interchangeable safe houses and storefronts throughout Goldgarden.

Zahnastaazjah and Xalo then passed the first quarter house of the former guard barracks, now sheltering a plethora of privileged criminal masterminds instead.

Xalo apparently took note of another of her underlords in their midst. "Dockjaw," he said, naming the respected smuggler. "Want me to flag him down to join?"

She pondered the dangerous man. Dockjaw was a Brutongan she had taken in from Tongatown. A large segment of their far-east civilization had pioneered in settling into their own designated district within the city-nation. His skin was more black than brown, almost as dark as the few Lunaril elven she had met. His thick raven locks were twisted into ropelike strands that hung to the back of his shoulders. The southeastern foreigner was likely in his midfifties, from her best estimate, but he displayed no signs of his age in his vitality.

Dockjaw had never been a part of a crime consortium before Zahnastaazjah had inducted him into the Stormtrees. He was a nefarious independent smuggler who contrabanded goods imported from the North Docks.

He was dreaded for his signature method of dealing with those who crossed him. The ruthless Brutongan would strap his adversaries horizontally and facedown to the piers, with just their heads projecting over the dock to face their doom. He fastened them to a thick plank over the length of their entire bodies and strapped their necks to hold their heads upright, facing the horizon, leaving their jaws at the mercy of the rocking jolt of whatever hard boat was moored to the wharf. These were never small boats, and it wasn't always an immediate death, but when the waves crashed right, the victim did indeed feel the crack of their jaw. Sometimes it was instant, right into their throat, but more often than not, it took a few hours upon the twilight of tides for the small ships to do the deed. Dockjaw was a man of honor, however, and had gained quite the following from the North Docks with his conduct.

"They all know they're joining—no need" was all Zahnastaazjah responded to Xalo.

Just as she finished speaking, it was as if Sundown, another of her underlords, had heard her assurance and confirmed it with his presence right alongside them. She never even saw or heard the master of stealth, nor knew what direction he may have approached from.

The plain-looking, black-bearded, raven-haired man was a master at blending into crowds and shifting into disguises. He controlled a vast network of spies and thieves that operated only after dark in both the North Commons and Midway districts in Goldgarden. They were simply known as the Night Street, and for the past decade and a half, they had worked for Zahnastaazjah as her faction specializing in espionage and other affiliated trades.

Zahnastaazjah, Xalo, and now Sundown pressed on, with a visual of the Stormtrees' final two underlords patiently awaiting them in the distance.

Devonduer was one of the humans born into the posterity of the modernized, multimixed lineages, often referred to as "mutts" by those of traditional elemental descendancies that remained purists. He didn't even remotely have talent as a fighter, but that wasn't his purpose as the chamberlain of the guild. He was blessed with insight on all matters relating to money, social connections, and local politics. The charismatic man armored himself like a warrior in iron mail, but it was his mind and influence that had augmented the Stormtrees to the status they remained fortified in today.

The pretty young man always became nervous when he got near Zahnastaazjah or Xalo for daily formalities, and he had an impossible time in hiding the fact. He pulled his long brown hair back in a tail, tying it in place with a small strand of cloth, and shuffled his feet habitually, as if he had been holding in his piss for hours but was afraid to move.

"Scarless. Xalo." Devonduer bowed.

Xalo pulled his spellblade halfway from its scabbard, staring down the man with a glower of promised death, prompting a green ring to flash around his right eye. "You want me to do this here, Scarless, or off the main streets?"

Zahnastaazjah saw the poor mutt's face go gaunt white, his eyes wide in sheer panic, and she believed she might have smelled a bit of that piss now. She shook her head, annoyed at Xalo's ridiculous antics, which she was used to but far from fed up with.

"Devonduer, calm. You know he is joking. When I kill you, I'll do it myself." She smiled and patted him on the shoulder, aware that it would not console him, but that was the point. All her men had to remain in check. *Especially the smart ones. Especially the strong ones. I know how this life works with you human thugs. No different from the Terollar alphas.*

"Let's see this mage," she said, and she looked at her final underlord, standing nearby in front of the doorway to her private guildhouse.

Atrick had been in her employ since that fated day in the Flush when he had turned on his own gang, the Copper Jacks, to help free Xalo. That unanticipated act had saved the man's life. She didn't trust him or like him, but she did rely on his obvious nature. He wanted to live and to live well. He would never betray an employer who paid better, was more unrivaled, and commanded more repute and fear. And so far Zahnastaazjah had no competitors in sight. Atrick was a capable henchman and a natural delegator of lesser men. He wasn't leaving her side anytime soon.

"Pyphan is ready, master an' custodian," Atrick said obediently and simply.

Zahnastaazjah caught Xalo out of her peripheral vision, seeing if the forced titles would coerce the never-smiling spellblade at least into a smirk, but nothing came of it. One of Xalo's demands for his agreement to comply with joining the Stormtrees and allowing

Atrick to live was that during his new employ, Atrick would be forced to refer to him as the custodian, in some poetic justice enacted on the formerly cruel slave handler.

And Zahnastaazjah had never demanded that Atrick refer to her as "master" or ever implied a reference to the title, but regardless, the ex-Copper Jack had stuck true to it since, ever humbled and grateful.

She expected Xalo to come nose to nose with the man and say something intimidating or witty, but nothing transpired this time. There was always half a chance he would. Her Elothian lover was just that unpredictable.

The five of them entered the guildhouse. Zahnastaazjah had refurbished the entirety of the Goldguardian keep. What had once looked like a place to bunk officers, utilized to hold militaristic assemblies, had been transformed into a place of conglomerated ideals and a surplus of vain trophies from successful exploits in the rise of street prestige. The keep of the old North Garrison had been renovated into a hub of leisure for new recruits, promotion celebrations, and the honoring of the elite of her organization with private reward parties.

Hog-tusk necklaces taken from slain Boarneck mercenaries defaced the wall over the hearth. On the adjacent wall hung several daggers with blue ribbons spiraled around their grips. These represented the former members of the Blue Blades who had conformed to become Stormtrees and died in honor through their service. The wall opposite this showcased many Oathemic Cabal knives, with green tassels at the bottom of their hilts, and polearms collected from the fallen Centron Spears. An excess of engraved copper tokens filled a large cauldron over an unlit firepit near the east door. It was up to the brim with signature souvenirs taken from the nuisances of the Copper Jacks gang. And along the wall connected to the entryway, several other mementos of victory were displayed from the luckless gangs that had dared to cross the Stormtrees.

They made their way toward the old sergeant's room, up the stairs. In front of the doorless chamber stood the only elvan in her party—Uubakrath.

He was a Terollar, like her, approaching almost seven feet in height. His light-blond hair was brushed to the back of his scalp, reaching the bottom of his neck, with half his locks twisted into braids interwoven with the rest of the loose strands. His fair skin, pointed ears, and pale green eyes matched her own.

In truth, she knew that Uubakrath was the only individual in her syndicate that she had no real control over. Terollar were rarely seen in Goldgarden—the city that pardoned and welcomed any race from across the wide realm of Penthara. He had randomly appeared to consign himself to her some couple of months back, at the beginning of the new Cycle of Kingfall, right when the Dawning season had begun. Uubakrath had given a cryptic message that he was a gift from her father, Khomo'Jhuvonus, and her son, Sorovronus, but had given little to no detail on the pair's covert machinations in the north, which she had escaped and left as part of her past.

All she knew was that she was stuck with the rather unfamiliar elvan enigma from her homeland—and that he was deadly, which she liked and found useful to her own schemes. She had heard the repute of his name growing up. Uubakrath was known to be over three centuries old and the most famous elvan archer the Glazjhendun of the Glace Isles had ever had. Her father and son had done her a great favor in transferring the celebrated hero to her, and she had no idea why.

"The mage is here waiting, Zahnastaazjah," Uubakrath pronounced in her native tongue. He never spoke in the Civil and never addressed her as Scarless either.

Inside the former North Garrison sergeant's room, she found the man she had been anticipating. Pyphan—the first mage to be inducted into the Stormtrees.

The young man before her appeared to be a mix of northern and maybe Elothian lineage, but one could never be too sure with a mage. While his eyes were green like hers, there was something significantly different between the shade of green in Terollar eyes compared to mage eyes. Hers were dark and natural, while his were vibrantly light with a luminescent halo around both irises. Around his eyes, he had fancied to apply black makeup, enhancing their color, which actually stood to make him appear more sinister rather than feminine. He had the eastlander eyes, but his hair was raven black, which he wore pulled back tight against his scalp and tied behind his head, forming a short tail that touched the top of his spine. His goatee, styled with no mustache, was long and twisted down to his chest. Magemarks resembling golden-hued tattoos ran across his exposed upper body and arms, up to his neck and down his hands, marking his binding to cast tairan elemental magic of the Dawning season.

Pyphan didn't wear much, as if he was prepared for a spell battle in which he would unleash everything inscribed upon him at a given moment. It was known that the rare magic users could only invoke their powers if their magemarks were not concealed by any means. The more powerful in tier a mage became, the more their body became marked with such arcanic imprints.

The mage stood from the empty sergeant's seat and gave a humble bow upon her entry. The man was slight and short in stature, but his body was lean in musculature, the like of which she had never witnessed. Thus were the fables of the mages proven true, as the more powerful they were, the more their bodies were honed to supernatural forms of human fitness.

"Scarless, of the seed of the Glace Isles khomo." Pyphan titled her beyond the Goldgarden regularities. "It is my honor to meet and serve you."

"Pyphan the Dawner." She offered him back a rather mundane appellation, since *Dawner* was the common city slang term for Dawning mages. "The man with no background, the only mage ever to elect to come to our grand city of mass corruption and not join the Mage Ward." She was hinting at her suspicions concerning his obscure history and the fact that he was the only hunder-touched she had met who had chosen to volunteer into an obvious gang instead of conforming to the ensured safe haven of the Mage Ward.

"I actually hate mages even more than he." The green-eyed man inclined his head toward Xalo.

Xalo nonchalantly shrugged, expressionless. "I don't hate mages. I just kill them. Always. And often." There was no joking inflection in his tone; he did well to dominate the hungry sword's desire to possess him into a frenzy to assault the present mage, as Zahnastaazjah was aware. "But I am doing well to resist as of late."

"I know little about you, next to what Devonduer has told us," Zahnastaazjah admitted as she moved on, confident that Xalo was the master of his sentient weapon with his disciplined skill, not the other way around, as with novice spellblades. "But we do not judge men for their pasts here. Your merit with us begins now. I would simply know why it is you have come from afar to seek me out."

"I've met the magic wielders of Mageholme and from your city's district," Pyphan elaborated. "I wasn't born blessed with my gift to dally in peace havens or squabble about arcane theories in fancy schools. They are not me. Nor is the Oathemic Cabal, of whom I have felt the tireless pursuit. I have heard of one place on the mainlands they cannot penetrate, thanks to Scarless, the Crime Queen of Goldgarden."

Zahnastaazjah said nothing for a moment and just stared the magemarked boy down. He was seemingly barely two decades old. She was analyzing him for signs of fear and judging his intent in seeking her out. He may very well have been a spy sent from any one of those associations he had just mentioned. "Dawning mages are the most prized magic users at present. You say you run from the Oathemic Cabal, but they would take you in with open arms. You would be protected by the most untouchable order in the realm. Then there is the Green Byway, the company of fast-travel mages specifically catering to Dawners, all of which are notoriously wealthy beyond what I can offer. I hear they are paying a king's share in gold for new recruits of your kind who can manipulate the tairan. I need to understand why you—"

"I told you. I simply hate mages," Pyphan interrupted—something no one ever did to her. "I am no mindless assassin like the agents of the Oathemic Cabal, who wish to sell their souls to the ranks of perpetual ambiguity with no knowledge of their purpose. I will also never demean myself as a land ferryman for the Green Byway and waste away my talents. The streets talk highly about Scarless and her Stormtrees. You can pay me just as well, and you will."

The mage was dangerously audacious and strikingly confident. She had decapitated men for less. But she was entirely interested.

Pyphan went on to enhance his proposition. "You only endorse the most clever, the most feared, the most trusted killers in the region. But no guild or gang in Goldgarden has ever attained a mage in their ranks."

"Mm-hmm," Zahnastaazjah cooed in interest, but she was still not done with her interview. "What can you do for me, then? I hear you are a tier-three mage. Correct? Explain, and sell yourself."

"Advanced in tier-three, yes. Best you will find in recent times."

Zahnastaazjah was aware that all mages suffered from what was called Transbernation —the need to magically hibernate the season after the one they were bound to, to avoid rapid aging or worse. She knew that all mages had a primer season, a bound season, a slumber season, and the other two following were considered null seasons. Mages could only use the full amount of their spellpower in their bound season and limited amounts of their spells in their primer season, the season prior to the one they were bound to. During her many years alive, she had also come to learn that the rare tier-five mages, sometimes referred to as the archmages, didn't need sleep during their slumber seasons — they just couldn't cast during them, or they would suffer consequences the same. The archmages were the only mages who could utilize their spellpower to some capacity in their null seasons as if it were their primer seasons as well.

Pyphan continued to sell himself as urged. "While I do not boast it, I can cast Traversement for fast-travel services the same as any Green Byway mage. I can carry up to two individuals at a time. I am further revered as an artist in my element, specializing in the manipulation and manifestation of it for combat practicality, rather than in the more popular practice of tairan-forming for utility purposes," he elaborated. "Also, while most Dawning mages can conjure or amplify the effects of poison—"

"Let me stop you there," Zahnastaazjah interrupted.

"She hates poisons," Xalo answered for her. "Medicines and such of any kind, actually. Doesn't trust them. You won't ever use them." She hated when he did that. But she would make no notion of her aggravation, to avoid implying dissent from her authority.

Pyphan studied his new employer and nodded his compliance to her wishes. "I was going to say that I can heal most poisons, and your wounds as well."

She puckered her lips in interest and lowered her green eyes, scanning the Dawning mage up and down. "This will do. Can you do something for us, then?"

"Anything, as you deem fit," the mage replied.

"I need you to help me kill someone."

On her prompt, her five underlords began to filter into the room around her and Xalo. Atrick, Sundown, Devonduer, and even Usurp and Dockjaw now joined, having taken the hint from her earlier passing to join in for the induction of such a powerful new recruit. Uubakrath still manned the door, eyeing Pyphan with a threatening gaze, as if the archer meant to put an arrow through his heart if the mage dared to back out now.

"I am a stranger to you, but no stranger to death-dealing," Pyphan admitted. "What is your bidding?"

Zahnastaazjah assessed Pyphan, studying the deadly faces staring back at him in the old sergeant's chamber. *There is cold in your soul. You do not fear us, do you, Dawner? I have never employed someone who did not fear me.* She contemplated this uneasily but then caught Xalo in her eye, standing beside her. *Aside from this one.*

Zahnastaazjah slid her palm across the tip of her bloodrime spear, cutting her hand open, and held the weapon out toward the mage in the ritual for guild initiations. Pyphan reciprocated the gesture, and she pulled his bleeding palm into hers. She held their grip until she could feel her Terollar impower repairing her new wound, and then she released him and displayed her fully healed hand for Pyphan to see.

"The others carry the scar. You will as well. Pyphan the Dawner, I now recognize you as a Stormtree."

On that prompt, Pyphan bowed low to her and repeated his prior inquiry. "I am honored, Guildmother. Whom am I to kill?"

Zahnastaazjah grinned with a snarl on her lips. "Oh, only the most powerful man in the city and everyone employed by him."

SYMBELLE & FYHEIR (I)

TAIRANCHULA

Look at us, Symbelle. We are beautiful. Accept it ...

She could not accept its pleas. She ignored the incessant voice inside her mind.

Give in and embrace what we are ...

Her eyes twitched between the hourglasses. There were twenty-five, to be exact—the same as there were hours in a full day. The perpetual motion of the sand ebbing toward its downward destiny was the only distraction for sanity in her newfound prison.

Two hourglasses were depleted, and it was on to the third. Time proved that every time one's sand was fully at the bottom, the complex apparatus each vial was connected to would trigger the next to count down another hour. Atop each was a candle that seemed to have a wick purposely designed to expire after an hour as well, so the room became just a little bit darker as time waned.

She sat and fidgeted with her darkened bifocals over and again, rocking in the lone chair furnishing the strange, makeshift room.

You need us. You cannot do this alone. We promise to include you next time ...

She disregarded its insufferable taunts and rocked in her seat some more. She rocked for hours. But she had to know. Curiosity was breaking her weakened resolve. She risked squinting at the image staring back at her in the mirror. She had never been a fan of how she looked, and being forced to gander at the depressing double only made her all the more uncomfortable.

Her short black hair was messy and spiky, not at all what the current trends and stereotypes would consider feminine. Her skin was pale, and her petite build stretched barely five feet high, but there were truly no aesthetic hints about her obscure lineage. Her strange eyes were another story in themselves.

Her otherworldly violet eyes were an ever-shifting nebulous of shades that clouded her pupils and sclera the same perpetually, randomly radiating into a glow out of her control, which she tried to keep in check by her tinted bifocals.

She had been born a hyperi—a phenomenon that occurred in the rare offspring of two tier-five mages. In her youth, she had always assumed she had simply been born with some form of cursed sight, but as she had matured, she had come to know at least the half-truths. The plethora of occasional ghostly lines she saw in the air, the glowing green balls in the distance at times, and that same eerie green aura emanating from certain individuals throughout her life—it was all a testament to the suffering to be endured by an untrained hyperi. However, Symbelle was only vaguely familiar with what her inherent condition was called, known as hypersight, which was an impower afforded only to the hyperi.

She was educated enough to understand that her kind were so rare that long centuries had passed to where no hyperis were reported to have existed at all. She was further apprised that by record number of historical accounts, she was one of the three hyperi alive in the realm on this current day and age, though she was familiar with none of the others, even by name.

Symbelle was unlearned of whom her obviously powerful parents were, or why the absence of their role in her life was so obscured. She was conscious of her hypersight, and that it permitted her to see the ethereal in things, wisps and magic and the unnatural perversions of the elements, but she did not know how to use her ability, nor had any aspirations to discover so.

Symbelle studied herself more with the mirror's afforded opportunity. She didn't like her own face. It was especially unpretty and plain, she inwardly dwelled self-consciously, though such had been her take even before she had suffered horrid scarring.

The particular shape of the mutilation was known as a fool's frown. The marring was something that had been popularized across Az'Eloth by the cruel regional lords in league with one another to make a point to the traveling carnival gypsies accused of cheating the locals with their one-sided games to win hard-earned coin. The lords had eventually had enough, and in the defense of their people, they had sent out militias to capture and punish the carnival masters and their main attractions by marking them with the fool's frown for being thieves, and thenceforth, they had been heralded as dark jesters for all to see their ill intent.

Poor Symbelle had never been a cheating thief or dark jester, yet now she was marked like one and had been since the age of just fifteen years. And while those mentioned were typically carved up by a thin knife, hers had been done drastically differently, with a blunt, burning blade. The shape of the fool's frown remained the same, however. Out of the right crease of her lips was an upward scar in the shape of a forced smile, while the left side turned downward, like a dramatization of sadness. The wound was deep and permanently lifted with a pinkish swell.

Her body was skinny, and her clothes were baggy, never fitting properly or matching, as the concept of modern fashion was lost on her oblivious taste for personal aesthetics.

You are unworthy. That is not what we look like. Why do you make us suffer so?

Symbelle knew she needed her wits about her in the unknown environment. She could not let the voice take over her now, as she had surrendered to it time and again before. But time did not cease. Another hourglass was gone, and then another.

Symbelle shifted from the seat back and forth, then finally tossed the chair into the corner. She began to pace with her eyes to the floor, but the image of herself was still there beneath her feet. Her heart rate had her sweating profusely, and her breathing was as if she had just run uphill through the countryside.

She removed her glasses, hoping that would at least blur the simulacra in the tiny room. There wasn't just one. There were hundreds, maybe thousands. She had never seen a room constructed like this. The ceiling and floor were made of reflective glass, while there was no end or start to the walls, just jutting triangular mirrors that arranged her replicating clones into eternity.

No one came. Time stretched on. Ten hourglasses emptied, and still all was quiet. Except for the voice. It would not stop haunting and teasing, no matter how hard Symbelle tried to ignore it.

Release us, and it can all go away.

Symbelle realized how thirsty she was. She couldn't recall the last time she had a sip of water or bite of food.

The time can pass, and all will be fine. You just need to find us in the mirror. We are right here.

Symbelle didn't like giving in to the voice. All went black when she did, and nothing good would ever come from allowing it to take over. Drastically bad things always occurred when she allowed the voice its turn. And it was becoming increasingly greedy, needing more time in control in latter years. It was becoming ever more dangerous as well. She could never remember what had transpired when it consumed her, but she had been told stories.

Symbelle decided the only way to endure the test was to cheat the voice and the mirrors. She closed her eyes and let herself slip into nostalgia, to fortify her resolve and to blind herself to the duplicates in the room.

She had always been an introvert and could have it no other way. She was terrible with crowds and became nervous and awkward in almost any social scenario. She was even panicking with anxiety in a room full of herself, even though all were quiet recluses, with not a single one speaking to another.

Before the age of six, life had all been a bit of a blur for her. She only knew that it had been spent with her mother and that she had never seen her again since. It was a befuddled, overimagined conception of whatever a child could hold on to at such an age. She remembered people, lots of people, a school, she thought, and colored tattoos on everyone, and the green eyes—many green eyes, and some that had radiant halos in them. She remembered the enchanted fires around her home, impossible to explain.

She could recall nothing about her mother's face other than it was loving, and only that her voice was soft and sweet. Her mother had the mage tattoos on her skin as well, everywhere and in red. Her hair and eyes were vividly burned into Symbelle's memory. She had green eyes like the others, but at times they were pure fire, yet not the kind that burned to hurt someone—the kind that invited one into its comforting warmth. And her mother's hair … Her hair was fire. Harmless strands of fire in every shade that the natural element was, through orange to bright yellow at the ends.

Symbelle recollected the significant toy her mother had given to her on her bornday's sixth anniversary. It was carved from a drakeroot, painted in the likeness of a miniature scale of herself. She had named it *Fyheir*, limitedly inspired as a child by the word for *Flame* used by the extinct Ibyssai elvan race. It seemed that everything in her past, including the subjects she was taught at an early age, revolved around the element of fire.

For whatever indistinct reason against her memory, Symbelle had been stripped from her mother by the same ambiguous individual that had come and gone throughout her life ever since. He was an enigmatic man who talked little and would sometimes appear with seemingly no other purpose than to check in on her. She recalled that he strangely had no face, always hidden behind a hood of impenetrable shadow, with glowing green halos for his eyes, and that whenever he came to visit, it was always cold—unnaturally, unbearably cold.

The first place he had brought her was a large farm just north of the town of Darrowden, in Az'Dayne. The man who owned the farm, Broderick, had a son named Pyphan, two years her junior, whom Symbelle had been taught to refer to as her brother, though not by blood. As Symbelle had grown a little older, she had begun to realize that Pyphan was the same as those she recalled in her early childhood around her mother. Her hyperi sight picked up a special glow about him because he was hunder-touched, which meant that he had been born with a special constitution that permitted him the preconditions to one day become a mage and wield elemental magic. No matter what games they played with one another, she could always seek out and find Pyphan, being drawn to the presence of his inborn wisp.

The area around Darrowden was especially prominent for the enriched soils that offered an abundance of unique plants not found anywhere else in the country. Such vegetation was harvested by the farmers to extract the largest variety of herbal remedies exported by the Az'Dayne Dominadom. It was a common practice for the inhabitants of Darrowden not involved in such agricultural trades to commission themselves as apothecaries or toxicologists.

Symbelle had come to see Broderick as her foster father, just as Pyphan had felt like family for her as well. Broderick was a master in experimentations on a variety of poisons and remedies, both local and foreign. It was through his meticulous teachings that she first learned this practice. As she grew older, she caught on to the fact that he had many business dealings with the same clandestine order and that each time they visited, she was strictly bidden to hide and remain silent.

Then one day, when she was fifteen, it all came to an end. Armed agents in silver cloaks stormed the farm by surprise, strung up and hanged Broderick in front of her, and gave her the fool's frown for resisting during the tragic episode while she had been forced to watch. The men tried to kidnap Pyphan in the process, but they were rescued by the mysterious mage who had kidnapped her from her mother, who finally introduced himself as Coldborn. Her memory had faded of what had occurred, as if it had been forced into a forgotten pocket in the back of her mind, but she did remember what happened next.

It was then that she had finally been told by Coldborn what she was, a hyperi, and of her special inborn sight, but he had gone into vague detail of what it all entailed for her. While Pyphan remained with Coldborn, never to be seen again after their departure, she was escorted a bit more north to the hidden academy of Tairanchula. This was an unpublicized university of the alchemical arts and advanced engineering, sanctioned by a powerful, clandestine organization never disclosed to her.

The professors there were expressly given instruction to keep her presence at Tairanchula secret, but to deliver the highest level of private tutoring so that she could master the crafts in which she excelled. Symbelle had developed at a genius-level rate for retaining knowledge and innovating new theories. She understood how to weaponize certain projects between chemical compounds and their apparatuses, including mastering pyrotechnics and reagent experimentation.

Instead of being treated as a prodigy in the many sciences, however, Symbelle gained no favor from her envious and bewildered professors. This opened the doors for Tairanchula's ensemble of resentful mentors to go against the behest of the shadow mage who had brought her there in the first place. Symbelle had been injected into the public settings of the school by her twentieth year, where she fast ascertained that she was the only female at the academy.

She had tried to embrace her life in the surreptitious college, but it became clear to her that she would not be accepted by her peers. Her glowing violet eyes left her shunned as an outcast in a region where anything resembling magic was loathed and castigated, giving no aid to her already asocial tendencies. She was a target for malice, heavily bullied and beaten by her male schoolmates, allowing their pride to treat her as a rejected oddity, remaining prey for easy victimization. She ignored the abuse to the best of her repressed ability, immersed in a passion over her craft. As the malevolent acts of her colleagues continued, she clung like a child in search of solace to the one relic left by her mother, the only token of sentiment in her possession—the tiny drakeroot toy, Fyheir, which never left her side.

But then one day her inhumane peers took their violent pranks too far. It began with her mulled wine being spiked with an untested herbal blend, each component known to inflict excruciating abdominal pain. The ingredients imbibed felt like fire in her throat and gut, and the internal agony that followed was harrowing. She remembered that even the projectile vomit had felt like scorching steam, and the water in her body had evaporated to leave her in a state of near-lethal dehydration. But it didn't kill her. It kept repeating in phases as she curled and twitched, writhing and dying, pleading and praying. And then they came in—all the cruel boys of her class.

They started by stealing Fyheir and burned the little root doll in front of her. As she somehow clung to consciousness against her will, something inside her mind forced her to remain awake and watch.

The bullies stripped her of all clothing, with a hungered look as if they meant to defile her, but they whispered to her that she was far too ugly ever to be touched by a man or a woman and that all would now see it. They took the torch to her naked body between her spread legs just long enough to blister her skin into more permanent aesthetic ruin. Just before it all went black, she heard the pleading and praying, but it was not to any known god or goddess. It was to another name. And that was when the voice came to her for the first time: *Shh, shh now, Symbelle … Your Fyheir is here to save you …*

And Fyheir did. By some unknown miracle, Symbelle survived the fits of the untrialed poison. She was not saved by any ethical regret from the young brutes. She was not found by the professors. There was no hero to help her. Only Fyheir, and Symbelle's destiny was thenceforth entwined with its power over her.

Things had forever changed for her that day. Symbelle had no vengeful desires to retaliate against her adolescent tormenters, but Fyheir always did. Still, Symbelle remained focused on her interests and studies, trying to resist the incessant persistence from the new voice of chaos inside her mind. When Fyheir first came to her after her near-death experience, the voice was subtle when it introduced itself. But as time progressed, it became louder and tougher to mute. It came often, almost constantly, as a copossession of her body.

Symbelle was an intelligent individual with the flaw of being weak-willed in her resolve toward stronger personalities. She could strive to resist the dominant character residing within her, but it was becoming more challenging.

Release us. Thirteen hourglasses gluttoned of sand in their bellies. This is a test from the unknown. Let it pass.

She was so thirsty. She was so tired. She just needed sleep.

They will feed us when we wake. Let us quench the thirst we feel with pure fire. Embrace it.

Symbelle closed her glowing eyes and placed her bifocals over them. She blindly walked to the edge of a mirror in the small room and slowly placed her palms on the glass, leaning wearily against it. She took a deep breath, preparing herself for the transition.

Yes, Symbelle, look at us, Fyheir whispered inside her mind.

And she did. When Symbelle opened her eyes, a manic smile spread across her face, and her eyes went wide and mad with excitement. She was now Fyheir. And as anticipated, it all went black again.

* * * * *

Symbelle came to after her spell of possession had washed away. In fact, she woke just as the last grains of sand emptied from the final hourglass. Hour twenty-five was over. A whole day in a room full of thousands of herself and Fyheir.

Suddenly, just as the last candle wick burned out and the glass room went dark, a dim hue from sconce torches returned a faint light to the obscure chamber. A familiar shadowy figure appeared before her, shrouded by a hood: Coldborn. She half expected Fyheir to say something snide due to his chilling presence, but the mage's power seemed to stifle her internal conflict into silence. Coldborn didn't speak at first, purely making an assessment of her. Glowing green halos rimmed his eyes. The matching aura of green that enveloped him was so strong, it seemed it could light up the whole room. But it didn't; only absolute darkness existed beyond his back. *No natural eyes can see what you see. The green in all things – the magic. That is our sight alone,* Fyheir reminded Symbelle of her impower.

His deep voice echoed back with a cold mist escaping his mouth. "Welcome back, Symbelle."

"Coldborn," she whispered, astonished, fully recognizing the cryptic watcher from her past.

The tenebrous mage scolded her tone. "You voice that name as if you know who I am, though we both know that you have never known." He shifted tangents with no pause for her to argue. "Do you know where you are?"

She glanced in all directions around the mirrored cell. Strangely enough, Symbelle only now realized she had no idea how she had come to be here. "In an eternal prison of myself?"

The obscure mage riddled back. "You are not free, Symbelle, and you never have been, but this does not make you my prisoner. I ask again, though. Do you know where you are? Do you know who I am, truly?"

"I do not know," she answered in defeat.

"Good. If you did, then we would not be who we are," he replied in his incomprehensible nature, with no suggestion of whom the word *we* was implying. "What is the last memory that you recall?"

"My graduation ceremony at Tairanchula. I was being called by name to come forward." Symbelle recollected at least that, but nothing after she had reached the altar with her professors and peers.

"Keep going." With each word, the frost in the air thickened, as if he were standing on an open tundra of the north. A sheer aura of cold emanated from him, like he was some manifestation of raw shadow in the flesh. "What happened next?"

"It all goes black. It happens to me. I have a …" She paused, unable to explain it.

Do not tell him about us. It will go bad for you.

"I have contracted a condition. The next time I came back to myself, I was here."

"Your condition is a consequence of maturing as an untrained hyperi. Your internal suffering stems from adversities that I did not anticipate. It is quite complicated, but the time is nigh for you to learn," her calculating mentor elaborated.

Coldborn then continued to enlighten her on subjects far beyond anything she had been taught before. "If your fractured memory serves, before I brought you to Tairanchula, I briefly explained what your hypersight can do. You were born with the phenomenon of pure perception. You can see the elemental descendancies and impowers within another, including the hunder in living elven and traces of wisps from dead elven, among other arcane effects or magic anomalies in your vicinity. Essentially, from diligent practice, you could even track down elven, mages, spellblades, umbran, qindrid, and other hyperis if I decide to have you trained by the one person I know that can. But trust is a scarce commodity in the cycle we live in. I am not the only one who has known of this power within you. I have ensured your safety by keeping your whereabouts unknown to those who still seek you out, to exploit you as a tool for their own ambitions. The most dangerous one especially." He paused for far too long before revealing whom. "Your mother."

"My mother!" Symbelle's voice squealed out, more a protest than a question, but she collected herself. The concept of her mother had been fractured into a distant phantom remnant of her youngest years, barely conjurable to mind. "You did take me from her, I remember. But who would steal a child from their—"

"A father would. *Your* father," Coldborn interjected in a monotone admission void of any sentiment.

Symbelle was paralyzed. Fyheir was silent. The world and time itself seemed to have stopped for her to attempt to digest the information that was not meant for the average individual to consume in one sitting. She did not even realize her mouth had spoken the words aloud. "You are my father ..."

"Your parents are not the subject of today. You asked instead about Tairanchula." He deftly dodged from emotional detours like a callous professional.

"Very ..." She struggled to comply, still dumbfounded and unsure how to feel. "Very well, Father. I do not know what to ask. What happened to me after my graduation? How did I get here?"

"That was six days ago," he said, surprising her.

"Oh." Again, she was at a loss for what to think or say. She searched for Fyheir for illumination, considering her alternate personality to blame, but the voice remained mute for now. "It has never lasted that long."

"You killed them, Symbelle," her father disclosed. "Every one of them. Tairanchula is no more."

Shh now, Symbelle. If you had only asked, we would have told, Fyheir taunted her in its typical sadistic manner.

Coldborn further clarified. "I learned that you had become maltreated and exposed, which compromised my preconditions with the academy. My agents subdued the students and the professors, but that is not what wrought their deaths. You unleashed something growing inside of you — a volatile version of yourself. You burned them and the university into a mass grave of ash."

A darkness washed over her eyes. Her head felt twice the weight of her entire body. The room began to spin.

Yes, Symbelle. Let it take you. We will protect us, Fyheir coerced.

A flashback of images flooded and fled her mind. She was afforded a glance at the many men attired in all black, with their horrifying black masks that made their stone faces appear as if they were ripped open bug hives. She also saw the fire and heard the screams and smelled the burning bodies. It was just a memory that Fyheir was allowing her to relive, though now that she did, she knew she could never again forget the smell.

"I ..." she stuttered, "I am sorry. I am not a killer." She bent over and vomited, confirming the sincerity of her statement. The wooziness overcoming her was only escalating as reality settled in.

"The ghosts of Tairanchula would argue otherwise, that you *are* a killer," Coldborn replied as a torch above went out.

Symbelle felt Fyheir jerk inside her.

Her father moved closer to her then. He seemed to be an avatar of pure darkness. Even up close, she couldn't distinguish the contours of her father's face behind his hood. Two glowing halos hovered where his eyes should have been, floating in a void underneath his garments. She was sure it was simply a trick of her delusional mind.

"A normal person would need time to let the impact of emotion and confusion pass, but you are not a normal person, are you? And we do not have the luxury of time. So you must evolve for me. Are you ready to try?"

"I will try," she meekly declared with no confidence in herself. "Pyphan, my foster brother, went with you over a decade ago. Where is he?"

"Pyphan has been one of us since that day, a part of the organization," he expounded. "The last you saw him, he was merely hunder-touched. He is now a capable and dangerous Dawning mage, and through our tutelage he is also an assassin for one of the orders under my control."

The pieces he was insinuating were in play were linking together in Coldborn's puzzle, but that did not mean Symbelle was ready to accept it. She wanted to ask more about the revelation of her foster brother being a mage assassin, but nothing was coming as a surprise to her in the bizarre scenario.

"You are to be my greatest assassin of all, Symbelle, just as was always intended." Her father admitted what she did not want to hear. "But you are a unique marvel in our industry—in fact, so rare that only a select few in my waning circle are even privy to your involvement."

Symbelle's heart calmed, and she felt the sweltering sweat on her chest and brow diminish to an uncomfortable chill. "You want me to kill someone." Her voice was hardly audible. She comprehended that he had just boasted she was his greatest assassin in the works. "You want me to kill much more than a single someone."

Coldborn produced a single small scroll sealed with black wax and a green diamond seal. "This is a writ. A writ is a legal contract, either scribed by me to represent the organization or penned by those empowered to make judgments for Az'Dayne, that will bind you to complete it once opened. These writs will drastically change the circumstances of those within, typically by fate of death, but not always. The names or groups you receive in the writs must be handled with thorough efficiency unless absolved by me alone in the process. Do you understand?"

She timidly heeded his encouragement and opened the writ without saying a word.

Target: Oldan Boldandgold, founder of the Boarneck Company
Last Location: Bridgeville, Goldgarden

Target: Amethyst, Seat of the Red
Last Location: Seven Seats, Goldgarden

"But I do not know how to"—*kill,* she wanted to say, but did not—"carry out a writ. Look at me. What did they do to deserve to die?"

"What they deserve is irrelevant. When they die is inevitable. Why it is you who will complete this writ has been determined. You cannot undo the path I have set you on," he riddled coldly.

She swallowed so hard she felt the lump she choked down had caused an instant bruise in her throat. "How then?" Symbelle dared to entertain.

"You will become a triple agent, through the Stormtrees, and then the Boarneck Company. You must infiltrate the largest gang in the city, and manipulate their leader, Scarless, Crime Queen of Goldgarden, into killing Oldan and Amethyst herself. And this must all be done in public with witnesses, so as not to appear that our organization had any involvement," her shadowy father elaborated on the impossible. "Pyphan is already in place within Scarless's guild, working to secure you a position to join him in due time. After your initiation with us has been fulfilled, your brother will come for you."

Symbelle emboldened her will to counter with some ground of defiance. "I am no prisoner, yet I am not free. You are my father, yet such is not an eligible topic. I am an assassin, yet I have not been trained to kill, nor wish to be, but my destined targets and new affiliates sound to be just that—straight killers. And I am indebted to an organization I do not even know the name of?"

The images of her clones in the glass began to fade in the dimming light, only faintly illuminated by the violet glow in her hyperi eyes. One torch remained defiant, clinging to life.

"Symbelle, you are in the Oathemic Cabal."

She heard her father's voice in every direction as blackness swallowed the chamber, and all went blind in its perpetual emptiness. And somehow she knew that Coldborn had vanished from the room.

ATHANIEL (I)

AN ASSASSIN'S LIFE

Death was on the palate tonight. And though he was trained to hold no penchant toward it, to be an emotionless dealer of such pre-chosen fates, he admitted to himself that he secretly needed these days.

Life as a silent killer made one more numb than even the most battle-hardened soldier. Battle-bred fighters saw their enemies as a means to an end. They lived with their dying screams in their dreams and shared the spilled blood of those they felled in their own open wounds. They hated their foes because those foes hated them back, for no other reason than that their commanders and countries told them to, with reasons justified by a history of strife or other causes deemed worthy. But an assassin's life was different.

He had no enemies, and none alive could call him one back. He heard no screams in his dreams, because his victims never had a chance to utter a sound. He had no open wounds from a single encounter, and not a drop of blood had ever defaced his garb. His foes were not foes, but faceless targets instead. They could not hate him, because they did not know him, and he did not know them. Ending their existence was a cold and simple unquestioned duty. Nothing else.

He was Athaniel Chandoss, an assassin of the Oathemic Cabal, assigned to a specific faction of stealth-oriented killers, known as the Hive Order, who were always paired with a partner.

His intuitive eyes clung to every detail on the bustling port promenade. Hopeless imitators of highborn citizens drenched themselves in rank perfumes, commingling in the company of filthy fishmongers and crabbers. Half the ships in the harbor seemed hardly river-worthy enough to make it even to O'Spice, the next port westward down the Triune, but he knew better for the merited reputation of the border city of Uslar.

Every boat on their docks and each sailor manning them were weathered but hardened representations of what true experience looked like. The Uslar vessel crews were known for their nautical caravans, traveling everywhere along the coast of the Conqeron Sea, and all throughout the Tairancian, Daynish, and Elothian river systems, as well as Taira's Scar. The tradesmen were no strangers to fending off pirates and other hostiles, and they were even keener to be news heralds from coastal town to coastal town.

It was one of these well-traveled harbingers that was marked for death today: the first mate of the ship *Silent Knight*. But there was nothing silent about Athan's target at all. Solomon Gunter was the mediator between the Silverbacks' main Tairancian outpost and their enemy agents infiltrated into key cities throughout Az'Dayne.

The Silverbacks had at first been nothing more than a provoking thorn in the side of Az'Dayne's Pentagogue infrastructure, but in the past few years the enigmatic opposing organization had multiplied in number and influence. Being a step ahead of the Oathemic Cabal was an impossible feat none could boast of to date, but the growing clandestine guild of the Silverbacks remained relentless in their recruiting and reach. To make matters worse, they used similar tactics of elimination as the Cabal, even utilizing mages and spellblades in their ranks. In fact, the Silverbacks were so efficient as an enemy, it was almost as if there were a leak, or several, within the Oathemic Cabal's own ranks. Their methods were swift and competent with never any trace for discovery.

The true leaders and motives of the Silverbacks had so far eluded the masters of Athan's guild, but the Cabal's informants had recently uncovered many principal exposures about the whereabouts of the Silverback agents on Az'Dayne soil and of the delegates they reported to.

Solomon Gunter would receive no questioning, no torturing to extract information, not even any apprehension whatsoever. That was not what the Hive Order did. If the Oathemic Cabal deemed it necessary to dispatch members of such a sect, then assassination was called for, with no hope for recourse.

Often Oathemic writs issued for group victims included the utilization of at least one mage from the Hunder Order.

The Hunder Order was the first faction to exist upon the

Oathemic Cabal's origination. These were the mages, the ones who chose not to run and hide in the sanctuary region of Mageholme. These were those of their kind who were oathbound to their sovereign country of Az'Dayne.

There was a supplementary reason for the Cabal's deployment of Dawning mages during the cycle's first season: their power of Traversement, enabling them to enter into an ethereal state and fast-travel throughout the local regions, transporting the assassins with them.

The Hive Order assassin pair never knew the born name or face of the mage they were being teamed with. The mages were only differentiated by their individually designed masks, always shaped as some type of fabled monster. Athan and his partner, Daerlem, always recognized the mages assigned to them, due to their signature masks. There were not many mages left in the order, so the few capable Dawning mages with Traversement capability were not that difficult to distinguish. The assassins gave their affiliated mages nicknames, as forfeit to ever learning their actual identities.

It was Stoneplay assigned to them today. Even without Stoneplay's custom mask, Athan could tell by the awkward way he walked and talked, by the way he never looked at people, only the plants and flowers, only the trees and stones. He was a most passionate acolyte of the tairan element, a true specialist in utilizing the element when taking out specified targets on a writ.

Stoneplay was nowhere in sight. He was hiding in the adjacent alley behind the barber's house, waiting for Athan and Daerlem to finish their project.

Athan could see his partner, however. Daerlem Black was a northman orphan, Barredish by blood, raised in the Oathemic Cabal since the age of ten. He had first been assigned to the Nectar Order, the faction of writ-runners, watchers, and informants. By the age of eighteen, he had been promoted to the Hive Order, having proven his stealth prowess and skills with a blade.

The assassin was in his midtwenties, had short-cropped black hair and dark brown eyes, was smooth in the face, and was always sinister in mood, with an incessant enthusiasm for wickedness. He was quite the opposite of Athan in his professional disposition. There wasn't a bone of compassion in Daerlem's body. Some boys were just born with an affinity for cruelty.

Daerlem's guise as a painted jester for the kill to come was probably the most fitting for his demeanor. Athan never thought the roaming city clowns were funny in the least. Their larks were intended to be jovial and make others laugh, but they were always done at another's expense, always derogatory, foul, repulsive humor that Athan found unamusing. Daerlem seemed to think his own detestable antics were acceptable, and they were at best tolerated and ignored.

Athan himself played the opposite role for this writ. He sat in silence as a rag-patched vagrant, hooded and hidden among the bustle of other lowborn transients. He stroked the false beard glued to his clean-shaven cheeks. The dirty blond thing was itchy and long, contrasting with his red hair, concealed beneath his cloak's hood.

One always acted as the observer, while the other focused on diversion. And just so, Athan watched, as he had done for two hours. The Oathemic Cabal assassins were meticulous in their craft—instant in their kills but patient in preparation.

Some fumbling minstrel could be heard failing on the chords of his psaltery while his half-man companion tried to keep rhythm on a small tabor. It was annoying but not distracting.

The same wayward teens kept drunkenly stumbling over Athan's feet, obstructing his view as they obnoxiously conquered the boardwalk. But his focus was unwavering. They were frustrating but not upsetting.

An oyster peddler intoned a repetitive chant in a circle for over an hour without skipping a beat. A group of fishermen offloaded their catch from their ship to their shop in a human chain of a decem dockhands, all working in trained unison to get the day's quota fulfilled in time. A chubby and scarred harlot tugged her way through the desperate sailors that had been out at sea for too long, testing her luck. He heard her price herself down three times once he started listening.

It was all quiet noise, faint smells, and hazy sights as the late sun waned on the horizon. His vision was tunneled in on the fated victim in his issued writ. Solomon Gunter was in front of him, and Athan never lost sight of the dead-man-to-be.

Solomon was about as mutt as it got, with so much obvious mix in his heritage that Athan deemed the poor sod more exotic for it.

Solomon was dirty, yet he showered in tried class and had been raised on the hard streets, but he carried an aura of cunning about him. His brown hair was long and beautiful, like a woman's, and his eccentric beard was carefully sculpted at an angle that made his jaw seem strong and triple its length. He was a man who spent half his coin on grooming and fashion, with the flaw of pretending he had been born above his lowborn station.

The assassins had already been made privy to the fact that Solomon's first stop in Uslar's port would be the man's favored barber, as it evidently always had been when returning from voyages from around the other coastal harbors. All was already arranged. And it was time.

Solomon was finished with his business with the captain and crew of the *Silent Knight*, and he was now making his way to a routine visitation for his typical grooming session and scheduled meet with the other Silverback agents, who would be nowhere to be found. The barber was in the Silverbacks' pocketbooks, as were the clients that visited on this hour. But there was no barber now. There would be no clients. The day had been bloody and busy for Athan and Daerlem not long prior to the waiting game for Solomon.

As Solomon made his way off the boardwalk toward the barber, the two assassins knew it was time to initiate the ploy. Daerlem, as the painted fool, broke into an elaborate flaming juggling act. It was evidently so impressive that even their mark turned around to take notice before leaving the vicinity of the docks.

It was only Athan who followed for now, though. His partner might have played the role of a joker, but Daerlem was a king in the game of capturing attention. The two had played this act in their rotation time and again, and Athan knew what came next.

Solomon rounded the alley corner, oblivious to the silent, shrouded vagabond close on his heels. But Athan took no chances in his stealth practices. The distance to the kill closed.

Solomon's head tilted upward toward the obvious diversion just over the adjacent rooftop, coming from the seaward promenade they had all just been on. Daerlem's intended fire was already blazing, and the smoke had taken over the skies. The city watch and every citizen in the harbor district would be momentarily mesmerized by the sudden inferno.

Solomon then shot a glance at the unexpected speaker on the

barber's porch, standing just outside the open door to the purged venue front.

"Three coins for your trouble?" Stoneplay, cloaked and concealed, appeared in the corridor to the unmanned shop, tossing three signature tokens in the vicinity of the agent's boots.

Stoneplay then disrobed, displaying his bare upper body and the golden magemarks across his throat, arms, and torso. Over his face was his mask depicting blocks of stone over his skin. An arcanic glyph flared up green in the middle of his chest as he activated a detrimental spell to open the ground to swallow and crush Solomon's feet up to his ankles—such was a common tactic used by Oathemic Dawning mages.

Solomon's wide eyes, etched with pure dread, were focused more toward the monetary pieces in front of him than his crippled state, it seemed. "Three-coined? No," he pleaded to stall, cognizant of the inevitable outcome. It was a popular kill token to be *three-coined* by Oathemic assassins before they executed the victims from their writs. "Oathemics. Wait!"

Athan, having seen it happen over a hundred times, still couldn't help but watch in fascination the way Stoneplay invoked his power, drawn from the tairan element. The mystery of magic would never cease to amaze him, and he was numb toward his victim's pleas for mercy.

Solomon's eyes caught all three assailants just before it ended. The mage stood his ground, unmoving. Athan rushed forward, still dressed as a street vagrant, but he had now donned the infamous mask of the Oathemic Cabal's death-dealers to seal the deal. Daerlem suddenly appeared, sneaking up just behind the man, wearing a matching mask.

The grey masks of the Oathemic Cabal's Hive Order were void of any humanoid feature except for the blank semblance of the lips. Appearing similar to rips in the face were vertical patterns that resembled openings to a nest of something sinister manifesting underneath, as yet unhatched. Even though Athan was one of the assassins himself, he had to admit he had never before witnessed anything more unsettling than the design of the intimidating mask.

The Silverback agent went to pull a simple knife sheathed at his belt, turning quickly to face down Athan first, but that was when Daerlem's punch gauntlet opened up Solomon's lungs from the back with the small blade that was fitted to the fist.

By the time Solomon's surprised, dying face could twist to look upon Daerlem, Athan's identical bladed punch gauntlet had entered through the man's chest, bursting open his heart.

The three Oathemic agents quickly arranged the man's body in a trademark display of Silverback victims slain by the Cabal. Stoneplay opened up the ground once more to sink Solomon's corpse up to the waist. His torso was leaned back, with one of the token coins cupped between both palms across his chest and the other two coins over each eye. Solomon Gunter's writ was complete.

With no time wasted, Stoneplay put his left hand on Athan and his right hand on Daerlem, channeling his power of Traversement. Several seconds after activation, the two assassins were rapidly moving in an incorporeal blur out of Uslar in Tairancia toward Orlaithe in Az'Dayne, their next destination for the follow-up writs issued by their order. Within twenty minutes, they had traveled close to two hundred leagues along the Triune, past the Cidarian Keeps and down the familiar bank of the AzXander River.

Orlaithe was a thriving city in Az'Dayne that stood as a historic testament to the Dominadom's defensive capabilities when pressed by their former neighboring enemy, the Elothian Empire. The famous Cidarian Towers that surrounded this region may not have survived the brutal wars, but the fortified castle city itself had never fallen. The eastern front between the city main and the river harbors had been fully renovated, with bustling life and new villages, expanding the populace three times over since the Daynish had defeated the Elothians, absorbing their lands into two separately seized countries—both Az'Eloth and Old Elothia. There had been relative peace with few local uprisings since Athan's country had usurped their homeland—at least nothing worth noting since Athan had been alive.

But Athan cared little to reminisce about the history of wars and politics. He was a man of simple tastes and complex tasks. The kill writ involving Solomon Gunter was a contingency contract. There were still more that needed to die today.

Through the gates of Orlaithe, the three Oathemics fluttered past every oblivious citizen in their way, seemingly hovering, deftly navigating around every man, woman, child, or obstacle in their way. Split-second stalls were made for the mage to investigate waypoints where secret signs had been placed by the Nectar Order, leaving an incognito treasure hunt toward their next destination within the city.

Athan knew when they reached it and had already deemed it obvious before any further clues were given. In the oldtown district of Orlaithe, down the most unvisited street in the city, was the front that was the Silverback safe house that had just been discovered. The two-story shop sported a crooked placard over the post just outside, which read MOOR AND MOOR BAUBLES, representing a boast of miscellaneous trinkets and novelties hauled in from the unappealing region of the Sevenmoors. This store wasn't meant to draw a single type of customer, and yet it remained open.

The Oathemic Cabal had ascertained the truth about the front shortly after uncovering the information on Solomon. Their fates were intertwined. Athan had carried out this bloody procedure many times before.

A ragtag boy, freshly in his teens, played with a bouquet of colored weeds from a nearby urban orchard. He appeared to be blind, with a patch over each eye, but Athan knew it was all a practiced pretense. The kid was a stranger to the three in front of him now, but no stranger to the Cabal. Athan could always discern an Oathemic watcher agent when he saw one.

The Cabal referred to them as *vultures*, just as the assassins' guild titled their young spies as *rats* and their couriers as *crows*. The vultures were the middlemen between the rats, crows, and assassins of the Hive Order. These vulture boys were rightly named for the way they circled around the soon-to-be dead marks that the Cabal had issued a writ out for.

The boy never even glanced at Athan, Daerlem, or Stoneplay. He just tossed weed after weed on the ground by the basement hatch, and then both of his eye patches in the same pile. *Nine Silverback agents inside. Not fighters. All spies. Asleep for now. Take the basement.* The codes were simple to decipher. *This is their safe house on Az'Dayne soil.*

With any regard for gratitude, the Oathemic assassins dispersed from the vulture acting as a blind boy and moved to make their way inside the safe house through the basement. Athan and Daerlem afforded one minute to discard the disguises they had used in Uslar and donned concealing black garb, fitting their Hive Order masks back in place.

The hatch door downstairs was accessible, with no hindrances, seemingly prepicked by their young associate nearby. Together, the assassins shot a glance at the empty dusk-lit street before entering downstairs into the basement. The city watch in Orlaithe doubled in number with their patrol at dark and tripled in the more dangerous oldtown district. This had to be fast.

Stoneplay left his robe at the base of the stairs and silently trailed them with his torso bare, exposing his gold magemarks to easily access his tairan-based spells.

Other than the excess of crates of odds and ends, there were eight basic cots toward the staircase on the far side of the room that went to the first level of the store. Only two of the reported nine enemy agents were in their beds. *All sleeping at this hour?* It didn't matter now. They were inside. The deed was getting done.

Athan crept up beside one of the sleeping Silverbacks, and Daerlem matched him, standing over the other in his floor bed. Athan didn't look at the man's face as he did it. He never looked at their faces. He pushed his long dagger into the slumbering agent's heart while Daerlem completed his assassination with his typically more gruesome overkill, a muzzling pillow over the man's head and several stabs to the side of his neck. The assassins' kill knives, with green tassels attached to the ringlet pommels, were left in the bodies as a signature of the Hive Order's presence.

They didn't waste a minute without movement on a mission. Directly up the stairs, on the store's ground level, the next two victims came into sight. Fortunately, though, both were sleeping in their chairs. The element of surprise was still on the Oathemics' side.

The closest one had his back turned to the intruders, slumped in his seat with an empty bottle and a handful of spilled dice, never having time to wake from his dream as Athan slipped a wire garrote around his neck, swiftly strangling him before his eyes could ever open again.

The other Silverback across the room had his feet propped up on one chair as if it were an ottoman, and his back reclined awkwardly in another, facing the front door, which Athan noticed was barred from the inside. He was armed with a loaded light crossbow resting across his lap—a weapon he never had the chance to use.

Daerlem had made it more than halfway across the store's

gallery, almost upon the man, when the first woken Silverback stumbled into the gallery from a back room, utterly unaware, by ill-timed happenchance.

The oblivious, unarmed Silverback barely got to catch a glance at Daerlem before Athan let loose a precise throwing knife that planted itself underneath the man's chest cavity. One of Daerlem's throwing knives followed suit without delay, impaling the unfortunate just below his right collarbone.

The dying agent gave a surprised shriek loud enough to wake the entire shop and fumbled to collapse to the wooden floor, but when his body found the floor it was no longer wood. It had been magically transmuted to a cushion of soft mud. Stoneplay was there in the background, ready to remedy any shortcomings or uncertainties they might come across.

The Silverback crossbowman in the chair suddenly stirred but only awoke in time to witness Daerlem's blade slashing across his throat. The enemy informant slumped back into the same position he had been in just moments prior, lifeless, as if nothing had changed.

The agent in the mystically made mud squirmed and pleaded for life in unintelligible mumbling but only received Daerlem's boot on his throat, slowly crushing his windpipe, as a mercy. Athan's partner retrieved their throwing knives from the dead agent's torso and returned Athan his once the Silverback lay still.

The three Oathemics progressed through the back room and then carefully up the steps to the second story of the safe house. Athan, taking the lead, caught sight of one of the men fleeing to the master office at the end of the hallway, where he could hear the panicked whispers from the remainder of the Silverback informants inside.

"They are here—two Hivers and a Dawner!"

"That means the Oathemics have gotten to Solomon. It's too late."

"They may take us in if we talk. Their numbers are thin. We have ten to their one in our growing ranks."

"We should kill you where you stand! Traitorous talk!"

"Fools! If that's two Hivers outside the door, then there will be no talk!"

"I hear these things can't even fight face-to-face. They're just backstabbers and sleep takers. Cowards with daggers in the shadows. If they come through that door, let's rush them!"

"And what about the mage?"

Four different voices. Two weapons drawn. Three moved to the door. Athan signaled back to Daerlem, and the two edged toward the cracked entryway leading into the office. They stood on either side of the door, waiting to initiate the attack that would conclude the assassinations for the day. They just needed the signal.

The green glow emanating from Stoneplay's golden magemarks meant it was time for the finale. The door in front of them shattered into splinters, the wooden shrapnel bursting inward like a bomb throughout the office. And in they went.

A half-blinded assailant flailed a saber wildly, but simultaneously the two synced killers proved their martial reputation of not being able to fight face-to-face untrue. As Athan plunged his dagger into the Silverback's kidney, Daerlem struck him in the lung, with Athan instantly following in the liver. Then Daerlem slashed deep underneath the bicep toward the armpit, and finally, Athan gashed him open on the upper inner thigh. The dying agent was bleeding out from several places, with few seconds left to live.

Their unison strikes didn't stop there; they opened the neck and heart in many places at once on the second armed agent. The two were dead before the third and fourth could register their demise.

But Stoneplay was already on those. His tairan glyphs glowed over his exposed body, and the wooden floor divided in a variety of directions. The Silverback nearest the fragmented door rode the ride, sliding back all the way to the wall, with a plank from the flooring flying up to mold around his waist, fastening him in place as the plank melded with the wall. The other Silverback simply had the floor beneath him open up, forcing him to fall back to the first floor, where he landed hard on a broken ankle and twisted knee.

"Please!" the agent trapped against the wall cried. "I know much about the whereabouts of other safe houses in Az'Dayne! Hallion's Harbor, Redlake—"

"We already know. They are being purged the same," Stoneplay stoically responded to the rattled man's vain appeals for clemency. The mage's gold glyphs fired up green again, and multiple floor planks arose from their fittings to wrap around the agent's skull and crush the life out of him.

Daerlem nimbly leaped down to the first floor and broke the neck of the final, crippled agent in two places. Athan landed surefootedly next to his partner, and the two assassins glanced up at the mage standing over them.

"Finish up," Stoneplay directed as he tossed down another writ for Athan to catch, stamped with the same orange wax seal of the Az'Dayne Dominadom as the others he had just completed. "We are done in Orlaithe. I part ways with you here. Your next writ begins now. The seasons of Kingfall are going to be a busy cycle for the Oathemic Cabal."

Athan and Daerlem did as instructed and plunged one of the green-tassel daggers into each corpse to mark the Cabal's work. He looked at his hands, caked in sweat but steady as a rock, not shaking at all, even with the waning of adrenaline. Athan slowly opened the new kill contract and inspected its brief contents before passing it over to his partner. He gave a long, deep sigh and decided his break was over.

And that was how it was. The life of an assassin. Their work never ended.

ADYSSAIRA (I)

THE MASQUES WE WEAR

It was not a typical day at the luxurious estates of House Chandoss. Every servant, manor hand, and paid guard, man, woman, child, and even the elderly had been put to work. Everyone performed their appointed tasks frantically yet efficiently, with a purpose to finish in the time that was strictly allotted to them. Such a day was a momentous occurrence that every noble family in Az'Dayne only dared dream of.

The very prince of the Az'Dayne Dominadom himself, Izayus Az'Ampion, had already arrived, barely less than an hour ago, visiting for a very special purpose that would change the fate of House Chandoss forever.

It was even more significant for Adyssaira's family specifically. Their family name had been widely considered a disgrace since their notorious predecessor, Nikayle the Firstnamed, her great-grandfather, had fallen rapidly from the high favor of his position in the court as the imperial bodyguard of the dominarchs. Nikayle's status for his prowess as a capable spellblade had been eminent throughout the nation, and he had been heralded as a beacon of strength in every Daynish city. This had been during his time under the prior Goldfyre kings, however, before the new Ampion rule.

Almost three hundred years ago, the far eastern territory of Az'Dayne had been officially proclaimed as Chandoshia, after the elevated founders of the well-regarded bloodline. The fertile lands east of the Aemenus River and Lake Chandoss, north of Taira's Scar and south of Az'Eloth, were considered the entitled subregion. Through generations of territorial battles, the lines of succession within the Chandoss name had conquered the biggest emerald mines on all of Penthara, which supplied a major export to Elothia and Goldgarden.

In addition, the mineral-rich lands provided more gold mines than any area in the country. The Chandoss name had risen fast as the most monetarily influential in the empire. Daughters of the lineage had been in high demand for political marriages, and the men had held powerful positions within the court.

Nikayle the Firstnamed's own great-grandfather, Aemenus Chandoss, had been the first Daynish spellblade recorded in history. Before then, only Elothians had been eligible to be spellblades, since their culture contained the original master smiths who crafted the magic swords. Aemenus had secured the secrets of the spellblade craft through expert diplomacy, and ever since, the mystic arts of the arcane trade had matured as an evolving weapon for Az'Dayne in past generations.

Nikayle had represented House Chandoss during the high-point years of their prominence. He had been highly celebrated not only for his position as High Bloodguard of the Crown but also for founding Az'Dayne's first university, the Syrene, based in Chandoshia, specializing in the higher learning of the musical, literary, and performing arts. The college attracted students from many cultures across Penthara, both humans and even some approved Zandaryn elven.

Thirty years ago, though, the last Goldfyre monarch had been forced out of power by the rise of the Dominadom, an adjoined empire between Az'Dayne and Khalimia. The Ampion-Hazhalah intermarriage alliance had taken over as the first of the dominarchs, titled equally rather than as king and queen.

Nikayle had kept his position as the trusted imperial bodyguard to the new rulers in power, just as he had for the Goldfyres. But this was before the descent of how spellblades were perceived in the Dominadom. This was before the Chandoss Curse had struck the family line. It had all happened rapidly, without any known justification.

It was two decades ago, the year Adyssaira and her two sisters, Valaythea and Odysserae, were all born at the same time. Something her great-grandfather had done wrought their once-noble name into excommunication from the Dominadom. All those born of his direct heritage were then labeled as lon'Chandoss, meaning that their bloodline was shunned by the nation, by both the aristocrats and commoners.

Nikayle the Firstnamed met a rather convenient and mysterious death shortly after. His spellblade was returned to the estates, and from that time on, not a single lon'Chandoss or person in their employ was allowed to set foot on the lands of Khalimia or Az'Dayne, outside Chandoshia.

The Chandoss Curse may not have been something supernatural, as it was often gossiped to be, but it was real. Several members of the family had passed to illnesses or unexplained disappearances, and others had suffered swift business ruin at the minimum. Adyssaira's own father and uncle had all experienced their share of calamities from the curse since the death of Nikayle the Firstnamed. Since his passing, the lands of Chandoshia had been governed by Nikayle's younger brother, Count Valdean, her great-granduncle. Valdean endured his own shortcomings with the unanswered peculiarity of never marrying nor producing any children of his own.

But then, after so many years, and her family giving up on any futile aspirations of redemption, today was an anticipated reality that proved the gods were listening to their prayers for atonement.

The dominarchs who had ruled the Dominadom for the past thirty years, Vaximus Az'Ampion and Sriyah Hazhalah, were revered as timeless avatars of the Five and Five deities by the common people. It had been decreed that any of their royal offspring would be honored as the Imperiar. And thus far, there was only one such, a son named Izayus, Prince of Az'Dayne.

Izayus Az'Ampion was the biggest name in the ever-expanding empire next to the dominarchs themselves. It was considered a grave offense to His Imperial Highness for any female in the realm to consider themselves his equal. An Imperiar did not marry traditionally, to join with a wife or a husband, but instead acquired legally bound paramours—five, to be exact.

Every year after his twenty-fifth bornday, Izayus had been able to elect a new paramour of a specific elemental descendancy in order of the Pentagogue's choosing. His first year was a woman of Khalimishe descent, Persillia Ashahd. His second year's paramour was Fairyn Highstone, of Tairancian lineage. His third was a Psage named Ruminae, strangely of no assigned surname at birth—such was their culture. And his fourth and last paramour to date was a young Barredish girl, Tamantha Bayn.

Each of the four paramours chosen was strangely of a fallen

house, formerly of very powerful influence in her nation. The rationale behind the Pentagogue's selection of these fortunate women, giving them the opportunity to redeem themselves for the sins of their ancestors, was lost on those who did not have the same insight into the Five and Five as the omnipotent religious order held. If the Pentagogue judged one's son worthy to become a paramour to an Imperiar princess, one did not refuse. If the Pentagogue determined one's daughter was worthy enough to become the final concubine of the prince of the Az'Dayne Dominadom, one thanked all five gods and all five goddesses for the rest of one's days.

And as such, Adyssaira and her family had been doing just that, with high blessings to the Five and Five, since Izayus had chosen her sister, Valaythea, for his final paramour.

Adyssaira, Odysserae, and Valaythea were the well-known lon'Chandoss Triplets. Adyssaira and Odysserae were born identical, except in hair and eye color. Valaythea, on the other hand, while born at the same time, had a slightly different facial structure. Some might argue that she was considered the prettiest and the most curved in a desirably proportionate way of the three.

Valaythea, the prize of the sisters, had wavy red hair, long and voluminous, down to the middle of her back. She had piercing amber eyes, plump lips, and a round face that everyone considered both adorably cute and beautiful at the same time. Her petite body was naturally athletic, and she walked with the grace of a noblewoman who had never fallen from favor, even though none of the girls had yet known what that life might be like.

Adyssaira's poor identical sister, Odysserae, on the other hand, had been raised as the odd sheep of the mix. She had been born near-deaf, only able to communicate in the gesture language of Hands. Odysserae could read lips and understand some speech if she was looking at the speaker, but she could not talk back. If she tried, the words came out muffled, with an inflection most had a hard time interpreting. Odysserae hadn't ever cared much for her own looks or for the attention of the local males. Her red hair was trimmed short above the gape of her neck, against the behest of their father, and always disheveled as if she had been bedridden for days before every occasion she was compelled into. She mostly kept her soft amber eyes pointed to the ground or out of a window in her own thoughts, far away from her depressed place of feeling cornered in life.

Adyssaira felt largely responsible for the ailment Odysserae had been born with. She only knew the story from her father, as he had finally told them in full detail just five years ago. Their mother, Valenteal, had died during childbirth, precisely due to the rare scenario when Adyssaira was being retrieved from the womb by the midwives. Just moments after Valaythea was delivered, as their mother was trying to give birth to Adyssaira, the midwives in the room all claimed they saw the same thing—the same thing her father saw from the outside.

A glowing green wisp had rushed through the open window past her father, straight through the split in the curtains to the bedroom. One didn't have to have encountered one of the strange wisps before to know what the spiritual entities were. The stories were as old as the histories of the continents themselves.

A wisp was a derelict hunder, a dead elvan's roaming soul, that had chosen not to drift into the afterlife to the great Beyond. Why these reluctant wisps would choose whom they did, Adyssaira had never been educated, but it was a fact that when one of them did interfuse with a human, it was always within a season before the baby's birth or within a season after the infant had come into the world.

Adyssaira had been born as one of these rare hunder-touched, with her bright green eyes and a faintly golden arcanic imprints on the back of her neck and over her heart in the middle of her chest, otherwise known as Dawning magemarks. Her hair was not red like her sisters', but golden blond. She wore it long and magnificent, like Valaythea's, always fancying her prettier sister's modern sense of fashion, as if she were an older, idolized peer she aspired to be more like. But she was also forced to wear it thus to veil her magemark and prevent others bearing witness to it. In her earlier years, Adyssaira remembered that her father had tried to obscure the magemarks through methods of burning or surgical excision, but the arcanic imprints would always heal back unscathed, so eventually he had retired from those cruel and futile solutions.

Adyssaira knew that the unique occurrence during her birth of being interfused with the random wisp was what had caused Odysserae's hearing impairment while still in the womb. Her sweet sibling had never expressed resentment toward her, however, and treated her like a best friend. If anything, Odysserae was her shadow anywhere and everywhere she went. She felt an eternal responsibility for her protection because of destiny's cruel hand put over them both.

But Adyssaira had been born into an even more dire situation than her deaf sister. Hunder-touched were all potentials to become mages. In the prejudiced jurisdiction of the Az'Dayne Dominadom, mages and those with the capacity to become mages were all sentenced to public execution. Certain young hunder-touched were sent early on for eligibility to join the Oathemic Cabal, but these were always male candidates. She had never heard of a sanctuary for female mages within the empire.

Athaniel, her older brother, was in the Oathemic Cabal, but he was neither hunder-touched nor a spellblade. She rarely saw him, and she knew his commitment to the guild of political assassins was far greater than the love he held toward his estranged family. Athaniel may have known and kept her secret, but he would never help her. Furthermore, her brother was the only one of their house that was permitted to go by the surname of Chandoss without the disfavored *lon* prefix.

Adyssaira was also aware of what her father had done that day after she and her sisters were born. She hadn't come to learn it right away, but as years had passed and she had grown wiser, she had puzzled it all together. He loved his daughters more than anything and would let no possible harm come to them. It had been no surprise to slowly discover in her adolescent years that he had each of the midwives involved in her birth immediately killed, along with any others throughout her upbringing whom he had grown suspicious of for their awareness of her condition.

Ethiass lon'Chandoss had become an overly paranoid man, by all accounts, especially concerning Adyssaira. Protecting her all these years and being discovered for it would no longer just jeopardize her life but also his and likely those of the rest of the family.

To secure Adyssaira's safety through her childhood, Ethiass had devised a mass facade to present to everyone in the Chandoss Estates. From the day she had come into the world, after he had the midwives murdered, he had pretended that she had been born blind. He had kept a blindfold over her eyes, and that was how she had been raised, never able to see or walk without aid. Only in the most private areas of Castle Chandoss, where she was safe from the scrutiny of servants, would her father allow her to take off the encumbering sash.

Only six people alive knew about her secret, and none of them were outside her closest family: Ethiass, her father; Nikayle the Thirdnamed, her uncle; Athaniel, her older brother; Valaythea and Odysserae, her sisters; and only recently, her cousin in the household, Emberalda. Adyssaira had been stringently instructed to trust no others, even of the Chandoss name. Her father had even forbidden her from visiting certain areas within the estates, constantly monitoring her whereabouts with scheduled recesses between her studies and duties.

But today was not about Adyssaira. Today was about her sister. Today was about her family's elevation back to its proper prestige, as it had been just before her birth.

Both Daynish and Khalimishe custom after the rise of the Dominadom through Az'Ampion and Hazhalah had gradually adopted the use of masques for those of favored aristocratic bloodlines. Masques were as unique as a house banner, each carefully and artistically constructed to represent the personality and visual representation of the "face" of the noble line for the public eye to recognize, though all masque applications had to be evaluated and approved by the council of the dual thrones themselves.

In the latter years, more than just the privileged highborn of the empire had been allowed to wear the masques. Certain merchant guildmasters and their high-ranking officers or the middle-class families of jumped-up reputation were even allotted the privilege of altering their surname to be born anew and bear a masque of individuality as well. But those were always quarter masques, and they were never allowed to be as elaborate by design as those born into nobility.

Masques, by definition, were symbolic guises that partially covered one's face, designed specifically to signify house representation and political status within the socially biased Dominadom. They were the single prerequisite accessory for all nobility and those of honored middle-class houses, to adorn themselves with in public settings or when accepting formalities from others of the same prestige, whether domestic or foreign.

The members of House lon'Chandoss had been prohibited by

the dominarchs from wearing their original masques from their time in the favor of the empire. The formerly aristocratic bloodline had been forced to be as exposed as the commoners of the region. But today was different. Upon Valaythea's official nuptials as the final paramour to Prince Izayus, they would be restored into the good graces of the Dominadom.

There was only one last act to perform. Her father, sweating beads the size of pumpkin seeds, lined up Adyssaira and her two sisters side by side. Odysserae was covered in sweat as well, having just returned from the penultimate performance, enacting a mock battle with a rope dancing martial art that specialized in using a rope dart and lasso.

Each of the girls were vigorously trained their entire lives in the performing arts: various styles of acrobatics, specific martial arts that displayed flamboyancy for crowds, and even weapon dances. Valaythea's specialty was with fire tools, a category called *solesce*, and *ejahra*, a Khalimishe word that translated to blade-dancing. Odysserae's proficiency in the rope dart, lasso, and other close-combat rope techniques was referred to as *wyrkenido*, an old Elothian martial art. And Adyssaira's, the least brutal of the three, was actually nothing oriented around fighting or weapons at all. It was all about enthralling attention through slow and majestic movements using ariel silks and poles. There was no name for it like the others, but the art of it arguably was innovated by her ancestor, Elexius Chandoss, almost two hundred years ago. They were the products of their father's obsession with perfection and his ambition to return to power.

The groomers anxiously patted the sweat from Odysserae's head and touched up the triplets' faces as beautifully as they could imagine to capture the attention of a prince of an empire.

Adyssaira was mindful that their makeup, hair, and attire had already been styled and ready more than a few hours ago, yet still her father seemed to second-guess himself and panic with constant minor alterations to what he had originally planned.

The contours on their faces were drawn identically to make all the sisters appear at one and the same from far away—even Valaythea. Where visible, and not veiled in costume, each had bright red lips, jet black around the eyes, rosy cheeks, and a pale-powdered brow and chin. Their hair was fashioned down, robust and wild for the purpose of the act.

Valaythea wore an all-red Sunder dress of many thin, ruffled layers, matching the natural color of her own hair. Attached to her shoulders like a long, draping cape that trained across the floor two feet behind her, were thin translucent Savatarm silk fabrics that shimmered between yellows and oranges, mimicking flickering flames when she moved in the light. She was meant to represent the embodiment of the fire element in the Daynish descendancy and the country of Khalimia in her part of the play to come. She was armed with a single curved wooden sword, painted green, to portray a spellblade. Her role was to personify old Az'Dayne, before the Ampion rule.

Odysserae was adorned in an elegant silver gown with an extra-long train the length of her own body, and she had been fitted with a grey wig of hair in a similar style to that of her sisters. She was meant to symbolize the undecided and the great unknown.

Adyssaira herself was outfitted in a more practical choice of garments for intended mobility. Her yellow corset and silk gloves contrasted with her blond hair and golden tights. She was to portray new Az'Dayne with the expansion of the Ampion rule, through the tairan element.

Each girl was barefoot and costumed with one other identifiable accessory. Valaythea bore a red sash over her mouth, tied behind the back of her head, while her other sister had a black sash formed into a bandanna over her ears and the top part of her grey wig. Adyssaira's own sash, of course, was secured over her green eyes, as always, of cloth dyed correspondingly to her corset. But her sash was made of the expensive Savatarm silk, and she could see through the translucent fabric on her side.

We are the Chandoss Triplets. Adyssaira swallowed any fears, reinforcing the reputation of her and her sisters, regardless of her bloodline's disfavor. *They want to love us. They always have. And today we give them their chance.*

"The other acts are finished. It is time," her father declared, biting his lip while fretfully peeking through the curtains of the massive stage out at the intimidating audience. "He is on the upper left, in the Sun Balcony. None look at him during the performance, as rehearsed. At the end, Valaythea, you, and only you, stare at him. Take our new masque off, just for a tease. Then return it in respect to the mandate. Adyssaira and Odysserae, you two shall not even glance once. Just bow and gaze to the Ampion-Hazhalah flag." As Ethiass spoke his demands, his fingers moved in certain gestures, translating into Hands so that Odysserae could understand.

"We know, Father," Adyssaira and Valaythea returned simultaneously, practiced to the point of it being impossible to blunder.

Odysserae was slightly late on the reply, but she responded in Hands. "*We know.*"

"I love you each. Save the family. For the Chandoss legacy."

Ethiass kissed each of his daughters before him on the forehead, then left the stage. The other backstage aides departed from the performance area as well, until it was just silence and darkness, just heavy breathing and shared hearts beating.

It is time.

The girls took to their positions for the final act. The curtains lifted, and the anticipant murmurs of nobility far and wide within the theater were utterly hushed. The stage was set, and all eyes were on them.

In the center background of the theater was a massive pipe organ, at which Odysserae sat and began to skillfully play, regardless of her handicap. Adyssaira's sister had memorized the notes and could feel the vibrations from the sound resonating through each push of the keys. The intro of the haunting instrumental melody began as a tease of a dark tale to come.

The lighting slightly obscured Odysserae, with its focus prepared on the foreground of the stage. There, Valaythea advanced forward to command the attention of the audience, making dramatic steps in a dance-like maneuver to the lone prop on the stage—a makeshift campfire with kindling over a fireproof slab.

She went to try to light the fire but struggled, and she caught a flicker of movement in the shadows around her perimeter. Actors in white martial robes and long blond wigs appeared, charging at her with their wooden swords drawn back to attack. She enacted her practiced choreography in a theatrical fight sequence to bring down the five Elothian pretenders, then imitated an injury taken during battle just after.

Cold and wounded, Valaythea tried again at the fire, to no avail. She silently cursed and kicked and finally curled into defeat around the stack. The lighting darkened around her as the focal light shone on a beacon from above, lowered from the theater's ceiling.

Adyssaira descended over the campfire and tossed an invisible token into the tinder, instantly setting it ablaze. This caused an eruption of impressed gasps throughout the crowd. The ariel silks attached to Adyssaira horizontally flew her down to gently invite Valaythea from her supine position and stand her up.

Adyssaira's feet touched stage, and together the two stood hand in hand facing one another as sisters, very different, but one and the same in that moment. On cue, Adyssaira lifted Valaythea under her arms, and the two spiraled into the air toward the ceiling of the theater.

Odysserae's song shifted continuously to suit the mood of the performance, with an uplifting crescendo rising from the morose tune of the intro. The odeless ballad coerced a beautifully unique aerial dance, with Adyssaira swinging from different rising and falling levels across the stage, holding Valaythea by the wrist, and then an ankle, once by the back of her neck, her waist, and both hands, then her feet, dramatically almost dropping her time and again for the maximum effect on the entertainment of the awed spectators.

There was no nervousness between the two sisters, in perfect sync with one another. No one in the crowd existed in their moment of flawless presentation, not even the Prince of Az'Dayne. It was just them, the music, and the silks. Valaythea trusted her life in Adyssaira's hands more than she would in those of the strongest knights in the realm.

The hovering dance went on for some time, but it was time for the story's climax. The control silks lowered Adyssaira to the stage, and she used some crafty sleight of hand to quickly detach herself from them, with Valaythea gracefully released back onto her own feet.

Adyssaira moved to take the fiery cape that Valaythea carried on her back, but her sister defensively pivoted away, flashing one of the pieces of cloth up to strike her hand. Adyssaira reeled back, as if burned, and stole her wooden spellblade prop. Seeing it as a motion for hostility, Valaythea engaged with her sister in mock combat. They dodged and struck and weaved around each other majestically, sensually mesmerizing, with their lithe bodies barely touching one another, intending to seduce any of those who watched.

And it was working. They didn't need to pause to gaze out to know that the crowd was entirely enamored of their erotic physical finale.

By the end, the two had traded who wielded the wooden sword several times over. Valaythea's fire cape had been shed, most of the layers of her dress discarded, and apparently, she was defeated of the two. But just as Adyssaira pulled back the spellblade to plunge it into her sister's abdomen, the most unexpected act of all occurred.

Valaythea grabbed the handle of the sword, holding it with Adyssaira, and shoved it into the air above their heads, pulling Adyssaira in with her other hand around her waist to a playacted long embrace on the lips. After the deep kiss, the two in unison set the spellblade in the fire and watched it burn away.

The entire audience erupted from their seats in an ovation, thinking this the end of the marvelous drama, but there was more. As so much focus had been on the blond and red-haired sisters, all had forgotten about the one in the background with the grey wig.

The light, as originally, put emphasis on Odysserae, no longer with her pipe organ. Hidden trained attendees had wheeled it off in a timely manner beforehand. The soft music that remained came from instruments in the shadows, played by unseen minstrels.

The way the stage was set, it made Odysserae appear in an optical illusion as extremely far away. Fake snow began to fall over her, while the fire near Valaythea and Adyssaira simmered down to coals as they approached the distant version of themselves. The closer they got, the more Odysserae revealed her true self. She slowly undressed from her elegant silver gown piece by piece, revealing black and gold undergarments of lace and leather underneath. And when she finally reached the two, she disposed of the grey wig to display yet another, but of all black. She was now the embodiment of the future of the Dominadom—the political absorption of Barredom, of the shadow and tairan descendancy.

And together the three denied their father his desperate demand before the play had begun. They decided to finish it how they had intended to all along. In unison, the triplets found the Sun Balcony and undeniably the face of the prince of the Az'Dayne Dominadom. Adyssaira assumed she could chance her false blindness being exposed in service of the rehearsed act. The stage was dim except for a spherical accent over the three girls. They didn't break their intimate gaze on him as all three leaned in simultaneously to kiss.

But then the stage went pitch dark, to the audience's obvious dismay, with a series of blind huffs and sullen murmurs. The girls had anticipated exactly that for the theatrical ruse to finish the play. It gave them just the time they needed for the stage help to do the necessary changes unnoticed.

When the lights came back on, Adyssaira was veiled from head to toe in an orange robe, and Odysserae was in a hooded black robe. Valaythea, though in her same loose red dress, was now wearing the new House Chandoss masque.

The masque took up three-quarters of her face. Black and exquisite with intricate details in design, it covered her lips, curving up the left side of her face, curling more like a crescent moon to divide her brow. As it came down to the bridge of her nose, the right eye was encircled by a black ring of the leftover masque, leaving the rest of the right half of her face exposed from cheek to temple and most of that side of her forehead. Valaythea's eyes were elaborately painted like glowing green fire, with a burst of tiny sequined emeralds around them. The mouth of the masque was carved into a radical open frown from years of sadness suffered. And finally, and probably the most striking addition that set the facial covering apart from the more typical found throughout the local aristocratic norms, was the frayed plume of five phoenix feathers sticking out of the left side.

The phoenix was a rare, magnificent bird of revered symbolism for the fire element, thought brought into extinction by the Thrench Empire when the Ashenwave had drowned out all life on the Sundorion Isles, killing off the Ibyssai elvan race and all manner of species that resided there. It was the phoenixes that were the first of the animal species to rise from the Ashenwave's total annihilation wrought on the isles. Now one could only find the exceptional defender birds being sold for a king's fortune by the Behemon pirates or held in protected aviaries in the Solaril elven territories. Their feathers were a vibrant, fiery orange, and they shimmered as if they were aflame when they took flight. They were twice the size of the Tairancian day hawks and Elothian eagles, but they couldn't stay airborne for long with their small wingspans. Other than for their elemental cosmetics, they were mainly known for defending their families and territories through fearless measures, regardless of consequence to their own lives. Such were appropriate, iconic beasts of emblematic representation for House Chandoss in recent times.

But there was still one last thing to do to conclude the epilogue of the performance. Their coordinated plan all along was to do as their father had initially intended.

Suddenly, in a violent motion, Adyssaira ripped at the left side of Valaythea's red dress, tearing off a large piece of the top. Odysserae repeated the same action to the right side of Valaythea's top. And one by one, in sync, they took turns ravaging what remained of their sister's fine gown until it was a pile of ruined fabric at her feet.

Upon finishing the aggressively erotic scenario, Adyssaira and Odysserae uniformly turned to face the audience with Valaythea, and discarded their robes to the ground. To the crowd's pleased surprise, the triplets now identically matched for the first time since coming on stage, having a secret outfit underneath to unveil.

They wore red leather corsets with black frayed skirts, studded knee-high red boots and elbow-length black gloves. They each had matching golden chokers, embedded with fire opals. But only Valaythea modeled the new official masque of House Chandoss as the first of their bloodline to publicly introduce it.

Odysserae went to one knee and set her eyes to the stage floor. Adyssaira followed, mimicking the gesture. And finally, Valaythea finished as the last of the three, the same as her sisters, but that was not how it ended.

Valaythea slowly rose back to her feet, lifting the new Chandoss masque to reveal her unmatched beauty for all to judge.

Time had stopped. All went silent. Every eye in the theater, including those of all three sisters now, inexorably pointed to one divine man standing from his seat in the Sun Balcony.

It was time for the imperial decision of acceptance. There could be only one judge to determine the fate of the fallen House lon'Chandoss. And his name was Izayus Az'Ampion.

VALAYTHEA (I)

FINAL PARAMOUR

She was sure her heart had stopped beating some several minutes back. *Or has it been an hour now ... or only one minute?* She had no way to be sure.

The only thing Valaythea was sure about was that she couldn't break from the paralyzing gaze of the prince of the Az'Dayne Dominadom, who was leering over her from above. His hard amber eyes were like molten fire on her naked face, instigating a surge of glistening sweat across her flesh that she had no control over.

She could hear the heavy pants of exertion from her sister Adyssaira, kneeling behind her, breathing heavily from their performance, concluded only moments ago. She could feel the stares of hundreds of Daynish and Khalimishe nobles in the crowd weighing down on her. And she could sense the insecure convictions of the four regal brides at the prince's side, whom she forced into obscured silhouettes by refusing to shift her focus anywhere but entirely on him.

She wouldn't dare look away at anything or anyone else. Izayus Az'Ampion was as celestial as an avatar in mortal form sent from the Five and Five. It was a surreal experience even to earn such an idol's attention, as profoundly divine as he was. That this day would even come to pass had recently been a dream she had never actually believed would come to certainty. She had fancied that the news was just some grand delusion of her father's vain aspirations for their bloodline's redemption, or perhaps some one-sided comical tease from the deities, who obviously loathed the lon'Chandoss house. She fully anticipated some malicious plot twist to strike her down on the spot in the middle of the stage.

She still hadn't breathed since the play had stopped; she was sure of it. But at least now she knew she was somehow still alive.

When Prince Izayus finally smiled down at her, the heart that she had been convinced was no longer working was now pumping and fluttering in overkill to make up for lost beats. *He is going to kill me if he keeps doing this … Father, what do I do?*

Prince Izayus took his leave of the Sun Balcony, obliging his four prior paramours to remain, and he began his trek down the spiraling stairs to the main theater floor with a small paladin escort in front of him.

Father, where are you? Valaythea's eyes incidentally shifted to her flank, scouring the backstage hideaways as she desperately searched for Ethiass. He was always there, but not this time. She instantly felt ashamed and weak even for succumbing to the need for her father in her true moment of adulthood as a woman. She was twenty years of age, no longer a little girl for quite some time now. She needed to do this on her own. Her eyes fixed back on the flawless prince.

His strawberry-blond hair was perfectly groomed by clearly the best barbers the realm could afford, styled voluminous and wavy down to the back of his neck. His masculine jaw and sharp cheekbones were like some unfair image out of every girl's fantasy. And while she had expected his face to be immaculately clean-shaven, it was not, with just a slight tint of purposeful stubble, fashionable yet razored to a degree. His body seemed masculine yet capable of gentle touch with whatever lay underneath the exuberant costume he had adorned himself in for the occasion.

Izayus was clad in vestments of the finest regional fabrics, dyed appropriately in orange dominance, most impressively blending into shades of bright red the lower his tunic extended below his torso. His pants and boots were black but appeared made of a decem layers from all manner of leathers from various beasts whose hides had been that natural color before being skinned. The golden laces through the middle of his shirt matched the rings on his fingers and the necklace that hung to his exposed chest. Ruby gems, both fitting in size and of flamboyant proportions, found their way into his well-placed jewelry as well. And he was coming onstage now.

Valaythea had spent the past several pentdays dwelling on how she might feel in this anticipated moment. It was like spinning a stick to point at one of twenty possibilities, but now that the time was upon her, any possibility was proven invalid by the single emotion that overshadowed the rest: fear. Valaythea wasn't sure if it was from the aura of shared anxiety from her sisters behind her or if the angst was all a manifestation in her alone. But it was real now. Not just a hopeless ambition of her father's, not simply a futile prayer to the gods from the people of Chandoshia to lift the bloodline's curse, and no longer a child's whimsical notions.

He is touching me … It was definitely real. All the warmth had left her body, and she didn't know why. She felt as cold as ice. As stone-still as the dead. But the prince put his hands in hers, and as his soft fingers closed over the tips of her own and he drew her body in close to his, the heat surged back through her veins hotter than ever. She felt more of a puppet to his desires than when the silks had been attached to her in the play, being controlled by the stage masters in the rafters.

Unexpectedly, Izayus pulled her hands down beside their waists as his body firmly pushed against hers, and he pressed a long kiss to her lips, which she did not reject. Her mind was numb, no longer on Penthara, and the life in her knees completely broke, yet somehow she miraculously managed to stand upright still and not collapse. Valaythea was sure she was quivering, but her soul felt as if it were outside her body, looking down, and she appeared calm and still. She was at his mercy to do with as he pleased.

Finally the kiss ended, and she risked opening her amber eyes, matching his own, venturing to surmise his own emotions in the moment. Her head was swaying from the light-headedness induced by the effect of the alluring power he invoked in her, but she attempted to read him nonetheless. *Nothing. You are empty. And as scared as me. But you don't want to be, do you, Prince?*

Valaythea shook that absurdity from her mind, vowing never again to conjure such thoughts. This was Izayus Az'Ampion. He was imperially born, the dominarchs' only son, raised as the most untouchable, glorified individual alive in the realm. How could he possibly feel fear or understand the concept?

Izayus brought the back of her hand to his lips and raised it high in the air, turning their bodies to address the crowd of the Dominadom's nobility in the Chandoss theater. He was officially accepting her in front of those who were considered anyone for all to see.

"All see her before you, not as before, but reborn, as chosen by the Five and Five, for my final paramour! The first of pure Daynish descent, matching that of House Ampion, which none can deny. Valaythea is now restored to her unfallen Chandoss name and will be treated with the highest esteem, which will surpass even that of her previously well-regarded ancestors," Izayus proclaimed loudly and clearly.

Valaythea couldn't stop staring at him, still in disbelief that this was her new reality. He seemed sincere and actually proud to be next to her.

"As for the rest of House lon'Chandoss, an imperial ceremony of atonement at the Pentagogue will be held to bestow unqualified absolution for past transgressions committed by those carrying the bloodline. When our dominarchs return from the north, in the first month of the coming Sunder of Kingfall, we will formally recognize the estates we are honored to visit today, after so many lost years, as the venerable House Chandoss once again! I will have it that they are all now treated fairly until such comes to pass."

The aristocratic crowd in the theater stood and began to clap in full approval.

"It is time for the pentamony and marital feast of the conjoining! Let the Bronze Ball continue!"

And with that, Izayus and Valaythea migrated to the next stage on the evening's matrimonial agenda. She was afforded a half-hour respite to quickly change from her theater wardrobe into more appropriate attire. Her father had gifted her with her mother's old wedding dress, only worn once and maintained in pristine condition. It was a stunning orange gown fit for a princess, low but classy at the bust to feature her as more alluring for the prince. The palace help ornamented her with complimented jewels everywhere they could place them as well: in her pierced ears and around her neck and wrists.

When she returned, she could finally see her father, eagerly ushering royal patrons and attendants toward the assigned Chapel of the Fives. Prior to the arrival of Izayus, Ethiass had had time to carry out renovations in expanding the wall to the small chamber of worship, enlarging its audience capacity tenfold for the prince and his entourage's visit.

Here Izayus and Valaythea were formally conjoined in imperial pentamony before the Five and Five, and it became official by all laws in the Dominadom that she was now Valaythea Az'Chandoss, never again just lon'Chandoss. They kissed again by custom after the ritual was completed, and it felt half as awkward as before.

Next, they commenced the celebration feast of imperial conjoining. Having been ever prepared for this moment to come to fruition, Ethiass had preset the banquet hall with food made by the finest chefs for hire in the region and beyond to entertain the insatiable palate of Izayus Az'Ampion's exotic appetite.

All of her family from Castle Chandoss were present at the table closest to theirs: Valdean, her great-granduncle, the Count of Chandoshia, her father Ethiass of course, her triplet sisters, Adyssaira and Odysserae, her gorgeous cousin Emberalda, and even her little half-elvan sister by blood, Sashka. Her father's Zandaryn elvan bride, Taizsha, was amidst the human congregation as well, along with her Uncle Nikayle who had managed to make it to the feast in his wheeled chair.

In the center of the table lay a queen scorpion, over two feet in length, procured from Hera's Desert, decorated with juicy fresh lobsters brought in all the way from Watergem. An assortment of spiced and cheese-covered shellfish from Lake Oyster lined one side, next to a rack of the finest fish caught throughout the channel of Taira's Scar, which segregated the countries of Az'Dayne and Savatarm. On the other side was an arrangement of land-animal delicacies. The largest edible item on the table was a pig specifically chosen from the best farm in Chandoshia, saturated in signature sauce and garnished with a surplus of fruits to add to the presentation. Minced venison soup, smoked rabbit, aged and marbled rare beef, bone-in bison flanks, and whole lemon-doused turkeys supplied the rest of the display.

On a smaller, more elevated counter behind the entrée table stood a presentation of many desserts. Cream-colored icing, chocolates of every shade, and rose-hued oddities of mouthwatering enticements teased from beyond for a delectable aftertaste following a dinner fit for kings and queens.

Izayus and Valaythea indulged just as a prince and his subsidiary princess might have, with plenty of dramas, comedic parodies, and routines of acrobatic skills organized by the Chandoss Estates entertaining throughout the imperial banquet. Izayus remained most attentive to her during the celebratory ordeal, constantly kissing her softly, hand-feeding her sweets from the dessert presentation, and awaiting her approval after each performance recited by his own actors brought in from the capital for her enjoyment.

Izayus was more than she had imagined he would or could be. He was a true gentleman inclined toward the highest regard in respecting his lady beside him. He seemed romantically disposed, adept in chivalrous honor lost by so many in the modern era.

In the middle of one of the ballads sung by a group of minstrels, Izayus even coerced her into a dance, taking over the banquet room, obliging all eyes to fix on them as if it were just him and her back on the theater stage.

During the last course of the banquet, gifts from each of the royal houses in the Dominadom were presented to the new couple. All across the expanses of Az'Dayne, Khalimia, Az'Eloth, Tairancia, and even now Barredom, she was told, even noble families that could not attend, as they lived afar and abroad, had sent their respects as monetary gifts or endowments in the form of sacred relics. Valaythea had never witnessed such a spectacle of insinuated power.

The conjoining ceremony was nearing its end, leaving just one last segment to complete: the actual act of the conjoining. She was prepared for this part and had not been able to take her mind from it during the latter half of the feast, hardly able to touch most of the lavish dishes pushed in front of her.

Izayus grabbed her by the hand and walked equally beside her as the two were guided by the house help to the bedchamber prearranged by her father. Only select heads of the invited noble houses were permitted to follow the duo any farther as the highborn entourage leisurely paraded down the echoing stone halls of Castle Chandoss.

This was Valaythea's home, all familiar territory to her, but she knew that Izayus, and likely every chosen lord and lady trailing, had never set foot on any ground inside the Chandoshia border. *Well, perhaps some might have*, she thought, second-guessing herself as she regarded a few of the more elderly aristocrats following them.

Ethiass purposely led the prince through the east-wing corridor of the palace, expressly ornamented for the occasion of his visit.

Armored Chandoss sentries lined the walls, with one stationed below each torch sconce. Each guard fell to one knee and bowed low as the Prince of Az'Dayne passed him by.

The high-arching glass ceiling of the east wing was open to the starry heavens of the late-evening sky. Expensive, rare paintings from famous artists depicting just about anything, from the abstract to Daynish war heroes, the current dominarchs, the Pentagogue, concepts of the Five and Five in the flesh, various fortresses or historic battles, littered the walls as if the hallway were a tunneled museum of the best art in the realm rather than just another passage in the palace.

Valaythea couldn't help but notice Izayus's evident interest in the strategic decor her father had placed. It was popular knowledge that Izayus had a pronounced passion for the visual and literary arts of his homeland. She took note of the way he squinted in disgust when eyeing one particular set of artwork, nearest to the chamber they were approaching.

They were five portraits of Nikayle the Firstnamed, all life-size, and on each canvas, his head had been defaced by slashes of red paint, along with the same red coat vandalizing the images of his spellblade in hand. Izayus then leered at the back of Ethiass and subtly shook his head.

Do you disapprove, Prince? She hadn't been expecting that. Was he upset that they even still exhibited the illustrations of the eschewed luminary of their bloodline, or was he reproachful of the disfigurement cast over them? Valaythea hesitated on how even to begin to ask, then dismissed it altogether.

In front of the door to the destination chamber stood two armored individuals she did not recognize. Both were in full blackened plate, one fit for a man, while the other was an obvious woman in curvature and stature. By the design of their helms and the signature dawnstar weapon across each of their backs, she recognized the figures to be a paladin and a veritan, but she had never heard of those in their order donning such colors.

Ethiass moved aside and let Izayus and Valaythea approach the two knights. A chill rushed up her spine as if something eerie were present and all might go awry on a spit. Even the prince's majestic presence did nothing to set her spirit at ease. But she kept her discomfort to herself and dared not a whisper.

"Prince Izayus Az'Ampion, only son of Dominarch Vaximus Ampion and Dominarch Sriyah Hazhalah, you stand before a shadow paladin and shadow veritan." They spoke in unison. "And Valaythea, daughter of Ethiass of House Chandoss, and Valenteal, pray her soul to have found peace in the Godslands. Kneel for the Five and Five so that you might rise reborn."

Valaythea went to kneel, still hand in hand with Izayus, somehow expecting him to bow with her, but she found that he did not budge. *Of course he does not have to kneel before the Fives. He is their equal.* She kept her eyes closed and aimed at the floor, not showing any sense of perturbation at the unanticipated ritual of the evening.

The shadow knights continued in practiced concord. "You have been recognized by the five gods of the elements and the five goddesses of the seasons. You are absolved from the sins of your ancestors. By their divine grace, the Five and Five have chosen you to conjoin with Izayus Az'Ampion in pentamony. Do you accept this conjoining, as deemed worthy by destiny?"

"I do," Valaythea promised, keeping her eyes shut.

"You are now Paramour Valaythea Az'Chandoss, conjoined in equality with Paramour Persillia Az'Ashahd, Paramour Fairyn Az'Highstone, Paramour Ruminae Az'A, and Paramour Tamantha Az'Bayn, and conjoined beneath Prince Izayus Az'Ampion. Rise now, anew, reborn as highborn!"

She did. When she opened her eyes, she found that the paladin and veritan had already moved away from the door, allowing Izayus and her entry to the chamber.

The prince wasted no time on dallying for more formalities and led her inside, gently closing the door behind them for privacy at last.

She watched his curious gaze scour the cylindrical room with a bit of puzzlement in his eyes. He never even looked at the bed placed in the middle of the chamber, obviously brought in only for one purpose. This was no place intended for slumber.

Bookshelves wrapped around the circular wall, lining it up three floors high, with tall ladders on tiny wheels latched onto certain attachments in higher sections. The domed ceiling was made of glass, just like the ceiling in the corridor outside. The abundance of white stars and the luminous half-moon provided plenty of light to set the tone in the makeshift bedchamber. But as if that weren't enough, an elaborate chandelier constructed of colorless crystals and elk antlers hung from the center of the glass dome, partially lit to allow one the ability to read but not to hinder the amorous mood.

Throughout the shelves were decorative wreaths made from a variety of flowers and other colorful vegetation. On the lone nightstand beside an oversized plush chair were three golden decanters filled with the highest-quality wines from across Penthara. Ethiass had spared no expense on this evening's elite guest.

"You brought me to the Chandoss library," Izayus stated with a mild assertion toward questioning her.

Valaythea was nervous. She tried to appear casual yet confident. *It is just like a play. You are an actress. Just act.* She was already enhancing her gait toward the wine, measuring her steps one at a time. "I may have done my research on you, Your Imperial Highness. Popular gossips say your biggest passion is for reading and all fine arts."

She made it to the table and the wine. *Thank you, Five and Five.* She was already pouring out two goblets from the decanter.

"So you think we will be reading tonight?" Izayus said, smirking and seeming amused by her antics.

She felt rude that she was already taking a healthy swig of the bitter red vintage without offering him his chalice first. But she couldn't help her nerves and hardly knew what she was doing. Valaythea coughed when she caught herself and turned around with wine spilling down her chin. She awkwardly wiped it away with the sleeve of her dress, spilling more wine from her own goblet in the process. *This is embarrassing! I am behaving like a peasant.*

She collected herself and walked toward him to hand him the wine she had poured for him. "I do not think we will be reading tonight," she admitted, somehow unable to make eye contact with him.

Izayus used his free hand to softly lift her chin, forcing her eyes to find his own, of matching color. He touched his goblet to hers and grinned, putting her at ease somewhat. "Valaythea, sit down. Drink your wine. Get to know me."

She grinned back and whipped around to go and sit on the corner of the bed and began sipping her wine rather rapidly. She saw strands of her bright red hair blurring the vision in her left eye, and she unconsciously blew air toward the annoying lock, which did nothing to fix the issue.

"I may have done my research on Valaythea of House Chandoss also," he hinted, to her astonishment.

She went to sip her wine some more, but the goblet was empty. She frowned and looked at the dry chalice as if it had just betrayed her. "Me? What possible interest could any have in me? What is there even to learn?" She couldn't help but giggle at the revelation. *Why did I just laugh? Get it together.*

She fidgeted with the empty goblet in her fingers as Izayus expounded. "Oh, I have many eyes and ears and busy hands that work for me, though I ask for none of them. Yet they feel the need to inform me all the same. Perhaps you can relate."

Valaythea completely related. She was already back at the wine, pouring more. She didn't even realize she had gotten up. She discovered she was actually woozier than she had expected, having forgotten how much she had already drunk over the extravagant twenty-course feast.

"Ask me anything," he demanded, ignoring her jittery conduct.

"Why me?" She had to know that single answer.

"Of course," he said with a beautiful smile, as if it were the question he hoped she would ask. "Do you know the imperial policy of acquiring a new paramour?" He didn't wait for her to respond. "I have you until the end of the Dawning. Just you. My other paramours must stay in waiting until the end of this season. At the beginning of the Sunder, you will join with them. But it will be too late by then."

Too late? But she didn't ask this aloud, as he repeated it much more sinisterly.

"Far too late."

Izayus pulled an odd extendable pipe from inside his vest pocket. He sat down his goblet of wine and then retrieved a pouch from the opposite pocket and began packing the pipe with the herbs as he made himself comfortable on the large red chair in the library.

"You want me to ask, 'Too late for what?'" Valaythea boldly dared to call him out. The wine was thick in her veins indeed.

Izayus lit his pipe on a nearby candle and took a few puffs, soaking in the smoky substance it produced. "I am going to tell you all that there is. And I am going to tell you why it had to be you."

She again walked to her safe corner of the bed and sipped her wine, now too intrigued by the mysterious prince's words to talk. It was clear from the gloss that appeared over his now-bloodshot eyes that whatever he was inhaling from the pipe was a drug of sorts that was numbing his senses.

"Your family ..." He paused as if it was difficult for him to finish. He took another puff. "Your family's curse is being lifted. But at a greater cost than you can imagine. And it cannot be revoked," Izayus warned. He mumbled something under his breath after, but she thought she picked out the words.

Did he just say my father sold his soul and all of ours?

Izayus smiled and looked all around the bookshelves, and then straight up with his chin targeted on the judging moon vertically above. "Valaythea, if you must know two things about me, know these." He choked on his words as he spoke them. "I know too much. And I am not a good person. I was born in the Know, and because I cannot let others know the Know, I have succumbed to a privileged life of selfishness, and therefore I can no longer be considered good. I now care about only one thing, you see." He took another, extremely long inhalation from the drug pipe, but this time not exhaling it. "I care only about the escape. And so will you."

Valaythea was so bewildered by what the prince was going on about and disoriented from the state she was in. *I am just drunk. And he is too, and from whatever is in that pipe.* She tried to conjure the more sober and practical version of herself back into the room.

She remembered a time when she and her two sisters and cousin had all gotten hold of her uncle's ale-cellar key when they had been just fourteen years of age, and how they had rambled on all night long about the strangest things that made little sense. Somehow she had managed to remember that experience, and it made her reminisce in this moment.

"You were quite the perfect gentleman tonight, Your Imperial Highness. I had no idea how chivalrous and romantic you might be." Valaythea spoke out of turn, as if she had not heard a word Izayus had been saying. Perhaps, Valaythea thought, she wanted to play ignorant and just coast through naiveté until at least the end of the previously dreamlike evening. He could wake her to the cruel hard facts in the morning.

Izayus's visage shifted to one of anger and irritation, but his inebriated smile remained the same, shifting down from the starry firmament of the solarium to scan over the abundance of books in the respectable archive. "Oh, so you choose not to listen, my beautiful final paramour. You choose to escape. Like me." He wasn't grinning anymore but was fully serious as he trained his stare through her very being. "So many sugar tales and pretty songs. I have read and heard most. I recognize them all. Romance and chivalry, gentlemen and ladies, and proud knights and their wives."

Izayus took another breath of his drug through the smoke pipe. "If you hoped this might turn into a love story, then you are reading the wrong book." The prince tossed his pipe to the stone and enticingly invited her to approach him with his pointer finger. He fixed a seductive gaze over her. "Prepare for a dark tale where all are the many hues of grey and where any might not be as they seem …"

SCARLESS (II)

SEVEN SEATS

She sat at her designated seat, the Seat of the Grey, at the northwestern point of the heptagonal table. There was no display of her usual attire, as was the covenant for attending the Conclave. When appearing at the secret council meetings of Goldgarden's Seven Seats, the appointed delegates must only be seen in robes that signified what they represented. Her grey gown was thick and heavy, mundane with little regality to it, and her hood was drawn low over her brow, mimicking the other six members in the sacred chamber. The Seven Seats was a clandestine political organization. Though each knew the others by name and affiliation, it remained custom to be obscure.

To her left, at the north point of the table, was a man she knew as Thederick Tyme, robed in all black, the voice of the Seat of the Black. She suspected he might be of Psage lineage but could not be certain, since she had never seen him with his hood pulled back, or outside this very room. Thederick was the foreign overlord who represented the relations and allocations of all spymasters involved in matters north of Utamia.

To Zahnastaazjah's right, at the most western point of the table, sat the oldest representative on the council. Baldric Whereway was a proud and pure Goldgarden-born native and a soldier at heart. His house name of Whereway supplied the only members ever to sit on the Seat of the Blue. He stood as the overlord in charge of the city-nation's navy, port policies, import handlings, and the trade and peace pacts maintained with the western sea powers of Throng and Vellyon.

The next seat counterclockwise around the heptagonal table was the Seat of the Gold. Arro Gemenis was the other Utamian overlord in charge of local matters. His entrustment was jurisdiction over merchant guildmasters, municipal fiscal matters, the mines, exports, and monetary relations throughout not only Goldgarden but the mainlands of all of Utamia, as well as Tairancia and the Tairanheart. Arro was also the public's voice for the world-renowned Pentharam Bank. Concluding his many responsibilities, the prominent magnate was the overseer of the metropolis's defense force, the Goldguardians.

Baldric and Arro's positions on the Seats of the Blue and Gold were indeed the most locally influential on the council—even to be fairly considered as the true leaders of the overpopulated city-nation—but Zahnastaazjah and the other five seats shunned that impressment of total authority, favoring that the Seven were intended to be an overall balance of campaigning that benefited the most powerful city on Penthara.

Next in the rotation of distinguished seats was the Seat of the Red, a Khalimishe who went by Amethyst, accountable for information discovered within the politically formidable Az'Dayne Dominadom. Ever since Zahnastaazjah had joined the council, she had somehow established an exasperating enmity with the confrontational woman.

On the east corner point of the table was the Seat of the White, in which sat Serafinelan, an Oriyan born in Goldgarden, who represented its recently passed Sho'Lonese delegate. Serafinelan had been appointed as the intermediary for the far-eastern human nations such as the segregated Sho'Lon Empire, the mysterious Vistsplit isle of Oriyen, and the Brutongan territories.

The Seat of the Green on the council was the illustrious Sunder mage of Savatarm, Shypriss Sol-War. Zahnastaazjah had met her before their placement on the seats. She was Psage, naturally hairless from scalp to toe, beautiful and tan with flawless skin despite her middle age—such was the blessing of youth afforded the hunder-touched, especially the more powerful they became. Shypriss was the only tier-five Sunder mage alive in the realm, as far as Zahnastaazjah had been informed, and was easily the most dangerous individual in the entire city, especially when in season.

It was just under a decade ago that the Seat of the Green had been opened for Shypriss, at the exact same time as Zahnastaazjah had been instated as the first to sit on the new Seat of the Grey. That fact and their being already familiar with one another before their official inductions into the city council, without the statute for wearing concealing robes, had imparted an emergent sentiment of sisterhood between the two. But like all siblings, they often found themselves at odds with one another, and all the more frequently as of late.

The Seven Seats were the secret rulers that governed and controlled all of Goldgarden. No one in the vast city exactly knew whom the ambiguous parliament consisted of. Each member of the Seven was allowed to choose only five, and no more, to be privy to their part on the secret seats. But the chosen five of each member had to be disclosed to each of the other delegates of the Seven in case there were suspicions of unpermitted compromise of classified information or causing other complications to the securities that made the city of Goldgarden so impervious to corruption.

Zahnastaazjah's entrusted men were Xalo and four of her underlords: Usurp, Sundown, Dockjaw, and Devonduer. There had been others in the past, but she didn't take compromise or complications lightly. She had quite the reputation for making her point in the most savage public demonstrations for failure and betrayal among her Stormtrees.

She actually inspired a new standard even for the rest of the Seven on how to discipline those who would jeopardize their confidentiality. She was the only elvan on the council, among six other humans, and a Terollar at that, a breed quite notorious for being particularly barbarous. She owned the stereotype instead of being vexed by it, wearing it like a proud badge to encourage disinclination in her would-be foes.

The scheduling of the Conclave was set such that the Seven Seats would congregate twice a season, and always on different days, so that no parties outside the secret council might suspect any member was a part of Goldgarden's ruling parliament. They never arranged to assemble during the obvious times, such as during the seasonal furrows or at the commencement of a new cycle or on celebrated days. It was always seemingly random, but prearranged for the year beforehand by the consensus of all seven.

Furthermore, each of the Seven Seats had their own officially appointed representative who could be a voice in their stead should minor meetings need to be convened that all the members did not need to attend. Typically, most issues that were to be tended to were between two or maybe three of the factional seats, and they did not call for their overlords to be directly involved in such easily handled matters.

But there were instances in which a member of the Seven deemed it essential to summon all delegates for a sanctioned meeting outside the schedule. It was quite rare, in Zahnastaazjah's experience, but it did occur. And this particular conjuring of the Conclave was precisely one of these instances, with their second official conference in the Dawning season only having been concluded nineteen days ago.

Thederick Tyme, of the Seat of the Black, had sent word of momentous news that might directly affect certain members on the council, and so they had each responded to his call to meet without question—such was the way of respect between the Seven Seats.

By tradition, when one member summoned such an impromptu Conclave, the other six overlords would have their turns to speak first, should they have updates to the current news.

They went around the table clockwise to the Seat of the Green, to the White, to the Red, to the Gold, to the Blue, and then Zahnastaazjah's Seat of the Grey, before finishing with the Seat of the Black.

Shypriss reported her complaint that several of her Dawning mages had taken extravagant bribes to leave Goldgarden to enlist as fast-travel guides for the Green Byway's new movement formulating in Tairancia, evidently matching the bulletins for the same enlistments popularized in Mageholme, again only for Dawning mages. Shypriss also claimed that a new mage named Pyphan had been seen in the city, but he had refused to join the Mage Ward. She was still researching his undetermined agenda.

Zahnastaazjah just peered across the table, glaring a hole into her friend's head, which Shypriss refused to match or take notice of. *You clever woman. You know exactly where the mage is now.*

On to Serafinelan. The Seat of the White updated with further matters on the eastern fronts with the expansion of the Thrench Empire. Evidently, the Emmonost army was amassing a navy on the western banks of the tropical country of Julkunda, which the Thrench had renamed as New Throng. Several harbors now dotted the seacoast, aiming northward to Blood Beach, with nearly a hundred ships already sighted.

This is not news. We've heard this same routine for months. We get it – the Thrench are destroying the elven of the east, my people most of all.

Amethyst told of the conjoining ceremony of Izayus and his sanctified final paramour, Valaythea of House Chandoss, and of the possible future of the formerly disparaged estates of Chandoshia. She also informed them of the status of the distant dominarchs, Vaximus Az'Ampion and Sriyah Hazhalah, who were still away from the Daynish capital, in Barredom, on other political matters concerning the conclusion of the qindrid war in Aggedon.

Arro Gemenis elaborated on the bank's clients who owed debts, which Zahnastaazjah completely tuned out, incidentally still dwelling on Shypriss Sol-War's possible scheming against her now.

Baldric Whereway had more to apprise them of on the Thrench, informing them that Emperor Djediheth Emmonost was asking the city of Goldgarden for a substantial loan from their bank reserves to further their war efforts in the east. Arro argued with Baldric in a brief exchange that it was his place to deal with the city banks as overlord of the Seat of the Gold, and by the end, not a single conclusion had been made about what answer to give to Throng on the matter before the table was passed to Zahnastaazjah.

As Overlord of the Underworld, of local and foreign territories, Zahnastaazjah had her turn to capitalize on recapping news of her habitual topic of concern.

"The Boarneck Company continues to absorb and control the northeast of the city. You cannot step around one corner in Bridgeville or Canaltown without running into one of them. They have been an influx in Little Worest for some while now, now running Outsider's Ring in full. With Boldandgold's regionally widespread propaganda thanks to the draw of the Monodrome, they have taken complete control over the flow of the city. The theater-arena's attractions break all of our laws, yet the Goldguardian Watch now tarries and turns a blind eye to it. Their influence has also infested the thick of the North Docks, smuggling more immigrants in pent by pent from Worestaschia. These Boarnecks now own more housing property than any citizens in the Midway, and they own every shop in Bridgeville. Their wealth proves to be boundless, and in essence, I am telling you that this mercenary company is fast growing into a threat that will soon have the ability to gain power over the isle once their Cavaliers return even richer than before."

Arro Gemenis shifted uncomfortably, aggravated by the ill mention of his Goldguardians, but it was Amethyst, as always, who chose to counter with a debate of her own.

"This is an absurd supposition. Oldan Boldandgold has been a most generous supplier of food to the isle during our most impoverished times in the past. He is practically revered as divine in all of Worestaschia. His and his son's Monodrome has elevated our city's unorthodox reputation, acting as a beacon for popular modernists to come and get a sense of our many wonders."

This Khalimishe cunt's always got something to add.

Zahnastaazjah interlocked her fingers and leaned over the table, glowering at Amethyst. "You would be a supporter of them. But you would not care to share the reason why with the other Seats, it seems. What *she* no doubt knows is a further disconcerting fact I have uncovered. Tristostopher Boldandgold and his subsidiary branch, the Boarneck Cavaliers, have been commissioned by General Randon Roth of Barredom and packed off north to aid in ending the war in Aggedon. We all know Barredom now kisses the heels of the Az'Dayne Dominadom."

"The entire Boarneck Company is comprised of mercenaries. They get paid for a job, and they go to where the job lies," Amethyst returned. "The Boarneck Cavaliers have been hired by other kings in other countries, and no one has stirred a bone. So because a northern warmonger hires their services, you are implying that we should feel some threat from the southern empire?"

Zahnastaazjah burst out in sarcastic laughter. "They have not been a southern empire in quite some time! Az'Dayne is conquering more land in human territories than the Thrench Ashenwave has across all the elvan isles! Do you not see it? The Dominadom now has the Boarneck Company in its pocket. They have been wanting a piece of us since Vaximus took his throne. Oldan Boldandgold is the gatekeeper to Goldgarden City's downfall."

"Far-fetched conjecture again," Amethyst dismissed.

Anyone else in this fucking room? What's your reason for backing the Boarnecks so fervently, Amethyst?

"Since the Boarnecks settled in, the vacancy in northern districts is near zero, and there has been new construction every month. Any shop or house they sell, they raise the price, and a wealthier version of the middle class moves in, improving the state of these wards and the status of our city as a whole," Amethyst defended.

"Why is the Seat of the Red such an advocate of the Boarneck Company suddenly? Have something you wish to share?" She finally had to call Amethyst out.

"I could ask the same as to why the Seat of the Grey is uncharacteristically playing the farce of some feigned vigilante," Amethyst challenged. "Go back to pandering and stick with what fits your skin. Besides, I am surprised we are not turning this on you. You have been blind to several traitors in your naive employ, Crime Queen. Are you even aware that your overman Sundown has his only son employed by the Boarneck Company? He has been the one recruiting the mages from Shypriss's Ward to the Green Byway. Is Sundown not your very own spymaster? I think you are losing grip on the throats of your thugs."

Sundown? Impossible. But it wasn't impossible that her spymaster had finally turned coat. Sundown wasn't the first traitor she had had to filter out of the Stormtrees, and he wouldn't be the last. *Looks like I'll be having a Purge of the Yard sooner than planned. But how is Amethyst coming by this information before me? No doubt Shypriss's mages spilled this leak to you to openly challenge me in front of the Seven. This is Shypriss's way of punishing me for recruiting Pyphan without discussing it with her first.* Zahnastaazjah bitterly pondered.

But Shypriss Sol-War did not play along. The prestigious mage may have been a fire starter in her own way but was never prone to temperamental outbursts in the way Amethyst got out of hand. The Sunder mage instead just brooded and built for probable explosion once tested to her limits. Zahnastaazjah had heard stories and seen minor examples of her ashen aftermath in the past.

The three women on the Seven Seats—Shypriss, Amethyst, and Zahnastaazjah—were all at odds in separate dispositions toward one another, but somehow they managed semicordiality throughout a Conclave.

As if cued, Shypriss Sol-War joined in the squabble. "There is more on the report of these Boarnecks, I fear. Their influence has spread. They have double agents all throughout the Midway and North Docks now in their pocket. I tell you this as a courtesy."

A courtesy? Such a consideration indeed to undermine my control over my own territory in front of the Seven Seats, Zahnastaazjah fumed in her mind. *Dockjaw's territory is the North Docks. You too, old friend?*

She did not want to swallow the possibility of his duplicity as well. "And how might have you come to this conclusion about the Midway and North Docks?"

"Because I was kind not to formerly mention openly, but it has been your men, paid by the Boarneck Company, who have been acting as liaisons to recruit my Dawning mages for this Green Byway," Shypriss said. "Your overmen who manage these turncoats should be reprimanded, of course, not you. It is not your fault you trusted untrustworthy men."

Zahnastaazjah chuckled at the clear jab. *You just openly called me incompetent in front of the Seven Seats. Xalo, where are you at? Get in here and take the green out of this mage.* "Convenient," she said instead, collecting herself, taking a deep breath before speaking again. "And why would my Stormtrees be doing this? Would one of you two like to educate me?"

"Well it is clear that you simply are not able to pay them well anymore since the Boarneck expansion," Shypriss taunted further. "You do not need to be the Overlord of the Underworld to hear that rumor abound on the streets."

Zahnastaazjah turned her head away from the council to glower back at the door she came in at, hiding her building rage, and seeing if she could feel the draw of her bloodrime spear for if she was able to return it to her grasp from such a distance. *Too far ... Too far.*

Thederick timely intervened to break the three women apart from each other's throats, and shifted to a different subject to keep the peace, being that it was him that called this Conclave in the first place. "Scarless, have you discovered any more news from your contact in Frostdale of what we were looking into privately that you wish to share?"

That I wish to share with this loathsome lot? You think I will ever impart anything I learn to any of you here? It is clear I am the outcast because I am the only elvan and none of you want me here, she vented her frustrations in her mind. Her contact was her son, Sorovronus, who had somehow manipulated his way to becoming the High Chancellor of Frostdale. How he pulled that off, being a Terollar elvan, she could not fathom.

Sadly, however, Zahnastaazjah had not been returning the correspondence. Sorovronus was an advocate of her father's, on his timeless lifequest waging strife against the Neveril elven.

Her father, spawned as just Jhuvonus, was the fifth born male son with five female daughters born between each male birth; symbolized with the widely believed superstition of destined good for the elvan race, as it embodied two parent lifemates of perfect balance in their hunder. Her father's parents were even titled "the Balanced" by the Arastarianar Sentinels, who involved themselves on the eastern attacks against the Caelduyan since the nation had turned to the Qindrid Transcendence by introduction of the umbran on their borderlands.

Jhuvonus was raised in an era of war, as the Terollar had been dubbed by the Sylvanil Sentinel Order the first race of official hunters to seek out and destroy their own elvankind —the Shiniryn and Wyldenar umbran, and the qindrid they turned, as the abominations went against the Balance of the elvan faith.

Two hundred and fifty years ago Jhuvonus's father was slain by Neveril assassins in Zsolindal with organized stoneborne qindrid backing them in a failed approach on the heart of the Aggedonian empire. This was the first time the Neveril were recorded to be an enemy of their fellow elvan race. Immediately following, each sibling of the Balanced was blessed by the Sylvanil Sentinel Order as *Khomo* or *Khema* respectively whether male or female as a prefix to their name, meaning "chosen voice of the people."

The offspring of the ten chosen siblings were promised no such royalties unless certain prerequisites from Arastarianar were met. Jhuvonus was ordained as Khomo'Jhuvonus thenceforth, honored with the such a title as Chosen before he ever even met his lifemate, which was a historical first amongst all Terollar, much less all elvankind. But it was from that day and onward that Khomo'Jhuvonus would impose all of those affiliated with him to entwine themselves to his violent saga to purge the Neveril from Penthara's hidden pockets.

Zahnastaazjah had all but forgotten about the Neveril elven and their irrelevance to her current circumstances until Sorovronus had begun dispatching letters to her hinting in code of their return.

Beloved Mother,

The ghosts of our destiny's charge lie beneath the cold hearth you chose not to come home to. The white cats father was looking for are for sale in the black markets of Az'Dayne. Perhaps you can find him one there. If not in Az'Dayne, then perhaps you can find one of the white cats in Goldgarden now too. I hear they are becoming more popular. Father misses you and says to reach out.

Your Forever Son

It was just one of the many attempts her son had tried to whet her interest. The ghosts and white cats were code words for Neveril. The "cold hearth" she "chose not to come home to" was implying the Glace Isles, and encompassed Barredom and Aggedon where her father's efforts had been concentrated. He continued to imply that the Neveril elvan were spreading beneath specific human nations. The conspiracy theory her father obsessed over was not anything she wished to entertain; in fact, it was the very definition of what she had cowardly run from so long ago, when she ventured across half the realm to come to Goldgarden.

But the truth was, she did entertain it. But she would not give her father or her son the satisfaction in knowing just yet. Her position on the Seat of the Grey as Overlord of the Underworld entailed not only the dealings in such jurisdictions as Goldgarden, but also foreign, where she had gradually managed to expand her spy network to. She began with the Savatarm Provinces before expanding to Khalimia, and just recently, within the year had breached a foothold in Az'Dayne, impregnating even the capital Everdawn itself.

Fortunately, her doomed spymaster, Sundown, was not privy to this private sector of the Stormtrees. Other than Xalo, no one knew that they even existed other than Devonduer, whom her lead espionage operative reported to through agents of his own. His name was Threpetoe, and the sector was titled the Cobra Collective, which was an entirely separate division that Scarless kept secretly funded through her Stormtrees. Almost every agent of the Cobra Collective, other than the highest officers, were not even aware of their affiliation to her guild.

And Threpetoe's enterprise of intelligence gathering had been utterly effectual. His plethora of ciphered messages came back with similar content as what Sorovronus had sent. There were indeed Neveril elven beneath the main city streets throughout Az'Dayne and Khalimia. And his most recent reports even suggested some form of shape-changers involved as well, taking part in the political scope of the Dominadom.

Scarless let what Thederick inquired from her marinate for a moment in her mind — *have you discovered any more news from your contact in Frostdale of what we were looking into privately that you wish to share?* She glanced at each cowled figure in the room, all shrouded in separate colors, and reminded herself that she liked nor trusted not a single one of them. "Nothing yet," was all she curtly lied back with.

Finally, with all side business settled, Thederick Tyme chose to take the floor to apprise of news in the north, the reason they were all here today out of schedule. "In spite and in light, then, my fellow brothers and sisters." Thederick held up two fingers to motion for silence, and all eyes fell on him. "But now for the true reason for summoning you all to this particular Conclave. I have heavy news to burden you with. Some it will impact more than others."

Zahnastaazjah already had a sick churning in her gut as she felt the man robed in all black was insinuating her. She glimpsed his neck slightly turning to his right to aim his gaze at her when he finished his sentence.

"First, Aggedon is falling. Strange reports hail from all across Barredom that the entire army of qindrid that occupied the Fourteen and guarded the land bridge of Continents' Kiss has bizarrely vanished. As have many other clans within their towns. And no one knows why or where to."

"Magic, maybe?" Baldric questioned.

Shypriss confirmed the facts of history. "Mages have never been known to aid the qindrid. They actually even warred against them when allying with Barredom, but that, as you all know, was generations ago."

"The dominarchs of the Az'Dayne Dominadom, as Amethyst established at the last Conclave," Thederick continued, "are now in Barredom, at Frostdale. If these stoneborne and greyborne are indeed gone from the north completely, this will give Az'Dayne control not only of Barredom but Aggedon too. Khalimia, Az'Eloth, Psaegora, half of Tairancia, and the list is growing. When will their reach and expansion end? I agree with Scarless that we need to get involved and discover their endgame, or we will find ourselves wedged between the two powerful empires of the Thrench and

Az'Dayne, making one our enemy over the other, or becoming absorbed ourselves to bow just as low as Barredom was forced to."

Many eyes looked at Amethyst, who was the overlord whose sole responsibility was keeping them apprised of the Dominadom's advances.

"I will personally involve myself with my contacts in the region to find those answers by the next Conclave," Amethyst vowed.

"And that is not all," Thederick went on. "The leader of these qindrid—this Last Umbran, as they call her, Lilealah—was captured. And she has been brought into Barredish custody, in their dungeons. What her fate is from there, I have found out no more as of yet."

"Go on." Zahnastaazjah could sense his hesitation, because he was just staring at her now. A few seconds went by, and for whatever reason, he gave all attention over to her alone. "Finish it. I am ready to hear it." But she knew she likely wasn't.

"In the capture of this Last Umbran, General Randon Roth of Barredom also managed to apprehend a large group of Terollar from the Glace Isles, known as their Glazjhendun," he declared.

"I know what the Glazjhendun is, Thederick." She was not trying to hide her annoyance and desire that he get on with what he wanted to say.

"Your brother Zuulzinj—Kind-Eyes, they refer to him as—was in the party. He is being brought to the Frostdale Deeps for interrogation set to be carried out by the Royal Inquisitor, Honorah Bayn. She has ..." He paused again.

Damn this man!

"A reputation."

Zahnastaazjah was about to interrupt and ask something, but Thederick finished his spiel with what he had obviously been reserving all along. "One death did occur in the apprehension beforehand, however. The king of the Glace Isles was executed by his own, they say. Khomo'Jhuvonus has been officially heralded as dead across the north."

No other words came from Thederick. The room went as still and silent as a crypt. Zahnastaazjah's poor brother was about to die a slow and horrible death unfitting for an elvan warrior. And her father ...

She counted back how many cycles it had been since she had last seen him. *Twenty-two cycles.* It felt like a lifetime, even in elvan years. *En khomo naso rahsee'ahsee.* It was a famous saying on the Glace Isles. The tribesven were a superstitious lot that had come to revere her father almost like a god among their ilk. They believed he could not actually die for good. In truth, Zahnastaazjah admitted to herself, she had come to see merit in the popular chant as well over the years and was convinced her father actually was a Chosen of the Balance, invincible to permanent death.

She didn't know what she was allowed to feel in the moment, but she did know that none of these other six in the room was worthy to witness a weakness in her emotions. She needed to leave.

Zahnastaazjah found herself standing now, both palms clenched around the edge of the table in front of her seat. "I am indebted to you for the news. Conclave is concluded for today. I will excuse myself."

And with that, she bowed and took her leave of the chamber in a rush to be out of her robe and back in Scarless Square, where she could breathe and feel again.

There she found Xalo and Devonduer patiently waiting for her as instructed in her designated tunnel, which led back underground and would navigate them all the way to their ward in the city. She discarded her grey robe on a wall mount nearby and didn't slow her pace one bit as she pushed through between them.

"Anything we should know, Scarless? Tell me what you need us to do." Devonduer trotted to keep up beside her.

"Yes. Call in the men. Every one of them."

"Okay. I can do that for you." Devonduer looked nervously at Xalo and then back to his guildmother. "And then what are we going to do?"

Scarless was approaching her bloodrime spear, which she had placed at the doorway to the Hall of the Grey, which led back into the Flush. She lifted her empty right hand as if beckoning to it, and the weapon instantly flew from its perch into her grasp.

She chose to kick the door open, with its busted latch, instead of reaching for the knob. *Then the traitors in my employ die.* She trusted no one at this point. Not even Xalo or Devonduer. She answered with the only fact she was willing to admit to her own. "Then we enact the Purge of the Yard. We are going to clean up."

SYMBELLE & FYHEIR (II)

FIRST OF A KIND

Symbelle stood on the top floor of the broken bell tower, surveying the lay of the forbidden ground as if it were deadly molten lava. The air of the scourged village was so thick with pestilence that she felt as if she could almost see it. Languid townsfolk infected with marks of the plague and pox streamed in and out of the dilapidated shacks.

The Plaguefolk Villages were all that this peculiar locale had ever been known to be named. There had never not been a putrid disease in its citizens for as long as the small community had sat on the edge of the Mekohan Forest, now dubbed the Sickwoods due to the state of the villages. The history of what had happened to the people was an enigma, but one fact remained: no visitors ever came.

Symbelle had just learned that this was for good reason, however, and all part of the facade. The entire purpose of the Plaguefolk Villages was to act as a front for the entrance into the Oathemic Cabal's central hub. The ailing people roaming about its withered streets had voluntarily taken the sickness induced through shadow magic cast by Coldborn, the founder of the organization. The surface effect was merely aesthetic, causing no real harm to their perfect health. In fact, it magically reinforced their constitutions against contracting an illness of any kind whatsoever. The citizens of the Plaguefolk Villages were just normal people bound to the same oath of secrecy as she was.

She had come to learn that the mysterious man who had identified himself as her father, the founder of the Oathemic Cabal, was a royal named Endrith Goldfyre, the single Umbra archmage on all of Penthara. The members were strictly told to refer to him as Coldborn and never by his real name, since there was a severe penalty for ever mentioning the Goldfyre name or those of its bloodline, by the Dominadom's ordinance.

Coldborn was an obscure individual of unknown but indisputably unparalleled power. Making matters more politically complicated, Endrith should have been the rightful occupant of the Az'Dayne throne, if lines of succession had been appropriately handled by law, disregarding the stipulations of mage prejudices, and if there had been no sudden ascendance of House Ampion.

Before the Ampion enthronement of Vaximus thirty years ago, the Goldfyre lineage had ruled all of Az'Dayne and its outlying provinces for nearly five centuries. The bloodline of the Goldfyres was as close to the original Dayne heritage that had begun the cross-descendancy of tairan with the Tairancians and fire with the Khalimishe in the ancient past. House Goldfyre was the royal embodiment of what it meant to be Daynish at its core, between the tairan and fire elements.

But the latter generations of the Goldfyres had begun a marriage alliance with the northern Barredish, those known to be Aggeans of the tairan-shadow cross-descendancy. What had begun as a pact to establish peace, power, and trade with a foreign war nation had gradually stimulated discord among the opposed aristocracy throughout Az'Dayne.

It was known that when a cross-descendancy interbred with a different cross-descendancy, one of their elemental lineages would eventually bleed out. It would begin with the tairan element as the first to be diluted out, followed by the fire element, then the sky, and then the shadow, and never the water element if it was at all involved in both parties breeding. After five generations of different cross-descendancies, the seed of each descendancy was said to bleed out completely in this order. As both the Daynish and Barredish had tairan in their elemental lineage, and fire came before shadow in the order, it was obvious which would bleed out for the Goldfyre line.

The fire element had essentially dissipated from their descendancy, and the royal bloodline had become practically Barredish with strong ties to the tairan element. Insurgencies had arisen, blaming Barredom for a conceived scheme that had taken one hundred and twenty-five years to somehow usurp the throne of Az'Dayne from the inside out. The last of the royal line in power was Endrith, the elder, and his younger brother, Kythaeus.

But Endrith had been born hunder-touched and proven as a mage early on in life, rapidly growing in renowned power. During Endrith and Kythaeus's upbringing, it was established by their father, former king Anderon Goldfyre, that Endrith would not be subject to the same punishment of the typical hunder-touched. He was allowed a royal privilege to create a special order for those half cursed, half blessed. This was the founding of the Oathemic Cabal.

Coldborn had created a covert haven for the magic-bound would-be exiles discovered within Az'Dayne's vast dominion. King Anderon saw the advantage in utilizing mages and spellblades in the nation's interest, as long as they were kept under control, and who better to do this than his elder son? This was his reasoning. Anderon capitalized on Endrith's matchless cunning to construct a network of intelligence agents and sanctioned assassins like none any nation had dared to create before.

The Oathemic Cabal was not meant as an authority under the nation's king, current or in the future. Its purpose and power were elevated above the monarchs. They were the true protectors, watchers, and silent soldiers of Az'Dayne's best interests, as well as the realm's security as a whole against growing power in human nations and elvan movements, whether territory-expanding, magic-involving, or supernaturally enhanced altogether. It was Coldborn's resourceful information ring that kept those in power over Az'Dayne informed of any potential threats. And it was his specialized assassins who were assigned to effectively eliminate such threats. The order was an unrivaled fraternity that stood as a critical asset for Az'Dayne's strength.

The long-lasting Goldfyre reign did finally end, with King Anderon and later his son, King Kythaeus, the last ruling monarch of the bloodline. They succumbed to tragic fates that were publicized as the will of the Five and Five by the Pentagogue for mortal sins committed against the faith. The details of how Anderon and Kythaeus met their ends formed an obscured subject of exaggerated hearsay and eccentric theories for the common folk far and wide across Central Taira.

Even King Kythaeus's infant son was claimed to have been discovered dead the same day Kythaeus had been pronounced deceased. Coincidentally, the ill-fated babe had been born within the same month as Izayus, the only son of the rising new rulers of Az'Dayne, Vaximus Ampion and Sriyah Hazhalah.

But with all the Goldfyres down the line finding misfortunes of ruin and demise, there was one Goldfyre who found himself immune. As the Cabalists liked to sometimes whisper, "the Forgotten Unforgotten," in reverence to their founder. Endrith "Coldborn" Goldfyre remained invulnerable to the penalties wrought on his royal house, with the backing of his deeply entrenched agency of death-dealers.

Symbelle's father had taught her much before she was turned over to Master Claydius, who had acted as her educational chaperone since she had first arrived. Coldborn had been scarce ever since the initial briefing in the mirrored room. He only checked in for follow-up lore sessions as she turned in for the evening.

Claydius was a tier-four mage, a class of mage whose members were universally dubbed sorcerers. He was bound to the Dawning season, with a mastery over the tairan element. He had remained entirely obscured by a green robe and featureless black mask with emerald stones scattered about the face, resembling pockets of pestilence. The telltale halos around his green irises were strong and vibrant.

Symbelle had been forced to don her own custom mask as well, crafted of her own engineering. The leather-and-metal breathing apparatus was fitted over her nose and the lower half of her face, with dual filters and respirator valves on both sides of her mouth. Her goggles locked in just above, making the entire design quite modern compared to anything her peers had attempted to devise.

After the morning lectures on the lore of the Oathemic Cabal, she would be escorted through the intricate layers of the clandestine organization that was now her new home, a haven of highly trained killers and masters of espionage. Understanding the central hub's layout was a chore of the mind in itself.

Day by day, Symbelle had come to learn more from Master Claydius concerning the different factions within the fraternity.

The first faction the Cabal had been founded around was the Hunder Order. These were the exonerated mages of Az'Dayne's jurisdiction, under the protection of Coldborn's immunity. Those of the Hunder Order each wore a unique monster mask, individually fashioned for the agent to symbolize whatever element they had control over.

The Hive Order comprised the infamous assassins that carried out the legal execution writs approved by the Pentagogue and the Imperial Throne of Az'Dayne. Their daggers they left planted in their victims, decorated with a green tassel hanging from the butt of the hilt, signified the work of their faction.

The merciless Hive Order wore the masks that Symbelle recalled in her flashbacks of the massacre of Tairanchula. Their unsettling design was like something out of a nightmare. Their faces were grey, their lips as still as stone, a cross between something human and something insect underneath.

She had yet to interact with the Nectar Order but had heard of them. This was the faction of writ-runners, watchers, and informants, a widespread network of espionage on different levels. The spies were referred to as rats, while the couriers were called crows, and the field agents that interacted with the Hive and Hunder Order were known as vultures.

Symbelle noticed a pattern in the masks and ranks throughout the assassins' guild, even before Master Claydius had explained the significance to her. The Nectar Order's rats, crows, and vultures, the Hive Order's insectoid masks, and the Hunder Order's monster masks, they were all symbols of dark tidings or things the world saw as omens of death.

Other than the Keepers' Order that consisted of the guild's supervision, the last order of the Oathemic Cabal she was aware of was called the Dayne-Web. They were the guildhouse defenders, the stewards, and the collectors, who would meet with privileged contacts from above. Their faction could be identified by their black masks covered in menacing gold-painted webs across the entirety of the face. They never left the confines of the hubs.

Hours of silence had passed and the darkness of dusk had begun to settle over the deteriorating rooftops. At the bottom of the bell tower, they came upon a hidden hatch door that led to the winch lift they had arrived in the village on. Once on the platform, Claydius rang a small bell that resonated down the cylindrical well, and the lift began to vibrate and slowly move.

Claydius drew up the sleeve of his robe to reveal the gold Dawning magemarks across his right forearm, and one promptly began to glow. She could tell that the lift had suddenly changed direction, moving horizontally now instead of vertically.

"You are casting tairan magic, are you not?" She was inquisitive, never having actually witnessed magic being cast in front of her to her memory as an adult. "Just as Pyphan can now. Will I, as a hyperi, acquire the ability to channel magic also?"

"As mages, as Coldborn, Pyphan, and I are," he began, "we are merely conduits who have been interfused with a wisp since birth, able to pull from avenues of elemental magic bound to our season. You, on the other hand, are a hybrid form of raw magic itself in the flesh. Your power comes from within your senses. But you have never learned much of this, which is why we are here today."

Symbelle hesitated for advice from Fyheir, but nothing came. "You asked to speak to me alone. I was waiting on you to begin."

"Alone," Claydius began. "That is the question of the hour. Are we alone though Symbelle?"

"I do not understand Master," she blurted ignorantly.

"But I think you do," he challenged her honesty. "You can see what we others cannot. Your father. Is he here?" Claydius began to peer at each corner of the enclosed lift as if Coldborn had magically merged with the shadows. "With us, or nearby?"

She squinted her glowing violet eyes to the same shadows, seeing no traces of anything magic in the vicinity other than the palpable green aura that radiated over Claydius himself. "I cannot use my hypersight as well as you may think I can. And my father, though his aura is stronger than anyone I can ever remember," she put herself in check from finishing, apprehensive from revealing too much about her ineptitude.

"You can speak plainly with me girl," Claydius coerced in an annoyed tone.

"He is able to hide it at times, almost entirely." Symbelle knew her explanation was even more ambiguous than the empty shadows. "But no, I have not sensed him here in the hub within the last few days. I believe him gone."

"Yet the next question still remains," Claydius teased as his forearm glyphs flared up green once again and the lift abruptly stopped altogether. "Why would I be curious if he is here or gone?"

Breathe. Fire needs to breathe if it wants to live, Fyheir surfaced with simple advice. And Symbelle did breathe finally. "I am at the mercy of your enlightenment Master."

"I serve Coldborn. Know this. I have served him since the first days of the Oathemic Cabal's origination," Claydius assured, shifting seemingly nervously as he took caution elaborating. "Times are changing rapidly however. There is a predator bird hovering above the new nest you have fluttered into. Our guild is not what it once was. The Az'Dayne Dominadom has a heavy hand over our creed's old ways. Policies are being challenged. The throne has sent in agents to join us by our consent, but Coldborn has found ways to eliminate or convert them thus far. They have also breached our guild with a new breed of infiltrators, ones that can change the way they appear entirely — skin-changers. Your father has discovered and expelled those as well."

Your master mage here is flirting with an insurgency. Let him play his hand. He is subtly proposing an offer for us, Fyheir counseled in her mind to stay her tongue and let Claydius continue.

And Claydius did. "To speak more plainly, the trajectory of the Oathemic Cabal and the Dominadom have been diverging since the Ampion rule took the throne from the Goldfyre reign."

"But Coldborn saved me. More than once. He is my father." *If you were fathered by shadow, let it be known you were born from a mother of the true fire that is I.* "I will do as he bids me, as I should?"

"Did he save you though?" Master Claydius debated her rebuttals again. "He plucked you from your mother where you were far safer. He hid you away your entire life, and then injected you into a home of assassins without training you to kill or use your hyperi talents. You are special Symbelle. You are important, more than you know. The hours near when you must decide."

We were correct. Entertain him. Do not be weak little girl. "That sounds like betrayal to my own blood." Symbelle ignored Fyheir's condescending guidance. "Are you betraying him? Is this a test?"

Claydius violently cast down his mask and robe to the floor, bearing nothing but his breeches and shoes. His infuriated face showed his age, likely later in his fifth decade, his beard and hair a mix between greys and white, but his body was more muscularly defined than she imagined a human could possibly physically achieve. She was at least educated enough in magic lore to know that the physical attributes of mages greatly enhanced the more powerful they became, and Claydius was professed as a tier-four of his kind.

"A test or a trick? Everything anyone ever ask of you from this point forward in your life will be a test for you I fear Symbelle. I am merely showing you the doors that you can open. Death exists in either side."

He is threatening us. "My death?" She had to know, now worried for her life.

"The doors are these," Claydius held a hand up towards one side in the lift, and a glowing green line forming an ethereal door began to take shape.

"Upon choosing to enter the first door, you will be presented with a writ to eliminate two dangerous high-profile targets — Scarless, Crime Queen of Goldgarden, the founder of the Stormtrees, and Xalo of Spellspire, her spellblade bloodguard. Scarless and Xalo are the main barriers between us and our necessary permeation throughout Goldgarden's infrastructure. Scarless is planning to embed a spy network of her own within Az'Dayne's jurisdiction, and she has slain agents of the Cabal during her reign over the Goldgarden underworld," he expounded on the familiar subjects.

He is oblivious of the writ you received from Coldborn. Symbelle conjectured that as well without needed Fyheir to point it out. She kept that fact to herself, and shifted instead, "How many has she killed?"

"If I told you it was one, that would be too many," he stated bluntly. "She has killed many more than just one."

The magical door began to fade as Claydius continued. "In order to accomplish this, you will be reunited with your half-brother Pyphan who is already implanted within their ranks. His role as a double agent is not unlike your own. He reports to me that he is currently securing you a place for your specialized talents in the Stormtrees to ensure her fall goes smoothly, without knowledge that the Cabal was ever involved at all. You have received this writ already haven't you?"

The writs she received from her father were for Oldan Boldandgold and Amethyst to be assassinated, not Scarless and Xalo. She was tasked to join the Stormtrees and perform as a triple agent, gaining affiliation with the Boarneck Company to manipulate Scarless into doing the assassinations in public herself. It was all similar, but far the opposite, contradicting the fates of one side to another. It was not until this moment that Symbelle truly understood that Coldborn and Claydius were aligned differently.

Symbelle meekly nodded in affirmation to Claydius's question, not feeling comfortable with lying to someone of his power and station, fearing he could read through her.

"You hesitate and counter in silence not because you do not wish to see Pyphan. No," he paused to muse and study her. "It is because you are not yet a killer in your mind. You want another way, don't you Symbelle? You want the other door?"

She watched as Claydius created another makeshift magical door on the opposite side of the lift as the one before. She removed her own breathing mask and goggles finally, matching Claydius's style of bare vulnerability. The small enclosed cubical lit up with a violet hue even brighter from her exposed hyperi eyes. "Tell me of my other choice."

"No killing on your part at all. No direct death-dealing by any means," he offered, feeding into her misgivings for violence. "No writs."

"How? But Coldborn —," she was interrupted.

"Is not here today," Claydius finished her sentence. "And might not be on the morrows. The doors are in front of you."

The first ghostly door began to take form once again. "The second door leads to a path only a hyperi can take. Your presence here is now known and the word has spread afar, and far too fast. You are being requested to Spellspire by Mesdarro."

Symbelle was confused, trying to keep up with all of the strange new names. "I do not know who that is."

"Mesdarro is the Magistrate of Spellspire. He is one of the only other known hyperi in the realm, next to you and one other. Mesdarro wants to train you on how to use your hypersight, as an advantage for our guild and Az'Dayne itself. It would be a greater benefit to the Oathemic Cabal for you to choose this door. It would be a safer path for you."

Why her father did not mention this as an option for her she could not comprehend? Why would he not want her trained as a hyperi, but instead was rushing her into a suicide quest even for the most highly trained assassins to pull off? "How long do I have before I must decide?"

Master Claydius's low voice softened and he smiled, trying futilely to lighten the grim mood. "You are the first of a kind within our guild. The first to be excused from taking the oath that we all had to. The first female in our strict fraternity. The only hyperi."

He let his last words trail and resonate and there was a long gap between the next words spoken. Symbelle glanced long at the first door and then the second. She did not want to make an enemy of the father she had never known, a man even more powerful than Claydius. But Coldborn's path led to death, many others and almost unavoidably her own. And the other path ...

Unleash the fire. Let Fyheir fill you whole. I will protect us. Tiny Symbelle need not fear the first door. The second door will not close for us.

"What do you suggest I do, Master Claydius?"

Magemarks blazed green across Claydius's muscular torso and suddenly his body merged into the lift, vanishing from sight, and taking the light from the formerly glowing doors with him as they dissipated after him.

"Choose the right door," his voice echoed from within the walls. And then it went quiet as the lift started down again.

ADYSSAIRA (II)

GIFTBEARER

This used to be her favorite part of the pent: the Teaching Hours. But that had been when Valaythea was still present. It had only been two sessions since her sister had been absent, called away from the estates, sworn to her new role as a paramour to the prince of the Dominadom, but Adyssaira had not recovered from the loss of her best friend's presence at Castle Chandoss since the night of the betrothal.

And though her home was referred to as a castle by name, all who visited the grandiose estates in person knew that it was unequivocally a palace. Not a single defensive structure could be found around the premises. *Palace Chandoss* would have been a better term to describe it, she had always felt. It was the most extravagant royal residence in all of Chandoshia, outrivaling every other palace in Az'Dayne, arguably next to a few found in Everdawn.

Four golden onion domes marked the corners of the massive architectural marvel, with a taller one erecting from the center of the palace. Atop their bulbous steeps a finial was formed from each, painted and shaped to resemble a flame. The five domes altogether symbolized massive candles, manifesting a certain aesthetic and religious attitude that identified with Az'Dayne's elemental descendancy between the embodiment of tairan and fire.

She and the rest of the girls restlessly sat waiting for her uncle to begin in the solarium of the palace. The glass-domed study chamber brimmed with artsy decor that was both eccentrically exotic and traditionally historic, whether elvan or from human regions overseas, from the Daynish homeland and its neighboring territories. Each abstract sculpture, each defined statuette, each precious bauble, they were all gifts that had once been given to House Chandoss by other great houses of Az'Dayne or nations and races that had held her ancestors in high esteem at one time.

The circular room maintained enough furniture for two decem individuals to lounge comfortably in its ample offering of plush couches and chairs, but it never needed that many seats. Only the family's most immediate members were ever allowed within the sacred chamber. Not even the guards or servants were permitted to enter, with a most severe punishment for trespass.

And that was all for the single reason of the lone item it secured—Nikayle the Firstnamed's spellblade. The magnificent dormant magic sword effortlessly stole the attention of all the other striving splendors in the room. Its potential power was unmistakable. Fastened just over the mantel above the fireplace near the doorway, the sheathed spellblade perched untouched on the only wooden wall in the sunroom, as it had remained since its last chosen wielder's unexplained demise.

Adyssaira had always feared the Chandoss Spellblade. It was an evil, sinister thing of death to her, for both those who were cursed to hold it and those who got in its way. The sentient weapon was comprised of elvan bone in the hilt, a gold-inlaid guard shaped like a winged serpent, an allegedly indestructible glass blade that was practically a phylactery for elvan souls and devoured mages' spellpowers, and a sharp emerald far more exquisite than any she had ever seen come out of any of the Chandoshian gem mines.

The sun was at its brightest point, gleaming through the curved panels of masterfully crafted glass that windowed the outer walls of the solarium. It was high noon, the time the Teaching Hours always began every five days. The name given to the tutoring sessions was a bit misleading, as the girls did attend a form of schooling every day, but that was from routine visits to the library to pore over designated tomes scheduled in advance.

The Teaching Hours were different. Adyssaira's uncle, Nikayle the Thirdnamed, summoned the girls to the solarium every pent to play the role of their lecturer for a five-hour course on countless educational topics. As of late, he had tried to make his sermons more entertaining, but he seemed to be losing his touch or running out of new material to teach. Adyssaira had started to feel as if she had read the same hundred-something books three to four times over. But the fact that her uncle even devoted such unwavering adoration on the girls to provide the Teaching Hours made him more fatherly in that aspect to them than their often-secluded father, Ethiass.

She sat against the window in her preferred chair, the only one she ever sat in, an overly large thing of incredibly plump orange cushions that could have fitted at least three of her in it. A skinny end table made of twisted brass separated her and her sister Odysserae, who sat directly across from her in a comparable chair of sun-yellow cushions.

Adyssaira attempted to play foot kiss with her sibling under the table out of sheer boredom while they awaited their tardy uncle, but Odysserae seemed in a particularly distant mood. Adyssaira's silent sister had always been a bit incomprehensible and definitely withdrawn from social engagement, but today she seemed even more estranged. Adyssaira held an empathy with her identical sister even more than with Valaythea.

Odysserae just stared out across the serene view of the Aemenus River meeting the mouth of Lake Chandoss. Her soft amber eyes were glossy, as if on the verge of tears, and they fixated on the small island of Carolelle, nestled not far off the castle harbor. She seemed so innocent and vulnerable in the scene of it all. Her short red hair was fixed in no style of intended direction, and her habitual pout made her appear about half a decade younger than she was. She held both of her hands together, palm in palm, not moving a muscle, as if she was comforting herself with her own touch.

Adyssaira removed a slipper from her right foot and squeezed two of her toes to pinch her sister around the exposed part of her shin.

"*Stop,*" Odysserae waved in the silence of Hands.

At least Adyssaira had gotten a reaction out of her. *What is wrong, Oddy?*

The girls all had their short names for each other: Ember for Emberalda, Val for Valaythea, and Addy for herself. But if any of the nicknames were specifically fitting, Oddy for Odysserae was on point by definition. Adyssaira had always deemed the moniker a bit cruel when said aloud, but it had stuck with her peculiar sibling since she was a teen nonetheless.

As if Odysserae understood her inward sympathy, she just looked back at her and shook her head in reluctance to open up and turned away from the glass to grudgingly gaze back into the room.

Sitting on her rump with her legs bowed and rocking on the floor in the center of the sunroom was their youngest sister, Sashka, holding several books, ready to begin the day's lessons. She was only twelve years old to Adyssaira and Odysserae's twenty and of a different mother than their own. But Sashka was more than just a half sister; she was half-elvan as well.

It was a popular yet abominable practice many of the neighboring Zandaryn elven were notorious for: engaging with the local Khalimishe and Daynish not in favor with the Dominadom. It was called the Taboo of the Quasi, as quasi were elven who had irrevocably disconnected themselves from their lifetrees in order to mate with humans. In fact, the Savatari, of the provinces in between the two power nations, even openly endorsed the detested communion to breed the rare hybrids of a quasi and human. Such half-elvan crossbreeds were known as the Z'shun, and the main elvan race that was known to commonly commit to that path of the Taboo was the Zandaryn from Zandabar.

Little Sashka's ears were almost the same size as a human's, barely longer, but ended in definite points, which peeked through her thin yellow hair, braided quite chaotically in different patterns that her mother had fashioned, just grazing the bottom of her neck. One of Sashka's eyes was orange in the iris, while the other was more of a pale gold. Her skin was the bronzish tan shared by both Daynish humans and Zandaryn elven.

Ethiass and Sashka's elvan mother, Taizsha, had committed to their hushed affair not long after the death of Adyssaira's mother upon the triplets' birth. Adyssaira and her sisters had just assumed the pleasant Zandaryn woman was her father's fair-faced, exotic chamberlain, whom he had inducted into the services of managing privy estate details while the sisters were growing up. They had been kept in the dark until they had come of appropriate age in their early teens, finally being enlightened that Taizsha had become a quasi.

But such news hadn't been a secret for quite some years now. Ethiass and Taizsha had been proudly "married" for six years, openly flaunting their officiality, even though their matrimony was considered unsanctioned by the laws of the Dominadom, which did not recognize such unorthodox unions. As the region of Chandoshia had remained its own, ignored within the empire nation, her father did not seem to hold a care for the Dominadom's snubs of his own personal decisions for peace and happiness.

Adyssaira picked at her irritating blindfold as she frowned at her half sister across the room. She was indeed accustomed to wearing the thin Savatarm silk sash to conceal her green eyes, and such an expensive fabric was transparent enough for her to see through without others gauging the color of her irises, but it was still a vexing hindrance she wished she didn't have to endure. Typically, in this area of Castle Chandoss, she was permitted to be free of it, but not within the presence of Sashka, who was kept in the dark about Adyssaira's hunder-touched condition.

After a little over half an hour, the girls' tutor for the day did finally show. Their uncle, Nikayle, was a crippled, rotund man, but not long ago he had been respected for his swordsmanship and known to be quite nimble on his feet. But that was six years ago, before his misfortunate fall from atop Valdean's tower, just outside Castle Chandoss. Nikayle never talked to the girls about what had happened the day of his accident, but the whispers around Chandoshia were that he had attempted to take his own life after suffering from depression in mourning for his wife, Delphine, who had passed from the plague. He had since been completely paralyzed from the waist down and was barely able to move his neck without excruciating pain.

His daughter, Emberalda, Adyssaira's elder cousin by one year, rolled him in on a wooden wheelchair to the center of the room, against a table prepared with a stack of books for the day's lessons.

Emberalda was blessed with the recognized Chandoss beauty, like the rest of them. Her long hair was the lightest of browns, almost fading into blond, and it was worn like the local elven instead of in the modern regional fashions. Emberalda's amber eyes were always set to a mischievous intent, matching the smirks soon to follow. She was often classified as the instigating rebel of their familial clique. Her cousin was a few inches taller than Adyssaira and her two sisters, more angular in features.

In fact, with Nikayle the Thirdnamed being the elder brother of Ethiass, and Emberalda being a year senior to the triplets, it should have been more politically correct to incline the Prince of Az'Dayne to seek her hand as his paramour instead of Valaythea's. But her cousin had ultimately stained her legitimacy the moment she had chosen to openly present herself as taking the same path as Ethiass and Taizsha.

Taizsha had two male bloodlinks who would visit her throughout the years in Castle Chandoss. In human vocabulary, *bloodlink* was simply the elvan term for "sibling," and in such translation, Taizsha's brothers of mention were Timmurian and Sundorion.

Both Zandaryn elven had a reputation for investigative habits, prying and researching too deeply in places they weren't always welcome and creating a wake of enemies in the lands they traveled through.

The younger of the three Zandaryn, Timmurian the Lorebringer, had concentrated his efforts close to home, in Khalimia, Savatarm, and only recently in Chandoshia itself, as he had decided to move to the Chandoss Estates to be nearer to Taizsha.

Sundorion the Cosmopolitan, on the other hand, was vastly more experienced in his exploits. He was a well-traveled archaeologist who held relics and stories from several corners of Penthara that he claimed to have ventured to and through.

The illicit relationship between Emberalda and Timmurian behind the scenes was a hushed fact between the family, and the few that were aware blamed the obvious indirect encouragement from the standards set by Ethiass and Taizsha. But no one had really tried to stop the disdained liaison either. Adyssaira's beautiful cousin and Timmurian were relatively restrained about flaunting their romantic endeavors in public.

Adyssaira squinted at her uncle fumbling through the two old tomes he had brought in. She found her attention drifting back to the spellblade over the mantel. It was a macabre-looking thing sheathed completely in bone. Other than its magnificent emerald pommel and its shining golden guard, all that could be seen of the magic sword was its bone hilt and matching scabbard, crafted from some dead elvan's spine. From the stories she had been told of the northern Terollar elvan tribes, she had always thought the weapon seemed more fitting for the barbaric trolls than any blade someone of her own blood might have wielded once upon a time.

But it wasn't the only spellblade in the family. Her lost cousin came to mind—Emberalda's older brother, her uncle's son. Nikayle the Fourthnamed had been around the same age as Adyssaira's older brother, Athaniel. Nikayle was now a reviled runaway whose name none was allowed to utter all throughout Chandoshia. Adyssaira recalled her cousin's reluctance to show much affection or interest in much other than his own schemes, which he had kept to himself.

Nikayle the Fourthnamed had been a bit of a prodigy among the bloodline, as he had somehow acquired his own spellblade and had not attempted to wield or pilfer the famous family heirloom, the spellblade of Nikayle the Firstnamed. It was the first time in the history of House Chandoss that two spellblades existed in the lineage. The sword before her, of her great-grandfather, had remained dormant ever since his demise.

The blade that chose her cousin was from Delphine's family line, the Barturons. In fact, after the Barturon Spellblade had become bound to him, and he absconded from the estates, she remembered her uncle telling the girls that he had even abolished going by his own given name, titling himself by both his surnames henceforth, Barturon lon'Chandoss. When Adyssaira thought on him, she no longer even conjured the name Nikayle the Fourthnamed to mind, only thinking of him as Barturon now.

"I have a surprise for you today, girls! Books I have never shared with you, from the vaults of our great library at the Syrene." Uncle Nikayle began by laying out two books across his paralyzed lap. "Though I know you are all sad that Valaythea is not here to join us and has left the estates."

We are, Adyssaira thought, instantly becoming depressed more than she had realized she was.

"We are, but we are happy for her. And for what it means for the family," Emberalda admitted for them all.

"For what it means for the family." Uncle Nikayle reiterated his daughter's words. "Never forget what is most important. Let that be today's first precept."

"So what are our choices for the Teaching Hours, Uncle?" Young Sashka was stretching her little neck far to catch a peek at the covers of the rare tomes brought in, intrigued about the lessons of lore more than the others, as usual.

"What say you to hearing about the lost elvan races of the realm, the ones vanquished by the Thrench Empire?" Nikayle held up the first book and then the second. "Or perhaps the mysteries of the Vist, the human nation of Oriyen, which exists between the west and the east, and the great Thrench Ashenwave, which crossed it with their indomitable navy?"

While they were indeed both intriguing topics, the silence in the room expressed the girls' combined disappointment in their choices. *What about magic?* Adyssaira wanted to ask. And the look she glimpsed from curious Sashka insinuated that her half-elvan sister likely felt the same.

But learning about magic or its potential wielders with the capacity to hone its power was forbidden knowledge in Az'Dayne. It was illegal, with the penalty of long-term imprisonment or even death, depending on the severity of the information provided by the guilty teacher of such a subject.

The books did still exist in Az'Dayne, however. They had not been destroyed, presumably because the wise sages still needed a historical account for facts concerning elemental science tied to the concepts of how magic functioned in the realm. To forget the secrets of magic would only make the nation weak should mages ever become an issue against the crown again.

Barely one year ago, Adyssaira and Odysserae had snuck into Syrene's prohibited chambers to steal away one of their tomes on magic. Odysserae had no care in the world for the book. She had merely come along to prove that she could pick the locks and get out without being caught. Adyssaira had gotten a quarter of the way through it before her father had recovered the hidden book from her room and scolded her for it.

She had learned much about the differences between a hunder and a wisp, why an elvan might reduce itself to a wisp in the first place, and why a wisp would ever choose to interfuse with a human baby at all.

A hunder was an elvan's soul. Elven believed that when they passed on into the afterlife, which they called the Beyond, their hunder safely traveled into the Vist to become a sentient part of its symbiotic fabric, which enveloped the material realm of Penthara. The complexities of what faculties a hunder had within the Vist in its afterlife was not in the sacred tome, *Of Wisps and Whispers,* that Adyssaira had read.

Concerning wisps, these ethereal elvan entities were much more tangible than a hunder. If an elvan died by natural means, then its hunder would pass as described. But if an elvan died due to the

Severance, which was an ability all elven had that could be best described as disconnection from one's spiritroot and one's living body—it was a form of instant suicide for the elven—their hunder would then transform into a wisp instead, which appeared like a hovering, radiant green ball about the size of one's fist.

Reasons for an elvan to commit Severance were many. Perhaps they had lived a long life, hundreds of years, and felt they could no longer experience fulfillment, and they wished to travel and fly around the realm in their new, invisible, semicorporeal state. More commonly, the elvan might have entered into incurable depression after losing their lifemate, no longer wishing to live, or maybe the elvan had become a wisp to escape torture. Even more rare, the elvan may have purposely wished to interfuse with a human babe or young animal, in the case of undergoing Animayan Transfusion.

In regard to the Balance, the elvan race's universal system of belief, wisps and human infants were the polar opposites in the spectrum of life on Penthara. In accordance with this theory, this was why wisps were undeniably magnetized by humans in their newborn form.

During the last five months in the womb and the first five months after birth, the infant was most susceptible to drawing a wisp of their shared elemental descendancy within the correlating season through involuntary interfusion. An infant of such eligibility would draw a wisp toward them if the wisp was within a horizon away. The wisp would then become visible and vulnerable and entrapped within the sight of the infant for the duration until the eligible infant was over five months of age, and then the wisp was free to roam as it pleased again. Many wisps, however, chose to succumb willingly to the interfusion during this time window, or, alternatively, they could be captured and forced into the infant while the wisp was debilitated in a vulnerable state.

Certain factors could change conditions in the Balance. If eligible twins were in the womb and would be born within the season of their elemental descendancy, then the draw they had on a wisp within distance would be much greater. In addition to its tangibility, the wisp had no ability to refrain from interfusing with the eligible newborn on its own. There were methods of deterring a wisp from interfusion by physical means in its tangible form, however.

Greater adverse effects were said to occur if more babies were in the womb in such rare circumstances. In the event that there were more than two babies, such as in the scenario of triplets, then nothing could stop a wisp within a horizon's distance away. The wisp would be forced into an incorporeal state to interfuse with the eligible infant. The impact of the wisp would always kill the mother of the infant, but the wisp would not enter unless it was certain it would survive the birthing after the mother passed. Typically, it was recorded, this would also injure one or more of the other babies in the womb in the process. This theory explained exactly what had happened during Adyssaira's and her sisters' births, with their mother, Valenteal.

It was not unheard of for a wisp to volunteer to live interdependently in a form of passive reincarnation through the human they had woven into. This was a sort of sleeper phase of synergetic existence within the human, in which the original wisp could feel through all senses of their host, living all their experiences. This wisp also had an impact on the hunder-touched individual's personality and dreams as they matured.

The original wisp who interfused with a baby was known as the genesis wisp. Any spellpower granted by the genesis wisp could not be afforded the hunder-touched until they were interfused with their second wisp, referred to as the catalyst wisp, allowing them to officially transcend into a tier-one mage.

Adyssaira recalled seeing more passages discussing ancillary wisps and eldritch wisps in the forbidden tome as well, but her father had confiscated the book before she had been able to delve any further into understanding these arcane concepts.

"It sounds like you mean to corner us into learning more about the Thrench, or to learn more about the Thrench," Adyssaira blurted, glumly nostalgic about her yearning to understand more about magic.

"But those are the same thing," Sashka argued, not catching the sarcasm.

Uncle, you always have a motive for teaching us certain topics in the Teaching Hours. What could the Thrench have to do with us all the way in Chandoshia? Adyssaira pondered as she studied him flipping open one of the volumes.

Emberalda stepped away from her father to lounge in a supine position on one of the many couches. She sighed dramatically as she plopped down. "Are we not going to talk about why we all just saw Sundorion traversing the halls like a raging magistrate? What is he doing here?" It was a shift in subject, to be sure, but her tone sounded sincerely concerned. "Surely the rest of you are not blind and noticed."

Why did you directly look at me when you said that?

Her uncle's loose grin transformed into a frown the moment the door opened to an unanticipated visitor. It was as if Emberalda's implication had invoked the itinerant Zandaryn elvan from afar.

Sundorion appeared in all his foreign glory. The Zandaryn was bedecked from head to toe in exotic cloths and multicolored leathers from everywhere and anywhere Adyssaira could imagine. Random trinkets hung from his neck and were fastened around his wrists and fingers. His yellow locks were spiked and flared back like a natural fire frozen in time, and his vibrant orange eyes complemented perfectly his bronzish-tan skin.

On a leash with him was a small black tiger cub, seemingly no older than a few months. Black tigers were a rare species native to more urbanized regions in Zandabar. They typically grew only slightly bigger than mastiff dogs, but reached full maturity in size within about half a cycle's time. The black tigers looked quite the opposite from the jungle tigers, as their fur was black with orange stripes, instead of the other way around. They were by far smarter than their more feral, larger cousins, and generally carried a rather domesticated disposition. It was because of this that the black tigers had become prized possessions as novelty companions or guardian pets for the Zandaryn elven with the riches to buy one.

It had been years since Adyssaira had last seen the fabled mystery explorer. His tragic story had inspired the hearts of local bards all around to tell his sad tale. Sundorion had originally followed in the footsteps of his parents, as part of the Avanthyl.

The Avanthyl were the Zandaryn elvan reformists throughout Zandabar, Savatarm, and Khalimia, advocates of the new-age Az'Dayne Dominadom and unbelievers of the traditional spiritual creed of the elvan race. They chastised devout elven as archaic radicals, and they fully supported the Taboo path of the quasi for humans and elven to partner and mate, with their offspring, the Z'shun, being a beautiful blessing of revolutionary coexistence.

Sundorion's love for life among the humans had fast faded after his parents had passed into the Beyond and his lifemate and daughter, Sheyelle and Carolelle, had been viciously beaten by a mob of elvan racists at the Chandoshian college, the Syrene, twenty years ago—the same time that Adyssaira's mother had died during childbirth. For Sheyelle and Carolelle, it was said they had been a public display of brutal torture for all to see before they had died.

After hearing the appalling news, Sundorion had never been the same. He buried himself in the exploratory endeavors of learning lost secrets and discovering forgotten artifacts, as had been the passions of Sheyelle and Carolelle in life, and he did so anywhere but in Az'Dayne. He had forsaken his affiliation with the Avanthyl, just as he had his faith in any human-and-elvan cohabiting reform. The only humans Sundorion still held any mild fraction of a soft spot for seemed to be the Chandoss girls, as he demonstrated on his spontaneous and rare visits to the estates.

Now here he was in the flesh, unannounced, which was very unlike the flamboyant elvan.

"I say good choice to either topic of the Thrench, little ladies! You will understand why it is so imminently critical sooner than you realize," Sundorion hinted.

"Sundorion the Cosmopolitan! To which cruel gods do we owe this surprise visit, then?" Nikayle grimaced in his question. Concerning elvan racists, none were more vocal about their discrimination more than her uncle had been for as long as she could remember. Whatever reason he had developed such prejudice, she had never ventured to prod into. Nikayle always expressed his bigotry in his witnessed exchanges with Taizsha, but he never treated Sashka as anything lesser, perhaps holding pity for her.

"Today you may call me Sundorion the Giftbearer," he said with a fun demeanor while walking the tiger over to Adyssaira and handing her the leash's loop.

Even though Adyssaira could clearly see the baby tiger through her transparent sash, she did not falter in her act of impairment from a lifetime of practice. Adyssaira fumbled around at the end of the leash with her hand outstretch to search for the exotic little creature. "He is for me?" she asked while petting it.

"It is a she," Sundorion corrected her. "And yes, she is. For you and Oddy. They say black tigers make great guides for the blind and hearing impaired, better than the best-trained dogs! Did you know the old tradition? The gifting of a black tiger from a Zandaryn elvan to a Daynish human began as the most trusting gesture between the royal houses of the two cultures."

"Oh, wow." She beamed, feeling honored with being given such a random gift, caressing her new pet, already purring up to her feet. *Will Father even let me keep her?*

Adyssaira's deaf sister reluctantly patted the tiger, seeming unenthused. *"Thank you,"* she gestured to Sundorion in Hands.

"And I trust you will give this to your sister when the Prince of Az'Dayne decides to let her return home to visit," Sundorion said to both Adyssaira and Odysserae as he laid down a sealed bag on the table between them. "Inside is a most precious seerstone. But do not open it. It is only for her to decide when to use it."

"What about me? My turn!" Sashka impatiently exclaimed with excitement.

"And it is your turn, little Z'shun." Sundorion spun around to open his satchel and pull out a large, pristine tome, so fresh Adyssaira swore she could smell the parchment's glue from across the room. "*Of Wisps and Whispers*, and it is the newest edition of the tome, updated by the scribes of Mageholme, which should make obsolete any copies in those dusty archives your peers tell you to read in that joke of a school your countrymen call the Syrene."

The book! That is the book! Adyssaira wanted to scream in elation, but it was not her gift. All she had received was a chubby baby tiger. *Maybe Sashka will trade.* Her half-elvan sister's eyes were paralyzed so wide with wonderment that Adyssaira was sure she had forgotten the ability to blink. *Maybe not.*

"Never stop digging, Sashka. Never stop learning," Sundorion instructed in a serious manner.

Finally, the generous Zandaryn elvan made his way over to Emberalda and teased his last gift, waving a tied scroll in front of her within reach to grasp. "And for you, my not-so-coy dear, you only get yours if you can tell me where my beloved brother is hiding. Give me the whereabouts of Timmurian, and this is yours—the deed to my mansion on the coast in the Savatarm Provinces. You and he can move there and fuck out ten baby Z'shun just like her for all I care." His tone took an angry, accusing turn, and he pointed the scroll back at Sashka when he mentioned Z'shun. "I just want to know where he is."

"Stop badgering the poor girl!" Emberalda's father demanded. "She is just as in the dark as you are. Look! You are bringing tears to her eyes!"

And Adyssaira could see it. Her cousin had started to cry at the mention of her mysteriously missing lover. But Emberalda countered by snatching the deed out of Sundorion's hand and snapping back, "I will take that anyhow, and we just may move!"

"Are you quite finished with your children's parade, sandling, or do I need to call in the guards to have you removed?" Nikayle threatened. "Girls, thank him or ignore him. I do not care. But back to the Teaching Hours. Where were we? Discussing the Ashenwave, correct?"

Sundorion clearly chose to pay no heed to Nikayle's warning to dismiss himself. The arrogant elvan took control of the tutoring himself. "The Ashenwave. The legendary elvan-killers." Sundorion spun around to directly face the elvan spinal bone of the sheathed spellblade over the fireplace, then theatrically spun back to face his young audience in the solarium. "Would you all rather hear my latest story about my escape from the Thrench instead of the drab tale Nikayle is going to blunder while reading from one of those?"

"Yes! Oh, yes, Uncle!" Sashka shouted to Sundorion.

Sundorion moved to continue without a pause for Nikayle to protest. "I was imprisoned on a Thrench ship just off the coast of Mageholme, with the son of Brigatha Emmonost, the Torrent archmage, and Imaniko the Palestorm, the Reaping archmage. The son is a most curious violet-eyed boy called No-Name, born a hyperi, which are the exclusive offspring of two archmages. His story is most remarkable but too long for my time today. He will remain unnamed until he is granted his Uedonvyor, his great destiny of a glorious death, from the Thrench emperor. He freed me and departed for his parents' funeral ceremony over the Conqeron Sea. Brigatha and Imaniko were assassinated by sorcerers in league with a foreign adversary. There is no current tier-five Reaping mage or a tier-five Torrent mage. The only archmages alive are the Dawning, the Sunder, and the Umbra."

The Titan, the Dawning. Shypriss Sol-War, the Sunder. Coldborn, the Umbra, Adyssaira recalled the names of the other tier-fives respectively, before shifting focus. She found herself utterly infatuated with the idea of the strange unnamed boy, but by the look of equal interest on her cousin Emberalda's face, she wasn't the only one.

Nikayle shot a glare at Sundorion. "What is the actual meaning of this intrusion? Last I heard, you were half a world away in Tundura or some such place."

"Tundura? Haven't been there in more than a cycle. I don't report my whereabouts or whenabouts to anyone. I am where I am, when I am. That is all you need to know," the snide elvan shot back before adding even more insult. "I just thought these girls could learn from an actual teacher for once, and not from some outdated old tomes written by corrupt scribes who like to fabricate history with falsities, or from the mouths of those who lack the ability to walk the realm for themselves."

Sundorion's words were spiced with a malice that Adyssaira didn't remember from him, and she could see it in her uncle's flushed face that this conversation was swiftly going awry.

Nikayle tried a different tactic to pacify the mood of the room. "Perhaps you need to address your misapprehensions to your sister, then. This is not the time or place for it. If you are looking for your brother—"

But Sundorion interrupted. "You know damn well that is exactly why I am here, and that I will be confronting your brother, Ethiass, instead. Who do you think sent for me to find Timmurian if not Taizsha herself?"

"You like hearing yourself talk, don't you, sandling?" Nikayle said with the derogatory term for a member of the Zandaryn race.

Sundorion seemed unperturbed and just shrugged. "Something everyone but you seems to have in common with me, actually, as we all like hearing me talk. I only speak hard truths learned through real experience."

The egotistical elvan turned to address each girl then, instead of Nikayle. "Would you all like me to return for the following Teaching Hours to tell you actual facts across Penthara and give poor ol' Nikayle here a break for a season? It seems I may be around for a while."

"Yes, please! We would love that!" Sashka cried out of a naive lack of sensitivity to her other uncle's plight.

"Okay, Sun." Nikayle grinned, with no love held behind his scouring eyes. "Let us talk outside, and I will tell you where Ethiass and Taizsha are. But as to your brother—your bloodlink,

Timmurian the Lorebringer, as he is now calling himself—he carries the same curse as you."

Hearing such a provocation toward his bloodline may as well have been fighting words, it seemed, as the Zandaryn promptly approached Nikayle, crippled in his chair or not. "Cursed, are we? How so?"

"Curiosity is the greatest curse of all." Adyssaira's uncle spat on his own wheelchair and shot his eyes back at his daughter. "Ember, take me into the hallway! Follow me." He motioned to Sundorion.

Adyssaira watched Emberalda wheel her uncle out of the room with Sundorion following, and her focus shifted toward the open tome about mages and magic on the table where Nikayle had left it.

As if her sister could read her mind, Odysserae got up from her perch and invited Sashka over with her new book in tow to share its vast contents at their table.

Her mute sister slyly faced the open tome toward Adyssaira so that she could secretly sneak a reading from it from underneath her blindfold at an angle.

Adyssaira then felt a pinch on her shin from what felt like Odysserae playing back at foot kiss. *Stop,* Adyssaira conveyed through a playful scrunch of her face, reversing roles. But when the girls looked under the table to find the actual culprit was the baby black tiger playfully teething on her lower leg, they both just giggled and then simultaneously looked out the window.

SUNDORION (I)

THOSE WHO DIG

Sun had traveled a long way south, straight from Mageholme, after receiving the disturbing news of his brother's suspect disappearance. Timmurian and Sun had been exchanging correspondences by code in their letters from afar for the past several months with growing concerns of foul forces at play, not only in Chandoshia, but seemingly throughout the entire Az'Dayne Dominadom. Even more suspicious was that their sister Taizsha was involved, or at the bare minimal, at least aware of the ongoing conspiracy. But being that Sun's last letter came from Taizsha, and not Timmurian, with a beckoning to make haste back to the Chandoss Estates to save them both, left most of the censored details to his cynical imagination. He returned by the fastest means necessary to exploit his brother's plight and uncover Taizsha's mysterious involvement in *the Know*.

The concept of what the Know actually was and the interpretations of the ultra-confidential Umbran Pledge were sometimes paired almost synonymously with one another. To the few that were privy, or to the rare outsiders who discovered the truth, the term of defining someone in the Know meant that they had been apprised to understand the scope of association between the Neveril Empire and the Az'Dayne Dominadom.

To be in the Know meant one knew that the old Az'Dayne empire had shifted from power after the fall of the Goldfyre line with the rise of the Daynish House Ampion and the Khalimishe House Hazhalah; enthralled to the tyrannical Neveril Empire, secretly lorded over by the clandestine elven dictators. To be in the Know further testified to the awareness that the Imperial Throne and the Pentagogue were fully entangled in the vast scheme of the Neveril that was spreading like a pandemic to infect the most influential citizens in Az'Dayne's reach.

The Umbran Pledge was the next step in the depth process for those in the Know — an oath of sorts to bind the affiliates that were the most enlightened of the Neveril Empire's connection to Az'Dayne political infrastructure. The oath was clearly enforced through brutal extortion and intimidation threats. Sun knew little yet, only the assumptions in the name of something classified as the Umbran Pledge, that the Neveril now had umbran of their own that they embraced favorably into their society, or that the empire had perhaps made a pact with the Wyldenar umbran of the north or the Shiniryn umbran of the east.

One fact Sun was sure of however, was that Timmurian had uncovered more than he was prepared to handle in his shared allegations that the Chandoss Estates was heavily immersed in the Umbran Pledge. His last reports confessed confirmations of Taizsha's participation, and at least Valdean and Ethiass being pledged in, along with the Chandoss Guard and likely more.

To get back in time to save Timmurian from whatever fate he had dug himself into, Sun paid the hefty toll for the expediting services of the Green Byway, whom he had been investigating for their latent commitments with the Neveril conspiracy as well. The Green Byway was an organized enterprise of sanctioned mages throughout the western parts of the realm. They offered their fast-travel faculty through Traversement at an extremely high price that only the wealthiest could fathom to afford. They employed only mid-to-high-tier Dawning mages, which meant the current season in the present cycle was ripe for their thriving company's commissions.

Fortunately, Sundorion the Cosmopolitan was secretly one of the wealthiest elven in the south. He and his siblings had been bestowed a mass of riches from the deeds of their parents.

Zandaryn elven were unique from the other elvan races when it came to procreation restrictions. Female Zandaryn could carry seed once per cycle as opposed to the significantly slower constraints of other elven. And while all elven were bound to one lifemate, Zandaryn were adaptable with a polygamous impower. Males could in fact have multiple lifemates; limitless in fact, if the partnered elvan lifemate was not bound to another. Because of this fact, there were substantially more Zandaryn elven throughout Penthara than any other elvan race.

Sundorion's father was no different with his endeavors in accepted Zandaryn polygamy. He had two other lifemates before binding himself to Sundorion's mother, having one child from each. Timmurian and Taizsha were indeed his bloodlinks, but had each had different matriarchs. Their parents had been well-established treasure hunters, all four traveling together, who had settled in the Savatarm Provinces. They had become key activists of the Avanthyl. When they died together on a perilous expedition, their accumulated hoard of found artifacts and banked coin had been bequeathed to Sun, Timmurian, and Taizsha. Each used their new fortune for various aspirations, but for Sun, it was more than just wealth to feed his ambition and support a lifestyle, as it offered the capacity to appropriately pursue his lifequest and complete a legacy in the making.

Sun stared into his sister's matching orange eyes with pent-up malice as she came marching fervently toward him through the eclectic sculpture gallery. The average guest touring this section of Castle Chandoss would surely be in awe of the masterworks in all shapes and forms around him, but Sun had seen it all. His feet had touched the soil of thirty countries in every direction, including beneath the surface. The rare wonders he had uncovered throughout his archaeology exploits had made him numb to the normal fascinations of the vastly unlearned populace.

Taizsha's posh gown was apple red and so thin it seemed the slightest wind could shred it. The slit in her dress was so high that he could see the top of her right thigh with every step. Her bright yellow hair stayed fixed like a torch blazing from her scalp, only a little longer than Sun styled his, slightly over a hand in length. This fiery cut was common for Zandaryn aristocracy and only made his sister appear even more heated at that moment.

But her guise of ire was a pretense in front of what was apparent as absolute fear. The two Zandaryn siblings just jousted in a staring war for a while longer, their pent-up malice ready to be unleashed. Taizsha won the exchange with an irrelevant inquiry whose answer he knew she could not care less about.

"Have you come all this way to cause waves through Castle Chandoss and hand out pointless, extravagant gifts to the girls before you disappear again?"

He knew exactly why he had given the girls what he had, as a proactive peace offering for what was to come, but that information was for him to know and no one else for now. Sun wasted no energy on answering and started his own interrogation. "Where is he?"

"Damn you to the Vist, Sundorion, tunneling in quicksand and swimming through lava!" Taizsha cussed through grinding teeth. She was in his face, now turning redder as she bottled up her frustration.

Sun knew his approach in sensitive matters was always on the brash side of the spectrum for proper investigation. This was why he dealt better with lost artifacts than with missing persons. He had only been at the Chandoss Estates a few hours, and already he had a trail of guards and house spies everywhere he went, as he openly strutted and gave no regard to hiding why he was there. Every man, woman, and child who caught his suspicious eye got questioned on the spot, and he was not afraid to barge into the many chambers throughout the palace and college, whether it was prohibited or not.

"Is that the same warning you gave Timm, sister, just before his vanishing?"

Taizsha coyly shot back, "Well, so locally cultured now, are we, brother? Careful—we may call you one of us again soon." She was implying that he was conforming to the popular racial reform of the Avanthyl, which she and Timmurian still fully sponsored, but Taizsha well knew that Sun had fervently renounced that fruitless path for the past twenty years.

On the whole, the elvan race frowned upon the human lazy disrespect to one's given name by calling others by shortened derivatives. And elven referred to their siblings and cousins as bloodlinks, rather than brothers and sisters and the like. But for Sun, it had nothing to do with his support of the Avanthyl's modernization movement. Sun held himself to no particular doctrine, by old tradition or new beliefs, but instead strictly to facts and logic discovered through science and travel.

One of "us." I will never again be branded as a follower of the Avanthyl! Sun fumed in his mind, feeling utterly offended by the implication. "I've already foretold this. And yet you continue to bed the snakes. I was getting him out of this soon," Sun barked back to her, wanting to keep the conversation focused on Timmurian.

"You mistake me for someone who ever had control over him. Want me to go digging as deep as you and him? They would have me banished, crippled, maimed, or killed," Taizsha said.

"Exactly. Who is 'they'?" That was the real question. "Those in the Know — those bound to the Umbran Pledge? Or your masters beneath? Timm was onto something."

Taizsha snarled and slammed the door shut in front of her, leaving herself in the art gallery while Sun stood befuddled in the hallway just on the other side, without any answers.

"Damn you, Sun! I am in it now." Her voice was muffled through the closed door, and she opened it again. She yanked at his tunic hard and pulled him into the room before closing them off from potential eavesdroppers. "I am in it. Do you see me shaking? Look at me! Look!"

He did look, and her hands were quivering, but he maintained an unimpressed semblance. "Yes. My assessment deems you almost as fucked as dear Timm, but it seems you are well and free, while his fortune lingers in the merciless hands of the Balance."

"You judge me as if I am unlearned in news of you too. I well know you no longer follow that dying creed that is killing our race." His refined sister called him out on his bluff. "My reasons for abandoning the Balance may indeed be classified as my weakness in conformity. I will not argue. But yours ..." Taizsha paused to contemplate how to navigate her own assessment of him. "No, you are educated, Sun. You have seen the corners of Penthara. You have wined and dined with the advisers of kings and queens of both human and elvan countries, and you've touched shoulders with the qindrid from the north and east. Spent seasons with the mages of Mageholme. You've even met umbran and been introduced to the Neveril nation, haven't you?"

Sun smiled, fond of her company in the moment, despite the heat of the exchange. All was true except the latter. He had never seen an umbran or dared any invasive measures against the Neveril to date. "Busy, busy ear you have. I should say you obviously listen well, but it is clearly selective. One more time, else I make enough noise to insinuate you are in league with Timm and I against your precious Pledge. Tell me, Tay, where is he?"

Taizsha's eyes and mouth went wide in terror.

You aren't lying. You are truly frightened, aren't you? It is far worse than I expected.

She brought him away from the door and hushed him, coercing him into sitting in a chair as she whispered. "Do not talk about them aloud. There is no turning back for Ethiass now. If I push further, he will put a blade through my belly before he loses another night of sleep over my reservations and decisions. Valaythea is now joined with the very prince of the Dominadom himself, Izayus Az'Ampion."

"You know I know this too," he whispered back matter-of-factly.

"Nikayle just broods and pretends nothing is changing, obviously more scared than any of us," Taizsha went on in her quieted tone. "He has seen things, Sun. You would do well not to rile him. Your approach should use more delicate tact in these dire hours—something you are too proud to attempt."

Sun huffed and stood back up, refusing to play the game of hushed voices any longer. "Advice heard."

"But not heeded," Taizsha hissed.

"Because it's not needed," he countered defiantly.

His sister unexpectedly pressed both her hands to his face to embrace him in a sudden kiss on the lips. "Then goodbye to you too, Sun. With my quasi curse, I have sullied myself out of ever meeting you in the Beyond after all of this."

"Enough." Sun withdrew awkwardly, half angrily, but more genuinely worried for the first time. "No talk like this. Tell me all you know. I can see it in your eyes that time is of the essence. I will find and save Timm. I will get you out of this, Tay. You and Sashka."

Taizsha began sobbing, appearing to have lost her ability to meet her brother's judgmental gaze. "Ethiass is withdrawn lately. He spends more time alone, in secret meetings with unfamiliar agents from the capital, and rarely involves me in what is going on. Only months ago, everything was completely different. All changed once Valaythea was chosen to be Izayus's final paramour."

She wiped her rainy eyes on the back of her hand and proceeded with her plight. "Count Valdean still controls everything from his tower. Ethiass goes in to visit him with visible tremors for his life, and he always comes out even more pale as death. The count is untouchable and has his heavy thumb over everything that goes on in the estates. This is where Ethiass is now. He is summoned to the tower more often than ever."

Sun went to reply with some consolation for it all, but apparently, she wasn't finished.

"And it gets worse. I've seen the death scroll on Sashka. An assassination writ."

This changed everything. Any residing animosity he held toward Taizsha for the poor choices that had led her and Timmurian into this grim predicament fled his mood. "What? What has Sashka gotten into? If there is a writ on her, it may be too late. I cannot stop this. We have to leave today!"

"It gets more dire," she confessed. "They wanted me to see it. It's a contingency writ, but nothing endorsed by the Oathemic Cabal. It comes straight from the Neveril themselves. It specifies that Sashka should be killed if I interfere or speak out against the Pledge. They have made me take it too, Sun. The things you think you know, they are even worse."

"Then you risk much even doing this, Tay," Sun earnestly insisted. "I'll tread more carefully; you have my word. Tell me why you wrote for me? What can I do?"

The worried look Taizsha shot him next was one that paled her face as gaunt as death. "I was going to ask you, but you just answered. How did you know what happened to Timm? I never dared write you but you think I did?"

What? I was baited here. No doubt Valdean is involved. "This revelation changes everything, yet essentially changes nothing," Sun said through his teeth looking away from her to contemplate his next decisions cautiously. "Someone wants me here. Whether to dispose of me as they did to Timm, or someone we are unaware of that used the identity of you through the letters that perhaps believes I can save Timm yet."

Taizsha shook her head violently. "Then you are gone too Sun! They will do exactly that, dispose of you. You should not have come."

"If they want me dead, I am not hard to find. It would have been much simpler to send assassins before I ever stepped in this palace. No, it is an ally who wrote, but who?" Sun truly had no idea who was manipulating him. "I will get Timm, Sashka and you out Tay."

"I don't want out. Ethiass would hunt me and find me wherever you took me. He has contacts and sources now that I fear you cannot outrun. But Sashka, she is ignorant to anything behind the curtains so far. You can still save her. Take her, and do not dare even tell me where to. Just keep her safe, Sun!"

He shook his head, not fond of the choice to allow his sister to simply condemn herself to defeat. "I can do this. But I cannot take my leave until I know the whereabouts and fate of Timm."

"The Umbran Pledge doesn't kill elven," Taizsha explained. "Only the Neveril themselves will execute another elvan. But they are here. Let me make that clear. They are very here. But Sashka, being a Z'shun, is not safe from this restraint—half-breeds and quasi are not recognized as elvan by them."

The grumbling and armored marching of three men down the hallway could be heard approaching the door of the gallery. There was no sneaking about the high-ceilinged, stone-walled halls of the palace, as everything sent an echo from room to room.

Sun knew they were looking for him specifically. "Let me work on Sashka. I'll have her out before the end of the month. Tell me where you think our brother is."

"Sooner for Sashka, Sun. Sooner, please," Taizsha begged with a doomed look in her eye he did not recognize. "I will tell you, but then you have to go. Timm has chosen to become quasi, as I have. I know you despise the Taboo, but he is set in his ways and hasn't had your guidance to deter him. He has even lied to Emberalda, his lover—she thinks him away in Savatarm on some short expedition for research. She does not even know he did it for her." She paused to listen as the sound of the guards came closer. "But he showed me the truth, wanting my support. Immediately following his quasi Transcendence that he had me accompany him for, he went to investigate Count Valdean's tower and never came back. He believed it linked to Neveril tunnels below, where Valdean has been meeting with them as a liaison. You need to go."

The guards were just outside the gallery door, poorly attempting to snoop before they intruded. Taizsha lowered her voice and spoke as softly as she could into Sun's ear. "One last thing. Odysserae, the deaf triplet, visits the tower. The only one allowed inside it other than Ethiass. I believe her innocent, but she knows much. Start with her."

The door dramatically flew open, and one palace sentry stepped in, hand eagerly gripping the sword on his belt. Three-quarters of his face was covered by a plain brass masque that was shaped like a small flame at the hairline. Only his eyes, mouth, and right cheek could be seen. It was the same mandatory masque Sun had seen on all the house guards. The stranger eyed Taizsha with stern disappointment, then shifted his focus to Sun with absolute prejudice. "Sundorion the Cosmopolitan, we have been looking for you."

"Yes? And you've found me." Sun left his sister's side and boldly moved with intent to exit the room unimpeded. "And who is it that has found me and stands in my way now?"

"The Chandoss Guard," the sentry officer announced. "We have been instructed to show you to your room and apprise you of the forbidden wards of the palace and estates. Some have changed since your last visit."

"On, then. Apprise me." Sun kept it short, letting the guards know he disliked their company just as equally. He resisted the urge to turn back once more to his sister to offer her silent solace, as he would risk no more in these unpredictable times.

He followed the armed escort out into the hallway and down several others. He had visited Castle Chandoss enough times before to hold no interest in its featured decor. These were amateur distractions failing to obscure the true intrigues in each room. *The Chandoss Guard – you are a piece in the puzzle, and have been for years.*

Sun had no intention of being so foolish as to stay in whatever guest chamber they had prepared for him, but he entertained the tour nonetheless. It permitted more time to spy what he needed to find while complying with the sentries instead of skulking about or causing a scene to draw attention. *I imagine I won't even find myself alive to see the morning if I stay here. Do Neveril assassins await me in the night? Or will I be restrained and taken to where Timm is being held? Is that my best chance at finding him, and do I play along?*

They passed twelve guards between the gallery where he had met his sister and the great hall they were leading him down now. All stood obediently frozen in position but wary in their eyes, never taking their gazes off him when he passed. They were leading him outside the main palace.

This guest chamber isn't in the palace, is it? Someone doesn't want me in here.

They were almost out, approaching the massive main doors, four times his height at least, when Sun's ears caught a feminine squeal to his left. Instinct turned his neck to catch the scenario.

It was Odysserae, just the girl Taizsha had told him to locate and investigate. She looked older in the eyes than Sun remembered her, much worldlier for experiencing the crueler side of life than an innocent young woman.

I am surprised I didn't take such notice of you in the solarium.

If his math was correct, the triplets were around twenty years of age now. Odysserae's short red hair was awfully disheveled, matching the condition of her tousled garments, as if she had just gone toe to toe with a pack of street dogs that played far too rough. And her fiery amber eyes were filled with checked fury in a distressed face. *Her eyes … She's been crying. Not in fear, but in disgust.*

She jerked herself free from the grip of one of the sentries but was caught in the grasp of an adjacent guardsman right away.

"Make it like you did yesterday," the masked deviant ravenously whispered in her ear.

They likely didn't expect Sun to hear the words, he assumed, but they were unwise to think it not probable. All elven had far superior senses of hearing compared to humans.

What is this? How is this being allowed? Do Ethiass or Nikayle or your sisters even know?

Sun was an expert researcher, but it didn't take one of his skill set to discern Odysserae's tragic predicament. His ethics prevented his feet from moving any further toward the exit, and he stood his ground to openly disapprove of the rape about to take place as another guard manhandled the deaf girl back behind the curtained alcove.

He heard the sound of swords leaving their sheaths, and by the time he turned around, his escort of sentries was now armed, ready to strike at one wrong move.

"We hear you are quite the digger," the officer guard spoke in a browbeating tone. "And we want you to know that your profession has no place here in Castle Chandoss. You can retire your spade until you leave. Understood?"

The implied threat was real enough for him to comprehend the dilemma he had now ventured into.

I am sorry, Oddy. I cannot save you just yet. Timm, Sashka, Tay, I will save you all. But not just yet. It seems I have come to the right place at the wrong time.

VALAYTHEA (II)

EVERDAWN

Her eyes hadn't hit the pavement in over an hour; she was sure of it. The soreness in her neck was even more painful this morning compared to the severe crick she had endured over the last few days. There were just too many splendors to see in all directions, and the deeper they trod into the urban valley, the worse she suffered from her own irrepressible infatuations and wanderlust.

It was an endless parade, with all eyes on Izayus and her, the most celebrated luminaries throughout all of Az'Dayne. Rows of citizens stood on either side, visiting from all across the country, cheering and chanting praises to their new union through every sector of the capital city. They were both masqueless throughout the entire ordeal, as instructed, which made the tribute custom even more popular with the common folk.

Valaythea had never seen so many people and truly never fathomed this many existed in the wide realm. Regardless of the books she had read from the Chandoshia libraries and college, she knew she had still been very sheltered and preserved quite naive. After just one day of the welcoming celebrations, they all looked the same to her. The multitude of Daynish and Khalimishe men and women and children blended into a repetitious blur, and their faces and sounds began to hold little interest for her.

Valaythea took a break from the city sights to mindlessly stare at the backs of the two grey elephants pulling the Imperiar Coach. She had never seen an elephant before Izayus had introduced her to them, but after the last pent, enduring the all-day excursions in the carriage, she definitely felt she was due for a break from being towed by the massive beasts.

Elephants were endangered animals on this continent, originating in Elothia and into eastern Tairancia, commonly hunted for their beautiful ivory tusks and thick leather hides. They were known to be the third-largest land animals on all of Penthara. The Az'Dayne Dominadom had issued a public order to cease poaching of them, with a punishment of five years' incarceration for violating the law, declaring elephants sacred creatures in memory of the fallen Elothian Empire.

House Az'Ampion, as noble as they were for the decree against hunting elephants and establishing repopulation farms, made themselves also appear quite hypocritical by enslaving the majestic animals as trophy pets and embellished coach haulers, Valaythea judged. But she voiced that criticism only in her mind, not daring to express her true feelings to her new spouse.

Her eyes caught his, gazing through her from across the spacious two-floor coach. The gold-plated imperial carriage was absurdly extravagant.

Mirrors were fitted to the ceiling of the first floor, and sequins of genuine rubies and topazes and black opals were even stitched into the tassels of some of the cushions littered about the sectional sofa. The lavish couch took up most of the room on this level, which was served by a skinny Khalimishe eunuch who acted with the single purpose of answering the beckonings of Izayus or Valaythea should they desire anything—food, drink, drugs, stops, privacy, and route alterations for the whip, the man directing the elephants. A custom table was prearranged every morning with a sumptuous arrangement of various fruits, cooked meats, raw, cleaned shellfish, cheeses, and wine decanters. In a locked chest on the butt end, next to the ladder up to the second floor, Izayus's drug dependence was kept secret. Valaythea had come to learn throughout exploiting him that his drugs of choice were called yewr root and fey petal.

The second floor of the coach was filled with barred windows over the sides. One plush bench was fastened to the front and another to the rear, facing each other. A few history books and street maps were strewn about the central table separating her and the prince.

Izayus's moods shifted often and without warning. For half a day, he may seem the most chivalrous and romantically sensitive man in the realm, and for the other half he stood more aloof, even narcissistic, like a tangible avatar of the deities. But more often than not, the disposition of the prince got much darker. That was when he escaped to his smoke pipe, mixing the herbs to inhale and distance his mind from whatever reality haunted him so deeply.

But on his good days—or more often, simply his good *hours*—Izayus did appear genuine in his affections toward her. On the journey from Castle Chandoss to Everdawn, the two had been afforded much private time to get to know one another, though they had been transported by a train of ten paired horses pulling the Imperiar Coach then, instead of the elephants.

Izayus was always focused, wholesomely engaged and sober, when he requested a story from her past. Valaythea told him all about her sisters, Adyssaira and Odysserae; her half sister, Sashka; her older brother, Athaniel; her cousin Emberalda; her father, Ethiass; her uncle, Nikayle the Thirdnamed; her Zandaryn elvan stepmother, Taizsha; Timmurian; and even her runaway cousin, Nikayle the Fourthnamed. She poured on about the Syrene, the famous college of her ancestral region. She spoke of Castle Chandoss, and every detail of the towns and points of interest in Chandoshia. She felt she couldn't stop herself from talking when the prince flattered her with displayed appeal and curiosity; it still hadn't settled in completely yet, lingering between the concepts of true reality and a fanciful dreamworld.

But one thing was for certain: Izayus Az'Ampion never whispered even a single tale of his own enigmatic story. Valaythea could not imagine the life of the prince of the Az'Dayne Dominadom growing up in the capital in such an eminent light. He was almost the most important name on the mainland, only superseded by his parents, the dominarchs, Vaximus and Sriyah.

Izayus was a profoundly troubled soul, disturbed by the secrets he had carried with him his entire existence. In the moments he turned to his drugs, he mostly did so in a panic attack, as if he had been struck by some epiphanic revelation from his memories or knowledge of the future, needing a diversion from the affliction of levelheadedness that accompanied sobriety.

And this was evidently one of those moments. The daily charade of Izayus pretending to be a noble paragon of righteous perfection was taking its recurring recess. The prince blazed up his pipe and puffed away his internal demons. His pupils dilated quickly, and his head began to appear too heavy for his neck as it bobbed more with every raised cobble that the wheels on the coach passed over.

He regarded Valaythea in silence, in a foggy haze; such habitual behavior was becoming normal for her now. Not many days prior, she had viewed the square-jawed Imperiar as faultless and exquisitely handsome, like all the other ladies who had been privy to his actual face, but gradually she was losing that attraction toward him. He was just petrified and pitiable and detached. Any strong-willed features exemplified by him were all an act for the public.

Why will he still not lie with me? Valaythea strummed the conundrum in her head. On the night of their pentamony, her last day in her lifelong home at Castle Chandoss, Izayus had not bedded her, which was not only his right as her royal spouse but also a precondition for the pentamony to be recognized as official before the divine judgment of the Five and Five. Fortunately, her reputation had been salvaged and all embarrassment avoided, since not a man or woman in the entire Dominadom would dare to ask Izayus himself for such details about his intimate activities, and so it was just left as assumed.

Look me in the eye while you do it. Valaythea remembered that bizarre night of their official conjoining so vividly. *Do not ever take your eyes off mine.*

He had said the same line on more than one occasion since then—actually, on several—as if he was bored and too lazy to come up with more provocative lines of foreplay, or as if he had altogether lost memory of what he would repeat due to the overuse of smoking the numbing fey petal and chewing on the psychedelic yewr root. Izayus refused to show any interest in actual copulation with Valaythea. The way he explained it to her was that he only wanted her mouth. He had trained her in how he wanted his oral fix and never laid even a finger on her below the waist, leaving her technically untarnished, by royal standards. He was gentle in his submission to receive it yet demanding in how he directed her.

Valaythea would do her duty to her imperial partner, as any paramour would for such a prince. But with his needs sometimes exceeding three times a day, she was gradually becoming numb in her role before it had hardly begun. Her superficial lover was a weak-minded figurehead in an overpoweringly strong position, and apparently he needed a release from his undeniable stress with more methods than his pipe provided.

Valaythea decided not to match Izayus's stare this time across the Imperiar Coach, not eager to be so close to him this hour in the day. His cloudy look and intoxicated sway invoked an annoyance within her that she kept checked.

Her eyes went back to the elephants before she allowed her focus to settle back over the great valley city of Everdawn. This was the fifth day of the tour, and it was still so mesmerizing to her. They had passed through six of the ten sectors of the enormous cityscape, now finishing the seventh.

The first day had been spent throughout the northeastern district, in Uptown Sector and through half of the Capital Hills Sector. These were the residential wards of Everdawn, each with the capacity to be a respectable city in its own right. Uptown Sector retained the main entry gate into Everdawn and housed the plethora of middle-class citizens throughout its stacked residences and small, homely shops.

Capital Hills was an extension from the Capilon Mounts, against the western wall. It segregated Uptown and the High Market Sector all the way to the wall of the city's central and most principal area, the Dominadow, which held three sectors. Capital Hills was constructed over a mildly sloping plateau, riddled with professionally cared-for landscaping and planted trees that had not originally been seeded there. The highborns' rolling bluff was teeming with grandiose mansions, manmade oasis ponds and waterfalls, and faultless brick roads. This was the habitat of solely purebred Daynish lineages, of the most upper-class nobility and especially wealthy in all the Dominadom, only matched, by argument, to Valaythea's own house and ancestral worth in Chandoshia.

The escapades in the High Market Sector started in the latter part of the second evening and consumed the entirety of the third day of the city tour. Valaythea had been practically secluded her entire life, almost imprisoned in Castle Chandoss and occasionally the local college, the Syrene. Sure, she had read about Goldgarden, the megalopolis almost three times in size and ten times in populace, but Valaythea had never seen or imagined anything like the expansive bazaar that was about as vast as a large town. If there was a market for any type of bauble or gadget or imagined item whatsoever, then there was an adept who could make it and sell it here.

It was during their stint sightseeing in the Everdawn market ward that Valaythea started to feel lost in the prince's company for the first time. They had halted the coach to explore the many diverse shops on foot, and his gentle hand would never leave hers as he led her through decems of lanes of eye-catching venues. Izayus wasn't too timid to properly introduce her as his wife, not even just as his paramour, to strangers who greeted them or shopkeepers they came upon. He seemed infatuated with her, never shying away from flaunting deep affection and attraction, as if she were the most beautiful jewel in a sea full of spectacular trinkets.

But those moments were fleeting and expired as fast as they began. The third day had ended charmingly and seemed normal, but by the fourth day, being split between the dock wards, Scar Harbor Sector and Bronze Bay Sector, the prince had already shifted back to his customary stately demeanor.

Scar Harbor proved to be the military district, accommodating the bulk of the army and navy of Az'Dayne. There seemed to be a barracks or small training fortress around every other corner.

Valaythea learned that Bronze Bay was actually the home of Izayus, where he resided most of the time. This was the imperial district, where the high thrones of the dominarchs were set inside the Ampion Imperial Citadel. Any flaw she had discovered in Izayus's waning armor was invisible while he was in Bronze Bay. His pipe remained hidden in the coach, and he appeared as abstinent as a statue while he played the unimpeachable part of the peerless prince of the Az'Dayne Dominadom.

Izayus made sure to steer the Imperiar Coach clear of the citadel and strayed from lanes that would direct their course to anywhere of significance that might stall the marital tribute procession. The only sites of relevance in the Bronze Bay were utterly avoided, and the rushed excursion through the sector came to an end rather more swiftly than any of the others.

The fifth day, they traveled through the Elothian Sector. Elothia was the eastward neighboring country, and its surviving people were now nothing more than a hardened but broken lot of lesser refugees allowed to live under the merciful sovereignty of the great Dominadom after they lost the final war. The humans of Elothia appeared much like the westwalkers hailing from lands like Sho'Lon and Oriyen. Elothians had more naturally tanned skin, but they still had more of an oval shape and narrowness to their eyes, straighter hair, and sported no body hair, unlike other mainlanders from countries as far north as Barredom and those as far south as Khalimia.

The Elothians that were permitted into Everdawn were the most privileged of their culture, those of the highest bloodlines or contributions in recognizing the rule of Dominarch Vaximus and Dominarch Sriyah. There was an inevitable segregation that could not be cured between the Daynish and their kind, but by imperial order, the two lived with each other now in bitter peace as part of the inflexible law.

Izayus expressed that he never felt comfortable or safe in this particular ward, even having recurring nightmares that some Elothian hero would brave to rise to the occasion and assassinate him just to stake his claim in history as the slayer of the prince of the Az'Dayne Dominadom before he was inevitably executed shortly after. The dreamed silhouette was as real to him as any one of the subjugated enemies roaming about the sector now, as far as he was concerned.

They ventured into Hallion's Crater the same day. This unique area was especially sacred in Everdawn, and the archives told that it was the exact reason for the settlement of the great city, long before it had become the nation's capital, back in ancient times when there had been no Az'Dayne but merely an extension of southern Tairancia bordering Khalimia.

Historians told that long ago a fiery black rock had fallen from the night sky and impacted the middle of the continent of Taira. The collision had been so powerful that the land had imploded with an underground shock wave that had divided the surface in catastrophic landquakes, parting the sea to swallow what had formerly been part of the continent. The aftermath had become what was now known as Taira's Scar, the large channel separating Az'Dayne and Savatarm and Khalimia from each other. The large rock that had shot from the stars had entered the skies with a trail of smaller shards accompanying it, and evidently, one such shard was what had caused the cosmic basin that had become a sector of Everdawn, Hallion's Crater.

Hallion was the father of Az'Dayne, the city of Everdawn and so many others. He had orchestrated the construction of the Pentagogue from the otherworldly debris of the giant black shards, the material of which no wise man to date had been able to analyze.

Now Hallion's Crater sadly appeared as nothing noteworthy or remarkable. It was just a barren valley of society's gutter trash and marked sinners, a place to exile condemned citizens. Psage humans roamed about the broken dirt alleys, offering fortune-telling and religious atonement for coin, and paladins sentried the main road that passed through on the way to the Dominadow district.

They were approaching the Pentagogue now, which wasn't far into the central area of the Dominadow. The Shadow Sector would be on the north side, while the Fire Sector was at the southern point.

Valaythea found herself completely entranced by the Pentagogue's design. She had witnessed the extraordinary architectural marvel in full from the bluff-afforded view a few days back, when being guided across the Capital Hills Sector. It was the tallest, most eccentric structure she had ever even read about, but to see it in person ... *It looks ... almost evil. Not divine,* she thought. But from several other high roads from which Valaythea and Izayus had taken in the city, the top of the temple's unmistakable shape could still be seen.

The builders who had designed it must not have been from this time, she considered. The dawnstar mace was known to be a symbolic icon in Az'Dayne, used even by the paladins and veritans as their sacred signature weapons. The Pentagogue itself was shaped as a colossal dawnstar mace sprouting from the central foundation of the city. How many floors high the shaft of the tower rose, Valaythea could not possibly estimate or gauge. But it was enough that she could no longer even see the top from so close.

It was said that only the most divine-blessed beings, chosen by the Five and Five, could join the paladins and veritans at the top, in the ball-like edifice that crowned the imposing building. Valaythea had also learned of the innovative chain lift that could move individuals to different levels and that it even went far below the surface, where more chambers of the Pentagogue had been built for the purpose of housing Az'Dayne's Paladin and Veritan Orders.

Izayus tapped his empty wineglass against the table upstairs in the coach and watched impatiently as the eunuch servant came scrambling to his needs. "Leave us. Get down and instruct that we are to turn around immediately. Back to the Bronze Bay. The tour is over."

The servant did as bidden, and gradually the wide Imperiar

Coach veered in the other direction.

"I am ready now." Izayus spoke hazily after a long period of silence back through Hallion's Crater. His fingers lethargically beckoned Valaythea over.

I knew it would be time soon … She kept her hesitations to herself and approached him obediently, getting onto her knees before him to do her duty as his paramour.

"No." Izayus put both of his palms atop her hands when she placed them on the laces of his breeches. "I am ready to tell you what haunts me." He fished around for his stowed pipe. "Why I try to escape what I know."

After finding his drug apparatus, he just gripped it tightly with eyes filled with hatred and disgust, before his focus drifted outside the window to the knights lining the road. "Look at them. Charlatans. Face changers. All of them."

How can you tell? They don't even seem to show a personality to act as fakes and frauds to me. She scrutinized the armored and helm-concealed paladins.

"We live ruled by the ghosts beneath us, dwelling among the blind and naive, or the frightened and obedient. It's all some grand scheme. Generation after another, we suffer and follow the course to extinction. And here I sit with my great curse, that I was born in the Know." He reached out to tenderly pull her hands so that she sat in his lap. He stroked her hair with the fingers of one hand while the other caressed her cheek. "Oh, Valaythea, it had to be you. And you will know why soon. But be sure of this: they will make us one of them soon. Our turn comes next. On the return of my father and mother, at the birth of the Sunder of this Kingfall. There is no more postponing it. It is our turn."

A burning in her cheeks swelled with the sheer terror of the horrid gibberish the prince was issuing. Tears formed, and she didn't even know why. "You are frightening me, my prince."

"Am I?" Izayus chuckled and kissed her cheek. "Sweet wife, if I am what frightens you, I feel you won't survive the next story." His voice whispered as low as it could go into her ear. "You can never unhear it. I am about to tell you about the neverborne."

A shiver shot down Valaythea's spine at the mention of the unfamiliar word, and she prepared to listen and weep her predestined fate away.

SCARLESS (III)

THE PURGE OF THE YARD

Zahnastaazjah strummed the veined shaft of her spear, eyeing the ground sconce it sat in beside her. She stood on the brick terrace overlooking the Yard, which acted as a focal podium in the square training court that now served as an auditorium.

There are birds and breeze in the clouds today … This should be a good day. She vainly tried to pretend to still care about such things that reminded her of her Terollar sky descendancy, but she simply didn't. It was a bad day, and she was ready to be done with it before it had even begun.

Every member of the Stormtrees who could fit was there before her, segregated into their smaller factions. To her right, Xalo judged the nervous crowd of criminals, while farther in the corner, Uubakrath was poised with his bow readied to rain death on any who stepped out of line, with a litter of countless arrows surrounding his feet. In the opposite corner, to her left, was her new Dawner, Pyphan, shirtless, with all his Dawning magemarks revealed across his neck, torso, and arms, appearing like golden tattoos. The only other Stormtree on the platform was her chamberlain, Devonduer, announcing her underlords and their tenures.

"All see the mighty Usurp," he went on, explaining that the infamous tyrant had been in Zahnastaazjah's employ since the original Blue Blades for next to three decades now, longer than any member in the Yard. Usurp was also the only underlord who could boast overseeing more than one faction—the leftovers of the old Blue Blades, the converts of the Centron Spears, now the Centron Guard, the Tolltakers, who levied taxes on half the sites on Festival Row, and the Ironarms, who muscled over Turftown. Usurp held more citywide fear than anyone in the underworld next to Zahnastaazjah herself. He had remained her ideal commander for dictating necessary coercion and collection practices for the guild.

"All recognize Dockjaw, overman of the Salt Lords, masters of the North Docks, overseeing our smuggling operations," Devonduer broadcast next.

Zahnastaazjah felt a pang of sadness swelling in her throat as she contemplated the decisions she had already made about the dilemmas she faced today. She found herself unable to make eye contact with the loyal Brutongan she had known and trusted for so long. The conclusions of a guild purge were hardly ever enjoyable for her, and today was going to hurt the most. The severity of what was about to transpire in the Yard had never been seen before in the Stormtrees.

"Dockjaw has been with the Stormtrees for sixteen years, the longest next to Usurp."

What a waste of life, old friend ... Why must you make me take this from you?

Her distraught thoughts turned to a musing of fury as Devonduer spieled on to the next underlord in her employ.

"Now all eyes on Sundown, for you may get no fair chance otherwise," Devonduer teased with a double meaning. Sundown was an adept in professional duplicity, always determined in the Stormtrees' favor against the many foiled adversaries and avoided uprisings they had endured throughout their many years affiliated with one another.

Jon Elwine. How long has it been since someone has called you by your bornname? We both know that answer.

"Overman of Night Street, masters of the Midway and North Commons after dark, overseeing our espionage, sabotage, and recovery operations." Devonduer granted the traitorous stealth expert his due credit. "Sundown has been with the Stormtrees for thirteen years, third under Dockjaw and Usurp."

Zahnastaazjah focused her green eyes on the serrated tip of her bloodrime spear. She decided not to look at the man until the deed of his execution today was ready to be carried out. Of course, she had prearranged that he and no others had any idea, aside from a rare privileged few —only Xalo, Devonduer, Usurp, Uubakrath, and Pyphan.

Jon Elwine had once been a military intelligence officer for the Goldguardians. It was said he had been a prodigy for his age at the time he had forsaken his duty to them and become a fugitive by law of desertion. Somehow the elusive manipulator had managed not only survival in thwarting their many hunting parties, but also masterfully maintaining discretion in running his operations as a freelance ganglord of thieves and spies and saboteurs.

Night Street was not a chosen name but a given one. It had just become the popular rumor that if one stepped out after the sun went down between the districts of the North Commons and the Midway, one was entering "Night Street" time and territory. Even the local city watch was aware and simply dealt with it through bribery, fear, or ignorance of the sheer clandestine skill set of the members. And thus was how the name Jon Elwine had swiftly dissipated into forgottenness, and the alias of Sundown had risen in notorious influence.

We both left our bornnames in a past life. Jon Elwine the Goldguardian and Zahnastaazjah the Terollar are dead. Sundown and Scarless have thrived since. Zahnastaazjah pressed her thumb in a flick over the blade of her almost vertical mounted weapon, just enough to see her finger bleed and rapidly heal.

She thought on what the Seven Seats had pointed out about Sundown's ongoing betrayal and his son's employment with the Boarneck Company, recruiting Dawning mages from Shypriss's ward or any newcomer prodigies who entered the city. Sundown was now nothing more than a mole for the enemy within her inner operations. After being enlightened by the revelations of Amethyst and Shypriss in the last Conclave, Zahnastaazjah had decided to do her own investigations into the allegations. And it was all true, yet far worse.

Not only had Sundown defected from the Stormtrees as a full informant for the Boarnecks against her guild, but his actions had further fueled the Boarneck Company, which had once been just an oppressive annoyance in Bridgeville, into a real threat that had the potential to take over the eastern districts of the city and overpower the Stormtrees easily by numbers alone.

She had learned that the Boarnecks were dabbling in something sinister with a major connection to the Az'Dayne Dominadom, and somehow they were accessing new subterranean avenues even deeper below the sewers of the Flush, meeting with unidentified contacts. The growth of the mercenary company was seemingly directly linked to this hushed enigma.

You and yours, all of Night Street, are lost to me now, Elwine. None of you gets to live to tell another lie. She condemned him silently in her furious thoughts.

"All recognize Atrick." Her chamberlain paused, as if he felt he was rushing the rituals of a full guild meet. Her underlord of public relations was a perpetually uneasy character, sometimes nervous for the most unwarranted of reasons.

Fucking Atrick. Why couldn't it be you? Zahnastaazjah wasn't even thinking about her most loathed recent associate. Her mind tunneled in on a decem different ways in which she wanted to butcher Sundown in front of her entire guild.

"Overman of the Copper Jacks, masters of Copper's Side, overseeing underground trade relations and exotic live exports. Atrick has been in the Stormtrees for three years now."

Devonduer continued to the last of the underlords. "And finally, all recognize Amaris, newly promoted as the Stormtrees' first overwoman. She oversees the affiliate venues and third-party connections, along with the guild safe houses."

Devonduer paused to take a swig of water from the wineskin around his shoulder. "Now, as to why all of you have been summoned to gather today. Because Zahnastaazjah, progeny of the fallen king of the Glacial Isles—" He stopped and jerked his head back at her in a sincere look of mortified apology.

Glace Isles. She almost threw Devonduer off the terrace onto the stone slabs below for the mistake. *Half this lot is an embarrassment.* She could see it in the horrified man's eyes that he knew he had misspoken, but instead of torturing the poor sod, she just waved him on to continue and shook her head at her fellow Terollar, Uubakrath, in annoyance.

"Because our most beloved Scarless, guildmother of the Stormtrees, Overlord of the Underworld, has deemed it necessary, and we do not deny her respect!"

Zahnastaazjah subtly held out four fingers on her right hand, just long enough for Xalo, Uubakrath, Usurp, and Pyphan to take notice, and then she stepped forward for her own broadcast.

"Thank you all for your attendance. I would address you all as Stormtrees, but it has come to my attention that more than a few of you have chosen no longer to be so. We have traitors at our table who share the same ale and wine with us. This simply will not do.

"Some of you have been with me long enough to experience what we refer to as the Purge of the Yard. For those who are new, prepare to witness the custom."

Zahnastaazjah briefly scrutinized each group below her and the henchmen who led them. The disloyalty in those of them who would be judged today brought a rot to her gut that made it churn. She narrowed her green eyes at one individual and pointed at the guilty-faced man. "Atrick, step forward."

Atrick looked back at Usurp as if he expected his skull to be bashed in by the burly brute, who stood several paces away in the rear with his own men. His eyes were wide in apparent dread at hearing his own name called out, glancing back and forth between Zahnastaazjah and Xalo. "Scarless, why me? I ain't done a damn thing to ya nor any Stormtree here! I swear on the fuckin' Fives!"

I know you didn't. But I like to watch you squirm. And it's all part of the game. She resisted looking at the soon-to-be-dead man, Sundown, not far behind him. "But the rats tell me that you whisper nasty things about your granted position in the guild. They say you pray curses on my name and Xalo's. That you still call for your old master, Copper King. What do you say to this?"

As rehearsed, Xalo nimbly leaped down from the low terrace onto other platforms below until his feet were level in the Yard with the rest of them, and the spellblade immediately commenced a brisk walk toward the Copper Jack overman.

"What? No! I love Xalo! I mean ..." Atrick stammered, tripping over his rant of thoughts, "I love ya, Scarless! Guildmother! Ya both! I only sing praises! Fuck Copper King! I'll spit down his corpse's slit throat again, same one I gave him for ya!"

"But you know something, don't you, Atrick? Something you have not brought to my attention that you learned on the docks. Doesn't he, Xalo?"

Xalo pulled out his spellblade as he continued to walk closer to Atrick. "That he does."

"Okay!" Atrick took a step back and held his hands up in defeat. "I've only heard rumors of the northeast docks bendin' to the Boarnecks, but nary a snake slithers in my garden! The Jacks are clean!"

Xalo slowed his walk slightly while Zahnastaazjah pressured Atrick. "The North Docks are the jurisdiction of Dockjaw. Are you accusing him of conspiring with an opposing organization?"

Atrick shook head and arms frantically. "Didn't say Dockjaw's name, Scarless. Not implyin' nothin' of the sort! Just sayin' what I hear an' that it wasn't me. I'd never betray ya! I thank every new day's sun an' moon for the mercy ya showed me!"

Even Dockjaw is getting nervous now. Good. She caught the Brutongan shuffling in place at the insinuation of his plausible incompetence over his own district. But her focus was still on Atrick. "You know what I like about you, Atrick?"

"That I don't fuckin' lie?"

Zahnastaazjah let out a chuckle at the obviously blameless man and his pleas. "That you are transparent. And with transparency comes trust. I know you will not betray me. You fear the consequences of disappointing me. I like to call this proper motivation." She snapped her middle finger and thumb together above her head.

On cue, a large arcanic imprint on Pyphan's torso flashed a fiery green. The luminescent rings around his irises burst to fill his eyes with the magical green glow as he aimed his hand with outstretched fingers in a spreading motion toward where the Night Street had positioned themselves, and he unleashed his first spell.

The magemark on Pyphan's body dissipated back to its golden hue just as the ground around Sundown rumbled in a violent shock wave so strong that it knocked almost every man in the Night Street to the ground.

Pyphan threw out his other hand in a similar manner to the first spell, with a different magemark emitting its glow on his skin. Another magic effect of the tairan element erupted in the Yard. From the ground beneath the Night Street, unnatural hands made of gripping roots and hard soil clamped the men down in place where they had landed, whether by the ankles, wrists, neck, or waist. The spell did not seem to discriminate or have a pattern in binding them.

For Sundown himself, the area he stood on rose up in a cone, which swallowed his body up to his thighs.

Before the horrified spymaster could retaliate with a word, Zahnastaazjah was already speaking. "Sundown, on the other hand, has chosen to dump thirteen years of service to the Stormtrees down the Flush."

The first casualty came with a loud crack as Usurp crashed his heavy war maul down on one unsuspecting victim's skull.

The second and third men fell next to each other with well-placed arrows to the chest coming from Uubakrath's direction.

The fourth made the entire Yard echo with his predeath wailing. His arm was awkwardly braced by Pyphan's magic roots, now broken at the elbow from his futile attempt to escape. He held out his other arm to pointlessly shield himself from his executioner, nearly upon him. Xalo seemed to take the man's fear as motivation to choose him specifically. Xalo swung his glass sword in a quick underhanded arch several paces away, never ceasing his walk, and unleashed a glyph's power within the blade, which hurled a thin wave of fire that struck the trapped man in the face, ending his woes for good. The rolling flames didn't stop there, and they spread over two more nearby victims, setting them ablaze to burn and die the same way.

"Guildmother! What is this madness?" Sundown entreated Zahnastaazjah at the top of his lungs, with frantic focus on the dying men of his faction instead of on her. "Because of the deal with Oldan in the Midway? Have you even thought to hear me out?"

"She *is* hearing you out. Your seconds on the horizon are waning, Sundown," Xalo retorted. "Seven ..." The Elothian thrust his sword through another victim's heart. "Eight ..." Another member of the Night Street met the spellblade's edge on the side of the neck.

"Nine!" Usurp shouted as he hammered down in sequence with the unmerciful massacre.

A few more fell to arrows as Uubakrath almost lazily aimed and shot at the ensnared men. Zahnastaazjah recognized each casualty by his dismayed face. She knew everyone in her guild by name and story. *They almost don't seem confused anymore. They understand. Don't you all? Just scared to see your Godslands is all ... A pity. A waste of damn fine infiltrators and informants.* She surveyed the Purge of the Yard, toying with the foreign concept of conjuring sympathy that she did not feel.

"The Night Street were acting as double agents in your stead, to infiltrate the Boarneck Company for weaknesses in their ranks. We weren't keeping any smuggling profits from the North Docks, only keeping your cache quiet. You know me, Zahnastaazjah! You know how I operate—silence and shadows until it's over," Sundown defended. "I have always come through for the Stormtrees!"

Why is he still talking? was all she could think when Sundown continued to impose some justification for his betrayal. "Your activities have doubled, and your return is the same. That alone is suspicious, Jon."

He seemed perturbed by her calling him by his real name, something that had not been done in public for as many years, but he had started the debate by referencing hers, so the trade was fair at this point. "This is my guild for life! What are you doing?"

"On to the second and third points: your operations are not smuggling, and the ambit you were encroaching on was designated to Dockjaw. Well known facts," she reprimanded him.

"Waning, Sundown, waning." Xalo taunted the helpless spymaster while he cut down more of the Night Street all around him.

"Twenty!" Usurp shouted an updated body count.

"How far does Oldan's reach go? If you tell me it's just Worest, the Bridge, and Canaltown, I vow to the Beyond that I will pull your guts up through your mouth and have this Dawner keep you alive to watch," she threatened.

Sundown hung his head in defeat and admitted, "It's true the Boarnecks have been buying up the Midway, even pushing into North Commons from the leads at the docks, going straight around you. Even making friends with Tongatown and them braggarts on the Bluffs. They're archon-rich as fuck, bleeding coin and shitting gems."

"A few more questions, then you are free to go," she promised, ready to be done with the prolonged interrogation ordeal.

"To go? How so? To the Godslands? Don't fool me, Scarless, please!" Sundown begged to deaf ears.

"Where do they get their men and wealth? It wasn't from the city." Zahnastaazjah ignored his pathetic appeals. *If you know me at all after all these years, Jon, then you already know you are a dead man by the end of this exchange.* She sighed, getting annoyed.

"Mostly Worestaschia in the beginning." Sundown pointed out the obvious about the Boarneck Company's state of origin, which every uneducated sod in Utamia already knew about. "Then they started across all of Utamia, recruiting on the bounty boards. They purposed their routes to and through where word told them there would be stables full of strong steeds, and they muscled and got their mounts, one way or another. Then they played the same across the Tairanheart and Tairancia, and lately they took near half the refugee Elothia eastfolk who had half a mind to fight and could ride. How they're affording it? Lost on me still from Oldan's backstory, but raiding, pillaging, and star-high contract jobs with kings and queens have been kind to their late momentum. They got enough power even to snub buyouts from Az'Dayne, I've learned."

Uubakrath did not stop languidly loosing arrows at the prone former spy network, while Xalo and Usurp continued with the slaughter of every faction member of the Night Street they navigated past.

"Why are they still killing? Tell them to stop!" Sundown screamed—an empty demand again. "I'm telling you all I was gonna tell you already!"

"No, you weren't." Zahnastaazjah silenced him. "The North Docks—which men under Dockjaw were aiding you? Had to be the border-block men."

"Dockjaw didn't know shit. Sorry for the shade." Sundown looked across the Yard at the Brutongan smuggler with a regretful semblance. "Those eight, standing tight. They were the border-block men. The ones assigned to—"

"That will do," Zahnastaazjah interrupted, and she threw a nod at Pyphan, adjacent to her left.

The Dawning mage didn't hesitate to invoke the same spell as his last one. Similar tairan hands erupted from the ground beneath the accused members of the North Docks, crushing their ankles as Pyphan gestured with his hands in a gripping motion.

Dockjaw just watched, seemingly unaffected and unsurprised, while Sundown blustered on with his never-ending fit. "I keep spouting truth, Zahnastaazjah. If you are done with me, just be done with it!"

Fine, then. You won't enjoy this last part. "How long has your son been under Oldan Boldandgold's heel, working for the Boarnecks? Almost two seasons now, right?" Zahnastaazjah condemned. "Tell me, was he the one in charge, enlisting Goldgarden mages for whatever the Dominadom is plotting to further scheme against us, or were you his boss? Or did it get confusing at times?"

She could see his reddening frustration transform into a paling terror. Sundown recognized the tone, and didn't miss a meaning behind the purposed past tense inference. "Was? Were?"

Usurp answered what Sundown was too afraid to ask. "He did at least fight, cryin' for Daddy till the end." Usurp pulled Sundown's son's severed head from a sack he had been carrying the whole time, then tossed it at Sundown's feet.

Sundown looked through the meager remains of his ill-fated son, suddenly glossy-eyed, as if he were staring through it all into the very soil. The convicted traitor began to cry with an uncontrollable flow down his cheeks, but his expression was etched with virulent rage. "Fuck you to the forgotten abyss of the Vist, troll!"

All went silent, as if the world had cast them all into deafness. Zahnastaazjah let the seconds before the finale play out far longer than necessary to build anticipation. Sundown knew he was a dead man standing.

In one astonishingly fast motion, she took her spear in hand and hurled it across the Yard, straight into the center of Sundown's chest. It snapped his spine with its sheer momentum as it bent the man over backward in half, with his head touching the fastening mound Pyphan had created. Xalo was already in position, directly next to the spymaster's corpse, and decapitated him in one swift strike. Zahnastaazjah held her hand up, and the bloodrime weapon yanked itself from its fleshy host, pulling Sundown's headless body back upright, and her spear soared back through the air into her grasp.

Xalo walked across the Yard with the severed head in hand, held by the hair, and once close enough, he hurled it up to the terrace for her to catch. In front of everyone, she spiked the skull of Sundown on the tip of her spear and replaced the weapon back into the sconce, leaning it over the Yard for all to see.

Her merciless eyes then pierced the eight crippled men from Dockjaw's crew squirming on the ground. "I believe our newest member of the guild now needs no formal introduction. Let this be it. All now recognize Pyphan the Dawner, first and only mage of the Stormtrees."

She pointed to call the master of the Salt Lords out next. "Dockjaw, step forward!"

"Guildmother." Dockjaw humbly and obediently did as instructed and dropped to one knee in subservience. "I did not know any of this."

"Your innocence in this matter is unquestionable," she said with a tone of genuine consolation. "However, your competence is."

Xalo trekked over the Yard, this time straight up to Dockjaw, who remained kneeling, demonstrating a fearless acceptance of his sentencing. "Your former guildmother wishes me to act as her voice to convey that you will be missed."

The spellblade conveyed the passing of judgment, and Zahnastaazjah turned her back on him to face the wall, away from her Stormtrees.

"You are no longer a Stormtree, Dockjaw," Xalo intoned. "You will not belong to any guild within the authority of her reach on Goldgarden Isle. You may reside as an unaffiliated citizen in Tongatown, or you may leave the city entirely. But your time here has expired, and you need to leave now."

Xalo walked away from Dockjaw to weave in and out of the crippled defectors next to him. "The guildmother wishes for you to escort these eight turncoats back with you. They are condemned to crawl about the North Docks for the rest of their lives, bearing one of the many signatures for betraying her."

"I kept a tight grip on the neck of my men," Dockjaw plainly said to Zahnastaazjah alone. "I never intentionally forsook my Stormtrees guild, nor yourself, as my adored mentor and master. I would never betray my own. I am sorry I lost you along the way."

She caught Dockjaw in her peripheral vision as he stood up and bowed to her back. And just like that, the Brutongan left the Yard, ushering the group of cripples from the vicinity.

Zahnastaazjah faced the remainder of her guild members, taking a long pause to allow Dockjaw to completely disappear from sight. Behind her stone-cold visage, she could feel somber eyes in hiding. *The birds and breeze are gone from the clouds … I knew it would be a bad day.* She took note of the skies above.

Xalo had not been lying to the former Salt Lords master. He would be missed. He and Zahnastaazjah had a long history—in the beginning, even intimate, many would whisper, until their quiet relationship had played its passionate course into a stoic duty of dull professionalism as timeworn as the old Brutongan.

There was only one more thing for her to say, and then she could be done with this damnable day. "The Purge of the Yard. New promotions and territory assignments are to be announced soon. You are all dismissed."

SYMBELLE & FYHEIR (III)

THE ALCHEMIST

We are going to let you see it.

Symbelle's memories writhed from the darkness of the force-forgotten abyss that remained a pit in the back of her mind. They appeared like smoking hands, dripping with burning flesh, and they sounded like wailing wraiths from the bottommost hells. Their faces came forth from the ashen fog. They were confused and angry. They were horrified and helpless. They were innocent ... most of them.

They were food for the fire that is us. And we dined well this night, Symbelle. Do not let the shadow take over. See it.

But she was done seeing it. Fyheir was forcing her to remember Tairanchula pieces at a time, but she resisted. Her focus took in the last point of concentration she had had before the trance of Fyheir had abducted her. The scroll on the table in front of her was illuminated by a faint violet light from the radiance in her strange eyes, beaming even through the opaque goggles she chose to wear. Her ever-shifting, glowing orbs made it impossible to hide her nature as a hyperi.

Ink was spilled across the half-filled page, full of innovative recipes with the ingredients of her most unconventional concoctions. At the edge of the table, a red blaze swallowed a bundle of folded garments that she recognized. They were hers.

More of the scene from the reality before her began to settle in. Her clothes were not burning. Nor was the table, shining with a coat of transparent wax. She was naked, even bare of all accessories, except the goggles, and she felt very strange. Her own skin glistened from the oil it was coated with, reflecting the fire.

The fiery display over her garments was no natural element but the product of igniting a grain-like material known as blast salt. The greased table was armored by a substance formulated from the blubber of the western Peromeise whales, the sap from southern ember trees, and the herbs harvested from three separate northern plants. She called it burnguard.

And the lubrication was painted on her skin, protecting her from the heat and incinerating effect of the fire, was something she had officially termed cinder oil.

Symbelle told her legs to stand, but the only muscles that acted were in her neck as she surveyed the complex chamber. Other tables were set in no certain pattern of asymmetrical chaos throughout the dark room. Only the accompanying fires provided light to the windowless workshop: the fury of the forge behind her, the blaze underneath the cauldron in the corner, and the red radiance from the tireless blast salt failing at feeding on her discarded but fortified clothes.

There was a mortar and pestle or two there, and random alembics strewn about next to compound apparatuses. There were vials and decanters made of glass or ceramic, filled or empty or missing a portion of their contents. She saw tairanware crucibles among a plethora of labeled herbal ingredients. This was a place she was well familiar with. This was an alchemist's abode.

She found a vacant bedroll cot in the corner opposite the boiling cauldron, and even more of her recollections came back to her. She had been here for days. Pentdays, maybe.

Master Claydius had been assessing the training in alchemy she had received at Tairanchula. He had been testing her resolve in certain scenarios, navigating her through methods of deterrence to avoid her weaknesses rather than strengthen them. She had been educated in Goldgarden politics and Utamian history and in matters crucial to the Stormtrees crime syndicate's interests, the Boarneck Company specifically. She had been given full tours of the clandestine facility that had proven to be the Oathemic Cabal's headquarters.

The blood in her veins found the stability of her hips, and her hips found the strength in her feeble legs, and again she found herself able to stand. Her mentor appeared directly in front of her. His robe cast an illusion, as if he had been conjured into the room and formed from the stone tile itself. The glowing halos around his irises, which complemented the supernatural green in his eyes, were all one could see of his face.

"Welcome back, Symbelle," Master Claydius rasped. He was aware of her returning from her blackout, no doubt a repercussion of the blast salt's explosion. Fiery aftermaths had taken their toll on her ever since the event. "Look around you. Does any of it seem familiar?"

Symbelle scrutinized her customized laboratory once again. She recognized it all now. Blast salt, burnguard, cinder oil—they were each her own development in the misunderstood art of alchemy, between the realm of science and magic.

"It does," she uttered. "They are all my creations."

Symbelle took notice of the tincture of undersight on the copper nightstand behind her. Such a tonic afforded those who drank it the ability to temporarily have sight in an alternative vision, seeing different emissions of heat produced by the living. The only downside was suffering from periodic disorientation and mild blindness afterward. But she had formulated a remedy for that side effect in preparation.

She then gazed past the heap of yellow powder packed into leather release pouches. She had named it skinny dust. It was a supplement. In small doses, it would suppress the appetite, boost the passive ability for losing unwanted weight, and make one's aggressive tendencies subside. However, when used as a weapon, in an abundant quantity inhaled, skinny dust could cripple the strongest and most willful individual. Severe dehydration would follow, with muscle enervation, and an eventual mental breakdown with an overwhelming sense of fear.

"You invented everything you see in this room. Every potion. Every oil. Every powder concoction. Every remedy tincture. All that you see. You have managed to achieve that which no other known alchemist has come to attain, inside and outside the order," Master Claydius rasped.

Her final innovation became more visible under the luminescent beam cast wherever she turned her hyperi eyes. Symbelle could not recall how she had made it, nor how she had discovered its abstruse components. She only knew the luminescent purple powder in the distant glass vial was precious and so rare that she could not ascertain its formulation. This was an achievement of Fyheir that her alternate psyche would not share with Symbelle. Symbelle had dubbed it as wispbane.

"You have a dangerous mind that you share."

She could only assume that the master sorcerer was suggesting one thing. "You mean with Fyheir?"

"We have met Fyheir," Claydius informed her, insinuating others of the order had as well. "But truly, have you?"

Truly, no, she had not. "We speak. But it has yet to let me meet it," Symbelle admitted melancholically.

"Hyperis are complex creatures. What blesses you is also your blight. You are the weapon we need and choose, but we need you to be the one in control, not it. Have you put more thought into my offer to meet Mesdarro? He can train you proper."

Meeting Mesdarro and not having to perform any writs was actually all that she had thought about since Claydius proposed the option to her that day in the lift.

What if we promise to be good? Fyheir severed her train of thought. *What if we promise to let you see with us this time?*

This was a first. Fyheir had never granted her such a luxury. Or perhaps Fyheir was her undying guardian, shielding her from suffering through the horrors of the fiery deeds it had done.

"It … it …" Symbelle stuttered, "it wants to answer for me."

"That is not an answer. Do you wish to learn to use your hypersight? We must act fast. I can override your writs, reissue them to someone more capable and willing," Claydius reiterated harshly.

Shh, shh now, Symbelle. Rest now and join our audience.

Symbelle felt her head grow heavy. The familiar warm and woozy wave washed over her mind, and her vision became spotted with white dots before the vacuum devoured her. She felt her body go limp and lifeless and embraced the inevitable escape. She expected to wake hours or days later, at the mercy of whatever toll Fyheir was about to exact from her.

But that was not at all what occurred. The blackness dissipated. Symbelle was still present. But she was no longer controlling her movements. Her body twisted from the shy and slumped broken self that she was into a being of sheer confidence, postured straight and sure. A new special sight became available, and green traces of ghostlike lines in different directions trailed throughout the chamber. Even the magic aura over Master Claydius was amplified into a strong green glow around him, as if she were under the influence of some psychedelic drug.

She felt a grin stretching her fool's frown across her cheeks as she rose and casually walked to the table with the undersight vials. She saw her own hand bring one of the small vessels up to her mouth and could feel the bitter liquid pouring down her throat.

Fyheir?

Symbelle was now the voiceless conscience, albeit with no influence over her alter ego. This was an unanticipated experience.

As the heat-seeing potion was imbibed, she watched herself follow with the necessary chaser to null the adverse reaction that coupled with taking undersight. A deep whiff of the pungent steam put off by the boiled plumhead mushrooms halted any potential vertigo or impairments to sight.

Fyheir closed Symbelle's eyes and cracked her neck from side to side, using no hands. *I did not know I was so tense.* When her glowing eyes reopened, peering through the thick, heat-resistant goggles her own hands had crafted, her sense of sight had changed altogether. She could see heat emanating from three living bodies in the room: Claydius in front of her, and two men in the corners, and then a hint of a fourth individual just on the outside of a hidden wooden door behind the master.

I can see them ... No ... Not just see them, but I know them. I can see who they are. How? Somehow Symbelle knew the identities of everyone before her, yet Master Claydius was the only one she had ever met. She even knew his family name, which had never been revealed to her. The being on the other side of the door was glowing differently than the others. She was female. Symbelle could see it had a spiritroot, through the trail it left that must trace back to a lifetree. She was an elvan, a Neveril. *This is not the potion. This is you Fyheir? This is my hypersight?*

Fyheir did give an answer. "We do not need Mesdarro to train us in the sight Claydius Orlaithe. We have Fyheir. You can tell Athaniel Chandoss and Daerlem Black to come out of the shadows and show us Nextaiya of Morvlanyun."

"Impressive feat, hyperi," Master Claydius confessed with convincing approval. "This is your Entity with us again then? Very well, Fyheir. Athaniel, Daerlem, bring in the lesson."

The two assassins moved in unison to reveal the concealed cubicle by shifting small wooden latches to the side and sliding open the secret doorway. On an upright gurney of sorts, with small wheels toward the feet and handles at the top, they rolled in said enemy.

She was a petite little thing, albino of skin, with sharp ears protruding from an obvious eccentric wig made of outlandish material the likes of which Symbelle had never seen. The slumbering elvan's fake red hair protruded upward like frozen fire on a hearth. A soft green glow emanated from within her, from where her heart lay, and Symbelle could only guess this might be her hunder, made visible by her enhanced hyperi sight.

May we touch her? She is beautiful.

"You seem to know much, but do you know what this is?" Master Claydius always had a way with imposing lessons.

Fyheir didn't have to scrutinize the white-skinned elvan to know how to reply to Symbelle's master. "The lesson," Fyheir candidly declared, lithely making its way toward the restrained victim. Symbelle felt humiliated, registering again that she was still without clothes, but Fyheir didn't shy away from displaying its host's nakedness, posing like a goddess in the flesh. The way Fyheir even talked with her own voice, but in a more sophisticated accent was alluring.

Claydius further explained. "This is a Neveril elvan. Some would have you believe they are behind the downfall of Az'Dayne from the inside out. Once you complete your current writs, you will be brought into the Know. For now, get to know its face. The face behind it all. This one is a deserter of its own kind. It is an enemy of ours as much as it is an enemy of theirs. The lesson today is to show me you can take its life."

She is so beautiful, though. Symbelle gloomed at such a macabre notion.

"The time can be now or then," Fyheir seethed with no remorse in its tone as it removed the sleeping elvan's wig to fit it over Symbelle's own short-haired scalp. The thin strands of hair moved at Fyheir's touch, staying straight, almost too easy to style in whatever eccentric fashion seemed appealing.

Still so beautiful, Symbelle thought of the now-bald elvan.

"Fire does not discriminate," Fyheir said.

"Unfortunately, you will find that fire does. The Neveril and their own creations do not burn so easily," the sorcerer corrected it.

"This is not the way."

Fyheir didn't seem to agree. It produced an uncorked bottle of wispbane.

When did we grab this? Symbelle had never noticed her own hands doing it earlier, too infatuated by the Neveril. Her peripheral vision caught a glimpse of Claydius judging her with a puzzled semblance as Fyheir brought the wispbane to the unconscious elvan's mouth and poured the glowing powder down her throat.

What are you doing? We do not even know this one!

Fyheir chose not to heed her, just as Symbelle would ignore it. She could only imagine the role reversal was a critical bliss for Fyheir in the moment, hearing her futile pleas.

As the albino elvan began to choke and cough, slowly waking up from her slumber, Fyheir had already walked away. Now back at the table with the blast salt, it took a small bellows device in one hand and another of the small lantern spheres in the other.

The Neveril girl seemed young, blameless, and afflicted with misfortune as her only sin. Symbelle could see the elvan's piteous red eyes desperately fighting against the substance in her veins that had forced her to sleep in the first place. Symbelle didn't want her to die. *Let's save this one.*

Fyheir stood halfway across the room and aimed the bellows with both hands to spray whatever filled the canister attached to its nozzle, and Symbelle watched helplessly as its contents were released in a stream to coat the prisoner in blast-salt granules.

"If this is my enemy," Fyheir fumed with baseless hate, pausing only to drop the bellows and poise with just the fiery sphere, "then they will all burn just fine in the end."

The small ball lantern acted as an igniter bomb as it was tossed onto the torso of the elvan victim, and the blast salt exploded in full effect. In a flash, the red fire blazed up so bright it lit every corner of the room, disintegrating the flesh and bone of the Neveril before she could even scream.

Claydius had been proven wrong. While the Neveril elven were known to be born with the impower to resist fire, the wispbane clearly nullified that unnatural immunity rather rapidly. The Cabal master and two assassins too seemed in awe at the display to utter a word.

Only the sound of flesh and bone still crackling echoed in the alchemist's chamber. Fyheir was satisfied, and Symbelle found herself saddened for no apparent reason at the sacrifice of the elvan stranger.

She felt herself slipping into the inviting void. She didn't want to see any more of what Fyheir could or would do. Her evil counterpart allowed the escape, and Symbelle crawled back into the familiar black hole until it was all gone.

* * * * *

When Symbelle awoke from her time lapse, she was nowhere near the confines of her laboratory. She was standing in an open field under the twilight stars, staring at what resembled the outskirts of the Plaguefolk Villages in the distant valley. Beside her, a lone looming boulder sentried the hill like some statuesque watcher over the horizons below.

But the only thing that kept a claim on her attention was the young man standing over her, assisting her back to her feet. His shirtless body was chiseled with muscle and covered in golden arcane glyphs. His black hair was tied back tight to his head, and his goatee was long and braided to his chest. His green-rimmed eyes gave him away for what he was, as well as his green aura, which she could see due to her hyperi sight. He was a mage.

Somehow she felt like she recognized him, and that was even before he confirmed it with his introduction.

"Sister."

Symbelle could barely believe her own ears and eyes. Before she could assimilate the full impression of their long-awaited reunion since childhood, she blurted ecstatically, "Pyphan!"

It was then that she also realized Fyheir had left. The presence had completely waned from within for the moment. It was just Symbelle and her foster brother, united once again after coming full circle in similar destinies, which they had never had any control over, evidently.

"Coldborn says you are ready," Pyphan said coolly.

Pyphan seemed cold and callous and full of detachment from anything other than duty. He wasn't the jovial package of innocence she recalled from their earlier years. Perhaps that was what happened when little boys were abducted from their happy homes and plunged into assassins' guilds at ten years old to be raised as killers.

"To begin the two writs?" she could only surmise.

"Four writs," Pyphan corrected her as he handed her an Oathemic writ, stamped in the Az'Dayne orange seal.

Target: Zahnastaazjah of Jhuvonhuthala, progeny of the lifetree of Khomo'Jhuvonus and Malindhi, alias Scarless, Crime Queen of Goldgarden, leader of the Stormtrees
Last Location: Scarless Square, Goldgarden

Target: Xalo of Spellspire, Son of the Crimson Clouds, spellblade bloodguard of Scarless
Last Location: Scarless Square, Goldgarden

Symbelle had come to learn that writs came in a variety of categories: target writs, which were for single individual assassinations; recovery writs, which were seize-and-return missions; faction writs, which were specific group-based kill contracts; and finally, general writs, which were broad instructions for whom to eliminate on an indefinite schedule to continuously and actively seek out.

"We walk between the lines now, you and I. The Oathemic Cabal will emerge in one of two ways by the time we are finished. Either the old way, the way that Coldborn created and intended. Or the way that no doubt Claydius is pushing on you, to evolve for survival. Our choice is simple. We complete both Coldborn and Claydius's writs."

"Simple?" She scoffed at her brother's downplayed logic.

"I said our choice is simple. The process is complex." Pyphan elaborated on the agenda before she could respond. "Scarless has just executed her spymaster and his entire faction, along with banishing her overseer of smuggling operations. She has weakened herself. Opportunity is nigh. I will present you as a candidate to join us, to fill the rifts imposed by their loss."

"But I have no training in this," she admitted, feeling habitually fretful and clammy with sweat. She fidgeted with each sentence, noticing that the goggles had been replaced with her dark bifocals. "I know nothing of espionage, as you do. Mastery of that trade seems to be a prerequisite for all within the Cabal but me. I am no actress," she stammered.

"We do not need an actress. We need a timid genius. We need an unsuspecting killer. I know all about you, sister," he explained rather tenebrously while complimenting her potential.

"And I know nothing about you, brother," Symbelle replied despondently.

"You will. We have a long"—he paused as if to find the right word—"walk. Take my hand. Come with me."

And as an indebted apprentice assassin, she did just that. She took her brother's hand in hers and let his Dawning magic run its course. She didn't feel so nervous all of a sudden. The spell of Traversement cast her into an incorporeal form, and her feet lifted from the ground, as if she had become a specter of the afterlife.

Her body traveled westbound into the unknown. She was leaving the Cabal, with which she was barely familiar, alongside a sibling from whom she felt estranged. All that she did was on a whim of hope for survival against the strong, as she was the weak. She desired to be accepted, as she was the unaccepted. Only her Entity embraced and cherished her the way she mutually felt.

Shh, shh now, my love ... Fyheir will never leave you.

ADYSSAIRA (III)

BORN BLIND

Robust primroses and rainbow hyacinths comprised the main attractions of the elaborate hedge maze. Daffodils, tulips, crocuses, and carnations were planted in certain divisions of the bushes, which were shaped in the form of various small animals. They matched their living counterparts roaming the park atop the hill that constituted the regal gardens dubbed Lovers' Labyrinth.

Adyssaira and Sashka casually meandered through the floral maze on the perfect, cloudless day, mostly griping at the curious baby black tiger running off in every direction that tempted her fickle attention span. This was Adyssaira and her half sister's favorite respite away from the drab daily chores around the castle, only about a fifteen-minute walk from the outer estates up the north side. Tiny white birds with pink-feathered wings and cream-colored crests trailed behind the duo in a spiraling flight as they chirped their joyous songs.

A small grey rabbit and her mate, along with a stork bathing in the fountain, scrambled for seclusion the moment the girls and tiger cub made their way along the last hedge avenue, approaching the impressive centerpiece of the garden.

The extravagant fountain had a pitted stone rim encompassing it, lined with coal and unlit lamps due to the hour of the day. It had five layers, with the first being the circular firepit around a moat, which made for an enchanting ambience in the evenings when the park servants came to ignite it. The next tier, gradually waning in circumference as it got higher, was teeming with schools of rainbow fish. The middle level was also filled with water, but it flowed with inviting cascades that carried down to each tier below in a continuous vertical stream. The fourth was the only one with no water at all, brimming with a sea of orange flowers that had black stripes ornamenting their wide petals. And the last tier was filled with drowned coins of all kinds from the many visitors who had been permitted to grace the core of Lovers' Labyrinth and leave a token in exchange for a wish, a tradition since the fountain's creation.

In the very center was a tall well of sorts. A sculpted rock stairway wound up around the cylindrical reservoir, with two small stone totems at the top, one shaped like fire and painted as such, and the other cut and colored like a flawless emerald. At the wellhead was a small platform, which served as an observation point for curious onlookers to view the grandiose Chandoss Estates from an ideal vantage.

At the sight of the fountain, the little yellow-haired half-elvan sprinted up to it and high-stepped her way up the tiers to uproot one of the orange flowers from its perch. Sashka ran back down as fast as she had climbed to present it to Adyssaira to continue with the guessing game she had insisted on playing.

"And what is this called?"

Sashka believed Adyssaira had been born blind, as everyone did, with the exception of a very select few in her immediate family. Of course, Sashka thought she could not see which flower she had picked next, but Adyssaira saw everything, as always. Her yellow Savatarm silk sash was tied over her eyes, affording her clear enough vision to discern her surroundings but shielding the shade of her hunder-touched green eyes. When all the world believed she was blind, she found that those around her acted more like themselves than they ever would if they thought they were being watched and judged. In her meager twenty years of life, she had caught many sins being openly committed. No one was scared to do wrong in silence around a blind girl.

Adyssaira took the plucked flower in her hand and brought it up to her nose to smell, pretending she had to in order to surmise its classification. After a moment, she reached her verdict. "Tiger dawnling."

Sashka laughed in astonishment and reached down to pet the lovable black tiger now at their feet. "You are always better than me at this, and I can see them!"

The tiger dawnling must have been the tenth flower her half sister had made her guess today. Adyssaira may have been better at the puzzles in Lovers' Labyrinth, or a few other trivial subjects, but

Sashka was miraculously far more educated in matters of importance, such as history and cultural differences. Even at twelve, Sashka retained an enthusiasm to train her memory in such things.

"You are better than me at that." Adyssaira pointed at the wishing tier of the fountain, purposely aiming her finger off its mark, to the left a bit.

"What, making fake wishes and pretending they will come true?"

They both chuckled at that sarcasm.

Adyssaira's little sister was smart for her age. *I wonder if it's like that with all Z'shun, or if you are just a special breed,* she considered.

"No. Making wishes that could come true," Adyssaira corrected. "Tell me a new one. One you have never told anyone."

Sashka took a moment to contemplate the request, then finally responded in a troubled tone. "I wish Timmurian were back. I miss him."

You and everyone else. No one seems to know where your uncle is. "I said tell me a new wish," Adyssaira whispered in sympathy, realizing the fun had expired.

Both of the girls said nothing for a while. Adyssaira imagined they let half an hour transpire under the serenity of nature's blanket cast over the manmade retreat. She escorted her sister to the fountain, then around the perimeter of the stone, up the stairway that led to the top of the well. Once they had reached the observation platform and still no words had come, she grasped that Sashka genuinely had no other wishes. Her half sister truly only wanted her Uncle Timmurian back.

Adyssaira, on the other hand, had many wishes she fantasized would come to pass. She had been urging Sashka to spend more time around her than ever as of late, ever since she had received the book *Of Wisps and Whispers* from Sundorion. Adyssaira could not openly pretend to read in front of Sashka, and her little sister had proven she wasn't letting the prized tome out of her sight or locked room anytime soon. Being an annoying inquisitor for every tidbit she could get Sashka to spiel on about was the best plan she could muster.

Adyssaira had learned the difference in her two golden arcanic imprints. The one over her heart was the actual magemark of her genesis wisp, evidently. If she were ever to become interfused with another wisp, the arcanic imprint of the catalyst wisp would appear over her left chest. Future ancillary wisps would run up her arms and shoulders, and even around her upper back. One could even obtain another catalyst wisp once tier-three, through a special practice that was basically a promotion of a currently interfused wisp.

The color of her magemarks mattered as well, signifying which element and season she was bound to. Adyssaira's golden-hued magemarks clearly classified her as eligible to transcend into a Dawning mage, with spellpower over the tairan element. Red magemarks would imply a Sunder mage, with the capacity for fire magic, as white would mean one was a Reaping mage of sky magic, and black for an Umbra mage, with shadow magic, and finally blue for Torrent mages, with water-aligned spells.

The smaller glyph on the back of her neck was something found on all hunder-touched and mages. This symbol stood for the impower of Transbernation, which was the necessary hibernation all mages had to observe after their bound season had transpired. In Adyssaira's case, as a potential Dawning mage, if she ever transcended into such by interfusion with a catalyst wisp, her Transbernation would always need to take place in the following Sunder season.

A mage's body would become physically taxed and internally coerced to succumb to the magic-induced slumber, but if the mage were to resist the Transbernation and try to cast spells during their post-season, they would encounter dire consequences. The casting would instantly age the mage by years, depending on the tier of the spell invoked, up to enough to kill them if the spells were too much to withstand. When entering Transbernation, the mage would gradually undergo a partial transformation by conjoining and melding with a specific form of their element, and they would remain in immobile repose throughout their post-season for the purpose of rejuvenation of their spellpower for the next cycle.

There were altogether five impowers a mage would acquire as they advanced in tiers. Other than Transbernation, the others were Telecommunication, Transfusion, Traversement, and Tranquility.

Telecommunication was the impower to commune with a genesis or catalyst wisp, or even enable either of those wisps to complete unfinished goals in their former life. Invoking this impower was essential in order to ascend to higher tiers as a mage or receive augmentation to certain spell veins. This ability also allowed the mage to leave vocalized messages inside objects related to their element for another mage to hear.

Transfusion was the impower to draw on and dissect wisps in order to manifest them into specific spells, or magic-storing glyphs through spellforging for magic weapons, as in the case of the creation of spellblades.

Traversement was the power of fast-travel, wherein the mage's body entered an ethereal, hovering state. This allowed the mage to traverse at rapid speeds certain terrain affiliated with their element, allowing them to transport up to two individuals the same way.

Lastly, the Tranquility impower, available only to high-tier mages, allowed a mage to stop aging altogether during their bound season, as long as they relinquished their link to any spellpower, by a form of magic disconnection, for the entire cycle.

Adyssaira truly believed she had no ambition to become a mage, especially due to the complications of living in Az'Dayne, where she would most definitely be discovered and suffer a capital penalty. But the learning of the illicit practices and vast mysteries of the arcane arts was something for which she found her appetite was growing insatiable.

Adyssaira caught sight of Emberalda down the hill, approaching on the path that entered the hedge labyrinth. She knew the role she had to play, however, and allowed Sashka to notice her first by accidentally nudging her out of her reflection.

"Emberalda!" Sashka cried with full glee. "She may have good news! I know she misses Timm too!"

They watched as their cousin fervently made her way through the maze. Emberalda's ecstatic smile was clear to see even with Adyssaira's eye sash causing mild obscurement from such a distance. They were privy to her secret romantic involvement with Timmurian. The bonding between Daynish humans and Zandaryn elven may have been more popular as of late, but it had never been accepted among the noble houses. Those who took part in the practice were disdained down to the bottom of society, just above mages and spellblades.

By the time their beautiful cousin reached the fountain, she was completely out of breath from her enthusiastic pace, barely able to utter a reason for her intrusion between labored gasps. Emberalda squealed in surprise as the chubby cub awkwardly fumbled to greet her, and then shouted, "I may be married soon!"

What? I don't see Uncle Nikayle or any local priests approving of this. The incredulous look on Adyssaira's own face matched the disbelieving semblance Sashka showed, though her half sister at least had an obvious sense of optimism behind it.

"To someone even more powerful than Val married," Emberalda confessed unexpectedly.

Sashka and Adyssaira didn't know a response to that confusing update, but Adyssaira spoke for the two of them anyway. "Who is more powerful than the Prince of Az'Dayne? Dominarch Vaximus himself? Did something happen to Sriyah?"

"What about Timmurian?" Little Sashka chimed in with the only way her young mind could comprehend such an intimate betrayal.

"Shh, Sashka. I cannot bear to think on that right now." Their cousin fretted as she flipped her hair back from her sweaty face. Her brownish-blond locks were not braided on the side and puffed up in the front, as she usually wore them, in Zandaryn style, but instead, she wore her hair quite traditionally Daynish for once, long and voluminous down to her midback. She did well in her attempt to hide the emotion in her reddened cheeks and glossy eyes at the mention of her late lover, who she was poorly brushing off.

Emberalda straightened back up, wiped away her perspiration with her handkerchief, and snubbed her way back into her snobbish demeanor. "No, Addy. I forget how pitifully sheltered and unworldly you are. It is no fault of your own. I still adore you! The suitor is no Daynishman. In fact, he is no one who hails from the Dominadom or anywhere on Taira. He is the nephew of the most powerful emperor across the wide realm, from the west to the east!"

Without even conjecturing a possibility for who that might be, Adyssaira blurted out a rather predictable response, based on her cousin's recent antics. "Um, is he an elvan?"

Emberalda scowled at her as if Adyssaira were the most untutored peasant in all of Chandoshia. "Fuck the Fives, silly lily, no! He is Thrench! He is the son of Brigatha Emmonost, sister of Emperor Djediheth Emmonost of the Thrench Empire, and he is arriving at our estates this very next Fourth-Day. I shall forgive you because I know you are quite limited, my dear, broken cousin." She inadequately tried to sympathize in her own condescending way.

She is talking about No-Name, the one that Sundorion mentioned during the Teaching Hours.

Expressing her mirrored thoughts, Sashka said, "You are talking about the one called No-Name we heard about?"

"Well, that cannot be his real name. So I plan to find out what it is." Emberalda beamed with confidence.

Adyssaira knew her cousin's hopelessly romantic behavior was just an emotional defense to cope with losing Timmurian.

"He and his ships are docking at Emerald Point soon!"

Sashka's entire demeanor changed from fun-loving child to truly cultivated adolescent wonder. Even her tone became more serious. "Because in order to equal the status Valaythea has achieved in marrying Prince Izayus Az'Ampion, you would have to marry one of the sons of the Thrench emperor. From eldest to youngest, they are Dominykus, Donderek, and Drythe. Djediheth also has a daughter, named Danuella. The former Thrench emperor, now deceased, Djerath Emmonost, also had a public consummation with Queen Ji-Jy Thainwu of Oriyen, and she became his imperial paramour through her country's submission to the Thrench invasion, which brought about the birth of Brigatha Emmonost. Words over the waters say that this upset the former Empress Nicretta, the wife of Djerath, so much that she returned to Throng, to her Castle Iskandon, instead of taking her place on the throne beside her husband, which caused much discord among the Thrench houses."

Emberalda placed her hands on her hips in irritation at being corrected, and she shook her head at Sashka. "Well, thank you for the pointless history lesson!"

"Not pointless." Sashka prepared to clarify. "You see, Brigatha is only half Thrench, half Oriyan and only the half sister of Djediheth Emmonost. And she married Imaniko the Palestorm, who is fully Oriyan. So really, No-Name is only a quarter Thrench. It would be correct to label this unnamed son, who has been kept obscured to prevent discussion in recent Thrench history, as technically of Oriyan origin. And if Sundorion is correct, that both Brigatha and Imaniko are now dead, then it seems this No-Name coming to our shores has no claim or rights to anything to elevate your situation. And furthermore, it is quite public that you prefer to lie with elven, and the Thrench race do kill elven for a living. He is traveling with the Thrench and has their blood in him still, so I only imagine he will look down upon you as tainted."

Please don't push her down the well. Please don't push her down the well … Adyssaira prayed as she stared at the building frustration in Emberalda's smoldering eyes. This wasn't the first time Sashka's aptitude for retaining knowledge had come out like word vomit.

"Did my father teach you this too?" Her cousin attempted to hold it together behind clenched teeth.

"No. Timmurian did!" Sashka happily explained.

Emberalda huffed in defeat and threw her hands in the air as she walked a small circle in place, and she broke down in convulsive tears as she neared them at the narrow observation point. "Damn him," she cursed between sobs. "Damn Timm! He left me. Told me he would make me his lifemate, then fucking left me to fend for myself," she choked out. "My name is now ever sullied and my reputation spat upon!"

Zandaryn elven males are known to be polygamous with their lifemates. I doubt Timm is any different, Adyssaira thought to add the known fact aloud, but chose not to rile her dramatic cousin.

"Where do you think he is, Ember? I pray he is safe," Sashka whined in a soft tone, expressing the concerns they all felt.

Emberalda mustered up the strength to answer her question between sobs and rage. "Oh, he is safe! He just took my heart and lied to me is all! No one wants me, and no one especially ever will now! You do not have to read your damn books to understand this!"

As her cousin's tears began to calm, Adyssaira decided to step back into the exchange for reasoning. "I'm sorry, Ember, but might I ask, what were your hopes with this No-Name—" She cut herself off short. "What were your hopes with this Oriyan boy of Thrench imperial blood? Why is he even coming to Chandoshia? I have never heard of either Throng or Oriyen coming to Az'Dayne."

The history of the Thrench Empire was nefariously renowned for its violent exploits against the elvan people of the western and southern island nations that no longer existed. Through the long Emmonost rule the Thrench had brought the Forlore, the Tortharan, and the Ibyssai elven into utter extinction off the face of Penthara, and had forced the Vistaryl into endangered reclusion, scattered to the seas or wherever they could hide, with the conquests of the Ashenwave invasion. They were a militaristic naval nation of elite soldiers, honed into perfect killers at an early age, that crusaded to eradicate the elvan race; though as for whatever originated their bloodthirsty motivations to begin with, only speculations could be conjectured by the rest of the realm.

"I do not know," her cousin admitted. "Maybe to escape and be taken far away on his ships. As we should all be plotting to do from this cursed Chandoss name we bear. Nothing feels right here anymore either, and I know you all know it too."

Emberalda wiped her face dry and collected her composure. "But if the Thrench Empire wants to visit and send imperial delegates, no nation will dare to oppose that. Your father, my father, and Great-Granduncle are prepared to meet with him on arrival."

"I want to meet him," Adyssaira said in fascination at the idea, keeping an eye on the whereabouts of her baby tiger pet, now chasing butterflies.

"Oh, don't you worry, sweet cousin. They've already arranged that! We are coming," Emberalda assured her.

"What about me? I want to go!" Sashka was beaming at the idea of getting to leave the estates.

Emberalda put a comforting hand on the young half-elvan's head and cast a compassionate grin. "Believe it or not, I actually adore you also. And because of that, there is no chance you can be near them. Just as you said, the Thrench despise elven. They might take you from us, Sashka, and I will not let that happen."

"But he is only a quarter Thrench, and I am only one half elvan," Sashka tried to argue.

"The men on his ship will be full Thrench. This is your father's decree as the Chandoshian ambassador, not mine. Not another word about it."

They didn't argue with their cousin's sound logic concerning the probably dire scenario. The three held hands and looked out over the horizon from the lofty platform at the top of the well, assessing the scenery of the Chandoss Estates below.

They all seemed to catch an interest in the same individual leaving Count Valdean's tower and making her way back in the direction of the palace main. There was no mistaking Adyssaira's sister.

"What about Oddy?" Adyssaira found herself asking before thinking that she may be giving herself away to Sashka.

Emberalda ignored the implication, well aware of her grand ruse since birth. "Do we have to? Maybe she won't hear us leave?"

It was a bad joke about Odysserae's impairment, and Adyssaira didn't approve. "Maybe I won't see you when we leave you. Or maybe she and I will introduce ourselves to this royal prodigy of a man first and let him decide the fairer Chandoss before you get the chance to meet him. I am sure it was my father who arranged the official greeting, anyhow," she jabbed back, knowing Ethiass held the political sway of the household, not Uncle Nikayle.

Emberalda nudged her hard and hissed to mimic an angry serpent. "Ew! A spiteful snake, are we not? Just a bad jest, Addy. Curse the sun!"

Her cousin threw one arm around her to force her into a sideways embrace and proclaimed, "Yes, she has to come too."

"Speaking of elven and the Thrench, though, how do we hide him?" Adyssaira asked.

This time Sashka did look at Adyssaira in skepticism. Emberalda was boring a hole into her head in disbelief at the act of sheer stupidity she had just committed.

I am an idiot. I may have been pretending to be blind since birth, but I wish I were mute instead!

She had been indicating the sight of Sundorion skulking about on the trail of Odysserae, not as stealthy and out of view as he no doubt intended. Adyssaira knew she had been caught and was honestly tired of hiding it from her innocent half sister. Maybe this was the time to let her in on the secret so few knew. "He isn't exactly the type that hides." She stated the obvious about Sundorion, not even trying to explain how she had seen him.

"Well, then," Emberalda said in a grim tone, changing her manner while staring Adyssaira down. "He will have to learn to hide better, or he will die."

Adyssaira wasn't sure if Emberalda was insinuating that because Sundorion was an elvan, he was in danger due to the impending arrival of the Thrench, or if her cousin had just given her a very real warning, using him to cover her chastisement for her failure in portraying her feigned blindness.

Adyssaira looked back on her cousin in a new light, suddenly with a wave of fear washing through her veins.

The girls said nothing more to each other. They just stood and watched the bustle of the estates in silence until the sun fell, each with her own agenda for her own future security to put in motion.

SUNDORION (II)

THE TOWER

Tick. Tick. Tick. Tick. Tick. Tick. Tick. Tick. Tick. Tick ... Sun must have listened to the noise ten thousand times over by now. *Tick. Tick. Tick. Tick. Tick. Tick* ... The tiny gears in the handheld clock he had obtained from his exploits with the enchanters at Spellspire ticked time away through the water trapped behind the glass face. The Elothian inventors called it a water-watch, but he called the cherished ultrarare tool Old Patience. It was an identical design to the watch he had commissioned for his missing younger sibling, Timmurian, which they had named New Patience as a jest.

There was something special about the two water-watches. Both were infused with enchantment magic from Torrent mages. When properly invoked, the bearer of the watch could slow down time, once every ten minutes, to almost an absolute standstill, from the perspective of the holder. The world and its living or moving entities could not actually be slowed, but the time that Sun had to evaluate them could. It could make one minute of actual time take as long as a day to transpire from the watch wielder's perspective.

The tool was most often used for leisurely purposes, as when playing a game of pawns against Timmurian. They would both use their magic water-watches to carefully contemplate most of their moves so that the game did not take up the entire day. Sun also used it for study purposes, when devouring tomes for his research, or for meditational purposes, when he needed to clear his mind and reset mentally or emotionally. He knew that in the right, or wrong, hands, Old Patience could be utilized for combat purposes, enabling calculated efficiency to counter or defend against an attack from an opponent in battle, but fighting was not Sun's way of getting things done.

Sun had done nothing but lie low since his foreboding encounter with the Chandoss Guard, completely out of his typical character, and study and memorize the schedules of the estate sentries, of Ethiass, and especially of Odysserae. He knew them all now, understanding when and where they would all be based on the tiny hands of Old Patience, signifying the minutes and hours. They were all creatures of routine and duty. They were boring, but they were consistent.

Stealth had never been Sun's forte. Even in all his explorations, he had never found the need for it. Sun ensured he was always welcomed in his travels by sending fair word to the appropriate regional dignitaries to allow him access wherever he fancied to go. But this circumstance was different.

This was not some lost Zandaryn relic he sought. This was not some ancient heirloom he needed to recover, or any archaic ruins to discover to further his research. For once, this was no thing or place but a person he sought, and it was the only time he was bluntly being told he was not welcome to look or ask questions. And the individual that had gone strangely absent was his only brother, his bloodlink Timmurian.

Tonight was the night. The right guards were on shift, and any capable officers would not be. He only needed to follow one small girl, who he believed would lead him straight into the heart of the mystery. *Are you the one who wrote for me, pretending to be Taizsha? If not one of you, then who?* Odysserae was about to begin her routine and leave the castle to head toward Count Valdean's tower. *One shouldn't need much stealth to stalk a deaf girl,* he thought, amusing himself as he sat up and stimulating himself into added confidence.

Tick. The hands on Old Patience matched the position of the moon he remembered it would be in. Already fully dressed in over-anxious anticipation, Sun sprang up from the bed in his designated guesthouse outside the walls of Castle Chandoss and eagerly opened the door to put the humble abode behind him.

There at the foot of the entryway lay a bizarre token he had not expected to find. *Yellow scythellin flowers ...* It was a symbol of significance very familiar between himself and his two bloodlinks. This type of flower was gifted as a sentiment of deep apology for betrayal or disloyalty to a loved one throughout Zandabar, though the custom had spread even to the humans between Savatarm and Az'Dayne in recent times due to the influx of Zandaryn elvan immigrants. The three Zandaryn elven were always getting themselves mixed up in scenarios where their curiosity got them caught up in troubles and they needed one or the other to aid them. And the secret code they would use to send to the other without raising suspicion from unwelcome meddlers was yellow scythellins, delivered with a note hidden within.

No note in these. Tay, are these from you? Or, Timm, are you trying to reach me?

Sun looked around the outside of the guesthouse, considering his sister's involvement. The only person in sight was the young stableboy from the Chandoss Estates down the hill engaged in his evening duties. *Fabian?* Sun was good at recalling the names of anyone or anything he had run across in his past. The perk was well-practiced through years as a fact-finder. He did not have time to spare and dwell as his feet took him down the hillside toward the path that led to the tower. He had donned a black hooded shawl to help conceal him under the cover of the clouded night sky.

The shoreline of the hillside path offered a vantagepoint of the island to the south on Lake Chandoss. Sun pretended he could see the shrines from where he stood. He took a few steps toward the cliff's edge and it was as if he had hit a wall of shame in his heart. *I am sorry, Carolelle. I cannot this time.* Tears welled in the corners of his eyes as he murmured another excuse to his daughter, as he always did. Taizsha had constructed two shrines on the island across from Castle Chandoss to memorialize his lifemate and daughter. Sun was aware that when the blind triplet, Adyssaira, was old enough to hear the sad tale of their fates she had dubbed the island as Carolelle Isle and said that was where her little wisp was resting in peace now. No one took the blind girl serious at that time, some ten years ago about, but Sun had always secretly clung to a dream of hope in that fantasy, that his daughter had found peace in the afterlife in spite what happened to her. He hadn't been by the isle in years out of sheer shame.

Sun had met his perfect match in a lifemate early on. Sheyelle had shared his fervor for uncovering the unknown, and they had passed the same investigative appetite on to Carolelle, with whom they had done everything. The three of them had lived a split life of travel between the fields of the foreign and the tombs of the ancient, and back in Chandoshia, at the Syrene, learning all they could from the vast archives at the university's library. They did not render their archaeology services for a fee, as they were not deprived of money by any means. They did what they did because they believed that by preserving the facts of history, one could navigate toward a better future for all cultures.

But when Sheyelle and Carolelle were cornered and killed at that same college that had promised to accept and protect all races, Sun's favorable views of the Avanthyl scattered to the wind. Any hope he had had for humanity was then more lost than the deepest forsaken relics. He had thenceforth made a point, from two decades ago, when the tragedy had occurred, to shake the foundations of all cultures, both human and elvan, for their flagrant iniquities, no matter the cost. And he did this through exploration and discovery; through truth-seeking and fact-finding.

Being Zandaryn, he could have taken on more lifemates as a distraction, but he never did. Zandaryn elvan lifetrees did not live as long as the other elvan races' lifetrees. They lasted around one hundred years before suffering the aging. But Sun believed that even if he could live for centuries that Sheyelle was the only lifemate he would ever be committed to.

Sun's steps continued to his predetermined post behind an ominous, dark-leafed willow tree, awaiting the regular time when Odysserae passed. And on expected schedule, she appeared on the path to the tower with a large satchel full of unidentified contents around her shoulder.

Sun found the silent Chandoss sister a bit of an enigma. She wasn't like the other girls in the family, not seeming to put any care into her personal upkeep. Her short red hair was spiked in some areas, flat in others, and her baggy clothes were fit more for an adolescent boy than a young woman, especially one of aristocratic heritage.

Why does Ethiass allow this for you, yet he forces the other two triplets to shine? Unless he wants you hidden and unwanted. Sun pondered Odysserae's full story, which either no one knew or none spoke of.

At the entrance of her destination, a lone guard blocked the door. He said a few words, and she simply responded with a small pouch, the normal procedure, and he moved aside for her to enter.

Sun contemplated the sensible purpose of the tower's origin. It wasn't tall enough to serve as a true vantage point for surveillance, since it only stood three floors high, and it wasn't set on the highest of hills within the estates' perimeter. Furthermore, there was not a single window, leaving whatever lay inside utterly devoid of any view to the outside.

It also wasn't protected enough by the typical Chandoss Guard to seem as sacred as it was made out to be. Only one armed individual was ever posted to block the way in, and even more bizarre was that it was always the same tireless man on duty. From dawn to dusk and back to dawn, day after day, the guard never changed. *This alone is an investigation in itself. What manner of being could endure such?*

There was a hole in the supernatural sentry's diligence, however. The twenty-five hours in a day were separated into five sets of intervals for one to better describe general time ranges, beginning with the five Dawning hours in the morning, then the Sunder hours following in the sun's prime, then the Reaping hours throughout the evening, with the Umbra hours during the introduction of nightfall, and the Torrent hours after midnight until it started all over. Each night, a brazier was lit atop the small tower by the guard at the beginning of the Umbra hours, and it stayed ablaze for five hours until the Torrent hours began. Then he would climb the ladder on the opposite side of the tower to the door and relight the brazier, which lasted until the new dawn's sun arose.

With the time afforded by this ritual, and the fact that the guard would spend some several minutes of recess eating the delicacies from the pouches Odysserae would routinely bring, Sun knew he had a window of opportunity to follow her further in.

Tick. Tick. Tick. Tick ... Old Patience ticked on. The feeling of anxiety from the wait had him sweating now, with his heart racing with a combined sense of nervousness from fear of the unknown and exhilaration from anticipation of the same. Such was the rush he lived for in all his adventures of discovery.

Finally the time came, and the tower roof's brazier dimmed to blanket the hilltop in darkness. The unsleeping sentry stayed true to the plan and left the doorway to do his duty and relight the flame. Sun did not hesitate the second the guard was around the back of the tower, nearing the ladder. He had forgotten he even knew how to run—it had been so long since he had felt the urgency to apply his feet in motion that fast. Sun was at the door and inside before he expected the sentry even to have gotten to the rooftop.

I am in. Please tell me there are no other super sentries in here, Sun prayed to no deity in particular, prepared ahead of time for that exact scenario to be probable. He hoped the rumors were true, that Count Valdean was very much the extreme hermit that the local gossips of the estates liked to portray him as. Sun had thought it through on every question he planned to interrogate Valdean with once he had him cornered. The old man would be temporarily powerless without his Chandoss Guard present, and there were a variety of contingencies to enact based on how that conversation went.

Sun had already deduced that Valdean's tower was no normal tower, but he was not prepared to see what he saw now, even with his research and Taizsha's confession of House Chandoss's deep involvement in the Umbran Pledge. He stood as still as a statue, mesmerized in terror at the scene above him. *Fuck the Vist and Void. Timmurian, what did you bring me into*?

From wall to ceiling, the inside of the tower held no separate floors, only sheets of otherworldly ebonice, which was impossible to maintain in this southern part of the realm. In the frozen black stone walls, and hanging from the ceiling like miniature stalactites were random red-hued crystalytes, dimly illuminating the vacant hollow of the three-story tower. There was only one place where this type of crystalyte was said to be found, and as an esteemed explorer and master archaeologist, Sundorion was well learned of it. *The Neveril are here. I should leave. This is folly and death.*

He found his hands slipping down his hood to reveal his Zandaryn elvan heritage in full, and his feet involuntarily defied his fears to turn around. He moved forward, hoping his education on the incomprehensible subterranean elven and those in their Umbran Pledge held merit. *The Neveril will not harm other elven. They are zealous defenders of our race. They press their human puppets, sworn into their Umbran Pledge, to kill Terollar on sight, but that is the extent of the threat. That does not apply to me. I am safe from them. Timm is alive …* Sun forced himself to test the facts of his learnings to boost his willpower onward.

It worked. He was already moving into the further unknown. There were steps that led downward, underneath the tower, winding their way into a tunnel that appeared partly manmade and partly natural, made from bricks, packed clay, and soil.

Every step of the way was lit by the unsystematic clusters of crystalytes in their red radiance, planted here or there in corners of the ground or in the cracks in the brick walls or spiking down from the low dirt ceiling. They were everywhere, in no particular pattern. Sun was a hobbyist of strange geology, and the Neveril lighting system had always held a fascination for him, but he was not here to indulge in the eerie enigmas of glowing rock. Priority ushered him along on his way deeper in after the girl he was supposed to be following.

The slope of the tunnel descended gradually away from the surface. He checked his watch periodically to maintain a sense of time passed. His unease felt like a tangible swell in his throat, and he was sure his face was flushed and his hair was drenched in perspiration. *Oddy, where are you?*

The moment the decline leveled out, and the passageway turned to bend his direction around a corner, he saw the girl he had been hoping to catch up to. "Odysserae." He almost shouted it but kept the volume of his voice in check, with the heavy echo stealing his words down the tunnel system.

Strange thing. Why is she just standing here, as if waiting for me? The Chandoss girl was about thirty paces down the passage, postured in place with no particular purpose, staring back at him with her shoulder satchel slung across her side. *How long have you been here?*

Sun suspiciously looked behind him, half-expecting to be apprehended by the door sentry from above, or even Count Valdean himself. He dared a few cautious steps forward with his palms harmlessly displayed out in front of him. "I am unarmed. I do not mean to intrude. I implore you, there is no need to tell the count. I just want to find my brother."

Odysserae just blinked back at him with no reaction to his explained plight. He felt all the more stupid for his futile attempt when he realized he was trying to speak to a deaf girl. *I heard you are quite well versed in reading lips, though.* More dramatic with his enunciations this time, he spoke more slowly. "Timmurian. Have you seen him? Is he here?"

She gave a subtle nod. She did understand.

"Is he alive? Tell me as much!" Sun felt his heart jump with hope.

"What is this here that you are delivering?" he said after a long, blank stare from Odysserae. Sun motioned his fingers at the satchel.

"Is this for Count Valdean?"

Odysserae responded this time simply by turning around to continue walking down the tunnel to wherever she planned to take it.

"Where are you taking me? What is your family involved in?" As he spoke to the back of the deaf girl, he shook his head at his own continual ignorance.

He allowed her to walk a bit farther until she came to a wide, circular soil chamber that split the tunnel into a fork of paths for the first time. The walls still held the luminous gem clusters, but the low ceiling was dark here. In the ceiling directly above his head were narrow-carved tunnels, perhaps barely wide enough for a small individual to squeeze into if they could reach them.

"Stop!" He reached out and seized her by the shoulder. He gripped the bag strap and purposely pulled hard enough for it to slip and fall to the ground. Unfortunately, the lip of the satchel remained closed, keeping the contents inside sealed against his prying eyes. He spun her around to force her to read his lips again. "I am going to ask you a question and judge your answer by your eyes," he warned, daring to feel in control of his fate by the end of this. "Have you heard of the Umbran Pledge?"

She could not hide it. Her eyes struck the floor with worry, but her head did not move.

That is a yes.

Sun knelt on one knee in a semblance of submission and looked up into her soft amber eyes, whispering, "You know I can try to save you too. It is not too late."

Odysserae locked her focus back on him as if she was willing to hear his promise out.

"I can save you and the girls. I just need the truth and to get Timmurian back," he pleaded.

She began to look around her in a circle and peered down the two darkened tunnels, which housed no visible crystalytes.

Are we expecting sinister company soon? Sun wondered at the mind of the quiet girl.

He found a snapped root on the ground and retrieved it to use as a drawing utensil in the dirt beside their feet. He shaped out each letter boldly, hoping she felt more comfortable communicating this way instead, since he had never learned the language of Hands.

IS HE NEAR

Odysserae's eyes betrayed her reluctance to admit to anything, but then her focus shot down the tunnel on the left. That was progress. He wiped his boot across the words in the dirt and used the stick to etch out another question for her.

CAN YOU BRING HIM HERE

She took the stick from him and did the same, smearing the soil back to a clean slate before drawing out:

YOU SHOULD NOT HAVE COME

"Why?" he demanded defiantly. *I must know one thing.* "Are you not the one who sent for me with the letters to Mageholme?"

She hesitated before she drew out the next sentence, scribing each letter almost apologetically, as if she were guilty of some foul deed.

I DID NOT WRITE FOR YOU

YOU ARE NOT WELCOME HERE

He began to assume as much before seeing her finish the words, but he could not bring himself to heed the warning. She finally opened the satchel to reveal the hearty amounts of food within and the flowers she pulled from on top.

Yellow scythellins ...

Odysserae presented the apology flower used between him and his siblings in an unexpected twist. "What? This is a custom to be given before an act of betrayal."

She nodded to confirm the intent of the flowery token as her eyes moved upward to the ceiling just behind him.

Sun turned around just in time to see something grey in skin color dropping from one of the tunnels above before a sack was thrown over his head, and he felt the impact to his face that cost him all consciousness and maybe his life.

SCARLESS (IV)

MIND OVER MUSCLE

Zahnastaazjah eyed the yellow-painted symbol next to the ladder that stretched up to the hatch to the surface world of the Midway ward in the city. It conveyed that they were standing underneath the East Basin. *This is precisely the same location I met you in three years ago,* she mused as she stared over at the athletic figure of her spellblade lover.

Her right foot was tapping the begrimed tile in no particular rhythm. Her green eyes shifted from the rat-shit-coated corners of the stone ridge she and Xalo stood upon and then back to the tunnel from which she expected her company to join them shortly. She found the butt of her spear now matching the drum of her foot in juvenile impatience. It was annoying. She was annoying herself. She was edgy and had no idea why she was displaying such uncharacteristic anxiety.

Her sarcastic lover was just staring at the side of her head in his typical readied ridicule, just waiting to pounce with his witty quips at the first opportunity.

Don't fucking say a word, Xalo, she thought. She asked him a question, demanding a response regardless. "What do you think about this mage?"

He casually looked down at his spellblade with his usual overly smug semblance and withdrew the sword ever so slightly from its scabbard, just enough to where there was a blank space on the glass—room for more spell glyphs on its surface in the future. "Mixed feelings." He smirked and sheathed the spellblade, and the green halo around his right pupil vanished as fast as it came.

I don't need your damn opinions, she lied to herself. "Think I made a mistake?"

The Elothian ex-gladiator just shrugged as if he didn't know, but he delivered his opinion regardless. "Sundown was a traitor. Dockjaw proved he was incompetent. The mage is a mage. We're the only gang on the isle with one."

Short and sweet and all true. She didn't like his derogatory insinuation about her guild, however. "They still call the Stormtrees a gang?"

Xalo just smirked again, raising his eyebrows incredulously at what he seemed to consider an absurd question, but he said nothing back.

"The fuck does that face mean?"

Xalo looked her in the eye and sighed. "You want me to say something that pleases you, but I promised myself a long time ago I would never lie to you. So you get this face instead."

That reply was unsatisfactory. "I want some damn facts spouted for once."

"No. You want a damn opinion," he retaliated.

If you had read my mind ten seconds ago, you would know I don't. She thought to interject but let him go on.

"And one against which you will argue, as always, and I will just nod and bow after and let it be. Pointless energy expended by both parties, so I just do this," he finished and made the same face that had upset her in the first place.

She hated that she loved him. "You make me want to stab you, you know?"

"I know. But you won't." He leaned over quickly to plant a kiss on her cheek. "Because I don't heal too well when you stab me, and you love me. But I might stab you if you keep at this game. You do heal, and you seem to like the experience." He blew her another kiss.

This man is impossible. She stood and brooded about the fact that she wouldn't get a moment of seriousness out of him if she lived another ninety years.

Instead of continuing the incessant arguing, the two just chose to become mesmerized by a lone rat wandering the filthy ledge, no doubt in careful contemplation of where to take its next shit.

Minutes passed in boredom before Xalo gave in to defeat and spoke again. "My opinion is that Sundown needed to go down as he did. But only after planting another spymaster in his place. Now we have none. As for Dockjaw …" He shook his head in disagreement. "You let him live. Mistake. He is influential and will now be extremely bitter. He will become an enemy. If you wanted to keep his name in some form of dignity, you should have had his throat slit behind the scenes and told some false story to save his status on the streets. On the mage topic, Pyphan is an unknown, and so is this sister of his he is bringing today. That is a good thing for what you plan to propose, but bringing them into our fold is still a great risk. We know little about either of them."

So you can be serious? Can we see this side more often? She believed she nodded in agreement but wasn't sure if her stubborn head moved at all.

"Also, concerning the Purge of the Yard," Xalo added, "the morale of the Stormtrees is at an all-time low now. I agree with a little fear tactics to properly detour potential turncoats in the guild, and don't get me wrong, I enjoy our methods, but we should have wrapped up that day with some positive reinforcement. We cannot afford to have more men and women second guessing their commitment to us or considering employment elsewhere during such a critical season with what we have underway. You need to remedy this soon."

You think I don't already fucking know this? I can feel it in their faces when I walk past. I've regretted it ever since. "I disagree," was all she opposed with a bold lie instead.

No you don't, Xalo's smug glance shot at her, but he said nothing.

The roof of the sewer chamber clanged as the metal hatch to the East Basin and Midway was moved to the side above, and a familiar brute started climbing down the ladder. "Usurp is here."

"He's going to say something stupid because you are bringing in a girl as our mole to replace Sundown's crew," Xalo surmised realistically.

"Since when doesn't Usurp say something stupid?" she joked back.

Her burly henchman leaped from the ladder onto the ridge when he was just halfway down, accurately stomping the life out of the meandering rat in the process, not seeming to pay any heed to the hapless critter. Usurp was a serious competitor for the title of the ugliest human Zahnastaazjah had ever seen, inside and out. The big black tooth at the front of his goofy smile did nothing to remedy his repugnant appearance. In fact, his nickname in the Blue Blades had been Blacktooth, for obvious reasons, before he had stolen the more nefarious alias of Usurp. He was now embarrassed of his old nickname and was known for having killed more than a few who had accidentally referred to him by it.

There had been times Zahnastaazjah had questioned herself why she had elevated such a blood-lusting half-wit to a prominent overman role in the guild, but then she would silence herself, since trust was a rare virtue in this day and region. *Hard to top almost thirty years of loyalty. More than any in my lot can boast.*

Proving her and Xalo's point about his tactless mouth in a timely manner, the portly ruffian stroked his massive beard as he hastened over with rowdy enthusiasm. "All right, let's meet this green-eyed bitch!"

Xalo just smiled and turned to watch Zahnastaazjah's reaction, staring at her own green eyes. She said nothing, just seething and breathing as she watched Usurp clumsily attempt to correct his indelicate comment.

"I meant the hyperi girl we're meetin'. I hear their eyes glow green, you know! Not like yours, Scarless. I know you have green eyes because you're a tro—" The word blocked his throat before it was too late.

Were you really about to call me a troll to my face, dead man?

"A Terollar. But ..."

Zahnastaazjah said nothing, standing face-to-face with him, just shifting her bloodrime spear's lean back and forth between her hands.

"Honestly, I like the color green." Usurp still stammered on in a plea for his life after insulting his guildmother.

"Stop making noise come out of your face," she said.

"Hyperis eyes glow violet, not green," Xalo corrected. "Violet is the eldritch side of magic gone awry, while the green glow you see in mages and myself is magic's natural color, the same that appears in wisps."

Usurp just looked ashamed and stupid down at the ground. The three were quiet for a bit as they waited in uncomfortable stillness.

Finally the sound of new footsteps echoed around the corner of the east tunnel in the crossway. Devonduer and Pyphan had arrived with the mage's sister in tow.

"Everyone play nice now," she commanded.

Devonduer didn't waste any time the moment his toes hit the drained ground of the crossway. He opened his arms wide and announced, "Scarless. Xalo. Usurp. Pyphan has someone to introduce to you!"

"My sister, Symbelle, the master alchemist." Pyphan presented the girl, moving aside to let Zahnastaazjah take in her newest recruit unimpeded.

Symbelle was a tiny little thing. Zahnastaazjah was certain she could snap the young woman in half with her hands if she cared to try. Symbelle's boy-cut, spiky hair somehow made her appear even more unimposing and vulnerable. Her skin was pale, as if she had lived her entire life in a dark room, and her eyes were strange and eerie, shifting like fiery violet clouds. *Eldritch indeed. I've never seen a hyperi.* Her timid face was flawed by a nasty scar Zahnastaazjah was familiar with in her profession—the fool's frown, where a blade was used to cut one curve upward at the crease of the lips and another curve downward at the opposite crease, making it appear as if Symbelle were stuck in a perpetual emotional struggle between dramatic happiness and depression.

The petite alchemist was dressed in fitted black garb, capable of easy concealment at night or while carrying out any fieldwork that required stealth. A harness was strapped around her waist and across her body like a bandolier, with several loops to secure flasks of reagents or whatever manner of contents her trade necessitated to be kept on hand. Around her back was an exceptionally full backpack with a large set of bellows protruding from the flap. *What manner of peculiarities are in there? I'd better find no poisons in your arsenal. I know your devious kind likes to employ them in your work.*

"Gr–greetings. I have long waited to meet you both," Symbelle stuttered, clearly shy or distressed. "I mean, you three," she said as if she intended to include Usurp's presence in the opening flattery.

"Oh?" Xalo took the initiative to speak for her first. Zahnastaazjah hated when he did that. "We hadn't heard a thing about you until two pents ago. Are we that popular in your parts? We try to keep ourselves a bit of a secret. Are you implying that we are doing something wrong, Symbelle?"

Zahnastaazjah could have enjoyed watching the girl squirm for an avenue out of Xalo's verbal torture session, testing her resolve and ability under pressure, but she was feeling rather impatient to get on with business and learn about what had fascinated her when Pyphan had proposed Symbelle. "Your foster brother here tells us you burned down a secret school in Az'Dayne, full of alchemists, engineers, and assassins in training. Tell me why you did that."

"She has a condition with her memories," Pyphan explained in her defense. "She doesn't always—"

Xalo slid his sword halfway out of its scabbard and cut Pyphan off. "Do all mages interrupt? Or just the ones who like to piss off spellblades?"

The underground chamber fell quiet for a moment.

"They …" Symbelle tried in a hushed tone, with her demoralized semblance finding no particular focus at their feet. "They were mean to me."

The hyperi's tone insinuated a plea for sympathy, but Zahnastaazjah couldn't control the burst of amusement that escaped her lungs, and she caught Usurp sharing her cheer in hysterical laughter beside her. Devonduer awkwardly mimicked them, seeming not to understand what was so funny.

"Oh, yeah, they were mean to you?" Zahnastaazjah said. "Good, because the Boarnecks are being mean to me. Maybe we can just burn them too?"

Symbelle looked up at the blatantly targeted sarcasm and spoke in all sincerity. "I know they are. And I plan to do just that for you."

Zahnastaazjah glanced at Xalo to see his eyes just as wide as she believed her own to be, and she calmed herself down from her moment of mirth, back to the gravity of the conversation.

"She's serious," Xalo remarked.

"Pyphan has made you aware of what I am in need of," Zahnastaazjah said. "I need a mole to exploit the Boarneck Company's weaknesses. Someone who can competently present themselves as a capable candidate to join them, someone they will accept and divulge their secrets to, and then report them back to me to be used against them."

"Pyphan has made you aware of what I am, then." Symbelle spoke with rising confidence in her tone.

"Some genius in the alchemical arts and pyrotechnics, born a hyperi. I know nothing about your kind, though. You, Xalo?" She turned to her partner, who always loved to hear himself speak.

Xalo shrugged, leaning nonchalantly. "Unstable prodigies born from high-tier mages. They sense out wisps and hunder-touched individuals, even spellblades. They call it hypersight. Mind-over-muscle types. Crazy and dangerous is the rumor."

Zahnastaazjah had been apprised of that much. "I will make this clear, Symbelle. You must do the impossible. I currently trust no one, but you must somehow make me trust you. Convince me that I should employ you and that you would do this for the Stormtrees. What have you against the Boarneck Company?"

It was Symbelle's moment to sell herself or get disregarded entirely. "The Boarneck Company is making a name for itself with its utilization of the combustible compound known as blast salt. It has taken credit for it as its own invention. But they are all thieves and liars, butchers and bullies." The alchemist's personality began to shift as she proceeded. "You see, I am the inventor. It is time I introduce them to Fyheir."

"Who is Fyheir? I recall that word. Which elvan tongue is it in though? It translates to Flame, no?" Devonduer asked for them all.

Usurp guffawed and looked at her as if this were preposterous. "The crazy bitch has herself a pet name, hopin' to intimidate!"

"Yeah, and I am sure your mother named you Usurp at birth," Xalo cynically struck back.

"Sure, sure." Zahnastaazjah joined the irony to shut the silly side subject down. "Just as my parents named me Scarless. Just because she claims a street name doesn't make her crazy."

It was as if Symbelle wasn't hearing any of the exchange though, as she was clearly too busy arguing with herself under her breath.

Xalo tapped his lover with the back of his hand on her arm and motioned. "That shit there kind of does, though. Just saying."

"Fyheir and I are not crazy," Symbelle heatedly retorted.

"Clearly, nope," Xalo mocked.

Zahnastaazjah took control of the tedious charade to bring it back to current concerns. "You are here for tactful infiltration and perceptive information extraction. Not a repeat of what transpired at Tairanchula. We will not be responsible for setting an entire district ablaze. You are only to proclaim yourself to be the true architect of their famous blast salt in order to gain recognition for hire within their organization. To begin, you will acquire their attention by auditioning in the Monodrome for the Kingfall Ball by use of the pyrotechnic skills you boast. Understand?"

Symbelle seemed confused as she focused on her mage brother. "Pyphan, you won't be with me? We've only just reunited."

"Aw, y'all are some cute fucks, ain't you?" Usurp said, mocking the open display of sentiment.

"Truly adorable." Xalo added fuel to the fire.

That was a soft comment, girl. Reunions can wait. "Your brother can escort you to the Monodrome. I am aware of your unfamiliarity in our great city. But Pyphan will ultimately be staying with me in the Square. You don't get to be seen with us until all is finished. This explains your challenge." Zahnastaazjah handed over a scroll contract. "Read it in front of me."

Symbelle studied the letter and tried handing it back when she had finished, pointing out one small section she needed clarification on. "What's this part at the beginning about?"

"That's the part where I come in." Usurp snatched the open scroll out of her hand and shredded it in half. "Gonna ambush y'all your first time out with them pig-necks—give you a proper street fuckin' as initiation! You down t'go down, girlie?" The obnoxious brute grabbed a full handful of his member between his legs and rolled his disgusting tongue across his bearded lips.

Usurp hadn't the time to show his ugly black tooth with a smile before Zahnastaazjah's spear smacked him with the flat of its blade, catching him completely unawares. The Vellyan hit the ground on one knee with the unexpected force of her strength, and after her boot caught his chin and his body was supine, Zahnastaazjah didn't cease from slamming down the butt of the weapon into his face.

When enough blood was pouring from his mouth and nostrils, and Usurp's black beard was painted in a fresh coat of red, she stopped and stated through gritted teeth, "A gang they call the Stormtrees still. Formerly known as liars and thieves, and butchers and bullies." She kicked Usurp once more in the gut, utterly disappointed in one of her most prominent overmen. She nodded to Symbelle in sympathetic respect as she repeated the line the girl had recently expressed. "It is time we evolve our own name. If anyone in the guild proves incompetence with this mandate for growth in our repute, then I will carve them into chum for the sharks when it's all settled."

She jumped down from the overlook ridge into the crossway, approaching Symbelle and ushering her forward to move beside her. She set a sisterly hand on the small of her back. "Walk with me. Talk with me."

Zahnastaazjah lifted her chin in the air toward Pyphan to signal him to follow as well. As they departed the crossway and entered the east tunnel, through which they had first approached, she continued. "In order to gain the Boarneck Company's attention and trust, you must share blood with them immediately. They don't hire your kind."

"My kind?" Symbelle was confused. "Hyperis or alchemists?"

"Women," Zahnastaazjah said simply. "Unless you're fit to be a whore, and you're far too cut up to ever try that trade. When you make your claim about the blast salt, they will be more likely to gang rape you and leave you drowning in your own blood."

No one gave a response for several seconds as they progressed down the tunnel away from the others.

Zahnastaazjah picked the topic back up when they were far enough away. "That your gear? Pyphan told me about all you can do. Most impressive."

"What do I get for doing this? When it is all through," Symbelle uttered, exposing some hint of human greed in her veins after all.

A fair common concern. I owe you this much. "Freedoms you have never been given, from what Pyphan tells me of your backstory. Life in luxury, which you have never had. What you desire and deserve. I'll give you a teaser before it's all done. This is my promise to you," she said to her new prodigy.

"I want this. I agree," the scarred alchemist replied eagerly. "How do I begin?"

Zahnastaazjah held out her spear, the signature gesture of an official induction into the guild. "Grab the blade of the spear."

The hyperi girl stirred nervously and reluctantly set both of her tiny hands over the weapon's jagged edge. Zahnastaazjah then slowly pulled the spear back to draw a thin wound on Symbelle's palms before replicating the ritual on herself and drawing blood from her own hands. She opened Symbelle's injured hands and set her bleeding palms in hers as she said, "You are my blood now, Symbelle. You are a Stormtree. Do not ever betray me, or I'll burn you alive."

"Heal her hands," she commanded of the Dawning mage, not paying too much heed to the looks of sheer bewilderment between the two siblings. "The Boarnecks cannot discover that scar. Take her to them and ensure she gets inside safe. I'll set Usurp in motion."

She watched Pyphan escort Symbelle back down the tunnels, which waned into darkness and faint echoes. When Zahnastaazjah was proven to be alone, her Terollar bodyguard stepped out from the shadowy corners he had been hiding in all along.

She didn't look at Uubakrath or his menacing bow, which remained in his steadfast hands. She didn't need to. The elvan from her homeland was a tirelessly loyal soldier who relished doing her biddings.

"If things go wrong" — she squinted down the sewer tunnel in the direction the mage and alchemist had disappeared in, contemplating the worst in unsettled paranoia — "you know what to do."

SYMBELLE & FYHEIR (IV)

FIRESTARTER

Symbelle clutched her brother's hand beside her for a futile sense of comfort in the unsettling locale. At least she thought she did. She noticed that her hand hadn't moved a single finger, paralyzed with disinclination. The bench she sat on was too hard, and the commotion in the raucous theater was too loud. She felt lost here, and Fyheir had been ignoring her so far today.

She was ready to interrogate Pyphan about his upbringing, since she had last seen him when they were but children, but this place and time just did not seem fitting for such a recounting.

The two siblings sat shoulder to shoulder in their designated seats in the regionally renowned arena known as the Monodrome. Oldan didn't boast that his famous amphitheater was the largest in the world, but he did brand it the largest indoor entertainment venue in the realm. The domed stadium was even more wondrous than Symbelle had imagined, housing up to fifteen thousand patrons, not including the vast back-of-house apartments for the multitudes of workers it needed to function.

One of the most prominent features it was famed for was its mechanically efficient rotating stage, which could instantly shift between transitional sets without the need for a drop curtain or tedious intermissions. Symbelle had heard of its tireless stage attendees, who labored over that task during their performances.

The seating was shaped in a semicircle, not unlike amphitheaters, but it was obviously built with a specific interest in catering to a wealthier caliber of patron. It had a variety of tiers, with the lowest for standing guests closely fitted together, and as the stadium climbed higher, the sections were segregated to afford actual bench seating and even chairs and beverage bars on the top tier.

The highest levels in the Monodrome were the skyboxes, each

with a lavishly decorated and fully serviced balcony that offered the best vantage for taking in the theater's shows. It didn't take five minutes after entering for Symbelle to discover that the first skybox, nearest the stage's left side—and the only one with a door to some upper level backstage as well—was permanently reserved for the owner. No doubt this would be where Oldan Boldandgold or his son, Tristostopher, sat in the event they would attend a show.

Today was the last audition day, a day on which the Boarneck Company lined up each of their applicants to potentially participate in the upcoming festivities celebrated on the eastern city side. This forthcoming event was no normal play or arena show that the Monodrome put on; it was a once-in-a-cycle affair, always named after the current cycle. The Kingfall Ball, the Maestro called it.

The main events had already been secured earlier in the season, but today the Maestro would be evaluating the side performances to be hand selected to work in as a prelude or fill in the gaps during intermissions. Today was the third day of the third pent of the third month of the Dawning season. Pyphan had arranged to get her here just in time, and she was now on the roster, signed up to audition.

The well-organized mercenary outfit would advertise their talent casting widely across the city's overpopulated urban expanse, as well as off the isle on the mainland, into Worestaschia. It didn't stop there. Their marketing influence for the company's notorious moneymaker stretched into the countries of Utamia and the western towns in the Tairanheart and Tairancia, and even throughout the Silverlakes.

Symbelle had been given ample education on the man behind the scenes, in charge of it all. Oldan Boldandgold was a self-made maven of all things pertaining to making money and the conquering of business across the regions he touched. No one ever got to meet him face-to-face, which gave him a nefarious status as a dangerous phenomenon.

The mercenary company of the Boarnecks, which had started as nothing more than an avaricious family of pig farmers and hog hunters along the coast of Utamia's western region, Worestaschia, had fast expanded into the most feared freelancer association between Az'Dayne and the north. They were opportunists. They were exploiters. They were capitalists. They were all butchers and bullies. And they all answered to Oldan, the mystery man Symbelle had been dispatched to kill.

But she doubted it would be easy to pull off such a miracle stunt on her first trip into Boarneck territory in Bridgeville. She had to bide her time, knowing she wouldn't be meeting or even seeing Oldan Boldandgold today. Today she would be dealing with one of his lieutenants, Terrib Ango, Maestro of the Monodrome.

Terrib Ango was an industrious old Utamian business connoisseur with a sour disposition and not a single hint of sentiment in his corrupt soul. He was the iconic representation of how the city life could infect an individual who seeded themselves too deeply into the roots of Goldgarden's abundant pleasures. His face was gaunt and pale, as if he hadn't seen sunlight or a full meal in decades, and the wrinkles on his features were almost as deep as the lines in the constant scowl that stained the skin around his eyes. She could tell the stringy grey hair that hung to his shoulders was dying faster than he was and that his hazel eyes were as cold as the far sea. His overly ostentatious sleeveless robe was made of some golden sheen silk, and he had bedecked himself in a ridiculous number of gems around his neck, fingers, and even around his skinny arms.

He was going down the list, announcing which numbers from the series of audition candidates would be participating in the impending performances.

Symbelle squeezed the tiny token notched with the number eleven in her clammy palm. Her other hand was still paralyzed, seeking to muster the strength to grab her brother's as she watched Terrib announce and judge each of the decem auditionees before her turn to take the stage.

The first to audition was a young and feeble-looking male Terollar elvan, appearing like some discarded runt of the Glace Isles, Symbelle imagined. He had let his hair grow to an eccentrically long degree, braided in a mess of blond locks that swept the floor like a cape behind him. His gimmick was to charge patrons to come onstage and cut off different parts of his limbs, from his fingers, toes, hands, elbows, knees, and even his private member or hair at set prices, while the visitors got to watch the spectacle of everything growing back.

"Same ol', same ol', but these sick fucks love it every time, Limbo! Opening act." Terrib approved him and referenced the elvan's stage name. "But we'll do it right before dusk and leave the roof open until the sun's hit the sea."

The Maestro of the Monodrome pointed to the retractable dome ceiling of the theater and then commanded more than the negotiated prices for the opening event. "Twice more than usual: one moon coin per finger or toe, two moon coins per hand or foot, three per limb above, and one full sun coin for your cock, but they get to keep the cock! Souvenirs like I keep in my bedroom jars." The decrepit playhouse master cackled, although no one else did. "You keep half; the Monodrome keeps half."

Surprisingly, Limbo didn't haggle and agreed on the absurd arrangement for such a macabre spectacle, being an evident regular of the Monodrome.

He was followed by his affiliate, an Aggedonian stoneborne who also charged customers to do harm to him. Patrons would pay a certain approved amount to come onstage as the prelude to the actual event, riling up their most depraved appetites, and attempt to knock him unconscious with one punch per payment collected. They could pay even more to borrow a small club if they wished a better chance at drawing blood from his impower-thickened hide.

"Yeah, yeah ... Rocker, follow Limbo. Eight coppers per punch, two moon coins per club. We take half. You got five minutes or twenty ticks, whichever comes first. Don't waste my time past it." Terrib waved the stoneborne on.

The third contender to make a name for himself in the Kingfall Ball was a Z'shun bard more prettied up in makeup than the harlots in line behind her. The flowery-dressed troubadour presented himself to sing comedic parodies about the adverse politics of outlying countries, such as Az'Dayne, Barredom, Throng, and Khalimia, among others.

Terrib had stopped him halfway through his flopping attempt. "Hate it. Stop it. Kill him." His last words made the entire theater pause, including his own mercenaries, trying to gauge his seriousness as the Z'shun stood pissing himself onstage, awaiting the end of his life. "Eh, let him kill himself instead. Break his harp and throw him in the bay. If his queer legs can kick him to the docks outside the district, then all the Fives' power to him. Next!"

A set of auditionees came on in a group of seven: six Brutongan women and a very muscular man who led the flawlessly rehearsed choreography. They proved to be gypsy fire dancers, each using different impressive tools or weapons set ablaze for the mesmerizing composition. Symbelle was most certain this would awake Fyheir inside her, but strangely, her sinister counterpart uttered nothing. Symbelle was getting worried.

"Nothing special. Nothing fucking special at all. But perfect for the follow-up to the prelude. Make it last ten minutes. Don't worry what I charge. Your take is your gypsies get four moon coins apiece, and I'll throw you two sun coins if you make it worth my stake!"

An ebony-skinned elvan approached next, with the most unique midnight-blue hair and dark blue eyes. She introduced herself as an escapee from Starfell, a Lunaril elvan fugitive from the slavering Thrench. In her work, she was guarded by four competent-looking giant Vellyan marauders. She was open that she had no special talent, but she had valid tales of the indomitable Ashenwave, House Emmonost, and the Thrench Empire.

"Hmm, you seem boring," Terrib mused aloud to the Lunaril, "but I bet my entire wager on this ball that you won't be. Don't know where to put you yet, but you're a first of your kind. I like those."

Symbelle sighed in relief, hoping this meant success for her own attempt to infiltrate the Boarnecks.

"I will decide on placement and price for you by the Fifth-Day of the following pent. You're in."

The sixth aspiring performer came forth holding a strange geode broken open. He was a middle-aged Psage, completely bald on the scalp and in the face, as all of that human lineage were. He was adorned in rather impoverished attire, as if he hailed from the urban slums instead of the bustling Psage Coast, where most of his culture were well off after the merging of the Insurmounts with the Az'Dayne Dominadom. His bizarre proposal was to sacrifice his life onstage, in a onetime ritual of consuming the mystical geode, which he referred to as a seerstone. It would take his life in exchange for granting him the clairvoyant foresight to see another's entire future. The seerstones' arcane abilities to forecast the future was a debatable topic among pragmatic scholars, but none could deny that every Psage who had ever partaken of the contents of the stones had been proven to be correct in their prophecies to date.

The Psage man's pitch to be accepted seemed fair for a just cause, with a helpless plea to save his disadvantaged family in Everdawn, the capital of Az'Dayne, who lived under thorough scrutiny and prejudice. He wanted to secure a contract with whatever buyer implored him to take the seerstone that would allow the Boarnecks to collect the bargained funds and transfer it for his family's well-being, to save them from their deprived state.

"So you die after you do this? Accepted, as long as the patrons get to see you undergo it," Terrib elatedly agreed, smacking his gluttonous chapped lips. "Do you a deal I don't make, since you die in the process. Thirty-seventy—me the less, you the more. Proceeds to your family, good sir. Good sacrifice. My treasurer will see you signed. Now move aside … Next!"

A mole-stricken witch from the Sevenmoors came onstage now, with an entrepreneur Behemon pirate after her. The witch was turned down for being boring with nothing more than parlor tricks of fortune-telling, and the Behemon man was shunned more harshly with the accusation of having a shop already established in Canaltown competing with the jewelry sales the Boarnecks had taken over in Bridgeville. Terrib forced the Sevenmoors witch to come backstage and tell him his future through her card readings, which halted the auditions for around half an hour, and the witch was never seen again. The pirate, on the other hand, was robbed and beaten in front of the whole lot of auditionees, with no heed paid to discretion, before he was tossed, broken, into the streets.

Number nine was a beautiful, and evidently popular, Zandaryn elvan prostitute who was a repeat Monodrome attraction. She charged customers by the turn to have at her sexually on two-minute sessions, with a ten-man minimum per show.

"Alceyse, to think I would ever exclude you! My dear favorite," Terrib wheezed with a phlegm-gargling purr. "Top coin, a silver per sesh on that honeypot. Give me my quarter and my special cut." He blew her a kiss and rubbed himself but ultimately failed at coming across as anything more than a debauched deviant. "We'll work you in real nice at the end as usual!"

Symbelle was numbered after the next one called. An exotically dressed Wyldenar elvan came to the stage, offering the same performance as Alceyse had, but she proposed twice the coin per turn, with a fifty-man minimum, and a promise to naturally change her hair color for every patron who had at her, to spice the show up.

Terrib seemed to fall in love with the newcomer, who called herself Ravage. "Alceyse, you're out. Go back to your parlor shop and suck off your sailors on the docks. Ravage gets the spot!"

Alceyse went on to argue that she was the most elite courtesan on the city's east side and that he was making a mistake not including her in the ball. Eventually, the three worked out a deal to coordinate the two perverse acts into one, with the same fifty minimum of men to prepay at the door in order to participate. Terrib decided to correlate their team activity of fornication as the closing sequence following the event's epilogue as the guests were leaving, hoping to make a return on more coin spent to join in the sex act and on the alcohol being served.

Symbelle found herself sweating profusely, utterly discomfited by the subject, being a virgin and quite naive when it came to such explicit content. How on Penthara was she supposed to follow that duo and hope to impress Terrib? Nearly the entire room of hungry onlookers, even the theater workers, had stopped what they were doing, becoming enthralled by wild fantasies about the two elvan whores.

"You have to follow that," Pyphan whispered next to her, mimicking her exact discouraging doubts.

"Eleven! Symbelle the Grand Pyrotechnician of Tairanchula, you're up! Take the stage!"

"Get up and do this," Pyphan urged, commanding her to find her resolve. Her foster brother was concealed completely from his neck down to his feet by a large robe to cover his magemarks, and his hood pulled low to hide the halo in his eyes.

"Fyheir, help me," she entreated under her breath.

Before she registered that they were doing it, her feet were walking toward the stage. She was sure her shoulders had gone as petrified as her spine, since she couldn't move her arms, not even her neck to turn and beg for her brother to steal her away from this absurd plan. Symbelle was not her counterpart. She was not the Entity that controlled her confidence.

"Fyheir, save me, please."

Symbelle took her alchemy pack in hand and kept her back turned to Terrib and the other judges. She was on the playhouse stage now, and there could be no turning back. "My arms are working again." She realized she had whispered this aloud. She could hear the Maestro of the Monodrome shouting behind her, but the world around her had faded into silence. "Fyheir, are you here with me?"

She felt a wash of heat surge through her veins, flushing upward into her cheeks, and she suddenly felt unbreakable. "Thank you."

Symbelle slipped on her goggles and filtered breathing apparatus. When she turned around, her hands were full of glass flasks and clay bombs, matching the assortment of potions plugged into the compartments stitched across her bandolier harness, and the similar tiny vials slipped into custom holsters in her bracers.

The harness and bracers were made of the same material as the breathing mask—the hide of a behemoth. Behemoths were exceptionally large reptiles from the Behemon Isles, as tall as an average man's torso and often over four times the length of someone lying prone. They were especially known for their thick leathery skin, which was impervious to fire and sustainably light when wet from aquatic environments.

Symbelle faced her audience with full confidence restored. Fyheir was within her. It had never left.

Slowly, she began to peel the clothing from her body in no particular order until she was completely naked, except for the mask, harness, and bracers. Terrib rolled his fingers for her to continue and move on with it, seemingly impatient yet intrigued.

She doused herself in an entire flask of cinder oil from head to toe, rubbing it in all over her exposed flesh and into her hair. She then pulled out two larger glass vials and dumped them in a wide circle around her, drenching the wooden planks of the undecorated stage in her vicinity.

Finally, Symbelle dropped her first bomb, which exploded in an eruption of smoke that filled the entire stage. She could no longer see Terrib or any of the spectators, but their exhilarated oohs and aahs were motivation to continue.

She pulled out more tiny bombs from her bandolier and lit their short wicks with her finger flint, then flung one here and one there, and another there, right next to it, while the last one landed just across. All four exploded in a series of different-colored sparks—one gold, one blue, one green, one red. The pyrotechnic display screamed in short-burst whistles as the fireworks spiraled upward in random, chaotic patterns.

When the smoke began to dissipate, and Symbelle came back into view for her captivated audience, she did not hesitate with the finale of the show. She pulled out a small pouch full of the highly combustible granules and sprinkled them around her in a circle as she rotated in place and then followed by slamming down her last bomb directly beneath her bare feet.

The fire flasks shattered, and up came the instant blinding red blaze that engulfed her and the entire circle of the stage within the burnguard radius. The explosion from the incinerating heat of the blast salt was wholly absorbed by the cinder oil she had coated her body in. When the fire disappeared, Symbelle stood dry as a desert, the cinder oil expended on impact from the blaze, and the burnguard was smothering the life out of the deadly aftermath as well, leaving both herself and the stage unharmed.

Symbelle removed her mask, pulled her goggles up to her forehead, and bowed to her audience. The show was over.

A couple of delayed light claps ensued at different intervals around the theater from chance viewers she could not pinpoint. The judges seated with Terrib just looked at her in awe, not knowing what to make of the fiery display they had just witnessed.

"What the fuck kind of performance was that?" Terrib scowled disapprovingly, standing from his formerly lounging posture on his plush perch. "What did we just watch? You could have torched the damned theater down!"

"That was not a performance." Symbelle wiped the sweat from her brow, answering rather coolly.

"Well, the fuck, then? This is Audition Day! How am I supposed to use this in the Kingfall Ball? You'll scare half the crowd and likely burn the other half!"

"This was my audition," she countered, "but not for the ball. I want in the Boarneck Company. Not the Monodrome. I am an alchemist. Better than any you have seen before."

The entire theater fell silent, and all eyes fixed on the exchange between Terrib and Symbelle. She could see that the Maestro of the Monodrome was assessing her even more than ever now.

"Was that blast salt?" he asked.

"My own invention. Your pretender, Jonan Riveiros, is a thief. He stole what was mine at Tairanchula, and I am here to redeem my name after I turned the school to ash."

Terrib cackled in wide-eyed, evil elation at her macabre boldness, seeming to approve. "He will kill you for this when he returns, you know!"

"Fair assumption. You can stop paying me after that, then," she returned with a sharp wit she did not recall being equipped with before. Maybe Fyheir had been working through her all along.

The laughs of Terrib and the others echoed off the walls of the domed auditorium. "I like this sick bitch!"

Terrib began walking briskly down the steps toward her, finally reaching her onstage, and tossed her a boar-tusk necklace that slid between her naked feet. "Get some fucking clothes back on, and wear this."

As he got closer, she could tell he was entranced by the violet radiance in her otherworldly, shifting eyes. "What's wrong with your eyes? You some kind of new mage type or something?"

"Hyperi," she corrected as she slid the Boarneck talisman around her neck.

"Don't know what that is. Don't care. You're in. Meet me backstage, Symbelle."

Symbelle felt a surge of air in her chest, so much that she could hardly contain it to breathe it back out, taking in the victory of the successful ploy.

"Fyheir, we did it," she whispered to herself with a smile, hoping to hear her voice once again.

"Pyphan, we did it," she whispered the same instead, looking back to the stands to find her brother nowhere to be seen, vanished from the theater altogether.

No one was with her now. This was her test alone.

Symbelle felt a pang of sadness at her brother's absence without a goodbye. She hadn't even gotten to ask him about their father.

VALAYTHEA (III)

FORGET THE UNFORGETTABLE

The cold was so unbearable, it was paralyzing. The ice in her veins stung like a thousand tiny needles coursing through her body, and her mind felt frozen to any act except the simplest of instincts—just to survive. Her senses were blanketed by pure shadow, and she had no idea where she was or how she had come to be here. A lapse in memory was frozen in the far reaches of the immeasurably vast dreamscape she felt induced to succumb to.

Indecipherable voices reverberated off the invisible horizons in the void world she found herself indefinitely trapped within. They sounded angry. Both of them.

"You will find yourself dead or replaced, like the rest of them. Your imperial name does not make you immune to their schemes."

"I know what is at risk for me. I have always understood. But I beg of you, stop doing this to her. Please Coldborn! Give her this instead!"

"Your drugs? I will not poison her with the same as you have weakened yourself with over time. My allowance for your free will has proven to be your only ailment. I am considering taking it from you."

"I will do better. I am finally ready now. Before the dominarchs return, may we begin this?"

One voice was her internally anguished lover. She had never heard Izayus speak to anyone as if they were his superior. And to her knowledge, the only beings in the realm that could claim such a status were the two dominarchs of Az'Dayne themselves. But this was not his father, Vaximus, or his mother, Sriyah. The name Coldborn had been spoken. She had heard the moniker before, but in her frigid miasma of numbing darkness, she could not swim toward an answer of significance.

"May we begin this, you ask me now? It has begun because of what you have done. They will kill her. They will not hesitate," came Coldborn's icy tone again.

"She is different than the other four, just as you said. We cannot let that happen. She is the one I have chosen to come with me when I go. I think I may love her."

He does? He does not show it.

The bickering came and went. Izayus was losing this battle of dispute. It all phased into an unintelligible conglomeration of murmurings as a building blizzard materialized in her incorporeal vacuum of a reality. The storm of snow swept through and crashed into her, rendering her utterly comatose.

She woke up from the nightmare gasping for air and aid, shrieking in fright, with her hands impulsively clutching the arm of the yet unseen next to her. She could feel the ice-cold perspiration pouring down her face and covering her collar line, drenching the skin between and underneath her breasts. She felt thirsty, with a mouth as dry as sand.

Izayus was eagerly sitting to her right on a peasant-worthy motley bed. She noticed that she had drawn blood on his upper arm with her fingernails, dug into the surface of his skin.

What she found on her left made her shake her head hard to ensure she was fully conscious. Her eyes went wide in disbelief seeing her left hand frozen in a glove of ice shards, perfectly fitted around the unharmed forearm of the other speaker in the room. She could tell the man was older, yet his skin and face carried the unblemished appeal of perpetual youth. He was incredibly muscular, more so than any individual she had come across, even more so than the best artists had been able to sculpt on any statue she had seen around Castle Chandoss. And his bare arms, exposed from his sleeveless tunic, were painted in spell glyphs that looked a bit like tattoos on every piece of flesh.

Coldborn? Valaythea had an epiphany. She remembered the name when she saw the green-haloed eyes of a mage. Her uncle, Nikayle, had said his name before in their studious Teaching Hours. *The grandmaster and founder of the Oathemic Cabal. What is he doing with us?*

Valaythea looked at her frozen hand again in a new plight of dread. A panic attack gradually rose in her lungs, heaving into a terror of rapid breaths. She started to scream, imploring Izayus with her eyes to save her from the assassin overlord.

"Calm," Coldborn warned as he put his palm on her chest and the rims around his irises began to glow. "Or I will put you under again."

The magical ice on her frozen hand dissipated in a dry melt without a trace of water left over. She retracted her freed hand to place it over the mage's across her torso, and she didn't know why.

The archmage assassin looked at her, puzzled by the unexpected gesture. He looked down at her hard, with seemingly no ability to display emotion whatsoever. "What do you remember?"

"Do you remember the Pentagogue, anything about it?" Izayus anxiously chimed in.

We never went in, Valaythea thought, quite confused by the implication, unless he was just asking about her knowledge of the gargantuan temple of Everdawn in general. "You turned the coach around, Your Imperial Highness. We never made it past Hallion's Crater."

The prince exhaled in evident relief, grinning hopefully at Coldborn for him to take that as some form of good news, but the archmage did not return the sentiment.

"Do you remember meeting the other wives?" Coldborn asked instead.

"Paramours," Izayus dared to correct.

The archmage was unflinching and just stared at Valaythea for an answer. "We have not yet been formally introduced. I was told we would not be until this Dawning's passing." She ended the statement more like a question to Izayus, now definitely confused.

"She does not remember anything she saw in the Royal Harem or the Pentagogue. See? It is done. We can stop this now." Izayus stood up, pleading with the unconvinced mystery mage.

"Tell me, girl," Coldborn insisted, "what does the word *neverborne* mean to you?"

Valaythea now sat up in the bed, realizing the shoddy, thin mattress may as well have been nonexistent. "Just some interest of my love's that he alluded to." She honestly didn't remember the day, assuming the abundance of strange wines from the prior evening had gone too much to her head. "He was going to tell me yesterday, but he has not yet. What is this about, fair sir?"

Coldborn helped her off the bed and onto her feet between them. She glanced around the tiny room, devoid of any decor or other furniture, and noticed that its doorway was most bizarrely only an apparent hatch in the corner of the wooden floor. *Where have they brought me?*

"She is telling the truth," Izayus insisted, sure of her honesty.

"She is," Coldborn declared, but again he displayed no sign of direction in his mood. "Your memories of what you have come to hear or see recently are gone, Valaythea. You will not recall them. For now."

"But I do remember everything," she argued. "My prince and I, we were just on the Imperiar Coach, touring the great capital. He brought me to his ..." She stopped herself at a wave of dizziness flowing through her. She realized she had a contestable recollection concerning whether she had even partaken of any alcohol. It was all faint, in a fog of questionable oblivion, from the moment they had left the coach ride.

"I have cast a spell over you. You have no memory of anything you have learned in the past ten days. The invocation is temporary, and all will return in vivid detail, and all at once. I have set it to end once the furrow of the Sunder arrives. I have saved your life, girl, by making you forget the unforgettable," the Umbra mage cryptically explained.

Valaythea felt a tingling sensation of nervousness all over. She was beginning to wish the Prince of Az'Dayne had never chosen her as his final paramour.

"It seems you two have started the clock without me." Coldborn bristled, with his green eyes condemning Izayus and not her. "This was all set to be in motion at the time it was supposed to be. But it will inevitably occur sooner than anticipated."

The intimidating mage then gazed back at her. "When your memories return, you must tell only one. Your uncle, Nikayle lon'Chandoss the Thirdnamed. He will instruct you as to what to do. Time will be of the essence, and your life, among many others, will depend on it. Do you understand, Valaythea?"

"No," she replied in all truthfulness.

"Good. If you did, then I would not be who I am."

His arcane answers continued to make no sense.

"Why Uncle Nikayle? How is he involved?" she asked. She felt she knew before she even finished the question however. She was aware that her uncle had a history with the Oathemic Cabal since even his earliest of days. Nikayle had been inducted into the assassins' guild at the age of ten and became part of the Nectar Order as a crow, and then a rat, and eventually a vulture as he was promoted. Eventually, at age sixteen, he was transferred to become elevated as a junior scholar for the Dayne-Web.

Nikayle had made an impression with Coldborn and the masters over the next decade, as by age twenty-six he was endorsed to relocate to his home in the Chandoss Estates to become a journeyman scholar under the direct tutelage of the professors of the Syrene, with a coordinated curriculum for him to navigate rapidly into a regent for the university. Over time Nikayle became tenured to such a title as Grand Regent of the Syrene. Valaythea was just now piecing together that Coldborn no doubt held political influence in such a decision to ensure Nikayle's placement of power over her homeland's university.

Nikayle had been quite open with his story to the girls, filled with tragedy over what happened to his wife, Delphine, and his unfortunate accident to make him a cripple. In truth, her uncle had played the role of a father toward her and her sisters better than Ethiass ever did. In some ways Valaythea had even convinced herself she was lucky that with the absence of her mother, Valenteal, since birth, she was instead blessed by two fathers to counterbalance the loss.

"Once one takes the Oath, one is bound for life. Nikayle will never retire from his obligation with the Cabal," Coldborn answered to solidify what Valaythea realized.

"What do I do until then?" she asked.

Coldborn stood in front of Izayus, looming directly in front of her now, making it as if only the two of them existed in the small room. "Izayus has jeopardized your well-being and the fate foreseen for our great nation of Az'Dayne to end in a favorable outcome for us all. It has been prophesied through the seerstones by the Elderlocks on the Dendrallthae. The role you will rise to will be paramount, Valaythea."

"What? I don't want any of this," she meekly admitted, futilely trying to back away in the confined space.

"What you want will have no impact on destiny's complex

weave to save the realm from a break in the Balance," he scolded, with a hint toward the elvan neutral religious doctrine of the higher elemental belief system being somehow involved.

"You must now be separated from him until I can plan an auxiliary to salvage all of this. You will be returning home to your estates just in time to join your family at the Suntide Faire. Seek out your sisters there, and leave all that you know of this between only us within this room."

She felt Izayus's hand holding hers by the fingertips as the prince forced himself back in front of Coldborn to look upon her before their departure. A sting of happy tears welled in her eyes. Valaythea shivered with her body temperature shifting from cold to hot and gasped a sigh of elation at the words. She let go of her spouse's hand and hoped to never hold it again. She was going home, and she prayed to never leave it.

ADYSSAIRA (IV)

LIE WITH ME

The boats were sleek, clearly built for the purpose of battle, as best her mind could imagine for what naval vessels might have looked like for an ocean-bred, warfaring culture such as the Thrench Empire. The banners above the kraken figurehead on the prow of the small ships matched a similar representation for the sigil of House Emmonost and their Ashenwave army of sea soldiers. The flags held a backdrop of grey waves with a blue kraken on the left side, its tentacles stretched out north, northwest, south, southwest, and full west. The tentacles protruded in from the right side of the banners as well, as if the sea monster were reaching from the west and across the east of a map, the same as the Thrench were historically notorious for doing in recent times, breaching the western Vist and invading the eastern shores.

As they disembarked at the harbor of Emerald Point, Adyssaira finally got her first glance at the legendary Thrench.

Their light armor was tanned from the exotic shablue material—the hides typically stripped from sharks or rays, tailored for nimble body armor, and dyed dark blue. Their sun-reflecting white helmets were made of the ultra-rare Starfell steel; the ore was only found and mined on the Lunaril elvan isle of Starfell, and then manufactured into steel by the Thrench master swordsmiths. The ocularium on each helmet was a narrow slit around the eyes, with the brow of the metal protruding slightly to serve as a visor, shading the wearer from the potentially blinding glare of the sun on the open waters. There was no metal guarding the lower half of the face, except for a fixed piece resembling long shark teeth extending over both sides of each man's mouth. A fish-fin crest, opaquely marine blue in color, ornamented the top of each soldier's helm as well, known to be taken from a slain swordshark.

Fastened over each soldier's back was a scabbard that sheathed a Starfell longsword, with a blade of pure white steel—the universal weapon of the Thrench Ashenwave.

They marched in flawless unison down the jetties of Emerald Point's wharf in double file, as if they were set on subjugating the Daynish harbor town. Adyssaira could see the brown skin of their muscled arms glistening with the salty splashes of the bay. She had trouble differentiating between the foreign soldiers. They all looked identical, she thought, with the exception of the different burn markings the men carried on their sword arms, or the occasional white stripe here and there. Adyssaira recalled her uncle's teachings of their culture. *White stripes ... They are honored with the thin tattoo per Neveril elvan they prove they have slain. And the other marks, the burn scars, they are badges of other elven they've killed.*

She counted what she thought must have been at least four hundred soldiers trooping in from the docks, lining up parallel to the harbor's boardwalk. At the very last, two decorated men walked beside a smooth-faced boy who looked like he was at the end of his teens, a little younger than she was.

The man on the left was obviously of Thrench bloodline, wearing the same armor as the rest. But his white helm was shaped more boxlike and had two fins down the middle instead of one, and he carried a cumbersome tower shield and a war trident instead of the single sword of the other warriors.

For the heritage of the man on the right of the boy, she could not determine it, but she assumed he was of Oriyan origin. He had green halos in his eyes, like a mage, but they were thin and narrow, similar to the eyes of the Elothians she had met. His skin was more tan rather than the dark brown of the Thrench, and his hair was a perfect blend of honey blond and brown. Furthermore, he dressed himself in no armor, but a turquoise robe instead, which paired well with the water-agate rings that decorated his long goatee.

There was no doubt concerning who the boy was; his identity was made no less evident by the way in which Emberalda was impatiently shuffling beside Adyssaira.

"My Fives, that is him," her cousin uttered excitedly.

His radiant violet eyes were not from this realm, seeming something divine, between the concepts of magic and wherever the sun existed in space. His orbs appeared to gleam and move with his every step. He wasn't just hunder-touched or a mage; this was something else entirely. His brownish-blond hair was pulled back tight in a topknot.

His vestments were a noble blend of the Thrench design and the exotic garb of the goateed foreigner. He wore a shablue tunic and boots, but fashioned more for luxury and not armor. His turquoise breeches were baggy and seemed fit for comfort, as was his open laced white shirt. His waist had a simple rope belt with a water agate as the buckle. And he carried no weapon that Adyssaira could make note of.

"He is looking straight at us," Emberalda gleefully squealed as the trio got closer. But he wasn't looking at them. He was looking directly at Adyssaira.

Adyssaira snatched the hand of her sister, who stood next to her, nervously squeezing her harder than intended. Odysserae tried to jerk away, to no avail. Adyssaira could feel her cousin's incredulous gaze on her, scanning back and forth between the Oriyan-Thrench boy and her in disbelief.

"He is looking at you, Addy," Emberalda confirmed, as if she couldn't trust her own words.

Why, though? Why would he stare at me? Adyssaira spun around to turn her back to the wharf and readjust her blindfold, feeling as though it must have dropped to expose her hunder-touched eyes. But the silk sash hadn't moved. She slowly pivoted back to nestle between Odysserae and Emberalda.

Count Valdean, at the last minute, had other foreign business to attend to, and did not join the greeting party. Her father and Uncle Nikayle eagerly poised for proper introductions at the foot of the jetty, and formalities were exchanged. The heavily armored Threnchman with the shield was the boy's bloodguard, whose fate was entwined with the boy's for life. His name was Thoravus Hlelvig. The Oriyan man in the robe was presented also as the boy's protector and protégé of Imaniko the Palestorm, and he asked to be addressed as Inkomway the Skycaller. Adyssaira expected she might discover the boy's true name, but she wasn't surprised when she heard him announce himself quite decisively as "No-Name" instead.

You are the one Sundorion told us about. Seeing him in the flesh was even more of a reason to swoon than her fancies had been fostering in her mind. And regardless of his lack of regard from the Thrench emperor, she found him entirely regal and handsome.

"You should pray for sight for just ten breaths to take this man-boy in. He is delectable." Her cousin expressed a shared opinion.

She knows all too well I can see him. But I have to pretend I can't. Fives give me the strength to do so.

"Let me borrow that sash." Emberalda gave a joking tug at the knot of her blindfold. "It does make you look darkly mysterious."

Adyssaira's father and uncle, along with No-Name, his two chaperones, and a contingent of fifty soldiers disappeared into the town hall built a block down the city's boardwalk, leaving the three girls and a few of the Chandoss Guard outside with the rest of the army and nosy Emerald Point citizens.

It was still the fresh hours of the dawn, with the morning mist blanketing the bay gradually dissipating up into the cloudy heavens as the sun climbed the sky. Half the day was consumed by Emberalda, fascinated with the sound of her own blabbering, and Odysserae constantly strayed off and returned, doing whatever it was that her odd sister did. *You're some secret spy for the Pentagogue or something, aren't you?* Adyssaira would often jest to herself when pondering the random wanderings of Odysserae.

With hardly any effort spent in prying, the girls had incidentally discovered the reason for the unsolicited Thrench visit to the shores of Az'Dayne. It evidently had to do with the Chandoss family's renowned gold mines throughout Chandoshia, from which they needed a substantial loan to appease the extravagant debt the Thrench Empire owed to the world-renowned bank of Goldgarden, the Pentharam Bank. The Thrench were attempting to occupy far more territory than they could manage, having sent the majority of their fleet and army with the Ashenwave war efforts across the Vist to the eastern battlefronts. They had offered House Chandoss and all citizens of Chandoshia the protection of the Thrench Empire, with a pact formalized by a marriage union between Brigatha Emmonost's son and a suitable partner from House Chandoss, to be decided. It had been vowed that if House Chandoss agreed to the gold trade, then No-Name's legitimacy would be granted in all rights by the power of the Thrench Empire, that he would be consecrated with a name chosen by Emperor Djediheth, and honored with the Emmonost surname until the end of his time.

As the day waned, it seemed Emberalda had hit her threshold of tolerance for boredom. "You girls be good. I'm going to steal me some big bad Threnchman—see if the rumors are true about how wet they can make it!"

Emberalda pressed her bosoms up in her shapely corset and grinned devilishly as she insinuated some sexual connotation Adyssaira did not quite comprehend with her lack of knowledge of such a vulgar subject. She was sure the analogy had something to do with the Thrench being of water descendancy, but she had no idea what the "it" was that they were going to make wet.

Her bold cousin flamboyantly flung herself into the town hall, leaving Adyssaira and her sister alone on a bench. Even the Chandoss Guard had been infected by the tedium of waiting, and they lost themselves in conversations about the Thrench soldiers or whatever rich stories they fancied to better pass the time.

Adyssaira was half-glad in the moment that her father had decreed against her cub pet being brought along to Emerald Point. She imagined the trouble it would be trying to keep the little thing from startling citizens or roaming off and hurting herself. *I need to name you, don't I, girl?* she mused, thinking on what would fit for a black tiger.

Adyssaira decided to escape from the curious eyes of the public with her sister for the remainder of the day, but she frowned when she found an empty seat in her stead. *Gone again? Now where?*

Adyssaira stood up to look around but did her best not to make it too obvious. Many of the harbor city's townsfolk were staring at her as she poked with her walking staff to migrate down the alley that led to the back of the city center, toward the grassy courtyard. They all knew who she was—the blind spectacle of the shunned yet popular lon'Chandoss triplets. She could never escape their judgmental gazes everywhere she went in public, but under the guise of her false impairment, she could at least pretend to ignore them.

She assumed Odysserae may have made her way to the parklike yard at the back of the town hall. It was the most serene escape to be found in the bustling trade city, tucked away from the main streets and heavily patrolled at the four entry points, prohibiting those less than highborn. At its center was a small pond, just enough to give haven to a good number of fairwater fish and ducks. Around the natural pool's perimeter were decorative benches and a colorful variety of flower bushes.

Adyssaira gave up on her vain search for her surreptitious sister, and she was meandering toward one of the seats near the pond, staff over foot with each careful step, when a young man's voice addressed her in an accent she had never heard.

"Green-eyed girl! Come, lie with me!"

He cannot be talking to me. My eyes are covered, she thought, frantically looking around for the speaker and for a way to escape her doom if anyone heard the truth about her greatest secret.

Adyssaira found the culprit: No-Name. She pretended to still be blindly looking in the wrong directions, all the while clearly seeing his outstretched hand inviting her to lie beside him between two benches at the waterline. "Lie with you, my lord? My eyes, they are not—" She tried to fib her way out but was interrupted.

"Green? Hunder-touched? No, you do not have to lie *to* me. Simply lie *with* me instead." He innocently patted the grass, again bidding her to join him on his level.

Adyssaira had no ability to hide her ploy in the moment, feeling naked and exposed, half-expecting paladins to appear from around a bush or from an alley to apprehend her and put her to trial for being born with her cursed eyes. No-Name was protected by the indomitable Thrench, the bloodline of Djediheth Emmonost himself, the most feared human on Penthara. He did not distress himself over the prejudiced wrath of Az'Dayne and had impunity against the laws of the unbending nation.

"My lord, you are not from here," Adyssaira softly warned, feeling more unsure about his otherworldly glowing eyes when up so close, but his face was easy to look upon, and her curiosity outweighed her fear. "You do not understand. You cannot say such things about me. There are consequences in these lands."

"For having green eyes? Because of magic being rebuked as a sin?" No-Name asked in a tone that proved he thought the notion preposterous. He stood up in an instant and cupped his hands to the empty courtyard. "I have violet eyes, sir! Cursed with magic eyes from birth! Mage parents, the both of them!" He pointed to imaginary citizens in the quiet yard while he shouted. "I was born a hyperi! See the violet glow in my eyes? You sir there! Warn the Pentagogue, and bring the paladins and veritans! Tell all of Az'Dayne you've caught yourselves a magic-eyed boy!"

She grabbed one of his wrists and sternly moved it down to his side. She could feel that he put up no defense to stop her. "You seem rather blessed but naive. Things are viewed differently here. These are not Thrench waters you wade in," she cautioned.

"A fine quote. Please, tell it to my uncle," he snapped back sardonically before returning to lie again on his back and stare at the sky.

She shook her head, looking around for snooping onlookers but finding none. "What are you doing, my lord?"

No-Name tapped the ground again next to him and scooched over to make room for her. She sighed in defeat and timidly found her place with her arm and thigh against his, gazing up at the nothingness of midday's cloudy shapes. "Now what?"

"Truly open your eyes and look," he softly said.

I love your accent, she thought. He didn't say anything for a while. *Did I say that out loud?* She began to feel embarrassed and moved her thigh away from him ever so slightly.

"Do you see them?" he asked.

Adyssaira tried to entertain the attractive foreign boy. "Clouds. Trees. Rooftops. The sun," she replied, sure that she had failed to give whatever answer she was supposed to give.

"Close your eyes and sense their presence," he whispered more quietly. "In between that which you can touch and that which you are not meant to see."

She truly tried. She let the commotion of city life become less than a muted hum. "The sea," she admitted. "I hear the waves."

He didn't say anything for a while again.

I got it wrong, didn't I?

She found herself turned to face him when he talked again. "Are your eyes still closed?"

"They are," she lied.

"You are using your ears and trying to listen. You must feel it deep. Try to drown out even the sea. You should know how."

She complied and closed her eyes. As she did, she felt the touch of his fingers interlocking with hers. His voice was barely audible this time, but something tingled and changed throughout her core with his touch. "Now feel and see for the first time."

And it all became clear to her, as real and loud as the outside world. A drone of ethereal echoes in every direction around her.

They were all trying to speak at once, but not in a language she had ever learned. It was all in Elvan, but ancient, not of the modern tongues she had heard. She dared to open her eyes to witness the multitude of incorporeal trail lines leading every which way that could be, out from No-Name's body. They all held a faint green glow. Of the hundreds of possible wraithlike umbilical cords, only one of them branched from her body into his. He made sure she saw it and then squeezed her hand hard and sat up, withdrawing his touch.

"What did you do?" she demanded, feeling sweat down her brow and heaviness of breath.

He explained, "I am a hyperi. We have a sense of hypersight, meaning we can see that which others cannot. We exist between the realm you know and the realm we were born into. The people of Mageholme call it the In-Between. It is where the hunder dwell."

Adyssaira looked all around her, searching for the fading green cords. *Are these a form of elvan spiritroots, or something else from the hunder?* She contemplated the mystical anomalies concerning the complex theories on elvan souls. She then looked into No-Name's strange glowing orbs, which shifted like violet smoke. "We learn about much in my house, at Castle Chandoss." She decided to fully stand back on her feet. "But magic is a forbidden, arcane knowledge in this country. You are Thrench. You are obviously spoiled by a life that knows no fear."

"Only partially Thrench," No-Name corrected, "or so my mother's side of cousins and my uncle like to remind me. I am more Oriyan than Thrench. I was raised on an isle in the Vist beyond the shores of Oriyen." His story should have seemed like a fabricated tale from a boy with a wild imagination, but somehow she knew it was all true. He stood up to match her stance, scowling unapprovingly at her side. "And just to clarify, I am all too familiar with the concept of fear."

He began to walk in front of her through the lush courtyard, exaggerating with his hands as he spoke. "Imagine being born into a family that bears the most legendary name on Penthara, but you grew your entire life without seeing its privileges, hidden on an island to be raised by monks instead of your parents, an island that exists between the east and the west, a nowhere land, where there is no sun in the day and no moon at night. There is no blue sky, only the ethereal fabrics of the In-Between. And when you finally get to see your family, after ten years of age, your father and mother only use you for your power for acts of violence.

"They used my hypersight to hunt and kill other mages across the realm. They used Traversement to soar through the skies and sail across the seas with me in hand to witness all that they did. I was just a boy. By twelve I was made to watch them both conjure up the largest magical storm ever recorded in history to rain down upon their enemies.

"And I didn't even meet a Threnchman until I was thirteen, when I was first introduced to my uncle, Emperor Djediheth Emmonost, and my cousins. They made it clear in my early years I was not one of them, eventually sending me to Mageholme. I am told I cannot claim the Thrench side of my bloodline until I complete my Sojourn and discover my path to achieve my ultimate Uedonvyor.

"To conclude all of this, imagine just recently hearing that your parents have been killed, having to attend their funeral without their bodies present to lay to rest in the sea so that they might find peace in the afterlife beneath the waves. Imagine all of that."

Adyssaira felt as if she were listening to the grandest bard's book ever written, about some epic hero in the making who could not possibly have existed. If it had not come from this peculiar boy's mouth, then it would have sounded all so unbelievable. "I cannot imagine that" was all she could sincerely admit as she used her cane to navigate next to him again. "I am sorry."

"It's okay, Adyssaira."

How does he know my name? "Lord, you know of me?"

No-Name cast her a shrewd grin, apparently quite proud of himself for taking her by surprise. "I did my research on the famous lon'Chandoss girls. I once shared a trading ship with an elvan traveler who had come through Chandoshia."

He is speaking of Sundorion, she mused, but she did not interject.

"He told tales of three sisters born at the same time, similar in appearance but each far different from the others. When he spoke of the beautiful blind girl, I listened more, and he told me her name."

No-Name turned to face her and dared to put a hand on her blindfold. She let him. "You see." He tried to slip it down to reveal her eyes. She continued to let him. "I, too, have felt blind, with the sheltered upbringing I was imprisoned in. I knew I had to meet you one day."

"I ..." *Did he just cast a fire spell on me? It is too hot. I cannot breathe.* She quickly pulled back and fixed the sash back over her green eyes. "I am flattered. But I think I need to leave. I need to find my family."

As she turned to walk away, No-Name trailed her with an argument for her to stay. "Your sister has already found you. She's been right there, watching and listening to us the whole time."

Adyssaira chuckled in disappointment at her clever new friend and glimpsed over at Odysserae, who was skulking around the corner. "She hasn't been listening. I thought you said you had done your research on the lon'Chandoss girls." *I think you only learned about one lon'Chandoss girl,* she mused, and grinned. "I do have to leave, though, kind lord. Thank you for ..." she stammered awkwardly. "Thank you for the company!"

Her feet propelled her faster than the walking cane could realistically guide her, in the direction of her sister, but No-Name did not seem satisfied to conclude his long-aspired-to meeting with her.

"Wait! Don't you want to know my name, since I know yours?"

"You don't have one yet. Your uncle won't grant you one until you complete your Sojourn," she tossed back with a little tease as to her own investigations.

No-Name put both hands on his slender hips and cocked his head to the side in total amusement. "And how did you come to know this?"

"Oh, I did my research. An elvan traveler once came through Chandoshia and told me of the famous violet-eyed 'No-Name' boy from Oriyen. I hoped I would meet him one day." She looked back and bowed to him before sprinting effortlessly now to Odysserae's side to leave the yard.

"Adyssaira, will you be permitted to see me again?" No-Name inquired in a tone that seemed almost panicked and distraught in anticipation of the wrong reply.

"No, never." She lifted the Savatarm silk sash from around her eyes to take one last glance at his regal figure and handsome face. She smiled and blew him a kiss. "I cannot see, remember?"

SUNDORION (III)

POWER OF PAWNS

The rusted cage creaked with every slight move as he tossed and rolled. Consciousness was a taunting ceiling far too high to climb to. Between darkness and vertigo was the new purgatory he existed in. He saw the silhouettes of replicated phantoms going in and out of the door to his hanging barred cell, and even the mirage of his brother in an identical predicament across from him, but he paid the illusions no heed. He was sure that whatever was causing this spell had something to do with the pain in the back of his head, and even more to do with the numbing he felt coursing through his tingling limbs.

Hours, days, he wasn't sure of the lapse of true time, as the abstract realm of dream preferred to lapse with elusive continuity. Eventually, the shadowy state of reality merged into a grey fog that tantalized with a light just over the imaginary horizon. The perpetual ticking of Old Patience matched the rhythm of another pocket watch nearby. He could feel his hunder drifting steadily toward it. And at last he reached it.

A blast of air hit his lungs as if he were coming up to the surface from beneath the suffocating sea. Sun opened his eyes in a panicked pant. The entire room was lit in a red radiance. He was awake.

There was a Zandaryn elvan just across from him, balled up on his rump, holding his knees with his head hung low and his long yellow hair hanging to hide his face. He was unclean, skinny, and half-naked, with a filthy shirt tied like a belt around his ragged breeches. His shoes were off, and around his neck was an unmistakable water-watch pendant like Sun's own. *New Patience!* It was Timmurian.

"Timm!"

His brother parted his frayed hair to reveal his face and prove it was him. A weary grin and nod were returned as a reply instead of words.

A pungent whiff of excrement overpowered Sun's nose, and somehow he determined his next question took precedence above all others. "That smell? What ...?"

He looked around his cell and found a bucket full of dung stains, flies, and maggots behind him, and he nearly gagged out whatever remained in his starving belly.

Timmurian answered with the obvious. "Shit. Piss. Mine. Yours. That of whoever else dwelt in these cages before us fools."

"You live, though." Sun tried his strength to stand in his tight prison, surprised to see it was just tall enough for him to do so without a crouch.

"I dare call this living," Timmurian said cynically.

Sun glanced around the barren cylindrical room, not inclined to find any reason to contest that statement. There were no windows, with the only source of light for the room being red crystalytes set inside sconces along the wall. Other than the two steel cages, the only pieces of furniture present were the table between them and the table behind Timmurian, along with one chair and an unlevel table with a few unrolled parchments atop it by the stairwell, which Sun could see led up as well as down.

On the table behind his brother were pieces of bread, likely a day in age from the looks of them, some cheese, and a bowl of basic fruit. Four pitchers were in the middle, with contents Sun could not quite discern from his angle, but he noticed that all were easily accessible to Timmurian.

Their cages were suspended about a foot off the floor, each hung by three thick chains that were fastened into rings protruding from a steel frame that went from wall to wall across the ceiling. It was apparent that the locked door to each confined cell was through the top, not the sides.

The table between them was much lower than the taller table with the food. This one was rectangular, only as high as the floor of the cage. Strangely, atop it was his and his brother's favorite pastime. It was called pawns, a strategy game that consisted of several squares chiseled into a stone board, with several wooden figurines with different abilities. One player's pieces were painted red, while the other's were black.

"Where is this place?"

"Not the tower. Something beneath it. A dungeon of sorts no doubt nearby," Timmurian replied, seemingly knowledgeable of the fact that Sun had tried to enter Valdean's false tower to arrive at this fate. "You were daft for following, Sun. As learned as you are, you could not see the people at foul play on this one?"

Sun was in no mood for mockery or an argument, only answers. "Something took me. Grey skin. Saw it out of the corner of my eye before I was struck. You?"

"Ise'andahr, a rogue-elvan. These rogues, the umbran progenies, have tainted grey skin, as you are learned. He is the progeny of Zsa'vauge, the umbran Architect over Chandoshia. It is true—the Neveril are here. And it is Zsa'vauge that pulls the strings. I have only seen Ise'andahr twice, and if you get the chance, you will get little out of him. His upbringing and rogue state have his mental capacities rather limited. I've yet to meet with Zsa'vauge, but I know my time is ticking. They work through Count Valdean as a topside liaison. We are in his prison until they take us."

"Zsa'vauge. The umbran over the Chandoshian territory." Sun recalled the Neveril's name all too well from Timmurian's letters to him of boundless theories. "You've been after this one for a while. Why keep us captured instead of just killing us outright? They are the ones with the answers. We have nothing to give but trouble. And how much power does the count have with them?" He knew about the political structure of the subterranean elven better than most. It was risky to dig too deep into that which wished to remain unknown, but digging deep into unknowns was what he did.

"Rest assured, the count works for them, and he has no authority to take your life. Humans under the Neveril's Umbran Pledge are not permitted to kill elven, aside from Glace Isles Terollar and the quasi, as far as I have learned." His brother alluded to information Sun was already educated in. Timmurian squeezed the watch dangling around his neck where it rested over the middle of his chest. "Which is my exact predicament."

Sun averted his eyes from his brother's before he could judge the shame in Timmurian's disposition to confirm what Taizsha had forewarned. "You idiot. You did it, didn't you? Tay warned me, but I shunned the idea that you succumbed to the Taboo and became quasi. You are as fucked as she is."

"Aye, it seems accurate to say so. And the Balance is punishing me for it now," Timmurian uttered.

"Fuck the Balance," Sun blasphemed. "You are simply being incarcerated for digging into their business, nothing more. We will be given a choice to comply with the Pledge before they finalize our fates."

"Am I? The Neveril adhere to no Balance either. The underrealm's far-reaching empire holds on to something new. The only Taboo path they revere is that of the umbran. Now that I am quasi, without a connection to my spiritroots, I am as good as human to them. I am considered tainted, just as they view Tay. And any seeds I would pass to Emberalda, as my human lifemate, they would consider abominations, just as they view all Z'shun, fit for a quick death, just as they plan for little Sashka."

Sun stared at his recalcitrant sibling with his mouth agape, hesitating to condemn him further. Sun thought to remind Timmurian that he did not have entertain bearing children with Emberalda if he took her as a lifemate. Zandaryn male elven had the unique impower of being able to pass seed onto their other lifemates, if Timmurian ever bound himself to one of their own ilk. Even as a quasi, Zandaryn could have full elvan progeny if they had another elvan as one of their lifemates.

"As much as I would love to hear a sermon from my elder about the ramifications of my decision to follow our sister's choice in becoming quasi," Timmurian continued in a cynical tone, "we were not done with the more pressing topic—Valdean. The Count of Chandoshia has been given a deadline to fix all loose ends before the dominarchs of Az'Dayne return from their business in Barredom. If he is unsuccessful, then the entirety of his house and his affiliates will be slain, save for a few who have current immunity."

"Let me guess." Sun was sure he could surmise who, other than Valdean himself, would be absolved from such a final sentencing. "The mute girl, Odysserae. Likely Ethiass as well. I have always suspected his role. And of course, obviously now Valaythea, due to her union with the Prince of Az'Dayne."

"Ethiass, no. He will be the first to go if all fails, and he knows it." Timmurian unfolded. "Valaythea, yes, is now under the protection of their shadow through her conjoining with Izayus as an imperial paramour. And you forget Athaniel, in the Oathemic Cabal.

He is untouchable. But the other girls …"

The way he let the sentence trail off into silence sent a chill down Sun's spine. These fiends planned to kill young, innocent girls like Adyssaira and Emberalda. "Oddy is not safe? She baited me here, ensuring my capture. But why?"

"Oh, she is in. She is safe. That one is vile, Sun, with a heart as black as bogbile. But she, too, is just a pawn in the grand scheme of this neverborne pandemic plaguing the realm." Timmurian huffed and flicked his middle finger on the top of the pawn piece on the game board between them, knocking it over.

"Neverborne? Is that a qindrid term, as in stoneborne or skyborne?" Sun was not learned of the term in his latest research.

"It was too risky to speak of it in the letters, even in code. Telling you of Zsa'vauge I even regretted the moment I sent it. But yes the neverborne, the qindrid of the Neveril. You will wish to unhear it if I divulge it to you," Timmurian warned. "But we are not going anywhere. I can promise you that. You fucked us good here now. I was counting on you to get me out of this, not barge in beside me."

Timmurian reached behind him to take the pitcher of water from the food table and took a healthy swig before handing it through the bars for Sun to get his fill and hydrate as well. "The neverborne are altered humans, as all qindrid are, but they are more. They have a special faculty through their shadow descendancy that permits them with an impower to be shape changers …"

Timmurian went on to explain that Count Valdean, as chief surface informant for the Neveril implanted in this region, had gone to Emerald Point in a shapeshifted form with Ethiass and Nikayle to investigate the unanticipated arrival of the Thrench on Chandoshian soil. The Neveril elvan race evidently feared the Thrench Empire as much as any other elven did, as they should.

I want to tell you, Timm. I truly do … I invited the Thrench here. They will be our one savior in what I've set in motion if all aligns as intended. But now that you are quasi, you are subject to being tortured more than I. I cannot risk you breaking and telling. You will just have to wait and see. Sun kept certain prudent thoughts to himself, allowing his brother to be the conveyor of news instead.

Timmurian had been digging too, but instead of going realmwide, like Sun had, his brother's focus had been exclusively localized. Timmurian's qualms concerning the presumptions that

Az'Dayne's higher powers were being gradually supplanted by imposters infiltrating their political and most influential ranks made him one of the pioneers of the original truth-seekers. He was the one who had sparked Sun's interest in the first place, from chasing artifacts in faraway ancient ruins to raiding underground tombs to debunking farcical myths from country to country. As of late, all Sun had cared about was what his younger brother had initially set out to uncover, the most hushed and speculated-on myth there had ever been, with conjectures about the Neveril Empire.

His brother had learned from Valdean that Taizsha's and Sashka's fates were to be entwined with their own. They would be saved from a sure death or brought in to be executed by the Neveril, depending on whether Timmurian and Sun joined the Umbran Pledge and aided the cause of the ominous order instead of further exposing it, hindering the Neveril scheme to subjugate all of humanity from the inside out.

The discussion moved on to other points, at first concerning his brother's feelings toward Emberalda. Timmurian committing the Taboo to life as a quasi and choosing her as his lifemate seemed a rather impulsive whim of romance with no long-term logic factored in. The elder Chandoss girl was known for her lewd antics and it just made no sense to Sun that Timmurian would do something so detrimental if his typically pragmatic brother had no ulterior motive. Whether he did or did not, Timmurian did not indulge that information yet, as he shifted in reminiscence of loved ones lost, like their parents, and then of Sheyelle and Carolelle, and about how they were still soundly buried under their statues at the sacred shrine that House Chandoss had built to honor them as condolence after their deaths.

Sun shied from the uncomfortable subject, feeling guilt for not visiting their graves, but he wondered now if he would ever be able to again.

He brought up the rations left for them, and the empty slop buckets. Apparently, Odysserae was a regular who visited the tower once a day, cleaning out the buckets and resupplying sustenance to keep Timmurian alive. But the silent girl had gone with Count Valdean to Emerald Point.

Timmurian explained that by proxy their cell keeper had been Ise'andahr, the rogue-Neveril who captured them, and that the hangover Sun was experiencing was induced by the aromatic reaction the candles produced when the wax melted, for whatever strange reason.

After apprising each other of their recent whereabouts and hardships, Timmurian suggested they pass the time with a little leisure over a match of pawns. It was a popular strategy board game with their elvan people in Zandabar, and as far north as Barredom.

The board was set with ten squares by ten, with a total of one hundred spaces a player could move to, and each player had twenty game pieces to start: ten pawns, two ships, two catapults, two horsemen, two traps, a spymaster, and a king. Pawns could be promoted to a variety of other pieces in the game, including an assassin piece. If a king was put in jeopardy to lose the game on a player's next turn, this player could alert the other with "King call." If a player won by trapping the king in jeopardy, then they would call out, "Dekinged." And if the player received a victory for promoting at least five of their pawns, then they would shout the ultimate victory of "Up-pawned!"

"You would have gotten yourself killed, Sun," Timmurian said hours into their first game. They had mostly held a tactical silence for the purpose of concentration. "For being the smartest hunder I know, you are a brash and brazen idiot."

Just like a human might refer to another as a *person,* the elven termed each other a *hunder*, a synonym for a member of their race when used in context. This was not to be confused with the same term used to refer to an elvan's soul, which carried impowered properties, connected to their spiritroot and lifetree.

They were nearing the end of their first session, Sun could feel, and his confidence in his long-game strategy was more sound than ever. They were both leveraging the time-slowing power of their magic water-watches to capitalize on swifter minutes spent during their move assessments. Sun knew he was brash, but he had never been an idiot, as his brother claimed. "Pawn me," he commanded as one of his pawns reached the other side of the board.

Timmurian placed one of Sun's casualty pieces back on the board in a free space of his choosing, at the end of the board nearest him, and Sun put this ventured pawn on a space in the row nearest him.

Several more turns transpired, and finally Sun killed his

brother's spymaster. "Exposed," he declared.

Timmurian revealed his assassin pawn and smirked, seeming amused to conjure a subject. "The power of pawns. Speaking of ..." He made his next move before finishing. "Oddy—"

"How far turned is she?" Sun substituted his own subject. "She seems innocent."

"She's turned, Sun. They are going to make her one of them." His brother implied the Transcendence into one of the neverborne. "But she is all we have to work with in our current circumstances."

"Pawn." Sun made another move toward his surefire win. "Perhaps she is, but she wants out."

Another few turns passed, and Timmurian seemed to gain ground in putting Sun's spymaster in jeopardy. "That's not all. The blind one, Adyssaira, she isn't blind. Emberalda cannot hold a secret to save her life. She told me it has been a cover-up staged by Ethiass since Adyssaira's birth. She's hunder-touched. No one but Ember knows that I know."

Sun glanced at the time passed on Old Patience. "Just now bringing this to light? This isn't good for the girl." He pretended to be concerned by the revelation but actually felt it to be a serendipitous spin in the positive direction for what he had prearranged before his arrival in Chandoshia, with No-Name on his ship. Some things he simply could not indulge Timmurian with yet, though. "If she becomes further interfused with any derelict hunder, she will be impowered as either a Dawning or a Sunder mage."

"I know my lore in elemental descendancies, Sun. Even when it comes to magic," Timmurian retorted, seeming insulted by Sun's assumption of his ignorance.

"Not doubting your erudition in the magical sciences, Timm. I'm enlightening you on nondomestic happenings, since you've had such tunnel vision on this region of Az'Dayne alone," Sun corrected before opening up. "If Addy becomes a Sunder mage, they will have her put to death, unless the Oathemic Cabal suddenly begins accepting women. But if she becomes a Dawning mage, there is something else entirely they will force her into. On my last visit through Mageholme, I was in the process of uncovering something new with the Green Byway. I am positive they have been bought out by a higher power. They are conscripting Dawners with exorbitant contract prices, and this just began in the Cycle of Kingfall.

These Dawning mages are taking up the contracts, but they aren't being seen thereafter in the company's travel service. They disappear. And my sources whisper that the Neveril are involved."

"This makes sense," Timmurian said in deep thought, while also studying his next move on the board. "I knew the Neveril were using tairan magic to literally expand their underrealm reach, but I did not know how. They use their own people like slaves, assigning them to the roles of drudges, stripping them of their bornnames during the conditioning phase. The Architects are the engineers behind the tairan-forming."

"Warrior," Sun stated, promoting another veteran pawn after its kill and fathoming the convoluted scope of House Chandoss and all its intricacies.

"Exposed," Timmurian proclaimed after he took Sun's spymaster with pride. "Two and two, Sun. We may have found a way to get the girl to listen. We have to act on certainties. And the certainties are these. The Neveril are behind the Az'Dayne takeover. They are utilizing mercenary mages this season to capitalize on aggrandizing their underrealm through tairan magic. Odysserae will be returning to the tower to tend to us as Valdean's assistant. And she will have a soft spot for her hunder-touched sister if we threaten to expose Adyssaira's birth secret to Valdean, or even Zsa'vauge. The Chandoss family is not yet all completely under the burden of the Umbran Pledge. Some of them can still be saved and have a chance to escape the grip of the Neveril Empire. Odysserae can still be saved, but only by aiding us in our escape, and she must come to believe this. And soon."

Sun heeded fact after fact laid out by Timmurian before activating Old Patience back into its time-slowing effect to finish the game. He carefully deliberated every option there could be for his brother to escape the fate he was about to press upon him in the game, all the while weighing everything they were discussing. Sun deactivated the enchanted water-watch's power and disclosed his assassin piece to the board by placing two gold-painted coins underneath the gemmed pawn. He then retaliated with his final move to end the match. His exposed assassin jumped over one of the opposing horsemen, leaving Timmurian with no option to move his king in any direction out of jeopardy. "Dekinged!"

His brother was clearly in shock. "I thought this one would be your assassin." He gestured to a different piece. "The pawn in play is not always who you might think it is."

It was clear that they both viewed Odysserae as a tool they could hopefully use in their favor.

Sun matched his brother's smile and nodded. "Indeed. Such is the power of pawns."

SCARLESS (V)

PARK DAY

Zahnastaazjah clutched the sealed scroll in her hand, parted from the white-billed raptor's talons as it had flown in and swooped out of reach from any hidden poacher's grasp. It chose to perch on a branch on the wide banyan tree above her head.

The large predator bird was no normal example of its class. This particular raptor had a recognizable glow of green in its beady eyes, a faint hint of a wisp infused within it. This was an animayan, a beast permanently possessed by a self-sacrificed elvan's wisp, reincarnated into its spirit. Any animayan Zahnastaazjah had encountered in the past were always of her own Terollar ilk, and she somehow indubitably knew this raptor would be no different. This was a messenger bird sent by her son, Sorovronus, whom she had fully anticipated receiving correspondence from the moment she visited Goldgarden's park districts again.

She nodded to the brown-spotted bird and spoke—"*Thank you, tree of my tree*"—in her native tongue, offering it a common phrase of respectful gratitude for the Terollar elven.

Zahnastaazjah surveyed her surroundings around the lofty retreat on the vertex of Centron Park. This area of the island city served as a fair sanctuary for all types of urban beasts that moved in and took over, such as packs of wild dogs, hordes of small vermin, and even vagrants of the worst kind—the human kind.

A blind woman in her late years was not far away, sitting on a large root with her back against a banana tree, feeding a handful of berries and morsels of some kind of meat to a pair of badgers. A way down the steep climb, a lost fawn just stared up into the trees, pondering life's curiosities. Six throws to her right was a mentally broken drifter she was acquainted with. She called the shabby man Mumbler, as all he did was ramble on to the birds and plants and furry creatures, babbling on in nonsensical gibberish.

Zahnastaazjah took a deep breath and turned her eyes down to the contents of the opened scroll.

To My Progenitor,

By now I am sure you have heard the news. I am sorry you had to find out the way that you did, and not by our tribesven. It was a necessary decision you will come to understand. The grief you suffer is a debt we will repay. Go with these parting encouragements. The role you play in your great city will have a larger role to play in our greater wilds before long. Remember your kind. En khomo naso rahsee'ahsee.

Your Forsaken Forwoken Progeny

The words from her son resonated in her heart. *En khomo naso rahsee'ahsee … He cannot die.* She mused on the popular concept held by her culture about her father's legendary prowess in remaining invincible against all attempts to take his life in the past, made by his enemies and by traitors among his own kind the same. *Everyone can stop saying that now. You are gone, and you are not coming back this time.* "The king of the Glace Isles was executed by his own, they say." She invoked the grim news from Thederick Tyme of the Seat of the Black. *An ironic end for you, Father. You spent your entire life trying to save the elvan race, only to be sent into the Beyond by your own tribesven.*

Zahnastaazjah briefly thought on Xalo and then each of her overmen in the Stormtrees, feeling confident that any of them could and would turn on her at any bleak sign that she was losing strength in her guild, any display of the slightest trace of weakness.

But park day was not for ruminations on business. This was where she went to escape the drudging stress as guildmother of the Stormtrees. This was where she went to remember her roots, not as Scarless the Overlord of the Underworld, but as Zahnastaazjah the Terollar instead. She closed her eyes and conjured a reverie of her deepest memories to the surface.

She was ten cycles of age, just meeting her father for the first time. She recalled hearing stories of the name Khomo'Jhuvonus in her youngest years, before she had ever registered that the fabled legend was also her progenitor. He was not cold and scary, like the tales of Teralloe told. He did not seem like some ruthless killer or savage warlord. When she was finally honored with meeting him, he appeared as she had hoped he would—as her proud and venerable father.

He presented her with a feathered bone spear known as a *skarpaka* in her culture. It was not intended as a true weapon but rather as a ceremonial token that was always bestowed upon a daughter of the king of the Glace Isles on her tenth cycle, her coming of age. She learned it was the same spear that had been wielded by her six elder sisters during their tenth cycles as well. She carried the spear with pride everywhere she went for those five seasons. It was the Cycle of Westwars, she recalled.

Her hazy nostalgia then focused on what seemed like a lifetime ago, her graduation from her edification and discipline tutelage with the Sylvanil Sentinel Order, as was custom, to discover the lifequest she remained uncommitted to. Sometime after her early twenties in cycles, she had then been taken from her race's homeland of Teralloe by her mother, Malindhi, to join most of her older sisters and brothers in Helderak, with the exception of Zuulzinj. This was instead of joining her father, in his violent escapades, on the Glace Isles.

This had been a direct violation of her father's aspirations for her upbringing. Helderak was a broken, barren country of bygone endemic strife between the Terollar and surface armies of the Neveril elven. During those years, Zahnastaazjah remembered quieter days on her end, just observing, listening, and absorbing everything. She watched and said and did nothing as her lifemate, Drevlijhun, fell feeble to the enticements of the gradual Neveril suppression. Her brothers, too, Kavajin and Jhukamwi, conspired with this subterranean domineering race to overthrow the strong interference her father was causing in the Neveril expansions in the northwest throughout the undergrounds of Aggedon. She even sat idle when her sisters became enslaved as concubines for the uppermost echelons of the Neveril Empire.

She was such a coward then. None of it inspired her. Not her father's campaigns as a Chosen of the Balance to end the Neveril reign. Not her lifemate and brothers' ambitions to join what they believed was the necessary lesser evil in the Neveril Empire's master plans for the evolution of the elvan race. She had no wish to save her mother or persuade her against betraying the core tenets of the Balance, for which she had been raised to live and die by.

She was numb when the news arrived about Kavajin's and Jhukamwi's deaths. Their challenge to their father had ended promptly by his own hand in a bloody and brutal duel. And she was oddly relieved at finding out her aloof lifemate, Drevlijhun, had died alongside them in the failed attempt to usurp the Glace Isles throne.

And now Khomo'Jhuvonus was dead, like the rest of them, enslaved to his own life's destiny, which had wrought his ultimate demise. He had spent his entire existence on tireless crusades for his ingrained faith in the greater good for the elvan race, to eliminate those of his ilk that would enthrall others through oppression and mass deception.

Her father had been hated by more than the few who revered him, but he had died with one legacy. Nearly every soul on Penthara had heard of his dreaded name. His renown for inspiring fear and loathing had become his fame.

The crash of two monkeys falling off the banana tree nearby and squabbling in a tussle over the shredded morsel of ruined fruit broke Zahnastaazjah's trance of reminiscence. The blind woman and badgers were nowhere around. She wondered how long she had been adrift in her ponderings. The sun hadn't moved much, but her mouth had gone dry, and her mood had spoiled.

Her intuition caught another elvan skulking up the hill behind her. *Uubakrath*. Of course it was him. Xalo may have held the reputation as her public bodyguard, but it was the Terollar archer who never let her out of his sight. Truly, he intimidated her, and that wasn't a feat any other being had managed since she first set foot in Goldgarden. Perhaps it was his incidental reminder of her true heritage and of what her higher purpose in the realm could be. She pretended not to notice Uubakrath, ignoring his approach.

I am still a coward now, she reflected in a check of all current reality. Zahnastaazjah knew she had grown vexed with the petty position she had ascended to in her urban distraction. Bossing around lowlifes and meaningless up-jumpers with no birthright credibility or impact on history's future chronicles was about as wretchedly trite a way to suffer a slow death as there ever could be. She could feel her hunder yearning for more than just this absconded state for survival and a false sense of purpose. Soon it would be time to chase down greatness, whether adored or reviled, like her father had.

She had once been a part of the same tree as he had been when she had cocooned into this world. She needed to start acting like it.

Zahnastaazjah could hear Uubakrath directly behind her now, even feel the heat of his heavy breath against her neck. It sent shivers down her spine, but something came over her. She felt elvan again. She felt alive again.

"*En khomo naso rahsee'ahsee,*" she uttered aloud.

VALAYTHEA (IV)

SUNTIDE

"Oh my, Val!"

Valaythea was weeping from joy long before she even heard Emberalda's sweet voice, having seen her cousin and sisters from a distance before they caught a glimpse of her.

She was already shirking her way past the lines of pedestrian traffic, weaving through the jubilant crowd of revelers at the Suntide Faire. She was overly anxious to reunite with her three best friends, whom she hadn't seen in what felt like an eternity made of only two months, if even that. She felt blessed by the Five and Five to be able to call her closest family members—Emberalda, Adyssaira, and Odysserae—by such a cherished, genuine bond.

She nearly lost herself to laughter when she saw her cousin yank Adyssaira's hand so hard to sprint forward that it toppled her down to the ground. Odysserae didn't skip a beat in aiding their sister back to her feet, assisting in adjusting her blindfold back into place as well. All four of them were stained by smiles from ear to ear.

"Emb—argh!" Valaythea tried to hurl her cousin's name out as she embraced her in a hard squeeze. She chuckled at the welcome affection and exchanged hugs with her sisters too. "Addy! Oddy! Oh, the Fives only know how much I missed you all!"

Odysserae was trying to relay something with finger gestures, but Valaythea, with her focus spun into an ecstatic frenzy, unfortunately didn't catch it, and so she simply nodded and smiled gleefully at her deaf sister in hopes this would suffice.

"We wept to think we may never see you again," Adyssaira confessed, an absurdly glum notion.

You are supposed to be acting like you cannot see me, regardless, Addy!

"Or at least for a long while, and only maybe if we were

pardoned to come visit you in the imperial court!"

Valaythea stopped to consider if indeed the House lon'Chandoss name had been absolved of its past condemnable iniquities now, or if that was something even Prince Izayus had no power over. Her detached spouse had mentioned such to be the case, but as for official formalities with which to first indoctrinate the Az'Dayne locals, he had neglected to mention if it would be postponed until Dominarch Vaximus and Dominarch Sriyah returned.

"Quickly, ladies! We were trying to catch the last act of the—" Emberalda stopped herself midsentence, seeming to rethink her agenda for the regional cyclical fair. "Wait, what am I saying? Val, to the five hells with that! You must spill all the nectar about Prince Izayus to us!"

Valaythea turned to see the mounted imperial escort that had returned her home fading into the background along the perimeter paths of Fairetown.

The four lon'Chandoss girls merrily roamed the extensive grounds of the festival together, sharing stories about the latest gossip or exaggerated updates in their own lives. Most of the attention was turned on Valaythea and her experiences with the exalted prince and the formerly forbidden capital.

She was cautious in her restraint in divulging any true detail of what she had endured—the parts she could remember, anyhow, before the strange spell of partial amnesia had been cast over her. It remained her biggest fear for the invocation to fade, just as Coldborn had warned her it would, and for the force-forgotten memories of what she may have actually discovered in those ten shadowed days.

For the most part, she just deemed it necessary to lie, telling her probing kin about the fictitious, stereotyped version of Izayus Az'Ampion, refraining from indulging them in the ugly actualities of his tormented character flaws. She elaborated on the countless splendors of Everdawn, the luxurious dresses and exquisite jewels she had been endowed with, and the finest-flavored dishes and wines she was treated to taste. The more she spoke of her pampered new lifestyle, the less she seemed to dwell on the haunting truths of her undiluted opinions.

Emberalda tried to act hard and pretentious, as always when she was in her emotionally defensive state of mind—Valaythea knew her trigger mannerisms better than any. Her melodramatic cousin couldn't stop talking about other happenstance liaisons with boys around the faire or obviously made-up men to be smitten with. But clearly she was still overly enamored of the one they knew her to be—Timmurian, her elvan lover, whom she talked about more than any of them, even though it was mostly negative in the insinuations for his unexplained absence.

Adyssaira slipped when pressured about some half-Thrench boy Emberalda confessed to first. Evidently, the Thrench Empire had arrived in Chandoshia, and Valaythea was only just now hearing about it. Her sister stayed modest on the subject and shooed away any prying attempts to get her to admit her fancy for the foreign bastard boy. Her defensive tactic to stray from lauding him seemed to be to resort to the subject of her new pet black tiger, which she couldn't wait for Val to meet.

Odysserae, while usually quite disconnected and unsocial, stayed attached to Valaythea's arm the entire time they meandered about the faire's delights, smiling and happier than Valaythea recalled her ever being. Unlike the other two, her quiet sister had nothing new to disclose that would be of particular interest to the group.

The boot-beaten dirt of the festival fields was so packed from the mobs of jolly townsfolk tromping over it that it had turned from its original loose soil into a surface that was hard enough that it may as well have been a massive paved road. People from all over Chandoshia, from Fairetown, where the faire was located outside town, from as far north as Emerald Point to as far south as Toil, were a part of the cyclical Suntide Faire's citizens who operated it. But folk from all over the eastern regions of Az'Dayne made sure to visit the famous festival as well. Aggressive tradesmen from Savatarm and Tairancia and farther afield also never missed the opportunity to exploit such a congregation of the weak and the curious.

Makeshift shops of all kinds, trade circles, peddler tents, and barter booths were a common sight. Games for sport and coin and entertainment for children littered the vast area. Intermingled sounds of minstrels' songs, hawkers' screams, and visitors' conversations accumulated into a single noise of pleasant pandemonium. The sea of life was coupled with the succulent smells of so many varieties of food, dominated by sweet cakes and smoked meats.

The Suntide Faire was rightly named for the significant midway point in every cycle's Dawning season, between the last cycle's Torrent season and the coming Sunder season. The principle behind throwing the festival during this time was to cherish the severities of a person's past, which had made them who they were today, and to celebrate the fresh new future in front of them. It was a Daynish tradition living on in Chandoshia, just outside Fairetown, rightfully dubbed as such, for the past forty-something years.

The girls talked and ate their fill and even partook of far too much cheap wine and potent Firebrandy than their petite bodies had the stomachs for. Valaythea had never seen Odysserae actually drunk before, and they all shared the mirth watching the hilarity displayed by the typically timid sister.

Valaythea excused herself after some time to vomit some of the intoxication out of her system, taking a short recess from the other girls to sneak behind a pair of conjoined tents with raucous vendors arguing with one another about nothing discernible—her senses were far too dulled.

She kept her hair lifted as she wiped her mouth on the sleeve of her dress when she was finished. When she looked up, she swore she must have been even more inebriated than she had assumed.

"Athan!" Valaythea swayed in disbelief of her own eyes. "You are home early?"

Somehow he looked unchanged and yet entirely different at the same time, if that made any sense. But she deemed it senseless, because she was simply drunk. His spiked red hair and handsome, clean-shaven jawline were just as she remembered. But in his eyes, there was something callous that lingered in the limbo of a world of cold death and dauntless souls. *Those eyes ...* She thought she reached out to touch them in her stupor, but she didn't. They changed everything about him.

"You are home early?" *I think I just said that.*

"You know why, Valaythea."

"Coldborn?" She didn't even know at this point what she was saying aloud, but the words kept spewing out regardless. "He sent you to protect me?"

"Assassins of the Oathemic Cabal are not sent to protect people," he said, as still as stone in every feature.

Valaythea grabbed at nothingness behind her, grasping for the tent nearest to her back or anything tangible to hold her upright in her sudden imbalance. *My brother is here to kill me for what I know.* "What are you saying you are here to do, sweet brother?" She could no longer breathe. In fact, she was sure she hadn't breathed since he appeared. How she hadn't fainted from lack of air yet was a miracle of the Fives, surely.

"I haven't been your sweet brother since I was ten." Athan put a coercing hand on the middle of her back to usher her back to meet with Emberalda, Adyssaira, and Odysserae. "Just keep smiling and moving. I will be with you until the spell fades and your memories return."

She had to know. "And then?"

"I will ask you a question. You will know why I am here based on the answer you provide," he said with finality. It sounded like an ultimatum that would decide whether she lived or died by her own sibling's hand. Such was an absurd and nightmarish notion, she could not comprehend it.

"I cannot do this anymore, Athan! I don't want to. I don't know what to do." Her defeated tone slumped from a high pitch to a low murmur.

"Yes, you do. You will just keep smiling," he commanded, but this time it felt like his shepherding hand held a knife blade at her back. "And keep moving."

ADYSSAIRA (V)

OMEN

The whole mood of impervious merriment among the girls had been subverted by palpable unease. There seemed to be no strategy for recovery, and their leisurely meandering had become awkward ever since Athan appeared in the midst of their company. The uninviting aura he exuded ensured every bit of that.

Valaythea had unexpectedly returned with their older brother some two hours ago, yet he had uttered hardly a word and expressed no normal sentiments of a family member who hadn't seen his dear siblings in the past two cycles. The last time Adyssaira recalled seeing him, he had already taken a turn in his personality, which had waned from warm to cold, but this time he was near unrecognizable. If he hadn't been wearing the face of the brother she loved and thought she knew, then she would have sworn the young man beside them now was an imposter wearing some magical mask.

Truthfully, Adyssaira was scared of him. There was something dangerous about him. And she told herself she would still have held that opinion even if she hadn't been privy to the fact that Athan was an assassin of the Hive Order in the Oathemic Cabal.

While her sisters and cousin were all outfitted accordingly in festive seasonal dresses for the occasion of the faire, Athan was garbed from neck to toe in black leathers, with a hood drawn low to cover his brow and visible knives in sheaths on his belt, boots, and armbands. If she had been a guard commissioned for security measures on the festival grounds, then she imagined he would have been a prime target for her to investigate as suspicious, with his conspicuously unscrupulous appearance. But either the Suntide sentries were lazy and didn't care or they were somehow apprised of who he was, a mortal of immunity in Az'Dayne, and steered clear of confronting him.

They tried visiting some exotic-animal unveiling to lighten the ambience, but Athan never budged a muscle in his semblance, not even remotely entertained. Adyssaira tried telling him about her black tiger cub, left back at the estates, but she could tell he had no interest.

At dusk there was a firework show near the lake, which they all found absolutely entrancing—other than him, of course. He just stared blankly at the impressive display like the seemingly lifeless husk he had become. Emberalda was the only one audacious enough to futilely attempt banter with him, but her words fell on ears obviously more deaf than Odysserae's.

The only activity Athan participated in was stealing away Odysserae, his favorite of the sisters, for a short moment to sign up for a quick knife throwing tournament. They came back with Odysserae beaming the biggest grin, and surprisingly Athan smiling as well, which was an impossible feat to witness. Odysserae was bragging away in Hands explaining how they dominated the competition, and at the end she received an audience and applause for her display of skills on the targets with a makeshift rope dart she made on hand. Her detached brother showing any signs of mirth, however, was short lived soon after he reunited with the group.

Adyssaira was fatigued not long after, ready for their scheduled escort back to the inn on the route back to Castle Chandoss. As they were leaving their last carnival dome for the day, making their way toward the southern exit of the fairgrounds, she could hear one final pusher pitching his gimmick.

"Fortunes! Get your fortunes! Come see Omen and get your fortunes here!"

The crier was a young Psage boy likely in his early teens. The bald peddler was wearing far too many clothes for his skinny body, and all two sizes too big for him. He smacked a small rod around the inside of an iron triangle to draw attention to him like a bell. "One silver star, and her sight is yours! Omen's cards never lie!"

Adyssaira was numb to the annoying hustlers by now, and she was sure the rest of her party was as well. They had all learned it was best to avert their focus and never make eye contact with any of them to dissuade the aggressive vendors from pushing them too hard. Adyssaira was lucky in that her blindfold afforded her the ability to glance at all of them and not fall victim to such tactics. Either every festy knew who the lon'Chandoss girls were, for the most part, or they looked like an easy target of well-dressed rich kids roaming the spiders' webs.

"You, girl." The Psage crier boy pointed at Odysserae specifically when they started to walk past the fortune-teller's caravan. "Come, show me your star. Meet Omen inside. Your fortune awaits!"

Speaking to the wrong sister. She cannot hear how galling you sound. Adyssaira felt grumpier than she had in a while. All this walking all day and into the late hours of the evening was not in her normal curriculum. Her hand went up defensively around Odysserae's shoulder to shield her deaf sister from the crier.

"That is Odysserae," came an elderly voice as the rickety door to the caravan opened, and out came a blind Psage woman wearing a tight handkerchief around her scalp in place of hair. She then made the oddest gesture, saying "*Greetings, special one*" in Hands directed at Odysserae. "House Chandoss has arrived."

The wheeled wagon had a large sign leaning against its side: *Seerstone Read for a Fair Price*. The word made Adyssaira clutch at the gift Sundorion had intended for Valaythea, which Adyssaira had been carrying all this time. She had forgotten to give it to her sister but had brought it to the Suntide Faire for the exact purpose of doing so. Sundorion's seerstone was safely away in the satchel around her shoulder for now.

They were already a few paces past the caravan and could have gotten away free if they had just chosen to ignore the woman, but Emberalda seemed to be feeling rather feisty, as usual.

"I'll pay a star, but you must first tell me which of the Chandoss family we are," her cousin challenged.

The white-eyed soothsayer crossed her arms and accepted, spilling out her answer in her raspy old voice. "The last generation. All but the Z'shun and the runaway spellblade. Sashka and Nikayle the Fourthnamed are elsewhere, but it will cost you to know where."

Emberalda did not seem the least bit convinced and answered for all of them, ushering all to continue along. Athan evidently hadn't stopped moving and was far ahead now.

"She's a pretender," Emberalda shot back. "She's faking her blindness. Just another fool's parlor trick. Let's move on. Everyone knows of us around these parts."

Do not goad her! She will call me out for mine. They all heeded their bold cousin until the seer countered, repeating her remarks and fingers toward Adyssaira, exactly as she had feared. "If I am a pretender, then so is she. She is faking her blindness. Just another fool thinking she is fooling us not-so-good fools, it would seem."

"I don't like this caravan," Valaythea said. "Let's go to another."

Omen took a couple of steps down the railed stairs that led into the open caravan, calling them all out. "You richlings don't want the mundane. The cards are too lackluster, but they come without risk. This cannot do. You want the seerstone the sandling gave you, which has not been given to you, Valaythea. Take it. It was meant for you, as it was meant for me." Omen pointed at the satchel Adyssaira was carrying, calling her out.

Adyssaira knew it was time to show her sister what Sundorion had gifted her. A great feeling of reluctance overwhelmed her as she realized she did not want to see her future, if that was what Omen was proposing. "Yes, Val, I meant to give it to you. Sundorion gave us all gifts. Yours is this seerstone, if you want it."

She revealed the multicolored split rock to present it to her sister, and Valaythea accepted her belated gift. The melon-shaped stone was a geode of sorts, mixed with yellow-golds, orange-reds, silver-whites, grey-blacks, purple-blues, and bright greens in that order toward the center. Adyssaira had done strictly as Sundorion had bidden, and she had not tampered with Valaythea's gift. She had never seen a seerstone before this one, and she imagined neither had her sisters or cousin. But all of them had heard about the mystic properties of the unique tairan pieces, which the Psage culture was reported to mine in their homeland for visions of foresight.

Psages were the ones who named the upcoming cycles, by tradition during the Umbra season of the current cycle. Nearly every nation in the wide realm adhered to whatever came out of Psaegora by utilization of the seerstones. This had been a western tradition for over two centuries, and in more modern times it had caught on with the eastern countries as well. Before, the names, cycles, and years were more simply recorded in numbers followed by a suffix abbreviation in the timeline of things. For example, the Cycle of Kingfall, which all were currently within, was also known as Year 1515, Cycle 909 CTS, which stood for the Cataclysm of Taira's Scar.

Adyssaira remembered the specific cycles of her life, for the most part. The last before Kingfall had been the Cycle of Longstars, named rightfully for the bizarrely continuous shooting stars throughout those seasons. Earlier than that had been the Cycle of Southmaw, validated by the fact that it had been the era in which the Az'Dayne Dominadom had peaceably subjugated Barredom and seemed hungry to devour all that lay between. Then there had been the Cycle of Coldsight, for reasons unlearned by her. The next, the Cycle of Bluetrees and the Cycle of Firetides, had directly referenced the Thrench Empire's war to conquer the jungles of Julkunda, held by the Neveril and their Terollar allies. The territory had eventually become what was now known as New Throng after the Thrench had succeeded. Then the Cycle of Silverpeace came to mind, when Adyssaira had been around ten years of age. It had been a rare time of coin shortage across the major highways and capitals, which had brought a diplomatic amnesty among neighboring enemies. The Cycle of Skycrowns had been when the Thrench had decimated the now-endangered Vistaryl into reclusion. Then there had been the Cycle of Mistdrowned, when she and her sisters had been born. For some reason, Adyssaira could not conjure the names of the cycles in her first few years, before she had turned seven.

"That will kill her if she consumes the whole thing," Athan said, suddenly appearing beside them again and taking an apparent interest. "They are not meant for the untrained to attempt, and they are not meant to divine more than a single person's path. It is a precious and rare thing."

"This hag is a caver," Emberalda snapped, using a racist term for Psages. "Why would we care if it does? They are nothing but a blight on Az'Dayne."

Adyssaira joined in. "I hear they cost a king's penny to buy, and almost as much to read." A *king's penny* was a term of sarcasm for something absurdly expensive.

Omen, with her ruined and clouded eyes, just stared patiently through the lon'Chandoss siblings with an eerie grin, while the crier boy stood next to her.

Athan, being the obviously worldlier in such matters, answered. "Typically, yes. Usually used for a favor, not coin. Most Psages are gifted them by their family lines, passed down."

"This one, by name of Athaniel," the oracle stranger said, "he knows of the divination rocks. Seerstones are mined in Psaegora, from underneath the Insurmounts, or found in the frozen pockets of the Dendrallthae, where the Dendrar Elderlocks are whispered to harvest them."

Adyssaira could not believe any of them would actually consider partaking of such a morbid proposition. "You are offering to sacrifice yourself for us and consume our … Valaythea's seerstone?" She was staring at Omen now, not faking her blindness for the seemingly all-seeing augur. "But why for us?"

Omen moved inside the caravan, inviting them in to join her. Reluctantly, one by one, they did.

"The cards and bones have spoken to me," the old seer rasped, motioning to her grisly display on the table in the middle of the domed wagon.

There were seven cards laid face-up next to a stack of several others facing down. Three of the cards looked similar, with young feminine cats of different-colored fur that were crowned like princesses, and each with a different expression: one of fear, one of sadness, and one of anger. Another was a fox in a dress with a sly smile. And another card was a young sun owl with its eyes focused on an open tome. And the last two seemed to be opposing one another, one a black viper holding a dagger in its mouth against a separate card with a green cobra with a sword gripped in its tail.

"They have shown me your faces, the lon'Chandoss Seven, and that it is my destiny to show you each your own," Omen said.

How did she know we would even accept her invitation to see such, and furthermore attend the faire at all? Adyssaira felt perturbed even trying to fathom the phenomenon of clairvoyant precision versus such impractical probabilities. She wondered which of the cards was supposed to represent her and inwardly guessed the cat in the middle, the one with the pale lynx coat and green gems on her crown.

Also on the table, arrayed more like an altar than a surface for dining, were a set of wooden, leafy animal bones with a kind of green-tinted ichor seeping from them, and an eyeball and its stem in the middle. Adjacent, in a brazier the size of a plate, were various tiny vital organs that had been burned black prior to their arrival.

All around the inside of the mobile abode were different types and shapes of crystals, eccentric-looking rocks and roots, strange reagents, and jarred powders on shelves. Adyssaira saw a spilled mortar and pestle there and a foul-smelling bubbling caldron on a portable stove over there. Nothing in the caravan matched—so many different dyed fabrics that contrasted with the decem or so overly plush square cushions, and triple that many in specific candle arrangements.

Emberalda's disgusted semblance at spying something grotesque made Adyssaira look to survey the same. In a wicker cage hanging above the couch, which was fitted between the walls at the far end of the wagon, was a living creature unlike anything she had seen before. It was comparable to whatever had been dissected and broken apart on the table. At first glance, it almost resembled a squirrel, but it was more like the skeleton of one, yet its bones were made of true wooden stems, and diminutive sprouts of leaves ornamented its head and tail where there should have been fur. It squeaked and frantically moved like a squirrel but appeared more like a magically animated plant. She had heard Sundorion tell tall tales of strange plant-animal hybrids before, but she couldn't remember for the life of her what he had called them.

"This is witch shit," Emberalda declared. "Makes my skin crawl. And I don't like her face," she said with an acrid grimace.

"How ..." Valaythea uttered in a hesitance, "how much? What is the cost for such an ultimate service?"

"Two thousand doms," Omen stated with an air of confidence at the fact that together the wealthy, privileged lot could rally the outrageous sum.

Emberalda was not having it. "Ha! She's no witch! Just a bitch. A conning, conniving, greedy festy, just like the rest touting their wares from tent to tent. Athan, you should take her false sign. Two thousand doms is no fair price!"

Athan seemed to affirm their cousin's opinion in his own way. "I don't need to see your version of my fate. I already know I die young and that it ends in blood."

The old oracle appeared to have all the patience in the world to await their answer. *Or perhaps she already knows our answer,* Adyssaira uncomfortably presumed as she took another glance at the witchcraft paraphernalia all around them.

"I think I want to know," Valaythea admitted as she reached out to grab Adyssaira's hand in her own.

"We should vote on it," she half-heartedly agreed.

Odysserae went to join in and grab Valaythea's hand on the other side, as a sign of her concurrence.

"I think it would be fun to know," Adyssaira fibbed, but then she brought up the more pressing dilemma. "But we don't have that kind of price on us."

"Fuck it," their tactless cousin puffed out. "I'll pay to watch the witch kill herself in front of us. Most excitement all day. Fittingly dark." She reached into her fancy satchel to draw out a handful of extravagant trinkets and flawlessly cut gems. "Tell me what these treasures are worth."

"Ember, where in the Fives did you come by—" Valaythea tried to inquire, but Emberalda was fast to interrupt with an explanation.

"Timm. When he left me. He clearly didn't want them, so I took them as a parting gift." Her voice slightly cracked with masked sorrow. "I hoped something in this dull faire would be worth their loss."

Adyssaira turned the attention back on Omen. "Why do you want all of this if you are only going to the Godslands after? You cannot take this material stuff with you."

"Oh, dear, innocent Adyssaira." Omen turned in her direction, looking through her with those disturbing white orbs. "I am not going to the Godslands after this. But I am going to die indeed. This will buy my family out of the streets in Az'Dayne and save them and their children's children from a lifetime of poverty."

Omen clapped her hands. "Simban, come in here."

The crier boy rushed in so fast, he nearly tripped over. "Grandmama?" Simban's eyes began to well with tears. "Is it time?"

Omen looked over toward Emberalda now, then scanned the caravan to find each of them, not answering her grandson's dire question. "Is this what you wish? This feat is final. You may not wish to hear what I come to see. It may forever change each of you."

Emberalda ignored the seer's warning. "It won't change me. But yes, I am securing this trade for your sacrificial services, witch."

As Adyssaira's cousin handed over the satchel of valuables, Omen did face her grandson one last time, and she handed the purse directly into his possession. "You know what to do, my darling boy. Take it. Go now." She kissed Simban on the top of his hairless scalp.

Adyssaira was sure that if Omen's ruined eyes still had the capacity for tears, the old witch would have been crying herself in that moment. "Thank you all." Omen addressed the lon'Chandoss group in sincerity.

"Grandmama." Simban kissed his elder's hands and tiptoed up to place his lips on her open eyes. Then, strangely, the crier boy turned to kiss Emberalda's hands as well, which Adyssaira was surprised her cousin did not flinch from. "Thank you."

Omen hobbled over to retrieve the seerstone from Valaythea, then navigated to the lone couch, which sat at the perfect height for the low table that displayed all the cards, wooden bones, and fleshy guts. "Whoever does not wish to take part in the seerstone experience, you should now leave."

She paused as she carefully sat her weary body down and began tossing out large cushions to the floor on all sides and corners of the table. "Those who wish to stay, sit now."

Each girl sat on a different-colored cushion in the order of Emberalda, Odysserae, Adyssaira, and Valaythea on the end closest to Omen, the same as Emberalda but on the opposite side.

Athan hesitated, looming over them. Adyssaira could tell he was contemplating all scenarios for what might go awry in this incomprehensible act of foretelling. Her brother put one of his knives down on the table, with the point facing Omen, and then took his seat opposite the seer, moving Odysserae and Adyssaira to sit between them. "Be careful in confessing what it is you think you see."

Omen responded without a sliver of fear. "My life can no longer be threatened. My words will be tied to the vision of the stone. You will hear, and you will all heed," she promised, and then looked directly at Adyssaira. "And you can remove that sash from around your eyes now, girl. All in this room know I am the only blind one here. See without fear for once."

Hesitantly, Adyssaira did just that, removing her blindfold after judging the acceptance and permission of her family around her. Then the door suddenly shut, making all but Athan jump and gasp. The ritual was commencing.

Omen took the seerstone in her hands, her fingernails so long and yellow they resembled claws, and she began prying away seven chunks from the geode in the size of small dates. She only filed away the orange-red and yellow-gold conglomerations that were connected to one another at first. Curiously enough, the segregated crystal masses began to glow brightly once removed from the geode. Omen then stripped the green centric pieces from the geode, which seemed to be made up of something much more brittle than the rock. She grabbed the pestle to scatter the green substance over the pulled pieces put in the mortar and ground everything down to a spongy crystalline powder.

"Let this represent the seven Chandoss children. Touch the powder and let it stain your fingers; then hold hands and do not let go until it is done. Athaniel, Emberalda, Valaythea, Adyssaira, Odysserae. Two others, not present, Nikayle the Fourthnamed, hailing himself as Barturon lon'Chandoss now, and Sashka the Z'shun, we will see their fates as well."

They all did as bidden and let the oracle continue.

"It has not been done by any Psage I know, this many at a time. Be prepared for the worst," Omen forewarned.

"Get on with what I paid for" was all that Emberalda had to say as the voice of the group.

The old witch whispered as she took all the pulsating crystal mash in her palms to bring it up to her mouth. "Omen's final omen," she rasped just before devouring the powder like a famished fiend.

The soothsayer's ravenous feasting on the edible glowing rocks was alone enough to steal the nerve from the party within the enclosed caravan. She crunched and chewed, eventually shoving the contents of the entire mixing bowl into her careworn mouth, which evolved into an impossibly wide, inhuman-looking gaping maw.

"Change," Omen uttered as the veins in her neck and arms began to protrude. "Great change in the blood sisters." She started to tremble in a fit just before spitting up bile and blood, which landed on three similar cat cards below.

Um, I think one of those is me.

"In the Z'shun, gone she is now. Gone she will remain. Gone she must stay," Omen forewarned.

"Barturon lon'Chandoss," she went on to insinuate their runaway cousin, "his destiny realigns with two in this room. One he will train. One he will confront. The outcome is evitable."

Adyssaira felt Athan shift uneasily at the mention of Nikayle involving two of them. It had been so long since she had seen Nikayle that she often dismissed if he would ever play a part in their future again. *Train one of us? Train us how*, she wondered.

"For the assassin," the seer began to rock her woozy head in a slow rotation as if she had just suffered a dizzy wave. "Ah, I can tell you —"

"Skip the assassin," Athan interjected promptly. Adyssaira had never heard her brother's voice sound so stern. "Do not say it."

He was breathing heavy and his palms had become sweaty to match Adyssaira's own. Omen sat quiet for some time, locked in whatever portending avenues she had succumbed to through the seerstone, forcing Adyssaira to hear the other girls' panting uncomfortably as well.

"For these four," Omen shuffled the three cats and the fox together one by one over one another. "For these four," she gasped and winced in pain. She pulled the handkerchief from her scalp and laid her forehead down to the table to rest inside the mined geode.

For what felt like a minute, nothing came. Only the sound of Omen compulsively shuffling the cats over the fox in no particular method to her madness. Adyssaira looked around at her siblings and cousin, all seeming to share the same sentiment of general disappointment. The five remained holding hands around the table, not budging, however.

"Murder!" Omen awoke from whatever vision she had passed into. Her neck writhed upward, and her head swayed in circles with her eyes to the ceiling. "And more murder," she squealed, as she shoved the fox card inside her mouth and began chewing it to shreds.

"Who the fuck was that?" Emberalda insisted, wide-eyed and appalled.

"I," Omen started, "it hurts," she twitched, "must choose … a path … before it takes me. Before," she grunted in agony, "you die. So much death." Her bald head plopped so hard to the table it shook the owl card completely off.

Is she dead? Adyssaira glanced over at her brother, hoping he knew all the answers to decipher the witch's drivel, but Athan let Omen continue.

"What? Murder?" Adyssaira blurted, not caring if she was interrupting the seerstone ritual.

"Who dies?" Valaythea squeaked as well, visibly covered in fear and confusion.

"All but one in this room ... All but one will die by the Kingfall's Torrent," Omen's voice was barely audible, but the words were unmistakable, with her face and lips still pressed hard to the table. The seer's head rose and slammed to the table again so hard, blood began pooling out of her nose and mouth. The gnawed-up card in her mouth began to slide out with the blood.

She is definitely dead now. But Adyssaira refused to be the first one to release her hands. She assumed it would be Emberalda, but her cousin was relentless in her curiosity now. Her eyes were as bewitched as those of Adyssaira's sisters next to her. Athan's face, on the other hand, was stained with a scowl of annoyance.

"Oh, my fucking Fives! Who is the fox?" Emberalda pleaded, trying to pull her hand free of Odysserae, but the deaf girl's strength prevailed. She seemed more focused on Omen's foretelling than any in the room.

"Silence!" Athan barked, squeezing his grip hard.

Ouch, Athan!

"Let her finish," her brother demanded.

Omen slowly rose as her spine elevated her posture back up, but her limp neck seemed dead or asleep, making her head awkwardly tilt to the side. "Betrayals." She spoke with spatters of blood spraying from her mouth as she attempted to convey the seerstone's revelation. "I am sorry."

The strange oracle broke her hands free from the circle and suddenly snatched Odysserae by the wrist and then Emberalda by her wrist at the same time. "I am sorry!" Omen's eyes fixed on her cousin's horrorstruck gaze in the same terror.

The Psage then turned her judging glare in fury on Odysserae. "Tell her how sorry you are!"

Before anyone had time to process Omen's antics the seer did the same to Valaythea and Adyssaira, grabbing them both by the wrist simultaneously. "I am so sorry," Omen sobbed while facing Adyssaira. "I did not mean to! I am sorry, I am sorry, I am sorry, I am sorry," she repeated and cried so dramatically that actual tears formed down the Psage's cheeks.

I don't like this, Adyssaira's eyes mirrored the look of concern in Valaythea, both perturbed by the bizarre scenario. *Who is sorry?* She felt like pleading for someone outside in the faire to come to the witch's aid, but she continued to sit as still as stone. The seer's white orbs had sunk slightly in their sockets, and the sockets ... *My Fives, are they getting larger?*

Her eye sockets were indeed enlarging, and her orbs were definitely vanishing into her skull. Veins were bursting beneath her skin. Her grip then clamped down to couple Valaythea and Odysserae together in her nonsensical charade.

"Forgive me!" Omen shouted at Odysserae.

"No," she seethed back at Valaythea.

Omen's bugged-out eyes were so sincere when she begged Odysserae again, "Please!"

"Never!" Omen defied back on Valaythea in livid vehemence. The next words choked on a glob of more blood, which was projected across the table.

Adyssaira was too horrified to dare move at this point. She wanted to study the faces of her family around her, but somehow she couldn't take her paralyzed gaze off the rapid deterioration of Omen. It was sick and scary, but she could not turn away.

"Change," Omen tried again, but her body's failure under the seerstone's lethal effects was draining her frail frame of all life. "Betrayal." Blood came pooling from her orifices. "Murder," she gurgled her last words. "You ..."

Suddenly Omen stood up and attempted to grab both of her palms around Athan's, but her brother was deftly quick. Athan parried the unsolicited vision by thrashing the seer's arms back down at her sides. The momentum only sent Omen forward toward the center of the table where her head collided, and somehow they all knew it wasn't coming back up this time. There would be no more words to divine. There was just silence. Silence and family.

Adyssaira felt like crying, but no tears came. She believed she had sweated them all out into her hands, which were still holding on tight to Valaythea's.

Somewhere in all the chaos the five of them had taken it upon themselves to stand beside one another, no longer sitting in the circle. Each transfixed by their own look of bewilderment, they uttered not a sound as they stared at the dead Psage. They didn't let go of each other's hands. Omen's omen was too much to dwell on.

SYMBELLE & FYHEIR (V)

ADVERSARY ASSESSMENT

The small vessel carrying them seemed to be crawling at the same speed as the pedestrians on the streets above them on the leisurely ride through the water roads of Canaltown. The propulsion was provided by one man standing at the stern with an excessively long pole in both hands. He rarely sat to use his paddle. Other than him, it was just Symbelle and five other men.

All had been strangers just a few hours back, before leaving Bridgeville, but by the night's prime, Symbelle was sure she could have sold each of their exaggerated stories of the hard sellsword life to a broke bard for a handful of moon coins. She didn't care to remember their names. She knew most would be dead at the journey's end, and whichever one was allowed to survive would likely be picked at random. The only one she cared to recall by name was the one sitting next to her, with the most repugnant breath. It reeked of sour ale, old food in his teeth, and maybe even a little shit. He had introduced himself as Samsey, and he had introduced himself twenty-odd times already. The other Boarnecks she just nicknamed for their looks or bad habits: Spitter, Gawker, One-Thumb, and Blisters.

The anticipated ambush couldn't come soon enough. Symbelle had received word that Usurp's thugs would be lying in wait at the pickup point and that they had been instructed to put on a show to assault her but not hurt her. What they didn't know was that Symbelle had been given strict orders by Scarless to kill Usurp's men and that even Usurp knew about it. They were just fodder to be used in the sick game played between gangs and killers.

The ploy was to have the Boarnecks believe they were picking up a shipment of rare medicinal supplies that only Symbelle, with her expertise, could identify, and they were to commence the ambush then and make it look as real as possible. For peace of mind, she had been informed that Usurp and Uubakrath would be on-site, in hiding, for her safety in case things went awry.

At least one Boarneck had to survive to tell the tale of her skills, in hopes that she would soon be awarded an audience with the mercenary leader, Oldan Boldandgold himself. Ten days in, and she still hadn't been honored with an audience. She had been drudging away throughout Bridgeville, getting to know the lower ranks of the local Boarneck sellswords and paid-off city guards.

It had been eleven days since she had heard from Fyheir. It should have been a peaceful concept to contemplate, that perhaps she was finally cured of her internal, malicious alternate personality. But that was not the case. All Symbelle could dwell on was how she must have affronted or displeased Fyheir, or how she had somehow accidentally acquired the willpower to permanently suppress it to where it could not conjure itself back to the surface of her mind.

Symbelle had never fought before. She had no formal training in combat whatsoever. She had never killed anyone and wasn't sure she could bring herself to actually do it. It was Fyheir who had burned all the people at Tairanchula. It was Fyheir who had killed the Neveril in the Oathemic Cabal's laboratory beneath the Plaguefolk Villages. It was Fyheir who had to be here to do this.

Symbelle got more nervous as they neared the docking point, now in sight. She had had all day to dwell on a hundred ways in which she might try to kill whatever strangers lay in wait on the streets ashore just ahead—strangers that were Stormtrees who believed she was their ally and had no inkling that she was about to betray them.

"You are going to betray the Stormtrees anyway in the end, you idiot," she whispered to herself, hoping the rocking of the boat and sounds of the city were enough to drown out her words. She needed all the self-reassurance she could muster to go through with such treachery. She had well known her mission all along as a new agent of the Cabal was indeed to eliminate Scarless, as well as Oldan of the Boarnecks and Amethyst on the Seven Seats council. This list of writs before her was something more fit for a team of veteran assassins. And here she was worried to kill just one or two lowly thugs.

"Lowly thugs," she uttered to herself, warming up her hands by rubbing them over and over each other, even though the night was absent of any chill. "You can kill lowly thugs."

"Ye just called me an idiot unner yer breath earlier. Now y'said a low thug?" Samsey demanded with a blast of hot air assaulting her nostrils.

"No" was all she could fail at intelligently outarguing him with. She stared in defense back at the lot of them looking at her in the cramped, narrow boat. Gawker just gawked, while Spitter spat, and One-Thumb chewed on his only thumb, and Blisters picked at the scabs of his blisters.

"Fee for a wait? Fee for a ride back?" The boatman ignored the probable debate in front of him as he steered the group up to the water-road stairs, which served just as well as a dock.

"Oh, ye're waitin'." Samsey slapped a couple of coins in the boatman's palm, then slapped down some more with his other hand. "And ye'll keep that mouth shut if ye like that throat and wakin' up in the mornin'! We got cargo comin' on. Keep yer eyes down, paddler," he warned.

And as One-Thumb used his thumb to gesture slitting his own throat, the boatman did just that and stuffed the money away in his pockets and didn't take his focus off his feet.

They disembarked onto street level up another flight of steps and only had to walk one block to get to where Symbelle had been told the false rendezvous would be—behind the alley between the abandoned cobbler's shop and house on the corner of Segmon Street and Roach Street.

Symbelle checked over her gear—the bandolier harness, vial-pocket bracers, and belt—for the thirtieth time in thirty minutes. *Blink bomb – one, check. Smoke bombs – two, check. Skinny dust – bellows, check. Blast-salt vials – six, check. Sparkler sticks – six, check. Screamer – one, check. Flash bomb – one, check.*

"Fyheir?" she queried quietly, checking for her most vital missing weapon.

And there was a flame. In the distance, at the end of the alley, a lantern had been sat on the ground by a wagon that had a few visible crates in the back. "Tell me that is you." She tried again, barely making the words audible, now begging for her friend to return to her in her dire time of need before it was too late.

"That's gotta be the mark," declared Samsey eagerly.

The oblivious Boarnecks rushed forward on Samsey's tail as Symbelle trod cautiously with her eyes on the rooftops. She reached for the undersight potion in her belt, and her heart stopped when her fingers fumbled at the missing flask. "Wait. I didn't pack it." She didn't even realize she was still whispering aloud. "The undersight. I … I need it! I can't see in the dark. We have to … to go back," she stuttered, suffering from heaving anxiety now.

Spitter, holding a torch, shouted behind him, unconvinced. "Then light a fuckin' fire. I thought you were s'posed t'be some fire witch that can see shit everywhere, anyway."

"Where the fuck's the dealers?" Blisters asked in worriment.

"Hey!" Samsey shouted, inspecting the suspicious crates filled with only hay in the lantern-lit wagon as the mercenaries surrounded it one by one. He seemed to be addressing a lone shadowy figure of extremely tall stature standing in the corner nearest the wagon. His hand stayed on his hand axe at his hip as he probed. "Ye our dealer? What's all this?"

Symbelle didn't like it one bit. She closed her eyes, knowing it was about to start. She reopened them to the flash of the shadowed man's own torch flaring up to reveal who he was.

"I'll be your dealer, dead men," Usurp said, throwing his torch into the hay on the wagon.

"Stormtrees! Ambush!" Blisters shouted out just in time to catch Usurp's heavy war maul hacking down directly onto the crest of his skull, splitting it wide open.

The wagon was set ablaze, and it began.

Usurp's thugs came pouring out of the cobbler's abode with murder on their faces. The first in line was unlucky enough to get his baggy vestments set on fire by Spitter's torch, which he was thrashing about like a weapon.

There were eight of them with Usurp included. Symbelle had no idea how they intended for her to survive this encounter with at least one witness and pull off any sort of realism to be reported back to the Boarneck Company to boost her reputation, as intended for the grisly drama.

It was too much chaos to keep track of for the untrained martial practitioner or someone who had no rough street experiences. She could barely keep track of who was fighting whom or who was winning or losing. She could see that the Boarnecks were seemingly better experts in this field than the lot Usurp was throwing at them, which was at least affording her time to do something with her hands, which hadn't moved yet.

For some reason, none of them were approaching her yet, and she wasn't complaining. She forgot what role she was even supposed to play as she became mesmerized by her first scenario of battle and bloodshed. This was why she never saw Usurp's hand coming. It gripped her around the neck and lifted her petite frame like she was a feather.

The brutish Vellyan tossed her just inside the doorway of the cobbler's old home and didn't skip a heartbeat to prove his point. He had dropped his maul to use both hands. He placed one of his massive palms over her mouth to silence her and control her head, while the other cupped the back of her neck, forcing her to drop lower until her eyes were staring just below his waist.

"You think I would forget that backhand I got from Scarless 'cause of you? I did say you were gonna go down today, didn't I, skinny?" Usurp took his hand from her mouth to plug her nostrils with two of his massive fingers, forcing her to finally take a gasp through her mouth, and then began to simulate humping, thrusting his member into her face while his pants were still on. As he started to fiddle with the laces to loosen his breeches, he continued. "When I'm done cockin' this ugly face, maybe my bull milk'll give you some wits to stop pissin' like a fairy and kill somethin' out there!"

Do you miss us, though?

"Fyheir!" Symbelle screamed in mercy as Usurp dropped his pants.

But we have a lot to talk about. Tell us you miss us, and mean it.

"I miss you!"

The Stormtrees overlord started laughing, stilling just for a moment to look down at her, flattered but entirely confused. "You say some weird shit before a proper face fuck, skinny. Now shut up and open back up. I'll still let you win this fight if you swallow right."

We've missed our Symbelle too, Fyheir purred in Symbelle's panicked mind. *Rest now. You can watch. We are here.*

Symbelle willingly relinquished control to allow just that, and she could feel Fyheir taking control of her emotions and body. The voice would be Symbelle's, but the tone was clearly Fyheir's. "Wait! I need my goggles on. To see you better."

Usurp scowled down at Symbelle with an impatient countenance and took his hands off her so Fyheir could proceed with placing her protective goggles over her glowing hyperi eyes. Fyheir looked up at the Vellyan with a mischievous grin, and he matched it, feeling an invitation to the sexual crescendo. But he could not have anticipated Fyheir's intent.

"Don't ever lose eye contact. Stare back at me."

And when the gullible miscreant did, Fyheir acted in an instant, with a flash-bomb flask shattered between his feet. It burst into a blinding white light over the entire house and out the door.

Fyheir did not hesitate to escape the Vellyan's unquestionably overpowering strength as he now blindly flailed about, searching for his dropped maul. And Fyheir was out the door as fast as it dared to strike him.

Gawker and One-Thumb are dead ... but so are two of theirs ... I mean ours ... I mean the Stormtrees. Symbelle considered her confusion, not quite sure who she even was anymore.

Fyheir ignored it all and did what it did best—killed without mercy in a ruthless fashion.

Fyheir palmed two of the blast-salt vials and threw one to shatter on the back of the Stormtree thug that was still on fire from Spitter's torch. He nearly disintegrated before Symbelle's eyes in an instant red combustion of melted flesh and bone. The other vial Fyheir tossed into the back of the burning wagon to cause an explosion that shot fiery shrapnel through the back of another casualty.

Two other Stormtree assailants charged at Symbelle with knives out, as if they didn't care to heed the warning only to rough her up, after witnessing Fyheir's fatal intent. Fyheir pulled up the bellows with the skinny-dust canister attached to the nozzle and squeezed them with perfect timing to catch them both in the face before they reached Symbelle. Both men went down choking on the abundance of the drug, instantly overdosing with a mind-crippling effect of fear and energy depletion.

Symbelle just watched as a spectator as Fyheir controlled her every movement, grabbing the nearest of the men by the jaw and effortlessly prying open his mouth. Fyheir's eyes were manic with gratuitous aversion to the stranger. It shoved one of the smoke bombs inside his mouth and pulled the cork before slamming his jaw shut and shattering the glass flask to bring the contents within into reaction. The man futilely heaved for air when there was only a surplus of smoke to choke him down to death.

The other Stormtree was just quivering in dread, looking up at Fyheir. No longer able to stand, he was balled up on his knees from the effects of the skinny dust already in his nerves. Fyheir bent down to his horrified face and rubbed Symbelle's thumb across her fool's frown from both sides of her lips, as if the gesture was to initiate the insane smile that stained her face after.

"Run," Fyheir commanded, still grinning so much, Symbelle could feel the pain of her cheeks stretching.

And strangely, the man did, hobbling straight into the fire, to choose death by burning rather than be near the monster of Fyheir that Symbelle had transformed into.

There was only one left besides Usurp, who she presumed and hoped was still inside the house, disoriented from the flash bomb. When Fyheir turned around, Symbelle saw Spitter trying to recover from apparent unconsciousness and Samsey fleeing the scene back to the boat. The last Stormtree thug was already on her, slashed his long knife across her right shoulder, missing his mark—her heart.

Fyheir almost dropped the bellows to try to wrestle the stronger goon off, but it didn't have to. A random stray arrow shot down from one of the rooftops caught him through the lungs, ending his fight. Fyheir peered through the darkness to find the archer, who Symbelle assumed was Uubakrath, but the stealthy Terollar elvan was nowhere to be found.

Spitter was now back on his feet and rushing for the boat the same as Samsey, and Fyheir joined them just behind. The city watch could be heard already hastening to the fire and small massacre. Fyheir produced a small chemical-filled stick from Symbelle's bandolier, ripped out the string at the end of it, and threw it as far as Symbelle imagined she had ever had the strength to. It soared threw the missing window on the top floor of another dilapidated home. Within seconds, the screamer stick did exactly as she had designed it to do—it began wailing and whistling like mock cries of agony from inside the house.

She hoped it would cause enough of a diversion to allow their escape back to the canal. And fortunately, their attempt to flee went unimpeded. They reached the boatman and hurriedly embarked on their journey back down the water road.

No words came from anyone for several minutes. Not even from the boatman, who seemed too scared to know too much from the three of them. Samsey and Spitter just stared wide-eyed at her in fear and respect.

"Ye just take down Usurp in all that?" Samsey had to ask aloud to believe it.

"This bitch took down almost all of 'em by 'erself," Spitter attested.

Be sure to report that back to your leader, Oldan. It is time I get my audience with him, she thought she said.

But Symbelle was still Fyheir. And Fyheir didn't say a word back to them. Fyheir just sat displaying that same eerie, wicked grin.

VALAYTHEA (V)

TO KNOW THE KNOW

The Echo Wing was rightfully named by the firstborn daughter of Aemenus Chandoss, Emberalda, whom Valaythea's cousin was named after. The legend told that little Emberalda died at just nine years of age due to a collapse in the shoring during the development of the substructure that Aemenus was building beneath the main palace. Whatever plans Aemenus had intended for the vault levels of Castle Chandoss, no one had ever come to find out, as the construction of it died with his daughter that same day. As generations aged the Chandoss line honored the behest of Aemenus, and ever since, the Echo Wing remained an empty, almost-forgotten underground corner of the palace.

The moniker remained in tribute of what the young girl had nicknamed the sublevels to be. And the echoes were there, amplifying the sound of every step Valaythea made as she hasted toward the only source of light at the end of the fragmentary corridor.

The hall was as wide as the courtyard and the vaulted ceilings arched above her head as high as the palace gates, likely some four floors tall she guessed. There was no fine ornamentation as seen in the rest of palace, just drab brick that smelt like dust and old death. There were several recesses on both sides down the hall that went up wide steps leading to a vacant dais, as if something glorious was intended to be on exhibit but never got its chance to be seen.

She was armed with only a lantern, but she now wished she had intreated with the Chandoss Guard for an escort. Valaythea was aware that such a request would be vain though. Not a soul in Castle Chandoss was permitted into the Echo Wing other than Count Valdean himself, unless he invited you. And she had been invited, which may as well translate to being commanded.

Valaythea, with her siblings and cousin, hadn't even passed

through the outer farms on the Fairefare Road, returning from Suntide, when she received a courier's message from her great-granduncle to meet him straightaway before she even considered to settle in from the long ride. Upon arriving at her home palace, Valaythea could not help but feel a tinge of resentment toward Valdean for rushing her homecoming back with no warming welcome at the gates. She wasn't even permitted to clean up or change from her riding attire, but instead was whisked away by familiar stewards who ushered her to the forbidden Echo Wing.

As Valaythea neared the only room in the subterranean great hall she was again haunted by the inauspicious spectacle she had just witnessed with her family at the faire. The omen of Omen was easily the most nightmarish ordeal she had ever encountered in her life.

The way the Psage seer's face contorted into a dramatically agonizing death was not even the most horrific part of it. It was the witch's foreboding words of a dark future looming over each of them. The way she was apologizing, insinuating and heralding murder and betrayal between her sisters and cousin was something she kept trying to shake from memory. If only Coldborn could appear again and cast another shadow spell on her to take that whole evening from her mind as well, she knew she would be as blissfully indebted.

During the ride back from Fairetown there was hardly a word uttered from Adyssaira or Emberalda. They were as silent as Athan and Odysserae, which was a hard feat to accomplish. It was an awkwardly long canter south with all mirth sapped from the seerstone seance in Omen's caravan. It remained an unspoken understanding amongst the five to never speak of it again.

The end of Echo's Wing on two sides of the wall was nothing more than an impassable mass of stone rubble that had never found a use in the discontinued expansion of Aemenus's derelict lair. But to Valaythea's left, outlined in red glowing crystals, was the only door in the wing other than the one at the entrance she came in at. The crystals brightened the closer she approached the door, as if they were feeding off of her body heat. The way the translucent spiked rocks were asymmetrically placed around the door almost seemed chaotically natural, as if they were growing from underneath the frame, rather than fixed there by man. Valaythea had never seen anything like it.

Valaythea hesitantly opened the door. The first face she saw was Odysserae's, instantly making her more at ease to step inside.

Her sister was standing beside Valdean as he sat at a desk littered with blank parchment, rolled scrolls, and scribing utensils. Odysserae too was wearing her same attire from the ride of course, but how she could have possibly beaten Valaythea to the location, and without Valaythea taking any notice, was an enigma to question. Her strange sister had always been the quiet one, and "full of more secrets than the Cabal" was the common family joke.

Valdean's hideaway itself seemed to also be keen for keeping secrets. It may have been the lone room in the Echo Wing but there weren't any echoes escaping its wall. Overstuffed leather pillows were stitched together in a diamond checkered pattern throughout the entirety of the wall and ceiling. While one cushion was red, the next would be black, and so forth repeating.

One could argue the purpose of such a bizarre composition for the refuge was to serve as a sound dampener, but it was clearly more of a heat trap Valaythea realized as she wasn't in the room but for a few seconds before the sweat came on. There must have been half a hundred candles in the small chamber. They were lit on small stone altars in the four corners, and a few on the desk. Other than the illuminated shrines and the center-placed desk, the only other furnishings to note were the chair Valdean composed himself in, and the one across from the desk on the other side.

The Count of Chandoshia. Valaythea said her great-granduncle's title in her head as a reminder to never forget it. The count was indisputably the ruler of the Chandoss Estates as well as the broad countryside from as north to Emerald Point to as south as Toil, but that did not mean Valaythea had ever come to know him nor feel any familial bond from the ambiguous man. He was an enterprising magnate who operated from the shadows since as far back as the histories mentioned him, and he seemed to be fine with that. Even when Valaythea still lived in the palace, it was not uncommon to go a few seasons or even a full cycle without ever crossing paths with her great-granduncle. He was where he was, and he did what he did, and that was the end of it. No one was ever allowed to ask.

Valdean's eyes never left Valaythea's as she entered, but she took note that his right hand remained inappropriately cupped to

Odysserae's hip, subtly fondling the shape of it up and down. She could feel the tiny muscles in her face inadvertently cringe while inspecting the open act of molestation, though she futilely tried to hide her distaste. Valaythea hoped to catch her sister's attention but Odysserae only despondently scrutinized the floor between them.

"Welcome home," Valdean initiated in his cracked voice and habitual meticulous tone. "Am I looking at a woman before me now, and no longer a child?"

As he asked the question his hand never seized from caressing Odysserae. Her great-granduncle matched his years in every bit of elderly appeal, just under eight decades old. His tan skin seemed leather tight, his ears and nose larger than the rest of his features, and his dark amber eyes studying; always studying. His grey hair was thin in the back and brushed back tight against his scalp that stopped just above his neckline. He wore a splendid robe with a high collar and embroidered lapel and cuffs that matched the checkered colors in the room. And around his neck hung a medallion, *the* Medallion of House Chandoss with their legacy symbol minted in.

"Count," Valaythea fumbled on how to properly respect him when speaking. "Great-Granduncle." She humbly curtsied.

"You look unwell," he bluntly called her out.

Because of where I am right now. And because of what we just dealt with at Suntide, her eyes pleaded to Odysserae to sympathize.

Odysserae moved her fingers to convey a message in Hands to Valdean. *"Sour pies from Suntide. We all had them. The ride went ill for most of us."*

"Pies?" Valdean glanced at both sisters suspiciously unsure.

"Yes, the pies," Valaythea confirmed the lie. *Thank you, Oddy,* she translated with her eyes to her sister.

"Leave us," Valdean gestured to Odysserae when he let go of the back of her thigh.

Odysserae bowed to Valdean and left promptly without a single look to her sister. It was no secret to every resident in Castle Chandoss that Odysserae had been Valdean's chosen servant for the past year, but the mystery still remained as to why. Valaythea never hated it for her until now. She wanted to help Odysserae, but had no idea how, or even what was entailed behind the scenes for her.

"Sit Valaythea," her great-granduncle asserted, motioning to the chair across from him.

She did, and he continued. "I am calling a banquet with the family at dusk. But before we delve into those pressing matters, you and I have much to discuss."

"Yes, sire," Valaythea respected back attentively. "What do you wish to discuss?"

"I want you to tell me everything you and the prince spoke of. Reveal to me what he revealed to you," he said with an eerie grin, while rolling an ink quill over between his fingers, one by one, almost as if he had a compulsion disorder to put his right hand to motion at all times.

"We took a grand tour through Everdawn," she complied, "all of the great sectors of the capital. Prince Izayus was most kind to me, and most generous. Just before I was permitted this hiatus to join family at the Suntide Faire, I was given the most exotic gift. A baby beast from across the eastern seas, brought in all the way from Majamn. He called it a giraffe. It has the longest—"

Valdean slammed his fist into the desk, snapping the dried up quill in pieces. His action was violent, his teeth were together, but his tone never shifted from calm. "I have never been a partisan of fools. I am not a fool. I strive to believe that none who carry my house name are fools. Why then should we treat one another as so?"

Valaythea shook her head, not sure how much she should tell him. *It is your duty to tell him. He is the head of the family, the Count of Chandoshia.* "I fear you will not believe the truth." *Why did you tell him that?* She berated herself the moment she did it.

Valdean sat back in his chair, sneering in a confident but conniving manner, assessing her like a master would a novice he was about to strike down. "I cannot chastise your reason to fear me. May you dream in peace knowing I have seen and heard more than I care to believe in a hundred lifetimes."

Am I supposed to not say anything? Coldborn and Izayus did not tell me. They said to speak to only Uncle Nikayle … "The truth is that I do not remember," she felt safe with that truthful answer.

"What an unsatisfactory reply," Valdean seethed, as he carefully began plucking a piece of parchment apart piece by piece in the most miniscule shreds. "What a vexing, unsatisfactory reply."

"I do not recall a thing," she stated assuredly again. "Something happened to make me forget." *You need to stop there. I have said enough.*

"This room is safe. Think of it as a chamber of secrets," her great-granduncle waved his arms outward and about as if there was something Valaythea was supposed to catch on to about the altars or cushioned walls. "I will come to learn yours before you leave, and you will come to know mine, to know the Know, as I have long yearned for you to."

When he put his arms back down, she could swear to the Fives that something was different about him. His grey hair wasn't balding in the back as before, and his nose and ears seemed ... *No, it is just the lighting. That is silly. Focus.*

"Great-Granduncle please," *I have to tell him. He will know if I lie. I have a duty to this family over the prince or Coldborn.* "A spell was cast on me. I dare not deceive you," she promised.

"A spell? Does Prince Izayus know?" Valdean seemed completely caught off guard with that unanticipated revelation.

"He was there. Yes. Someone named Coldborn. He is who," Valaythea stopped herself from revealing anymore, shaking her head in self-disappointment for the predicament she had cornered herself in.

There was a long silence in the room. Valdean was palpably concerned the moment she said the name *Coldborn*. It was obvious he knew who he was, not only from the archmage's famous sobriquet, but furthermore because of some deep history between the two.

Valaythea fretfully glanced around the room to the shrines, half-expecting the Umbra mage to appear from the shadows and smite her down with dark magic upon any second.

Valdean's hair seemed thicker and less grey in the light she thought when she looked back at him. "What did Coldborn want with the Prince of Az'Dayne?"

His inquiry was voiced with critical concern. However, Valaythea knew she was only going to disappoint again with her answer. "I do not remember."

"You do not remember meeting the other paramours? Talk of the Orchestrators? The neverborne?" Valdean badgered on with his interrogation.

"I met the paramours, or so Izayus told me, but that instance is in shadow too. He spoke of neverborne, but I —"

"Think child," Valdean interjected demandingly. "Think. The

Pentagogue? Did you go inside the Pentagogue on your tour?"

She did try to think of everything she could surface to memory. "He turned the coach around. He did not want me to go inside the Pentagogue. That is when it happened. Or not when it happened, as evidently, I did much more that day. Or days after maybe, I do not know ..." *You are not making any sense!* She closed her eyes and took a deep breath before starting again. "The coach turning around, detouring from the Pentagogue, and his words, '*I am about to tell you about the neverborne,*' are the last I recall before the shadow spell stole the rest. I dare not deceive you, my sire!"

Something was indeed off, she was sure it wasn't just the lighting playing tricks on her now. As Valdean contemplated over what all she had said, she was positive that his face seemed younger. His crows feet and wrinkles were almost gone and color had been restored to his hair. The old count had shifted from an elder in his late seventies to the restored image of a nobleman in his forties.

"You are entangled in this web now Valaythea Az'Chandoss. I need to know where you stand. Are you a spider, as I am, or are you what gets trapped in the middle?"

Both sounded appalling if they were her only choices. "I do not wish to be either," she countered candidly.

"You must understand my frustration," he softly conveyed. Even his voice had lost its croakiness. "So many powers moving and removing. Collusions inside conspiracies, intrigue and insurgencies, dark scheming, political manipulation, extortion and supplanting. A debilitating endeavor to even conceptualize the choices of words; a futile attempt to describe it all. Az'Dayne, House Chandoss, the realm beyond our borders. It is not changing before your eyes, no," he paused.

Ten more years had been invigorated into his features, now even arguably handsome, attaining the fetching appeal that the Chandoss bloodline was renowned for. "It has been changed all along," Valdean declared.

"My sire, your face," Valaythea didn't know how to address what mystic act she was beholding. "It has been —"

"I prepared Ethiass to match you as the prince's paramour, to discover if we have a place back in the imperial court. You were the ripest fruit in the garden, bearing the most potential as a proper dish to serve to the Dominadom that turned its back on us. But the possibility of Izayus collaborating with Coldborn behind his own parents' backs while they were away, and including you in the fold," Valdean balled up a handful of torn paper scraps to knock his knuckles against the desk in unease.

"Well, now I simply cannot trust Izayus. I believe this should be reported to the proper authorities, do you not agree?"

"He is the Prince of Az'Dayne. Who is an authority above him, other than the dominarchs? And Coldborn, an archmage assassin, the founder of the Oathemic Cabal. I dared not," she argued but trailed short, forgetting her place when speaking to her great-granduncle that no longer appeared as a *great-grand* relative at all.

"This imposes a new conundrum for you," he implied. "That perhaps I should not trust you either?"

Valaythea stood in defiance to defend herself at the accusation, and braced her fingers tensely on the desk as she contended. "But Great-Granduncle, I —"

Valdean abruptly stood and matched her stance as she shouted back her repeat phrase in a threatening pitch. "Dare not deceive me?"

He came around the desk in an intimidating maneuver to loom next to her paralyzed neck and whispered, "No. You never ever will."

Valaythea had forgotten about all the sweat from the candles in the heat-trapped chamber until now. She was uncomfortably drenched from hair to toe. It was hard to breathe, but not just from the temperature. She was in over her head at every angle her life had tossed her in. She didn't have the grit to look Valdean in the face when he was so close. Instead, she gazed down at the desk and meekly whispered back, "Never ever."

He traveled back around the desk, now appearing barely over her age, much more likely to be taken as a lost cousin of hers rather than the bloodline's oldest alive. His hair was thick and red and his skin was full of color from the sun and healthy.

"*Neverborne*. Izayus spoke this term to you," he said.

"He alluded to charlatans, face changers he called them," she thought on Izayus's exact words.

"Indeed. The neverborne can change their faces, among other skills," Valdean confirmed in his new youthful accent.

"You are one of them," she realized finally. "Izayus spoke

unwell of them. I believe he fears them. I believe he fears all that he knows."

Even though the discovery that Valdean was one of these neverborne shapeshifters, she still had no idea what they were or what they intended that had the prince so worried. "What are you?"

"I am the Count of Chandoshia, your great-granduncle, the same as I have been since the morning Valenteal passed into the Godslands and you and your sisters were brought into the world," he mentioned her mother's name. "I am the same man who saved House Chandoss from the imperial wrath that was at our doorsteps before the fall of your great-grandfather, Nikayle, High Bloodguard of the Crown. Some would say that I am not a good man," his chin shook emotionally as his tone pitched higher when he defended, "but it is I who has sacrificed his integrity for the sake of his family's virtue so that it may remain unsullied against the shadow the Dominadom has cast over us."

"Thank you," Valaythea stuttered, feeling she was supposed to give him the sympathy he was clearly fishing for, though she felt no sincerity in the deed. "Thank you for doing that for us."

"Sit back down," he insisted, seeming annoyed now, as he sat in turn. "Yes, I am one of them – the neverborne. Your husband is right to fear us Valaythea."

"Who all knows? Oddy knows?" She knew the answer to her second question without having to ask it, but she more needed to understand why.

The young version of Valdean nodded. "Ethiass and Nikayle. Taizsha is in the Know as well. Most of the Chandoss Guard and the palace stewards are as qindrid as I am. All that we employ within the estates are a part of it. Before the end of this Dawning, the others girls will be introduced if my master decides a place for them. The light that is the fire in the shadow will be learned, and those worthy of an invite will receive it."

Qindrid? Neverborne are qindrid? I thought that was what Barredish called cursed Aggedonian people, she mused, wishing she had paid more attention during her uncle's study sessions. "You anticipated that I would become enlightened in the capital through the prince," she comprehended aloud, "that you would not need to explain this to me. How long has this gone on for? Shapeshifters across the Dominadom?" Valaythea's series of impulsive questions had no sequence of order of how her mind was shoveling them to her mouth to spew. "How do you even become one? What do you and father, or the prince and Coldborn expect from me?"

She found herself tearing up and red in the face, overwhelmed with it all. "I do not want any of this! I do not want to know your damned Know!"

"I know," he grinned with an equivoque.

She heard the door to the chamber bar behind her, instinctively turning to see what intruder had entered. Hanging from the ceiling, *No, standing on the ceiling,* she registered, was a bald elvan standing where one of the cushions above had formerly been. The leather pillow was on the ground and now a hole disappearing into the unknown in its place.

The young elvan had grey skin, long ears, at least twice the length of Taizsha's, and his hairless scalp was carved with deep black scars that seemed to be a purposed design instead of something earned in combat. The ornate mutilations went into his forehead and cheekbones and down into his neck as well. His large grey eyes were stained in sadness, but that did not help assuage Valaythea's reaction of sheer startlement.

Without even realizing she did it, she flung herself to the other side of the desk to use Valdean as a shield in front of her. "What is that? Oh my Fives!" She screamed, and was sure she repeated herself two or three times maybe.

"That," Valdean motioned his hand out toward the unexpected visitor. "Valaythea, that is what I fear. He watches me. He has watched me daily for years and years. The son of the umbran who made me what I am. His name is Ise'andahr."

We need to call in the guards! I will shout for the guards! The notion seemed too preposterous to attempt, as the epiphany of the curtain dropped that the Chandoss Guard was in on the ruse all along.

Valdean spoke to bring the emphasis back on him, but Valaythea's attention never strayed from Ise'andahr. "I know you mentioned your husband was going to tell you about the neverborne. It seems he did without Coldborn's approval. Thank you for educating me on the stance of Izayus Az'Ampion in the scope of it all. This information you have provided will be essential for our house's rise of prestige."

Valdean spoke into her ear directly beside her, his voice

reverting to his elder inflection. "It is only fair that I now educate you in return. Coldborn is not here to save you from your memory of the Know this time."

"Let us get you comfortable." He gently guided her to take a place in his own seat, and then lifted her chin with a finger to force her stare away from Ise'andahr and back on him. "You are not going anywhere before dinner. You have much to learn until then."

ATHANIEL (II)

HOMECOMING

A decem servants scrambled around the family banquet room as flustered as if they would catch fire if even one fork deviated from its designated placement by the fine flatware set down. Wine goblets were filled with shaky hands in frantic haste. Of the twenty chairs the long dining table afforded, ten were promptly removed by the busy bees swarming in and out of each other's paths.

The whole spectacle of organized chaos might have been annoying or amusing to watch, but Athaniel Chandoss did not get annoyed or amused. He just existed, nonchalantly absorbing every detail of his surroundings.

This was an anticipated family meeting, called for by Valdean. It was a rare event in the Chandoss palace.

The placings were specific on where each member of the family was expected to sit. The high seat at the head of the table was of course designated for none other than the infamous Count of Chandoshia, Athan's great-granduncle. To the immediate right and left of the table's head sat his uncle, Nikayle, and his father, Ethiass, respectively. On the left side where Nikayle sat, down the line Athan found his own seat between his uncle and an empty chair secured for Valaythea, with Odysserae next to hers. On his father's side, Emberalda sat across from him with Adyssaira to her left. At the furthest end of the table, near the door, not permitted to sit next to them by strict instruction from Valdean, were Taizsha and Athan's half-elvan half sister, Sashka.

The purpose of Athan's homecoming to visit his family had many angles. He had an itinerary of directives to complete before he could report back to the Cabal.

The first was to act as the Oathemic Cabal's liaison in dealing with Valdean on matters pertaining to the Neveril Empire. He had already been made aware for the past few years that his great-granduncle was a propaganda distributor for recruiting more into the Umbran Pledge, as well as a mediator for the elvan subjugators staged underneath Chandoshia.

The second stemmed from Coldborn's fantasies in the divinations foreseen through seerstones consumed by the Elderlocks on the Dendrallthae. The archmage conveyed his superstitious beliefs in confidentiality that it would be Athan who would unlock the Chandoss Spellblade from its dormant state by attempting to wield it when the time was right. And according to Coldborn, the visions predicted that such a time was now, on this visit home. His great-grandfather's renowned glass sword had been nothing more than a decorative ornament in their palace solarium since he was just a young boy, after the passing of Nikayle the Firstnamed became publicized.

Athan did not share the same confidence as the Cabal's founder. It was kept hushed, but indubitably proven and known, that Athan's cousin Nikayle the Fourthnamed, his former best friend, had become a spellblade through his mother's bloodline, Delphine Barturon. Now his fugitive cousin had been dubbing himself as Barturon lon'Chandoss instead of Nikayle, and was rumored to be a crucial agent for the Silverbacks that Athan had been hunting.

Spellblades, the wielders, appeared within a family in which another spellblade had originated. History had validated that oftentimes the sentient swords themselves would not choose a new wielder within the family line in the immediate generation after the death of their former wielder. There had been no workable premise of confirmed requisites to meet in order to explain why the magic weapons chose this wielder rather than a another within the bloodline, or what made the difference between this generation or the one after, and so on.

But the fact that his absconded cousin had already acquired his own spellblade gave Athan all the proof he needed to rationalize that Coldborn was wasting his time in conjectures that Athan, too, would be worthy to wield the Chandoss Spellblade. Still, the unique occurrence of two living spellblades within a family line, and furthermore within the same generation, was a bizarre and impractical concept to swallow.

Other than the family spellblade and meeting with Valdean, the miscellaneous task from Master Claydius of the Cabal had been added to his agenda to discover the actual reason why the Thrench were now in Chandoshia, on Daynish soil.

Finally, Valdean and Valaythea entered the banquet room. His sister kept her head down, subservient and distraught over likely more than what transpired at Suntide Athan wagered. She timidly took her seat next to him, still reeking of horse from the ride in, resembling a beaten dog more than an Imperiar's noble paramour. *He did not even let you change,* Athan grimaced at his great-granduncle in disgust as the count took his high seat.

Athan studied his great-granduncle like he was dissecting a wild beast to gauge the location of its vital organs in order to more efficiently kill its kind in the future. Valdean had been the cause of the immediate downfall of their house name after the death of Nikayle the Firstnamed. The demise of the spellblade legend that had gained their house their prior fame in the imperial court was a mystery of convoluted gossip to most, but Athan, privileged and educated by the Oathemic Cabal, knew the truths in it all. Valdean was the poison to their legacy, tampering with any hope for redemption, and the puppeteer of the Chandoss Curse, which had befallen their bloodline so long ago. But Athan's purpose here today wasn't to expose his great-granduncle for such treacherous schemes committed long ago.

The servants finished the elaborate arrangement of appetizers and vintage pours for the reunion banquet, scurrying for the door immediately after.

Athan's father abstained from even trying to be subtle in staring over at his son, whom he had not seen in two cycles. Athan knew his appearance had changed little, yet he felt entirely different all the same, based on the strange looks he received from family he had once known so well.

Ethiass, on the other hand, hadn't changed. His father still brandished himself in the most spendthrift cloths and leathers that Az'Dayne or Khalimia could produce, and he never left his bedroom without adorning himself in more jewels than a queen on a coronation day. His false-red goatee and mustache were dyed an amplified color to mask the natural blond underneath, and his goatee was sculpted to such a point that Athan was sure his personal barber was paid twice daily for the upkeep. His father's slicked-back blond hair was packed with some kind of new-age grease that looked rather ridiculous, glaring far too brightly in the chandelier light.

Ethiass was weak-willed and always had been—at least from what Athan recalled of growing up. It was his uncle, Nikayle, who had mainly raised his triplet sisters and him in matters of education and anything relatively important.

While it was true that Valdean was the head of Castle Chandoss and the surrounding locale, it was Ethiass who acted as the foremost emissary in Chandoshia, and in accounts concerning the many gold and emerald mines of the land under Chandoss control. His recent promotion to ambassador, as the imperially appointed delegate for state affairs in the capital, could not be humbling to his already inflated ego.

When the heavy brass doors slid closed, and it was just the ten of them alone without the palace help present, his father decided to open up with informalities. "Ah my girls, so how was Suntide? You all look a little out of sorts. Especially you Val!"

Valaythea looked startled and off-guard on how to answer. *All of them are still shaken up from that witch's divination. They need to hide it better,* Athan silently reprimanded the girls with a scowl.

Valdean surprisingly intervened with an excuse instead, "Sour pies was it, correct Valaythea?"

"Yes Father," Valaythea addressed Ethiass more confidently, "that is all it was. I will feel fairer tomorrow, I am sure of it."

Sashka piped up from down the table, briefly stealing all the focus. "I wanted to go! Mother would not let me while the Thrench are here!"

But the little Z'shun's insignificant debate was discarded as if it had never been voiced. Athan's father did exactly what he hoped he would not do.

"Nice to see you well though Athan. A father's mind can be cruel and cursed with imagination when we do not hear from you."

"Uncle," Athan nodded to Nikayle. "Ethiass," he hailed his father, not returning any sentiment, nor even glancing back at him.

"Family," Valdean commanded the room as he stood.

Other than Nikayle, impaired in his wheeled chair, every Chandoss at the table stood on cue. But together they at least all honored in harmony, "Count of Chandoshia!"

Every Chandoss but Athan. He never budged nor spoke. He glanced back at Odysserae to witness her translating the reverence in Hands.

Athan could see that Valdean detected the disrespect from him, but no regard was paid, defiant to draw any care at Athan's open impudence. *I know you noticed though. So did everyone else.*

His great-granduncle had on the same exotic black and red robe as Athan recalled him always wearing. His faded grey hair clung slicked back to his neckline against his leathery tan skin, and his face was clean-shaven. His faded brows were bushy and ominous above his amber eyes.

Valdean was the type of imposing individual who exuded an aura of intimidation over the average person. It had served him well for his own personal advancements, which had buried him deep and secure in his underworld of vast scheming. But the old man's disturbing impression had no effect on Athan.

The insolent jab did not waver Valdean's unflinching composure, but it did shift his focus on Athan with a fake grin. "Welcome home. Your presence with us is quite unexpected, without any formal announcement."

Athan took a sip of his wine and methodically began to unsheathe different knives. From his belt, boots, gloves, elbow straps, knee straps, and tunic, ten blades with the Oathemic green tassels at the butt were set all around his eating utensils and plates. He knew the gesture was inappropriate and that was the point. He looked at Nikayle when he replied. "Formal announcements are not what my order does."

"Indeed, no," Valdean squinted his eyes and sneered as he took his seat, with the family following in suit. "And how long are you staying this time?"

This time Athan did glare back. "We will talk elsewhere."

Valdean returned the candor. "I am sure of it."

There was an awkward full minute of no talk at the table, just everyone shuffling to sip from their cups or go through the motion of nibbling on a morsel from the plates. All Athan could hear was the racket of gulping or chewing around him.

There was only one individual not sharing a taste at the table. It was Taizsha to break the silence first, who hadn't stopped scowling at Ethiass since they all sat down. "Ethiass, since you will not address it, I will. It seems we are two seats short. Where are Timmurian and Sundorion?"

"You know where Timm is?" Emberalda chimed in with a burst of mixed emotions in her anticipant eyes. "Sundorion found him?"

"Oh, I am sure he tried child, and ended up in the same place," Taizsha snidely commented, "imprisoned or dead!"

Valdean ignored Taizsha's presence as if she was beneath him, and eyed only Ethiass when he calmly directed. "Ambassador, I permit you to usher your wife and her abomination from the table. Their invite was a fragile one, out of respect for you. It has been revoked."

"No need husband!" Taizsha shouted vehemently, rising from her seat to slam down her empty plate that never received any food. "Farewell *family*," she said mockingly. "Take a good look at me. I know my time will expire before I see an exile! Ask your questions girl! You have more immunity in this cursed tomb than I do! Your lover is gone and is never coming back. Get it through your head!"

When she was done harshly advising Emberalda, Taizsha snatched her daughter by the wrist and dramatically stormed out of the banquet hall.

Valdean stood and tolled a small bell several times that was stationed on his corner of the table, which prompted four guards to rush in. The count's visage rendered his order to the guards as they trailed in the wake of Taizsha and Sashka who did not give them time to register what the issue was.

"We now have Thrench inside Chandoshia, soon in our estates, and we have elven and crossbreeds under our roof!" Valdean flung an accusing finger on Ethiass and then Emberalda. "You two will be the death of this house!"

He sat back down so hard Athan was sure he would bruise from it. Valdean rung the bell again once to sound for the servants outside. "Bring on the first course! Let us compose ourselves!"

The double doors opened and piling in came the obedient kitchen help. They eagerly introduced the first course of the dinner. It was an assortment of fine breads paired to be dipped in a brown broth with contents that Athan cared little to inspect. He was more interested in pertinent clues as to what was transpiring in his old home. *That servant has a small knife hidden in his left pocket. Far too athletic and well fed to be just a kitchen slave. And that one, I remember your face from when I was a child, running through these halls. I could never forget your face. You had that burn scar over your right eye. Now gone. Those do not heal without magework or something else. It is in the help now, not just the guards as last time I was here.*

His great-granduncle could not take his eyes off him. *You are nervous, Valdean. I make you nervous,* Athan thought with satisfaction, refusing to match eye contact while being scrutinized.

Finally Valdean did shift in his sit to face Ethiass. "Do not ever let me see you allow the Chandoss male line appear to be so weak again. The Dominadom may have entitled you as Ambassador now, but know your name is still Chandoss, and you reside in Chandoshia under my decree foremost," he warned.

Athan's father forced down a chunk of bread far too large to swallow in one go. Ethiass gave Valdean his full attention when he promised, "Never again, Count. I know whom I serve."

Valdean smiled cordially, a man of many moods, and raised his wine goblet in the air for a toast. "I would direct the attention on our fair imperial paramour returned to us, but Valaythea and I have already spoken. So instead, we shall focus on the topic of the Thrench for the remainder of the evening."

All took a sip from their cups to conclude the gesture, and mimicked Valdean when he set his down. All but Athan, of course.

"On our eastern shores we have this imminent concern. Of all powers that could trespass our borders, they are here, but why?" Valdean's tone was concerned and confused as he calculated his latest report, "Four hundred strong, armed to the teeth, with Oriyan mages."

"Five hundred. One hundred remained on their ships," Uncle Nikayle corrected. "Thrench are always armed. They did not fly the Ashenwave flag. If this was an armada sent by Emperor Djediheth, they would have sent thousands, and there would be no parley. We would already be dead. This is merely an escort entourage for the emperor's nephew."

"I was called away and could not attend, as you all know," Valdean explained. *To meet with Zsa'vauge, your umbran,* Athan kept his assumption to himself. "Ethiass, this is the first we have spoken of it outside of our limited correspondence. Tell me all you learned."

"They are desperate," his father assuredly determined. "And their timing here is impeccable, precisely when the dominarchs are away in Barredom. It is my belief that they intended to arrive before Valaythea was secured in a union with Prince Izayus. They want to unify with our house through a matrimonial pact between the emperor's sister's son and one of our girls, Valaythea having been the most probable choice. I believe the Thrench are overindebted to the Pentharam Bank of Goldgarden, too beholden to swim back to the surface."

Athan's father took a deep breath, animated in his momentous time to shine. "The realm thinks of the Thrench as mindless conquerors who island-hop and subjugate those who would dare to oppose their tyrannical demands, and while they still are just exactly such, they stretch themselves thinner season by season. Their Ashenwave army amasses in the east, in Julkunda, now where New Throng lies, which has left their western isles dry of capable ships for protection. Even their homeland of Throng only holds a skeleton fleet, a shadow of its former armada, they say.

"Without gold, they cannot appease Vellyon to help guard their Starfell mines from the Lunaril. They cannot keep the pirates off the Tortharus and Forlornedian Isles. They cannot maintain their trade alliances with the Behemons or monitor protection against pilgrimage of Solaril and Zandaryn trespassers on the Sundorion Isles. And they are about to be severed completely from access to Goldgarden's affluent pockets.

"The Thrench don't speak much about their numerous internal issues, but guess who does? The boundless gossipers of the biggest city in the world. Piss your reputation away in Goldgarden, and it doesn't matter how monstrous a military empire you might be—you are shit to the wide world then."

Athan had never hid his disdain toward Ethiass as a paternal figure, but he had to admit that his father could always be commended in the accuracy of his appraisals of current events. And his father wasn't even done impressing upon the table his vast insight on the specific matter.

Throughout the second course delivered with the lemon duck pies, Ethiass, Nikayle, and Valdean traded opinions on further Thrench civil matters overseas. Evidently, the complex union with the former emperor, Djerath Emmonost, and Oriyen's current queen, Ji-Jy Thainwu, had stirred much unrest across the capital isle in Throng. The oldest, most stubborn conservatives of the Thrench noble houses, especially House Iskandon, abhorred the sacrilegious union that was viewed as a slight on Empress Nicretta that brought Brigatha Emmonost into the world. No one dared to openly rebel against Djediheth and his feared Ashenwave, but the time was maturing for an insurgency against his insatiable conquest.

"We should only continue to give formal courtesies to these Threnchmen on our shores and send them on their merry way, or we can play with fire and water and watch ourselves drown while we burn screaming," was his father's advice as the third course was served.

Racks of lamb and roasted bison littered the table for the main feast, but Ethiass was too in love with his own voice to cease from airing his opinion on the Thrench topic. "Any new information we can find on weaknesses to exploit in the Thrench Empire can only elevate us within the Az'Dayne Dominadom, and all of this needs to be thoroughly researched, so what better time than now to invite these water lords to our very table?" Ethiass finished with a melodramatic motion with his hands to signify where more seats could be added back to the banquet table.

After the meat dishes were devoured, in came layers of sweet cakes and cream pastries before the servants did as commanded and barred themselves from the room to give the Chandoss family their privacy once again.

I know you too. Old but now twenty years younger. Athan recognized another of the kitchen maids from his younger years in the palace, and then another. *And you, once fat but now skinny. You are each one of them, are you not? But clearly not clever. Are the girls too daft to notice or too scared to talk?*

"The boy then, this No-Name," Valdean focused on the most pressing concern at hand. "The same way we impregnated our way back in court with Valaythea, we will do with the Thrench. This is something that has never been done before in the history of Az'Dayne. The Thrench want our gold. They can have it in a dowry, an exorbitant one, if they accept our marriage proposal to the emperor's nephew."

Ethiass expressly added, "We should suggest this to the crowns first before we formally do something so profound. Valaythea could send word for Prince Izayus to be present in the dominarchs' absence to weigh in on the decision."

Valdean waved his hand to dismiss that suggestion. "I will find permission another way, by inquiring with someone else, not the prince." He looked straight at Valaythea when he referred to Izayus. "We can at least plant the seed of interest with Djediheth's nephew before an official proposal. We will need the hyperi boy to convince the emperor regardless."

What did you tell the count about your husband Valaythea? Did you lie to me about not remembering anything? Athan scowled in silent judgment at his sister, pondering if she was shrewder than he gave her credit for.

"Both of my eligible daughters are disabled," Ethiass countered with the apparent dilemma. "Who do you mean to —"

Valdean interjected in his habitual manner. "Emberalda is the only choice."

The count then faced Athan's undeniably beautiful cousin. "You are the best equipped to seduce this Emmonost prodigy. You had better pray your tarnished behavior has not traveled asea. There may be redemption for you yet."

"He does not even want me," Emberalda huffed and pointed to her left. "He only looks at Addy. He even wrote her a letter saying he wanted to take her sailing on Lake Chandoss with Uncle Ethiass's permission."

All eyes aimed toward Adyssaira. The intrigue whirling around in Valdean's mind was evident. "Interesting. Adyssaira," he clicked his tongue in heavy thought. "Not as practical of a choice, but," he paused to contemplate the unexpected twist. "Is this true?"

Do not bring innocent Addy into this. She is the last good one, Athan shot a mean look at Emberalda as if she had just betrayed her cousin by exposing her to be thrown into the count's schemes.

Adyssaira shuffled uneasily in her chair at being treated like an adult, just as Athan recalled of her insecure antics. She even nudged the seat around eight times in various directions before even trying to answer. "He seems nice," she finally said. Her face flushed as red as Valaythea's hair when she shyly affirmed, "We spoke in private at Emerald Point. Yes."

"It does make more sense," Valdean's scrutiny over Adyssaira transformed into an appalled frown when his eyes fell back on Emberalda. "The Thrench can smell elven from a league away, and this girl reeks of it between her legs. I am surprised they did not cut you down at the docks."

Emberalda shot a conveyed plea of outrage at her father to step in and defend her from the vulgar insults, but Nikayle had already gotten the attention of the room when he slammed his plate on the table. Nikayle and Valdean just stared at each other in a non-verbal challenge for several seconds, tuning out the audience. The bad blood between the two had never healed and never would.

Nikayle's collected tone betrayed his threatening grimace as he asked, "What are you asking Addy to do?"

You and I should speak in private Uncle. He does not have to get away with this. Why we have let him live this long is beyond me, Athan considered overstepping his place in the Oathemic's directives not to harm Valdean in any way no matter what he had suggested to his superiors in the past.

The count just smugly grinned at Nikayle and turned back to Adyssaira. "What did you speak of with him at Emerald Point?"

Adyssaira made it apparent that being the center of everyone's focus was not her desire as she began fidgeting with her orange dress and special blindfold, still blushing uncomfortably. *Do not tug at that. Act blind better,* Athan wanted to warn her.

"Just his past," she said so soft it may as well have been a whisper. Adyssaira then tried to speak up more. "And he mentioned that he was here to gain recognition as a true Threnchman, to earn his uncle's blessing, since he is not full-blooded from his father's Oriyan lineage. He said he was here for his lifequest he called his Sojourn. Something about an *Uedonvyor.*"

That last word sat Valdean back in his seat in alarm. But it was Athan's father who spoke for him, his voice thick with worriment as well. "That changes everything. They are not here for gold. An Uedonvyor means —"

"Blood. I know what it means," Valdean interrupted on point. "It means they are here for blood."

How did the Thrench hear about the Neveril here? Even so, they are in a war across the eastern sea. I do not imagine Djediheth would send his nephew here in such a time. This No-Name is here of his own accord, without the emperor's blessing or knowledge. Athan realized he wasn't being as imperceptible with his thoughts as he intended, unintentionally measuring Nikayle with suspicion on the matter. *Why would they dispatch a battle fleet without having a leak to tell them about what was here?*

"What do I need to do?" Adyssaira dutifully asked.

"Is it not obvious. We need to learn more. Everything there is to know. You must couple him immediately," Valdean pushed, already having replaced Emberalda in his shameless plots with poor Adyssaira.

"Couple with him?" Athan's naive virgin sister was confused.

"Seduce him. Bed him. Let him enter you," Valdean uncouthly spelled out for her. "Do you need Ember to show you how to do it?"

Both Nikayle and Emberalda stirred from their seats so abruptly that the table shook Odysserae's empty chalice over. Athan's crippled uncle was clearly fed up with the slurs against his daughter, and Emberalda, now in tears, was at her breaking point as well.

"Count," she stood and stared down at her plate submissively, choking between syllables. "May … I … be … excused?"

The cruel count didn't even spare her a glance. He just shewed his hand in her general direction. Emberalda didn't give him another second to change his mind, as she instantly made her exit to retreat and cry elsewhere.

Nikayle remained pushed away from the table in his wheeled chair. "We three should talk about how to go about this more delicately," Nikayle's teeth were together when he carefully insinuated himself, Ethiass, and Valdean. "Away from the girls. Do you not agree?"

Unperturbed from any offense taken around the table, Valdean snubbed him off. "If it involves them, then they need to hear it. They are no longer little birds we feed from the nest. Time for them to fly or fall. If this No-Name is as loose-lipped as Adyssaira describes him to be, we need to crack him open like an egg to spill as much yolk as possible. He is the key to cultivating an assessment to apprise to who we answer to."

Now, even Ethiass squinted, feeling bold enough to dispute the count's motives. "You want to pawn her off even if they have come with hostile intent?"

Valdean interlapped his fingers between each other and leaned in Ethiass's direction. "You believe they sailed across the Conqeron Sea to initiate his blood quest on a twenty-year-old blind girl? No, they came to Chandoshia specifically for a reason, and Adyssaira will dutifully do her diligence for her family and country to uncover why."

Nikayle spoke for everyone, reiterating in a way that sounded more like a demand than a suggestion. "I believe all at the table have had their fill this evening Count Valdean. Perhaps we could all be excused, and you, I, and Ethiass continue this strategy in the morning. Athan and Val have had a long ride in."

Valdean didn't give Nikayle the satisfaction of a single second to make it seem as if the idea wasn't already his own. He stood without a breath to think about it. "Family!"

Again, all but Athan and Nikayle stood on cue, and shouted back, "Count!"

Even Odysserae joined in the gesture with her sign language. *If there is anyone that needs saving at this table it's you. How did you allow yourself to become his pet?*

The family began to eagerly make their departure from the banquet hall, with Ethiass coming around the table to wheel out his brother in the absence of Emberalda. Valdean caught Adyssaira by the wrist before she could take one step however. That was all Athan needed to reclaim his seat as he patiently waited, refusing to leave his sister by herself with the monster.

When everyone was gone from the room, and it just remained the three of them, Valdean and Athan just stared at one another while Adyssaira stood confused in the count's grasp.

"Sire?"

"I want to feel confident in you my dear," Valdean explained, giving her his undivided attention. "Comfort me and say it."

"I will do my duty. For the family," she sounded more sure than before.

"For the family," Valdean repeated in his overly-enunciating manner. "All that I do, that we all do, should be for the family foremost, above any power that supersedes us. In the end, we are all we have. Never forget that. No matter whom you lie with, whom you may marry into, your union to them does not trump your legacy as a Chandoss."

The only thing we have ever agreed with ...

"I understand," Adyssaira readily replied.

Adyssaira turned with her walking staff to eagerly guide herself out to rejoin the others, but Valdean wasn't finished.

"And Addy," he grabbed her fondly by the back of her slender neck, which made her jump in startlement "You know, I am glad it was you. Your sisters are in the Know now. It is time we remove the sash from your eyes. See this through, and through this you will see, and be blind no longer."

You still think her actually blind, don't you? As clairvoyant as you try to be, you may still be the blindest one yet Valdean.

Athan put his own hand on Adyssaira's shoulder and motioned her out of Valdean's grasp. "You are excused now sister," he promised her as he retrieved each of his knives to return them to their hidden compartments across his leather wardrobe. "Leave me with the count."

Valdean only smiled amused. "One does not deny an assassin his demands."

Neither one of them said another word until Adyssaira had left the room and the two were finally alone.

"You wished to talk elsewhere," Valdean remembered. "Where is elsewhere?"

Athan was depleted with his great-granduncle's feigned ignorance and was ready to get business behind him. "I believe you know. Take me there."

SUNDORION (IV)

ON DEAF EARS

Shapes and shadows, bad dreams and harsh hangovers—the day-by-day routine hadn't changed one bit.

The single exception was that he was sure it had now been three whole days since he had last seen Timmurian, but that was putting hard faith in a cloudy sense of time passed. The candles that kept being lit at night were putting him under a sleep-induced spell that seemed almost poisonous to his mind. He could never remember the hours before he fell into the forced sleep, and he always wasted a quarter of the day upon waking in agony from the excruciating headaches that constituted the aftermath. He had finally learned from his brother that such inflicted ailments were the effects of bugsthrone mushrooms. When the spores were cooked, or even exposed to high heat, just one candle's worth was enough to put someone under for hours and weaken their mind and body. Three candles' worth in a small room like his own was enough to drop a horse or stop a grown man's brain from functioning.

Sun hadn't used Old Patience to slow time in days. There was nothing about this predicament he wanted stalled. He was eager to accept what was next.

He was still in the same cage and same drab room, never having been transferred since he had first found himself confined to his new prison.

Sun had become much more enlightened about what his brother's research and recent discoveries had proven valid. Not only were the Neveril controlling the political powers of Az'Dayne and its expansions, but the mysterious elitist race was apparently overseeing the other umbran outside their Neveril ilk as well, including the Shiniryn umbran in the Sho'Lon region and the few Wyldenar umbran left in Aggedon. To make matters worse, they apparently also had a significant portion of the Terollar elvan tribes in their favor based in Helderak to fend off the Thrench Ashenwave invasion. How Timmurian had squeezed this knowledge out of Count Valdean he refused to elaborate on, but Sun presumed it was freely given propaganda to coerce intimidation and compliance.

Sun saw the same elusive faces by the day as well. Odysserae came and went, as did the same sentry as always, who he had come to learn was named Caven, and most definitely a neverborne qindrid. As it turned out, *Caven* was actually five different individuals all posing as the same person. The seemingly timeless guardian of the tower had proven to be a duty shared by a group of the skin-shifting qindrid.

Sun had seen the count finally as well, but only by a glimpse and recognition of his voice. And, just that very morning, an all-new face to the chamber, but not at all unfamiliar. The young man was Athaniel Chandoss, no doubt returned from his bloody exploits within the Oathemic Cabal, likely sent to conspire in Valdean's unscrupulous collusions as well.

Sun felt his body utterly drained of the strength it took to rise from the floor of his caged cell. Even his neck betrayed him in enervated paralysis as his skull pounded his throbbing brain. But his eyes were open. They had been open now for hours—at least, he assumed it had been hours. Perhaps it had only been ten minutes. But his ears were alive as well now, and that was all that mattered when the voices echoed clearly from the floor below, funneling up the stairway to sound as if they were all in the same room.

"Why is me witnessing this pertinent to what we must discuss?" the obvious voice of Athaniel began.

"Come, Athan," the recognizable old tone of the count returned. "We both know you were sent here to be Coldborn's eyes and ears on the happenings of the estates, specifically involving me. I am apprising you openly, so that you do not have to pry where you do not belong."

Their unfriendly exchange did not skip a beat with Athaniel following. "You are a blight on the house, Valdean. It has always been you. The curse began with you and will only end with you."

"The Chandoss Curse," Valdean scoffed. "An exhausting title for what I did for the survival of our bloodline in its entirety. Let me tell you, you would never have come to know such a life, as even meaner killers than you would have cut out your heart as a babe, and your sisters' too, if I had not done what I did to save the family. So let's end this charade of enmity that will get us nowhere swiftly. You stand there immune by the Oathemic Cabal, and here I am immune by the backing of something much more dangerous."

"You've become incomparably arrogant in your later years." The heated joust continued with Athaniel's turn. "We have one elvan here and another upstairs, who both wish to expose you to the realm, neither of whom you can dispose of, and yet you blather on without a worry in the world."

One elvan here and another upstairs ... Timmurian is on their level? Unconscious and injured? But alive, Sun surmised as he strained his ears to catch anything he could from the conversation.

"You were sent to see, so see you shall, but by my invitation alone," Valdean declared. "Timmurian and Sundorion are both induced into sleep. My contacts will come for them soon. Rest easy knowing that our words are mute to deaf ears in this sanctum."

There was a good pause between the two before Athaniel spoke again in a tone of skepticism. "I sense you are about to present a proposition, aren't you, old man?"

"You were always wise for your age. Your order must be dissolved. It is the most principal threat to these Neveril and the qindrid," Valdean explained candidly.

Sun found himself sitting up straight now, fully engaged in the increasing intrigue of the debate, and he wasn't sure when he had adopted this position.

"Dissolved? What are you even implying? Coldborn would have to die for that to happen," Athaniel argued, pushing back against the drastic absurdity.

"Coldborn," Valdean seethed disdainfully, juggling the name in his mouth with some form of implied familiarity. "Yes, the founder especially must die, as must all of the mages, save for the Dawning ones. Most of the likes of your special Hive Order must go also if you choose to resist."

"You are explicitly specific," Athaniel pointed out with skepticism in his tone. "Have these subterranean elven grown fond of Dawning mages for some withheld reason? Should we purge our ranks of neverborne imposters, because you know that we can see you? We have ways. We of the Cabal were the original infiltrators on this side of the realm, and we still hold more strength than any empire above and below can even come to fathom."

The count's voice came in response. "We can dally all day in this measuring of our allegiances' merits, but the subject has grown weary already."

"You tell me all of this in such faith. How do you know that I will comply and not relay it to have a writ penned for your own life, which I will beg to execute personally?"

Sun was on the same page as Athaniel's last retort, considering the same bleak outcome for Valdean with the unexpected presumptuous request, but the overconfident Count of Chandoshia was not deterred or intimidated in the least. "Coldborn has to get his writs approved by the imperial crown. They will not sign off on it, so it will not occur."

Again came the pause, as if Athaniel was carefully contemplating a volley of return fire, but Valdean seemed to be reading into the assassin's reluctance. "But why would you do this? What is in this for you?"

"Spit your spiel, Valdean."

The count complied with Athaniel's blunt demand. "You've always been an ambitious boy, Athaniel. You came back for that spellblade that you believe is yours. You have it in your head that you must earn its favor, as your cousin Nikayle, or Barturon, as he is calling himself now, cheated you on this. And by reasons beyond my understanding, you think climbing through assassination writs in your order is the only path to prove your worthiness in ever wielding the family blade. Do I have you sorted thus far?"

When no words from the other side, Valdean continued. "Your talent is but a copper in a coffer in the vast scope of the Oathemic Cabal, but allied on my course, with me, beside the Chandoss legacy I continue to carve"—the scheming count paused for accentuation—"you would be recognized. I do not mean by me, nor by those I now serve. I mean by the glass blade of Aemenus that sits above that mantel in the solarium."

Athaniel did not seem to be having any of it. "You want to confide in me to betray a fraternity I am sworn into for life. How hypocritically should we commence in this new trusting affiliation we are building? What you also imply would be suicide to even an army of Threnchmen. Kill *the* Umbra archmage, who is anywhere at any given time, with an unimaginable power like no mortal in history can boast of. That is, if I can get others within my unbending order to join with me, and somehow not have my throat slit for the very mention of betrayal."

Athaniel emphasized, "If the Chandoss Spellblade needs all of that for a worthy wielder, then it can sit on that lonely hearth for the rest of eternity."

"The girls. I will save them," Valdean riposted in an unexpected detour. "Those I can, anyway. I know you have a soft spot for them. Yes, they are inevitably to become part of the Pledge or be given a choice to become one of their qindrid—the neverborne. But I have been given an alternative bargain to present to you alone, one that could salvage their souls and keep them in the bliss of ignorance for the entirety of their days, if they so wish it."

Athan retaliated with his own logic. "Save them? Val is now untouchable, even to you. You refer to Sashka as an abomination, because the Neveril you serve view half-breeds as such. She likely won't survive past the Sunder. Ember, you would rather see fall from the Syrene and be done with her, hoping she does herself in after Timmurian is disposed of. Now you have Addy in your dark web of scheming against the Thrench, and Oddy has been doing your biddings like a beaten pet. They are each doomed. Do not lie to me again."

"You should not be angry with me about Odysserae. She wants the Transcendence. You should accept that. It is her choice."

"I do not accept that," Athaniel forthrightly disagreed.

"There is a way," Athaniel's voice rang with a sliver of hope and sympathy Sun had not heard before, "for Oddy. The Cabal has an affiliate order, comprised of all women initiates. I am forbidden to disclose any more to you, but I can to her. This is something she would want more than what you plan to do to her."

"More than giving her the ability to hear and speak like us? More than an ageless life like I have?" Valdean confessed, whether intentionally or not, that he was already a neverborne qindrid.

Yet you choose to remain in the skin of your own, as the old and wrinkled man you've aged into. Why not a younger version of yourself, if you can change your appearance as you say these neverborne can? All part of the master ploy, though, is it not? Sun had an epiphany. *Or are you sometimes someone else entirely and live more than one life? You stay elusive enough that you could manage such a feat quite easily.*

"Lies! He intends to kill them, not save them! Both Sashka and Ember!" An easily recognizable voice broke Sun's contemplation.

Timmurian? You are awake!

"I will end this reign, changeling! I will play the Neveril's game and turn them against you and see if they will listen to one of elvan ilk over your capricious breed of replacements, face by face by face. It's all the fucking same now, isn't it?"

Timmurian fiercely berated Valdean by the stairwell's echoes from the floor below.

"I will—"

His brother's words fell quiet after the unsettling sound of a loud thud. The sound of two men's footsteps rushing up the winding flight of steps followed, and Sun chose to instantly retreat back into his former position of mock unconsciousness to save himself a little while longer. When he wasn't molested and didn't hear the cage budge, he knew whatever Count Valdean was devising was something out of his control. The footsteps of four boots casually began to withdraw back down the stairs, and that was when Sun smelled the dooming stench. *The candles … bugsthrone …*

"We aren't finished here. I'll be back on the morrow's dawn." This was the last thing Sun heard Athaniel address to Valdean before the bugsthrone fast took effect.

One day … Athaniel will be back in one day … in the morning … And the unwelcome comatose state came fast.

* * * * *

When he came to again, the pain inside his head was surprisingly gone, and his lethargy had lessened. The chamber floor that served as his constant prison was clean, including his slop bucket, and the pawns board was perfectly put back together, with the missing pieces in place. They had been strewn about when he had accidentally kicked the board in his stupor a few naps prior. And the culprit of the tidiness was right in front of him, oblivious to his consciousness, filling the water pitcher and food plate on the table just outside his cage.

Sun sat up dramatically to gain her attention. "Speak to me." He spoke slowly enough, knowing the hearing-impaired girl had proven to be capable in reading lips.

Odysserae only scowled at him and frowned, but she did not look away.

Stupid choice of words … Say something clever before she gives up and goes back down! "You know what I mean." He tried to rectify his insensitive remark. "We can help each other."

Odysserae finished unloading her satchel of fruits and crusty bread, then stole back two plump grapes for herself, placing them in her mouth.

Sun regarded her boyish hair. It was shorter than he remembered, but perhaps that was only because today it was brushed completely down instead of spiked. And her clothes were filthy, as if Valdean had forced the poor girl to deep clean the entire underground sanctum.

"I have seen what they do to you." Sun dared to intervene in her chores. "The men in the castle," he went on, regardless of the glare in her fiery eyes. "Does he know?"

Sun had no idea how he was supposed to communicate with her, but he assumed they could find a way. Instead, his brief aspirations were shut down when she nodded and promptly turned to depart down the stairs.

Damn me! I've lost her now.

When she returned just a short time later with a quill and blank scraps of parchment, Sun was so flabbergasted that his expression of hopefulness could not suppress it.

Odysserae scribbled something and handed the parchment to him through the cage: "No more false hope."

His eyes said he was sorry, but his words repeated his last question aloud. "Does Count Valdean know what the men do to you?"

She scribbled back on the note: "He does know. He encourages it."

Sweet child, why would you not tell your father, then? How long has this gone on? Why not even your sisters, or especially your brother? It could stop. Sun could not fathom her reasoning for hiding it with such a powerful family at her beck and call. Surely, the Chandoss Guard involved or even possessing knowledge of the defiling would be gravely punished without remorse. As ambassador, Ethiass carried more external influence in Az'Dayne now than Valdean could hope to merely within the Chandoshian territories.

However, instead of writing all of that, he left it for her in ink with one word back: "Why?"

"He calls it my training, says that it makes me stronger" was what she wrote back.

She dipped the quill deep in more ink, as if she had had second thoughts on expounding upon more tragic detail. And what she wrote Sun could never have predicted in the vilest of scenarios.

"The count knows I am being raped, because he is one of them. He changes himself to his younger self. He calls it my training, says that it makes me stronger," she repeated on parchment.

Fuck the Vist and Void. This is sick! Sun did not know how to react. He wanted to reach through the cage and embrace her like an older brother might, to conjure some otherworldly strength to smite Valdean on the spot like a father might, but he was in no position to do either. Instead, he had to think practically, like a prisoner might, which was what he was. Odysserae was still clearly the enemy, working for the enemy. *Something to be used against her. Remember this.* He shifted his sentiment to a more logical sense. Sun was capitalizing on the return of his strength to utilize the minimal window he felt he had. He had to twist these intrigues and familial predicaments in his favor for his brother and him to escape.

"How exactly is he going to help you?"

Odysserae read over his question and began to write a response, but Sun had already discovered her reasoning beforehand from his eavesdropping on Athaniel and Valdean's most recent exchange.

"I will get to hear and speak like you all," Sun read, the most obvious answer he could imagine her giving.

He could not let on about any truths he had come to learn about the neverborne, so he played the game strategically as he best knew how: "What magic is this?"

She scribed back: "I get to become one of them. I know you know. It is almost time."

"The qindrid who change forms?" Sun wrote, playing dumb.

She gave him a dissatisfied squint and refused to take back the quill or take a fresh piece of parchment for her turn.

Sun did not hesitate in writing more, since he had been afforded the opportunity to goad her: "He cannot make you do that. Do you know this?"

She took back the quill: "Becoming one is one's own will. It is a choice. It has to be. And I know much more than you. Much more."

Well, this route is clearly striking a nerve. This girl has avenues to exploit. Test her, but do not insult her. "What if I ask you to help me escape?" Sun jotted the words down, goading her without a bargain into what he knew would be irrefutable denial.

She returned the parchment to him: "We are not in control of your fate. That is for the ghosts to decide. They will come for you soon. You will not escape. No one will."

Sun knew the continual references to ghosts pertained to the Neveril. He ignored her insinuated doom about his plight, and he struck back with his best shot on their shared scroll: "What if I tell the count about a secret I also know? About your not-so-blind sister touched by a wisp? There is a special place for mages of her potential capacity among the Neveril Empire's grand schemes."

That struck a nerve in Odysserae. She drastically held it in so forcibly that she seemed to forget the ability to blink as her face reddened in frustration.

You have a weakness for protecting Adyssaira.

Sun wasn't done. He pulled every piece of information he had learned from his mental pockets to break her down by bluff and ruse and coercion. "What if I tell the count you are planning to run away with Athaniel to join the new order within the Oathemic Cabal, an order that accepts women? It is real, and your brother is going to propose this to you."

As she scoured the words, appearing confused at how to feel about such a proposal, he put the parchment down and whispered with clear enunciation, knowing she couldn't hear him, but she could damn well interpret him. "What if I do everything in my power to ruin your chances of curing your ears?"

Defeated, Odysserae sat down and groaned in vexation, while Sun was already scribing his conditional note to her: "Just listen. I wish to know what they plan to do with my brother and I? And I want you to stop putting the mushroom spores in my candles. I will play the sleeping game, but let me be awake."

Odysserae took the parchment and quill and responded: "Do not tell my great-granduncle any of these things you say, and I will not use any more of the spores on you. If I have to, I will use goodcaps, another mushroom that reacts in the candles, as I did today, to give you a swifter recovery. Timmurian and Taizsha are both going to the same place as you. The ghosts will come and bring you all to the Under. It will not be long."

"Why do your sisters not know of the Umbran Pledge? Or do they? Who is in this among the girls?"

Odysserae read over his questions and responded with trepidation this time: "Val knows, but something happened to make her forget. They will not let me near her yet. They have plans for Addy with the Thrench that are here, but I fear for what will come of her once the count finds out about her eyes and condition. Ember, I do not know what he plans, but he does not like her. They do not like quasi elven. They consider their human lifemates to be the worst blight to have ever existed, Ethiass included because of what he did to Taizsha. Sashka will be used as an example. I cannot help her."

The girl has grown as cold as ice. She even refers to her father by his name. Sun read the new note several times over, taking in every clue that could be exploited in his favor. He weighed the profound risks he knew he was taking that would rile Odysserae out of any compliance. He needed to take advantage of the impending situation that could radically be turned by a little maneuvering with his new pawn in play. He used the fading opportunity to act like he was writing a new note, purposefully scribbling and grunting as he tore away a chunk of the parchment that held the first half of their conversation, in which she admitted in her own writing to being raped by Valdean and the guards, and in which she had declared her aspiration to take the Transcendence to become neverborne. He crumpled it up as trash and wrote a new note for her, hoping she would ignore the discarded ones. And she did, paying them no hint of heed.

He handed over the last of the used-up parchment and anticipated the worst as she scoured his last words: "Sashka will die. The Neveril Empire does not accept the Z'shun. Ember will be killed, as Valdean disfavors her and plots her demise, confirmed by hearing him speak to Athan about it. Val is a prisoner to the prince as his paramour, and hates it. Suicide is the only path I predict for her. And Addy will be executed as a mage candidate or will be forced into some form of slavery for the underworld expansion."

The silent rage emanating from Odysserae's countenance was deep now. Twitching with unpracticed fury, the lithe Daynish girl pitched her glare at him as if he were to blame for her current position, and likely her inherited impairment too.

"Your sisters and cousin are doomed unless you help me and Timm escape." He matched her infuriated stare with a determined one of his own.

But as expected, she snapped to fear instead of rising to heroism. Odysserae rushed for the candle and already had the bugsthrone pouch readied to pour the spores around the wick.

Sun had expected exactly such an outcome, and he used the distraction to shove the balled-up parchment in his cage into the tight waistline of his pants. Odysserae didn't see him do it. She hadn't held up her end of the bargain—refusing to use the candle to heat the brain-impairing spores—but that was all an intentional gamble. When the head-pounding sleep took him, he for once embraced it. *He'll be back on the morrow's dawn …*

* * * * *

"Why did you move him and leave Sun upstairs?"

"I did not move him. I was in the palace. Not far from you."

"Ise'andahr then? Will I meet him this time, or does he still fear me?"

"Do not goad me, and especially do not think to goad him. You think you are worthy?"

"You think I have never met a Neveril? You know little of us."

"I think the Oathemic Cabal has killed one or two. I would wager that yes, you may have killed one or two."

Sun recognized both voices echoing up the stairs. *Athaniel is the first speaker … Valdean the second.*

He felt wide awake, recovered from the ill repercussions of inhaling the bugsthrone spores. *Goodcaps? Oddy mentioned she would burn them as a remedy. Maybe she can be trusted,* he dared to hope.

Sun played the slumbering bear in hibernation with his eyes open just enough to keep a sliver of a view to spy those in the same room with him now. The young Oathemic assassin and duplicitous Count of Chandoshia soundlessly studied his faked deep snooze.

"The answer is no, Athaniel. You may not meet my liaisons of the Neveril Empire while I am here. Only I," Valdean answered candidly.

"These two are too high a risk to be kept alive. You could have slit their throats and been done with it if you hadn't already informed your superiors," Athaniel starkly reasoned.

"I hide nothing from Zsa'vauge," Valdean asserted. "It is a meticulous process, what needs to be done. Know that he will not appear until you have left the estates entirely. You waste your time."

"And you waste yours, wanting Coldborn dead by my hand," Athaniel said straightforwardly.

"And you will waste yours when you attempt to wield the spellblade. So much wasting away, you and I, yet it is I that will inevitably live longer. Should we keep playing this game?" Valdean teased at Athaniel's nerves.

As the count turned to lead the way downstairs, Sun purposely fidgeted just enough to draw Athaniel's attention, and he tossed over the saved balled-up notes from his and Odysserae's conversation the day prior.

The sly assassin caught it under his boot and didn't say a word to his great-granduncle as he retrieved the scribbled exchange to stow it safely in his pocket for reading later when alone, as Sun had anticipated.

Sun was confident that he had just got either himself or several others at the grisly minimum killed. He would just have to wait patiently and see how Athaniel, the merciless killer with a soft spot for his sister, was going to react when he read that Odysserae was being violated by Valdean and his men.

ADYSSAIRA (VI)

CAROLELLE

Adyssaira waited patiently with her black tiger cub by the familiar skiff beached at the edge of Lake Chandoss, close to her family castle, as she had been doing all day in nervous anticipation. More than a few servants had visited throughout the morning to keep her apprised of the busy dealings the Thrench delegates were having with her father and uncle. No-Name was with them, but she had already been made aware that their imminent courtship had been approved and arranged to happen today, at any given hour.

She inspected the small boat's single sail and the tiller at the stern, ensuring everything about the day would go as perfectly as she imagined. All this tarrying had her stomach grumbling—she was famished from being unable to eat all day. She considered rummaging through the small day pack she had stowed on board to retrieve a snack, but she had made herself a promise that the carefully prepared luncheon would be saved for her lover-to-be when he finally arrived, and not picked into a moment sooner.

"I still need to name you," she whispered to her chubby pet as she traced the orange stripes along the tiger cub's fluffy black fur. "Maybe I will do that today." Playing with the small, happy thing and coming up with what to call her helped the hours pass. The little black tiger wasn't so little anymore. She had already put on several pounds since Sundorion had introduced them, but she seemed to be growing more in girth than in height. Adyssaira found the fledgling predator to be an adorable companion, and she kept her by her side everywhere she went that her father permitted. And Ethiass was not here today, so she had already decided that the tiger was joining her on today's adventure.

The latest update had told that it wouldn't be much longer. They were finalizing whatever decisions would come to pass concerning the Thrench acquiring their credit with the gold contribution to aid in their eastern war efforts. Adyssaira had been stringently instructed on her part to romance the Thrench emperor's nephew to discover if any alternative schemes were underlying the reasoning behind their unannounced visit to Daynish soil.

Valaythea, Odysserae, and Emberalda had all made an appearance in the meantime to tease her about the day and pass the time. Each of them seemed to be much more educated in the matters of seducing men. Emberalda would not shut up about her advice, which often contradicted herself, between fancies of hopeless romance and shameless fornication. Valaythea was suddenly acting like an expert on the subject, after only experiencing a month of submissive acts with the prince. And even Odysserae translated her opinions on carnal lust and sensualism a little too detailed, making everyone feel uncomfortably hot and bothered. *What could you possibly know about it, Oddy? What books are you reading lately?*

Finally she saw the target of her intended affections approaching over the hill. He was just as handsome as she recalled from their introduction at Emerald Point. His brownish-blond hair was worn the same, pulled back into a topknot, but he had grown a slight mustache and goatee. The celestial radiance in his piercing violet eyes could be seen from afar. And today he wore black boots and an orange lace shirt to contrast with his colorful turquoise breeches. *Curious,* she mused. *Such a diplomat. Orange is the color of Az'Dayne.*

His heavily armored bloodguard, Thoravus Hlelvig, and Oriyan Reaping mage, Inkomway the Skycaller, were beside him until halfway down the knoll to the shore, where No-Name casually dismissed them to leave Adyssaira and him alone for their romantically inclined engagement.

"I am glad you came," Adyssaira said in greeting. She was out of breath by the time he made it down the hill, panting with a dry mouth as if she had run the entire way up to meet him. "Was it difficult to get away?"

"Surprisingly, no," No-Name replied with a coy grin. "They encouraged me to have the day to myself and explore the estates at my leisure. Besides, I made you a promise."

She remembered every word of the letter he had written her, which she had received on the road home from the Suntide Faire. She had read the thing close to twenty times over, she was sure. "To take me sailing, yes! I am ready for you to show me how Thrench you really are, good sir."

Adyssaira nimbly jumped into the small personal skiff, where she had already placed her black tiger to accompany them. She sat herself comfortably in the seat at the bow, arching her back as she grinned back at him. She imagined it looked alluring, having memorized the art of subtle and feminine movements she had seen her cousin Emberalda perform for men before.

"You do know Oriyans can sail just as well," he laughed, apparently entertained at least. "Just you and I and this little one, then? You have the boat ready and all, I see. I can manage this."

The unlikely trio pushed off and set sail on the lake, with No-Name confidently steering at the helm. When they weren't far out on the open water, and he had managed the sail to catch the wind, he took a seat at the stern to gaze back at her.

"I wanted to call on you sooner, but my time here is" — he looked away with a conveyance of disappointment — "demanding and short at best."

"I know. I do not dare flatter myself," she humbly returned, petting her tiger cub to calm her. The young creature was apparently nervous, panting on the open water.

"You really should, though. My time in Az'Dayne will expire, but my time with you ..." No-Name seemed to stop time itself when he stared into her, as if he could see her sparkling green eyes through her sash. "It does not have to."

She blushed and turned away from him, too flushed to counter with anything witty in the unaccustomed moment of someone fawning over her. She instead kept her focus on Carolelle, the looming isle in the distance.

No-Name broke the tranquility of the sound of the calm lake waves when enough silence had passed. "So, what intrepid adventure do we find ourselves on today, my fairest lady? That isle, I assume. What is on it?"

"Yes, that isle," she confirmed. "Just a spirit is on it. Or so I made up when I was ten. It has been trapped there since I was a babe."

No-Name burst into an incredulous laugh, coercing her to turn back to face him. "Seriously?"

His perfect smile was infectious, and she couldn't help but fix one back on him. "Seriously! Her name is Carolelle. They even let me name the island after her," she explained. "We are sailing today to Carolelle Isle!"

He exclaimed, "Sounds like a grand tale for bards to sing all around the wide realm!"

This time she laughed, unable to take the idea seriously any longer. She was sure that to an outstandingly well-traveled prodigy like himself who had been to every land mass around Penthara, it sounded quite silly to add Carolelle Isle to the list of his legendary exploits.

She decided it was also silly to keep the blindfold on when he was more than well aware of her ability to see and of her hunder-touched condition.

"That's much better," he cooed when she pulled the silk sash off and discarded it in the boat.

Adyssaira responded with no words, just a smile, before she tilted her neck to peer into the bright midday sun.

"But be careful, for that *will* make you go blind," he teased.

"At least I can finally feel something and see its effects on me without fearing some unknown consequence. I would rather look at it in the face and know its intentions." Adyssaira boldly stared into the intent of No-Name's soul without blinking.

When he had nothing to refute on that account, she allowed her eyes to drift back up to the sky, this time catching a colony of grey gulls flocking directly overhead. A glimpse of majestic pink congregated on the distant banks of Carolelle, with a squawking flamboyance of flamingos. "You are blessed to be able to embrace what you are," she said without thinking, not able to fathom actually being blind to all the beauty before her.

"Then you truly heard nothing from me when we first met at Emerald Point," he retorted with irritation in his tone. "I may not have to hide my eyes, because those who are magically adept are not killed on sight by the Thrench or Oriyans, but I could argue that I grew up even more cursed than you. No matter what I do on my Sojourn, and no matter how I achieve my Uedonvyor, I will still never measure up to a true Threnchman. I will never be what my cousins are. And my parents, who never treated me as anything more than a wisp-finding tool, are still dead—assassinated by other mages who sought their demise. They made many enemies in their time, and in doing so, they put my own life in everlasting jeopardy.

Are you sure you want to sail this journey with me?"

She felt stupid for her ignorant remark and tried to repair the damage she may have caused with a little bit of shared sympathy. "I will never be what my sister is either. She is now married to the Prince of Az'Dayne."

When that didn't do anything to erase the growing frown on No-Name's face, she tried another avenue. "But I am fine with not being her. I like where my path is sailing me."

"Az'Dayne." He spat out her country's name as if it were the vilest of profane words. "It is no Throng. The Daynish and Khalimishe and all their relentless scheming among each other. Most of your enemies seem to be within the same house bloodlines. It would be exhausting living here."

Adyssaira thought she should have felt offended at the obvious slight, but she was surprised in herself that she wasn't in the least. She accepted it and realized she agreed with him. It *was* exhausting. She looked down at her tiger and noticed she was finally sleeping, massaged into a snoring slumber between her feet.

Instead of debating a defense for her home nation, she probed the main topic enticing her interest. "Tell me about Throng, then. Tell me about everywhere No-Name has been, which seems to be everywhere that can be. I would know your story."

No-Name obliged her and expounded on the history of how he had come to be in more detail than he had done before on their introduction at Emerald Point. He explained how his mother's birth had caused much upset in Throng among the old houses, and how his grandfather's polygamous choice to publicly consummate a political union with the Oriyen queen Ji-Jy Thainwu had nearly caused a civil war with the more traditionalist Thrench highborn who completely opposed the atrocity of a union outside their people's bloodlines. The Thrench were an extremely prejudiced and utterly segregated culture. If you were not one of them, of the water elemental descendancy in full purity, then you were simply considered a lesser being.

In No-Name's earliest years, the political unrest caused by his mother's birth had eventually subsided over time, with no insurgencies coming to pass, but he was told that tensions were still rife in the capital of Throng. The noise of his own existence had been all but drowned out entirely, in fact, as he had been hidden away in a monastery on a secret isle that lay in the Vist that divided his realm for his first ten years of life.

He briefly expounded upon the actual details of the enigmatic Vist, which was something of a convoluted phenomenon of inconsistent theories from sage to sage, in Adyssaira's experience. He said that the Vist was Penthara's prime meridian, which divided the east from the west down the middle of the realm from north to south. It was recorded to be around eighty leagues wide in its southern half, but as one traveled more north, the expanse of the Vist became immensely larger, all the way to five hundred leagues wide at the northernmost points.

The Vist was the only place on Penthara in which the plane of the In-Between was visible. The Vist was also referred to as the In-Between by the elvan race when they were alive, and as the Beyond after they passed on after death. While there was no valid proof of any true afterlife for humans, regardless of their religion, for elven it was different. It was a universally recognized fact that when an elvan died, their hunder entered the Vist, becoming part of its otherworldly fabric. Much of the makeup of the Vist was the mass of wisp-like entities that interconnected with one another, able to reunite with loved ones lost through eternal telepathy or to teleport elsewhere within its vast confines to transfer feelings and knowledge with other hunder in the mass symbiosis of its celestial composition.

The way No-Name described the Vist's appearance was a great wall of green mist above and below the sea surface, with the occasional glowing green ball that was webbed to others, and it appeared identical for as far into the horizon as one could see. No living thing could see through the nebulous structure of the Vist, save for the nearly extinct Vistyzus elvan race and the rare hyperi humans, which was why and how No-Name had eventually been utilized to navigate the Ashenwave armada over from the western boundaries to the eastern shores, where the majority of the navy now resided.

He professed the trials he had to endure as a child into his teenage years, where his mental stability was tested by the only other hyperi he had ever met, Master Mesdarro of Mageholme. He was taught in the tales of the past failures of others of his kind who had seemed to lose their minds to the elements—those that they were hereditarily fused with due to a byproduct from their archmage parents. No-Name's own parents, Brigatha and Imaniko, were tier-five marvels of the water and sky elements. No-Name admitted he had felt the tug of an Entity developing in his mind on either scale of both elements but that Mesdarro's stringent tutelage had honed him to mastery over that pull that had become the downfall of other hyperi in the past.

No-Name briefly touched on the next few years of his life, in the custody of his power-hungry parents who used his special hyperi intuition to seek out and slay other ambitious mages who were consumed with taking their place. Since there could only be one tier-five mage of each season on Penthara at a time, there was also potential opposition from the tier-fours or others trying to elevate themselves in spellpower. One was never safe with the status one had achieved.

When his parents had found themselves so utterly depleted of energy from the magical storm they had wrought upon Cabernus, No-Name was introduced to the Thrench emperor, his uncle, Djediheth Emmonost. No-Name was put under the temporary care of his cousin Drythe Emmonost and underwent strict tutelage in what it meant to be Thrench and of the Emmonost imperial bloodline.

On his fifteenth year, just two years ago, it was determined by the emperor that he would remain away from his parents' care, but he was to be brought to Mageholme, back in the care of Master Mesdarro, to refine his powers and truly become trained in what it meant to be a hyperi. Mesdarro trained him in his hypersight through all functions in how to use the impower to its fullest extent. He even showed him how to sense out and find other hyperi, not just mages, existing in the realm, and how he discovered that another was present somewhere northwest, near the coast now, he believed. Eventually, and rather abruptly with no reason given, Mesdarro had departed from Mageholme to become the new overseer of Spellspire in Old Elothia.

Adyssaira felt he was withholding information concerning his purpose there, but she dismissed delving into those implications and chose instead to become lost in his wisdom about the foreign country in the north that embraced the practice of magic and protected those who had the faculty to hone its power.

Mageholme was secretly reputed to be the most formidable

place in the realm, a haven for hunder-touched individuals and magic supporters who could wipe out entire armies and turn the tides of any wars with ease if they wished to involve themselves in the affairs of other nations. But Mageholme rarely ever did. It remained a neutral zone for study and serenity, not conflict—quite the opposite of how life would have been for No-Name if he had been permitted to grow up on Throng or join the Ashenwave.

He also mentioned how he had met Sundorion and first learned of Adyssaira. No-Name had been scheduled to have a long-overdue reunion with his uncle to discuss his Sojourn. Sundorion had been on the wrong transport ship at the wrong time, in route to the Glace Isles, when it had been ransacked by No-Name's ship as it left Mageholme, full of Thrench marauders.

The Zandaryn explorer was captured and declared to be the one No-Name would duel for his first kill, as was the typical challenge when a Thrench highborn came of age, to slay his first elvan in an organized match of single combat. Thrench boys were supposed to spend days with their enemy before they dueled them in this way, to study their elvan opponents and discover any weaknesses they could discern.

But No-Name was no warrior, he admitted, and this had not been his wish. He could not bring himself to fight Sundorion, especially after hearing his stories. The day Sundorion told him about the Chandoss Triplets and No-Name first learned Adyssaira's name was the same day he devised a way to help Sundorion escape from his predicament.

No-Name had broken Sundorion out of his imprisonment and saved his life, and No-Name swore to Adyssaira that he had never told a soul—other than Inkomway, who had been involved in the escape—the truth until this very moment.

"The Vist. Mageholme. Both just sound like places no human is allowed to see." Her voice came out almost as soft as a whisper. She was half-lost in the ponderings of what such a place might be like to visit one day, or even perhaps live in.

"Mageholme is a place for only humans to see. Humans and wisps." No-Name disabused her of any false assumptions. "Picture a paradise that promotes that which we are, a protected place that encourages the practice of magic, an unparalleled populace that harbors the hunder-touched, just like you and me. Adyssaira, you must vow to let me bring you there one day."

I am sorry, Great-Granduncle. I am sorry, Father. I cannot do this. "I have decided I do not want to lie to you," she said aloud, unable to turn back now from what she was prepared to confess to the exotic, violet-eyed boy she was falling for.

No-Name chuckled and peered at her playfully. "It pleases me to know we are reestablishing that pact."

"No," she blurted. "I will not lie *to* you that they want me to lie *with* you." She knew the conversation sounded familiar to the one they had had when they had first encountered one another, but the implications now were entirely different.

"They? Who is 'they'? What do you mean by 'lie—'"

"Seduce you," she admitted. "My family wants me to seduce you and steal your secrets. They want to know why you and your Threnchmen are really here. And your Oriyan mages."

No-Name looked upon her with a different intent behind his eyes. He stopped moving the tiller as they neared Carolelle's bank, allowing the skiff's natural course to do the rest for him. He came to sit next to her on the bench at the bow and took one of her hands in his. "I don't think I want to lie to you either, Adyssaira. My family wants me to seduce you too. And steal your secrets."

"What a dilemma." She squeezed his hand before forcing it away.

Adyssaira stood up to grab her day pack and cradle her heavy tiger cub in her arms. She balanced her way across the small sailboat to leap onto the sandy shore of the isle. She set down her awoken pet and looked back at No-Name to prompt him to do the same. "Whatever are we going to do? Seduce each other and please our families?"

"Fuck my family," No-Name said, and then he jumped off the skiff himself, landing just in the water to sink his boots. He waded his way fully ashore to meet up with her. "My parents discarded me for half my life, used and abused me for the other, and now they are dead. And the rest of my family doesn't even claim me yet. They won't even give me a name."

"I can name you," she nonchalantly declared.

"The gesture is sweet, I am sure." He did not seem convinced. "But it will not be the same."

"As what? Earning it from a family you just rebuffed? No. I am naming you today," she firmly vowed as she took the lead with her wandering tiger to walk the isle.

No-Name let out a hearty laugh and tried to keep up with her fervent pace. "Okay, then, Adyssaira. You mean to tell me you *earned* your great name?"

"Babies don't earn anything. But my family did not pick my name either," she elaborated. "My sisters and I, the infamous Chandoss Triplets, we were named by Psage seers on our identical bornday after my mother passed during our birth."

"I am listening. Go on." His eyes spoke of respect and sympathy, but they also delivered the truth of his deeper curiosity. "Why did they pick the names you have?"

Adyssaira picked a spot to picnic and dropped her satchel of food, recognizing that it was her turn to tell a story—one she had never told before. She used her hands to draw imaginary depictions on the ground as she enlightened him.

"There are islands to the west of Az'Dayne. The three main ones are all named for their similarities on the outside, but how different they are once you actually explore farther into them. The larger one is called Valaythea. They say that island is the most beautiful, lush with more vibrant tropical trees and pretty flowers, and it has the most wildlife thriving on it. The one closest to the coast is called Odysserae. It has been a haven for renegades for as long as stories have been told of it. It is a place of secrets and shadows, quiet beaches and deep caves, but gossips say that the most valuable treasures are found at its center. Then there is the isle I was named after. Adyssaira." She took a pause and a deep breath before continuing. "My father told me the seers say it is a magical place, full of trapped wisps. They say that the elements of the nature within it are not like the norm you will find on other isles. They say—"

"I don't care what else they say," he interjected, unexpectedly pulling her to him by the hands with his strength. "It fits you. You are as close to what feels like magic as I have ever seen."

Her heart and body froze as she fell limp to his control, to do with as he pleased. Her eyes instinctively closed as his lips neared hers. *I think I am supposed to close my eyes. Is this how it's done?* She second-guessed herself and reopened them at the last moment, but her focus was distracted by a figure in the corner of her vision. *The spirit!* "Carolelle!" she squealed as she saw the mysterious wisp.

No-Name's lips were still half-puckered when he opened his own eyes back up, wholly confused by what had just transpired to rob their tease at romance. "What?"

"The spirit! I made it up, but it's real!" Adyssaira slapped her palms over her head, stunned is disbelief. "Carolelle. Right there." She modified her tone to a whisper as she guided his hand to point at where a glowing violet wisp was creeping behind a tree.

The docile orb just aimlessly floated about, between the two shrines that Taizsha had masons build for Sundorion's long-dead lifemate and daughter. The strange spirit was either oblivious to their presence on the lonely isle or entirely uncaring. The tiger cub seemed not to notice, and began jumping over the tall grass to playfully make her way to a patch of hovering butterflies instead.

"You didn't say it was an eldritch wisp. It has the violet glow," No-Name pointed out, as she just now registered that its radiant hue matched his hyperi eyes perfectly.

"I have never," Adyssaira was lost on what she was actually perceiving, "no one has ever seen that! I do not even know what it is! Eldritch wisp? I read that," she thought hard on Sashka's book from Sundorion. "I read that recently somewhere I believe."

Adyssaira remembered the last passages she had read in *Of Wisps and Whispers,* all concerning the topic of the rare eldritch wisps. If more than one wisp was within the right distance of an eligible infant, the wisps then became bound to each other. While only one wisp could interfuse at a time with one so young, the other wisp would become stuck in a place of familiar comfort until the genesis wisp they were bound to was activated by the mage's catalyst wisp later in life.

Eldritch wisps were altered from their natural green glow to a deep violet radiance instead, and they were permanently cursed to orbit the individual that their bound genesis wisp was interfused with. Any further information Adyssaira could have learned of the eldritch wisps had not been made available to her. Those pages had been torn from the tome, as if Sundorion had purposely done so himself before gifting the book to Sashka.

"You are able to see her because we are touching," No-Name gently interlocked his hands in hers even tighter. "I am the conduit that allows you temporary hypersight as I have."

Adyssaira realized they had not let go of each other's hand.

Something about seeing Carolelle in the moment bolstered her confidence, and she ushered No-Name back a few steps and softly breathed to him, "I am naming you. And I am naming my tiger today too."

He smiled at her. "The wisp inspired you?"

She was all too earnest, though. "Think of an island. We named this island Carolelle after her. I and my sisters were named after islands. Surely, the boy from the great Vist out of Oriyen, who has sailed all over the oceans with the Thrench, has been to some greatly named islands himself!"

"Well, let's see ..." He smirked, deciding to play along with her game. "In Mageholme, on Harkland Lake, like this one, there is an island that citizens visit just for nightly festivals all cycle around. It is a place full of friendly fires and shows and all sorts of revelry. It is called Luna Isle, which translates to the Moon Isle." He pointed to her tiger.

Adyssaira pondered the catchy name while spotting her cute pet in the distance. "Luna," she uttered with a smile. "That is perfect for her! Come here, Luna!"

The little tiger turned her head back to look at them, and they both laughed. And then Luna went back to happily chasing after butterflies.

No-Name continued with the endeavor to discover a name for himself. "Luna she is! Now for a name for me." He paused to contemplate. "There is Depyreoshlinyoq, the underwater realm of sea caves of the Oceanil elven. That sounds mysterious!"

"Yeah ... um ..." She scrunched up her face in a tongue-tied semblance. "I cannot pronounce that. I am pretty sure no one can but you. Next!"

No-Name conceded and moved on. "There are all kinds of spire-like, lofty islands throughout the Skystone Isles. Each has a name. The natives there are extremely cunning apes, almost as smart as humans. They can even fashion weapons and armor. It is quite impressive to see."

"You want me to name you after an island full of mean apes? No, thank you. You need to do better!"

No-Name chuckled defeatedly. "Oh, wow, you are taking this seriously!"

"It will be your name forever." She smacked his hand hard but playfully. "Yes, and so should you!"

He seemed to put a small amount of effort into thinking on it this round before answering. "There are the isles of the Westway, off Oriyen. We have named some of them. Though most foreigners just dub them the Westwalker Way as a whole now."

"Westwalker sounds tough." Adyssaira chewed on the flavorful moniker, judging it for a minute.

"I am pretty sure there is already a fellow roaming around the north claiming that one as a sobriquet, though. Evidently, he is a big deal or something in Barredom or Aggedon. Besides, *westwalker* is just an ethnic slur for what people in your lands basically call us Oriyans and the Sho'Lonese. It is not a good word. That's like me referring to you and your family as goldbloods."

"Ew, no." Adyssaira rebuffed the popular epithet. "I have always hated when the Khalimishe call us that. They call anyone north of Savatarm that because of our tairan descendancies."

"Well, okay." He spun around in place, looking off through the trees on the deserted island and across the horizon of Lake Chandoss as if his memory could invoke some resolution by doing so. "I could go over the many isles around Throng. There are several, and I know all of them by heart. There is actually—"

Adyssaira had an epiphany she could not keep silent. "The island you were born on! In the middle of the Vist, between the west and the east. You mentioned it."

No-Name smiled and nodded his head. "It lies between Oriyen and Vistyzus, between the west and the east, a place amid the great In-Between. They say that it alone played the part that saved the Threnchmen who vanquished the elven on Vistyzus during that conquest, when the Ashenwave first broke through the Vist on the other side. Their ships utilized this isle as a beacon to guide them."

Finally, something that sounded appealing and poetically worthy enough for him, she considered. "What is your origin island called?"

"My people, both the Thrench and the Oriyans, we call it Desdjlandar."

"Ah, it sounds aloud very similar to your uncle's name, Djediheth," she determined ecstatically.

He visibly shared in her delight at possibly discovering a defining name for himself. "My grandfather, my uncle, and my cousins all share the same in their given names, starting with a *D*. I do not know why, but I always envisioned I would be granted the same due to my imperial lineage."

"Does it have a meaning to it?" Adyssaira had to ask.

"Desdjlandar ..." No-Name considered the etymology of the isle. "It is in our Anshient tongue. Hard to explain, but its closest translation would be 'the one who is hidden now but is the hero later.' 'The unsuspecting champion' is another."

Adyssaira was beaming with the biggest smile she was sure she had ever had, so big that even her cheeks hurt, but she couldn't stop staring at him with a whole new sentiment.

No-Name, however, appeared confused by her display of dreamy emotions. "What?"

"Desdjlandar," she said to him, leaning up to his lips as she began to close her eyes again. "It is nice to meet you."

And she felt Desdjlandar's lips connect with hers.

SCARLESS (VI)

TO BECOME THE VILLAIN

The old mansion now known as Water Daisy's Brothel was a particularly bustling haunt today. With the approach of the Kingfall Ball, newcomers, both locals and those from abroad, were pouring in by caravan over Garden's Bridge and by boat into every north district that held a harbor.

Water Daisy's resided one block in from the docks in Little Worest, directly across a canal to Bridgeville. It was typically brimming with the same salty urbanites that meandered the ward, but on this evening, nearly every face within was a new paying patron. That was the way that Zahnastaazjah wanted it.

The Goldgarden district of Little Worest had been so named after the region of Worestaschia, which was where Oldan Boldandgold and his Boarneck Company of infamous mercenaries originated. Worestaschia had formerly been a state region of Utamia, taking up the area surrounding the mainland's coast directly east of Goldgarden Isle. It began as a simple but prosperous territory of farmland for beef, venison, pork, and poultry exports, but upon latter years of the expansion of Goldgarden's influential grasp, Worestaschia had become an extension of the city-nation, rather than still being considered part of the country of Utamia.

Most of Little Worest consisted of housing for the Boarneck sellswords or richer farm lords of the mainland, and it was a fact that Water Daisy's Brothel itself was owned by Oldan. But that hadn't deterred the audacity of Zahnastaazjah.

She had a very special meeting today and would not take any counsel to send an intermediary. Zahnastaazjah had brought a heavy purse to amuse herself during the two hours prior to the scheduled time to greet her mole within the Boarneck Company. And the hood of her cloak had not been pulled down one time, to hide the points of her elvan ears and the green of her Terollar eyes.

Zahnastaazjah was not typically inclined to the companionship of women, but it had been a while since her last experience. She justified it both with the cruelness cast from boredom and the overall scheme she had in place. In addition, what Xalo didn't discover couldn't hurt him, she reasoned. She had been done with the pleasures of the girl after the first thirty minutes but kept her for the full time, needing the well-paid harlot to act as her envoy.

Zahnastaazjah stood leaning against the entry frame of the small, intimate room, behind a sheer curtain that was placed to partially obscure the activities within, as no doors existed inside the brothel for the security of the working women. She kept her focus trained on the main lobby of the dim-lit establishment on the level below, just beyond the balcony rail outside her missing door. Eventually, the contact she was waiting for did show. Symbelle had finally arrived.

Zahnastaazjah turned around to toss the harlot two more gold coins and watched the buxom strumpet escort her shy spy up the winding stairs to her designated room. Symbelle seemed entirely discomfited through the hallway as she passed the other open rooms, filled with the wailings of compensated pleasure givers and peaking grunts of depleted men. When Symbelle reached the room, another coin was tossed to the harlot. She did her duty by humming a song in a sensual manner while seductively dancing in the curtains of the doorway as Zahnastaazjah retreated back inside to take a seat in a chair across from the bed.

The tiny, timid human fiddled with her dark bifocals for a minute before she even moved again, with her eyes shifting uncomfortably to the half-naked prostitute in the doorway instead of focusing on Zahnastaazjah. "A brothel? I've never been in one," Symbelle squeaked. "I did not think it would be you who would meet me." She sounded surprised in her soft tone, recognizing her employer beneath the hood.

Zahnastaazjah ignored the avenue for needless banter and got down to business. "How was it?" She patted the bed's pillow near her, implying that Symbelle should be at ease and take a seat.

Symbelle did, awkwardly sitting on the pillow, then in the middle of the bed, then back on the pillow, before finally sitting back on the bed with the pillow laid across her lap. "What did you hear?"

She sounded ashamed.

"That you are a scary bitch, Symbelle. People fear you. Usurp isn't too happy, though." She chuckled.

"I've learned some things already. Many things, you might say," Symbelle chimed in, but then she glanced back nervously at the harlot and shifted her tone lower again. "And I may be getting to meet Oldan soon."

It had been eleven days since the report came of Symbelle's impressive feats during Usurp's ambush for her intended elevation in the Boarneck ranks. Such was plenty of time for Symbelle to have learned much about what Zahnastaazjah was keen to learn. "Let's discuss Oldan first."

"He is meeting with Amethyst," Symbelle revealed.

Zahnastaazjah squinted her green eyes in suspicion at the way her mole answered that so casually. "You say that name like it is familiar to you," she stated without a hint of questioning.

Still, Symbelle readily defended herself. "It isn't. I have only recently heard of her."

You are breathing hard. Are you lying to me? Or do you get nervous in these settings? No, not just whorehouses, but around lewd women. Isn't that right, shy girl? Zahnastaazjah mulled over several scenarios in her mind, studying her double agent, whom she perceived she knew very little about. *You present yourself as useless and weak. And you, in this moment, even believe you are, do you not? But either you are a liar and a cheat, or you are as cunning and dangerous as an unstable mage.* She kept her head cocked to the side and aimed an unsatisfactory sneer at Symbelle to keep her uneasy.

"I know that she is provisioning the Boarneck Company's expansion needs, that she and Oldan are in the pocket of the Az'Dayne Dominadom. It ..." Symbelle stuttered before building up her momentum. "It is my assessment that with her on the Seven Seats, aware of who controls the city, and with the Boarnecks being the bridge that determines who is allowed in or off the isle, it won't be long before Az'Dayne has its hand in Goldgarden, the same as it does in the rest of the western mainland countries. Oldan has complete control of the North Docks too but is not exposing that fact. And worse, with the political guidance of Amethyst, it seems they are dipping into the Gem Docks and Southport as well."

Zahnastaazjah wasn't completely convinced by her infiltrator's uncanny success in the extraction of information, seeing as she was so inexperienced in such a deep field. "I find you remarkably confident and well informed in such matters for someone who has just joined this reticent mercenary lot. Not even the best of my spies could discover this for me."

"Your best of spies were in the Night Street, whom you executed in your latest Purge of the Yard," Symbelle retaliated with an uncharacteristic boldness compared to her former disposition. "What I am telling you is the best report you can hope for."

Zahnastaazjah secretly liked the alchemist's newfound wit but wasn't going to display this fact. She ground her tone into one more coarse. "I don't have a plan for Amethyst yet, but Oldan's reign over Bridgeville ends soon. I have an idea to accelerate your meeting with him."

She got up from her chair to grab the wooden pitcher of Tytainian Red—her favorite wine, which was distributed all over the city—and filled two bone mugs to the brim.

"Coin. As much as you need, I am going to give it to you to do what needs to be done. The Kingfall Ball is the most important event all cycle that Oldan runs, and there are more visitors pouring into the city to participate in its mass revelry than there have been for any spectacle put on before," Zahnastaazjah explained. "He prides himself on this exact type of demonstration of grandeur, and this is where we will get him. You may have earned his attention with the rehearsed ambush, but it is your pyrotechnics that will guarantee your getting in front of him. The fireworks display of the prior balls is something Oldan has always been celebrated for, and his reputation for outdoing himself means everything to him. I want you to use that hyperi mind of yours and contrive something new—the most impressive fireworks presentation that Goldgarden and all the wide realm have ever seen. Go down to Festival Row and buy anything and everything you can."

Symbelle smiled in evident relief at being tasked with something she had full competence in. She reached for the wine mug on the end table near Zahnastaazjah, but she hesitated and relented. Instead, the alchemist just elaborated on her task. "Give them something they have never seen before. I can do this. I have other favorable news to include." She gleefully changed her tune and did grab the mug, clumsily spilling a quarter of it all over her lap.

Symbelle looked down at the wine like it was her own blood for a split second, utterly aghast, and then shifted to put it behind her as if she bathed in it nightly. "They've given me full access to all of their blast-salt supply and control of the alchemy laboratory beneath the Monodrome," she chirped in her little-girl voice, squirming jubilantly in triumph on the hard bed.

Zahnastaazjah found the scarred introvert quite endearing in that moment, and she hoped she never had to kill her, as often as it had to occur within the Stormtree ranks. Some roles had a high turnover.

"How did you manage this?" She had to know this of the intriguing, industrial hyperi girl.

"Jonan Riveiros, the man who stole the recipe from me, is gone. He joined the Boarneck Cavaliers with Tristostopher Boldandgold, in the commission from Barredom's general, Randon Roth. They told me I had the lab and supplies until he returns, and when he does, I can challenge him to keep them."

Zahnastaazjah nodded and smirked, wholeheartedly believing that revelation. "They are sick fucks who would enjoy that spectacle. That will not come to pass."

She sipped her full-bodied wine and encouraged her new agent to do the same, but Symbelle still hesitated to make a move in partaking of the drink. *You think it is poison? I told you I hate poisons, alchemist.*

"The blast salt, then. That's the key to unlock their undoing. You must fill that lab with it, and anywhere else you come to discern is a point of weakness. I need not train you in how to construct an efficient bomb."

"We will be ready" was all that Symbelle said, with her mystically glowing violet eyes entranced by the provocative dancer in the doorway.

"Who? You and Fyheir?" She made the ultimate inquiry.

"Yes, Fyheir and I." Symbelle did not hesitate much, which had not been expected.

"Do you find this difficult or easy, Symbelle? To betray those you share a hearth and home with at night." Zahnastaazjah had to know to assuage her paranoia. "Those who now openly confide in you and have taken you in as their own. Did you lose sleep on the moons following what you did to your friends at that school?"

"I had no friends in Tairanchula," Symbelle said simply. She took her glasses off to reveal a cloudy stare at nothing in particular on the floorboards between herself and the chair Zahnastaazjah sat in. "I have no friends in the Boarneck Company. And to be honest, I had no friends in that ambush you sent either, Scarless."

Zahnastaazjah scrutinized the guiltless hyperi girl, evaluating her for possible motives for a long-game intent, to no avail. "You don't have any friends in all the Stormtrees either, Symbelle. Opportunities, but no friends, as much as I would like to consider us as such."

The alchemical wonder reached out with her free hand to grasp Zahnastaazjah's own. Symbelle's tiny hand was so small in her own. Zahnastaazjah wasn't prepared for the sincere gesture. "I think of you as my friend, Zahnastaazjah, if I may call you that."

Do not dare goad me into that web of weakness. She ignored the miscalculated tangent and shifted. "I'll ask you again. Do you find it difficult to betray?"

"For me, Symbelle, at the core of it all, I do. I could never deceive a soul. But for Fyheir, there is no difficulty in anything it does, I fear."

If you cannot control whoever you are insinuating Fyheir is, then I cannot control you, and those I cannot control I do not trust. She thought to give her assessment aloud but said instead, "If Fyheir has no difficulty in anything, then it appears to me that you shouldn't fear at all."

"What about Scarless? Is she fearless?"

It seemed Symbelle had turned the analysis session back on the analyzer. Zahnastaazjah already knew the answer, though, prepared after a human lifetime of contemplation in her elvan years of hard experience. "Scarless isn't real, just a villain in everyone's mind who meets what I present to them as real. Someone that isn't real cannot fear. Zahnastaazjah, though, at the core of it all ..." She paused and coerced Symbelle into contact with her eyes. "Oh, yes, she fears much."

Zahnastaazjah chugged the wine from her mug and then emptied the rest of the Tytainian Red from the pitcher into her bone drinking vessel and Symbelle's, which had hardly been touched. She half wished herself out of her Terollar impower in that moment so she could get lost in the stupor of the alcohol, instead of regenerating its effects away so swiftly, as always.

"My father, you see—" She stopped to impromptu toast Symbelle before expounding further. "He was famous for being fearless. He was born with a destiny to become not only the savior of my race, the Terollar elvan people, but also the hero that would bring the Balance back from the state of chaos the Neveril were imposing on it all across Penthara. He amassed countless attacks against the Wyldenar umbran and qindrid armies in the north."

Zahnastaazjah turned to watch the dancer in the doorway to make Symbelle feel more comfortable before going on with her story. "My brothers and sisters all found their doom the same way, failing by falling into the senseless path of their aspired-to righteousness, of no use to their people or the fucking Balance. But me, no. I embraced the villain within. I ran from my father's destiny to protect the old ways, and from my siblings' belief in the new reforms. I evolved. I became Scarless. And all the people alive around me loved me for it. And any who found themselves hating me soon found my spear or the blades of my guild of villains. No one can betray me, because you have to trust an ally or lover to be betrayed, and I trust no one. I just live life, and I thrive." She took another healthy swig of the wine. "Fuck destinies!"

"I am sorry for the loss of your father," Symbelle said softly in all sincerity. "I have only met my father a few times, and only recently discovered he was even my father at all. He is famous too, and fearless, and a believer in the greater good for the realm. I believe he thinks he is some hero of sorts, in his own way."

Zahnastaazjah chuckled at the similarities between the two histories. She decided that she liked Symbelle, as strange as the internally tormented alchemist was. She forced a toast with her mug against Symbelle's. "To our fathers, then!" But then she turned her mug upside down instead of putting it to her lips to dump the contents over the floor. She motioned for Symbelle to match the gesture, and she did.

"So, you are saying I should just let the Entity of Fyheir take control?" the hyperi guardedly asked. "Leave Symbelle behind?"

"Not quite, shy girl." Zahnastaazjah stood and took both mugs to place them on the end table and coerced Symbelle to her feet by taking her hands. Looking down, face-to-face with Symbelle, she stood a full foot taller than the tiny girl. "Never forsake who you are. Fyheir is not real. Just the villain you wear on your back. As long as you, Symbelle, stay in control, then all will be well. You just need to become the villain within from time to time, and live."

"Become the villain within." Symbelle took the phrase to heart.

Zahnastaazjah inspected the crooked fool's frown and felt sorry for the scarred girl in that moment. She wasn't exactly sure why, but she slipped her tongue deep into Symbelle's mouth and passionately kissed her in that moment between them before sharply turning for the doorway.

Contradicting everything she had just said about her sentiments on betrayal, Zahnastaazjah repeated a promise she had threatened Symbelle with before, when they had first met. "Do not ever betray me, or I'll burn you alive," she said in all seriousness and then exited the room as if the kiss had never occurred.

SYMBELLE & FYHEIR (VI)

BOLDANDGOLD

She kept her head low and her eyes focused from booth to booth down the bustling wayfarers' promenade. The entire city of Goldgarden struck a strange chord of clouded reminiscence of her earliest years of childhood, but that did not make it feel any less uncomfortable. Symbelle was still an unfamiliar foreigner here, and she did not like the turning head of nearly every curious passerby.

Maybe it was her radiant hyperi eyes, though their glow was softened in the glint of the midday sun. Maybe it was her dramatic scarring, but this was the busiest sector in the largest metropolis on Penthara, a place accepting of all manner of shapes and sizes and scars and deformities. Or perhaps it was because this was Festival Row she now traversed, the multiavenued, shop-filled, narrow ward of silver-tongued hustlers and coin-hungry peddlers, and she was carrying far too much conspicuous gold in the saddlebags of the horse she rode.

Symbelle felt a target for both thieves and swindlers, and she was ill-equipped in strategies to combat either. She wanted to finish this task and be done with it.

Pyrotechnic supplies to make the shells, fuses, powders, mortars, and colorful effects were carefully selected piece by piece for bulk purposes. Her contact wasn't here yet, so the purchases were on standby until he could arrive and no doubt bring several carts in tow for the impressive haul she intended to buy.

Symbelle tuned out the whistles and caws of the greedy merchants in their incessant beckoning, and she attempted to hone in on just her innovative musings for the future theatrics of the Kingfall Ball.

She dismounted from her steed, borrowed from the Boarneck Company, to approach yet another kiosk full of select minerals and powdered metals. She fiddled with a bit of raw sodium and copper salt before finally choosing the barium salt—the necessary component for making her fireworks explode in a green burst.

"Daughter of Endrith Goldfyre," came a strong Khalimishe accent behind her.

Utterly startled, Symbelle dropped the container of barium salt and spun around to address the invasive woman looming directly behind her, but she only responded with wide eyes and silence, agape.

The green-eyed middle-aged woman had the mage halos in her eyes that Symbelle was becoming more accustomed to seeing as of late. Symbelle's hypersight picked up on a strong green aura around the woman as well. She was well covered but not enough to hide the red magemarks across her throat and down into her bosom, which could be seen regardless of her ample clothing. The inflection in her voice was clearly southern, but she appeared as pureblood Psage as they came. "The hyperi of Coldborn's seed." She grinned and alluded to Symbelle's secret heritage again.

Symbelle glanced rapidly at everyone in her vicinity, as if they were all hidden agents of the Oathemic Cabal, testing her. She would not fail the test if it was one. "Milady, I do not ..."

"Know me?" the Psage woman finished for her. "But I know you. Or at least, I have always wanted to."

"I do not understand." Symbelle was intrigued but confused by the cryptic implication.

"My name is Shypriss Sol-War. I knew your mother. You might say I knew her better than anyone could."

Symbelle did not know how to take the unprecedented topic of her long-lost mother, whom she never even thought of anymore. She had left that faded memory behind long ago. And as such, that was where she decided to leave Shypriss as well—behind her.

In an awkward shuffle, Symbelle swerved around the mage blocking her path and walked back to her horse, but Shypriss called to stall her.

"Wait! You will want to hear this. I do not know who raised you, only that they were not your parents. Your father is one of the most powerful mages in the realm."

Symbelle halted next to the horse for a moment to retort. "So people like to remind me lately."

"But the one they do not remind you of at all is your mother. She, too, is a mage. Arguably just as powerful as Coldborn," Shypriss revealed.

"I assumed that when I was educated about my condition. It is what being born a hyperi entails," Symbelle said, feeling annoyed at the untimely subject and inappropriate setting for such revelations. "Lady Shypriss, much respect to your knowledge of my heritage, but now is not the time or the place for me to inquire upon this."

"We may get no other chance," Shypriss warned. "You've been a busy, busy girl with the Stormtrees, Boarnecks, and the Oathemic Cabal, haven't you, Symbelle? You should know that when Shypriss Sol-War requests for someone to sit and give her time, they are typically polite and oblige."

The mage was clearly accustomed to coming across as intimidating in her notorious position, renowned throughout the city. It was a soft threat to comply.

"I do not want to be caught," Symbelle said in full transparency. "What is your intent by this?"

"I made a promise that I would find you one day and protect you at all costs. You were taken and hidden from your mother as a child by your father. Time does not allow me to divulge to you all just yet, but if you permit me, I would love nothing more than to do you this kindness when we can speak again. My Mage Ward will always be open to you," Shypriss promised.

Symbelle heard a familiar wheeze and cough not far behind her. She grabbed her horse's reins and turned it around to see Terrib Ango, the decrepit Maestro of the Monodrome, cantering up through the narrow bazaar toward the mineral-compound stall he had predesignated for their meeting.

Beside Terrib was another man, mounted on an even finer steed. Symbelle knew next to nothing about horses, but the beast the stranger rode was easily the most impressive creature she had ever laid eyes on. Its white coat could hardly be seen underneath the thick leather barding armoring its entire body and head. Its mane and tail were dyed blue, and protruding from its custom helm were two elongated boar tusks, making it appear like the horse was some unnatural crossbreed.

The man atop it was old as well, but Terrib was still easily ten to fifteen years his senior. He had bedecked himself in the finest leathers that could pass for trend-setting fashion. His greying hair was short and groomed in the popular military style. And the most prominent feature, which no one could miss, was the obvious deep gash on his right cheek, the remnant of some old wound that had never healed properly, almost like a hole had once been made in that part of his face.

"He is coming. That's my contact." Symbelle shifted her focus back to Terrib. "I ..." she stuttered in consideration of the lie she was about to voice. "I truly don't need protection."

"You are embedded with enemies in all corners, Symbelle. You may come to change your mind on that soon. I will be watching you."

A shudder went up Symbelle's spine with the realization of it all. She did have potential enemies that would kill her in a spit if she failed any of them. She was a triple agent, acting for the Oathemic Cabal, pretending to be a mole for the Stormtrees to infiltrate the Boarneck Company. What was she thinking? She was not trained for this life. She looked back to see the mage had vanished into the crowd, and then she took another glance over the metal salts she needed for the upcoming pyrotechnic constructions.

Something inside her told her right then that she knew she should have just stuck to a trade making fireworks for the rich. Or maybe she should open a simple apothecary shop and join the sea of salesmen that thrived right here on Festival Row. She could live a safe life.

"There's our fucking star!" Terrib shouted from not far off. She was in too deep now. There could be no such fantasy as living a safe life. Hyperis came with powerful parents, who invariably seemed to have unpreventable plans and schemes.

"Getting everything you need?" Terrib inquired in his croaky tone as the two elder men loomed over her from their horses. "You're a resourceful little cunt—the only Boarneck that's never asked for a copper to do whatever it is you're doing!"

She was no actress, but she was becoming better at feigning it. She puffed up a bold facade. "What I'm doing is preparing the best fireworks show the isle has ever seen. I do have my sources. I don't need your coppers yet."

"Aye?" The other older gentleman judged her with a calculating gaze. "And what sources might those be?"

He beamed with an air of obvious authority, and his demeanor made her feel uncomfortable. She was sure she was outwardly showing it, but she wouldn't let her voice quake and betray her. "I have my own purse. Is there an issue in that?"

"You are speaking to Oldan Boldandgold," Terrib Ango warned quietly with a nasty glare cast down at her. "Might wanna retrace your next words to see if you wanna go there."

This was him. The founder of the Boarneck Company. Another target in her Oathemic writs to assassinate. In the middle of Festival Row, in broad daylight and among hundreds of lively citizens and ignorant visitors, was not how she had envisioned her first encounter with the mercenary tycoon.

"Me and obscurity have never been friends. And you, strange alchemist, are just that—bloody obscure," Oldan declared.

"Sir ..." Symbelle stammered while determining how to properly address a man of his station. "Milord—" She stopped herself again, realizing that was how the lower class enunciated it. "My lord." She embarrassed herself for a third time. "What do you wish to know about me?"

Oldan just stared at her for more than a minute before speaking again. His face looked half annoyed, half analytical as he interrogated her. "What's an obscure rich girl like you doing seeking out me specifically? What do you want with my mercenary company if you don't have need of my money? You haven't asked to talk about payment once, nor any shared commissions."

That was an amateur fool's mistake on her part, she realized. She didn't even know how she was going to finish the sentence she had already started. "I just ..."

Fortunately, Oldan interrupted her. "And if you sell me some bloody shit about just needing to be accepted in this cruel world, or that you're running from whoever bullied you"—he waved his finger to indicate her facial scars—"I swear I'll gut you myself in this very street as if we had never become friends. No offense."

The unfamiliar cannot offend us. No hesitancy. Say it, Fyheir commanded within her.

"I burned them all alive." She did say it, feeling emboldened by her symbiotic fiery spirit. "Those who bullied me. And being accepted in a cruel world is something I knew I was never going to be good at. So I changed my ambitions. If the world is cruel, then only the cruelest can rise and thrive."

Oldan grinned, seeming to accept her spin on the fate thrown her way. "And you seem to be thriving," he assessed. "You have gained my attention. Now, what will you do with it? Your pitch lacks luster. You aren't from here. Why Goldgarden? Why the Boarneck Company?"

She had practiced this conversation in anticipation at least. "The misdeeds of my recent past were done in Az'Dayne, and they have rewarded me with a writ on my life from the Oathemic Cabal assassins. Goldgarden has immunity from their reach. I have learned that the Stormtrees guild, which oversees this great city's underworld, has a reputation for keeping their agents out. And your Boarneck Company offers protection that I currently need, and it is an enterprise for me to exploit that which interests me."

Whether Oldan was sold on her intent yet or not, she could not discern. His seasoned eyes didn't flinch as he played along. "And what interests you?"

"Oh ..." She hesitated.

Say it! Say it!

"Fire. Only fire."

Oldan nodded in understanding and sounded prepared for her story. "The blast salt we patented as our own. That's your invention, I hear. You want recognition for it. What do you want me to do with Jonan Riveiros?"

In truth, she held no resentment toward the man who had stolen the credit for her chemical invention in Tairanchula and taken it public in the Boarneck Company, but all this was part of the ploy, and she could not retire from it. "Jonan was a failure in Tairanchula and a thief of my prestige in the end. He took my recipe and the acclaim. I have an idea of what I want you to do to him."

Oldan backhanded Terrib on the shoulder and pulled a blank parchment from his leather doublet. "Let it be done, then. Write it up. I will entertain the idea of you, if you are what you present yourself to be." He turned to instruct his maestro. "Send word to my son, Tristostopher, to dispose of Jonan Riveiros, the pretender, whenever they are done with the alchemist's skills for Barredom's commission in Aggedon."

Oldan reached down a hand to help Symbelle onto her horse,

but she politely declined, nodding back to the mineral shop. "Anything else you need?" Oldan asked. "You are the new Grand Alchemist of the Boarneck Company. It is official."

On the spot, Symbelle could not conjure the words to thank the Boarneck leader for such an honor or articulate what she could possibly need, so she simply responded with the most appropriate words to come to mind. "You mentioned we get paid."

Oldan and Terrib looked at each other, confused, and simultaneously guffawed at the preposterous contradiction to her former notions.

"Tell me, Symbelle." Oldan was still laughing and genuinely smiling with his yellowy teeth. "You mentioned the Stormtrees. If I had turned you down, would you have joined Scarless instead?"

Lying without thinking too much on it was the soundest insurance, she determined. "You wouldn't have turned me down. But yes. I know nothing about this Scarless, but the Stormtrees guild would have been my next attempt."

"A pity." Oldan puckered his lips in distaste. "I would have had to kill you and would never have met you."

"A tragedy on your end well dodged, then. No loss on either's account now," she countered with an uncharacteristic sharp wit she accredited to Fyheir's tutelage.

"I like her," Oldan admitted as he snapped his head toward Terrib. "You like her?"

"I hate everyone," the old Maestro of the Monodrome cackled. "I might hate her less, though."

"Last thing. Then we are done today," Oldan said. "How are you going to do it? How are you going to astound my spectators with the biggest finale in a festival that they have ever seen? The Kingfall Ball must outdo anything that has ever been. It must be everything to everyone who witnesses it."

"I will spare you on the pyrotechnics. All new devices, you will see. But we will use barges, not in the streets in Bridgeville, as I have learned you've done in the past," she explained, purposely vague.

"Barges?" Terrib challenged, unconvinced. "Why the fuck put 'em on water?"

"Mobility." She silenced any more contentions to her logic. "I'll line these projectile pipes, these mortars, up with fuse flares and set them to be lit at specific times. One hundred per boat, and as many barges as we can manage. They will come in from the Utamian Channel, down past the Monodrome, and push through every water road of Bridgeville and Canaltown, as far as you want the parade to stretch. The whole population in the city's northern districts will see its magnificence, Boldandgold's Fireshower of the Kingfall Ball!"

Oldan's eyes sparkled at the vision of it all as he fell for it. "Give her everything she needs," he commanded Terrib Ango. "Take as much time as you wish. You'll be beside me during that time of the ball, at the festival's finale, on my pleasure barge. I want to be in the middle of the show. This will be the event of a lifetime. Plan to impress me that night, Symbelle." Oldan licked his lips and shot a devilish grin at her.

Terrib lifted his hand high above his head and made a circle motion several times. Several carts came into view, pulled by teams of horses. He ordered the Boarneck drudges to load whatever she needed until their combined funds ran out, to ensure her promised showcase for the Kingfall Ball's finale transpired in the way she had promoted.

They had no idea what was in store for them that night. And as Symbelle took one last glance at Oldan Boldandgold, an unsettled feeling coursed through her fiery veins as she realized that neither did she.

SCARLESS (VII)

PLAY TO THE PLAY

The old North Garrison officers' table served ideally in Scarless Square tonight for a confidential meeting of the Stormtrees' overmen and elite. Zahnastaazjah took in each of them and weighed his worth to her as she waited for her last man to join them.

Xalo, forever by her right side, was the only human in the room that she would hesitate to feel confident against if the terms between them fell into unfortunate hostilities. The pretty Elothian man was a self-assured individual who knew he was the best fighter in the room, or in any room, no matter what seasoned fighter might be present. But the spellblade had one major weakness: he needed his spellblade in order to be competent whatsoever in a fight. The magical swords themselves were rather jealous sentient things that would not allow their wielders the use of any powers or other form of weaponry without permission. She felt Xalo's own ego would be his downfall one day, but the lingering thoughts of losing her late lover to such a tragedy stirred an emotion she refused to dwell on in the moment.

Moving on, there was the only being in her party that made her remotely nervous, and he was her single member who was no human at all. Uubakrath was not even actually one of her Stormtrees, just a guardian of sorts assigned to her by her father and son from the Glazjhendun of the Glace Isles. The veteran Terollar archer was more than just a capable hand to bolster the competence of her already intimidating array of street-tough specialists. He was the best marksman she had ever seen, or even heard of—the outcome of a trade practiced to perfection for over three centuries.

Beside the tall bowman sat Usurp, the burly Vellyan, just as tall as Uubakrath. Usurp was an odious fellow in all facets of his personality, but the bruiser's merit was irrefutable. He commanded fear and respect among the surplus of thugs throughout the city, and gangs simply bent to his will. His violent reputation was unrivaled, and surprisingly, so was his proof of loyalty displayed toward Zahnastaazjah in their many years in each other's professional company.

Then there was Atrick. He may have looked like a man, but he was as much a weasel, a rat, and a snake combined, if ever there could have been such a detestable hybrid. As much as she didn't trust the contemptable turncoat, she silently applauded him for his industrious skill set in finding and producing money. Atrick and his Copper Jacks had brought in more revenue to the Stormtrees in his short time with the guild than the rest of her overmen combined had managed in years.

The last person in the war room while they waited for Devonduer to arrive was her new mage, Pyphan. He had a history full of holes, but the mysterious deeds of his past were not nearly as important as what he and his enigmatic foster sister could do for her aspirations.

Zahnastaazjah glanced over each weapon laid bare in the middle of the table. It was a sign of trust when she called in such assemblies. Her bloodrime spear, Usurp's maul, Atrick's longsword, and even Xalo's spellblade—all but Uubakrath's Terollar longbow. The elvan did what he wanted, and she had no authority to sway him otherwise. He was there for her protection, but hoping he would comply with the policies and agendas of the guild was a fruitless exercise.

Another hour escaped them in patience-trying quips passed between Xalo, Usurp, and Atrick. Being elvan, Zahnastaazjah knew that such forbearance for the irksome tedium had been exercised with age.

Two pairs of footsteps could be heard charging up the steps just outside the door. Devonduer trampled over his own feet, out of breath, with Amaris, the Stormtrees' safe-house keeper, in tow.

"It's done!" Devonduer panted while pulling back on the tail his hair was tied in, as he always did when anxious. "All's in place."

"The safe house as well? How close did you get us?" Zahnastaazjah directed this straight at Amaris.

"One to meet your mole beforehand, and one for you after the play to the play is done. The old Ingid Manor on Cryptly Heights in the Midway and the abandoned timber warehouse in Canaltown, between—"

Zahnastaazjah waved a hand to interrupt Amaris, knowing she could neglect the details. She needed only directions and times, not particulars. "Good, Amaris. Get them ready. You are dismissed."

"You don't wish me to sit in this time?" Amaris dared to inquire, shuffling in regretful retrospection of challenging the command.

The room paused to consider how Zahnastaazjah was going to react. She just stood up and towered over Amaris, the short-haired woman's head barely coming up to her bosom. Zahnastaazjah stared down into her fretful brown eyes for a while before placing her strong palms around Amaris's face, a hand on each side. Zahnastaazjah gave a grin that somehow conveyed no sentiment of amicability, and she tapped her with two light slaps to Amaris's right cheek. "No, I don't wish you to sit in this time," she seethed.

Amaris backed away without delay and bowed before exiting the old war room, leaving Zahnastaazjah's chosen overmen and specialists to themselves.

She kicked out a nearby chair and physically coerced Devonduer down to make himself comfortable, which the Stormtrees' negotiator did in the most uncomfortable way. Zahnastaazjah then found her own seat again and returned to the conversation at hand. "Talk to me. How is she?"

Devonduer took in a gulp of air, then pulled out his waterskin to quench his gabby tongue before beginning. "She met Boldandgold. They've given her full access to the blast salt, and she will be directly coordinating the fireworks finale of the Kingfall Ball."

"Then it's in motion. The play to the play," she declared to the group. "Take a good look at the Square, everyone. Most of you won't be back to it for a while. There will be a brief war in the streets, and I'll tell you how it goes."

Devonduer coughed and knocked on the table with his knuckles just loud enough to steal attention. His voice was meek when he piped up. "Street warring is not really my particular specialty …"

"Being a squat-pissin' bitch is, though, we know," Usurp berated him in his gruff tone. "You'll just get in the way."

"I said most of you," Zahnastaazjah corrected in a scolding manner. "Devonduer, after we leave, I put you in control of the Square until the bloodshed is done."

She took the end of Usurp's maul and the hilt of Atrick's sword and positioned them on the table for the overmen to grasp their weapons. "Usurp and Atrick, you will do what needs to be done by minimizing the casualty risk of any innocent passersby. Only mercs of the Boarneck Company die the night we do this."

"That ain't what I do," Usurp huffed as he drew his massive hammer into his lap, looking confused. "Minimizin' casualties?"

She ignored the impudent Vellyan. "Atrick, you will take up a position in Dreamer's View, just over Garden's Bridge. Bring as many of your most competent Jacks with you as you can. Quietly dispose of any of Terrib Ango's solicitors for the ball and replace them with your own. Your goal here is to push visitors through Bridgeville with false information, so they don't linger in the district. You will lie and make it public knowledge that the Kingfall Ball will be held on Festival Row now. Dissuade any rumors about the Monodrome or Canaltown being an area of interest."

"Yes, master. On it." Atrick obediently submitted to his responsibility.

Xalo jabbed at his former custodian. "Don't look so sad that you and Usurp can't play with the big boys this turn."

But Atrick retaliated with not even a glance at the intimidating spellblade.

It was Usurp who struck back for him. "The fuck's that s'posed t'mean?"

Zahnastaazjah squinted her green eyes, annoyed. "Usurp, you're doing that thing again."

"What?" The Vellyan looked at his leader, bemused.

"Translation," Xalo simplified. "Shut the fuck up."

Usurp was a bold brute who didn't take much heed of the competence in Xalo's lethal capabilities. He would probably have openly challenged the Elothian right then and there and died if Zahnastaazjah hadn't ushered the tone of seriousness along.

"Extortion is your game," she told Usurp. "Do what you do best, but do it quieter. I want every ticket to the Monodrome the day of the ball bought up. If they're not a Boarneck or one of our implanted Stormtrees, they don't get in. Find any citizen or tourist who already has a ticket, and buy it off them. If they are proving stubborn, then make them … unstubborn."

The massive ruffian seemed keen to take on the role laid out for him. "Never met someone too stubborn," he patted his maul.

"Where does my sister come into it?" Pyphan joined in on the most prominent part of the topic.

"With us." Zahnastaazjah prepared to elaborate. "You, Xalo, Uubakrath, and I, we will go after Oldan and his guard. It's going to have to look like an accident with the blast salt and fireworks show. By the end of this, the Monodrome will be a pile of ashen debris floating down the canals, and the Boarneck Company will be left leaderless."

"Oldan's son, Tristostopher, will return one day, likely in a season or so," Devonduer said, announcing the results of research conducted by his network outside Goldgarden Isle. "He will be looking for the murderers of his dead dad. The war's basically over between Barredom and Aggedon. The Boarneck Cavaliers will be coming back richer than ever before."

Zahnastaazjah waved her hand, slating the tangent of Tristostopher for another day. "We will chop the head off that snake when it's time. That's a long way off yet. Besides, I may have a solution for removing the problem of the Cavaliers' captain after we end Oldan's reign in the city."

"Details, then, my Zahna. Let us do this." Xalo spun the emerald pommel of his magic sword toward him on the table before grabbing it to sheathe it.

He knows I hate that, she fumed at her agitating lover's audacity to call her pet names against her continual behest not to. But she declined to counter Xalo, for the sake of maintaining dominance in the room. "You sent me word that she has been given the liberty to roam freely for now?"

The question was directed at Devonduer, and he confirmed it. "Yes, Guildmother, to finalize her prep for the Kingfall Ball with whatever she needs."

Zahnastaazjah stood up and held her hand above her bloodrime spear, and the symbiotic weapon hovered up from the table and into her grasp.

"Then get word to her. Symbelle will meet us at the safe house before we set this city on fire."

ATHANIEL (III)

SECRETS AND SYMPATHIES

His brethren in the Hive Order of the Oathemic Cabal referred to it as the gargoyle game. Gargoyles were a creature of myth used primarily in Daynish sculptures. They were humanoids depicted as grotesque grey statues with demon-like wings and exaggerated features in the face, hands, and feet. The religion of the Five and Five said that gargoyles were humans who had chosen to become heathens, casting out their devotion to the Fives, choosing to embrace the tairan or shadow or sky element of their descendancy through some blasphemous ritual instead.

Even though there was some merit to the myth, with the grey skin and a sacrilegious path of infusing the elements into one's soul, the fable had become an outdated one since the popularity and validity of the qindrid cultures in the north and east had been proven. Now there was no talk of gargoyles. Grey-skinned, elementally enhanced infidels were all qindrid, period. And anyone identified as a qindrid may as well be considered just as grotesque as a gargoyle.

At least, that was what the world had taught him to believe as a child, and what the Oathemic Cabal ingrained in its members. But things were evolving fast before his eyes. Athan wasn't so sure what the future held in the way of drastic reform for what was to be believed or not anymore.

But he did still believe in the gargoyle game.

In the initial training of a killer for the Hive Order, the masters first exercised them into perfecting the five noncombative virtues of an assassin: surveillance, stillness, study, stealth, and subterfuge.

Throughout the game, the boys could pick any place in any random town or city chosen by the Keepers' Order. One boy played gargoyle, while the others were the hunters. The gargoyle had to choose five spots to stay in or guises to assume, and they had to stay in such a place or costume for one hour while the others tried to find them. If the hunters chose the wrong person, such as a non-playing citizen, then they lost the game and had to sit out until the next session. The way the gargoyle would win the game was to last five hours, moving between five different spots or guises without getting caught or have the hunters exhaust all their choices on the wrong candidates. It was a tedious but fun game that instilled patience in them before they were trained to be killers.

And so, sitting in the bedroom of his younger sister Odysserae for the past seven hours may have been a test to break the fortitude of most men, but for Athaniel Chandoss, it was just another day with a longer version of the gargoyle game.

The sun had waned some ten hours back. Dawn wasn't too far off. The latter hours of brightening twilight had made the many tapestries across her wall visible once more.

Odysserae had always been a fan of beautiful things—pretty art, pretty jewels, pretty clothes, pretty people. But she showed none of that outside the room he now found himself in, assessing his troubled sibling from the inside out.

The bedchamber was excessively large, like each of his sisters' private rooms, fitting for their aristocratic likings. Odysserae's ceilings were three times as tall as a man, and the room was as wide as most townspeople's entire houses. The wall with the tapestries on it had the large pieces of artwork on some sort of hanging rod, such that they could be moved to a variety of areas on two sides of the room, opposite the corner the canopy bed was placed in.

Athan hadn't moved a muscle to do anything more than blink in the past half hour. But when the door handle moved and in skulked his quiet sister, he did find himself fiddling with the dagger head he had specially made for her from the Oathemic Cabal.

He waited for the door to shut once more and for her to deadbolt it in three places behind her before he stood to catch her attention and whisper, "Hello, little sister."

Athan knew her impaired ears couldn't hear him, but she was adept enough at lip-reading to discern his careful enunciations. "Do not be scared. We have secrets to share with one another."

Athan utilized the respectful gesturing language of Hands for her to communicate back with him. "*Sit down,*" he motioned.

Odysserae was clearly startled, and regardless of his counsel to be at ease, it was the first time she had ever looked at him and conveyed a sense of actually being scared at all. *"I do not want to tell my secrets,"* she said back in Hands.

He beckoned her toward him with his finger. *"But you will."*

When Odysserae stood next to him, he put a calming brotherly hand on her shoulder and guided her to the bed to sit comfortably beside him. He gestured, *"But first, gift time? You like gifts."*

He tried to lighten the ominous mood in the air, but he was sure he had failed at that endeavor when she flinched as he produced the sharp weapon he was concealing to lay across her lap.

"For my wyrkenido," Odysserae ogled over the masterwork of the fine Abellagen steel with its wavy inlaid design. The rope dart's main ring that melded into the butt of the weapon had no rope in it at the moment. Athan was aware that the weight of the blade head was more balanced for lethal utility compared to the performance versions she was mostly adept with.

He nodded to her and softly set down a coil of thin rope and a wire garrote next. *"I know you have a passion with ropes. They are less messy. Do not be afraid to put them to use more than just on stage."*

As she fondled rope, tethering it through the eye of the dart in defensive silence, Athan played with the torn and crumpled scroll in his pocket, the one that Sundorion had thrown in his direction that provided the very purpose for his presence here in this very room now. Athan studied his grown-up sister's face, still deeming her the innocent and aloof child he would always remember her to be, with her short, boyish red hair and downtrodden amber eyes. He wasn't quite ready to show her just yet.

"When else would I use them?" she acted naïve. *"I have never hurt anyone. I have no reason to."*

"But you do have more reason to than anyone. To hurt those who keep hurting you. You want to, but you need me to show you how." Athan encouraged for her to trust him and reveal her plight.

"I want to." Odysserae turned her back to him and hung her head like a child who knew she was about to be scolded. She held out one hand behind her to make the gestures in Hands to spell out, *"What are you about to tell me?"*

Athan went to the nightstand to jot down a note on one of the many empty scrolls. He took the parchment and went to stand in front of her to gesture a response before handing it over to her.

"That you do not have to do what it is you are planning to do. You do not have to become one of them."

Odysserae acted ineffectively ignorant of the insinuation, so he forced the note into her grasp to read for herself what it said: "Do not succumb to become a neverborne qindrid. I know everything."

She tried to huff, but it sounded more like an awkward hiss as she disposed of the parchment in disgust as if it were covered in shit. *"What, then?"* Odysserae hammered out with her fingers and fist.

Athan explained on paper: "There is an affiliate order of the Oathemic Cabal. They are based in Savatarm. The Cobra Collective has a faction designated as the Quiver, comprised of women only. They are a branch of the Stormtrees guild out of Goldgarden. All you need to do is to get on the same boat we are arranging to smuggle Sashka out in. When you get to Savatarm, the first city is called Shellport. Find the market and ask any harlot where you can find the Quiver. They will bring you to them."

"Cobras and harlots? What about my ears?" She stood as she pointed to them and then opened her mouth dramatically to indicate inside. *"And my tongue? Will your snakes and whores cure those?"*

Things were getting serious, and the only logic Athan could counter with was blatant facts, with no more punches pulled. "What about your honor?" He spoke aloud clearly and pointed straight between her legs. "I told you we would be sharing secrets. Sit back down," he commanded without waiting for her compliance as he shoved her into the plush bedside chair.

Athan took out Sundorion's torn scroll, which Odysserae must have had with the Zandaryn in Valdean's sanctum during one of her recent visits there. The imprisoned elvan had known Athan would react exactly as he was now, and he was likely counting on some form of repayment in an escape plan.

Athan waited for Odysserae to finish reading her own writing, but he was sure she stopped halfway through, as she promptly sprang back to her feet to abscond from the bedroom and flee any further confrontation on this topic.

She didn't make it far. He put himself in her path, blocking every avenue she tried in order to detour around him. He had loitered the entire night for his stubborn sister, but the time for patience had expired.

Athan pointed a threatening finger at her, warning her not to dare try fleeing again. He briskly walked over to the tapestry wall and rolled three of them to a different section in the bedchamber to reveal what was being concealed behind them.

"These the men?" Athan demanded in Hands.

Odysserae showed sincere signs of concern when she inspected the hanging lineup. The rope-bound, ball-gagged individuals on the rollers were the ones he had captured and detained earlier in the evening. It hadn't been difficult to find the three boasting culprits in the household guard using subtle Oathemic tactics of extraction throughout Castle Chandoss. Beneath them each was a wash basin that he had confiscated to clean up the inevitable mess to come.

One of the three was already dead, punctured in every vital organ until he was bled out into the bucket below him. He had proven to be the least skilled in following instructions to keep quiet until told otherwise. The dead neverborne's features had returned to their trait colors with grey skin, red irises, red fingernails, and the blackest of hair.

The face of one of the other qindrid's was halfway morphed between a semblance of Athan's face and his own, appearing deformed and grotesque. *Skin-changers and shape-shifters. The art of the neverborne we now have to deal with,* Athan mused with no tolerance for it. "You did not understand the instructions either I see," he scolded in a low tone.

In a split second, he had one of his knives in hand and thrusted it upwards into the groin of the one with the semi-shifted face. He repeated the action six more times before anyone in the room had registered that he did. He could hear his sister's disconcerted gasp behind him, but he chose to ignore it.

The remaining living qindrid appeared like a normal man, in his natural pigments he likely had before he had undergone the Transcendence. The neverborne squirmed and issued muffled pleas in his bonds, as he stared horrified at the wash basin filling up higher with his comrade's blood spilling between his legs. But Athan's ears were more deaf to the pleas than his sister's.

Athan's intuition was on full alert. His focus honed in on the door of the chamber and for any motion in the room. Fortunately, his sister remained paralyzed in startlement. Athan waved her over to the small table for her to hurriedly scour through the message he had prepared before she ever stepped in:

"On this rising dawn, I will wield the Chandoss Spellblade for all of the family to see. It will not deny me. It has been foreseen in seerstone visions that it will be me who unlocks it. I would like you there to witness it. Immediately after, I will be leaving back to the Cabal. There will be a mage on the hill of Lovers' Labyrinth that will take me. His name is Elixion. You need to accept my invitation to come with me, or allow me to save you by sending you away with Sashka. Let me help you."

"What about Val and Addy? And Ember?" Odysserae simply scribed back.

"Our cousin is lost. You would do well to lose no sleep on it. But if that is what it takes to convince you, I will steal Ember away too. Val is part of the plan. My master, Coldborn, who sent me here, has plans for her that are in motion that I am yet privy to. She will be safe. Addy just got herself in a complication with the Thrench that I cannot intervene with until I consult with my masters. But you have my word, I will not forget her. I will come back if you let me take you from Valdean and all of this."

Athan watched her read over his words again, but this time she pushed away the parchment and resorted to the communication of Hands, which she was most accustomed to. *"But my ears and voice?"*

He consented to speaking in the gesture language with her. *"Coldborn is the most powerful mage on Penthara. If any living man on Penthara knows a way, he will find a way,"* Athan struggled to gain her trust with finding an alternative solution for her lifelong impairment. *"There is also another archmage locked away in Barredom. He is called the Titan. He is the tier-five Dawning mage with healing abilities like no other in the realm. Perhaps —"*

"You do not know another way," Odysserae snapped her hands together, interrupting him with her gestures. *"Coldborn does not know! The Titan is locked up! And no one can help me except Count Valdean! That is why I do what he says! That is who will help me!"*

This time Athan snapped, but he transferred his fury into a violent embrace over his sister, smothering her in his chest. He squeezed her so hard he could feel her struggling to breathe. She did not fight back. Odysserae only burst into a fit of sobbing at his mercy. He wanted to cry with her. He begged to his lost gods for the momentary ability to shed a single tear even for her. But he couldn't. Athan just slowly released his tension to hug her back and hold her for as long as it took to bring her comfort.

Fives, I do not pray you to. I pray to none now other than the cruel curse of this Chandoss blood in our veins. Release us now, please! Let me save just this one. Show me the way before I am taken away …

Odysserae pulled back and dried her tears up on her sleeve. Her glossy eyes tunneled in anger on the violator still alive that was bound to the wall.

"You do not have to join the Cobra Collective," Athan counseled in Hands, hoping to mollify the mood between them. *"There are other ways I can show you."*

Odysserae whipped toward to the bed surprisingly fast, and when her spin turned her back around she had already let fly the rope dart that pinpointed directly into the neverborne's throat just above the collar line. The bound qindrid writhed in pain and panic only for a few seconds more when she jerked back on the rope dart to volley it back into her grasp from across the room.

Athan stared in disbelief between his grim-posed sister and the last dead guard. *Was he your first kill?* Somehow, Athan considered it very plausible that he had misjudged her experience. *Who is training you? This Ise'andahr that hides in our walls,* he glanced over the ceiling corners of the room a bit uncomfortable about the Neveril he was aware of, but had never seen, *or is it pure hate that moves you so?*

They both had secrets, but she wasn't telling any more of hers and he was done telling his. The time for sympathies was null and gone as well. *"I will dispose of this mess. You can return in an hour."*

As she reluctantly dropped her weapon to the ground and scuttled her way toward the door, he grabbed her to try one last time. He didn't use Hands. He knew she could interpret his lips. "Be there tomorrow for me. Pack light. We can leave right after."

Athan imagined he should have felt some form of satisfaction in exacting such a revenge for his sister's honor on the qindrid that had defiled her. But instead, all he could dwell on was the fact that he was too late to redeem her. *There is a killer in you yet sister,* he mused to himself as she exited her own bedchamber.

VALAYTHEA (VI)

THE WIELDER

The palace solarium felt strange to her today, like an old friend from her childhood she had lost touch with and almost forgotten all about. *It has been months,* she realized, grasping how much time had passed since her last visit to its sumptuously snug staging.

The sun was what made its spacious opulence all the more grandiose. Without its celestial omnipresence, the plush conservatory would have just served as another room in the palace.

And today the morning beamed bright with the new dawn's glaring smile over the study chamber. The light was just vivid enough to blind one to the marvelously intricate detail of the many fine sculptures, paintings, and abstract artworks. But even the sun could not hope to outshine the brilliance of the most prized possession in the whole region of Chandoshia, the Chandoss Spellblade, which solemnly rested above the hearth mantel with its golden guard and bone scabbard.

It was the reason they had all been gathered today. There were no Teaching Hours about to commence with her uncle's educational sermons, for which she was accustomed to visiting the solarium. This time it was Athan who had summoned her family in.

But only a select few had chosen to join his monumental invitation. Her father and Valdean had Adyssaira wrapped up in session after session with the Thrench ever since she began courting the No-Name boy she was now calling Desdjlandar. And for whatever more prominent reason her clandestine sister had, Odysserae had opted to stay missing from Athan's substantial moment as well. And speaking of her elders, the only one from the household to show was Uncle Nikayle. Count Valdean, her father, and Taizsha may as well have spit in Athan's face. The disrespect of everyone's absence was not excused.

All Athan had been able to do for the past half hour or more was nervously pace the sunroom, making it quite clear that he was waiting for their attendance before beginning.

Nikayle had been transferred to his corner rocking chair, facing the group, so that he could enjoy a bit of leisurely mobility.

Uncle Nikayle. Valaythea glanced over at him, hoping not to catch his notice. She again recalled the cryptic words that the strange mage Coldborn had told her on her last night with Izayus: *When your memories return, you must tell only one, your uncle, Nikayle lon'Chandoss the Thirdnamed. He will instruct you as to what to do … Once one takes the Oath, one is bound for life. Nikayle will never retire from his obligation with the Cabal.* Though instead of pursuing a private audience with him to discover answers, Valaythea had entirely avoided her uncle. She wasn't ready for her memories to return—or ever would be, in truth.

She weighed on that last phrase in her mind one more time: *Once one takes the Oath, one is bound for life. Nikayle will never retire from his obligation with the Cabal.* Neither Nikayle nor Athan ever made eye contact between one another that she had took notice of, but for the first time, Valaythea contemplated how much the two knew about one another's involvements in the guild or with their individual obligations to Coldborn.

Emberalda had come in late but had still been present for the past ten minutes. At least her body was present, since her mind was anything but. Her cousin's pristine state of natural appeal had been done an appalling injustice. Her sandy-brown hair, usually kempt, looked like it had been tangled for a pentday, and the bags under her eyes provided proof of lack of sleep. Emberalda's dress was the same one Valaythea recalled seeing on her a few days ago. She had the shakes, as if she hadn't been eating, and she must have gotten up to sit in each chair in the room twice over already, unable to get comfortable.

Finally Valaythea attempted sympathy for her self-tortured cousin and pulled two overly large posh cushions down to the floor near the empty fireplace for them to sit together on. She forced her to stop her perpetual rocking with simple, soothing strokes of her cousin's hands.

"I cannot take it anymore, Val," Emberalda finally uttered. "He is still here. I can feel it. He needs me."

Valaythea knew she meant Timmurian, Emberalda's ill-fated elvan lover. She remembered her cousin having such resolve in being coveted, unwavering in rebuffing the surface affections and attractions of the decems of boys who had thrown themselves at her throughout her late adolescence. Not a single one of them had ever even remotely impacted her. The Emberalda she used to envy was impervious to such silly things. *I think the spell cast on you is far stronger than the one that's been put on me*, she mocked in her thoughts, but she shut down the insensitivity as quickly as it had come.

Valaythea spoke as quietly as her cousin's tone to keep Athan and Nikayle from eavesdropping. "What about Sun, then?"

Emberalda's face went sour with raw anger, but the volume of her voice was still just higher than a whisper. "You know it and I know, like Taizsha warned—Sun got too close and probably found Timm, and now suffers the same fate. I think they both live."

"Got too close to what?" Valaythea feigned intrigue, being the actress she was trained to be, but she was sure she knew after her private audience with Valdean.

"You tell me!" Emberalda snapped accusingly but quietly. "You're the one fucking the Prince of Az'Dayne! Do not act like you do not know more than everyone in this damn palace!"

Valaythea let go of her hands, since the allegation was offensive, but that only fueled Emberalda to huff and continue her attack. "And I know the count has told you more. You and Oddy are both the same, and now even Addy too! Everyone is in on it but me! Valdean hates me, and I do not know why. My own father will not even tell me!"

Valaythea watched her cousin's glare shift over to Nikayle as if she was condemning him for his own betrayals as a father. She found her tone mirroring the somber shift in mood of her cousin's voice with growing compassion. "What do you want me to say? If Timmurian is still in the estates, you know as well as I do where he is: in the tower. What are you afraid of? Valdean shows contempt to the whole family. He is a miserable brooder. What do you think he will actually do if you show up and knock? He lives for this family and its legacy. He will not kill you."

"He will not? Val, I know he killed my mother," she seethed between clenched teeth, speaking even more softly than before. Her cousin then nodded in the direction of her paralyzed father in the corner. "I know he did that to Father."

This dire revelation was not something Valaythea had ever wanted to believe about the rumors. "What?" She shook her head in disbelief at such an accusation of blood treachery. "I do not need to know this. I need another spell on me."

"Timm was going to do it, you know?" Emberalda ignored her plea to cease from enlightening her deeper down the forbidden burrows of the Chandoss Estates' dark secrets. "He was going to commit to the Taboo and become quasi, like Taizsha did for your father. He was going to do it for us. We were to be married." She choked up slightly in the wayward drift of improbable pleasant thoughts. "We were going to have baby half-elven, move to the Savatarm Provinces, live in the new world ..."

Valaythea could not refrain from raising an eyebrow in disbelief at the fanciful notion. "That sounds absurdly whimsical. You do know you are still a Chandoss. None of us are escaping this," she reminded her. "We are all cursed for life."

Emberalda's glossy-eyed focus tunneled in on the sheathed spellblade above the hearth, again fading far away to anywhere but here. "My brother ran. He got away."

It seemed so long ago that her cousin Nikayle the Fourthnamed had fled from the prison that they still called home. Valaythea had always imagined that he was off living in Savatarm or Goldgarden, thriving in modern indulgences with no aristocratic obligations that may as well have been dungeon shackles for what they had felt like.

But instead of saying something positive to reinforce Emberalda's fantasies of a better life, Valaythea was in an especially dour mood, and it showed in her retort. "And now he will live in hiding under a different name for the rest of his days."

"You think I give five fucks about my name?" Emberalda shot back. "Do you mean to tell me you are yet to know what it feels to be in love? If you did, you would not chastise my plight with such apathy."

"If only you could see inside my head ..." Valaythea paused a moment and let out a heavy sigh in contemplation. "You would sadly perceive that my answer is no. The purpose of love remains more foreign to me than those Threnchmen outside our doors."

"The Threnchmen outside." Emberalda accidentally said this loud enough to catch Athan's attention. "Addy should be here."

Her brother whipped around to them as if they were the standing accused in some magistrate's court. "They should both be here! Odysserae must be here for this! We wait for her."

Uncle Nikayle voiced his opinion. "No one else is coming Athan. You can get this over with and meet the mage outside to put it behind you for good."

Valaythea and Emberalda's quiet exchange was brought to a halt as Athan and Nikayle had the floor with their concerns now.

"Put it behind me? It has been seen Nikayle! I was told so by Coldborn himself," Athan's panged tone was clearly offended by his uncle's doubts.

"This is folly, Athan. You already know my take on this, but I will say it again"—he pointed to Emberalda, implying Nikayle the Fourthnamed in every way—"My son is already the spellblade for this generation in our family line. It is time you accept this."

Athan vehemently snapped back, kicking the leg clean off one of the end tables. "The Barturon Spellblade that my cousin now wields is not even tied to our Chandoss bloodline! Aunt Delphine blessed that weapon onto him, but this one, the sword of Aemenus, remains ripe and ready! Spellblades choose who is worthy of them within their line, period. That is the science, Uncle."

"Fair logic, I am sure. How cosmically convenient that you believe my son and yourself, both the same age, will be awarded one of the legacy swords bound to either side of the family lineage. You think its tallying your death count before it lets you? If that blade denies you, it will kill you boy!" He pointed to the glass sword.

"Where in the five hells is Oddy?" Athan barked to no one in particular in a frustrated burst of fury.

A familiar foreboding voice came from the doorway to the solarium. "She wanted me to tell you that she regrets that she cannot come. I will sit in for her instead." Valdean smirked as he pompously strode into the room in his customary robe.

For the first few days after the homecoming banquet, Valdean had taken up all of Valaythea's free time with incessant questionings any time he could get the chance. In her private quarters, over undisclosed dinners between just the two of them, catching her on morning strolls, practically anywhere he could find her at any given time. All was to no avail, much to his obvious dismay, as the majority of anything pertinent she was pressed for was still blocked by Coldborn's shadow spell.

"She cannot come?" Athan probed Valdean with revulsion in his heated eyes. "Why would that be?"

"I think your brief session back home has expired. You dabble outside the realm you are permitted to play in. Time for you to run along now." Valdean scolded her brother like a youth in his early teens.

"Why couldn't you allow Addy to come?" Valaythea heard herself asking aloud without thinking too much on why she dared to open her mouth in her great-granduncle's presence. She turned her next question to Athan, sincerely curious. "Did you invite her?"

"He invited her," Valdean verified before Athan could. "But she will not be coming either. She is doing her duty for the family, as would be wise for each of you. Adyssaira is sealing our deal with the Thrench."

Valdean glanced back at the solarium double doors and snapped his fingers. Following the simple command, the open entry was barred by the sentries in the hallway, leaving only those of Chandoss blood in the study chamber to their privacy.

Emberalda stood up defiantly, even when Valaythea tried in vain to tug her back down to the cushion beside her on the floor. "I doubt she even got word that Athan wanted her here," her cousin proclaimed. "She would not have missed this for you!"

"Do not act so noble, Emberalda," Valdean warned. "You shan't be staying either. I am ending this charade. Business is imminent. All must be in place before Prince Izayus returns for Valaythea."

Valdean pried an exceptionally large iron key out of some concealed pocket under his robe and tossed it across the room to bounce just past Emberalda's shoes.

"A key?" her cousin inquired.

"The key to my tower," he elucidated.

Emberalda grimaced at the sight of the cumbersome thing, snubbing it as if it were a chunk of rotting cheese. "Why would I want this?"

"You have my permission to leave." Valdean shooed her away with two fingers. "Permanently. Go find what you are looking for, and get them out of here before the Thrench catch on that we are housing and feeding elven under our roof."

"You have had Timmurian all along? And you took Sundorion?" Emberalda was stomping and screaming out the questions now, bolder than Valaythea had ever seen someone dare to confront the count.

"They would be our end," Valdean said, unperturbed, practically bored. "I was made aware that the Thrench were coming to our shores, seeking an audience with our house, but I did not know why. Those two are the loudest sandlings in the region and would be too stubborn simply to lie low. We cannot be affiliated with elven during these critical times. Taizsha is with them now as well."

"Where is Sashka?" Valaythea interrogated no one specific.

Valdean shot a fiery squint down at Valaythea and then shifted his inimical gaze over to Emberalda, clearly losing patience. "What are you still doing here?"

Her fragile cousin hesitantly began to veer toward the exit in the wake of their great-granduncle's berating. "Val?" She looked at her straight in the eyes, seeming scared and pleading for sound advice.

"Do not go alone, Ember," Valaythea cautioned. "I will come with you, right after this."

"My mood is a fickle thing as of late. Go now, else I may change my mind." Valdean proved his tolerance was sapped.

Emberalda apologized to Athan with her eyes as she scooted quickly to the door of the solarium. "I am sorry, Athan. I am so sorry!"

Her brother snatched her by the arm before she could react with another step. "Wait for me," he openly bade her, with a tone of compassion Valaythea had not heard in his voice in years. "This fiend has no intention of giving you anything but the same thing he gave your mother."

With Athan's dire insinuation of Valdean's malicious intent, they all took a long look at the aged man as if he were some abhorrent monster that roamed the palace.

"Ember!" Nikayle shouted after her when she broke her arm free of Athan and disappeared around the corner.

"I warn you now Count," Nikayle threatened Valdean, seeming as if he was about to shun his paralyzed impediment and rise from his chair, "not a hair on her head. I vow to the darkest gods, if you plan to —"

"Yes, yes, her hairs will be intact," Valdean snubbed Nikayle's weak warning, not taking her crippled uncle capable of any danger he could conjure.

"Get on with this, Athaniel," their great-granduncle huffed, and he motioned toward the sword on the mantel as he sat down, fatigued, in one of the chairs. "And then get on with yourself. You will no longer interfere with the affairs of House Chandoss. You are no longer a part of this legacy that I control."

Valdean's dispassionate words of riddance ignited Athan into action. Her brother strode across the room to yank the sheathed glass sword from its perch, and he did the previously unthinkable. He forced the Chandoss Spellblade from its bone scabbard and attempted to wield it for his present family to witness.

His amber eyes took on a twinkle of victorious glee that Valaythea had never seen before in them. But that only lasted a fleeting moment. The emotion on her brother's face fast warped into something entirely opposite: absolute dread.

Athan stared at his right hand as if it were betraying his command, and his cheekbones rose in an expression of sudden agony. "Argh!" He wailed as his knees buckled, and his neck pulsed with muscles clenched, like in every other part of his now-writhing body.

"Athan, let go!" their uncle warned.

"Keep holding on, boy," Valdean spitefully urged as Athan's red hair rapidly began to pale into an elderly grey, and wrinkles began to form at the corners of his eyes. "Prove yourself!"

"Let go, or it will consume you in full!" Nikayle shouted at the top of his lungs, again pressing him to submit before it claimed his life.

"It's killing him!" Valaythea screamed, now standing over her twitching brother, who was curled into a fetal position, and she did not even remember standing up. "Stop him!"

"Nooooooo!" Athan kicked for his life, defying their reasoning. "It was seen ... I would unlock this spellbla —" He was barely able to talk, but his eyes cast out a new hatred in the direction of their great-granduncle.

Nikayle slammed his fist on the arm of his chair, unable to remove himself to save anyone even if he cared to try. "Athan, accept its decision and let it go!"

"No ... It is ... testing ... me." His words were coming out softer, between long pauses as his body underwent spasms. His sword arm seemed scorched to a char, and his aging face appeared progressively older.

It came from nowhere—a headache like none Valaythea could ever even imagine. It struck her like lightning, and she swore her brain had imploded. Something inside her knew what to do without being told. It was just as if her soul had the knowledge stowed within it, hidden in some ethereal vault all along. Her right hand was moving, though she did not command it to do so. Her mouth was moving, though she had no idea what she was about to say or why she did shout the name of her famous ancestor. "Aemenus!"

And it was done. Her brother no longer seemed in pain. The cursed sword was free from his grasp. His supine body no longer convulsed, and he was simply staring back up at her now, utterly confused. They were all looking at her; Valdean and Nikayle were confused as well.

"Valaythea," Uncle Nikayle whispered, his eyes fixed on what was in her grip that she was too scared to see for herself. "This cannot be."

But she did look. Her eyes felt stretched twice as wide as she imagined she could make them. She tried to drop the spellblade out of her grasp, but it would not allow it. "I don't want it."

She meant what she said. This was all backward from the way life was supposed to have been mapped out for them. Athan was the warrior of the family. He had spent his entire adult life proving himself worthy of its embrace. This was his weapon.

"You do not get to decide that," Uncle Nikayle said. "*It* decides."

Valaythea saw a green glow flash in her right eye, and she felt her shoulder, elbow, and wrist possessed by some force within her to sheathe the glass blade back into its scabbard made of elvan bone. She dropped the entire thing to the floor the moment the spellblade allowed it.

"This changes everything," Valdean declared.

"But I am the prince's paramour now," Valaythea whispered, in denial of the impossible twist of fate.

"This does not have to be acted upon at all, Valdean. Let us forget it ever happened." Her uncle's tone was concerned.

"Guards!" Valdean shouted, ignoring him.

The solarium doors opened, and in came the two entry sentries, followed right behind by six more of the Chandoss Guard down the hallway.

"Escort Valaythea to her personal chamber. We have much to discuss." Valdean ushered her by the hand into the custody of two unfamiliar men.

"Athan's time in the palace is done. See him off the estates and safely back to his order. I have already sent word to the mage outside of all his dirty deeds." Valdean kicked her brother's boots just before he was forced to his feet to be dragged out by two sentries of the Chandoss Guard.

Athan would not stop looking her in the eye. The sentiment he expressed wasn't anger or sadness. It was void of all warmth, blanketed in cold, emotionless emptiness. And for some reason, even though she was certain she may never see him again, she was more scared of him in that moment that anyone or anything she had encountered before.

"Brother," she whispered, almost inaudibly, as if it were the sincerest apology.

"Oddy," he whispered back with his exhausted eyes closed from the arcane enervation that was forced through his body. "Save Oddy for me," he tried to beg her as the two of them were separated into different directions down the hallway and out of each other's sight.

SUNDORION (V)

QUANDARY OF THE QUASI

This was new. Sun woke today bound upright by the cold feel of iron links over his exposed limbs and waist, gagged tight and blinded. The clinking of turning gears and a chain mechanism in continuous motion resounded down a tunnel, letting him know he was still likely underground. His head jerked to the left with every jolting click of another gear's tooth being rotated into the next slot as the automated apparatus propelled him to an ambiguous destination in the next phase of whatever cruel reality awaited him.

After some unclear amount of time, the contraption finally stopped at its intended depot. The distinct smell came first. *A mine, maybe. Thick in minerals, thin in air ... Some form of metallic lubricant used for the device I am fastened to. The ceilings and floors are low – I can tell by the echo.*

There was no sound of footsteps or scent of another being nearby, yet the linen bag over his head was nonetheless yanked away from its position hindering his senses. His focus shot to the dimly lit area in front of him.

The rocky room was cylindrical, seemingly made up of a natural cavern, though obviously manmade. It had not been constructed for any considerably large person, as Sun noticed his feet were only slightly suspended above the ground, and his head was likely less than a hand's width from the rough ceiling. There were two sets of tracks built into the floor, with one set being what carried the mobile rectangular table on railway wheels he was bound to.

Sun could vaguely glimpse a dark avenue to his right, through which he had entered the obscure area, as well as one straight ahead, with a hint of a shadowy chamber just outside his own beyond it. But there was no sign of what might lie within or beyond the passage, due to the lack of light. The only illumination was the occasional red crystalyte conglomerations, which served just enough for Sun to see his own new cell as clearly as needed.

And that was when he took notice of her, directly adjacent to his right. "Taizsha?" Sun screamed in defiance at the improbability of his sister's presence. "Why?"

"There is no escaping this," Taizsha moaned in pain.

"The quandary of being quasi," came the voice of Timmurian, to Sun's left. All three elvan siblings were bound in similar fashion, shirtless and wearing nothing but pants for garments. "They are punishing Tay and me for our choices. There will be consequences for Tay trying to flee once in the Know, just as you and I will suffer for our invasive trespass."

Sun was able to extend his neck to inspect their shared predicaments. While he and his brother were chained into their seated positions at the table by the wrists and their ankles into the cart's floorboard, Taizsha's contrivance was much more sinister in design. Her bindings were made of metal wire wrapped around her wrist and ankles as well, but also around her elbows, knees, waist, and neck, all linked through a gearbox fastened to the back of her steel chair.

"All this for that fickle Chandoss trollop?" Taizsha did not relent in her condescending opinions. "The girl prances about as flippant as a cock-hungry, gold-chasing strumpet!"

"Ember has a history before me, but the antics of disloyalty you insinuate are an act she puts on to protect us," his brother snapped, great offense clearly taken. "There was a pragmatic motive behind it all you see. There is something deep-rooted in her father's role he plays in the grand scheme of things. I have discovered he remains employed in his position as a journeyman scholar for the Oathemic Cabal, bound to his duty for the guild, but he also doubles as an agent for the Umbran Pledge, reluctantly reporting to Count Valdean. He is a neverborne, just like the count, and most of the guard in the estates. Nikayle's crippled act in the wheeled chair is just that – an act now, as it has been for years. Ember is my lover, and I do not deny it, but she was also my spy."

All this time alone together and you never thought to indulge me on this vital revelation? Though I am a hypocrite to keep you in the dark of my invitation of the Thrench … "Damn Timm, as if the poor girl's life wasn't already jeopardized enough by seducing you into becoming quasi, which is a cardinal sin for the Neveril, you definitely fucked her the wrong way with this strategy," Sun expressed instead.

"She did not seduce me. And I did not use her. It was mutual. It still is," Timmurian's tone waned softer. "I regret it all now. I never meant her harm by antagonizing the Neveril. Just as I am sure Tay meant Ethiass no harm when she became quasi for him."

"Ethiass." Taizsha laughed overdramatically. "Oh, and what a wise choice that was! Timm, you are tenfold the fool!"

Timmurian was obvious in his unapproving mood toward her blatant sarcasm. "Again you goad me in this state. Do not."

"She doesn't even know," Taizsha threw at him, staring at Timmurian as if Sun weren't even between them. "Ember is tormented thinking you left her. If this was your choice, then why did you two not just elope from this tainted domain? Why must you and Sun always meddle in business that has nothing to do with you? Digging into Valdean, Nikayle, the damn Neveril Empire of all things!" Taizsha's eyes flicked back and forth, futilely seeking an answer from her brothers.

"Does it matter now?" Timmurian retaliated with a hint of growing exhaustion. "Does it really even matter? Our hunder will be free of our bodies soon enough."

"You're both fucked." Sun broke them up with a necessary tinge of uncouth candor. "We are dealing with the Neveril. You devalued yourselves to individuals tantamount to humans, whom the Neveril view as inferior to elvan ilk—so much that their empire began a realm-wide takeover to exterminate humankind from the inside out. But instead of running off to Savatarm or Goldgarden, or even back home to Zandabar, where such is accepted, you two decided to fall so in love with the inferior race that you cast yourself down to their level."

"Since when did you become so racist in your travels?" Taizsha said with disgust in her glare. "You sound like a zealot of their fanatical distortion of the broken Balance."

"Far from it. I just know how to think like the enemy. Let me paint a clear picture for you both," Sun said. "Z'shun like Sashka are the vilest abominations that can exist, according to the Neverils' creed. I hope you hid her well before you let this befall you, Tay. Any sort of deal you may have thought you had sorted with them is obviously null now. They will hunt her and give her a cruel death. And they view you quasi as perversions of the master elvan race, the creators of these half-human abominations, just as they revere their umbran as the highest ascendence a being can aspire to become by the benediction of their emperor."

The hard sound of the mechanical pulley system started back up, and a separate table on railway wheels came into view to maneuver to the center of the chamber. This table was circular however, and continued to slowly spin even when it stopped in front of Sun. The approaching silhouettes became tangible shapes when Ethiass and Odysserae came under the crystalytes' faint crimson illumination. Though seated and bound as well, their chairs were turned around to force each other's backs to one another.

"What is the meaning of this? I demand an answer!" Ethiass beseeched, his voice heavily cracked from apparently screaming to no avail for quite some time.

Sun looked over at Taizsha, expecting her to respond to her human lover's shared dilemma, but Ethiass had fully taken in the individuals present with him now. His neck even twisted so far behind him he was able to catch notice of his daughter.

"Taizsha? Odysserae? Why do they have my daughter?"

One, then two, then three and four half-naked albino elven with hairless scalps crawled into the chamber's dim lighting. They traversed the ceiling on all fours, wearing mining boots and gloves and ragtag breeches, but nothing else. They were morbidly skinny as well, as if they had been force-famished for many months. Not a one looked past the age of elvan juveniles, very young. *Neveril drudges.*

All eyes went to the corridor through which they had each entered. Crawling in on the ceiling, the same way the drudges had, was another young elvan, seeming of the same late adolescent age as the others. The boy seemed of former Neveril descent, with a naturally bald scalp covered in scars that went down under his grey eyes. His leather garb mixed with contours to camouflage with the stones and tiles. His skin was also grey, and his ears protruded flat and outward like an umbran.

Sun recognized him somehow and recalled Timmurian telling him the young elvan's name. *Ise'andahr. The one who captured me. The rogue-elvan progeny of Zsa'vauge, who was born here.*

"Ise'andahr!" Ethiass's voice shifted in excitement at his apparent familiarity. "Where is Valdean? Get Count Valdean!"

Ise'andahr slipped from the ceiling to land on his feet. He ignored Ethiass and fixed his cold grey eyes on Odysserae instead.

The gravity-defying adolescent elven ignored their prisoners, scurrying about like programmed slaves sent in to simply perform their tasks. They checked over the mechanics and hidden levers along the wall that Sun was just now taking note of.

"Fool husband," Taizsha scoffed so hard Sun swore she spit. "These drudges will not speak to you. And Ise'andahr is a tool of his father's, unbending and unbreaking. You turned one their precious elvan allies into a quasi and made her give birth to your Z'shun daughter. Zsa'vauge and his Neveril have hated you from the beginning, and always will. Your surface titles for Az'Dayne mean nothing to the true empire we are forced to serve."

"Why are you being so malicious? What have I done to you?" Ethiass appeared to be off-guardedly stung. "Other than secure you a place in all this, under their protection, once we conjoined and you did become quasi. I cannot tell you how many times I have saved you, and yet I spare you from the grisly details!"

"Saved me? I know it is you that turned me in when you couldn't find Sashka," her sardonic chortle erupted violently. "I made sure even I would not know where she was taken! I knew it was over the moment I saw him come for me," she finished with her eyes accusing Ise'andahr.

Ethiass shook his head confounded and defeated. "This isn't how they promised me it would go. The count told me —"

"I told you as I was adjured," came the familiar tone of the Count of Chandoshia making himself present. "I am not who passes the judgments. Meet who does."

Valdean entered the chamber with two other strangers trailing shortly behind him, stealing any magnificence he may have carried before.

One was clearly the umbran. The abomination was a faint trace of anything formerly elvan. He had grey skin, all black eyes as dark as shadow, and his long raven hair hung past his shoulders. He donned a maroon robe with a straight high collar that cuffed all the way to his drooping pointed ears. And on his forehead was pressed a cluster black gems the shape and size of his own eyes that almost appeared as if he had a plethora of alternate orbs to see out of.

"My master, the umbran Orchestrator of Chandoshia," Valdean

announced the transcended Neveril, "Zsa'vauge."

The disturbingly eerie umbran stared right at Sun as he walked up to the one empty chair placed directly across from table in front of him. His question was clearly to Valdean as his intrigued focus stayed locked on Sun. "This is him then?"

"Sundorion the Cosmopolitan, as requested," Valdean assured.

"Mesdarro?" Zsa'vauge broke his gaze to look back at the other human who came in with Valdean.

Sundorion recognized him now. Mesdarro, the Magistrate of Spellspire. He was the famous hyperi of the region. Anyone born in the past forty years had heard of him.

Mesdarro's glowing eyes radiated like violet magic. Sun only knew of one other hyperi to have existed in his lifetime — the nameless boy that was the son of Brigatha Emmonost and Imaniko the Palestorm that he met in Mageholme.

Mesdarro was much older than No-Name though. He appeared to be in his early senior years. His greying hair was styled in a military cut while his long and pointed beard was grown down to his chest. He wore a regal uniform of a tunic and trousers that represented the colors of Spellspire, of greens and whites, with a long cape that matched.

The elder hyperi man approached Sun and placed his right hand over his forehead. His violet eyes illuminated even brighter as the cloudlike substance in his orbs began to flicker while he analyzed the very lifeforce of Sun's hunder. Sun could see it but for a moment. There was a faint green line protruding from his body, stemming from his spiritroot, which was a thicker and brighter ethereal cord that Sun knew trailed back to his lifetree. The other was thinner, broken even, and went down the corridor ahead into nothingness. Alongside it coupled a violet ghostly line with it, not unlike the hue of Mesdarro's eyes.

"It is there. The eldritch trail," Mesdarro explained what he was seeing with his hypersight. "It is still dormant, but nearby. It can manifest itself as corporeal if you succeed in what we discussed."

Zsa'vauge appeared pleased by the affirmation, speaking in slow enunciations with his odd manner of speech. "Then by your theory there has been a hunder-touched in the estates for twenty years." The umbran turned to accuse the Chandoshian mogul. "Are you hiding something from me Count Valdean?"

"Never, my master," the count squirmed for the first time Sun believed he had ever seen from the cunning, unwavering man. "The only hunder-touched we have ever had in the region are the mages the Thrench brought with them just recently, and not by invite. I would never lie to you."

"Lying in beneath is you. Though the incompetence to not see a green-eyed child in your own home for two decades you are entirely proven capable of," Zsa'vauge harshly chastised before shifting his reproving glare to Ethiass behind him. "Who is lying to you Valdean?"

"I am not," Ethiass stammered, "I did not —"

"Your evaluation has not yet begun," Zsa'vauge interjected.

"The matriarch of this one's progeny is indeed interfused as a genesis wisp in the hunder-touched host." Mesdarro let go of Sun's forehead and took his place diagonal of the table in front of the elven, next to Valdean, and again stole the emphasis of the room's attention. "The eldritch wisp awaits the catalyst. You can proceed as planned Zsa'vauge. My duty to you is fulfilled until we return to Spellspire."

Zsa'vauge nodded in the direction of Mesdarro, seemingly satisfied, and then readdressed his primary focus. "Sundorion, things are about to become," he paused to accentuate, "complicated for you. Try to keep up."

"You are referencing them? Sheyelle and Carolelle?" His words manifested before he could even comprehend his own thoughts. He could have no idea why his lifemate and daughter were being brought into this. "How do you even know of them?"

"Oh, I have been here for some time now, haven't I Taizsha?" Zsa'vauge explained in his soft-toned meticulous enunciations of each word he said. "Sheyelle was my first contact while you were away. She was most helpful to my origin endeavors. She was most helpful, until she was not."

"What are you saying? They were killed. By a mob outside the university," Sun dared to argue the tragic historic occurrence, but he let his words trail short in doubt.

"You are going to become emotional today. First it will start with anger," the slow-speaking umbran calibrated his grim tone. "Then fear. Then grief. Then emptiness. Do not worry Cosmopolitan. I am here to take it all away from you."

"You had them killed?" Sun realized, interrogating Zsa'vauge as if they were the only two in the chamber, and the tables were turned with he and his prisoner instead. "How did this start? Did you use her as a source for information? Why kill Carolelle? Why didn't Sheyelle tell me of you?"

"She was planning to. Have you ever witnessed another elvan committing to the Severance in your lifetime? I have witnessed two acts of it twenty years ago," Zsa'vauge clarified with his grimace a semblance between a frown and a sneer.

"Elvan suicide of the soul," Valdean translated as if he were explaining it for humans.

"Most weak elven will turn to the option under torture. Or if being beaten," Zsa'vauge insinuated the fate of Sheyelle and Carolelle. "At least they did not suffer long."

No ... Sun's mind lamented on a decem different scenarios of how he could have saved them if he was only there for them. He felt as if time had stopped to allow him the anguish to dwell on what could have been done to prevent their deaths or to encourage Sheyelle to tell him about Zsa'vauge when it all first began.

"Proceeding," the umbran's articulated accent broke the silence. "This leaves a few dilemmas with House Chandoss. We begin with you Ambassador Ethiass."

As soon as he spoke Ethiass's name two drudges trekked down from the ceiling to unbind him and force him into the chair moved across from Taizsha at the table.

"Come. Sit for me," Zsa'vauge acted as if there was a choice in the matter. "Grab your wife's hands and look her in the eye."

Zsa'vauge placed Ethiass's palms over Taizsha's as she burst into a frightened fit. "I am scared! I don't want to die," his sister screamed. "Please!"

Sun looked at her wanting to cry for her, fearing her desires to live past today may be a vain hope. *I don't think any of us will live to see the morrow,* his eyes spoke as he glanced over at Timm after.

Zsa'vauge massaged Ethiass by the shoulders and neck as a lover might to their spouse. The gesture only made the umbran more intimidating as an individual with chaotic behavior. "You have three daughters and one niece. One daughter here, our candidate. Is all still in order for her to take the Transcendence?"

"Yes, master," Ethiass's voice was barely an audible whisper as he stared apologetically into Taizsha's weeping eyes.

"Your niece. Will I see her today?" Zsa'vauge continued.

"It is in motion," Valdean answered for Ethiass. "Yes."

"Your daughter, the imperial paramour," the umbran's questions remained targeted at the Chandoss ambassador. "Enlighten me of the news on her."

"She is," Ethiass hesitated, "unexpectedly, she suffers from," he fumbled and took a deep breath.

"He does not know," Valdean rescued Ethiass from further humiliation. "She is the one: the spellblade I just spoke to you of. I just witnessed it myself. Our Chandoss legacy weapon has chosen her. She is bound as the wielder. I would ask of you, what does this mean for her?"

"What? When did this happen?" Ethiass stole the words from Sun's exact thoughts. "It rejected Athan and chose her? I should have been there," Ethiass shook his head in a deep frustration only a failing father could feel. "You took that from me Valdean."

Sun held a nostalgic empathy for the despicable ambassador in that scenario.

Zsa'vauge assessed the revelation. "She has a higher purpose. She will meet with the Orchestrators," he decided after several seconds of pondering the surprising discovery. "When the Thrench embark from your shores, she will be brought to me. Her union with the prince will be absolved."

"And my other daughter?" Ethiass was expressly concerned.

"The other daughter," Zsa'vauge repeated Ethiass's words back to him as the umbran's black orbs narrowed in deep thought.

Adyssaira. Her plight of being born hunder-touched is no longer a secret. The poor girl has no idea what is about to change for her.

Count Valdean spoke up to impart the umbran of Adyssaira's present circumstances. "She is currently with the hyperi I promised you. She has somehow managed to seduce him. The Thrench soldiers and the Oriyen mages are in the castle."

"Brigatha's boy," Mesdarro recognized the mention of one of his own —another hyperi — likely familiar with No-Name from his time in Mageholme. "It is critical that I meet with him."

"We cannot risk your life if he is here on his Sojourn as reported," Zsa'vauge rejected. "We have no means to conduct any attack on Thrench and mages."

"An assassination would only fuel the ire of the small army they brought with them," Valdean warned. "They would murder my family and level the estates, and likely butcher the entire countryside before calling in more soldiers from New Throng."

"We will not be provoking the Thrench of the Neverils' presence," Zsa'vauge ensured. "Mesdarro has enlightened me that being that the boy is a hyperi, he has no doubt already seen that there are neverborne present. And that fact was solidified the moment you greeted them on Emerald Point."

"My other daughter," Ethiass audaciously ventured to return the subject back at hand to his primary concerns.

"Adyssaira," the umbran stared at the humbled ambassador as he explained. "I do try to remember names. Her unique position has elevated from moot to paramount. Seduce the boy, she must, and lure him here to Mesdarro. If she succeeds, I will have a place for her beside me."

"A place for her as what?" Ethiass reached for an answer.

"Alive," Zsa'vauge declared bluntly. "Is that acceptable?"

Ethiass just gazed emptily through the table in front of him, mentally distraught at the position he had cornered himself in.

"I do not trust you Ambassador. I do not like you. You are an exemplar of all that goes against the Neveril creed," Zsa'vauge admitted as he crept his face up against Ethiass's own cheek and ear while condemning. "A human who corrupts elven into quasi and breeds abominations. You did this to her," he pointed at Taizsha. "You started a movement that did the same to him," his finger shifted over to Timmurian. "You failed to deliver me your Z'shun. You have lied to the Umbran Pledge concerning your hunder-touched daughter. Should you die today, Ambassador? Should I judge you now?"

Ethiass began sobbing softly with his eyes closed as his voice quaked in terror. "I want to live today …"

Mesdarro intervened once again. "The contingencies that will commence following the awakening of the hunder-touched girl will be all that we researched. My theory is sound."

"Then it begins," Zsa'vauge decided. He stood upright and jumped to the ceiling, catching himself with his hands and replacing his feet to position himself invertedly balanced on the rocky surface above them. The umbran manipulated Ethiass's hands to grasp around Taizsha's skinny throat. "Prove to me how much you want to live."

"Ethiass, no!" Taizsha begged in a half-gurgled scream.

"No!" Timmurian echoed back just before the Neveril drudges appeared from behind to gag Sun and Timmurian simultaneously.

"I am sorry," Ethiass began squeezing harder while bawling his eyes out.

"Ethiass … you … coward," Taizsha wheezed between strangled breaths. Ethiass's focus waned downward in despair as she berated him. "Fuck … ing … cuh –"

"Do not apologize to this creature," Zsa'vauge seethed into Taizsha's ear in his upside-down stance. "Apologize to me, Ambassador. Feel sorry for yourself. You did this to you."

Sun tried to wail out alongside his brother to no avail behind their muffled pleas. Ethiass's eyes were closed tight as he endured choking his wife reluctantly between heavy cries.

"Please …," Taizsha's dying voice sounded like a trilling shriek with pure horror in her eyes.

"Do not disappoint me! Open your eyes and watch yourself kill it," Zsa'vauge raised his voice for the first time in fury and snapped his fingers to signal commands.

One drudge sprinted down the hall to initiate some other ill-boding sequence. Sun barely glimpsed the subtle movement of Ise'andahr in his peripheral vision, still there, inverted on the ceiling the same as Zsa'vauge. The rogue-elvan pulled down a lever on an intricate switchboard that activated the sharp wires in motion that were binding Taizsha to her seat. The gearbox behind her chair whirred and the edged cables rotated in a sawing rotation through the contraption, getting smaller in diameter as the mechanism utterly dissected Taizsha into pieces in a matter of seconds.

Wait! It all sounded righteous in Sun's head, as if he could pause or turn back time, but his mind ceased from spouting futility in the dreadful moment of his sister's last moments. And only Timmurian's gag had been pulled just then, not Sun's.

Sun registered the fresh spray of blood that stained Ethiass and Zsa'vauge, but it took what felt like a season of silence for him to notice that he, himself, was coated in his sister's own gore more than anyone else. Ethiass slumped down to the ground in a semi-conscious condition between life and mental numbness. Sun tunneled his vision only on Zsa'vauge, wishing to never glimpse the grisly scene to his right again. His own mind retreated into the same state of shock that Ethiass suffered.

Ise'andahr was releasing Odysserae the same as was formerly done for Ethiass, speaking in Hands to her and guiding her to move forward into the chamber ahead of theirs.

"Odysserae," Zsa'vauge spoke to the group instead of the deaf girl. "Her final trial of worthiness for the Transcendence is here. She has done all that we have asked. But she must prove her loyalty as well."

Whether Odysserae understood her test or not Sun could not discern, but the girl did move forward regardless with a lit candlestick in hand bestowed from Ise'andahr. She entered the dark vestibule ahead and did as she was instructed, lighting the chandelier ornamented with an excess of candles hanging above the lone podium centered in the small room. As the chamber brightened, Sun could now take notice of the bundle of yellow scythellin flowers placed on display. *Apology tokens ... The trap that got me here ...*

Odysserae was scurrying back into the main chamber when Sun glimpsed new clusters of Neveril crystalytes radiating almost blinding red in the vestibule with the flowers and candles, and down a long corridor leading beyond, which turned around a corner out of sight. There were only two ways crystalytes glowed that bright — by a non-Neveril's presence in the vicinity, or if poison hit the air. The familiar candlewicks must have been laden with bugsthrone spores, but enough to fell a room full of grown men.

Ise'andahr shepherded Odysserae to stand away, near the tunnel through which they had all entered, while the rogue-elvan returned to the switchboard.

"Timmurian the Lorebringer," Zsa'vauge boomed to bring attention back on him. "The time is nigh; I take from you everything. Your will to live. I will see your wisp stripped from your body from the Severance. You have been judged, quasi."

Ise'andahr flipped another set of levers on the switchboard. The walls separating the main chamber they were in from the smaller one with the poisoned chandelier began to gradually close in from four different directions: top to bottom, bottom to top, left to right, and right to left. The walls ceased from going any further when the opening was just large enough for those in the chamber to watch what was about to transpire in the candlelit room, but too small for anyone to possibly squeeze through.

The silhouette of a shapely female figure came into view from down the hallway. And then she appeared in the light, approaching closer. *Emberalda ... turn back.*

Sun never saw when it happened, but Timmurian had been brought to the center of the chamber, still bound to his chair, able to see through the large peephole perfectly as the drudges around him spotlighted him with torches so that one could see him through the corridor and small chamber on the other side.

"You are now permitted to scream," the umbran whispered to Timmurian.

"Timm!" Emberalda apparently caught sight of her lover as Zsa'vauge anticipated. "My Timm!"

And his brother did scream. "Ember, no! It is a trap!" Timmurian cautioned, his speech quaking when he cried out. "Run! Get out!"

His voice only seemed to motivate Emberalda's steps to quicken her fervent pace toward the unknown. "I thought you left me! They made me think you left me! I never thought —"

"Oh love, I never left you," Timmurian's shoulders slumped and shuddered as he broke down into tears.

Emberalda ran right past the flowers on the plinth and reached her arms through the square hole in the almost closed mechanical door. "I'm ... here ... my ..." was all she got out before the inhalation of the spores took effect. Her arm almost immediately fell limp through the door's orifice, and the sound of her body collapsing lifelessly to the ground could be heard in a solid thud.

"No .... I never left you ... no," Timmurian wept even more as he turned around to face the macabre remains of his sister next to Sun. He was promptly dragged back in his chair by the drudges to face in front of Sun with no time spared for remorse. The grief-stricken look on Timmurian's face appeared as though he had been sapped of his will to even breathe.

Don't do it Timm ... This is what Zsa'vauge wants.

The umbran appeared above them again, traversing the ceiling as if it were the floor. His face was adjacent to Timmurian's, facing Sun, as he talked into Timmurian's ear. "Lorebringer, I need you to listen carefully to my next instructions."

Zsa'vauge talked and walked in a full circle around Timmurian as if under some slow-motion spell to heighten the drama of it all. "You can go now."

Sun's brother looked at the evil Neveril confused by the false hope, and then turned his attention to Sun for an answer on what to believe. That was when Sun felt it. Ise'andahr had vanished from the switchboard, but he caught a glimpse of his grey hands when a bloody strip of Taizsha's gown she had over her legs was pulled into a noose around his neck, suffocating the life out of him.

"Please go," Zsa'vauge uttered back to Timmurian, staring sadly into Sun's bulging eyes that he felt would pop from his skull if he did not receive immediate air.

"Please go now, Timmurian," the umbran beseeched, mimicking sadness in his tone. "Through the only exit you have."

It was all black and white spots now, and desperate snorts as Sun frantically but futilely tried to stand or resist Ise'andahr from asphyxiating him.

"Thank you for trying to save me, brother," Timmurian looked up at Sun and finally managed a weak grin, perhaps content that the misery was almost over. "It seems it is my turn to save you."

"Yes. Save him fast," Zsa'vauge urged cooingly, placing his grey hand with sharp black umbran nails through Timmurian's head of filthy yellow hair.

"Goodbye now," Timmurian said sorrowfully, expressing his last words to his brother, turning to make eye contact with Emberalda's arm, which still hung from the corridor door. "I am going to show the Thrench where we are."

Sun regained the ability to think more clearly as he felt Ise'andahr's attempt on his life loosen up behind him. He tried to comprehend the meaning behind the message, but he ceased from any more thoughts when Timmurian began to fiercely tremble in racking convulsions. His eyes brightened with a green glow as his hunder surfaced into brief visibility, just before it snapped loose of his body, and his mouth gave out one final death shriek.

Timmurian's wisp shot from his body in a rapid course down the crystalyte-lit hallway through which Emberalda had entered, leaving an evanescent wake as it vanished around the corner.

Mesdarro's voice seemed so foreign and distant as Sun had forgotten the hyperi magistrate was still even in the room. "The catalyst wisp will find and bind to the hunder-touched girl. The eldritch wisp of Carolelle will go to her. Be ready."

Carolelle?

Sun felt paralyzed. Whether any further words were vented by Zsa'vauge, Sun was unaware, as his ears had entered into a delirium that muted all sound. He paid no heed to the drudges as they removed Timmurian's corpse from the bindings and discarded it on the stone floor as if it were spoiled meat. He ignored the same being indelicately done to the eviscerated appendages of Taizsha.

The faint images of Ethiass's limp but woken body being drug alongside his hysterically emotional daughter was just a shadow in the unhinged reality Sun was forced to exist in. Zsa'vauge, Valdean, Mesdarro, they all faded into the same shapeless obscurities as the rest of them. Sun had lost the will to live, not unlike his brother.

Sun took hardly any notice even when Ise'andahr pulled another switch, which jolted him into motion and retracted him along the tracks back into the darkness from where he had come.

ADYSSAIRA (VII)

HUNDER-TOUCHED

It had gone on for days. Their building infatuation for one another lingered even more thickly with longing desire when they were apart at night. The courtship between her and Desdjlandar may have been arranged, but it never felt forced. There was an undeniable sensation of fate-struck love that Adyssaira lost herself in, denying the grim drama in the air around Castle Chandoss. She preferred to exist only in the dreamlike rapture that her foreign lover induced in her.

And there was passion, an overwhelming amorous impression that came over her when she was near him that heightened some senses but numbed others. Her sight would become cloudy when he kissed her, but she could still see her desires more clearly than ever before. The scent of him was forever pressed into her memory, and his slightest touch would send shivers across her tingling skin every time. And the way he tasted—she could lose herself in his lips for hours without the need to talk.

She had eagerly surrendered her sacred virginity on that first day, when they had visited the isle of Carolelle. And it had happened five other times since, over the past two days. It happened again on Carolelle, and in her room after a private dinner. Then three times more in Lovers' Labyrinth: once during dinner over the fountain and twice more playing a rather lecherous version of hide-and-seek throughout the floral maze park that spiraled down the hill.

The young lovers had a new dining arrangement prepared for them on this engagement, atop the highest point in the castle wall walk that led to the northwesternmost tower. It overlooked the Aemenus River, and this particular spot carried for Adyssaira a great deal of sentiment about her past, which she had been reluctant to share with anyone new until now. But she trusted this boy across from her, and she somehow felt she always could.

She had left her little tiger, Luna, at the estates' farm with Fabian, the stable boy, who was her and her sisters' childhood friend. He had promised to take care of Luna for the evening, just as he had when they had been away at Emerald Point and the Suntide Faire.

She kept her back to the tower, with her hair pulled up, something she had never dared to do before in her own home, but there were none of the Chandoss Guard behind her now. The back of her bare neck bore her golden glyph, and her yellow dress was worn low at the bust to display her arcanic imprint from the genesis wisp that had interfused with her.

Adyssaira sat across from Desdjlandar, staring into his ever-phosphorescent violet eyes, which radiated even more ethereally in the hour of sunset. She realized she had taken hardly a bite of the courses, transfixed by his presence, fawning over the contours of his masculine jawline down to his strong shoulders, which she could hardly tame her impatience to be held by again. The only thing she craved could not be served on plates, as she yearned to disappear into the tower and do away with the Thrench entourage that hovered behind him. They always shadowed them everywhere they went, like the eternal guardians they were assigned to be.

Her foot was unconsciously stroking his calf up and down underneath the table that had been placed there just for their occasion of courtship. She glanced down at her fingers doing similarly, sliding over his free hand from knuckle to knuckle and every trace of vein down his forearm. She could tell he had already had his fill of food after the third set of plates had come out, and all he had been doing was playing with his fork rather than eating for the past five minutes.

"I want you to take that off," he whispered, smiling.

Adyssaira felt a flush of heat wash through her neck as she pulled on the neckline of her dress. But his eyes were on hers, not her bust. She blushed, embarrassed, when she realized he was talking about the sash still over her eyes. Her focus caught the few Chandoss Guardsmen still present in their midst, patrolling the wall walk down to the next tower. She had forgotten it was still there, since the Savatarm silk was transparent enough that she could see him and her surroundings just fine, being so used to the thin, obstructing material.

"Then finish so you can take it off me," she teased as she pulled on the laces of her corset instead of the insinuated blindfold.

Desdjlandar gave a roguish smirk and shot his eyes to the top of the tower behind her. "What is up there?"

I was wondering if you would ever come around to asking! "The highest point in Castle Chandoss. We call it the Nest of the Phoenix. Or sometimes just Phoenix Tower," she anxiously informed him.

"Can you take me?" He put down his fork and wiped his mouth, taking in a final swig of red wine.

She pouted when she surveyed the ten Threnchmen and Inkomway the Skycaller in their vicinity. "Do they have to come?"

He shook his head. "Not this time. Inkomway and Thoravus could use the respite," he said of the Oriyan Reaping mage and the bloodguard. "Just you and I alone."

Adyssaira jumped up so fast, she thought she might have bumped over the table in the process, the way it nearly tilted over. "Come!"

She snatched his hand in hers and escorted him into Phoenix Tower, up the winding stairway to the fourth level, at the top, where the balcony was set. She brought him over to the lone piece of furniture on the whole floor, a wooden chest, no doubt there for sentries to hold rations and changes of clothes. She turned around to pull him into her open legs as she hiked up her dress and sat herself on the chest. She tossed her blindfold aside, locking her thighs around his, and began to undo the laces on his breeches so that she could feel him. Their tongues collided as they locked lips, and she stroked him hard while they kissed with the tower breeze licking the side of her neck. Her legs were already shaking when he entered her.

"Wait. I want to, but this is not why I—" he tried to explain, but she shut him up by shoving his lips and hips back into hers.

When he finished in her, he was panting with his mouth agape in lustful awe of her, and she couldn't stop smiling as her racing heartbeat gradually tried to return to whatever normal felt like—she neglected to recall.

"You were saying?" She kissed his cheek, then his neck, then the other cheek. "Ask or tell me anything. I am yours." She kissed him softly on the lips.

"May we go up there?" His eyes went to the ladder that went to the tower's crest.

Adyssaira grinned and removed herself from the chest. She took him up the ladder that led to the splendorous view of Phoenix Tower. It had been a long time since she had visited this spot in the castle, for a very substantial reason. It was a place of sadness for her. But it shouldn't have had to stay such.

The Nest of the Phoenix afforded any onlooker a flawless view over the entire majesty of Castle Chandoss from an aerial perspective. The horizons across the river and over the serene Lake Chandoss, even down to Carolelle, could be seen. The numerous houses throughout the north and eastern estates were gleaming with the last bit of sunlight reflecting from their rooftops in the overcast of dusk blanketing down for the night. The temperature seemed to drop two seasons in advance at the tower point in the evening as well, with a perfect draft playing with her blond hair and the fringe of her dress.

Desdjlandar broke the silence of the magical setting with the most inappropriate and random topic. "Your mother, I would hear what you knew of her, before she ..." He awkwardly stumbled in his words. "My apologies. It is just that I have told you of my parents, and you have told me all about your father, but never her."

"You want to spoil this moment to ask me about my mother, whom I have never met and know little to nothing about?"

He seemed ashamed for even trying after hearing that retort. "No ... I don't know. Never mind, then." He made a poor attempt at trying to kiss her again, as if it could restore the mood.

Adyssaira cupped a palm over his chin and mouth to stop his advance and explained. "I will tell you one coincidental thing. It all happened right here. On this very perch. My uncle told me it all before. I never forgot."

She gently grabbed his hand and ushered him to the edge that had the tower balcony directly below it. "She learned some terrible secret right here." She pointed. "From my father. They never told me what it was. I decided I did not want to ever know. Whatever it was, it was so great that my mother tried to jump from that balcony with three babes in her belly. She was going to take herself, me, and my sisters all to the Godslands that day."

Desdjlandar kept his hand in hers, giving her just enough

strength in his grip to give off a sentiment of protection. "What stopped her? Your uncle, Nikayle?"

"He says he tried, but that is not what stopped her. That was when it happened, when the wisp entered her. Quite fatefully timed—divine destiny, some might say. She fainted from it, and that was how I became hunder-touched. Me, out of all my sisters. The wisp chose me instead of Val or Oddy, and I will never understand why."

A sudden burning itch flared up in the center of her chest as she finished her tale. The birthmark of her genesis wisp had never imposed such a sensation before.

"Are you okay?" Desdjlandar caught her as her knees buckled from the numbness coursing through her. "What is happening?"

She squeezed her eyes shut tight to make it go away as she rubbed over her heart where the imprint was, and then the back of her neck. "My marks itch. I feel tingly. That has never happened."

"You cannot be serious." His eyes fervently searched below for signs of something he seemed to expect to spy. "Do you know what that means?"

If he had told her before, in his many tutoring sessions about magic and the arcane properties associated with it, then she did not recall. "What?"

"What you just felt …" He paused to look around the lower grounds once again. "This means a wisp relative to your elemental descendancy is near."

Adyssaira was still confused as she looked down with him. The lantern lights of Castle Chandoss came out in full one by one as the servants carried out their routine diligence. "I do not see it."

"You will!" Desdjlandar spoke with rising glee, as if it were happening to him. "If it gets closer, and if it chooses to interfuse with you. This is exciting!"

"Oh, no." She let go of his hand, becoming worried. *Does that mean I will become a mage?* She paced to the middle of the tower crest and turned back around to face him. "What if I do not want it?"

"You cannot stop it. Only it can," he answered, confirming the inevitability of the impending outcome. "You will know its name when it hits you, the name of the elvan whom the hunder belonged to when it was alive. It will awaken and activate your genesis wisp." He pointed to the gold mark in the top center of her neckline, and then beside it to the side of her chest. "You will gain a new one here, imbued with this catalyst wisp."

"As in imbued with spellpower? I will be a mage?" She knew the answer but needed to hear it validated.

"Yes, a Dawning mage. The spells you acquire from the marks will be decided based on the strongest traits of the elvan's derelict hunder that also match your circumstantial emotions at the time it entered you," he clarified of the arcane science.

"Desdjlandar, I do not want this! You have to hide me from it. Why is it coming for me? I cannot become a mage! Not here!" She began to pace in random paths with no sense of where she could possibly flee to, a suffocating anxiety budding in her lungs. "When can you take me away?"

"I can take you away soon. Very soon." He grasped her by the wrist, this time a little too tight. He pulled her in close to coerce her eyes back to his, but this time it was his that were sad. "But not your family."

The truth comes out. I was afraid of ... "Maybe just my sisters and Emberalda, then? I have this other sister too." She hesitated to mention Sashka, seeing as she was half-elvan and he was of the Emmonost line of royalty, incessantly surrounded by Thrench soldiers. She ultimately decided she could not leave Sashka out. "My youngest sister, but—"

"None of your sisters can come," he interjected quite matter-of-factly.

There seemed to be no response with which she could counter the way he said it. The only thing she could surface was an "Oh ..."

"I am no good at this," he confessed, letting go of her to walk back toward the edge of the tower crest that looked down over the balcony.

She invited herself back up beside him to let him open up.

"I am no good at lying. To you, or anyone. But especially to you."

Adyssaira tried to comfort him by embracing him in a hug from behind and resting her head against his broad back. He was a hand and some taller than her. "You told me already. You were supposed to seduce me and learn all my secrets. But the only secret I have you already know." She paused to turn him around and look into his glowing hyperi eyes. "I am quite unremarkable compared to you in fair truths."

"Stop. I never want to hear you say that against yourself again." He lifted her dejected chin up and smiled at her. "But you were supposed to do the same to me."

"I like to lie to myself and pretend that maybe I did seduce you." She smiled back, assuming she was on the same page as what he was implying.

"No. You were supposed to learn all my secrets after you seduced me," he corrected.

"But you have been so open and told me all about you." She wasn't sure what possible secret he might still be holding. *But this is what Valdean and Father sent me here to do. Let him say it.* "What do you mean?"

"You have to promise me first. You must tell me how you feel," he demanded as a prerequisite.

"Like I never have before," she said in sincerity.

"Because I believe I am in love with you, Adyssaira Chandoss," he whispered, and he kissed her fully, as if it could be their last.

"I am in love with you, Desdjlandar Emmonost," she promised back. She believed she didn't care about her duty to her family. And she definitely didn't care to learn any more secrets today. She just needed to exist here and now with him and never lose this moment.

"Do not let what I am about to tell you change that, then," he said, clearly with an opposite agenda to hers. "Please."

She did not like where he was taking this. "You are making me nervous."

Desdjlandar pointed down below to the Thrench soldiers on the wall walk, where he and she had just been dining. "Look at them. My men. The Thrench helms. Do you remember what I told you they were made of?"

Adyssaira did remember but failed to understand the relevance. "You said it was Starfell steel from the Lunaril elvan capital isle. The one your nation controls."

"Indeed. Do you know all it can do?"

"Um ..." She made a face, slightly annoyed at his tendency to toss out serious subjects during the hours of brief passion permitted to them. "It doesn't rust? You said it was impervious to badwater."

"It also allows them to see through shadow," he said.

"They can see in the dark?" Now she was annoyed, but she tried to hide her frown. *Why are we talking about this? Go back to kissing me.*

Desdjlandar was clearly on a roll to explain his point, as he always had one. "All properties of the shadow element. Not just the dark. Including through illusions cast by Umbra mages. Including through the skin-shifting impower of the neverborne, the qindrid under the command of the Neveril elven beneath us now."

All remnants of romance had fled the air with no hope for redemption. "What are you saying?" She looked at him with a horrified grimace. "You are scaring me! Never-what?"

"I told them you were innocent." He gritted his teeth and shook his head. "I knew you did not know. I defended you. They are letting me protect you."

He reached back to take her hands in his, but she slapped them away. "Stop it now!"

"I cannot help your sisters, though. They are not so innocent," he morbidly said, and she felt her eyes glaring in anger at him for the first time since they had met. "So I need you to forgive me in the end. Because I do love you, and I know that you love me."

Adyssaira stormed away toward the hatch to the ladder down from the tower crest. "I am leaving now. The moment has passed, sir! I will pretend it was the wine making you so!"

But Desdjlandar was faster than her and blocked her path at the hatch. "It's too late now. You cannot leave. You can come with me or …" He hesitated and looked down at his feet before meeting her eyes again. "Well, there will be no 'or.' Once you become a Dawning mage, and it is known, your great-granduncle Valdean will steal you to be enslaved in the Neveril's underrealm expansion. Sundorion knows all of it. He is the one who told me and brought me here. Without him, we would never have met."

There was only one pertinent fact she needed his affirmation of. "What are you implying you are going to do to my sisters?"

The look on his face was one of accepted defeat. She knew before he spoke that she wasn't going to like the answers. "They are with the enemy now. They are set to become neverborne qindrid by the peak of the Sunder season. Your family, they have all deceived you and kept you in the dark as if you were truly blind. And in truth, you have been until now.

"Your family cannot come, because I am here to stop their Transcendence coming to pass. That is what they are here for." He motioned his arm back in the direction of where the Threnchmen had stationed themselves on the wall walk. "This is my Sojourn."

Adyssaira pushed him, far harder than she thought she had the strength to, as he nearly lost his balance and fell backward. "You are not touching my family! I will tell the guards! You can leave now!" She briskly took herself to the edge overlooking the handful of foreign soldiers below. "You and all your men can leave now!"

"I feel bad for you. I do," Desdjlandar called over the sudden gale that whistled up the castle heights. He casually strolled back toward her. "You cannot see what I can. I do not need a Starfell helm to see it. Such is the blessing and curse of a hyperi. The hyper-sight. Your Chandoss Guard and servants." He pointed out across the wall walk to where two were posted at the next tower, then to the maid cleaning the table where they had dined. "I could see them all along. Their grey qindrid skin, their red eyes. They appear in their real form to me, but you see something different, as if they were still human, before the turn."

I've known Perry for three cycles, since we picked her up in Toil. She recalled her introduction to the servant girl long ago. *Why is he lying?* Her words came out in vehement denial. "I am going to tell Father. Why are you ruining this? I am going to tell everyone!"

As she turned quickly to beat him to the hatch, she realized he did not follow to stop her this time. "Adyssaira, you will not make it that far," he warned. "On my signal, my bloodguard, Thoravus, is going to take you back to my ship. You will need to wait there until ..."

Until what? She dared him with her eyes.

"Until it is done" was all he said of the grisly matter.

She felt the instant lump in her throat, and the tears were already there. "Then take my sisters and cousin with me! Take us all!" She ran back to him and surrendered herself to his embrace, softly hitting his chest with the side of her fist. "Please," she sobbed.

"The wisp!" Desdjlandar proclaimed enthusiastically instead of consoling her as she had expected. He turned her away from him to face what he saw in a rapid change of subject. "It is coming."

Suddenly Adyssaira briefly forgot about the threat against her family when she saw it too. At the top of the gatehouse at the entrance to the inner bailey, a luminous green incorporeal ball seemed to slightly change in shape and size as it propelled itself upward along the wall walk of the castle.

"I see it," she said.

"The trail behind it. I will bet it leads to where the Neveril are. Where Sundorion is now," Desdjlandar speculated with confidence in his tone. "Unless that wisp *is* Sundorion."

But Adyssaira was lost on every point he had just mentioned. She squinted through the darkness of the dusk, to no avail. "I don't see a trail."

"I know," he returned, not needing to again remind her of his special hypersight.

Adyssaira's and Desdjlandar's focus stayed mesmerized by the wisp as it slowly progressed up the curtain wall of the castle tiers. "It is coming up the wall walk to us! Look!" Adyssaira exclaimed.

"It's coming for you," Desdjlandar disconcertingly promised.

The wisp was passing the last tower, where the Chandoss Guardsmen were, weaving through the oblivious Thrench soldiers. The mage Inkomway appeared to pick up on its presence, however, but Adyssaira did not wait to watch any more of his reaction.

"Desdjlandar!" She pleaded and tugged at his tunic for a futile miracle to occur. "Hide me!"

"If it has chosen you, then you cannot hide from it. It wants me to see this. It wants me to follow that trail." He seemed entranced, with his gaze scrutinizing below, down the wall walk, to trace whatever mystic, ethereal wake only he could see.

He grabbed her by the shoulders and stared into her with his penetrating, otherworldly eyes and whispered, "It is here."

And then it hit her. The left side of her bare chest flared as if it were on fire, and she swore she smelled the scent of singed flesh. In a chain reaction, the same sensation burned in the marks on her neck and the center of her chest. She squinted from the brilliant flash of blinding green light that burst from her new arcanic imprint, brightening the sky above the crest of Phoenix Tower. A surge of unnatural strength coursed through her veins and the very core of her being, forcing her eyes to close as she became helpless to absorbing the power being instilled within her.

When she opened them, a new light was there, and she could somehow see the glowing halo forming around both of her irises. A wraithlike voice whispered in her mind in an ancient language she distinguished as Elvan, and somehow she could comprehend that the wisp was introducing itself. *Timmurian …*

"Extraordinary," her lover's voice came. He sounded so far away, but she knew he was holding her upright. "Adyssaira? How do you feel?"

She slowly collected herself and her memory of all that had just transpired. She began to recall their heated exchange before Timmurian's wisp had appeared and interfused with her.

"We have to leave now. I will get you out safe. You have my word, my love," Desdjlandar vowed. "If Valaythea, Odysserae, and Emberalda do not resist, I will order them detained to come on board as well. Come!"

"Emberalda is dead." She had no idea how she knew it, but she did. She said it aloud before she could process the emotion of losing her cousin.

Desdjlandar looked entirely confused and shook his head. He went to grab her and speak, but she was quicker as something instinctively took over her initiative to act first. She screamed at him, "No!"

Adyssaira noticed the left half of her dress at the neckline up to her shoulder had been scorched away, exposing that she had been branded with the new magemark from Timmurian's wisp. Somehow she knew what spell it invoked as well. *Timmurian's remnant, his hunder, lies within me now.*

Before Desdjlandar could put his hand on her, the spell was already cast. The catalyst magemark lit up, and a green spiral of lights appeared around her feet as the stone beneath her on the tower's crest began to part in a whirling motion caught in the momentum of the magic. Adyssaira dropped immediately, and safely, down to the next tower level, where the balcony was.

"Adyssaira! Wait!"

She could hear Desdjlandar's cry.

She ran to the balcony, plotting her unfeasible escape, and looked up at him.

His eyes were not on her as he shouted, "Thoravus! Stop her! Do not harm her!"

His bloodguard was set in motion, along with the rest of his soldiers. Inkomway stayed on the wall walk and assessed the scope of the situation.

"I will jump!" she promised at the top of her lungs, ignoring the irony of the situation, given her mother's plight in this exact location in the castle.

"No, you will not!" Desdjlandar pleaded more than promised. "Just wait! I am coming down!"

"I am not coming with you!" she screamed back.

"Even if you got away, which you won't, I would be able to find you, Adyssaira," he warned, implying the impower of his enhanced hypersight. "You know this! You cannot hide from me. I am here to save you. Don't you see this?"

She could hear the march of heavy boots charging up the tower stairway. The Thrench soldiers would be upon her at any moment. Desdjlandar disappeared from sight, and she caught a glimpse of the hatch door opening inside, but she was done looking at him for a lifetime. There was only one way out of her predicament. Down. To her death. She believed in the moment that maybe she was ready.

Down ... or across. Again something inside her instinctively knew what to do and what her birth spell could conjure. The halos in her eyes flashed in tune with the genesis magemark over her heart, and her feet took flight in an impossible jump to the balcony of the next tower across the wall walk.

She didn't look back for a reaction from her ex-lover or the Threnchmen. She didn't need to. All she needed to do was get as far away from them as possible. And she used her new spells all night long to do just that as she dug and jumped her way to wherever she believed a hyperi could never find her.

SYMBELLE & FYHEIR (VII)

BEHIND THE EYES

The humid rain drizzled down, drenching the oversized cloak her brother had placed around her head and body to conceal her identity. Symbelle was being hastily ushered down winding avenues of the unfamiliar Midtown district. She believed she heard one collector call out the street name of Cryptly Heights, but she couldn't be certain with the muffling of the random downpour.

She almost tripped on the hill's incline that led from the paveway to the front door of the abandoned-manor safe house chosen by Scarless's agents. She could hear the recognizable voices of Scarless and Xalo, but the few others she was unacquainted with.

Pyphan directed her through a long hallway, forcing her head low underneath the cloak's hood, into some ghastly old banquet room. "I have her," he announced at last, handling her to oblige her to sit on the chair at the head of the table.

"Good. Everyone else out!" Scarless commanded.

"I'll keep my two sentries at the door for you if you need to call on me," a feminine voice answered.

"Amaris, why would she need your two up-jumped cat's-paws when I am in the room with her?" The obvious sound of Xalo chastised whoever Amaris was.

"No one stays in the room with us," Scarless corrected Xalo. "I said everyone out."

Symbelle just maintained patience, staring at her wet boots underneath the table, while Xalo made his discontent known. "Truly pained, my Zahna. Truly pained."

She could hear the drumming echo of several feet exiting the large dining room, and then Scarless's sarcastic counter of "I love you too" before the slamming of the door.

The Terollar street queen removed the hood from Symbelle's

head in a rather rough manner and shot a wicked grin down at her. "Hello, Symbelle."

"Greetings, Zahnastaazjah," Symbelle returned courteously. She adjusted her thick goggles and made a quick survey of the room. The ceiling was two floors high, with cobwebs amassed in every corner high and low. There must have been a second floor as well, because she could hear the outside precipitation showering through a leak in the roof, no doubt causing the lump in the warped wood bubbling above the doorway. The extensive banquet table had enough seats for twenty guests but was dressed with zero sets of dinnerware, and by the look of things, Symbelle imagined it had been as such for several months, or maybe even a year or longer. The mansion was a desolate hollow that still held a tinge of death in the air from whatever secrets its spectral walls had kept throughout time.

"This is the last time we meet before the ball. Tell me anything and everything I do not already know, and exactly where you will be with Oldan Boldandgold," Scarless commanded, all business in her intense tone, very different from the friendly spirit offered when they had last spoken, in the brothel.

"Where is everyone else?" Symbelle gambled to ask, and she wasn't sure why she thought her own questions would take any form of precedence in consideration. "Why is it just us in here?"

"I did not ask that," Scarless replied, even more annoyed than she looked. "I don't fully trust a soul in this realm, not even my own half the time. I'm not giving up my mole when I'm so close to ending an enemy's reign."

"Your mole." Symbelle frowned and removed the wet cloak completely to discard it on the floor. "Sounds so elevated."

"You aren't very good at wit and quips just yet, Symbelle. But you're cute, so I may keep you." Scarless omitted to counter with any sentimental tact. "Maybe I can set you up with Xalo to hone that uncultivated craft for you, if that's the route you wish to take."

Symbelle knew they likely had little time to spare, so she shooed away the idea of entertaining any pointless tangents. "I've convinced them to let me do the firework finale over the water on boats. Something new that's never been done before, utilizing their mobility in the canals to give every citizen joining the Kingfall Ball the same show as everyone else, no matter what street they're on in

Bridgeville or Canaltown."

"Admirable and interesting. And now I'm bored," Scarless snidely remarked, insinuating she wanted to hear something relevant to the mission soon.

Symbelle further explained what she had devised. "I've been personally invited by Oldan to join him on his pleasure barge. Each vessel on the water will have a different-colored display from specific fireworks. His barge will be the only one in the armada with green lights in the sky above it. I am sure you know more than I, but there are two bridges just before you reach the Monodrome, which connect the districts—a perfect vantage for Uubakrath, and for you, Xalo, and Pyphan to jump aboard when we pass. This is when it should happen."

"Clever," Scarless commended, this time with no sarcasm in her delivery. "On to the Monodrome. We hear you have access to their cache of blast salt. And that it is underneath the stage?"

"Depends on how you want to do this." Symbelle offered the options she had carefully weighed. "The festival can go on with the scheduled entertainment of the Kingfall Ball already set to happen, for more of a public statement, but this will bring a mess of casualties including many citizens and tourists, not just the Boarnecks. Or you can find a way to get them out of the Monodrome. Makes no difference to me." She was surprised by her lack of moral conviction toward the potential loss of innocent lives.

Fire does not discriminate, Fyheir reminded her.

"Fire does not discriminate, as a certain friend keeps coaching me."

"This Fyheir of yours?" Scarless probed, curious to learn more about Symbelle's mysteriously dark alter ego. "I am still waiting to meet it."

You will meet us. But you won't like it when it happens. We can already smell the sweet fire on your scarless flesh, which will not heal so well, Fyheir fantasized, coercing a sinister smile to spread across Symbelle's face. Fyheir wasn't taking over yet, though, just torturing her in the worst moments, like the typical malevolent nuisance it liked to be.

Scarless, obviously ignorant of the internal warfare going on in her mind, smiled back and continued about the protocols of the violent scheme. "The Kingfall Ball will not take place inside the

Monodrome. We are seeing to it to ensure that no performers or citizens outside the Boarneck affiliates die in this massacre."

"Then after Oldan dies on his barge, we can all move through to the Monodrome," Symbelle followed up. "It should be mostly empty, aside from Terrib Ango's investigators. He will be there, and the standard guard of the playhouse, but that shouldn't be a match for—"

"It won't be," Scarless interrupted. "Usurp will be with us too by then. And he will have a few of my vetted Blue Blades with him to dispose of any resistance."

That wasn't the plan. Symbelle and Pyphan were supposed to be assassinating Scarless and Xalo immediately after Oldan's death, somewhere inside the Monodrome during the final distractions afforded by Terrib's elite henchmen. She wasn't planning on having Usurp and more men in the mix to contend with as well. "I don't think there will be a need." She tried to dissuade Scarless from the scheme. "Seems a bit like overkill. Maybe Usurp and Uubakrath would be better placed topside for anyone trying to come in."

"I like overkill." Scarless shut down the debate. "Secondly, I will not dishonor my most loyal Stormtrees by subjecting them to the role of mere sentries at such a monumental hour. I like you, Symbelle, but do not mistake me as keen on your advice concerning anyone in my guild again. You are new here." The imposing Terollar elvan took a seat on the most adjacent chair and rested her writhing bloodrime spear across her lap. "Act new here," she warned.

"It won't happen again," Symbelle promised, fidgeting with her goggles impulsively again while staring at the intimidating weapon across from her. The haunting image of her and her brother's heads spiked on the point and on display in Scarless Square after all this was over flashed through her mind.

She ejected the nightmarish possibility from her thoughts and found her way back to the topic. "After we reach the Monodrome, I will lead you to the sublevel where the blast salt is kept. And there, I will ignite a timed explosion to erase the Boarnecks' prized arena from the map of Goldgarden."

Scarless's green eyes gleamed with elation at the sound of such flawless fruition. "A sight for all at the ball to spectate. The Stormtrees will be heralded as city heroes by the next morning. No one wants the Boarnecks here."

Scarless stood again to tower over Symbelle, still in the chair. She firmly cupped her under the jaw with the palm of one hand and said, "You need not wear this mask much longer. The burden of playing both sides, being torn in two, is almost over. I am ready to openly embrace you as mine." And without warning, Scarless bent down to plant a full kiss on her lips.

Symbelle let it happen – she knew she wanted it and had secretly craved it ever since Scarless had first kissed her in their private room at Water Daisy's Brothel. "Embrace me as yours how?" Symbelle challenged her intent, blushing uncomfortably when she realized she had incidentally acquired a lustful fondness toward her assigned enemy.

Scarless teased with a mischievous grin. She bit her lower lip as she lithely placed her right boot all the way above Symbelle's shoulder and set it on the top of the chair's stile.

Symbelle was dumbfounded, staring between the muscular legs of the limber elvan. Scarless was fully clothed in tight leathers, but Symbelle was flushing with fire in her loins from vividly picturing otherwise. She had never received the slightest degree of any living thing showing attraction toward her. Scarless, of all beings, was the only one. And Symbelle was beginning to believe she may have been growing far too close to the mark on her assassination writ to go through with it. She truly had no desire to see Scarless die, much less to actually be responsible for it.

Fyheir? Do we have to? Her evil inner half was allowing her to think for herself for once without imposing. *Must we kill her? Look at her.* Symbelle's mouth watered the more she ogled the Crime Queen's voluptuous build up and down. *I am barely in the Oathemic Cabal. I don't have to return to them. Scarless will protect me. Xalo can share.*

Scarless seemed to enjoy Symbelle's helplessly paralyzed display of obsession. She taunted her into further submission with the fingers of her right hand running through her red wig, to control her head if she so pleased. Symbelle closed her glowing eyes and hoped for exactly that to happen.

But as soon as she did, the futile fantasy was shattered with the crash of the door being flung wide open and an anxious woman shoving in with two lackeys in tow. "Guildmother, I believe we have been found! This safe house is no longer safe. We must leave!"

"How? Who? The Boarneck Company or someone else?" Scarless slammed her leg down from the chair and instantly broke back into character as the serious Stormtrees leader she was.

Symbelle recognized the voice as the one belonging to the woman she had called Amaris earlier. The closer Amaris and the two men beside her got, the more exceptionally off they appeared to Symbelle. They weren't human or elvan, but something different. Their skin was dark grey. Their hair was black. Their irises were red. And something about their bodies shimmered in the faint lighting, as if they were shifting between an illusion and reality.

She had to know. "What are you?"

Amaris ignored her curiosity, and Scarless seemed more concerned with the pressing warning.

"Where is Xalo?" Scarless questioned, loud enough that she may as well have screamed it. "The others? You shouldn't be in here, Amaris."

Amaris was staring and analyzing every detail of Symbelle, but Symbelle did not relent in asking again. "Your skin is grey," she said aloud, somehow understanding that her hypersight was taking over her senses as her violet eyes radiated brighter. "Are you all qindrid?"

That stopped Amaris and her grey-skinned men in their tracks. She even began to back away as she corrected her. "You are mistaken." Amaris chuckled nervously. "Check your eyes. Why would you say that?"

Xalo literally slid into the room behind them with his spellblade drawn as if there were an impending fight. "I love when you scream my name," he smugly said to Scarless. "Is someone about to be punished?"

"I've never seen a qindrid, but I have always wanted to. Are your eyes always red as well?" Symbelle continued with her fascinated interrogation, stealing the attention of everyone present. She also noticed a near-invisible green aura emanating from Amaris and her lackeys.

Xalo looked utterly confused with the situation, seeing the same puzzled semblance displayed on Scarless, who just stood and listened, but he couldn't help but join in the conversation. "You should visit the Grey Ward in the city, then. Don't know what I missed, though. Why are we talking about qindrid? One of you a greyborne or something?" He walked in front of them, inspecting their faces closely.

Amaris was clearly showing signs of poorly masked fear, and Symbelle saw one of the qindrid men pivoting toward the door like he intended to sprint to the exit.

"Guildmother, Xalo, please," Amaris implored, "we need to go now. Oldan's spies have learned of our location and are likely encroaching now with an ambush."

Scarless held her bloodrime spear out to point at Amaris with her right hand and raised her left hand with an open palm up. "Wait, what do you mean grey skin and red eyes? What are you seeing that I am not? Xalo?"

"No. Fair or tan skin. And their eyes aren't red either. But I'm not the one wearing goggles as thick as bricks either," Xalo replied, and he shrugged his shoulders, looking over Symbelle.

"Symbelle's eyes do not lie," Pyphan's voice declared from the doorway, where he appeared. He was referring to her hypersight. "She is saying they are neverborne qindrid."

On cue, all three of the alleged neverborne dashed for the door. Pyphan wasn't expecting the charge and was shoved hard to the side as the two lackeys muscled past him, unblocking the path out.

Amaris was not so lucky. Ever fast, Xalo snatched her by the back of the scalp and yanked her so hard, she was forced back in front of him. All in one smooth motion, he brought his forearm across her throat to collapse her into a gasping, curled-up ball on the floor.

The Dawning magemarks on Pyphan's bare torso flared up green as he cast a tairan spell on the floorboards and forced one of the fleeing qindrid back into the room. The plank the man's feet just happened to be on had grown around his boots, entrapping him, and the other boards on the floor all shifted out of its way as it moved freely to escort him into the center of the room.

The third had apparently gotten away, but his whereabouts did not seem to take precedence over the two qindrid that hadn't.

"What the fuck is a neverborne?" Xalo harshly asked Amaris, sticking the point of his sword on the middle of her forehead.

"I have an idea," Scarless said, making her way over to Amaris with a furious glare. "I have had an idea for a long time."

Fittingly, however, it was Pyphan who clarified what he was

already well studied in from the Oathemic Cabal. "The new breed from Neveril umbran. The realm doesn't know about them yet. They are skin-shifters. Conspirators that take out politicians and wear the faces of those in influence and power. I could spend a day apprising you all of this."

"Well-read Dawner." The neverborne that Pyphan had captured with his spell directed these words at Symbelle's brother specifically. "You a dropout from the Green Byway or a dual agent for the Oa—"

The qindrid tried to expose Pyphan, but Symbelle's mage brother was too swift with his next spell. A board in the ceiling became rimmed in a green glow. It took the shape of a guillotine blade and quickly dropped to precisely decapitate the neverborne.

"Wait! Scarless!" Amaris seemed motivated by that to reteach herself to talk between wheezing for her life. "I took this turn to live longer. I can explain. Please, I am not ready to die."

Scarless stood over Amaris now and nonchalantly propped one foot against the side of her head, putting a mild amount of weight on it. She placed the butt of her spear on Amaris's hip. "You sound like someone who enjoys life, Amaris. I enjoy life too. Let's pretend you love life so much that you still want to remain friends."

"It's Amethyst." Amaris readily complied to turn the outcome into a merciful favor. Symbelle recognized the name from her father's instruction. She was part of the contingency plan to become a necessary casualty by the conclusion of Symbelle's writs. "It's all in the name, just a code for who gets to sit on the council. The blend between the sea and fire, blue and red, Goldgarden and Az'Dayne. The Seat of the Red works for the Pentagogue of Everdawn. And the Boarneck Company has been bought out by the Dominadom, reporting to Amethyst. They are opening the gates to let Az'Dayne infiltrate and turn the city the same way they did Everdawn. The same way they are doing in Frostdale, in Barredom. And so many other cities."

Scarless tilted her head in scheming contemplation. "Where do you rank in this?"

"Amaris is just a code too," the former safe-house keeper replied. "I answer to Amethyst directly, and my umbran masters. I have no affiliation to the Boarnecks nor Az'Dayne, technically. I was told that you and your Stormtrees were our first obstacle to remove this season. Shypriss's Sol-War movement will be the last, planned for the Reaping this cycle. Shypriss and her Sunder mages were to be slain during their Transbernation."

Xalo started to draw the design of the Stormtree sigil in her forehead with his spellblade. "She likes to talk. But I don't think she wants to live yet. We waste time."

Uubakrath intruded on the room next, with his Terollar composite bow in one hand, dragging the qindrid who had fled in the other. The neverborne was clearly dead, with an arrow protruding from the middle of his back.

The tall elvan archer dropped the runaway next to the headless qindrid by Pyphan and spoke something in his native tongue to Scarless, who translated for the group. "He says the skin changed to grey after he put an arrow through it. Judging by your other friend here, it looks to be that your little trick fades after death, doesn't it?"

Amaris did not reply, slowly daring to raise herself from her prone position to her knees.

Uubakrath said something else in Terollar, which Scarless interpreted for him again. "There were more outside. This one got a few houses down and exchanged words with the spies lying in wait. We do need to move along."

"Let me be your double agent," Amaris beseeched of Scarless, glancing back and forth between the Goldgarden Crime Queen and Symbelle. "You have Symbelle for the Boarneck Company. Let me be yours for Amethyst! She will never suspect it."

"She won't do that." Pyphan crushed any vain hopes. "Whatever Neveril umbran turned her can see through her eyes at any time and find her. It's called cerebration. They can even control them if they are close enough. It would be far too risky for Amaris to betray her masters. She could simply turn coat again and inform Amethyst of what we know, and that we have a hyperi on our side who can see through their shadow guise."

Symbelle studied the dead qindrid with Uubakrath's arrow in him and dispassionately reminded them, "They may have just been informed about that anyhow."

"It's begun, then." Xalo sheathed his magic glass sword. "We move out."

Amaris was still determined to survive the night. "Scarless, keep me with you, then! I can shift my look to appear like another. I can pose as Amethyst and work with Symbelle to help assassinate Oldan. Bring me into the plan. I was dying of a sickness, only days left in my lungs, when I took the turn. I just wanted to live." The pathetic neverborne woman tried to invoke sympathy from the wrong party. "I am your loyal—"

"Hush." Scarless shut her up with a disgusted look. "I am not going to kill you."

The room fell silent for Scarless to elaborate, half-expecting a sharp ruse and for her to command Xalo to slay Amaris instead. "You are going to help me draw out your masters. The power of propaganda. Walk with me now and learn how."

Scarless manhandled Amaris to her feet by the back of her neck and thrust her into motion to start walking out of the banquet room. Uubakrath and Xalo joined in beside her to leave the safe house behind them. Scarless blew Symbelle a kiss as some form of farewell. "See you on the pleasure barge, Symbelle."

"Come, sister," she heard her brother say, but she didn't look at him. She was distracted, in a trance as she watched Scarless leave her sight. The green flash of Pyphan casting some spell to open the walls to lead outside came just before she entered into Traversement with him. They fast-traveled in a blur through the streets of the Midway back in the direction of Bridgeville.

There was no turning back now. As Xalo had said, it had begun. All Symbelle could dwell on was if she had it in her to follow through with Master Claydius's writ to assassinate Scarless in the next few days, or to incur the uncompromising wrath of the Oathemic Cabal.

ATHANIEL (IV)

INFINITE REFLECTION

The Room of Infinite Reflection was what the Oathemic Cabal called this particular uniquely designed chamber for meditation and escape in the order's principal hub beneath the Plaguefolk Villages. There wasn't a space on the wall, floor, or ceiling in the pentagonal room that didn't have a mirror fitted to it. It was a place agents went to for solitude, with their countless clones staring back at them from the panels in all directions. It was a place for uninterrupted internal contemplation, for agents to reset or discover themselves after enduring something that had adversely impacted their mental stability or to instill emotional detachment.

The mirrored room had five walls. In one top corner of the pentagonal chamber were twenty-five apparatus-activated hourglasses with a lit candle placed atop each one. Each candle had a different length of wick, which would dwindle and expire when its vessel's sand depleted to the bottom and triggered the next.

The only piece of furniture in the retreat of introspection was the lone chair that Athan sat upon. While there was no mandated time an agent had to spend once committing to the Room of Infinite Reflection, it was a general code of devotion to complete all the hourglasses and candles before stepping back out. Once one stepped in, there could be no recess for food or drink. To relieve oneself, there was simply a bucket by the door. A full day's twenty-five-hour revolution was expected to finish as the agent constrained himself to a fast that should not be broken during the meditation process.

It was also in the code of conduct between other agents, and even masters, not to interrupt an agent for any reason during their forgoing of the outside world.

Athan used the quiet time afforded by the course of the first hourglass to find his inner peace. The Room of Infinite Reflection was the first place he had visited when he had returned to the Cabal's capital base and been denied an audience to speak with Coldborn alone. He had not tried to seek out his partner, Daerlem. He had not alternatively sought out Master Claydius or demanded to speak to another master. He had come here.

His mind was racing. He was full of bottled-up hate, feelings of volatile anger that needed to be unleashed. He was embarrassed by the defeat of his pride, ashamed of his bloodline and the failures he had exhibited in front of them all. He was sad for his sisters. *No … I am not sad.* He was scared, he decided. He was sincerely scared for their fates being manipulated out of his control. He needed to clear his mind and still his soul.

When the first hour ended, he moved the chair to face the semicircular shrine of hourglasses and candles, like a throne of fire and sand. He sat with his back to the heat and suffered the deep sweat that swiftly took over his body. He wanted it to hurt. If he had thought he could survive the flames, he would even have considered setting himself ablaze. Anything to fix it.

Athan spent the next few hours searching each pathetic face on the walls, examining the wretched depictions of himself for signs of weakness. There were so many. It was no wonder his lineage blade had denied him. His hair had greyed, and wrinkles had formed on his face, and his right hand had been scalded into a horrid scar. By the time his great-granduncle had him escorted out of Castle Chandoss, Athan recalled looking and feeling like he had gone from his midtwenties to late fifties in age. The Dawning mage, Elixion, who had conveyed him back to the Oathemic hub had tried healing him after they had stopped, but Athan had denied the magic halfway through. He wanted the reminder.

The right side of Athan's face still looked older, heavy crow's feet in the corner of that eye, and his hair was grey and thin on that side as well, while the left remained youthful, with his healthy Daynish red locks. On his sword hand, there was still the remnant of the burn the spellblade had branded on his palm as well.

It made no sense to Athan why the spellblade of his ancestor would choose Valaythea and not him. Athan was the warrior of this generation in his family line. The only other who could even possibly contend with that claim was his cousin Nikayle the Fourthnamed, though he had been chosen by the Barturon Spellblade of his mother's family line.

But magic was strange, and Athan realized he knew nothing of the spellblades' arcane parameters, as he had thought he might from his time around mages in his line of work. The perpetual questions that had haunted him for so long resurfaced as much as he tried to banish them from his musings.

Thoughts of his cousin brought him to ponder on his great-grandfather, Nikayle the Firstnamed, infamous High Bloodguard of the Crown, who last wielded the Chandoss Spellblade that now fancied Athan's unworthy sister over him. If there had been any traces of doubt in his accusation of Valdean devising the assassination of his great-grandfather and defaming his name, there were surely no such reservations now. Athan hadn't been alive when the act had occurred, but his history with the Oathemic Cabal had provided more than enough research around the subject surrounding the ill-maneuvered imperial switch from Goldfyre to Ampion for him to determine his convictions.

Another hour passed, and Athan finally gave in to the unbearable heat. He began slipping his drenched attire to the floor until he was naked, sitting in a slippery pool of his own sweat. It felt like he could breathe again, being free of his clothes. Some impossible cold mist kissed the back of his neck, sending a shiver down his spine, ignoring the warmth of the candles. Athan glanced behind him, thinking it may have been Coldborn creeping in with his Umbra magic, but all he found was another hourglass done—that and those thousand images of himself staring back at him, patiently waiting to be judged.

He loathed what he saw, but he didn't want to. He needed to hate something, someone other than himself. He tried to funnel his ire on his renegade cousin. *Nikayle … Barturon Chandoss … Whoever the fuck you are …* But he could not keep his inner turmoil on him. *You earned what you are. The glass blades do not lie. It sees I am unworthy because I see myself as unworthy.*

He tried to hate his own father for failing in every avenue a father could. *I can only pity the pathetic. I cannot hate that which I do not respect.*

He channeled his fury on the thief who took the Chandoss Spellblade from him. *Val … You glory glutton … You pretend you do not want the attention, yet you somehow receive it all. I hope your pedestal bur* ... He stopped his evil wishes from surfacing. He didn't mean any of them. He loved his sisters. He was jealous of Valaythea's ironic glory, but he endured no enmity toward her for it.

My sisters ... Addy, poor Addy ... Valdean, do not touch her as you've done to Oddy. Oddy, he breathed uncomfortably heavy. *Oddy,* he breathed more rapidly in anger. *Odysserae!*

"Valdean!" Athan bellowed in fury as if he was conjuring the Fives through the ceiling.

"Valdean!" He became too consumed by his malice to focus on anything else. *Why did you do this to her?*

As many reflections as there were in the mirror, he began to contrive a different way to kill his great-granduncle for his great sins. *Why?* His spite ran so deep that Athan ignored his previous self-loathing. "Valdean!"

The sands in the glass waned heap by heap as the room grew dimmer with fewer candles lit. The passing of several hours was dedicated to the same dead-man-to-be. He funneled so much animosity through his thoughts that it drained him of all energy, mind and body. Within the same hour, his eyes could hold on no longer. The debilitation of long-needed sleep possessed his bones to collapse him into a profound slumber.

* * * * *

Athan woke to the sound of three coins hitting the floor in front of his face. He knew the sound all too well. Being "three-coined" was a signature of the assassins of the Hive Order when they were about to eliminate a victim on a writ.

He spun up to his feet in an instant, unarmed to properly defend himself, and blind in the absolute darkness of the room, but that didn't matter. It was too late anyway. He already felt the knife point at his back. Athan stood still as stone and braced himself for the next one to enter his heart.

But it never came. Only the familiar eerie accent of Coldborn. "That is how it will happen to you. This much is known. All that matters is what you decide to finish before destiny's inevitability comes to pass."

There were no writs on the three guards I killed. Nikayle or Valdean told Elixion, who brought me here. I knew this day would come for me.

Athan prepared his resolve to die as he turned around to inspect his execution by the founder of assassins himself. Instead of three coins on the ground Athan found likenesses of the tokens in makeshift shards of magic ice at his feet. And the dagger's blade proved to be Coldborn's finger, elongated into an icy spearpoint as well.

Athan didn't try to decode his master's riddles concerning his fate. Instead, his last thought lingered on the arcane mysteries he had always wanted to know, of how Coldborn could even consistently cast Umbra magic outside of the season.

But there was something strangely different about the shadow master this time.

"I am not here. You now find yourself inside a contingency spell. Time has stopped until this message expires," the flickering figure of Coldborn motioned to the infinity mirrors surrounding them. The archmage's illusion seemed to be a manifestation between pure shadow and raw magic, with the signature faint trace of green speckled throughout the ethereal fabric that shaped him.

The room was pitch dark, yet somehow Athan had gained the supernatural ability to see in it. He could see the endless images of himself petrified in impossible stillness even as he moved in circles to inspect the shadow magic in place. But Athan had seen a lot, and knew when the rare circumstance that Coldborn confronted him, whether as an apparition or in the flesh, it meant to provide an absolute of undivided attention.

"This is where it ends between you and I, as master and apprentice. By now you may know the extent of it. The Oathemic Cabal has been far too compromised and infiltrated. The ghosts and their puppets are in us now."

The Neveril and the neverborne, Athan surmised between his master's intervals in the magic message.

"By this Sunder, a month, less or more, you will witness the dissolution of our guild, with orders reformed or disbanded entirely. The Az'Dayne Dominadom will apply new masters to control the hubs, at which point most of our current agents will be replaced in an efficiently swift fashion."

Why are you not fighting this? Or allowing the guild to do so for you? Athan found that he was unable to speak, and realized the futility of the absurd notion regardless, being that Coldborn wasn't even present. *Maybe you did fight this. And we simply lost ...*

"New writs will be written. The first of which will be on my head. You will spearhead the hunt."

I will never kill you. I cannot kill you, he knew beyond a doubt, even if he was blessed by a miracle from the Five and Five. *No one can kill you.*

"My last act as Founder of the Oathemic Cabal has been to promote you to Keeper of the Hive Order. It is already known and done. Claydius and the other factions have been apprised and have accepted. The only way the Cabal survives is for me to feign its surrender, and turn it over to the assassins to lead it. The Dominadom will not harm you or the men you assemble, as you will be their only link to the spy network scattered throughout the regions. The new masters will expect you to choose who dies and who lives. This is a burden I cannot assist in."

But there has never been a Keeper of the Hive Order? Master Claydius is currently over the Hunder and Hive Order. Again, Athan was glad his ability to speak had been stripped from him, as he recalled the archmage's clear explanation of the forthcoming changes that were evidently being expedited throughout the guild.

"As I leave you now, I absolve you from your oath, with my permission to do all that they ask. It has been an honor watching you grow into the agent you have become Athaniel Chandoss. You are an instrument of Az'Dayne and the realm. Do not forget this."

Coldborn's illusion began to dissipate, and with that, so did the limited light in the room. He somehow knew his ability to speak had returned and that the time stop spell was fading as well.

"Your final official writs from me are in the mirror you are now looking at," were the last words spoken from the archmage before his simulacrum vanished completely.

Which mirror? Athan was about to ask when he glanced at one in particular just before the chamber went black.

And that was when it shattered in a chain reaction that took the rest of the mirrors with it in an explosion of glass shards that fell to the ground, pulverized into miniscule fragments the size of dust.

All that remained was a magic green hue around two scrolls above the pile.

"The writs," Athan whispered aloud. His duty in death-dealing had only gotten more dire.

VALAYTHEA (VII)

DANGEROUS DANCE

This was her favorite personal place in the palace, where she visited to clear her mind, sweat out the bad, inhale the new, and cleanse her soul. This was the performance studio constructed specifically for the lon'Chandoss Triplets, adjacent to the theater.

Valaythea, Adyssaira, and Odysserae had been trained in a variety of performing arts by masters of their crafts who had come from across the wide continent just to hone their talents with others at the Chandoss college known as the Syrene. Since they had been little girls, just old enough to walk, these artists had exercised them in routines of several styles of dance: Chandoshian ballet, Khalimishe belly dancing, Savatarm sensual, and Daynish contemporary, now just referred to as *modernesque*.

Adyssaira had been rigorously trained in a derivative of the Elothian aerial, enhanced by their ancestor, Elexius Chandoss, to incorporate pole dancing and graceful gliding from hanging silks. Odysserae specialized in the martial art of wyrkenido, which best translated to "master of the dangerous ropes" in Elothian also. Valaythea's dual proficiency was ejahra, the dramatized exercise of blade-dancing, and solesce, the practice of using a variety of fire tools for entertainment purposes.

The girls were drilled in how to integrate these acrobatics, martial arts, and dance forms into a single skillset on stage to better awe the spectators Ethiass invited to their lavish events.

But today Valaythea was in the mood for an innovated style she had not done since the Fire Festival last cycle. It incorporated the semblance of the Daynish solesce she was trained in and the Brutongan fire dances, which were the most hypnotically riveting performances to watch compared with any other culture's, in her opinion. Just mastering one of the special instruments to use in the fiery show was enough to mesmerize a king, but Valaythea had fervently practiced them all: the fire whip, the fire dart, the fire hoop, the fire box, the fire staff, the fire pois, the fire torches, the fire fans, and other variations of tools that the artistically pioneering Daynish had introduced into the different dances. And Valaythea had all of them at her disposal in front of her in the stone studio.

She had staged five diverse sets of equipment on five tall platforms, each nearby enough to allow her to gracefully leap to one after the other. She set the braziers atop each fireproof platform safely ablaze and prepared to begin.

Today she wore minimal clothing, exposing her skin in all the right places to entice a questionable balance between eccentrically erotic and practical. The entire length of her slender belly was exposed between her black leather skirt and cropped top, with leather straps snaking down her thighs and calves, matching the bracers over her forearms. Her fingers were exposed for manipulation of the tools, and her feet were bare for the purpose of the acrobatics to come. Around her neck was a leather choker that had a ringlet in front of her throat, which fastened a chain talisman that hung between the crease of her breasts.

She kept her red hair tied up in a tight bun and placed a double-layered sash of fine cloth over her eyes and ears, wrapped completely around her head to block out her sight and hearing. She was embodying her sisters in this dance, since they were unable to join her. Over her face, she placed the new House Chandoss masque, which she had donned just for the performance when she met Izayus.

The masque was symbolic for her to wear, but it also augmented the requisite drama of it all. The masque was black with an open frown and covered three-quarters of her face from the left side and whole mouth area. A fiery burst of green was painted around the left eye. And out of the same side of the masque were the eye-catching orange phoenix plumes that flared out from her head.

It had been two days since the evil irony of destiny had played its hand on her when she wielded the Chandoss Spellblade in front of her family, robbing her own brother of his earned right to be chosen by it. Count Valdean had all but locked her away in her bedchamber ever since, practically making her a prisoner to her own room, sentried over by the most veteran of the Chandoss Guard.

Everyone in her family had become curiously astray during the time being as well. She hadn't received a single knock from her sisters, nor from her father or uncle, and she had an awful gut feeling about Emberalda. Whatever her bullheaded cousin had gotten herself out of line with, relentlessly chasing after Timmurian, was costing Valaythea sleep and the appeal of her stress-ravaged nails. *She is fine. This is what she wanted, just to be with him*, Valaythea had to tell herself in order not to fret to death.

The only family who had cared to visit had been Valdean, with his incessant redundancy in futile interrogations. He wanted to know all the same answers, about when Izayus would be visiting the estates; which she did not know. He wanted to know this; which she did not remember. He wanted to know that; which she reminded him the same. He wanted to know all the *whys* and *whats*; which she was ignorant to it all.

But as with everything else lately in her life, that contemptable routine proved to be as transient as the rest of the queer events unfolding. Valdean had given her a respite, and even the guards had abandoned their post at her door. Rumors echoed down the halls that the Thrench were on the move, anxious and potentially agitated. Instead of seeking out family, the moment she found the opportunity to flee her personal prison, she had come straight to the studio and geared up for her own escape.

Izayus has his drugs. This is mine … Valaythea concentrated on a series of deep breaths to immerse herself into character and then commenced performing the dangerous dance.

Her eyes were blind behind the sash, but her sense of touch was heightened to detect the direction of the heat in the brazier. She did a cartwheel and came back up with the two torch props that had been there waiting for her. In a few spins, she turned to light their ends in the firepit and began her juggling dance. Halfway through, she connected the torches into a fire staff and finished the memorized routine before releasing the staff and nimbly side-flipping her way off the platform onto the second.

For this dance, she picked up two fire fans, fitted with several candles, which she immediately lit in the new brazier in a few swooping motions. This performance was much more sensual in the beginning and progressed more intensely toward the climax with faster twirls of the fans and her body spinning around. Each session of props was timed to last two minutes, and by the end of the fire-fans skit, she was already glistening with sweat from brow to toe, intent on controlling her breathing to finish the strenuous routine. She had taken too much time off from her exercises, indulging in the fineries of an imperial paramour.

Valaythea dropped the fire fans and did a flawless butterfly kick to land on the third platform, where she took up the fire dart and set its end aflame in the brazier. She wrapped its rope around her body and arms and danced with the small fireball. She swung the rope in circles outward from her on either side, around her waist, arms, and even her neck, spiraling the flame in wide arcs. For the final thirty seconds, she discarded the dart prop and kicked up a special whip, which she set on fire also, and dramatically snapped and cracked it in a whirlwind dance.

During her backflip to the fourth platform, Valaythea felt a wave of dizziness almost take her under. A biting cold stung her brain, and scores of images flashed invasively through her mind, of Coldborn and Izayus, but they were gone in a second, as fast as they had come. She did not let them affect her lead-up to the finale of the performance.

She picked up the fire hoop with her foot and set it on fire to continue. The vertigo crept back into her veins during the dance, but she felt her feet still staying true to the movements and spins. Valaythea exhaled a huge gust to eject the poison from her mind and regain composure for the last of the props in the routine, but she lost time entirely in perhaps the last minute.

Unsure if she had completed the fire-hoop dance or not, she defeatedly released the prop and went to flip to the last platform. But as her feet tried to leave the small stage she stood on, she felt her head become heavy, bending her body to aim toward the ground. This time it was a blast of frigidness imploding from within her, as if an explosion of raw cold detonated from her blood and bones.

It only went black for a moment, and then the light came. A flood of images from her time in Everdawn that she had completely forgotten about. They gradually matured into not just images but full scenarios of entire conversations and whole days' worth of recollections of vivid happenings that had transpired.

She watched herself meeting the other four imperial paramours in the Royal Harem, and the debauchery of the orgy that had taken place after. Men and women had crowded around in their full masques to watch the ordeal between Prince Izayus and his five subwives. She had been forced to take part in smoking opiates from hookah pipes and imbibing yewr root, which induced psychedelic hallucinations. She recalled walking barefoot through the private vineyards just outside afterward with the northern paramour, Tamantha Bayn, and establishing a bond of trust for what was to come.

She remembered meeting two heavily guarded, highly secretive, grey-skinned, black-eyed elven in the Royal Harem. Izayus had warned her that they were Neveril umbran and that she would come to know them very well in the coming season of the Sunder, when she would be coerced into taking the Transcendence to become a neverborne qindrid.

Memories of her tour through the Pentagogue came back. She had met so many paladins and veritans of every rank that day. Izayus had taken her up in the complex lift that rose to the top of the spire, over fifty floors high. The entire structure was shaped like a dawnstar mace, with the shaft of the lift appearing like the stem of the weapon and the spherical apex like the ball of the head. She had also been briefly shown that there were an additional ten floors that went below the ground level, which Izayus had made clear he was not permitted to show her quite yet.

But what her sudden reminiscence fixated on the most was the time she had spent beside the Umbra mage Coldborn and his discussions with Izayus. Valaythea had been implored into a confidentiality that no other paramours had been privileged to receive.

Both Coldborn and Izayus had enlightened her about what was in store for her when the dominarchs returned from Barredom. There was going to be a mass awakening of the public, called the Greyfire Revolution, in which some of the final pieces to transform into neverborne, from the most influential people in the power nations, were to take the Transcendence. And this was when the Neveril planned to make their assault on the Thrench Empire from all sides. Valaythea had learned that both she and her sister Odysserae were among the chosen to undergo the Transcendence, albeit with different umbran lifemates and on vastly different trajectories. Coldborn knew about Adyssaira's great secret and had explained that once she was discovered, Valdean would force her into an enslavement camp of Dawning mages the Neveril were using to create an ever-expanding underrealm beneath all of Az'Dayne and beyond.

But Coldborn had other plans of his own. He was always one step ahead of the plotters, since being the founder of the continent's assassination guild came with more perks than just being the mastermind behind a surplus of highly trained killers. The Oathemic Cabal had also evolved into a vast network of effective information gatherers that acted as the largest spy organization in the world.

Coldborn had stayed true to the tenebrous tendencies he seemed keen on portraying, never saying too much, to keep others in the dark just enough to navigate them as he chose to orchestrate his own endgame. But Valaythea had never had a political endgame herself, nor ever an actual fair start, if she was to be honest, so survival and an escape into some ignorantly perceived fantasy were an easy upgrade for her to accept.

Coldborn had proposed that Izayus rescue her when the time was ripe, before the dominarchs' return. There were so many factors to consider, manipulate, and prepare to sneak the very prince of Az'Dayne out of the land without the obvious open use of magic, and without being noticed by the watching eyes of Izayus's perpetual imperial guard and the neverborne spies. Izayus was supposed to take the Transcendence as well, but that was going to be impossible due to a complication with his hidden true lineage, which remained ambiguous to Valaythea. They had not explained.

Coldborn had insisted that Valaythea return to the Chandoss Estates and speak with her uncle, Nikayle the Thirdnamed, when it was time. He was one of his most loyal Oathemic agents, still sworn so despite his injury, and would apprise her of the contingency plan after Coldborn had secured a safe abduction for Izayus out of Az'Dayne with minimal resistance.

The last thing Valaythea recalled trying to bargain for in submission to Coldborn and Izayus's scheming was the rescue of her sisters and cousin in the clandestine operation. Either Adyssaira, Odysserae, Emberalda, and Sashka were included in the covert extraction from the shadow of the Dominadom, or Valaythea would not comply. That was when the Umbra spell had hit her.

Who did I dare to think I was to deny the wishes of Penthara's most powerful shadow mage? How am I even still alive? Alive ... Valaythea felt her eyes blink rapidly and some level of consciousness returning. *I am still alive? The heat from the fire, it … That cold in my mind, I did not realize it was there … It is gone …*

Valaythea felt strength returning to her arms as her palms braced behind her to sit her upright and remove her blindfold. Her eyes fluttered open to cautiously assess the practice studio. She half expected to find herself set on fire by one of the many props she had set ablaze. A solid knot in the right corner of her forehead reminded her of the nasty fall she had taken when she had been attempting to finish her fire dance.

She realized she must have still been dreaming in a comatose state, however, because her uncle, Nikayle, was standing over her, gripping the fire hoop she had last held with his hands in the flames, impossibly unflinching from the element.

Uncle, you don't burn? What is this?

"Memories coming back, Val?" he smugly inquired. "The shadow spell should have lasted longer, but I was going to have to find a way to break it soon anyway. I believe the heat of all that fire countered the cold magic. I should have thought of that."

"Uncle? Your legs …" She hesitated to finish and decided to examine him instead. *You were paralyzed. Where is your chair?* "You can …"

When her words trailed off, Nikayle took the opportunity to finish for her. "Stand? Walk?" He tossed the fire hoop back up onto the adjacent platform. "I know. Must be exhausting to find out that everything you have come to know and trust your entire life has gone to the hells in a matter of months, just when you thought everything was finally falling into place for all of us."

"My memories are back." She evoked an epiphany from her surge of recollections on the part her uncle was supposed to play in the plan imposed by Coldborn. "I was supposed to talk to you. I was told that you would know what I am to do from here. But that still does not explain your chair. Your back?"

"I am one of them, Val. I have been one of them," he alluded to the most disturbing possible explanation.

"The Neveril beneath us, who run this lost country, have schemes upon schemes, and advanced sciences that you cannot yet comprehend. The umbran who made me what I am now, their names are Zsa'vauge and Qaynethlith, can use a certain impower called cerebration to hear what I say, see what I see, but I have learned to feel when they are doing it, when they are with me, in my mind. They are not right now, so try to keep up, as I will talk fast."

And he did, not skipping a beat to swallow between sentences. "By taking the Transcendence to become a neverborne qindrid, you are reborn in a way, immune to disease, cleansed of any scar or injury you may have suffered, and it can even get rid of impairments in a girl who was born deaf." He shifted the topic to clearly imply someone very familiar.

No! Do not touch my sisters. "Oddy is going to take this Transcendence? This keeps getting worse. I need to sit down." Valaythea huffed in anxiety, trying to find her uncle's missing chair, but all she found was her rump still flat on the floor.

"You *are* sitting down," Nikayle bluntly reminded her.

"Then I need to breathe. I need out!" she screamed, and she stood up defiantly, shoving away her uncle's helping hand. "No wonder your son fled! Tell me where to, and I will join him now, I swear on my life to the Fives!"

"A fitting vow. You just may. We will revisit that," Nikayle obscurely replied. "Would you rather save your sisters instead?"

"How? Oddy wants to become one of these *things,*" she retaliated pointing at Nikayle, "that you and Count Valdean are! Addy is being married off to the Thrench boy. She will be rescued and outlive us all! And who in the five hells knows where you all have hidden Sashka?"

Valaythea stormed over to take a seat at the nearest stage; the one she assumed she fell from. She huffed defeatedly and couldn't place her eyes on her uncle.

"Sashka is your cousin. You do have another sister though. Emberalda has been your half sister all along," Nikayle revealed without detail. "We should think about saving her too."

Valaythea rubbed at the knot she felt throbbing on her forehead, and intelligently inquired without much energy, "Huh?"

"This is the best time for me to tell you this. By now, I know you are aware who the Neveril is that lives in our palace. Valdean and Ise'andahr are not here presently, nor is Ethiass," he explained. "There is a meeting with Zsa'vauge taking place in the tunnels beneath the count's tower."

Valaythea could care less about the Neveril and the umbran at the moment. It was too much to take in. She needed to know simpler things. "What do you mean Ember is my sister? But she is your child? That would imply that Ethiass —"

"I am glad you decided to sit back down," Nikayle stopped her, putting a fatherly hand on top of hers. When she looked back up at him in disbelief, he had tears in the corners of his eyes.

His voice was very gentle when he continued. "My wife, Delphine, was not a loyal wife. In the end, Valdean took her from me, as he takes everything from everyone in this family. I knew about it and she knew that I knew. Your great-granduncle single-handedly organized the deaths of your great-grandfather, your grandfather, and so many others. In the end, he even took Delphine's life to spite me for my noncompliance in withholding information as a double agent for the Oathemic Cabal and Zsa'vauge."

She didn't know why but she felt extremely cold in the instance, as if the blood had retreated from her limbs and into her stomach. *Maybe the spell is returning and I can forget all of this again. Please be true*, she prayed. But instead she dared to puzzle the pieces aloud, "You are my father?"

Nikayle gave no gesture of affirmation. He just elaborated more. "Throughout all of this, Ethiass's affair with Taizsha began long before your mother's death. It is not popular to admit to in respects for Valenteal, but we were all aware. Valenteal found solace in me, as I also confided in her. There was always something there, between your mother and I, that we feared to act upon. But we confessed our hate to the cruel fate that we were not paired together, and instead trapped in a bad dream with adulterous spouses. What we had was natural. I loved Valenteal. If humans could have lifemates, she was mine," Nikayle somberly admitted, sniffing back tears that he seemed to have been holding back for her entire life.

"Oh, Uncle," Valaythea squeezed his larger hands in hers, wanting to pull him in for a sympathetic embrace, but she didn't know how to respond. "I mean Father … I," she stumbled in her words, with her mind not sure how to navigate after such a surprise unveiling. *This means Athan is my cousin, no wait, my half brother. Sashka is now my cousin, and Ember … my half sister all this time …*

"Odysserae knows," he confessed. "She is the only one alive who knows. Ethiass is still ignorant of the affair, and I have never had the heart to break it to him."

Of course Oddy knows. What secrets does she not know? "But how could you know for certain," she felt a choke in her tone as tears had crept up on her as well, but she tried to shift from crying by inquiring logic. "How could you know we were yours?"

Nikayle pulled his hands back to wipe his eyes and compose himself back to seriousness. "Coldborn has ways to know through his magic. It is true and real Val. And as much as I wish we had time to let today be all about what I have had to keep hidden your whole lives, we sadly do not have that luxury. This is all we have time to go over."

He unfastened his belt to remove the Chandoss Spellblade from his waist and hand the sheathed family heirloom into her grasp. "Your destiny."

"My curse," she countered, ogling the weapon as if it was the most repulsive thing she had ever set her eyes on. She inspected the intricacies of the bone hilt and emerald pommel, up to the golden guard shaped like a winged serpent. She should have been in awe to hold such a magnificent artifact, but her face spelled out what she truly felt.

"Here it is Valaythea, and here it lies. You cannot deny it now," her father softly coerced her hands over the bone hilt.

"Prince Izayus is on his way here. I have hired the Thrench and the Silverbacks to plan his escape. You are going with him. You always were, but this does change the outcome."

What are the Silverbacks? And how do you hire Thrench? They are not mercenaries ... Valaythea checked herself from asking any of the questions overwhelming her, and to just allow her father to finish his premeditated resolution.

"You can stop considering him your cousin. My son, your half brother, Nikayle, will be who you are to meet. He will train you in how to use this," he motioned to the glass sword. "As you are aware, he hails himself as Barturon now, but he may be traveling under different aliases."

"But where is he? I thought no one knew," she returned with what limited information she had been imparted with.

"I am far from no one. Other than Grand Regent of the Syrene, I remain pledged in title as Journeyman for the Oathemic Cabal, which is a fancy term Coldborn uses to classify his main informants of a region. My jurisdiction is obviously Chandoshia.

"My son did not flee because the Barturon Spellblade chose him. I sent him away after it chose him. Spellblades have no place currently in the evolution of the Greyfire Revolution. I imagine they will either be executed, or used as bounty hunters to hunt problematic mages, such as Coldborn. And I imagine you neither want to die or futilely attempt to kill godlike mages.

"The leader of the Silverbacks is a man named Haelyn Rook, archon of the Silverlakes. He may just be the richest man in the central part of the continent. The Silverbacks are the assassination organization of the realm specifically intent on ridding this side of the world from the neverborne and Neveril involvement. They target members of the Pentagogue and even Oathemic Cabal agents who get in their way. You could even say they are the Oathemics' counterparts, and they have many of their insurgents in Oathemic ranks.

"You and Izayus are going to find refuge with Haelyn Rook in the Silverlakes on his return with his new bride from Frostdale, in Barredom. He should be back in the Silverlakes by the time the prince can get you there with his improvisations in travel. Your brother Nikayle will rally with you there, before or after, dependent on his own assignments to conclude. I am told he is gathering recruits into the Silverbacks' fold."

Valaythea put her right hand on her father's shoulder, bracing as if to feint. Ever since she had entered pentimonial union with the prince her life had been falling apart consecutively piece by piece. "Wait," she stammered to keep up with the influx of information, "Athan is in the Cabal, and so are you. Why is Nikayle," she reconsidered what to call him, "*Barturon* going against Athan? Going against you? What side is everyone on?"

"Oh, sweet daughter," he consoled, "I know it is too much at once. It would take sessions to lay it out for you, even if I could, but I am yet permitted but a taste to motivate you in motion."

"I am not motivated," she tried to nudge the spellblade from touching her, but her father put his hand down to halt its course from edging toward the floor.

"Coldborn foresaw the dissolution of the Oathemic Cabal. And the guild has been out of his complete control for some time. He created the Silverbacks to do the intent of the Cabal, and assigned Haelyn Rook over the new guild as a private figure to the new agents within. Athan is safe, to a degree, and doing as Coldborn intends within the Oathemic organization , and will be pulled when the time is right. He does not know what you know. And you do not know what he knows. It is all a rather ambiguous strategy for a divine end, you see?"

Of course, she didn't see. How could she? Not being able to foresee what the Oathemic agenda was is what made Coldborn and Nikayle so grand in their roles. The subject of Athan did bring her distress though. "Athan," she expressed his name in sympathy, remembering how bad she incidentally humiliated him, "he would sooner kill me the next time he sees me. I stole his honor and his sword."

"You wounded his pride," Nikayle reinterpreted. "The weapon was never his."

"Just tell me what to do. And that my sisters will be safe also."

Nikayle obliged to her humble requests. "Haelyn Rook is a spellblade also. In his estates, more protected than you could ever be here, you will be trained in how to master the Chandoss Spellblade and unlock its full potential.

"As for your sisters, I cannot stop Oddy from what doing what she is committed to. You cannot either. That is a hard farewell you are going to have to endure. I am preparing for Ember to join you when you leave, though she will be reluctant. As for Addy, she was a price to pay to gain the Thrench's loyalty before arranging their invitation. They were going to choose either Ember or her, and as it turns out Ember's reputation with Timmurian has stained her for life. The Thrench want nothing to do with someone besmudged from coupling with elvankind."

"What about Sashka?" Valaythea had to know. *You hid her?*

"The likelihood that the Thrench would have killed her on sight was high. I am still the Grand Regent of the Syrene, and I am owed favors of silence from each of the headmasters there. Her presence will be kept hush within the college, and she will be raised with the finest of private schooling that gold and position can buy. By her own request, not even Taizsha knows where I have placed Sashka," Nikayle confidently assured.

"The only one who thinks they have a clue is Athan, who believes Sashka is being smuggled into Savatarm. But that was only another poor ploy of mine, as a final attempt to get him to dissuade

Oddy from her decision to become one with the enemy, and to find a suitable means to satisfy her insatiable ambitions. Part of ascending as a master informant is the subterfuge of feeding misinformation as well."

It was no argument that her newfound proclaimed father was the shrewdest and most educated man that she had ever understood to have existed. Valaythea appreciated why Coldborn must have valued such a matchless agent of his incontestable facilities. There were several questions she wanted to pursue. "It is world-known that the Thrench pursue only violence. So, by what purpose did you send for them, aware of their war with the qindrid and elven; the Neveril in particular. If they knew what you were …"

"They are acquainted of what I am Val," he professed. "Even if I did not divulge them beforehand, they would have discovered the dark truth the moment they disembarked from their ships. Before we meet with them," he paused to emphasize, "which we damn well will soon, I will need to fill you in on a new Teaching Hour: covering starfell steel and the gifted sight of hyperis."

She was exhausted with the continuous diversions. Intolerable obscureness from Izayus and Coldborn, then relentless intimidation from Valdean with an imbalance of offered information, and now with Nikayle, her uncle-turned-father, surpassing them all in incomprehensible revelations.

Defeatedly, Val gave in and surprised herself when she pulled the sheathed spellblade back and readied it in her right hand. "Fine then. I am growing accustomed to having a shadow in my mind, and learning to trust no one. I have you to thank for that since day one evidently, *Father*," she jabbed harshly, but did not allow him a chance to recover.

"But what do I do with this?" She held the strange weapon out awkwardly, as if it weighed ten times what it did. "I have never even swung a sword outside of stage props."

"The spellblade knows how to wield you," he reassured. "Take caution, the power in the sword may possess you against your will. You will not be able to stop it until you are properly trained, which is why you must seek this archon, Haelyn, out."

A part of her wanted to drop it, but she hesitated, considering the priceless blade was made of glass. *You probably do not break so easily, do you?* she asked inwardly of the sword. *I know you are enchanted.* "What is it going to do to me?"

"Be more worried about what it will do to others. Stray far from any known hunder-touched. Do not go near a mage. The sword stays hungry for them. You could find your body becoming hostile while your mind is imprisoned, at the mercy of the magic within."

Nikayle delicately stroked the scabbard with his fingers. "Your dancing you have honed to perfection. You will discover that while you wield the sword, you will become flawless in your craft, making no mistakes. You will also acquire the martial ability of any other master swordsman who wielded the spellblade before. In the case of our family's weapon, this will include Nikayle the High Bloodguard of the Crown, and your great ancestor Aemenus, who first used the spellblade when it was created for him. All that is needed to conjure their abilities is to think their names in your mind, clearly and strongly. They may also come to take control of you if they sense you are in danger. The sword will not allow you to be harmed by others."

Valaythea dared to pull the sword halfway from its elvan-bone scabbard to expose the ovals where magic glyphs should have been etched into the glass. "What about these? They look empty." Upon doing so, she could see the flare of something bright illuminating from her right eye, startling her enough to shove the spellblade back in its place, and her vision returned to normal.

"We can fix that. Most of the spellpower is still locked within the sword from the mages that Aemenus and Nikayle the Firstnamed slew. They will change to glyphs of the elemental season once you conjure their names to mind. They are dormant now, but the spellblade may awaken them at any time if it senses the situation is critical, or if you find ways to inspire a remnant of a wisp absorbed from a mage killed by the sword. Summoning the names of the dead mages those glyphs belonged to works as well. For any new mages, it will help to know the caster's name first if you plan to invoke their stolen spellpower," Nikayle proved his expertise on matters around the artifact.

Valaythea snorted at that ludicrous and revolting notion. "I will not be killing any mages."

"The sword will not be asking your permission for a while. And you will be fighting before it is all done. Until then, call upon the weapon mastery of your ancestors to do the work for you if you find yourself in peril."

Valaythea hopped from sitting on the stage and started casually toward the door out of the studio to imply she was about done hearing anymore for the day, but Nikayle did not concede that they were close to being over, as he walked beside her and continued.

"Let me help you with a few last things. The ones I recall, anyhow. Do not forget these. One of the glyphs belonged to an Umbra mage woman named Saravelle. It will summon replicas of you to act as you in random to confuse your opponents." He pointed to one oval imprint of a dormant glyph and then to another. "And this one here belonged to a mage named—"

"Stop." Valaythea interjected and stomped in her tracks from going any further. She waved her hand to cast away the topic. "I do not wish to hear the names of murdered mages."

"Fine," Nikayle said, granting her wish, as he retracted from her to give space for her to leave if she so chose.

What kind of father does this? Twenty years of not telling me! And you choose now? Like this? Damn you! She could feel her mouth was curled in unspoken fury, but her eyes burned from pooling tears, and her chin quivered uncontrollably. *You called the Thrench here knowing damn well they kill qindrid, and you are one of them!*

"What is going to happen to you?" She couldn't stop the fit of tears that streamed after she asked. She dropped the spellblade, hoping the enchanted glass would shatter from the impact, and went to throw her arms around her father. "They are going to kill you, and you knew that, didn't you?"

"Shh now," he coddled her in a fatherly embrace. "I like to pretend I am a clever man with a few good ideas up my sleeve."

Her father put his hands on her shoulders and squared her away to look him in the eye as he instructed. "Everything will be fine. With you, and your sisters, I will get us all out of this cursed house and cursed life. I need you to trust me to know what is best as you always have. That much has not changed."

He kissed her on the forehead. "Go back to your room. I will be calling for you. The prince is almost here and you can leave soon. Know that I will never stop protecting you."

She did trust him; the man who had always acted as more of a father to her than Ethiass ever had. She retrieved the spellblade and turned to leave. *And I will never stop protecting you.*

SCARLESS (VIII)

POWER OF PROPAGANDA

She could feel the battle paint caked on her skin, over her forehead and around her eyes, over the middle of her lips and down her chin. Xalo, beside her, had the same white tree over the black paint drawn on his brow, with streaming lines over his eyes, while Uubakrath honored the sigil just above his left cheekbone, and that entire side of his face was coated in the black paint as well. Her last guild member with her, Pyphan, had chosen the dead tree sigil to be painted over his left eye, inside a black sphere.

It was the ritual of the Stormtrees to decorate their faces in this specific war paint before knowingly setting out to shed the blood of their enemies within the city. The sigil was the stormtree only ever seen in the small party by Uubakrath and Zahnastaazjah herself, as the supernatural trees only grew in their race's homeland of Teralloe.

They were strange white trees that appeared dead all cycle around, but during the Reaping season, they would act as impervious conduits for persistent lightning strikes, funneling electrical energy into the ground for fields around them. The trees were unremarkable and hardly noticeable for the other four seasons, but when it was their time to show their power, they did, and they did it with an awe-inspiring, spectacular show. The Terollar elvan culture had come to venerate the stormtrees as a symbol that stood for power through patience, and prestige through performance. And that was the mantra her Stormtrees guild lived by: *Power through patience, prestige through performance.*

The four trained killers tolerantly waited for their fifth companion to join them in their rented inn room in their enemy's ward. They all surrounded Amaris, former safe-house keeper and recent turncoat of the guild. She was sweating profusely and glancing at each of her potential executioners with an obvious aura of fear. Zahnastaazjah knew that Amaris was reluctant to participate but also that the shape-shifter did not want to die by the more immediate threat surrounding her now.

Usurp eventually came through the door and explained that his assigned tasks were done. There wasn't a single person in the city visiting the Monodrome's finale show for the conclusion of the Kingfall Ball. The Vellyan's specialty in extortion proved sound as he told that each ticket had been bought or bullied back into the hands of only designated agents of the Stormtrees that were participating in the raid on the Boarneck Company. The Boarneck agents would be amassed in the famous theater this night or underneath in one of the plethora of revelry rooms, and all most likely unarmed, unaware, and highly intoxicated. Usurp further confirmed that the additional seats, which outnumbered the combat-proficient agents he had brought with him, would be filled with the surplus of informants and spies the Stormtrees commissioned throughout the city.

Zahnastaazjah needed Usurp's competence in battle for this final showdown. Before she dismissed him to handle the loose ends at the impending Monodrome massacre, she granted him a brief moment of respect to briskly paint the guild sigil on his face.

Dusk was only an hour away. The six promptly moved out of the mid-district lodge. With the exception of Amaris, all of them wore long black cloaks, keeping their hoods down low. Zahnastaazjah and Usurp handed their spear and maul to Uubakrath to tote, while Xalo was able to keep his spellblade concealed within the shrouding garment. Pyphan, of course, remained always unarmed.

Amaris, on the other hand, was not dressed so covertly. Her garments were loud, intended to attract all eyes to her. She wore a bright yellow costume with long red feathers draping from the under part of the sleeves and train of her dress. Her masque matched, but the feathers splayed out from both eyes like crimson wings. And she was the only one in the group presented with a lit torch, for part of the plot.

This was the Kingfall Ball, after all, the one day per cycle everyone in Bridgeville and Canaltown was expected to adorn themselves extravagantly in dramatic new fashions and participate in the festivities hosted by Oldan Boldandgold's prosperous and ostentatious Boarneck Company. Of course, the prior cycle, it had been named the Longstars Ball, then before that the Southmaw Ball, as it changed in title every cycle.

The streets were far more crowded than usual. These weren't just local Utamians and Goldgarden citizens. This was an exotic mob of racial and cultural engagement for one single evening of private parties and public shenanigans.

Several Z'shun and Zandaryn elven were openly incorporated into the mirth with a heavy majority of humans, along with a few Lunaril immigrants, easily spotted by their ebon skin and blue-tipped ears. For the humans, Zahnastaazjah saw almost every human ethnic group in the realm other than the Thrench and Caelduyans. She dismissed trying to categorize the trivialities.

They weaved their way through performances on every street corner. Goldgarden termed them buskers. Some rented chalk-drawn circles by the hour, or large stage boxes for a higher fee. They were anyone who worked strictly for monetary donations and was approved to display some form of expressive activity. Bards, jugglers, sex shows, bestiality spectacles, animal exhibits, fortune-tellers, and really any variety of performance artist, skilled or inept, grossly vulgar or raunchily comedic, it was all here in Bridgeville during the Boarnecks' tasteless mockery of what a sophisticated ball might be.

The sun had waned from sight, and the full moon was now breaching the lower buildings. The early dusk was still bright enough, however, to cast a grim bluish-grey hue across the district. The street lanterns were being lit by men on stilts as well, further illuminating the creeping darkness before full nightfall.

The stage box that Zahnastaazjah had arranged to lease came into sight, and the act was put in motion. Uubakrath and Pyphan departed to gain higher ground for a strategic vantage point from the rooftops. Amaris was released to do her duty and step aboard the stage with her torch. Zahnastaazjah, Xalo, and Usurp took to a horse trough across the bustling street and utilized it as a bench to wait and watch for their foes to come out of hiding.

"Citizens! Visitors! May I have your attention, please?" Amaris began, to no avail. Her voice was far too small to contend with the mayhem of merriment in every cluster of life nearby, not to mention the competition from the other three corners across from her. "I want to confess to you the truth about the shape-changers that live among you!"

A few heads turned, but the momentum of their steps to wherever their destinations were did not allow them to stray from their courses.

"You there, listen here now! Do you want to know about the skin-shifters in your city?" Amaris pointed at a passerby, theatrically waving her feathered arms any time she used them for an eye-catching effect. "This is the era of the neverborne! They are the qindrid of the Neveril!"

"She's gonna get herself killed." Usurp tried to whisper the obvious, but it came out as loud as a shout as he elevated his voice over the festival's noise.

"This is why we try not to invite you places, big fellow," Xalo uttered quietly while patting the buffoonish Vellyan on the knee.

"Huh? The noise is too loud!"

"Someone is going to get killed, yes. That is the point." Scarless ignored Usurp's ridiculous last retort but gave an answer for his first. She scanned the roofs around her, even behind her, for signs of her archer and mage but found them nowhere in sight. *Good. I know Uubakrath and Pyphan are there. If I could see them, that would be a problem.*

"We call them ghosts for a reason! The Neveril! The subterranean elvan race that is white as snow, as silent as death! They walk walls and ceilings like level ground, immune to both fire and cold, heat and disease! They see through darkness like we do the light! The Neveril are here beneath us now!"

Amaris was receiving fairly negative responses from the light-hearted revelers, who did not want such dire reports from far-fetched doomsayers. She was told to shut up more than a few times and even had a drink flung across her blouse, and she had barely gotten started.

"They have taken Az'Dayne! Their Pentagogue of paladins and veritans are all puppets of their Neveril elvan masters, turned"—Amaris paused just a moment for dramatization—"no, transcended into these neverborne qindrid that are here right beside you!"

Amaris seemed to see someone in the midst of the crowd that made her visibly nervous. She made one step to retreat from the podium box and glanced in the direction of her dread, then over at her former guildmother.

Zahnastaazjah simply stood up from her makeshift seat and stared at Amaris underneath her hood. Amaris measured her options of how to die, and it was clear that Zahnastaazjah had won the game of competition when Amaris stepped back into position and continued.

"They have grey skin, red eyes, can wear your faces, and talk like your lovers! The way of the Neveril is to take the leaders first, or those in power around them, and then the citizens around the city that can contribute to influence or have the most to lose, to act as their spies and pawns!"

Finally a small group of bored couples strolling about, or perhaps lost, stopped to show Amaris some attention while one of the young men used the respite to reassess his district map.

"Goldgarden citizens and visitors!" Amaris seized the opportunity to capitalize on it. "Guests of the Kingfall Ball! May I have your attention now? I am a neverborne! I am one of them—the new qindrid! I am the enemy! Watch me change now, and believe it!"

Just as she had forewarned the anticipated gathering, Amaris's skin turned grey like the qindrid she was, and her eyes to red and her hair to pitch black. The volume in Amaris's delivery increased with confidence when more spectators ceased from walking away to witness her testament.

"Believe me now! I do not ask, but I demand it! Behold!" Amaris brought the lit torch under her left arm, setting the feathers and sleeve of the dress ablaze to validate her claim.

"I am about to tell you about the others! Amethyst, one of our own, member of the Seven Seats, our appointed delegate of the Az'Dayne Dominadom on the Seat of the Red, she is one of them as well! She is whom I answer to! But not today! Not anymore!"

Amaris was in a frenzy of determination now, ripping her burning clothing from her body until she was naked from the torso up, proudly displaying her flawless skin, undamaged by the fire. She pranced about and waved the torch at the amassing audience she had managed to captivate after all.

"The Boarneck Company as well! All of them are paid turncoats! They are helping Az'Dayne infiltrate our city with these fiends like me, to turn your city from the inside out! They did it to Everdawn, the capital of Az'Dayne! They damn well just did it to Frostdale, the capital of Barredom! And they are doing it to our beloved Goldgarden as I speak!"

Amaris froze in place, and her eyes became entirely white, iris and pupil and all. She stood in a minor fit of convulsions for almost half a minute but didn't seem to care to still when she broke back into consciousness. The effect only seemed to entertain her growing fan base more. "Oldan Boldandgold, leader of the Boarneck Company, proprietor of this district's famous Monodrome, orchestrator of this Kingfall Ball, is a traitor to the citizens of this city! The greatest city on all of Penthara! Or at least it used to be! Before my kind came through!"

"She's good. But she's a dead woman," Xalo commented. It was what Zahnastaazjah was already considering, rapidly investigating every patron in the streets that seemed keen on Amaris's doomsaying oration.

"My masters are here now too, the Neveril umbran who turned me!" Amaris audaciously pointed to her left eye with one hand to implicate what had just transpired—the ability of umbran cerebration—and she stuck the blaze of the torch in her other eye.

If this wasn't run by Boarnecks, you would probably win the day if they awarded buskers on performance. You own the block now, Amaris. Look at you. And she truly did. Everyone around was climbing over each other to steal a peep of the unburning grey-skinned woman.

"My masters are watching me! Watching you! You may be chosen next to take the Transcendence! Beware!"

Amaris kept on for a while longer with a tirade against the umbran and Neveril race as a whole, bashing the Boarneck Company and Kingfall Ball, until her eyes went white again and she stammered, incapacitated in place, seemingly against her will. Two men pushed their way through the mob and seized her by the arms, yanking her off the stage box. The condemned woman was applauded as she was carried off and away, and the crowd dispersed to find other marvels to entertain themselves within the vast street festival.

Zahnastaazjah didn't have to say a word to her own two trained men beside her. Xalo and Usurp hurriedly followed her as she inconspicuously stalked Amaris and her new captors to wherever they were heading. She could only hope that Uubakrath and

Pyphan could keep up if they were still on the rooftops.

Not ten shops down, her former safe-house keeper was guided around the back of a tanner's warehouse and forced inside. Zahnastaazjah stealthily crept to the door and frowned when she noticed she was still weaponless. She held her hand up to test the distance Uubakrath, who was caring for her spear, must have been from her. As expected, the bloodrime weapon came soaring from the roof of a workshop across the way, back into her grasp.

Uubakrath came into view with Pyphan, and Usurp's heavy war maul was returned to the Vellyan as well. She wasn't going to wait to let whoever, or whatever, was inside prepare. She knew there was a Neveril umbran inside, maybe even two, since it took two that were lifemates to create qindrid. She was educated in all matters concerning Neveril and umbran and qindrid from her father's lifequest against them.

Surprise and rush tactics constituted the only maneuvers to employ in this incursion. Zahnastaazjah gave a familiar nod to Usurp, indicating he should make the first move.

Usurp kicked the back door to the warehouse open, and the four killers of her assault team moved in beside her and spread out in search-and-slay formation.

There were only two faint lanterns lit in the dark storeroom, and no sign of any life beyond the shadows. Before Zahnastaazjah could think to improvise what to do next, Pyphan tossed his cloak to the floor to expose the golden arcanic imprints etched into his body. Select magemarks on his body flashed in a bright green light that matched the halos in his eyes, and as he gestured with his hands, the floor was manipulated in the areas in which he chose to move certain items where he wanted them.

He must have seen something she hadn't. A bucket of oil and a pile of fur pelts were positioned just below the lanterns in the center of the spacious room. The wooden beam that held the lamps then magically piled itself into the ground until the lantern shattered into the oil, and the fire blazed up, catching the pelts to create flames large enough to illuminate nearly the whole warehouse.

She could see it now. There was no sign that it had ever been a Neveril, save for perhaps its hairless head. The umbran's skin was grey, like that of Amaris. Its eyes were all black, like dark voids. Its former elvan ears were about twice as long as the norm, drooping outward instead of back against its head. Zahnastaazjah had never seen an umbran. She had only heard countless horror stories of their kind from those she had been raised around back in her old Terollar life, long before she had drenched herself in the indulgent escape of the corrupt human city she now called home.

The Neveril umbran was a male. He looked scared. They all looked scared—the other four Neveril elven beside him, the two henchmen that had brought Amaris in, and especially Amaris herself. She was sitting in a chair, halfway through being bound by rope, with absolute panic in her eyes, which were back to normal, no longer under the effects of the cerebration that had taken hold of her in the streets. The neverborne woman looked around at every individual in the room as if they were all in a competition with each other to decide who would be awarded her murder.

Zahnastaazjah did not tarry for the pleasantries that were never going to happen. She heaved her spear into the chest of the umbran before it could speak. When the bloodrime weapon returned to her, there were only a few seconds of confusion in the warehouse before the slaughter began.

Uubakrath immediately followed, launching a lethally aimed arrow straight through the nose of the closest albino elvan.

The three Neveril that were still alive appeared to be unarmed, but that didn't stop one of them from snapping the neck of Amaris, putting her misery for the inevitable outcome to rest. One other fled, while the third found some skinning knife nearby to defend himself with.

The two men who had hauled in Amaris charged at Pyphan with their shortswords drawn to eliminate the mage as a priority.

Usurp stood in front of Pyphan to act as a shield for his comrade, taunting the oncoming assailants with a war bellow. He raised his maul up high to smash the first one to come in range of his long reach.

Pyphan was already evoking his next spell, paying no heed to the obvious threat to his life. The Neveril trying to escape was running a zigzag pattern up the walls and then with his feet to the ceiling in a sprint to the exit across from them. The front door radiated with a faint green hue just before it exploded into a thousand pieces of wooden shrapnel, piercing through the flesh and organs of the hapless elvan.

Zahnastaazjah casually made her way to challenge the panicked, knife-bearing Neveril, but Uubakrath had already volleyed two more arrows into him before she even got close.

An arching wave of fire was flung through the air from Xalo's spellblade, hitting the two charging men across the eyes like a whip before they could reach Usurp's vicinity. That should have taken them down, or blinded them at a minimum, like it would any normal men, but it only seemed to disorient these two with a fleeting moment of annoyance.

Xalo wasted no time in trying to process how they hadn't been affected by the fire, likely presuming the same thing Zahnastaazjah already was—these men were neverborne qindrid, just as Amaris had been. The spellblade quickly closed the distance to his kills.

One of the unorthodox bruisers came in slashing his small sword in a series of impressive strikes that displayed his aptitude with the weapon. But Xalo's swordmastery was simply far better. He played a quick exchange of parries with his foe, then a fatal riposte with a slash that opened his throat.

Xalo was already spinning around to catch the last man standing, who must have considered himself a suicidal opportunist for a surprise back attack, but Xalo was quicker. A glyph on his magic glass sword flared up green as it struck his opponent's blade and shattered it into metallic dust. Before Xalo could end his life the same way he had the other, however, the man's head burst open when Usurp's two-handed maul collided with it.

Xalo stood blinking awkwardly, annoyed by the blood coating his face and attire. Usurp, towering over the Elothian ex-gladiator, just grinned sadistically and patted him on his shoulder in apology. "Too slow, little man."

Xalo didn't retort. He just pushed the Vellyan's palm away and took his place beside Zahnastaazjah, using his discarded cloak as a towel to wipe off the mess from his skin and clothes.

"That was only one of the umbran." Pyphan brought focus onto the ultimate problem. "There has to be two. Always has to be two."

Zahnastaazjah walked over to the corpse of Amaris, looking down at her grey qindrid skin. The dead men who had tried their luck on Xalo had also transformed back into their neverborne flesh tones. "Amaris did her part. We have their attention now. The other umbran can feel the life gone from its lifemate here. It will be near."

"Time to move forward in this. The umbran wasn't part of the plan," Xalo contended pragmatically.

She could hear Usurp saying something about heading out to clear the back entrance of the Monodrome and to wait for her there, as he had been instructed. She didn't say goodbye. She was too deep in her musing. The umbran was a part of the plan now. Xalo was wrong.

"On to Oldan Boldandgold" was all she replied in concurrence, though.

She turned to exit the warehouse with her deadly companions in tow, on to the next phase in bringing about the downfall of the Boarneck Company. And her thoughts shifted to the other agent they were all depending on.

See you soon, Symbelle. Do not fail us now.

SYMBELLE & FYHEIR (VIII)

PYROTECHNICALITIES

Symbelle stood anxiously on the edge of the quay where Oldan Boldandgold's pleasure barge was berthed. *You will feed the fire tonight, Symbelle. You will share this moment with us.* Fyheir quashed her swarm of hesitations on being able to follow through.

The city canals were especially gloomy after dusk, only enhanced by the murky ambience of the thin fog that blanketed the water and the lack of natural starlight from the day's cloud cover. She could still see a line of the other, smaller barges, however, which were brimming with her firework cannons for the show that she had solely orchestrated in its entirety, in design, timing, and pyrotechnic engineering.

From the vantage of the quay, she noticed that she would be able to see the igniters Oldan had assigned to her on the other vessels. The barge in front was arranged with blue fireworks, with gold fireworks on the one in front of that. Then there were boats with red and white and orange and purple, then always back to blue and gold, as they were the colors of water and tairan, which Utamians celebrated in representation of their elemental descendancy.

The only barge with green fireworks was the one in front of her now. The sight of the ninth bridge was her cue to light their fuses, when the Monodrome neared, signaling Scarless, Pyphan, Xalo, and Uubakrath to pirate the barge and take the life of any Boarneck aboard. The actual attack was prepped to be quick, but the leisurely ride to get to the ninth bridge would be anything but quick. It was about a three-mile jaunt on water from the first bridge, where Symbelle was now, against Tenttown, along the main water road that divided Canaltown from Bridgeville, and these flatboats were not built to move with any sense of urgency.

A small man dressed in clothes fit for a palace masquerade

rather than a boat deck approached Symbelle to escort her by hand up the ramp to the first deck of Oldan's personal barge.

"Welcome to *Indulgence,* Grand Alchemist." Oldan himself was there to greet her as soon as she boarded.

She took a moment to absorb her new surroundings. She had never seen anything like this. The pleasure barge was more lavishly decorated with furniture and fineries than she imagined the Prince of Az'Dayne's own private quarters might be. There were decems of well-dressed servants running around in composed posture, all displaying a different exotic dish or vintage with names she could not pronounce.

The uncovered forward portion of the main deck had a curious smoke hearth with large dual pipes protruding from it. The covered area of the deck had enough seating for fifty guests at first glance, and it had steps that led to a rooftop, which was shaded by an intricate canopy with the Boarneck sigil embroidered on it. Even though the wide vessel was propelled by teams of laborers with quant poles, it was clear Oldan did not choose to captain the boat himself, with an obvious navigator at the helm of the roof deck barking orders to those below.

"An honor to receive your personal invitation, my lord," she said after taking everything in.

"Take her things," Oldan instructed his steward as he extended his hand. "Come."

She reluctantly declined the courtesy and defensively squeezed her pack, which held all the alchemy gear she needed to complete the night's grisly agenda. "I would rather hold on to them. Nervous habit."

"Bloody nonsense!" Oldan snatched the pack and opened it to briefly investigate the contents. "Too much overprepped paraphernalia you won't even need! You're not working tonight, Symbelle, just signaling when the fireworks need to start. And I want you to learn the color smoker." He pointed at the device at the front of the deck that had caught her eye before.

But something else suddenly eclipsed her interest in anything else. The panic shook her bones so hard, she began to feel tingly all over. "Where are they taking the fireworks I ordered placed on board?"

Oldan looked back at his deckhands removing her hard work,

which was all part of the necessary plot to trigger the possibility of her rescue by the end of this. "I'm not putting bloody fireworks aboard my precious *Indulgence*." He frowned at her. "I'll have numerous dignitaries and rich merchants with far reach on our decks tonight. I don't want any of those fire engineers in sight. This is a party, Symbelle. Take time for yourself and indulge. Those are my only orders."

We will have to burn him and his barge down without the help of your new troll girlfriend. Should we try now or wait for an audience?

Symbelle shoved Fyheir's absurd notion from her mind and tried to intelligently construct a rebuttal to change Oldan's decision. "But it's just that the …" she fumbled, "green fireworks, they are—"

"Green. I know." The Boarneck founder stopped her. "I hate green, by the way. That's as good as me saying I embrace magic, and I damn well don't. No offense to your purple eyes, or whatever you got going on there," he pointed to her glowing orbs behind her glasses.

Oldan rummaged through her belongings and produced her alchemy goggles to throw them to her, insinuating she should cover up her hyperi eyes, which she did. "You do know that my Kingfall Ball is a Utamian celebration for our people of Goldgarden's realm-renowned accomplishments. The only colors on this vessel will be blue and gold, as it should be."

Symbelle had always considered that the level to which the majority of the world seemed to identify their elemental descendancies with a specific color and season were a bit overzealous and extreme. Humans were not like elven, who actually were born with impowers from the elements, and thus it made sense for their race to adhere to such staunch beliefs. It was no matter to humans where their elemental lineage lay unless, by her recent learnings, they were hunder-touched, with eligibility to become mages, or were aspiring to the Qindrid Transcendence.

Gold for tairan, season of the Dawning, with cultures based in the central regions of Penthara. Red for fire, the Sunder season, with races that found habitat in the south. White for sky, for the Reaping season, and those of the east of the realm. Black for shadow, the Umbra season, and the cultures that dwelled in the north. And blue for water, the Torrent season, and the people that lived on the western coast or island countries.

"Very well, my lord" was all Symbelle felt she could respond with.

"Ren, show Symbelle the color smoker! You handle it tonight, but I want her to learn the basics in case we have issues with the dyes or component side of things." He waved over a chubby fellow with half his hair missing and glasses not unlike hers. "That's kind of this bitch's thing. No offense for calling you a bitch," Oldan apologized in a half-assed way. "I barely know you."

"Easy breezy, Oldman!" Ren informally joked with the modified name of his employer, and he waddled over with an ugly smile fixed on Symbelle.

"Bring her to the roof after," Oldan ordered, and he left Ren and Symbelle to it.

Symbelle could not take her focus off her pack being taken away by the steward even as Ren guided her toward the smoker on the bow. She eventually gave the weaselly man her attention when he began going over the mechanics of the apparatus.

There was a powder paint to be put in a small capsule on either side, one designated for the blue paint and another for yellow paint. Once the stove-like hearth was fired up at the bottom, the powder would transform into colored smoke and rise out of the pipe. Ren informed her about a merging valve that could be turned as well, which would create an opening between the two pipes to mix the colors if needed, or to funnel one color into the other pipe if one of them became clogged. But he also strictly warned her that such was not a part of Oldan's agenda for the evening. Ren had been explicitly instructed to release only the blue on cue and let it smoke out its entire course before changing it to yellow, and then repeating in a cycle, utilizing only one pipe at a time and keeping the merger valve closed.

They practiced on the smoker for some time as the barges drifted down the canal, northward through the city en route to the Monodrome. They made a stop at the next bridge to pick up several noticeably aristocratic individuals of all kinds. There were bejeweled couples from local wealthy families, dressed in exquisite attire, among obvious foreigners in their eclectic senses of modern fashion. Others were fancy merchant lords in obnoxious outfits one could only get away with in public at such a ball as the one Oldan had put together for the city.

At the next bridge's stop, hand-selected entertainers and high-end courtesans also joined the blend of promised debauchery about to take place. And that was when Symbelle was told by the barge captain to signal for the fireworks to begin. She was given control to command anyone aboard Oldan's barges in her new position as Grand Alchemist. Even Ren did as she bade, commencing with lighting the blue on the color smoker and watching the flow exit high out the pipe, fanning out over the canopy of the barge's roof deck.

The fireworks began, barge by barge, ahead of *Indulgence*. Different colors exploded into the night sky. Eventually, even her precious green fireworks were introduced into the mix, sporadically timed to be lit on the other vessels.

By the time Symbelle was able to join the festivities at Oldan's beckoning, she could see that most of the boat's occupants had indeed indulged in its ample offerings, as its title implied they should. The guests were already well into inebriated antics. Some of the couples proved to have no shame with acts of fornication in the open, sometimes trading partners without inhibition.

"Symbelle!" she heard Oldan shout as she was coming up the steps to the roof deck. He was clearly feeling his drink early on as well, no better than his decadent invitees. "Pour her one!" he ordered a naked serving maid wearing nothing other than lewdly placed chain mail. "Pour her two! She has to catch up!"

When Symbelle got close enough, she was startled by Oldan grabbing her hard by the wrist and manhandling her into his lap. "My lord!" she squeaked. She couldn't say another word, because the buxom, chain-mail-wearing wench was already straddling her own lap from the side and forcibly pouring a hot white wine down her throat before she could resist—and she admitted she secretly didn't want the girl to get off her. In the moment, she even forgot that she was still sitting on Oldan, who was groping at her hips.

"Bony little bird, aren't you?" He insulted her in his condescending, grimy demeanor. "And you know, you aren't even too ugly after a few drinks. Even with the scars. No offense meant, but put on this wig anyway." He pinched the right side of her face on her fool's frown with one hand and pulled out her red Neveril wig with the other.

"You went through my pack?" She did not mean to sound so vexed in her tone.

"I go through every bloody thing that comes on my boat. I may go through you too before the night's done, if you're lucky," Oldan taunted in jest, but his perverse eyes spoke differently.

Everyone near them laughed at their host's obnoxious jokes. The chain-mail-wearing girl against her thigh crawled off and disappeared into the drunken mirth of other depraved magnates on board. Symbelle removed herself from Oldan's lap and slipped on her goggles and wig, beginning to feel more confident with the aesthetic transformation that she would gradually become Fyheir when it was time. She could feel the fire quietly building inside her, but Fyheir stayed silent for now.

Symbelle ignored Oldan's unwelcoming presence next to her and searched for anything to steal her interest. A Zandaryn elvan dancer in nothing but transparent, multicolored, flowing silk sashes mesmerized half the rooftop with her erotic routine to the music. Symbelle was sure she had never seen anyone so alluring. Almost anyone …

"Oh, so you prefer women?" Oldan took notice of her infatuation. He leaned into her ear and whispered, "It's okay. Me too, most of the time."

She didn't want to look at his creepy smile, which was leering into her peripheral vision. "Just one," she answered, implying Scarless to no one's knowledge but her own. "She isn't here, though."

"Whoever she is, she won't know tonight. Everything that happens on *Indulgence* tonight will be secrets between each other, yes?" Oldan nudged her with his elbow.

The masquerade continued on with Oldan and his festival moderators coercing the plethora of privileged highborn to spoil themselves in imbibing strong vintages and consuming small samples of fine dishes from abroad. Symbelle herself was force-filled more than her tiny body could handle with both wine and sweets. It made her head spin and stomach groan more than she had ever been used to.

"Third stop!" the barge captain shouted above the halted music at the fourth bridge. "Last stop before we reach the Monodrome!"

They had already picked up the privileged guests and then the entertainment party. Symbelle could not imagine whom else they needed to bring aboard, so she had to ask, "Who are we getting?"

"Shh," Oldan warned, putting his sticky finger on her lips to hush them. "We don't talk about the grey one in the hood," he said nervously, standing up to get a better look at the new invitees coming up the ramp. "The woman next to her either. They call her Amethyst. She is on the Seven Seats. You are going to learn a lot tonight, Symbelle, of who we are and what we do."

Symbelle woozily stood up with Oldan to take a gander for herself and judge the newcomers. She froze in terror at the sight of what was moving across the deck toward the rooftop. On first instinct, Symbelle blamed what she was witnessing on the likelihood that the alcohol in her blood was causing her to have drunken hallucinations. But then she realized what was happening. Her hypersight was overruling her natural sight, and she could see what others could not, beyond illusions from the shadow element.

It appeared like an ethereal green umbilical cord, linking four of the others and a central figure robed in grey. The mysterious individual also glowed green in the middle of their torso, visible underneath the cover of clothes. Two other robed enigmas walked beside the one in grey. Symbelle could see their albino skin underneath their hoods and on exposed hands.

The other five were not concealed by cowls and were outfitted to join the revelry of Oldan's private party, it seemed. A faint green light emanated from the Khalimishe woman in the middle and her companions, close behind the impressive train of her dress. Their skin was grey, each with raven hair, just like the neverborne imposters that had been discovered in the safe house with Scarless.

She recalled Uubakrath saying that one of the qindrid had gotten far enough to speak to others outside before he had shot the aspiring escapee down. But the thought that any word had gotten out about Symbelle's involvement as a mole for the Stormtrees infiltrating the Boarnecks made her too scared to gamble the chance of being seen by one of them.

"Move around," Oldan shoved her wrist away from his couch. "More important people need to sit now. No offense."

For once, there wasn't any offense taken. And Symbelle was already gladly retreating from anywhere near Oldan or people who seemed important. She rushed to the stairs down to find a better spot on the barge to avoid attention, but she nearly knocked the grey-robed figure down as she breached the way below.

It was a female. Symbelle surmised she was elvan by glimpsing her pointed ears beneath the hood. But they were longer than any elvan Symbelle had seen before, and turned outward. Her skin was grey like the neverborne. Her eyes were abysmal all-black voids.

The other two cowled figures proved to be elven also, but with red eyes, white skin, and normal elvan ears. She could see that the five qindrid trailing them on the stairs indeed had the trait of red eyes, confirming them to be neverborne, as she had presumed.

A shudder shot down Symbelle's spine, but she was too afraid to utter the consideration of an apology as she squeezed past the foreboding entities, rushing down the stairway. She pulled the strands of her Neveril wig in front of her brow to veil her face as she worriedly budged her way through.

Well, that may as well have been the best way to ensure you have all their attention now. Those two elven were Neveril, and you are wearing one of their wigs, which can only confirm you took it off the corpse of one of their affiliates. We may stay awake now just to watch you squirm when you die. Fyheir angrily berated her ironically ill-timed decision to flee.

The music stopped, and the mood was different, but the boat began to glide up the canal once again. Symbelle went to sit in one seat and then shifted to another, playing musical chairs in the muted scream of awkwardness enveloping the entire vessel. She could not find a place to drown out the warning that she had been exposed and needed to escape.

She surrendered her attempts to make it out of this impending doom undiscovered. She made her way to the chests where she had seen the steward stow her alchemist gear and frantically combed through everyone's belongings until she found her familiar pack. Some twenty chests later she had her gear, but she wasn't even sure where to begin on daring to use any of it with so many innocents on board, and against such a number.

There were thrice this many at Tairanchula. Let us guide you through it. Fyheir tried to stimulate a brazen act of suicidal courage, but Symbelle snubbed the foolish massacre into a forgotten pocket of her thoughts.

She caught something out of the corner of her eye. A dinghy was being lowered into the water by a rope and pulley, with the black-eyed elvan and the two robed albino elven. The grey one stared directly at Symbelle as the rowboat descended past her to touch hull to water in the canal beside the barge. The two Neveril with the malformed elvan looked at her as well, not with anger but with a gaze of curiosity and a glint of sadness.

The dinghy detached, and the three mysterious visitors rowed away toward the quay on the other side of the canal. The momentum of *Indulgence* picked up as the barge entered the final stretch to reach the Monodrome. The general carousal of the pleasure barge recommenced, with bards playing music and entertainers performing, gradually resurrecting the jubilant ambience.

Symbelle knew that something was now amiss with her presence among enemies, posing as a friend. Attempting to swindle people who were well trained in lifestyles of natural deceptive practices on a daily basis was becoming a preposterous aspiration. How had she fathomed she could manage as a triple agent for Coldborn, Scarless, and Oldan all at once and somehow miraculously come out alive?

She hastily made for the color smoker and found Ren diligently at his duty in selecting the next powder to sieve into the furnace. She looked up at the gloomy night sky above and noticed that Ren was feeding the right pipe burner to send up blue smoke on this rotation, leaving the yellow on standby for the moment.

An epiphany struck her with a feasible solution for her predicament of no longer having access to any green fireworks for signal flares. "Ren! The steward needs you above. I forget his name. Something for Oldan, I believe," she stammered, a blatant lie.

"Lawrus? Why's he sending you? That's his damn job to walk around and do other people's jobs," the grime-covered boat tinkerer spat with skepticism.

"I was expressly informed that if you were not manning the smoker, then I had to be. I do not know what it is about. I just do as I'm told," she explained.

"Aye, and I suppose you're suggesting I just do as I'm told too, eh?" Ren grumbled as he meandered his way up to the top deck and out of sight.

Symbelle did not tarry in acting on the opportunity.

I know what you are doing, Fyheir invaded.

"Of course you know what I am doing. You are me," she

whispered harshly back at her inner self.

You need a green signal in order to let us live. And the blue and yellow powders mixed together will make –

"Green! Yes. Hush." She tried to command her tormenting other half into quietude.

She put both flammable powders in at once, set them ablaze to channel the smoke through both pipes at once, achievable with a simple full turn of the cutoff valve. Nothing came.

The music stopped again, and Symbelle could feel one hundred eyes on her back. She was sure she was being overly paranoid, but she slowly twisted around to validate her certainty nonetheless. Oldan Boldandgold, the one she could only assume was Amethyst, and the neverborne men were all at the edge of the roof deck, peering down at Symbelle with condemning gazes.

"Come up here, Symbelle. I did not dismiss you from my party." Oldan's tone sounded less friendly now. "I just want to ask you something."

Symbelle fretfully looked back at the furnace to see the powder substance still burning in preparation to fully combust into enough smoke to enter the pipes. It was taking too long. "I …" she stuttered, "I would rather stay down here."

Oldan dramatically laughed and grinned an evil, full-toothed grin. "I will bet you would! We can do this from here. Tell them what you told me," he said as he set a hand on one of the qindrid beside Amethyst.

Motioned to speak, the neverborne answered, "That is her. The mole from the Stormtrees. Just before I watched my cousin shot down by their troll archer outside their safe house in the Midway, he had time to tell me that she was a hyperi and covered in face scars. He said Scarless was using her to scheme something at the Kingfall Ball on your boat."

"She sees us for what we are with her hyperi eyes," the stranger, Amethyst, proclaimed, as if she were some close friend who had known Symbelle her whole life and felt betrayed. "And she dares to bear a firecrown in public." She referred to Symbelle's exotic wig. "That is forbidden, only worn by the Neveril. They were not pleased. She has to die."

"You have anything to add to defend yourself? Being in the safe house with my bloody nemesis, conspiring with her to end my life."

Oldan gestured with his accusing fingers down at her. "The scars, that Neveril wig!"

"Maybe it was someone else who looked just like me? Coincidence?" Symbelle meekly shrugged.

Oldan clapped his hands, and Ren appeared behind her, more stealthily than she would have given the chubby man credit for. He trapped her with his arms and put a fish knife to her throat.

A flash of green light caught everyone's attention two boats ahead. Symbelle felt Ren turn her to witness it for himself. Xalo's spellblade, emitting the green magical fire from the edge of the glass blade, was casting fire spells and carrying out some form of apparent carnage, from the sound of men's dying wails aboard the vessel.

"Who the ...?" Oldan had stopped paying attention to Symbelle and was trying to pierce the gloom of night over the water with his gaze. "Who is that?"

An unnatural fog swallowed the barge that the spellblade had invaded, concealing everyone aboard. The screams of dying men did not cease.

"Scarless's man. Xalo." Amethyst confirmed her suspicions of the obvious. "There's some form of signal for which boat to attack. But this bitch failed."

Another green firework burst from the barge that was surrounded by fog. All eyes were on the bridge above it, which Xalo had leaped down from, and on the burst in the sky.

Oldan answered for all of them. "She wanted green fireworks on *Indulgence*. I removed them before we set off."

The look he was casting down on her now was the most malevolent semblance she had ever witnessed on a person. The Boarneck founder appeared like a fiend in human guise, a being of pure evil, promising her a long and brutal death. "Bring her up here now!"

Ren shoved her through the crowd of sobering nobles desperately finding corners to hide in. The pleasure barge became sheer chaos, with everyone scampering in different directions. One man even jumped overboard into the canal when more green lights flashed from beyond the bow.

Ren turned enough to allow Symbelle to see, just as they began up the stairs. On the barge just ahead, a single figure was glowing with different glyphs on his exposed torso. He pointed at barrels, which exploded at his gestures, followed by manipulating the splintered wood like a weapon to combat the Boarnecks aboard.

"Pyphan!" Symbelle cried, but she knew that her brother was too far away to hear.

Ren manhandled Symbelle all the way up the stairs. She was far too frail to overcome his strength, and even if she could, she knew there would be nowhere for her to escape to. Her alchemy tools had been left by the smoker as well.

Oldan was right up the stairs, waiting for her to reach the roof. He grabbed her by the back of the neck so hard, she thought she felt her spine move into her throat. He moved her from Ren to the edge of the deck to watch the magic massacre Pyphan was carrying out on the Boarneck crew with his Dawning spells.

"This one with you too? That Scarless's new mage?" He held her body leaning over the deck to make her watch ahead.

"The mage there is her brother, not by blood but by a fostered youth together," the neverborne confessor from the Midway meeting gone wrong verified.

"Kill this little expired tool, and pull this boat over, Oldan. I am leaving!" Amethyst demanded.

Oldan seemed awestruck by Pyphan's slaughter as he manipulated wood and metal to use as weapons to make short work of the men on the barge. The whole barge ahead of them was immersed in the radiating green fire of raw magic unleashed. *Indulgence*'s captain was already doing as Amethyst had commanded and directing the vessel to the nearest docking quay to escape the mage's wrath if he decided to turn his magic on them.

More highborn lords and ladies were no longer waiting to reach the urban shore. They fled to the water road, with no regard for their fine clothing or their priceless jewelry being lost in the process.

"What are you doing with her?"

Oldan looked at Amethyst to consider her inquiry and then whispered into Symbelle's ear through his foaming mad lips. "I'm gutting this trash fish. She's feed for the canal dragons." Unexpectedly, he bit half her right ear off and chewed it before spitting the flesh into the canal. Blood ran down her burning face and out of his mouth as he finished. "Blood makes them come swimming."

Oldan took the knife from Ren and went to do the gory work he had just sworn to do. But something stopped him. Surprisingly, he let her go.

Symbelle turned around freely to see Oldan on one knee, clutching the back of his leg where a huge arrow was protruding. Another arrow sailed onto the barge and struck Ren in the face, followed by a third hitting a neverborne through the heart.

She knew it was Uubakrath but could not find her Terollar hero anywhere. He must have had some high sniping point on one of the rooftops on the Canaltown side of the water road. She decided she would have to thank the elvan later if she were somehow to make it out of the dire scenario alive, but she did not have the luxury of time to linger in place now.

Symbelle ignored the pain pulsating from her half-bitten-off ear. Her left knee buckled in agony when she jumped back down to the first deck. She ignored that pain too. Whether she limped or sprinted, she wasn't sure and didn't care, but she got to where she needed to without any more obstacles. She could see the pipes had gotten clogged from too much residue, and she needed to find an instant solution.

Symbelle found her pack, pulled out a small fire bomb, and shattered it in the hearth. The blue and yellow powder exploded into both pipes to merge into a thick green smoke that trailed over the barge.

Indulgence passed under a bridge, eliminating Uubakrath's positional advantage to rain arrows down on either deck, and the captain pulled the vessel into the docking quay on the other side. Total anarchy bull-rushed the ramp off the barge, with people running over each other and even pushing their own spouses to the side in a selfish display of survival of the meanest.

The Monodrome was now in sight, but not a soul in the vicinity cared to even take a glance at the colossal architectural marvel. Their focus was either fastened to the dangerous mage annihilating everything that breathed in his path or to their own two feet in front of them as they fled in a tumultuous frenzy.

Oldan was barking orders from above, and every attendant aboard *Indulgence* that proved to be a Boarneck was urgently finding weapons to arm themselves with. Time seemed to stop, however, when Pyphan's spells came to a halt.

Symbelle's and Oldan's eyes locked onto each other, with him still on the roof deck and her by the smoker. Their attention went to the same thing, the green smoke, and then to the barge of dead in front of *Indulgence*.

Large stone bricks began to separate from the bridge above them and the pavement on the shore, taking some supernatural flight, highlighted in that familiar green magical glow, and they formed some makeshift arch of steps between *Indulgence* and the barge Pyphan was on. Pyphan emerged to take one step at a time on the blocks that sometimes flawlessly appeared just in time for his next one forward. He came in a sprint to land at the bow of the pleasure barge.

A section of her brother's golden magemarks lit with green luminescence to match the halos in his gleaming eyes. His long, braided goatee was coated red from the unfortunate Boarnecks who had tried their luck on him and failed. The black eye makeup and Stormtree sigil painted on his face were blended with blood as well, making him appear quite psychotic. Pyphan was a mage assassin of the Oathemic Cabal, not a simple thug in the employ of the Stormtrees, and it showed. In a disturbing musing over the entire grisly ordeal, Symbelle incidentally felt envious of her brother in the momentum of it all.

Oldan shouted something Symbelle didn't quite catch, but it was obvious when all the mercenaries on deck charged at Pyphan from all angles, weapons held with intent to show no mercy.

Pyphan menacingly stared them all down like fools beneath his talent's worth. More arcanic imprints lit on one of his arms, and the bricks he had just used as steps to come aboard *Indulgence* suddenly encircled him in a rapidly moving sphere of lethal stones.

The first two men who came close enough caught fatal bricks to the head, and their faces were pulverized on impact. That was enough to make the others hesitate at the perimeter of the magical tairan shield, evaluating how to reach the mage. One even threw his knife, but it was effortlessly parried by Pyphan with one of the flying stones. Two others tried to run, but Pyphan manipulated the deck to flip them back into his spinning shield of bricks, and they fell victim to it like the others.

It only took a few seconds for it all not to matter, as more glyphs on her brother's body glowed, and he gestured with his hands to control a surplus of the bricks at once. They seemed to follow his telekinetic command in the air. Every man that worked for Oldan on board *Indulgence* was dead with a shattered skull in less than two minutes.

Symbelle realized she hadn't seen where Amethyst or her few surviving neverborne had disappeared to, and she wondered if perhaps Uubakrath had succeeded in felling them too before the bridge had blocked his elevated vantage.

That detour of thoughts was short-lived. She felt a familiar grasp on the back of her neck and saw Ren's fishing knife back at her throat. Oldan had powered through his own injury and managed to take Symbelle back into his embrace to use her as his own shield to ransom his way out of his doomed situation.

"Three people need to live today, mage!" Oldan bellowed. "You! Your sister! And me! Do you understand this?" He drew a small slit of blood in her neck so that Pyphan could see how serious he was. "I don't know what that troll bitch is paying you, but I'll drown you a hundredfold in treasures and pleasures that Scarless could never dream to touch! I am the richest man in Utamia outside the city!"

The bricks gradually began to drop to the deck, and Pyphan's magemarks waned in light as he dropped his hands to relent in hostilities. But he said nothing.

"You listening, Dawner?" Oldan continued. "You're using unsanctioned magic in Goldgarden without the permission of Shypriss Sol-War. Every highborn that's someone just saw it! Scarless has cast you a short life, and you have chosen the wrong side! You're a bloody dead man come Sunder, Dawner!"

Pyphan did not smile. He did not talk. He just casually removed the least bloody long-sleeved shirt from one of the Boarneck corpses and put it on, concealing his glyph marks, hindering their ability to be used. Symbelle was not sure of his intent in doing so.

"Depleted or something?" Oldan shouted with a tinge of nervousness in his inflection. The gesture of Pyphan clothing himself so confidently did nothing to bolster his resolve, it seemed. "I am not calling a fight here. The losses are done. No qualms with it! Here is what happens. She and I, we are getting off right here. I am going inside my Monodrome. You are not. You let me go in with that door shut, and I will release her once I have a fair start. I can see you want no complication in this!"

Oldan dared to shuffle off the barge without Pyphan's permission, but her brother still said nothing. He just stared at her now and gave her a calming smile.

"Tools and fools, brother and sister!" Oldan shouted when he reached the ramp off *Indulgence*. Pyphan's silence seemed to be driving him mad. "You're being used by an archaic visionary of thugs and thieves! Scarless and the Stormtrees, and all the gangs of Goldgarden, are antiquated rejects of the past! Let me show you the future! We can schedule a proper sit-down!"

"There is no compromise." Pyphan finally spoke as he took one step forward, and then another, slowly. "We are not employed by Scarless. The Stormtrees mean nothing to Symbelle and me."

"Then tell me who." Oldan brought his knife down from her neck and moved himself beside her. She could feel how tense his muscles were in his stance. He was getting ready to strike when the opportunity was prime. "So that I can properly negotiate with you. Money is everything, mage! I can prove this to you."

Pyphan kept his unconcerned pace toward them at the ramp, defenseless with each of his golden magemarks covered up. "Life is everything," her brother revised. "Life is all there is in the end. I will prove this to you. You are speaking to an assassin of the Oathemic Cabal. The fact that I just admitted this to you should let you know where you now stand."

"Willing to watch your sister die for this writ?"

Pyphan answered with a shrug of indifference to the matter. He had been trained as an assassin from an early age, instilled with emotionless motive, and Symbelle knew that he would still do his calculated duty regardless of her fate.

Oldan took the opportunity of the closed gap between him and Pyphan to lunge with the fishing knife straight toward her brother's chest. He barely got a foot forward when a spear appeared in the air, soaring down from the bridge, and planted itself through Oldan's chest. The dead Boarneck magnate was launched overboard into the water by the strong force of the weapon impaling his torso.

Scarless jumped down from the bridge onto the canopy above the roof and then nimbly leaped from the top deck to the main to join Pyphan. Her bloodrime spear emerged from the water, cleansed of any remnant of murder, and returned to Scarless's hand as she lifted her palm to call it back.

Symbelle breathed for the first time in an hour—she was sure of it. Before any other words were traded between the living, she noticed Xalo running down the wharf to reunite with the party, and Uubakrath also, standing on the bridge above, where Scarless had just been.

The pain in Symbelle's half-eaten ear finally started to truly settle in just when Scarless addressed the group. "The Monodrome now. We made a lot more noise than we needed to here. This is far from over."

As the five of them all made haste for their final destination, Symbelle let the reality of that statement settle in. "This is far from over," she whispered. She was still supposed to kill Scarless and Xalo before the end of the night, and she began to ponder the consequences with her brother if she decided not to follow through with it.

SCARLESS (IX)

THE MONODROME

The city guardsmen were dashing on horseback through the crowd of confused cityfolk toward Oldan's pleasure barge. It seemed that the majority of the revelers that lined the quays were clueless about the magical mayhem that had just taken place on the nearby vessels in the canal. Most just watched in their drunken stupors, waiting like a paying audience before a theatrical show, ready to witness the next firework that might burst in the gloomy night sky.

But the fireworks never came. They were over for the evening. Fortunately, Symbelle's ingenious distractions had allowed the small assault team the needed diversion to sprint down the boardwalk fully armed with not a soul paying them any regard. Pyphan helped his sister, in her hobbled state from an injured knee, navigate as best they could to keep up. Xalo and Uubakrath did not shy from keeping their weapons ready, following Zahnastaazjah's lead with her bloodrime spear broadly displayed for any bystander to witness. There wasn't really a way to conceal such a sizable death-dealing tool.

The looming Monodrome commanded all eyes to its wondrous architecture. It was larger than any sanctuary of worship constructed in the Temple District. Its magnificent brass dome capped the palatial theater-arena. It took being this close to the grandiose entertainment venue for Zahnastaazjah to truly appreciate the realization of Boldandgold's flaunted opulence. It was hard to fathom that this area in the district had once just been a butchers' emporium with stockades for wild boar and pigs constructed underneath it, which were rumored to still be there. The Monodrome no longer appeared entirely round, as she had always believed it to be. It was now evident that the bluish-white marble walls were of a polyhedral design with hundreds of sides.

A fleeting wave of old memories washed through Zahnastaazjah of her old Terollar homeland. She remembered the Great Grove of Teralloe, guarded by the ancient mortali and their alliance with the Sylvanil Sentinel Order. Leagues of Terollar lifetrees blanketed the horizons of the Shevelokeval Knolls, which were embedded with sporadic clusters of stormtrees throughout the windy uplands. She recalled the private grove of her progenitor, Khomo'Jhuvonus, against the southwest coast. The entire region, named after him, Jhuvonhuthala, was blessed supernaturally by the tairan and sky elements as a place of perfect purity in balance between the two. White sand as far as one could see, yellow petrified trees that grew as high as Goldgarden's tallest spires, as thick as Az'Dayne's largest castles. *That is the difference between elvan beauty and what the humans revere.*

But now was not the hour for nostalgia. The time was nigh to finish off her local enemies for good. She had already cut the head off the snake. Now she just needed to burn down its infamous den. They had finally reached the destination she had never been able to get so close to before tonight.

Her massive Vellyan underlord revealed himself from the shadows as they approached the back entrance of the Monodrome. Usurp was covered in blood from face to boot, presumably from more than one Boarneck-affiliated victim who had gotten in his way. He had an antsy countenance and an injured lean in his stance. Through his thick raven beard, which hung down to his chest, it was fairly clear to see the mean gash in his cheek, and the stab wound he was clutching on the right side of his lower back was no doubt what was causing the stagger in his posture.

But the barbaric-minded half-giant rose—all seven feet tall and then some—in raw refusal to evince any sign of pain. "Guildmother," he called reverently with an instant shift in his impatient sway when her small entourage got close enough. "Boldandgold dead?"

"Oldandbold's dead," Zahnastaazjah confirmed, using Oldan's most popular street nickname. "Symbelle said Amethyst and the other umbran were aboard the barge. They escaped. We have to hurry."

Usurp's face said it all, that he was neither convinced nor pleased with the way events on his end had transpired. He waved one of his mighty arms back at the doorway behind him. "They're gonna trial us all for this fuckin' mess."

"Since when do you care about making a mess?" she called out her habitually reckless underlord, quite matter-of-factly. "No. Amethyst will not risk snitching about our involvement here now that we know what she is. She will just deny outright any accusations made of her affiliation with Oldan or the Boarneck Company." Just as Amaris had informed Zahnastaazjah before her demise, Symbelle had also attested that she had seen Amethyst in her true state as a neverborne.

"Someone said something about hurrying?" Xalo reminded her cynically. He took the lead to open the back door to the Monodrome and walk in without a fear in the world.

Zahnastaazjah ignored her witty lover and followed Usurp behind Xalo, after the Vellyan had tilted his war maul back into his grasp from where it was leaning unattended against the doorframe. Symbelle, Pyphan, and Uubakrath filed in too, trailing her inside.

"I need you to stay here," she commanded Uubakrath in their native Terollar dialect, which only the two of them could interpret. "No one comes inside. Your bow would be useless in these close quarters, anyway."

The old archer said nothing. He just bowed and did as she had bidden. He wasn't much of the talking type, she had come to learn. And she felt uncomfortable with that—and the fact that he had no true reason to show her loyalty other than their racial alignment.

"Where are the men?" She was expecting Usurp to enlighten her with something dire, seeing as he hadn't presented that pertinent point at the beginning.

"Sent most of 'em back," the bloody Vellyan readily explained. "Had to start without you. Fuckin' didn't run smoothly." Usurp winced slightly and switched his maul to his left hand, which caused Zahnastaazjah to take notice of his fresh shoulder wound, which she hadn't seen outside in the dark.

"They started catchin' on that no one attendin' was tourists or those local peacocks who watch this shit!"

"I knew this ploy was peppered with folly. Too many variables." Xalo groaned out his own logic to Usurp's briefing. "Too many people in the way."

"That was half the point," Zahnastaazjah reminded them all.

"Our finale for the Kingfall Ball is meant to be seen by the cityfolk, albeit with no casualty to them. Wait until we light this thing on fire."

Symbelle chimed in to timidly give her own reminder. "It won't just catch fire. The explosion over the districts on either side will be so bright, it will light the entire night sky in a red dawn."

Everyone looked at Symbelle as if she were some oracle of doom with the power to see into the future.

Xalo broke the transitory moment of pondering with another one of his wisecracks, repeating himself. "Someone said something about hurrying?"

You don't stop, do you? Zahnastaazjah cast with her eyes at the sarcastic spellblade.

The cocky glint he returned said, *You know I don't, and you like it.*

She rolled her eyes and cautiously continued into the delivery corridor of the Monodrome.

There was no resistance to be found down the hallway. Upon reaching the storage and prop rooms, they walked past a few dead men with their throats cut. The kitchen and small wine chamber were the same, with murdered cooks and servants. None of these seemed to be individuals who could have posed a threat even when alive, but it was clear that silencing all life was a must for the ruthless perpetrators who had done the deeds.

The employee passageways behind the scenes of the enormous theater-arena were more elaborate than anything Zahnastaazjah recalled being in before. She could only guess how impressive the stage and stadium area would be. Terollar didn't build things like this. And neither had any human she'd met before. *Oldan Boldandgold, you will be missed by some, I am sure.*

A green flash went off behind her at the rear of the line. She turned to spy Pyphan casting some minor healing spell on his sister's half-bitten-off ear while whispering something in it, then using his magic to restabilize the wobble in her hurt knee.

The mage had the capacity to regenerate nearly any wound, and for some reason, he seemed to take no interest in wasting his spells on Usurp, who was obviously in need. *You all dried up, mage? Or just being selective in who makes it out of this alive?* Zahnastaazjah contemplated the worst in her distrustful judgment toward the magic-instilled newcomers of her guild. It was in her nature and history to hold little faith in those with whom she kept close company. Sadly, she understood that she truly trusted not a single individual in the scope of it all, not even herself, since she had arrived in this iniquitous city of greed and duplicity in nearly every corner.

Usurp took the lead up several steps to reach the access area to the spectators' seats. And the grandeur of the domed theater was all that she had expected it to be and more. There were several different sections offered in a variety of tiers for guests to choose from, presumably from moderate to expensive in ticket cost—from standing, to bench seating, to chair seats, and even a higher tavern area for roaming socialites to meander while watching shows. They were on the ceiling level, just under the dome, with a vantage of each of the skyboxes. She was sure if she were anyone else, the entire brilliance of the great urban wonder would have enthralled to tour each one of the private balconies with such a rare opportunity, but the grandeur of the Monodrome was not what she was here for. And time was not a luxury they had to waste on such curiosities.

What did steal her attention was the litter of corpses throughout the stands and piled in a mound on display in the middle of the main stage. Men, and even a few women wearing the Boarneck token talismans had been bludgeoned, slashed, or choked to death. There was a small pyre of burning carcasses on one of the smaller stages, she noticed as well. *Those must be ours that fell. It looks like the Boarnecks were caught unawares. There isn't a single weapon in sight.*

"In case you're wonderin' where all the mercs are," Usurp said with a proud and ugly grin, "they're dead."

"I was," Zahnastaazjah muttered, still scanning the macabre scene. "And I assumed so." She knew this was only a few score dead of the thousands of Boarneck mercenaries that were alive and well, ignorant of all that was happening to their company's infrastructure while they were in the field or enjoying the outside festivities of the Kingfall Ball. But the loss of Oldan and the Monodrome would be enough to make the majority of the sellswords recant their contracts and go freelance.

"What of Terrib Ango, the Maestro, Oldan's theater operator?" Symbelle asked a good question.

"Him and a few other luckies are holed up in a vault with all that salt shit you need. There's a lift down through that door." Usurp pointed to the most opulently ornamented skybox, and the only one with a door on its terrace. "I left six of ours there guardin' the door he's got locked now. Harlow, Lavance, Primm, Korben, Goffrey, and Chem—all good men. Coulda hammered it down, but I didn't want the whole place to blow."

"Yeah, it does not blow from you hammering down a door," Symbelle clarified in a more annoyed inflection than Zahnastaazjah had ever heard the alchemist use before. "You can hit it all day with that thing, and it will just smear the substance. Only fire ignites it."

"Well, I didn't know that shit, bitch! Don't talk to me like I'm stupid," the offended Vellyan threatened.

"I always talk to you like you are stupid." Xalo provoked a challenge, but Usurp either ignored it or didn't care, as his intense glare on Symbelle was not shifting.

"I am just vainly educating the uneducable," Symbelle dared to goad further. "As Oldan Boldandgold would say—no offense."

It was apparent that tension, however, was only rising in the vehement Vellyan as he towered over the petite hyperi in a hostile stance. "Scarless, I'm gonna squeeze this cunt's head in with my bare hands if she comes down on me again!"

"The last time you were alone, you attempted to push her down on you, and you failed miserably and were checked." Pyphan opened his robe slightly to unveil his magemarks for instant activation in an insinuated challenge. "Yield, or I will also check you."

"You hearin' this? I've ripped tongues out for less lip, little man! And I don't let any fuckin' bitch one-up me! Get that story straight." Usurp turned his promise of violence on the mage.

Zahnastaazjah had had enough. But her obnoxiously ill-tempered underlord wasn't deserving of her scolding. She was tired of his unruly antics at the most inappropriate times. She stepped between him and the two siblings and confronted him with a bored stare.

"Scarless, not meanin' anythin' about you," Usurp stumbled, with a softening quake in his demeanor. "I am sayin' this bitch, Symbelle, and all the other bitches. Not that I mean you are also a bitch, though," he yammered on. "Because you are a woman, and women are sometimes bitches. But you are different. Because you are a tro—" He caught himself to correct his words quickly. "A Terollar elvan. And elven ain't bitches. Well, maybe there are a few elvan bitches, but you ain't one."

It all sounded so ridiculous, pathetic, and inarticulate that Zahnastaazjah questioned her own intelligence in ever promoting the brute into his position in the guild.

Xalo spoke her mind for her in his own way. "Can we leave him in here when we light the kegs?"

She shut the senseless friction down between her group by commencing toward the door to Oldan's skybox, and everyone obediently quieted and followed.

"You are sure that below here is where the quest ends? Where we will find the source to light the fire?" Pyphan inquired of his sister.

"I just fuckin' said that!" Usurp answered harshly.

"Down deep, below the surface, where the shadow and fire will meet," Symbelle riddled in a somber tone.

Strange exchange. That was a code, Zahnastaazjah thought concerning the two foreign siblings she realized she knew little about. *I dislike codes, and I've never trusted a secret I wasn't in on.*

Zahnastaazjah pretended not to be alarmed at anything conceivably amiss between the two, at some potential countercollusion against her. She opened the door to the lift, and the five of them entered the large cage that led down just underneath the Monodrome's surface. She flipped the lever above the cage, and the lift slowly began to descend.

Zahnastaazjah glanced behind her at the sound of Symbelle muttering something to herself. The hyperi girl looked conflicted and apprehensive. Even Pyphan, beside his sister, shifted in an uncomfortable manner, she thought she perceived.

She dismissed it and faced the door of the cage until she heard rummaging behind her feet. Looking back again, she found Symbelle now on her knees, garbing herself for anticipated violence, it seemed. The alchemist was fitting in place her bandolier and bracers of vials with whatever concoctions she deemed it necessary to fill them with. Symbelle then pulled out a modified set of bellows with a canister of some sort fitted to the nozzle. And lastly she put over her poison-resistant breathing mask with filter valves attached near both sides of her mouth. Symbelle's goggles and red Neveril wig were arranged around the mask's secure fit to her face.

Symbelle was talking to herself, whispering as if in some internal argument. The whole preparation and bizarre attitude returned the uneasy wariness in Zahnastaazjah. But it wasn't until Pyphan dropped his robe and cast a spell on himself, illuminating every part of his exposed upper body and face in some magical, faintly green glowing shield, that Zahnastaazjah decided to speak aloud her concerns.

They know something we do not. "You two expecting a fight?"

The lift came to a stop, and the door to the cage automatically unlatched to allow it to be pushed open. But no one yet moved.

"There is poison down here," Symbelle answered with a voice muffled by her breathing mask. She was now also wearing two different tinctures around her neck, dangling as if they were stylish necklaces.

What? I hate poisons. Zahnastaazjah's perturbed eyes translated all that she was concerned about. She knew her Terollar impower would keep her alive and heal her if she were ever exposed, but circumstances in her past had always given her a deep fear of the substances.

"Better be givin' me one of them potions, then, little girl." Usurp put a massive hand on Symbelle's tiny shoulder to encourage her to comply.

The evolved alchemist did not meet his bullying gaze down at her. "I will be giving you a potion" was all she promised as the formerly shy girl took the lead and pushed through the lift to progress farther in.

I am not liking this sudden change in you, Zahnastaazjah thought.

The narrow corridor area was well lit with torches on sconces in either direction. Symbelle turned left and guided the group, while Pyphan lingered in the rear.

Usurp was so tall, he had to duck his head slightly to avoid hitting it on the low ceiling. He stopped to point in the opposite direction and explain, "Back that way leads out. Not too far a walk. But you can't come back in once you go. The door locks. That's how I got back outside."

"You are correct," Symbelle confirmed while still trekking farther down the hallway. Even her typical awkward gait had altered. The hyperi moved lithely in a feminine stride.

Something is different in you.

"This poison is going to be in the air? What do you have for us? I see no point in all of us proceeding. Let's get Pyphan to get the door open and flush Ango out of the vault," Xalo rationalized to Symbelle, then turned to the mage. "Simple. Unless you have some spell to get us through whatever we are about to breathe."

"There is no more at the moment. Just a precaution," Symbelle assured him. "Just provisioning ourselves for a premeditated contingency."

"I don't know what that means. Turns out we aren't equipped to breathe poison. Can you answer something straight?" Xalo demanded with a hint of uncharacteristic anxiety.

Usurp barged up past all of them, nearly toppling Symbelle over on purpose when he took point. "You sound like a piss-pants man-bitch, Xalo. There ain't no fuckin' poison down here. I was just here!"

The entourage came to the vault Usurp had mentioned. Zahnastaazjah and her party were breathing safely in the enclosed space, but that didn't matter, as the whole scene in front of them was suspect.

"The fuckin' hells is this?" Usurp asked the question Zahnastaazjah herself was wondering.

The six men Usurp had said he had left to guard the vault were on the floor. Chem was curled up in a fetal position, shaking and crying. Lavance was in the corner, frightened for his life. Primm and Goffrey were crawling on the floor. Harlow was staring at the wall with wide eyes as if he were frozen in time and could not even blink. And Korben was bleeding from his throat with his knife in hand, an evident suicide.

The vault door that Usurp had said was locked tight was wide open. Inside, Zahnastaazjah spotted Terrib Ango and his few survivors in similar states as Usurp's minions, in mentally debilitated states of induced fear.

There were four blast-salt kegs with hoses connected to them that were engineered into the wall. Upon more vigilant inspection, Zahnastaazjah spotted several air holes in the wall just below the ceiling, lining the vault and just outside, where they were now standing.

Against her better judgment, she moved forward into the vault to further assess Terrib Ango and not shy from her reputation as the Stormtrees' intrepid leader. *The old thing is dead*, she saw, looking down at the Monodrome's disreputable maestro. Terrib's eyes were twice their normal size, open in shock, staring back at her, but his face was pale and his body was stiff. *Heart attack.*

The three other Boarneck mercenaries who had accompanied their dead supervisor were still alive, however, but helpless in incapacitating horror.

"Why are there only four kegs?" Xalo whispered right over her shoulder. "Where are the rest?"

Before Zahnastaazjah could give a guess to that peculiar fact, which raised new misgivings about the whole scene, the door to the vault suddenly shut, and a hiss of yellow mist sprayed from the holes.

Xalo turned to open the door, but it was locked tight.

The poison was working fast into Zahnastaazjah's bloodstream. Within seconds, Xalo was slowly slipping down to his knees, barely clutching his spellblade. There was a spyhole grille in the door, which she managed to get to as her impower of constantly regenerating kept her from fully succumbing to the toxin's effects. She felt weak, incredibly weak, but was able to negate the psychedelic reaction of fear that tried itself on her mind.

Zahnastaazjah found Usurp slapping at his head in a crazed stupor as the large warrior collapsed to his knees also. Pyphan's gold magemarks lit up green, and the mage waved his hands to magically shift the door to the vault away into some arcane space through the floor. Symbelle was glaring through her goggles, with her glowing violet hyperi eyes visible through them, at Zahnastaazjah, with her head eerily cocked to the side. The alchemist was aiming the bellows device straight at her and Xalo.

"For whom, then?" Zahnastaazjah addressed Symbelle with total surprise as to what had just occurred. "Why?"

Pyphan answered for her and threw down a scroll at her feet. "Zahnastaazjah of Jhuvonhuthala, progeny of the lifetree of Khomo'Jhuvonus and Malindhi, and Xalo of Spellspire, Son of the Crimson Clouds, your writs from the Oathemic Cabal have been served. Meet your assassins."

"Symbelle?" Zahnastaazjah's tone came out confused, more emotionally wounded than she intended.

"That is not our name," the alchemist assassin said. "Symbelle is going to sit this one out. Allow me to introduce ourself."

"Fyheir?" Zahnastaazjah asked. But she already knew the

answer even before Fyheir pushed down the bellows and the next batch of poison left the canister attached to it.

Zahnastaazjah breathed in the stinging purple gas and instantly felt her impower to regenerate cease from functioning. And for the first time since Zahnastaazjah had left her homeland, she did know fear.

SYMBELLE & FYHEIR (IX)

ALLOW ME TO INTRODUCE OURSELF

(TEN MINUTES EARLIER)

"You are sure that below here is where the quest ends? Where we will find the source to light the fire?" Pyphan initiated the rehearsed Oathemic code phrases for confirmation to execute the writs in sequence as planned.

Where the quest ends translated to Pyphan asking if they were entering the place to officially present their order's assassination writs to their targets before formally eliminating them. *Source to light the fire* was to be deciphered as her brother inquiring if this was also the location in which she had hidden the cache of blast-salt kegs, throughout the stockades.

Pyphan had not stopped probing her fading resolve ever since they had debarked from Oldan's abandoned pleasure barge. "Are we in?" he would ask in her ear every chance he could when the others were neither looking nor prying. "Or do I tell Master Claydius and Coldborn of one more casualty in the fray? I am about to begin," Pyphan would threaten, to remind her in different ways.

"I just fuckin' said that!" Usurp shouted in apparent offense taken by Pyphan even asking what he had already been enlightened of by his successful bloody raid.

"Down deep, below the surface, where the shadow and fire will meet," Symbelle returned to Pyphan in the Oathemic Cabal's code talk, referred to as Cipher.

Scarless, Xalo, and Usurp obliviously proceeded into the skybox lift that would take them below to where the established destination of their graves was waiting. Pyphan and Symbelle entered the cage just after them and watched the Stormtrees' matriarch pull the lever to descend onward to her doom.

You will not be able to do this. Fyheir doubted her inner tenacity. *Allow us to do it for you.*

Symbelle looked aside to her brother for forgiveness in failing the mission at its penultimate moment. She realized she had known very little of him since they were but children. The mage standing next to her was a cold killer who did not waver in the weaknesses of typical society. She did not doubt that Pyphan would add a fourth grave for her without a second thought if she proved to fumble when it was time.

You have taken a liking to her, Fyheir judged as Symbelle's focus shifted to the back of Scarless's head. *You question why betray her, the one person who has ever shown you respect, the only one who has ever shown you affection.* Everything Fyheir pointed out was striking the nerves in her very core so strongly, she could not argue back.

For whom, then? The Oathemic Cabal, because your father, whom you had never truly known, instructed you to, as your duty to him as an expendable pawn in his game? The same way he uses your brother.

"Yes," she whispered back, as if she were alone, uttering a soliloquy. "Why must we follow through?"

Because we do not do it for him or him. Fyheir insinuated Coldborn and Pyphan. *Or any of them. We do all for the fire. We were reborn from it. And the Oathemic Cabal is who made it so that we met in Tairanchula. We owe them this one favor. Then we may do as we wish.*

"My brother will not allow that. There has to be another way. We are running out of time." Symbelle was talking so low to herself over the cranking noise of the moving lift that she could barely hear her own words, but still her brother leaned from leg to leg in an awkward rebalancing as he tried to overhear what she was muttering. She continued to beseech Fyheir nonetheless. "We can warn her. She can run from us. I can stall my brother. He will understand," she dared to lie.

Scarless quickly glanced back at her as if she suspected foul play, but the imposing elvan only held regard of her for a second or two before turning back forward with her eyes diverted elsewhere.

Symbelle felt her body kneeling and removing her alchemy pack to carefully scavenge through it. She had no control over her hands and legs, and evidently not even her lips, as she heard her own voice whispering back to her. "This one does not run. Not anymore," Fyheir said with her tongue aloud. "And this one is a killer, just like you." Fyheir had implied Scarless at first and was now mentioning Pyphan. "His mind is in this; yours is not. But you have us to save you."

"Wait, Fyheir. Wait." Symbelle found that she somehow still maintained the will to overpower her dominating alter ego and speak aloud. "I cannot …"

But even as Fyheir was still allowing her to currently emit words, it became clear immediately that the sinister Entity had taken complete control of her body already. One by one, Fyheir was inspecting tools and vials from the pack and equipping Symbelle for death-dealing alongside Pyphan's wishes.

Her bandolier harness was fitted with a flash bomb, a smoke bomb, a rapid-healing potion, and three vials of wispbane. Her alchemist bracers, on the other hand, held a remedy tincture to reverse the effects of wispbane, another to grant undersight, an inhalable immunity elixir for skinny dust, and three extended vials of cinder oil. She had prepared more of the concoctions in case she had need of them, safely fitted in pockets stitched to the inside of her pack.

Next, Fyheir pulled out her bellows device with a small canister of gasified, compressed wispbane locked in to spray on those it was intended to debilitate.

And lastly, her leather breathing mask was fitted around her face, with her goggles and Neveril wig adjusted accordingly around it.

I had given you a chance, but you are still weak, our love. Fyheir warned her of the inevitable consequences.

"But you are not my love." Symbelle gave all her strength to try to stand and warn Scarless, even just one touch to get her attention once more. "She is …"

I know Symbelle. And Fyheir has become quite jealous of what we see, her diabolical higher conscience admitted.

Don't make me watch! I don't want to be here anymore, Symbelle pleaded, back inside her mind, as Fyheir completely resurfaced to take over. *Take me away.*

"Oh, no, our love. You made us watch as you cheated on us," Fyheir seethed under its breath. It was delighting in the opportunity to exact retribution as Symbelle felt her body rise back to her feet. "Now you watch as we take her from you."

Scarless turned back around with shock in her countenance upon seeing Symbelle all dressed up for danger and Pyphan casting some form of green aura over himself. "You two expecting a fight?" she asked.

Run, Scarless! Don't go down here! I'm going to kill you! Symbelle tried to say with every fiber of her being. But as the lift reached the bottom and the door opened to the vault corridors, Symbelle knew she no longer had any control to save Scarless. Everyone was now at the mercy of Fyheir's gluttonous hunger to consume life.

* * * * *

"Zahnastaazjah of Jhuvonhuthala, progeny of the lifetree of Khomo'Jhuvonus and Malindhi, and Xalo of Spellspire, Son of the Crimson Clouds, your writs from the Oathemic Cabal have been served. Meet your assassins," Pyphan proclaimed over the devitalized Terollar tycoon and her spellblade companion.

"Symbelle?" Scarless sounded so hurt and confused.

I am so sorry. It isn't me.

"That is not our name. Symbelle is going to sit this one out," Fyheir enlightened her. "Allow me to introduce ourself."

"Fyheir?" Scarless amended herself, holding out one hand to futilely shield herself from the inevitable.

Fyheir aimed the bellows straight at Scarless, barely a foot away from her face, and slowly squeezed them, spraying a purple mist over her and Xalo, further weakening their internal enhancements.

Scarless's reaction to grab her spear was dramatically lethargic from the fallout of the skinny dust. She looked as if she was trying to throw the bulky thing, but just holding the toxic bloodrime was enough to take another toll on the nonregenerating Terollar.

Fyheir grinned at their two contract targets wickedly. "That's the wispbane in you now." Fyheir went to safely remove the weapon from Scarless's strengthless grasp.

Fyheir caught Xalo, out of the corner of her eye, failing to lift and utilize the magic properties of his enchanted sword as well. "No need to try. You no longer have the capacity to activate those glyphs. And there is enough skinny dust in the air to ensure none of you can lift a weapon. All of you brave individuals have been introduced to what it feels like to live as the weak among the strong. Among those you will come to fear." Fyheir set down the bellows and produced a torch from Symbelle's pack, which it promptly lit, and it put the blaze right in front of Symbelle's face to stare into. "Like me!" it exclaimed.

An axe-head-shaped piece of the floor manifested to decapitate Primm and prevent him from crawling any farther, and beneath Goffrey, the floor magically warped into something similar as four spears formed up through his prone body and retracted back into the ground within a second. Pyphan began casually eliminating each of the living in his vicinity through his innovative use of tairan magic.

Symbelle's foster brother paused and threw his right hand at the wall that sealed away the old stockades on the other side. With another glyph activated, he effortlessly slid the barrier to ethereally merge into the others, revealing the big surprise.

Symbelle, imprisoned in the back of her mind, regretted that she had ever even involved Pyphan on this level of detail concerning the Monodrome. Her initial promotion to Grand Alchemist for the Boarneck Company had afforded her all the liberties of reconnaissance she had needed to be a successful triple agent.

The stockades area was constructed with hundreds of hog pens, now with not a single swine in sight. The former farm enclosure was now used as a secret housing department for the cache of blast-salt kegs Oldan Boldandgold had hoarded.

Fyheir went to the single half-hourglass, placed on a table near the entry to the pens. Beside it was a fixed candle with a wick lengthened to match the time of the apparatus's sand, the same as in the Room of Infinite Reflection, except this smaller one was set to finish its sand after thirty minutes. She flipped the half-hourglass over to start the timer and lit the wick, which was attached to a long fuse that led to a blast-salt keg by the table. Just one keg would cause a chain reaction to detonate the others in the largest demolition explosion that had ever been created.

"We are going to grant you a quick and more painless death, Scarless," Pyphan declared.

Thank you ... You remembered my request.

"Symbelle wishes to bestow a mercy, and I will allow it."

Arcanic imprints on Pyphan's body glowed once again as he channeled his magic to shape wooden hands from the floor. They dragged Scarless back to the nearest wall, while another set of hands formed from the floor planks seized her bloodrime spear and pinned her to the wall by her throat, holding the weapon either side of her head.

"The rest of you are food for the fire." Fyheir approached the horror-struck giant form of Usurp in a lithe gait. Before her body reached the Vellyan, Symbelle witnessed Lavance, in the corner, being lifted up the wall to his grisly death by some manifested stone hook that came out of the brick pillar. Pyphan was still picking apart the leftovers, taunting the strongest last.

Usurp was seated on his rump, flailing his huge arms to try to push Fyheir away from him while he desperately scooted back. Typically, one punch from the lethal brute could have ended Symbelle's life, but he was in no condition to harm a mouse with how much skinny dust he had inhaled. His only emotion could be fear, and the weight of his muscles was now more of a hindrance to further sap his stamina. He became more paralyzed as he attempted to use them.

Fyheir effortlessly caught one of Usurp's arms as he swung at Symbelle and shoved it back down to the floor, where it stayed. Fyheir straddled the huge man with her tiny body and shoved a blast-salt vial into his mouth, then forced his jaw shut to shatter it open with his teeth. Usurp was crying in fear, but that only fueled its infernal intent.

Fyheir stood up with one foot braced on his broad chest and the other balanced on the floor, and it removed Symbelle's breathing mask to discard it beside her. It pulled another vial from her left bracer, filled with a yellow elixir that granted immunity to the effects of the skinny dust, and breathed it in fully after uncorking it. Next, it generously drenched Symbelle's body in a flask of cinder oil, like she was shower-bathing in a perfume.

"I'm sorry," Usurp managed to gargle with muffled words between the blast salt coating the inside of his mouth, "I'm sorry!"

Symbelle could not see herself, but she could feel by the stretch of her fool's frown that Fyheir was smiling manically, and that her eyes were open far too wide in crazed excitement. Fyheir knelt back down and stuck her fingers in Usurp's nostrils up to the knuckles, until he opened his mouth back up.

"Your turn to swallow instead," Fyheir seethed in exasperated pleasure. It slipped the torch into Usurp's mouth and watched his head explode into a disintegrating combustion of blood, bone, and red fire that enveloped the rest of his charred body.

Symbelle's alchemy pack was sent sliding across the hallway from the blast, directly up against Xalo's side as he lay flat to the floor in hallucination spasms. The impact seemed to give the broken swordsman the will to act. Xalo rummaged through the bag to find the same elixir he had seen her inhale to negate the skinny dust coursing through him. The aromatic potion seeped yellow smoke over his face and seemed to instantly have an invigorating effect as Xalo rose back to his feet with his spellblade readied in hand.

Pyphan was using one hand to finish off the remaining lackeys of Usurp and Terrib with spells and his other to control the magic wooden hands that were choking Scarless with her own spear. Symbelle's brother almost didn't catch on in time that Xalo was charging at him, but his killer instincts were sharp and honed from his years training with the Oathemic Cabal.

Pyphan stopped the magic that was pinning Scarless to focus everything he had on defending himself from Xalo's advance. He summoned ethereal vines that burst through the floor, walls, and ceiling, creating a living web that came after the Elothian warrior from every direction.

Xalo managed to cut through several of the magic vines, progressing dangerously close to Pyphan, but he was eventually constrained by his wrists and ankles, neutralized as a threat.

Fyheir approached Scarless to stand over her and dropped the torch far aside while keeping Symbelle's bellows in hand. The formerly invulnerable Crime Queen sat with her back to the wall and feet outstretched, convulsing in writhing agony from the bloodrime taking its toll in her veins, coupled with the remnants of the skinny dust and wispbane that was still in her lungs. Fyheir indolently moved with no sense of urgency to switch out the wispbane canister on the bellows with one of more skinny dust and aimed the nozzle down at Scarless's terrified green eyes.

Please don't make me watch. Symbelle cried inside for Fyheir to possess her completely and take her into the forgotten void of subconsciousness like the evil Entity had done at certain times before.

Make it quick! She was nice to us.

But Fyheir seemed to be in no rush and ignored Symbelle the same way that Symbelle had often ignored Fyheir's pleas before. "You really must hear what we are forced to listen to. She really loved you, you know?" Fyheir referenced Symbelle while harshly speaking down to Scarless as if reprimanding her. "Symbelle does not even want to be here. But she is weak. She has always been weak." Fyheir squeezed the bellows to spray the skinny dust directly into Scarless's helpless face.

"Those like you and us, who have always been the strongest, we do not understand them, do we? The only way we can is to live in their bodies and feel what it must be like to be so pathetic," Fyheir went on as Scarless retreated back into a fit of tremors from the fresh batch of skinny dust settling in her.

Symbelle could feel her body kneeling as she feebly watched Fyheir commencing with its baleful motives. "That is what life is like as us. We live and we breathe in this weak body, day after day. Can you sympathize with us now?"

Fyheir! Stop teasing her! Just do it!

"She is begging us still. Are you going to beg us also?" Fyheir teased with a wicked sneer as it ran Symbelle's hand through Scarless's long blond locks. "You were beautiful, though." It then brushed her fingernails against Scarless's trembling face. "But you were stealing Symbelle from us. And we do not share so well."

Symbelle watched herself pour a flask of flammable oil all over Scarless. Fyheir massaged it into her hair and skin like a lubricious lover might. It then pulled out the remedy vial for the wispbane, an indigo substance. "There is a part of us that thinks you deserve a fight in this, to see if you can combat the hunger of the fire. Is the great Zahnastaazjah's ability to live stronger than the power of Fyheir? We will give you this warrior's challenge before we go."

Fyheir emptied the wispbane remedy into Scarless's mouth and watched her readily imbibe it all down her throat before standing back up. Fyheir aimed the bellows back at the elvan to spray her down with skinny dust one last time. It then traded the modified bellows for the blazing torch on the floor.

I will not watch this, Symbelle vowed.

"Oh, but you already are," Fyheir whispered back.

Pyphan was slowly strangling Xalo with the magic vines he had conjured, while also manipulating other strands to pry away his enchanted sword and point it back on its wielder.

"Grab the blade yourself," Xalo taunted, with difficulty in finding air to speak with his entangled neck.

"This will do just fine." Pyphan grinned in satisfaction at the twisted fate of ending Xalo's life with his own mage-killing weapon. "I thank you for this honor, Xalo. You will be my first spellblade."

Xalo smiled back. He never smiled. "You will be my eighth mage."

Xalo opened his left palm to reveal a flash bomb he had pilfered from Symbelle's pack and then dropped it to burst into a blinding light. The surprise flash caused just enough of a disruption in Pyphan's channeling to allow Xalo to loosen his hands and take control of the magic vines himself. He wrapped Pyphan's own hands and the spellblade together, forcing the mage to grab its hilt. The sentient blade became angered at the mage's unwelcome touch and rapidly began to age him.

Pyphan jerked and tried to release the cursed sword, but Xalo's determination in his strength on the vines was not budging. The only way Pyphan could escape the wrath of the spellblade's denial was to dismiss the vine spell. As soon as he did, Pyphan retreated back several paces to conjure his next tairan spell while Xalo promptly reunited with his spellblade.

Just as the two faced off to finish their duel, an arrow protruded from Pyphan's gut, loosed by someone from behind him down the hallway. No one needed to further investigate to realize that Uubakrath had joined the fight with Scarless and Xalo against Symbelle and Pyphan.

Pyphan ripped the arrow from his stomach and cast a quick healing spell to close the wound, and instantly he followed up by channeling his magic to slide the wall shut behind them to seal off Uubakrath and prevent him from setting another arrow loose. But the Terollar archer was fast enough to at least let fly one more arrow before the magic wall barricaded him on the other side.

Symbelle felt the pain flare up her spine as her leading leg seemed to burst into fire from within. But there was no fire on her, only a large arrow sticking out of her right thigh. Symbelle screamed and dropped her torch, and she understood that Fyheir had retreated back into the untappable void of her mind. "Fyheir?" Her dominant personality had fled when she needed it the most.

"Fyheir, where are you? Fix this!" Symbelle reached for the torch, but it was too far away, and she had no idea why she even still wanted it. She needed healing potions from within her bag. Before she knew it, she was crawling on the floor, struggling toward her open alchemy pack to find salvation. "Come back …"

Scarless gradually rose back to her feet, with her regenerative impower returned, bringing resolve back to her mind and body. The look on the elvan's face was one of promised wrath as Scarless took the torch instead and tossed it onto Symbelle's alchemy pack, destroying the contents within in a swift blaze.

Pyphan never got out his last spell as Xalo proved to be the quicker. He pushed his spellblade through Pyphan's chest all the way up to the hilt. The magic glass sword pierced through Pyphan's mortal flesh like butter. Pyphan's eyes glowed vibrantly green before the light left his skull and shot through the tip of the spellblade to find a place for a new Dawning glyph on its glass surface. The sentient weapon had absorbed a wisp from the mage's spellpower for its own use.

Xalo let Pyphan's lifeless corpse slide off his sword and sheathed it once the mage's spells had dissipated from the room, allowing Uubakrath to join him.

Scarless stripped Symbelle of the red Neveril wig and used the living hair as a rope to pull her from under the neck to the middle of the stockade pens in the center of the blast-salt cache.

"No, Zahnastaazjah! It wasn't me! I didn't want to!" Symbelle screamed as she was dragged against her will. "I cared for you! It was Fyheir." She began violently sobbing. "Please," she begged, aware of the futility.

"Fyheir." Scarless uttered the name like a curse between gritted teeth as she towered over Symbelle's impotent form. "Don't worry, Symbelle. I cared for you also." She turned her otherworldly spear around to stab it deep into Symbelle's other thigh, further crippling her. She left it there for a few seconds while glaring down with a condemning gaze.

"Zahnastaazjah," she cried in agony. "It was Fyheir that tried to kill you, not me."

Her elvan executioner cooed back in mock sympathy, now

visibly regenerated back to flawless condition. "If it helps, then tell yourself it wasn't me either. It was Scarless who killed you."

Scarless then opened her hand, and the bloodrime spear returned to her grasp. "Burn well, Symbelle."

Symbelle watched as Scarless, Xalo, and Uubakrath made haste toward the exit down the corridors to escape the inevitable boom that was soon to come from the blast salt that she had staged all around her.

She found that she couldn't move whatsoever, either because of the excruciating pain in her legs from Uubakrath's arrow, still sticking out of her right thigh, and the bleeding gash in the other from the bloodrime spear, or perhaps even because of the lack of will to still live.

Symbelle removed her goggles to see her fading world with no obstructions blocking her view. Her hypersight took over, and she realized she could see the faint trails left behind by the hunder within the two Terollar, and then a darker, more complex green line from Xalo's sword. She had never noticed them before now.

She thought to call after Scarless once more, tell her she loved her, maybe, but decided against it. Symbelle knew she deserved the fate that had been bestowed on her. The wick of the candle was down to the bottom. All was about to become bright before it became dark.

This was how it had all begun, Symbelle remembered, in the Room of Infinite Reflection, when she had first been introduced to her father and undergone the enlightenment of her induction into the Oathemic Cabal. Scarless hadn't killed her, she judged. Her father had. He had coerced her into betraying the one person who had ever been true to her, and this end could be the only fitting way to exit the pathetic story that was her miserable existence.

Symbelle could no longer see the wick. The flame was down to the fuse. It would be any second now. *The flame,* she mused in sadness. *Fyheir …*

No, it wasn't her father who had killed her either. It was only one Entity that had betrayed her in the end.

"Burn well, Symbelle," Fyheir whispered aloud, repeating the last words of Scarless, before the fiery embrace came to claim her.

SUNDORION (VI)

WELCOME TO THE UNDER

Sun slouched in a personnel mine cart, rebuilt to comfortably seat two individuals on either side. He hadn't budged a muscle in hours as the Neveril drudges directed the trolley to wherever they planned to subject him to more misery next. Everyone he had come to care about in his existence of incessant migration had perished by some calamitous end. He was dead in mind, hollow in heart, and numb in body. Whatever his enemies had in store for his next chapter could no longer do any harm.

"Why am I still alive?" Sun called out in a voice barely above a whisper, to no one in particular. He couldn't help but notice his clothes and skin still caked in Taizsha's blood.

There was no answer. He asked a little louder. "Why am I still alive?"

"Your cooperation will be needed for what comes next." The familiar voice enunciated each word all too melodramatically. The sound of Zsa'vauge adjacent to him subconsciously compelled his neck to lift his head up momentarily so that he could absorb his surroundings.

Sun glimpsed Ethiass and Odysserae, still in a trance of appalled shock themselves. He wasn't sure when Odysserae had taken it, but she was wearing Timmurian's water-watch, New Patience, around her neck, as well as Sun's own, Old Patience. She glanced back at Sun, almost in apology, before she vanished around the corner with her morally damned father.

This area of the underrealm seemed to be a cave-like lobby of sorts, with many things taking place at once, and a crossroads of tunnels to venture further in from this juncture. The signature red Neveril crystalytes illuminated the unnatural subterranean antechamber. Obvious mages, Neveril elven, and other conspicuously deviant characters with grey skin filled the rocky cavity.

"You mean participation," Sun countered at his oppressor's mention of cooperation. "Why would I aid in anything now?"

"You will willingly aid me in all that I require. Know this. And know this also: you will not survive this," Zsa'vauge promised in complete transparency, just before climbing into the small railed vehicle to join Sun.

You will not survive this. Sun repeated Zsa'vauge's dooming words in his head. He had already expected it. He had already accepted the inevitable of what he had surmised. But hearing the confirmation still sent a shiver not only down his spine but along every appendage he could move. His head ached, and his extremities stung. His eyes burned from dry tears, and his mouth was as dehydrated as the Zandaryn deserts of Wroth. He had nothing more to live for, but still Sun feared the finality of death and going to the Beyond.

Sun watched the conscripted Dawning mages at work tairanforming certain sectors of the large lobby before his eyes. Their half-naked bodies glowed green with their skin glyphs as they shaped and twisted the stone to their design.

Sun took notice of Mesdarro speaking to Ise'andahr and several grey-skinned, raven-haired humans in the chamber, whom he had surmised already to be the aforementioned, the neverborne qindrid in their natural forms, before taking on the likenesses of others. The hyperi Magistrate of Spellspire began to make his way toward their rail cart.

"Sundorion, you will be critical in what comes next. Therefore, in trade, I will impart to you all that you have always wanted. All that I know, you shall know. Just ask and I will tell," Zsa'vauge promised him in the most amicable manner he had conveyed yet, just before Mesdarro was close upon them. "I know that is your life's ambition, your reason for being, to be privy to all the shadow's secrets, big and small. I shall fulfill it for you before you comply to die, as you must."

"An ironic and proper end, then," Sun murmured, staring off in a daze, sure that he was growing more weary of the anticipation to be done with it rather than fearing the inevitable.

Zsa'vauge paid no regard to the sarcasm as he called over Ise'andahr, just as Mesdarro also approached. The umbran addressed his rogue-elvan progeny. "Count Valdean has sent Odysserae to lure her hunder-touched sister for what needs to be done about the hyperi boy. We need him alive, but not with his entourage. Stay with Odysserae and aid her with any diversions she will need assistance with."

Ise'andahr bowed to his father saying nothing. *The few rogue-elven I have met have lost the ability to speak with age. How far in are you?* Sun mused as a distraction from his melancholy.

Zsa'vauge reached from the cart to grab Ise'andahr by the wrist just before he turned away, sternly reminding, "No assassinations. No Thrench die. The hyperi's desire to come to Spellspire alone must be voluntary; to put his Sojourn on suspension. Ensure Odysserae sees her sister up to the task."

"She will be a mage now, bound to this season. Adyssaira, her name was you said," Mesdarro added with an arcane explanation. "Timmurian's wisp will have interfused by now to become her catalyst. She will further be able to draw upon her spellpower from her genesis wisp she was born with from this one's lifemate."

Sheyelle ... You are who entered Valenteal's womb on the triplets' birthing day. Mesdarro had insinuated the phenomenon in vague conjecture when Sun was chained beside his siblings just before their deaths were forced. But Sun did not register the magistrate's words at the time. The paranormal peculiarity of the mystic development from twenty years ago came crashing into him like a jolting epiphany. *You are the reason Odysserae cannot hear ... Why Addy is what she is. Hunder-touched because of you. You have been here all along my dear, with her ... And I was blind to see it, wasting time in buried corners of the realm away from you again.*

"Is this where you want her?" Mesdarro expressed concern in his tone, obviously implying Adyssaira's twisted role in all of this.

Zsa'vauge scrutinized the many mages in the vicinity performing their duty at tairan-forming. Sun counted eleven of the bare-chested, muscled men channeling their magic.

"Dawning mages," Sun whispered with pain in his cracked throat. So much of his invasive research had been verified. "Are they all members of the Green Byway? How many are in the Neverils' employ?"

"A mutually lucrative arrangement," Zsa'vauge replied to Sun instead of Mesdarro. "We have an established alliance with the

Green Byway. They are paid like kings and promised protection when the Greyfire Revolution begins. The others you see are mostly sellspells."

He took Sun's wrist to aim it toward another trio of shirtless humans strolling about, inspecting the integrity of the cave's ceiling. "No one can match our price, and they know that there is no safety in the realm for them outside Goldgarden or Mageholme. With us, they have a life of unparalleled luxury."

Mesdarro stared at the umbran patiently waiting on his question to be answered in turn, which Zsa'vauge did expound on. "Our new Chandoss Dawning mage will not be put to the expansions tairan-forming needs. As agreed, Mesdarro, we will only use her to draw the eldritch wisp. You can do what you wish in Spellspire with her after that. I will not default on our bargain."

"The Sunder is near. She will be collapsing soon, succumbed to Transbernation until the Reaping season," Mesdarro recapped the technicalities of the delicate dilemma. "Her door narrows fast for how long she has to get No-Name alone in front of me. We cannot have the Thrench provoked to follow to Spellspire."

"What is the Greyfire Revolution?" Sun involved himself in the discussion, letting them know he was still present. "What is the eldritch wisp you speak of?"

Zsa'vauge proved himself true to his word by revealing to Sun all that he asked. "The Greyfire Revolution commences this very coming season. The empire's first act of war. First, the final chosen of who all will take the Transcendence to become neverborne will be completed in a great ritual in front of the emperor – Emperor Zsinsinyrahn. And then all qindrid united, the skyborne of the east, the stoneborne of the north, the greyborne among them, and the remaining Wyldenar and Shiniryn umbran. All will join in the great offense against the Thrench Ashenwave. There are many allies to the cause as well on the forefronts. The Helderaki Terollar, the Kingdom of Sho Kung, most of the tribes of Brutonga, and soon to be the Caelduyans to name a few."

Sun soaked the information in, knowing he likely would not live long enough to make a difference or see the end of that Greyfire war, much less even the beginning.

Mesdarro climbed into the trolley cart to sit across from Sun, next to Zsa'vauge. The hyperi's otherworldly violet-clouded eyes emanated brightly enough to give the cart a purple hue.

"It is only fitting I elaborate about the eldritch wisp and your role to come," Mesdarro acknowledged. "The eldritch was," he paused to correct himself, "*is* your progeny that committed the Severance twenty years ago alongside your lifemate. The wisp we speak of is Carolelle."

"The eldritch wisp awaits the catalyst," Sun recalled Mesdarro's words spoken on the hour that Timmurian and Taizsha died. His mind had not registered it then. *"The catalyst wisp will find and bind to the hunder-touched girl. The eldritch wisp of Carolelle will go to her. Be ready,"* the hyperi had said.

Sun's eyes said it all, as his focus incidentally plead to Zsa'vauge for answers instead of Mesdarro.

"Try to keep up," was all the umbran replied, as he grabbed Sun by the chin to fix his attention on Mesdarro again.

"Eldritch are not normal wisp. They do not hold to the green glow that one equates with the signature hue of magic. No, the eldritch are more like my eyes," Mesdarro opened his radiant orbs wider, "violet, as the anomalous side of arcane forces.

"The origin of an eldritch is so rare, in that it can only occur when one wisp, who was linked to another wisp in life via their spiritroots from a shared lifetree, comes under certain shared conditions in the afterlife. What occurred after the Severance of your lifemate and progeny is that Sheyelle found itself drawn to the pull of the triplets in their mother's womb. When Sheyelle involuntarily interfused with the mother, it indubitably killed her. The child Adyssaira was born hunder-touched through Sheyelle's conjoining of its spirit.

"But you see, Carolelle's wisp was also being drawn this mother's womb the same. Once Sheyelle was absorbed instead, this altered the state of Carolelle, evolving into an eldritch wisp. The nature of these aberrations is quite complex. They lie dormant for years at a time, stagnant in a place of comfort for them in life, not far from their matriarch or patriarch's wisp.

"In such a case with Carolelle, Sheyelle had become Adyssaira's genesis wisp. It has taken Timmurian's wisp to further interfuse with the girl as a catalyst wisp to awaken Sheyelle from its dormant state inside her."

Sun was comprehending the sequence of relativities Mesdarro

was alluding to. With his eyes glossed over in a daze he barely registered what he was saying aloud. "Timmurian's sacrifice forced him to collide with Addy, initiating everything. By Sheyelle awakening, Carolelle is also …"

As his words trailed the unthinkable, Mesdarro added to the realized affirmation. "Awoken. Yes. In a sense, though be sure that they are not who they were in life. They are but a minute fraction of their essence. Wisps cannot speak, but there are residual memories that linger within them.

"Before I could see where the eldritch wisp of your progeny was, but could do nothing about it. However, Carolelle is now in a corporeal form. As an eldritch wisp it will no doubt find and cling to Adyssaira now that she is a mage."

"Why am I needed?" Sun feared he already surmised the possibilities without the need for such questions.

"Carolelle will now be anchored in permanent orbit around Sheyelle's active genesis wisp. Essentially, the eldritch facilitates deadly capabilities, acting as a defensive weapon. There is only one way to sever the orbit from the matriarch."

Me … His despondent frown said what Mesdarro avowed in follow, "The eldritch wisp must be redirected to orbit the patriarch."

Zsa'vauge grinned, showing his two fangs that all umbran were notorious for having. The umbran's grey skin, abysmal ebon eyes, claw-like black nails, and long black wig put him off as more of some demon from the hells than something that should be living amongst the mortals.

"You discovered a way to capture Carolelle by using me as a tool to do so," Sun said, more than inquired.

Zsa'vauge affirmed through the same fanged grin, "Precisely."

"But I am going to die during the process," again Sun was no longer asking, but telling himself.

"It will be better to show you," Zsa'vauge hissed while caressing Sun's knee as if it were a pet's neck.

"Why do you need Carolelle?" This time Sun did direct his demand to either or both of them.

The umbran and the hyperi looked at one another, obviously hesitant to reveal that part of the scheme at the time being.

"To Spellspire we go," Mesdarro answered ambiguously. "You will learn more than you wish to before we release you from your part to play in this matter."

Release me from my part to play … Sun narrowed his eyes to match the sneer that Zsa'vauge was casting over him. The umbran examined him with ogled fascination like an appetizer before a main meal. *My release is my death … What do they want with my Carolelle? How do I save her, if not myself?*

Sun tried to subtly avert his eyes to where he last spied Odysserae, but the girl and her father had vanished. He had no allies here, but perhaps there was still hope for her yet.

Four Dawning mages began making their way over to the small trolley cart as Mesdarro beckoned them to come. An exchange of gems was placed in each of their hands, and each man took a place on the corners of their ride. Zsa'vauge secured straps around Sun's lap while Mesdarro fastened his own, but the umbran did not place one on himself.

"You have been digging your whole life. Always seeking what was underneath it all," Zsa'vauge teased in his dramatic enunciations. "Well, it gets no deeper than this. Welcome."

Identical magemarks on the casters lit up green, and in an instant, the cart was moving forward at an impossible speed through the cavernscape. All appeared like a blur of blackness outside the trolley, with the occasional illumination afforded from clusters of red crystalytes that protruded from the rocky surfaces.

Even though Sun could not see the ground that the rail cart was connected to, he could tell by the pressure in his head and pull on his strapped-in body that they were gradually moving into an inverted position on the ceiling. Zsa'vauge remained unaffected, not budging in his seat.

They were moving too fast for Sun to truly appreciate or study the scope of the massive region of the underrealm. The trolley passed through a subterranean area so vast, it seemed like an entire countryside planted underneath the surface, passing over hordes of Neveril in every direction, with signs of house-like constructions throughout the expanse. He could only imagine it was somewhere beneath Old Elothia now, traveling toward Spellspire.

So, my introduction to it all is how it ends for me … Sun mulled on the ruthless irony, regarding his devious umbran captor who was gawking back at him with the same eerie impression he always had.

I did this to myself. Welcome to the Under, Sundorion.

ADYSSAIRA (VIII)

SISTER, SISTER, SISTER

Adyssaira wasn't sure how long she had been running. She only knew it had been days, maybe three now. The hours in hiding were bleeding together, tied up with the tedium of nothing to do and the delirium induced by lack of sleep and any real nourishment.

She was too scared to leave familiar grounds around the estates, but she could see that her family had sent out the Chandoss Guard to search for her. The Threnchmen were looking as well, though, so she didn't yet dare allow herself to be seen. She was able to access fresh water from the fountain atop Lovers' Labyrinth, but the only food she had put in her body was from stealing the stable boy Fabian's stale lunch the day before.

Being interfused with Timmurian's wisp had proven to be quite practical by allowing her the ability to navigate quickly and discreetly. She just needed to find her sisters and have time to think. Maybe they would have advice. Maybe they would flee with her. Maybe Odysserae would betray her and tell Valdean, and maybe Valaythea would write to Prince Izayus and have her executed for being a mage. Maybe she shouldn't trust anyone, she debated.

Adyssaira had quickly become acquainted with who her genesis wisp had been all along as well. Why she had not put two and two together long ago, she couldn't say. She felt quite imprudent. The hunder now had the capacity to introduce herself to Adyssaira after so many years in forced passivity. The wisp who had interfused with her in her mother's womb, consequently killing her, was none other than Sheyelle, the former lifemate of Sundorion, who had taken her own life.

And somehow Adyssaira could also feel that she had now awoken an inescapable draw from Sundorion's daughter, Carolelle, who had been cursed as an eldritch wisp for the past twenty years, ever since this horrendous coincidence had occurred. She had been idling in an invisible perpetual stasis near her gravesite until Sheyelle had been activated as Adyssaira's genesis wisp.

Adyssaira remembered the last passages she had read in *Of Wisps and Whispers,* all concerning the topic of the rare eldritch wisps. If more than one wisp was within the right distance of an eligible infant, the wisps then became bound to each other. While only one wisp could interfuse at a time with one so young, the other wisp would become stuck in a place of familiar comfort until the genesis wisp they were bound to was activated by the mage's catalyst wisp later in life.

Eldritch wisps were altered from their natural green glow to a deep violet radiance instead, and they were permanently cursed to orbit the individual that their bound genesis wisp was interfused with. Any further information Adyssaira could have learned of the eldritch wisps had not been made available to her. Those pages had been torn from the tome, as if Sundorion had purposely done so himself before gifting the book to Sashka.

Adyssaira knew that she couldn't stay home any longer and had to escape the wrath that Az'Dayne would decree upon her for her newly acquired spellpower. She couldn't just watch as Desdjlandar ordered his Threnchmen to annihilate her family and raze everything she knew to the ground either. She wanted to warn her father, but his whereabouts remained elusive. She had tried to get to her uncle, Nikayle, but she was too nervous to enter the palace after Desdjlandar had warned of what the servants and guardsmen actually were.

There was only one person she hoped she could trust who was sure to be free from any of the Chandoss Guard outside the palace. She had written a note apologizing to Fabian for sneaking off with his food and asked him to bring Luna to the top of Lovers' Labyrinth and not to tell a soul other than her two sisters, Valaythea and Odysserae. She almost included Emberalda as well but then recalled what she had felt from Timmurian's wisp, that her cousin had perished the same time as he had. The adrenaline and fear in her had thwarted the emotion of grieving from settling in just yet, but she knew the reality would impact her soon enough.

Adyssaira knew she risked much, but at such a point she was more afraid of starvation or of being found and detained against her will by the household guard than the unlikely possibility of any of her siblings actually deceiving her.

It was at the sun's high point on the cloudless day when Fabian appeared on the mazelike hilltop, at the fountain centerpiece that ornamented Lovers' Labyrinth. He smiled, genuinely relieved, when he saw Adyssaira, and released Luna off her leash.

Luna clumsily hobbled over in a gleeful manner, and Adyssaira embraced her in a hug, kissing all over her furry forehead.

"I am glad you are okay, my lady! I have lost much sleep," Fabian offered in a subservient tone.

"Thank you so much, Fabian!" Adyssaira did not try to suppress the biggest smile, feeling tears of joy forming in her bright green eyes. "My sisters?"

"Valaythea was with the prince. Prince Izayus. He is here, but in secret, it seems. I dared not go near."

Adyssaira thought a bit on the unanticipated issue of Izayus Az'Ampion's presence. *I know you are not leaving now. I cannot let the prince see me for what I am. I suppose this is goodbye, and I didn't even get to tell you.* Her transient moment of joy turned into bitter sadness thinking on Valaythea.

"Oddy is on her way here, which is why I came so fast. My lady, I must warn you, you need to leave with the Thrench," Fabian's tone was panicked and out of breath she just took note of. "You need to avoid both of your sisters and go now!"

You do not get to tell me what is best for me, and do not dare ever talk down about my sisters' intent! Her aristocratic upbringing forced a disdained glare over the servant boy the girls sometimes treated as an equal. *You forget your place,* she wanted to curse at him, but her eyes said enough. She was trained in conveying diplomacy through heated emotions from her father.

"You did well, Fabian. I vow on the Fives, one day I shall repay you." Adyssaira deeply hugged the teenage boy to dismiss him in a warm way. "I can start by doing this." She handed him a sealed letter. "It is signed by me to you, if anyone stops you. I am giving you permission to enter my room in the palace. Take anything of value you find in my jewelry box. It is yours now. You need to run far away, Fabian. The Thrench are here to kill us, not save us! Start running now!"

The stable boy looked entirely frightened, taking her warning seriously. He bowed to her and sprinted halfway down the way he came in before turning back around. "Forgive me Addy, you do not understand! Do not go near your sisters, either of them! You need to wait here. I will tell No-Name where you are! He will save you! It was arranged!"

"No, Fabian!" Adyssaira cried out against his ignorant betrayal. "Fabian! Run from the Thrench," she yelled at nothing as the boy was already long gone. "They are the enemy … Not my sisters."

She compulsively stroked Luna a while longer at the fountain base after Fabian left them alone. She nervously paced and passed the time waiting for Odysserae by praying to the Five and Five.

Fives, please protect me today and always. Please take me from this cursed place and deliver my sisters to safety with me. We will forever be your reverent servants. I pray to you for them, for they do not know the danger that I do. Please guide my sister Val to me today, find a way to bring her before me, so that I may save her, and perhaps she will find a way to save me too. Please grant Oddy the will to listen, to come away with me from this place. Please bring peace to Ember and Sashka … Fives, show me the path out of this life I live in now.

Adyssaira then recited individual elemental venerations to all ten deities in the Five and Five pantheon, one each for the Lord of the Land, the Lord of Fire, the Lord of the Sky, the Lord of Shadow, the Lord of the Sea, the Lady of the Dawning, the Lady of the Sunder, the Lady of the Reaping, the Lady of the Umbra, and the Lady of the Torrent.

She held Luna in her arms and uttered similar prayers over and again, whispering them aloud this time, hoping that if she repeated them, they would have a better chance of being heard. Finally, after the fourth or fifth time, she could see Odysserae entering the flower maze.

As soon as Odysserae reached the summit, Adyssaira evoked her spell from Timmurian, twirling in a rapid spin through the ground to reappear just in front of her sister on purpose to make a long story shorter concerning her present dilemma. Odysserae fell flat on her back in startlement, with terror etched all over her face.

"I know." Adyssaira sympathetically offered her sister a helping hand up, which she accepted. "I am scared too now. I am a mage." Her shoulders slumped defeatedly, and she began walking back toward the fountain, unable to meet Odysserae's judging gaze.

"What do I do, Oddy?"

Her deaf sister rushed up beside her and fretfully turned her around, communicating in Hands. *"Do not tell anyone. I can go tell Father. Or did you just tell him when you saw him? Or do you know yet?"*

What are you talking about Oddy? I haven't seen him to tell him, she was confused by her sister's last gestures.

Adyssaira respected her sister's impairment and translated into Hands as she spoke the actual words aloud. "No, do not tell Father! The Threnchmen already know. They are looking for me. Timmurian must be dead. I was beside No-Name when Timm's wisp ..." She couldn't stop the tears creeping into the corners of her eyes, interrupting her momentum.

"Oh, everything is wrong now! We are all in danger. The Threnchmen are here to steal me away and destroy our estates, palace and all. Our whole house bloodline! No one is safe! You have to get Val and find wherever Sashka has been. I feel something has happened to Ember too! We have to go!"

This time it was Odysserae's turn to start crying, as she hesitated before gesturing back. *"I killed Ember."*

"What?" Adyssaira refused to accept the horrific confession. She stepped back, up the steps that led to the top of the tiered fountain, all the way to the platform overlooking the well as an observation point.

Odysserae did not pursue her, staying at the bottom of the fountain's steps. *"They made me do it. I did not know,"* she gestured with free-flowing tears, mirroring Adyssaira with loud sobs now. *"They killed Taizsha. They made Timmurian kill himself. They made us watch,"* she admitted, shaking her head in denial. *"They took Sundorion away for the ritual, and no one knows where Sashka is."*

Adyssaira threw her hands in the air, not resorting to the sign language this time as she screamed, "Who? What is happening?"

Odysserae signed back, *"The Neveril elven beneath us, whom House Chandoss serves."*

Oh no, Desdjlandar was right. Oddy, not you too ... I didn't believe it. She shook her head so hard it made her dizzy. "Oddy, stop!" She rushed down the steps to push her sister back. "Stop it!" She then retreated back up to her safe position on the observation platform. "You are frightening me! I cannot hear this! I need your help." She decided to use Hands this time as she whimpered in hopelessness.

"Just go get Val, and let us leave."

"I want to leave too," Odysserae shot back with her frantic finger motions. *"They will not let me. They are making me become one of them – the shape-shifting qindrid. But I will get to speak and hear."*

She is lost. My sister is lost! Fives! She began to pray in her mind but changed her mind to voice it aloud. "Fives, I pray to you now more than ever, bestow on me true blindness and my sister's deafness, or safely take me far away now if you choose not to wake me."

As she dropped to her knees and closed her palms together, she felt the friendly licking of Luna's tongue on her leg. She had completely forgotten the little black tiger was even still there beside her.

Odysserae did not relent in her futile optimism. *"There is hope for you,"* she gestured in Hands. *"Since you are a Dawning mage, you can join me. They will accept you. You will not become transcended, like me, but they will hone your spells, and you will be treated like royalty by the Neveril. I have seen it."*

Adyssaira felt suddenly disoriented. The only spell she felt alive in her still was the vertigo in her woozy head. She considered that she might be delusional from the absence of true rest or any proper food. "I just want to leave this …"

"They just want you to do one thing to prove your loyalty," her sister still tried. *"You must lure your Thrench boy."*

"Lure No-Name?" Adyssaira asked in irritation.

"Did I hear my name?" The voice was all too familiar coming from the entrance to the flower maze. Desdjlandar began casually walking toward the two girls. "Or shall I say, my former lack of one?"

Something inside Adyssaira stirred with excitement at the sight of him, but it was coupled with the remembrance of why she feared him. She shouted his name in surprise with a mix of emotions. "Desdjlandar!"

He smiled, continuing to get closer. "My dear, I told you that the hunder-touched cannot hide from a trained hyperi. You can run and dig and jump." He paused for dramatization. "But I will find you always."

Her face flushed with anger, and she lost her fleeting sentiment of attraction toward him. "I told you, I do not want to go with you!"

"You want what your corrupt sister wants for you instead, then?" He pointed accusingly at Odysserae to condemn her. "Did she tell you yet?"

"Neither of you!" Adyssaira screamed at the top of her lungs, glaring down disgustedly at the two people she had once loved.

Her eyes spied Valaythea at the bottom of Lovers' Labyrinth. *She has the power of Prince Izayus on her side! She will know what to do!* Her thoughts raced with confidence to escape these nightmarish fates she had been cornered into. *My Five and Five, you listened! You brought her here to save me, didn't you?* "Val!" she called out as loudly as she could manage.

Adyssaira leaped down through the fountain's shallow water tiers to avoid Odysserae or Desdjlandar obstructing her path out, with little Luna ineffectually trying to keep up. She sprinted for the exit downhill as soon as her feet touched the grass.

"Wait, Adyssaira! She has the spellblade! Do not get near her!" Desdjlandar sternly warned.

Adyssaira spun back around to confront them both in a threatening stance. "Come any closer, either of you, and you will never find me again!"

But neither Odysserae nor Desdjlandar obeyed that caution, and the moment they took their first steps toward her, Adyssaira conjured her jump spell to place her halfway down the labyrinth. She kept shouting for Valaythea the whole way down as she used several spells to bypass the maze walls by magically digging underneath until she was standing in front of her savior.

"Val! I have something to show you, and so much to tell," Adyssaira gasped in panted breaths, holding on to both knees to regain air. But she could see something amiss in Valaythea's eyes. Her right eye was glowing green in a magic halo, in likeness to Adyssaira's own when casting a spell, and she had their Chandoss Spellblade readied in her hand to strike.

But I prayed for you to save me, she thought in confusion. "Sister?"

For some reason, she was still in denial about the danger even when Valaythea pushed the glass blade through her belly, and she felt her life being stripped from her body.

VALAYTHEA (VIII)

OF WISPS AND WHISPERS

(ONE HOUR EARLIER)

"Are you sure you want it to end this way? There could still be something arranged for you," the prince vainly tried again, offering disregarded alternatives for Nikayle to strongly reconsider. "I do not see why Coldborn would allow his most valued informant to just give up and die."

Hearing Izayus's voice again somehow roused her with a returned virginal feeling of hopeful security and hopeless romance. She had missed him but didn't know why, because she had been so ready to be permanently rid of him just one month ago, when she had been in his company last. She was undeniably attracted to him again but didn't know why, because she had been so thoroughly repulsed by his presence. But here he was in the flesh, as flawless as she remembered, humbly arguing with Nikayle in the palace stores beneath the old armory basement, which led to the stables outside.

The two of them and Valaythea had been at a stymied debate for a quarter hour and were getting nowhere, despite time being of critical essence. They now had a Thrench bloodguard in their midst, who stared at them as if their fates had been predetermined.

"I have made up my mind," Nikayle reiterated. "Besides, it is not up to you or me. Ask him." He turned to face Thoravus in their small, private huddle, fully armed and armored as if prepped for a war on their doorstep. "Is there a better alternative for me in all of this?" Nikayle asked for an answer he seemed to know would inevitably not be in his favor.

Valaythea was still not used to seeing Nikayle standing, free of the falsely advertised crippled state she had known him to be in for years.

"All the Neveril and neverborne must die. That was the arrangement," the Thrench bloodguard confirmed coldly in his foreign accent. "If he were to live, the umbran who turned him could find him."

"I accepted this some time ago," her father conceded.

"You will be given a clean death. And the last death, after we dispose of the Guard and others," Thoravus promised, as if his words were supposed to make anyone feel better about it. "I will even do it myself. You can choose any place in your home you wish to be when you meet your gods."

"My kind do not get to meet any gods," Nikayle reminded the stipulation of being qindrid. "We will discuss that later. Not in front of her."

There was a pause for awkward sympathies toward her father. Valaythea took the permitted moment to throw her arms around him and squeeze him tight, not caring if they were running out of time. She knew this was the last instance she would get to do it.

"You told me you were clever, and that you would never stop protecting me," she whispered into his ear, hoping only he could hear. *"Do not do this."*

"I will always protect you," he whispered back and slyly grinned, seemingly unaffected about the inescapable execution that awaited him. *"Do you still trust me?"*

It was all happening far too fast for Valaythea to truly comprehend how drastically the trajectory of her destiny was changing from what she had accepted and been trained for her entire life. She was no warrior, and no magic sword that had been cursed down to her due to her ancestral bloodline could convince her otherwise.

"Valaythea, are you ready?" Prince Izayus asked.

No, not at all. Her face said it all. She couldn't take her gloomy eyes off of her father. *I need more time ...*

Izayus ignored the pessimistic semblance and attempted to assuage her misgivings. "Adyssaira will be safe with them. You will meet again. Odysserae will not be harmed, only detained, if she does not comply. She will be with your sister."

You don't know Oddy. She glanced doubtful at her father. *She won't be detained either.*

Izayus continued to try to convince her. "Nikayle has vouched for Sashka's safety as well, and it has been taken care of. And Emberalda is set to come with us. We just need to locate her. Thoravus, please confirm."

"When I see Oddy, I will ask her to find Ember. I know where she is. She is coming with you," Nikayle confidently assured. "Barturon will take care of her when you reach the Silverlakes."

"Desdjlandar's command is that none of the girls will be harmed. All is in place now," Thoravus reconfirmed.

"I am ready," Valaythea lied aloud to herself for the sake of the others. "I just have to get the sword."

"Stay clear of Inkomway," Thoravus warned. The Reaping mage had stayed behind while the others were preparing for an onslaught on the Thrench ships docked down the northeast shores of Lake Chandoss. He grabbed her arm far too hard within the grip of his gauntlet. "I have heard what the spellblades can do." It sounded more like a threatening warning than friendly advice.

Nikayle elaborated to explain what she was already educated in. "Just do not draw the weapon near the mage. You are too novice as its wielder. It will control you. You should make no use of it anytime soon, until well after you reach the archon of the Silverlakes and are trained by Haelyn and Barturon."

Valaythea still felt she was in the dark on too many variables for what could go wrong. Before she committed to anything, she found it in her will to coerce her submissive tendencies to the side as she addressed the prince. "I just do not understand how we are supposed to get there with just you and me. How many leagues is it? It will take pents, even on swift horseback. And the escort you brought with you ..." She mused over the futility of trying to escape them. *I know they are neverborne ... Or if not qindrid, then they are at least in the Umbran Pledge to keep you under a close eye.* "You are the Prince of Az'Dayne. They will not just let you out of their sight."

Izayus grimaced and nodded, seemingly mindful of that pertinent fact. "They will not survive past the hour."

Thoravus followed his statement. "The blood of your escort in gets spilled first."

Izayus nudged her with a sense of urgency in his countenance to move things along. "Do you still need more details?"

"It will not just be you and Izayus," her father took the time to ease her obstinate worriment. "We have Silverback agents with your horses in place at the stables. They will be your protection out of Az'Dayne to the Silverlakes."

"No more questions. This begins now," Thoravus concluded, lifting his large tower shield from the floor to leave the huddle and bring the plot to action.

Izayus put his hand on Valaythea's lower back with a soft lover's touch. "Grab the spellblade, and find me at the stables," he instructed her.

They parted ways to do their part in the impending scheme. Spiritlessly, and with a looming fit of anxiety under her skin, Valaythea attempted to do the same.

Upon separating from the group, she glanced back to catch only her father still in the hall when Odysserae appeared flustered and in a fit. Valaythea did not catch what it was that her sister was hammering away in Hands, but whatever she conveyed it outraged Nikayle to new ends she had never witnessed before.

Nikayle erupted into á violent outburst. "What?"" he challenged Odysserae as he snatched her by the back of the neck like a child about to receive the worst flogging that a father's provoked wrath could deliver. When they disappeared around the corner from her line of sight, Valaythea instinctively spun to go and inspect the cause for the ire, but her impulses told her otherwise.

She then dashed straight to her bedchamber, where she had last placed the Chandoss Spellblade. Its perch on the mantel in the solarium was a thing of the past. The sword was destined to be at her side for the remainder of her days, however shortened they may have become now.

When she got to her room, she shut the door for a brief respite of privacy before embarking on a life on the run.

Valaythea found the sheathed sword out of the corner of her eye, almost too afraid to look at it as it sprawled across her clothes chest. She snatched the magic weapon up by its bone scabbard and went to stand in front of the full-length floor mirror to close her eyes and manage her irregular breathing with a meditation practice.

When she opened them, she saw the shell of a tortured soul trapped inside the body of what she used to think was a beautiful young woman. Her body was still shapely and athletic, petite in stature, and her lush red hair ran down over her shoulders in the front and down to the middle of her back. Her amber eyes were focused but nervous, perpetually unsure of anything anymore. And her face, she did not find it vain to acknowledge that she was pretty, but there were now bags under her eyes from lack of sleep.

My eyes, she mused, feeling a bit self-conscious about her looks now. *No, not both my eyes, but just this one.* Valaythea stepped closer to the mirror, inspecting her right eye, which felt like something was in it. *There is something there.*

And suddenly it flashed green as a magic halo formed around her one iris. She did not understand what had prompted it to do so until she discovered her right hand involuntarily holding the hilt of the spellblade now instead of the scabbard.

No, I do not want to wield you, she asserted in her mind. The sentient weapon clearly had a level of persuasion dominating her will. The trapped entities inside the sword were stronger than she was, just as she had been warned. Valaythea hurried to strap the bone scabbard to her belt, but as she finished, she could sense its power numbing her control, and she somehow knew how.

She could sense something. *Mages ... two of them nearby.* She recalled Thoravus mentioning the Reaping mage Inkomway the Skycaller. But for the life of her, she could not fathom who else could be a mage within the perimeter of the estates, unless another of the Oriyan mages had stayed behind.

The sentient sword was pleading to her in several voices to take hold of its hilt and unsheathe it just for a moment. Just for a moment—there could be no harm in that. It seemed logically pointless, yet somehow a great idea all the same. Before Valaythea knew it, her hand was already on the elvan-bone hilt of the sword, slowly sliding it free of its case.

Wait! My sister is hunder-touched ... Addy!

The moment its tip touched the air, she lost control as the spellblade possessed her with a hungry purpose of its own to seek and slay the mages nearby before allowing Valaythea to do anything else.

* * * * *

Stop it! Valaythea tried to stop her feet from moving forward but could not. *Addy, run!* She tried to scream, but her mouth never budged. *Wait!*

The sentient sword in possession of her was not listening. It was in control now, as it had been for the past half hour, since she had first held it.

Please! Addy, go! She futilely pleaded as she watched herself going through motions against her own accord.

"Val! I have something to show you, and so much to tell." Adyssaira stood not far in front of her now. She was obviously out of breath, hunched over and grasping her knees as she panted to recover from whatever she was running from. But she was running from the wrong people.

Valaythea wanted to tell her that the only person she needed to run from was her. *No!* she implored again, trapped as a prisoner inside her mind, even as she watched her hand wield the spellblade with intent to kill.

"Sister?" Adyssaira looked so sad and so confused in her eyes when it happened, in her innocent bright green eyes with glowing halos around them.

Valaythea felt no resistance as the green fiery end of the glass blade impaled Adyssaira's stomach and exited through her back. Her sister's flesh may as well have been air.

She knew Adyssaira was dead the moment the blade went in, and she could do nothing to stop the diabolical weapon from continuing what it had started. The sword wasn't just intent on killing a mage; it was yearning to consume something more. It was stealing something inside her sister.

The magemarks on Adyssaira's chest flared up green, and the magic flowed out of them into their new home, becoming engraved with a dual glyph representing the Dawning season on the surface of the blade. It was as if Valaythea could feel exactly what powers were within the fresh rune and how to summon them by name—both powers intertwined with her sister's name.

Somehow she even knew the identities of the wisps that granted the magic sword the spells absorbed from Adyssaira. *Timmurian.* Valaythea could not believe it but knew the tairan spell for the power he afforded her somehow. The other essence, Sheyelle, was someone at first unfamiliar, but it came to her — the wisp that killed her mother and made Addy hunder-touched and Oddy deaf.

A shrieking wail came from behind. When Valaythea turned to

see who it was, she saw Odysserae running down to the entrance of the flower maze to assess the horrific reality for herself. Valaythea turned. She was able to turn again. The blade was releasing its control over her.

"Adyssaira!" Desdjlandar shouted in horrified disbelief, trailing on Odysserae's heels. "Why?" His face spelled confusion, but his eyes cast fury.

"Stop! Stop!" Valaythea found her voice again and immediately retracted the glass blade from Adyssaira's limp form, which had fallen against her. "No!" she cried when her sister's lifeless body slid into a curled position at her feet. "No, this isn't real! But I didn't!" She defied the nightmarish reality settling in.

"Kinslayer!" Desdjlandar accused her. "Murderer!" he titled her with spite on his tongue. "She was trying to save you!" He then pointed to Odysserae and back to Valaythea. "To save you both!"

"The sword! The spellblade! I don't want this!" Valaythea tried to drop the evil weapon, but it would not allow her grip to release it. She screamed at the top of her lungs to nothing in particular, aimed at the cruel heavens above. "Take it back! Addy, no!" She could feel herself fast becoming hysterical.

"You will die for this," Desdjlandar promised her with a vengeful tone. "Your whole cursed house will die for this!"

The hyperi boy stormed off down the hill of Lovers' Labyrinth, looking back at the girls as if they were fiends conjured from the deepest parts of all the hells. "Thoravus!" Desdjlandar called to his personal bloodguard as he disappeared over the brow.

"I didn't mean to!" Valaythea burst into hyperventilating sobs. "I love you! Come back," she whispered to Adyssaira's dead body while cradling her. "Come back! Come back! Come back! Come back ... Come back ... Come back," she repeated desperately over and over.

She caught a glimpse in her peripheral vision of Odysserae facing off against her. She had a rope dart readied in her stance, seeming ready to end Valaythea's life with it.

Valaythea did not care if Odysserae truly meant to follow through with harming her or not. She could not shake her indifference to anything other than bringing Adyssaira back to life. Her own life meant nothing now. "Oddy, tell her I did not mean to. Tell her." She spoke so softly, it was barely an audible whisper. Her words were for Odysserae, but she said them directly into Adyssaira's ear with her lips pressed against her cold face. "I love her. I am so sorry!"

Her own face felt tight, as if her skin were warping in. She couldn't stop bawling and could hardly understand her own words as she tried to explain between trembling heaves of air. "It's … that … Psage … Omen … fr–from … Suntide." Valaythea recalled using the seerstone Sundorion had given her and what the soothsayer had foretold from her vision just before the mystical stone had taken its toll and ended her life. "You remember … what she said … would happen to us … that … she saw … in the seer … the seerstone?"

Valaythea finally tried to stand, unable to look at Adyssaira in such an expired state any longer. Her knees quaked with weakness, scarcely able to manage lifting her back up. "I was trying to save her also … To save … you too," she stuttered in her vehement whimpering in apology to Odysserae.

Valaythea was not expecting the fine rope dart that was thrown next. Odysserae was dexterously quick with it. Whether her sister's aim was accurate or not, however, did not matter. The spellblade, still in Valaythea's hand, sensed the danger and repossessed her body, deftly parrying the dart in midair, then followed by slashing through the rope, and sending the sharp head into a rosebush nearby. Before Valaythea could register what was transpiring, she noticed Odysserae already forced onto her back. The sword had taken over Valaythea's arms to use the blunt of the blade to sweep her sister helplessly down to the ground.

"No! She is my sister!" Valaythea managed to take control again, retracting the spellblade away from killing Odysserae in the same way as it had Adyssaira. She could see the fear and absolute hate in her sister's face and could not blame her.

"She is a Chandoss, like your wielder now." Valaythea found the courage to command the sentient sword. "Just as your wielder before, and your maker before him! You will not harm her!"

All went silent between the two living triplets for a moment. All was quiet until their concentration in processing the barbarous scenario was broken by the sound of an affectionate tongue against flesh beside them. Both sisters looked to find little Luna licking Adyssaira's cheek and trilling in confusion as to why her mistress would not wake up. This time, it was Odysserae's turn to relent and break down in tears, succumbing to defeat as she curled up to hug their dead sister in a sobbing ball of sorrow.

Valaythea could now only hear the unique whispering hum of the magical green fire that traced the edge of the spellblade. The wraithlike murmur haunted as a fusion of wind and breathing from several trapped souls; unlike anything remotely natural from the world of the living. So long as the sword was unsheathed, she took note that the green, shifting glow remained intact.

Valaythea's tears were far from dry, and her throat was not done convulsing with choking, and she felt herself forgetting the ability to blink. She just stared motionlessly at the macabre scene, as if she had stepped into a dreamscape where nightmares dwelled and reality was not a thing.

"Valaythea!"

The sound of her own name broke her grief-induced musing. It was Desdjlandar coming back up the hill of the flower garden with armored backup in tow. "That is her! Kill her!"

"That is not what we discussed," Thoravus Hlelvig, beside him, reminded him.

"That is my order! You are my bloodguard! Do as I command!" Desdjlandar had evolved into a bloodthirsty vigilante of justice in Adyssaira's honor.

Thoravus, an advocate of the sisters' best interests just one hour prior, turned toward Valaythea with a broadsword readied and his shield raised. "Come, girl! I must obey," the heavily armored Threnchman hollered. "I will give you a mercy. Stay just so."

The sentient blade in her grip coerced her focus to take notice of someone else precedent, just behind the brawny bloodguard. *The Reaping mage … Inkomway the Skycaller.* As little as she had been educated on the matter, she was somehow aware that Reaping mages could not wield their spellpower in the Dawning season. The competent Oriyan mage was just a man—just an unarmored man.

If Valaythea were to have it her way, she was ready to surrender to the mercy of a quick sword to the back of her neck, as promised by Thoravus. But the Chandoss Spellblade was not allowing such a possibility. She felt her entire body go numb once more and could see the flash in her right eye as the magic halo formed over it. The sentient sword was telling her to touch the single rune on its glass blade, the double Dawning glyph that had appeared after she had taken Adyssaira's life. The spellblade was psionically threatening that it would take possession again to conjure her sister's name to mind if Valaythea did not reach out to touch the glyph.

Her executioners were getting closer. Desdjlandar joined in bravely beside Inkomway, treating her as if she were some indomitable champion they had to devise an attack plan for.

"Adyssaira," she whispered, but the spellblade was not pleased, and she winced in pain the moment she finished her sister's name. *Adyssaira, I said.* She flinched again from the shooting agony in her sword arm. Thoravus was only a half leap away from her when it all came to her, and she said it right this time—not as a whisper aloud, not as a passing thought either, but as the concentrated invocation of the keyword to conjure a spell.

ADYSSAIRA.

Valaythea saw her body spin in a blurring cyclone through the ground beneath her, near instantly appearing back out of it in an entirely new location, directly behind Inkomway. With the spellblade controlling her movements, she watched the glass weapon plunge into his spine and through his heart from behind. She could feel his magic being stolen by her sword. She could feel the exact details of the newly acquired spell and could see the white Reaping glyph of Inkomway etching itself into the glass blade.

ADYSSAIRA.

She invoked her sister's name again and glanced at the glyph glowing before the dig spell from Timmurian's wisp brought her back underground and out the other side at the entrance of Lovers' Labyrinth.

Thoravus stopped his advance and looked about, confused, to survey what had just occurred, taking several seconds before even realizing that the renowned mage, Inkomway the Skycaller, had died just that quickly and so easily. Even Desdjlandar, with all his boasting of arcane education, seemed perplexed.

"I am sorry," Valaythea submitted meekly to them, surprised she was even able to talk again.

She felt her knees buckle to offer them her life in trade for the murders she was committing, but the Chandoss Spellblade was not having it. The magic of the sword's possession strengthened her legs, and she saw her body turn to sprint up the hill through the flower maze. She had left Odysserae and Luna, both curled up next to Adyssaira's poor corpse.

Valaythea reached the top of the hill and took a defensive stance near the fountain. She wasn't even remotely out of breath and could not fathom how. Thoravus, in all his armor, was not far behind as he apprehensively closed in.

She could not see the bloodguard's face, veiled by his Starfell helm. A starfell-steel broadsword and shield filled his hands as well. This was the elite of the Thrench, not a normal man. A normal man might not have thought it wise to contend with a spellblade in combat. A normal man would likely have fled after seeing a mage as powerful as Inkomway slain in such a manner. But Threnchmen were legendary fighters. They lived for their Uedonvyor, their life's destiny, to achieve the most glorious and worthiest death possible. To receive death from an actual spellblade warrior was a great honor for any of them.

Valaythea knew she was no warrior. Her spellblade ancestors were. Barturon and Athan were. *I do not want this,* she pleaded subconsciously to the sword, but it did not matter. The Chandoss Spellblade would not condone defeat.

The epiphany of another name of power came to her mind. Her uncle had told her it in the training studio the day she had regained her memories after performing the fire dances. *Saravelle,* she recalled. She had dismissed it then, not wanting to know the names of murdered mages, but the name of the dead Umbra mage the spellblade had no doubt killed and stolen a spell from seemed more pertinent than ever now.

SARAVELLE.

She called it to mind without even realizing she had. The formerly white oval of a blank rune space on the glass blade changed to the glyph of the Umbra season and fired up green with power.

Valaythea watched seven copies of her likeness walk out of her body. The illusions encircled her single aggressor, and she witnessed her own body fading into invisibility in that same moment.

It would have been the perfect opportunity to flee, but the Chandoss Spellblade dominated her will and prevented her from doing anything of her own accord.

Thoravus slammed his huge tower shield into one of the incorporeal illusions, with surprising speed for a man his size, forcing the simulacrum to blink rapidly in and out of existence, and his sword quickly finished what his shield had started. The remainder of the shadow phantoms assaulted the bloodguard on all sides, but the Thrench champion dispatched the clone images in lethally efficient clockwork.

Valaythea saw her body blinking back into place, visible for Thoravus to see. She knelt down on one knee, again astonished that the spellblade was even allowing her temporary decisions. She wanted it to end, and end quickly. The entire day was not real, and if it was, she would rather be dead than go on to live through the aftermath.

Prince Izayus is still waiting. It wasn't until Thoravus was upon her, with his sword held high to thrust down with a life-ending strike, that she changed her mind. She saw the glare from her right eye flash again when her sword controlled her free hand to touch the newest glyph, gained from Inkomway's quick death.

INKOMWAY. The Reaping glyph was highlighted in green on the glass blade, and as she rose up to meet the blade of Thoravus, her own sword struck his, and a massive surge of wind flung the sword from his grip and lifted the heavy man into the air to heave him several paces back and plant him hard on his back.

INKOMWAY. The power word of the Reaping mage was invoked again by her own command, but her body was the spellblade's to manipulate. Valaythea's body turned and arced her spellblade in a parallel slash from the ground, hurling another wind blast to crash against Thoravus's shield, flinging it from his arm which now appeared broken.

Valaythea felt taxed with fatigue and a nerve-jolting pain in a form of empathy from the sentient sword when she called upon Inkomway's name for the second time in a row. She was naïve to the rules of invoking its spellpower, but her instinct to survive conquered all sensations of anguish in the fight-or-die moment.

The emerald pommel radiated bright as the essence of Valaythea's great ancestor, Aemenus, the original owner and forger of the blade, took over her now.

Thoravus, injured or not, was still in the fight. With his sword arm still strong, he quickly retrieved his weapon to meet her blade to blade.

Valaythea held the spellblade in both hands, with a parry so powerful, she wasn't sure how her meager one hundred pounds could muster the might to offset the soldier over twice her weight.

She struck again and again with both hands, far faster than the well-trained killer, gaining momentum on off-balancing him.

Suddenly she could feel the shift, and the swirl of light in the emerald at the bottom of her sword acted like some volatile phylactery ready to burst. The martial abilities of her lethal great-grandfather Nikayle the Firstnamed, the last wielder of the spellblade, came over her to combat her foe.

Valaythea now swung her sword with incredibly swift one-armed blows. Most were feints, but it only took less than half a minute to cripple the bloodguard with a hamstring cut when she tumbled in a roll behind him.

But Thoravus was a tenacious brute. He advanced with a limp to default on his word to give her any mercy. He was almost on her when she noticed the glyph with the wind blast spell on her sword's transparent blade was still clear in color of the glass instead of white, as it was before she had cast the Reaping mage's power.

INKOMWAY.

She conjured it anyway and braced for the anticipated pain and drowsy wave that followed. Inkomway's glyph and the emerald with the readied strength of Aemenus stored to unleash radiated bright green, and the Chandoss Spellblade powered straight into the Thoravus's face. His Starfell helm ejected from his head, leaving him with a bloody broken nose and disoriented stance.

He bellowed in pain and hit both knees in defeat.

Valaythea could feel again. The spellblade was releasing its possession over her arms and legs to gradually allow her full control once more. She only took a breath to blink and scan her surroundings. She could have used the opportunity to flee back down the maze, but she was not ready to confront her sisters again—both the living and the dead. Valaythea retreated up the steps to the top of the fountain for the tallest vantage to survey the estates from ahigh.

When she reached it, she saw him. *Izayus.* She could see the stables clearly. Fabian, the stable boy, and several men atop her family's horses, with Izayus and her own horse, saddled to leave. The prince was anxiously inspecting every direction, looking for someone. *Me.*

Valaythea looked at the Dawning glyph attained after taking her sister's life, and it was clearly two runes, one over the other. The spellblade had a way of subconsciously conveying to her what to do. She touched the bottom fragment of Adyssaira's double glyph and saw the magic within ignite with green fire.

Her feet left the platform atop the fountain, and she found herself soaring in a supernatural leap through the air away from the Lovers' Labyrinth.

ADYSSAIRA.

She called her sister's name until the sword could no longer expend any more power, until her last leap took her in an impossible jump to land beside Izayus, on her horse, which would take her far from this hell she used to know as home.

The prince did not say anything to her. He saw the fear in her face and the tears still steady in her eyes, and that was all he needed. He urged the Silverback agents into motion to lead the way, and together he and Valaythea rode their horses deeper into the nightmare she would never wake from.

SCARLESS (X)

BLOOD TRADE

Finally she could see the high walls of the Square. Rich's Rich Hall, a warehouse turned gambler's hub, was the last commercial establishment in Copper's Side before anyone could reach her designated corner of the city, if avoiding the North Docks and the entrance from Centron Hills.

The street that led straight to the gated hold had been renamed Blue Carpet Lane due to the Blue Blades' use of the avenue years ago for their main assault to take over the former North Garrison, sanctioned by the council seats of Goldgarden. At that time, there had been heavy hearsay about the reputation of the city guard manning the North Garrison. Allegedly, they had become quite corrupt, practically branded cutthroats wearing the colors of the Goldguardians, extorting innocent citizens and operating a monopoly on the surrounding districts through intimidation by false representation of the law.

Zahnastaazjah and her local ruthless gang, the Blue Blades, had been granted their first sanctioned commission from the secret rulers of Goldgarden shortly thereafter. It had also been her first time to meet the elder council leaders from that age who were still present—Baldric Whereway, on the Seat of the Blue, Arro Gemenis, on the Seat of the Gold, and even Serafinelan, on the Seat of the White.

And Usurp. She drifted in the memories of her longtime partner in crime from her earliest days in the diverse city-nation. *As it was to be, old friend. Or were we ever even friends? Find peace if you can, where I never will. I don't believe peace was meant for our kind in life.*

Zahnastaazjah had never been one for inherent sympathy, due to her upbringing and history, and as such, the ephemeral emotion played out its short-lived course. After the death of her lifemate, Drevlijhun, the impact of loss had dwindled down to a waning numbness in her heart, barely a throb to remind her that she was still tainted by repressed morality somewhere deep inside her. She hadn't even shed a tear when hearing about the death of her father, or of her brothers, Kavajin and Jhukamwi, years before him. With all that she had suffered through, she especially wasn't expecting to lose any sleep over Usurp.

Why, then, was the betrayal by Symbelle upsetting her so much? Zahnastaazjah had experienced similar duplicities throughout her life, especially in her recent years as the guildmother of a massive crime syndicate full of impermanent members who chased coin and thrills over honor. The hyperi girl had somehow found a way to strike a spark in her hunder that not even Xalo could manage.

"Scarless!" She heard her street name shouted by a familiar voice. Zahnastaazjah had been staring up at the morning sky rather than the cobbles of the road, she realized. Being so close to the Square again after such a long night, and on not a single slip of sleep, was forcing her concentration to wearily glide into a reverie in the middle of her jog beside her companions.

She glanced around at Xalo, Uubakrath, and Atrick running beside her, but she knew it had been none of them. *Atrick? When did you get here?* Zahnastaazjah had almost forgotten in her haggard state when they rendezvoused with the man after she had sent him to Dreamer's View across Garden's Bridge. *Oh, yes, we waited at the …* She recalled it but dismissed expending any energy on the irrelevant point. She knew Xalo and Atrick were barely keeping up with her and Uubakrath's tireless pace. Their Terollar impower of regeneration was the only thing keeping them going. She wasn't sure what supernatural ability was keeping the two humans in the race to get home other than sheer discipline of mind over body, but she respected them more for it.

"Scarless! Scarless!" The shouts came again. It was Devonduer, of course, running up from the east gate of Scarless Square to greet them.

"Mages. Too many," Xalo warned between heavy breaths before Devonduer could speak first when he caught up to them. Zahnastaazjah was well aware of Xalo's spellblade perk of being able to sense the presence of magic users within a vast radius. "Unless you want a fight we cannot win, I have to walk elsewhere, and now."

Long fucking day. Please, no more today, she groaned inside her head, having no possible notion of why multiple mages might have invaded her urban territory.

As hoped, the frantic chamberlain explained to settle nerves. "They do not want to fight! It is Shypriss Sol-War and her Sunder mages."

"You don't want me near here. The sword's pull is too strong," Xalo urgently persisted.

Zahnastaazjah looked past Devonduer, scanning over what she was now close enough to, that she could gander at with her own eyes. There were several robed individuals standing across from one another lining a path inside the entrance, past the open portcullis. "Go where you need," she told Xalo with a nod. "We are done with bloodshed."

Uubakrath put his bow around his shoulder, and Atrick took his hand off his sword hilt. Xalo bowed and grudgingly walked off the street to lean against a dilapidated home, while Zahnastaazjah and the small group commenced toward the gate.

Once inside, Zahnastaazjah halted to assess just how many mages had trespassed and what her people were doing about it. The two hundred-something Stormtrees in the Yard seemed unsure but bolstered by the sight of their guildmother. Several fervent shouts of "Guildmother!" and "Scarless!" ensued, followed by the metallic clang of weapons being drawn.

Thirty mages, she counted, men and women. They dropped their robes to the ground and stood in a nondefensive stance, with their arms held high and facing one another. Simultaneously, the same arcanic imprints, in different locations on their bodies, lit up green, and an arc of fire was released from their palms to meet another's directly in front of them, creating a makeshift covered pathway formed by magic fire. Being that the Sunder season was pending soon, these fire mages had the ability to conjure a capacity of their spellpower in the Dawning as their primer season.

Her men against over a score of Sunder mages trained by Shypriss Sol-War did not seem like good odds, even though the Stormtrees in the Yard outnumbered them seven to one at that moment. "We are done with bloodshed! You will all stand down!" she bellowed to her guild, and then spoke to no mage in particular. "What is the meaning of this intrusion?"

The two mages at the end of the pathway, the closest to her keep, turned to make another arc, which traced the door, seemingly harmless, having no burning effect on the wood around it.

Shypriss is inside. Zahnastaazjah took the hint and felt confident that if the dangerous fire mage wanted her dead, it would already have happened. She led the way with Uubakrath, Atrick, and Devonduer trailing.

As expected, she found Shypriss in the war chamber, comfortably seated in Zahnastaazjah's chair at the head of the table.

"Zahnastaazjah!" The complacent Psage woman feigned surprise. "You live?"

"Unfortunately for you," Zahnastaazjah sneered, not hiding her annoyance, contemplating the most likely reasons for her visit. "Were you a part of this? Symbelle's betrayal?"

Shypriss didn't even have the courtesy to get up for a proper greeting. "Symbelle and Pyphan were agents of the Oathemic Cabal. They are no longer." She clarified the obvious.

"Because they are dead. We killed them," Zahnastaazjah bluntly admitted to the archmage, with no fear of consequence.

Shypriss just smiled smugly and said, "I will not be long," shifting on to business. "My presence will breed suspicion. I am here to broker a blood trade."

"Maybe you didn't hear me outside." Zahnastaazjah slammed her bloodrime spear on the table so fast it made Uubakrath draw his bow, with a readied arrow aimed to kill Shypriss in a second. "I made it rather clear. I am done with bloo—"

"You are far from done spilling blood, Crime Queen," Shypriss interrupted. "Let us have the room. You and me."

Zahnastaazjah nodded her approval to motion Atrick and Devonduer out of the chamber, and then she spoke only to Uubakrath in their native Terollar tongue. *"If I am not out in five minutes, get Xalo and start killing mages."*

Uubakrath bowed his concurrence and left the two leaders to it, shutting the door behind him.

Shypriss then got up from the seat and offered it to her as she moved around to the side of the table where Zahnastaazjah stood. They traded places at the war table, but Zahnastaazjah did not take her seat.

"The blood trade," Shypriss continued. "I would like you to kill my mages."

I did not see that coming. "You couldn't have told me that a few seconds ago? My Stormtrees are more than willing. And my man has room for several more marks on his blade." Zahnastaazjah implied Xalo's sword.

"Not these mages," Shypriss said. "Only the Dawning mages under my care that now reside in my district. They will be down for Transbernation soon. This is when you must do it. You know what that is, do you not?"

Zahnastaazjah had been around enough years to know many things concerning magic in the realm. If anyone knew a thing about mages, they had heard of Transbernation. "Your kind's fancy term for magic hibernation. The Dawners have to sleep after their season, throughout the coming Sunder."

Shypriss nodded. "That is in ten days."

"Eleven," Zahnastaazjah corrected her, "counting the furrow."

There was an uncomfortable moment of long silence between them, and Zahnastaazjah could not shake the semblance of palpable loathing that she could feel staining her face.

"You look at me as if I am the enemy," Shypriss said with an unperturbed grin.

Because the more I think about it, the more you remind me of her. Zahnastaazjah mused on the image of Symbelle again, as much as she tried not to. "The Oathemic Cabal sent agents to get me to openly massacre the Boarneck Company and burn their Monodrome to the ground on the busiest night of the cycle for every visitor in the city to see," she stated with a bitter taste on her tongue. "You want me and my guild to murder sleeping mages. You are both making me a public enemy on all sides. The Seven Seats will remove me and have my head before the next Conclave."

"The Seven Seats is removing you, but we do not want your head." Shypriss continued with revelations Zahnastaazjah was not prepared to concede to. "We want you to take another."

"I am being removed?"

"We want you to kill Amethyst as well." Shypriss had finally answered with something Zahnastaazjah was keen to commit to. "The Goldgarden council is greatly changing the way they do things. I will not have a place either."

No Seat of the Grey or Green? What is your motive, Shypriss? You are always five steps ahead in the game. "Why should I do all of this?" Zahnastaazjah inquired.

Shypriss went to open the door of the war chamber. Just beyond it, awaiting her signal, were two other mages, who escorted in a figure with familiar appeal. The former elvan woman had grey skin, all-black eyes, elongated ears that angled outward from her head, and long black nails. She was hairless, like the male one Zahnastaazjah had disposed of in the tanner's warehouse in Bridgeville just yesterday. *The other Neveril umbran … the lifemate of the other who was making qindrid in the city.*

"I found someone you are looking for. I have already asked all that I can. She won't break. They never do," Shypriss stated, and she pushed the bound umbran to bend over the table in a helpless position of submission. "Your turn to try. Or kill her. Our last Conclave to attend will not be long into the Sunder. Bring her head, and they will let you take the betrayer's as well. Amethyst dies by your hand at the meet."

"I am assuming you are not giving me a choice in this matter," Zahnastaazjah said to Shypriss, but she kept her curious gaze on the umbran, already wondering how to go about keeping her. "What will be my place in the city after this is done?"

"You will be taking a necessary recess from Goldgarden this new season. Details are to be given at the Conclave," Shypriss vaguely explained, just enough to give absolutely no real answers at all. "I only know this because it was my idea for us both to take our leave."

"Well, then." Zahnastaazjah opened her right hand to summon her bloodrime spear back to her firm grip, then slammed the butt of it on the floor. "It seems you are done here, Shypriss. I will take it from here. You can excuse yourself. I am sure you will be in touch."

"I will," the Psage mage affirmed as Zahnastaazjah approached the exit of the chamber. She intended to gesture them out, to have them leave the Square to her guild members.

Shypriss let Zahnastaazjah open the door before she added an implausible unforeseen condition. "But one other stipulation: you cannot ever again lay a vindictive hand on Symbelle. You cannot seek to finish what you did not end."

Impossible. "She burned with the Monodrome." Her words were almost as low as a whisper, in utter refusal to embrace this as true.

Shypriss shot her a smug smile again. "Did she, now?"

"You fucking saved her with your fire magic." She voiced the deduced into existence. "Why, though?"

Shypriss and the two mages she had called into the room made their way to exit the upstairs war chamber, leaving Zahnastaazjah alone with her new umbran prisoner. The prominent fire mage turned back to give her the unambiguous answer she needed to shed light on such an incongruity of bizarre events.

"Because I am her mother," Shypriss declared.

SYMBELLE (X)

FLAMELESS

Symbelle twitched and tossed and turned and screeched in pain from the unimaginable agony of fire dining on her skin, consuming her flesh and tissue down past the bone, into her soul, tormenting the innermost parts of her being into retreat from ever wanting to exist. She begged for death a thousand times over. When her pleas to Fyheir went unheeded, when her eyelids were singed from her skull, and when the fire's light was so bright it all became white in blindness before the purgatory of perpetual blackness took her, she prayed to other entities too. To water deities she did not know, to gods of mercy she fabricated in desperation, to the Vist and Void to bring her the gift of nothingness in the abyss of bodyless, mind-dumbed bliss.

She relived dying by fire in more dreams than she had endured her entire life, and still it would not end. Some being of incomprehensible evil was punishing her for her vile iniquities, for her treachery against the single person who had ever given her acceptance as a promising equal, and not seen her as a tool to be used and discarded when no longer needed. She tried to cry it all out, but tears could not survive in such hells, disintegrating the second they touched her fiery orbs. Her eyes …

My eyes … Symbelle reached up with both hands to touch them to see if what she saw was true. Her palms reflected a violet glow on them from her radiant eyes. They were not on fire. She was seeing again. Seeing things as they actually were.

My hands … There was flesh on her fingers. Unscarred skin down her wrists and arms. She dared not inspect any further, fearing it all to be too good to be true, another cruel joke made by Fyheir in collusion with the Lord of Fire and Lady of the Sunder.

She only turned her neck instead to peer at what her peripheral vision was teasing, toward a window in the afterlife chamber she now resided in. It was a man, not a divine nor a devil. His eyes were the giveaway. *Green halos …*

Symbelle was sure she sat up in panic, but upon noticing her viewing angle had not changed, she realized she must have still been lying supine on the plush bed.

The mage in the window seemed to notice some form of life awoken in her, however, and he looked startled. "She is awake! Go get her!" he shouted to some unseen steward somewhere that Symbelle did not care to take note of.

"Rest, destined one." The bearded young mage approached her with a calming hand on her sweaty forehead. A spell glyph glowed on the left side of his bare chest as he uttered, "You are alive, but …"

Symbelle's eyes opened. She hadn't even realized they had closed. When they did, the scene in the room had completely changed. It was dark outside instead of blessed by the day's sun. The mage was gone, replaced by a bald middle-aged woman. She knew her. *Lady Shypriss Sol-War …*

"Symbelle," Shypriss whispered hypnotically.

"I died. I watched myself." Symbelle sat up in the bed in a panicked frenzy, squeezing the sheets until her knuckles were white. "The fire … it …" She began rocking rapidly, looking at every crevice in the room for an escape. "I felt … It felt … I …"

She could not stop the suffocating feeling of the invisible smoke reentering her lungs, causing her to go into coughing convulsions. But somehow, when Shypriss laid her hand in her own, Symbelle's nerves and chaotic fit calmed altogether.

"The fire saved you," Shypriss uttered.

"The fire …" She thought on everything that had happened so fast. The moment the blast-salt kegs had exploded in the Monodrome, it had been over. It should have been over. *How did I …?* "Fyheir," Symbelle mouthed in addled recognition of the fact that for the first time in as long as she could remember, her thoughts were her own, and not those of the dissociative identity that had plagued her capricious personality. Fyheir had finally been extinguished through death by fire, and she knew it.

"It changed me. Fyheir tried to kill me." She gritted her teeth as her eyes settled over a lone candle atop the small chest of drawers at the foot of the bed. Symbelle abruptly flung the blankets off her in an impulsive rage, not taking her focus off the elemental enemy that represented the embodiment of her greatest foe. "I hate her! Get her out! Take her away!"

"This will take time," Shypriss said with a semblance of sadness. She snapped her fingers, and a small red magemark on her wrist lit up bright green, and the fire at the end of the candlewick vanished into a tiny smoke string. "But you are not done with fire, nor your *Fyheir*."

But she was. Fyheir's time with her had been doused into silence, and she was sure she would never lament over the missing internal monologue.

Symbelle surveyed the contents and decor of the room, discovering several remnants that sparked an anecdote from her past. *Worn orange sheets with the corner scorched black ... Red crystal flowers on the shelf ... The song box with the dancing Ibyssai, that was my gift, for my fifth bornday anniversary ... And that painted drakeroot on the windowsill. Just like the one Mother gave me for turning six, the one that was burned by the boys in Tairanchula ... I called it Fyheir. That was how we met.*

"I know this place. I have been here," Symbelle murmured, realizing her nerves had pacified, her curiosity piqued by the triggered nostalgia.

"You have," Shypriss whispered back as she took a seat beside her on the edge of the bed and held her clammy hands in her own. "This was your bed. Your room. You lived here for a time."

"My mother." Symbelle reminisced with a wave of repressed memories, which a young child might have compartmentalized. "This is the Mage Ward. I was so young."

"Your mother, yes," the Sunder-mage matron affirmed. "What did she look like?"

Even before Symbelle could speak, she knew the answer. *But she had fiery hair ... And her eyes were ...*

As if Shypriss could read her thoughts through her expressions, a sudden flame grew on Shypriss's bare scalp to shape into a full head of fiery strands in a blend of colors from red at the roots to orange in the middle to yellow at the tips. The archmage's eyes went from their inherent bright green to tiny balls of actual fire. Symbelle did not know why she hadn't seen it before, but she had never remembered her mother any other way than this.

"Mother?"

Shypriss smiled, rubbing a tracing thumb where Symbelle's fool's frown had formerly been. "You are scarless now." Her mother grinned with the purposeful pun. "Not a single mark of the fire, so that we can begin anew with one another."

Scarless ... Symbelle froze for a moment in disgust to dwell on her betrayal of her friend. Her eyes went wide as she was unable to fathom what she must look like now without the horrid marks. Both of her hands instinctively slipped under the blanket and between her bare legs to feel that Shypriss indeed wasn't lying. Her skin was as smooth as it had been when she was born.

"I have been looking for you your entire life, since they took you from me," her mother calmly stated.

Symbelle shook her head, not remembering a thing from the day she had been kidnapped from her birth home in the Mage Ward of Goldgarden and mysteriously brought to the farm outside of Darrowden in Az'Dayne to be raised by Broderick, her foster father, for reasons beyond her understanding that were never explained.

"I was different then. Your father was right in his judgment not to trust me, due to my selfish intentions to use your hyperi abilities for my own gain. I have had two decades to think on my actions and change." Her mother vaguely filled in the gaps of their history.

"But you are special, Symbelle. And I do not just mean that as my daughter. You are truly special, someone who could turn the tide of the war that is about to begin this Sunder of Kingfall."

"I am special because I am a hyperi, but for no other reason." Symbelle slumped back in the bed, dismayed.

"You are special because you are a hyperi, daughter of ours," her father's voice came from the doorway to the bedroom, not offering any sympathy to her realization. "It is time. You will finally be trained in how to use your hypersight. The decision has been made and the invitation extended. Mesdarro of Spellspire is coming to Goldgarden just for you."

Coldborn, in all his foreboding glory, stood across from her, robed in all black with the cowl pulled over his brow and a magically impenetrable shadow hiding his face except for the glint of the glowing green halos around his eyes. His presence created an aura that sent a chill down Symbelle's spine from both his ominous appeal and the perpetual cold that followed him around.

Symbelle recalled the name Mesdarro, Magistrate of Spellspire, as if it were yesterday she had just learned. He was the one Master Claydius had been proposing she seek out instead of following the writs to eliminate Scarless and Oldan and the rest. She sat quiet for a moment wishing she could take it all back and change her choice.

They both had many questions to answer, but she doubted she could get the two power moguls to answer any but perhaps one. "Why now? Why just now am I being considered to be trained?"

"Because Mesdarro is in league with the Neveril Empire. He works with the umbran, the enemy," her father enlightened. "Your introduction to him for your training will all be part of the ploy, that we are pretending to make a truce between the Oathemic Cabal, the Goldgarden Mage Ward, and the underrealm's grand scheme. Your role will be critical in securing the plot against them."

"We call it Sol-War," Shypriss stated as she released her touch from Symbelle and went to stand beside Coldborn.

"Sol-War as in your surname?" Symbelle was confused; she was aware that Shypriss's last name was the same.

"Sol-War is a sobriquet," her mother clarified. "It is the surname of every Sunder mage in my district who will be involved. You may consider it yours as well from now onward, as you cannot publicly go around announcing yourself a Goldfyre."

"Sol-War is a movement," her father went on. "The first part to take place will be the assassination of all Dawning mages in the Mage Ward here and those who are agents of the Oathemic Cabal. There has been an increasing demand for them within the Neveril Empire. They have already sunk their claws into the Green Byway. They have infiltrated my guild, and they have penetrated this city's Mage Ward also. They will go after Mageholme last."

"The other half of the movement is where you come in as the key to Sol-War's victory, Symbelle," her mother elaborated.

Symbelle stopped to consider if Pyphan was doomed from the start no matter what. It was clear his allegiance was unquestionable toward the Oathemic Cabal, and not against them as was being implied. "More killing?" Symbelle sighed heavily and cast her gaze down at the bedsheets. She was ready to go back to sleep, exhausted again already. "Who, then?"

"More killing," Coldborn confirmed with no sentiment. "You

are going to make what you did at Tairanchula look like child's play."

"My dear daughter," Shypriss concluded, "the primary focus of Sol-War is exposure. You are going to show all of Everdawn the truth about the Pentagogue. Every paladin, every veritan, every hidden skin-changer in the vile capital of Az'Dayne, and every Neveril who dares show their skin above ground. When your hypersight has defamed the Dominadom for what they are, we will use your alchemy skills to cripple their army with a plan they will not suspect. Every Sunder mage under my lead in the district, and every loyalist of Endrith in the Oathemic Cabal." She paused for emphasis. "We will be beside you."

But Neveril and neverborne are immune to fire, she considered and almost voiced aloud, but then she remembered otherwise. *Until I invented a way to change that.*

"Get some rest, Symbelle," her father advised. "Sol-War begins soon."

But she already was. Symbelle curled up and closed her eyes, futilely trying to drown out the fires of the haunted future she could not escape from. Even without Fyheir, she knew she would never find peace.

SCARLESS (XI)

THE PROGENY

The umbran's otherworldly eyes swallowed her own like pools of pure darkness, drowning out any avenue to elude her entrancing gaze. It was almost hypnotizing, almost alluring, almost a redefined level of eerie, but none in a single class, yet altogether a seamless synthesis of each in the same.

Umbran were known to be masters in the unnatural art of seduction. In the Sho'Lon region of the world, where umbran were first discovered to have manifested from the Shiniryn, the native people had come to call the female transcended elvan race of the umbran by the name of succubi in their tongue, and their male counterparts incubi.

That is what you are, isn't it? You are a succubus, here to try your shadow tricks on me and mine … But you have no effect on me, witch.

Zahnastaazjah matched the enchantress's stare, tuning out the others in the room. The metamorphosis that had taken over the former elvan was interesting to see up close, with her telltale grey skin, dark eyes devoid of any white, flat, outwardly growing ears, front fangs, and clawlike black nails. This was the closest she had ever been to a live one.

Her new prisoner was wrapped in a confining leather gown that had no sleeves for a purpose, with shackles around her ankles, left over from the North Garrison's jail cells in the basement of the keep they all now stood within. Xalo and Atrick stood beside her, but she had paid them hardly any heed for the past hour.

I could be torturing you for answers. Perhaps I should, Zahnastaazjah thought, cocking her head to the side as if she were speaking aloud to the umbran. *But it just never ends. I am weary of it all. My reputation be damned – I would hang this mantle of Crime Queen up if I could just sneak away, find another city, and start anew. I would do it differently this time. Maybe I will take my leave this Sunder and never return ... But what do I do with you? A quick death? Is that okay?*

Zahnastaazjah knew she was becoming enervated on the inside from the unending violence that had played out its course over the many long years she had been subjected to it. She noticed that her focus had left the umbran, however, and was now on the stairway leading to the ground floor of the keep, above their heads, where several pairs of footsteps were heard hurrying down.

Devonduer appeared in all his typical excitement, with Uubakrath behind him and a few of her guild agents beside them toting large burlap sacks. The men promptly dumped the unwieldly things at her feet, spilling out contents mixed with a variety of plunder: coins, trinkets, and art items of value.

"What's this?" Zahnastaazjah broke from her concentration on the new hostage.

"Dockjaw's cut," her chamberlain loosely declared, "but there is also something else to note."

Zahnastaazjah frowned at Devonduer, who normally was not so nebulous in his answers. Everyone was well aware she had banished her overman in charge of smuggling operations at the last Purge of the Yard for his incompetence in employing Sundown's turncoats right under his nose. "Dockjaw doesn't owe a cut. I will ask again. What is this?"

"He must not listen well or take you too seriously." Devonduer prepared to elaborate, as he customarily did. "He has not stopped sending money from his smuggling operations, which he evidently continued after you debarred him at the last Purge of the Yard. These aren't cuts from just the North Docks either. He is sending from Giant's Landing and Little Worest now as well."

Atrick spoke up with his crude sarcasm. "We call overachievers 'ass-lickers' and 'cunt-kissers' where I come from."

"I always lick her ass and kiss her cunt." Xalo didn't skip a second with his unwelcome wit. "I suppose I am the best overachiever in the guild, eh, Zahna?"

Don't fucking call me that, she said with her scowling eyes before she rolled them and shook her head.

Devonduer stayed on subject, speaking before she could. "What do you want me to do with all of it?"

"Well, we ain't fuckin' sendin' it back!" Atrick answered with some logic for all of them.

"Put it to the side for now," she directed. "I will decide what to do about Dockjaw's potential absolution. You said there was something else I should know?"

"Yes," Devonduer admitted. "There are men outside requesting an audience with you. Green-eyed men."

"More mages? Is this bitch Shypriss serious?" She couldn't believe the audacity of the woman so soon after the last trespass and harassment. "Can she not ju—"

"Not mages," Xalo intervened, drawing out his magic sword all the way to reveal the glass blade. Not a single elemental glyph or arcanic signature glowed. "I would feel it."

"They are Forwoken," Uubakrath answered in their shared Terollar language. He had been outside with Devonduer to witness and confirm. *"Your progeny, Sorovronus, has sent word. You should come up."*

News about her son trumped all else for her. "Everyone, as you were. I will be back," she promised.

She followed Uubakrath upstairs and out of the keep into the Yard where the Forwoken monks stood patiently. There were eight of them. Each was armed with the Forwoken's signature bladed-spear polearm, and they kept their heads covered with a full mask that concealed their ears and face, rather mundane and expressionless, painted all white. These particular travelers were in road leathers, though Zahnastaazjah had learned that the ones Sorovronus kept in his company around Frostdale were much more armored.

One stepped forward from the others in the group to orate as their speaker. "Zahnastaazjah, progeny of Khomo'Jhuvonus, progenitor of Sorovronus, whom we serve, we greet you with privy information from the north."

"Forwoken monks." She cordially greeted them back in the native tongue of her Terollar people out of respect. *"Whom do I address now?"*

"My name does not matter for those who are not inducted into our order. You may simply refer to me as Forwoken," the spokesman monk offered, as expected.

Zahnastaazjah nodded. "What does my son wish to tell me this time? He knows I care little for his Barredish meddling. Get on with it." She shooed her hand at them, pretending not to care. "My brother is dead, is he not? Joined my father in the Beyond?"

The Forwoken emissary said nothing for a good several seconds, enhancing the drama in her anticipation before he finally revealed, "Zuulzinj lives and is free. As does Khomo'Jhuvonus." He paused again to let that settle in. "He lives and is free."

"En khomo naso rahsee'ahsee," Uubakrath uttered in reverence, and he dropped down to one knee.

The eight Forwoken monks all did the same, repeating Uubakrath's respects to her father's honor. *"En khomo naso rahsee'ahsee."*

"En khomo naso rahsee'ahsee." She followed with the prevalent Glace Isles invocation as well, though she remained standing, taken aback and in a bewildered state at the unprecedented news.

"The Chosen of the Balance, Khomo'Jhuvonus, requests your aid. Your progeny has beckoned you to join our cause just this once." The emissary stood back up.

So this was all her son's bidding. "Rather auspicious timing Sorovronus has. Does he know I am being exiled from Goldgarden?" Zahnastaazjah shifted to Uubakrath as she finished. "I suppose we need something to do with our free time. I am listening."

The Forwoken monks began walking through the Yard of Scarless Square without any notice of why or where they were moving the conversation to. The one who acted as the emissary walked as if he had lived there for years, striding specifically to a private corner in the southwest side, under the old blacksmith's shed. Zahnastaazjah shadowed the group of elven with Uubakrath beside her to acquire some discretion, as the monks implied was needed.

"We need you to free the king of Barredom, Aerik Roth." The emissary reverted back to their Terollar dialect once privacy had been established. *"He has a doppelgänger in his place who is serving as an imposter for the Neveril Empire. The Frostdale Council and many of the advisers in the kingdom are qindrid who have the ability to shape-change, including the queen."*

"Neverborne," she whispered in the Civil, then shifted to Terollar. *"I have seen them."*

"Their reach is spreading further than we anticipated. I will relay this to Sorovronus." The monk seemed surprised to hear this.

"Why me?" Zahnastaazjah had to ask. *"If the Forwoken Order*

knows the placement of this imprisoned king, why not free him yourselves? My son is the most enterprising individual I know, and there are hundreds of you. Furthermore, you all know the lay of the land better than I possibly can."

"Those in charge of Barredom's qindrid are catching on," the Forwoken emissary explained. *"Sorovronus is under close scrutiny as the High Chancellor. He cannot risk his position, especially after orchestrating the escape of the khomo and the captured Glazjhendun. If they suspect anything, they will come for the lives of him and the entire Forwoken Order. We are all on the verge of exposure."*

Zahnastaazjah chewed on that development for a half minute, contemplating all that could go wrong if she agreed to get involved in the politics of the north, which she had always sworn to refrain from, but it seemed to continue to be the doom of all her family. "Next questions: where and how?" She knew it would come across as a form of disrespect to the elvan monks if she chose to speak in the Civil tongue of humans, but she was annoyed by her son's timely manner. He seemed to have known just when to ambush her into helping a cause she could not care less about. "Where do you believe they are holding the king? And how in the Vist and Void am I supposed to sneak myself in, being a Terollar, with a spellblade and another Terollar by my side?" Zahnastaazjah spoke of the very real predicament of the unsubtle presences of Xalo and Uubakrath.

She would wager that if the emissary hadn't been wearing a mask to conceal his features, she would have witnessed his irritation at being coerced into talking outside his native language, but there was only a small inflection of discontent in his tone. "He is being held in Komak Keep, which can be accessed underground through way of the Hjaergn Fjord, out of IceBathed, Barredom's westernmost port. If you can get a ship to transport you through, you can do as is needed. We were hoping, with your multiple resources in the city, you perhaps knew an expert smuggler who could accomplish this."

Dockjaw. She couldn't help but smile at her old friend's opportune moment to resurface into her favor. "We know a smuggler," Zahnastaazjah confidently affirmed. "Who is to be my contact, then, on arrival, if not Sorovronus or the Forwoken?"

The emissary inquired, "Are you familiar with Honorah Bayn,

the Royal Inquisitor of Frostdale?"

Anyone who has heard of Barredom or the infamous Frostdale Deeps has heard of Honorah fucking Bayn. "I am fortunate to admit that I am familiar with the name, and perhaps even more fortunate that we are yet to be introduced. I am sure it will be pleasant to make her acquaintance," she retorted sarcastically. She did not expect to ever hear that the uncompromising torture master of Barredom was considered an ally to her race, with the ruthless reputation that preceded her.

"She will be under a new title, more humbled, and more cooperative than the rumors of her history tend to imply. You will see," he said. "Are you in, Zahnastaazjah? Give us something that suffices as a vow that your word is—"

She cut him short by promptly drawing her spear and slamming the shaft of it down between them as they stood face-to-face. For the sake of restoring a code of manners, she answered him in Terollar again. "*My word is bound in my blood, and my blood is Terollar thick and true, of the root of the Glace Isles king, Khomo'Jhuvonus. I am the last progeny of the Balance's Chosen of our race.*"

Zahnastaazjah clutched the end of the bloodrime spearhead until blood poured from her palm, then extended the spear to the Forwoken emissary to match the gesture. "*Do you accept and trust this binding vow?*"

Her son's messenger returned the motion, cutting his palm open on her spearhead. He honored the pact by firmly sealing his bloody hand to hers, and the two held their grip until their Terollar impower regenerated their hands back to their original, scarless states.

On the approaching Sunder season, Zahnastaazjah and her carefully selected crew would be on the cold shores of Barredom.

VALAYTHEA (IX)

HAPPILY NEVER AFTER

They sat under the blanket of stars amid the unpopulated Cidar Tower Ruins. The remnants of the old strongholds were now just dismal hollows filled with sad memories of the dead who had fallen there from the Az'Elothian War in ages past.

The moon was a beacon of heavenly judgment casting its dooming gaze down upon her soul, which she was well aware would now be deplorably damned in the afterlife soon to come, if she could even be so fortunate. She truly wanted simply to die and be done with it. Her life held no more meaning for her.

It had been a hard few days' ride north to escape her homeland of Chandoshia. They had taken succinct breaks and stretched the horses to their limits. This was the first stop they had come upon that Valaythea was certain she would find sleep at. Her mind could bear no more weight from a single emotion. It had diminished into an empty shell, with depleted tears and the exhaustion of a damaged essence that had formerly been so full of joy and hope. Her shattered heart was just as heavy, and she had come to find out that she was having a hard time even mustering the will to speak lately. Perhaps she was dying. Perhaps the Five and Five would be kind and allow her such a mercy to take her in the night once her eyes were closed.

The seven Silverback agents who served as the escort team for the prince and Valaythea had set up their tents farther up the hill for a surveillance vantage. They made no fire and no sound, and their meals were all the same: jerky and one raw, shaved potato.

Fabian, the stable boy of her home, had chosen to join the outlaw crew with no argument from anyone when he had followed behind on Adyssaira's steed. He was more hysterical than even she was when he found out about Adyssaira's death, and how it happened.

He mourned her and Emberalda's death at the top of his lungs each night, in defiance to accept the unthinkable tragedies. Valaythea never knew Fabian to care so deeply about them. She wanted to go to him, to beg for his forgiveness, but she was a coward with no ability to plead for pity in her desolate state.

Izayus and Valaythea had their own tent, nestled in the valley against a leafless tree that seemed as expired as the broken buildings peppering the gloomy horizon. The prince's tent was large enough to comfortably fit a decem guests for leisure or respite, but that still didn't stop the newly wedded couple from choosing opposite sides to rest on for this somber night.

There was nothing in between their separated bedrolls but an arrangement of lit lanterns and rations laid out on a rug, which neither had the appetite to eat. The warm air from the outside crept through the flap, reminding them that the Sunder season was to drop in less than a pentday.

"I can offer you no words." Izayus attempted to provoke her into conversation with sympathies again. He had been trying for days to no avail, barely managing to get her to say a word or two before her grief would possess her into fits of crying. "I do offer my promise, on my life's legacy, that I will do what it takes to heal you in time and help you find your way back to peace."

There will never again be any peace, Valaythea said with her sorrowful eyes, but her lips never moved. She stared at the unsheathed Chandoss Spellblade in her lap, sitting with her knees bowed to the side, rocking away her tormenting worries. She could not take her focus off the connected Dawning glyphs she had witnessed appear on the glass blade immediately following the murder she had committed of her own sister.

Seeing as Valaythea was not going to join in any exchange with him, and that Izayus seemed to be growing unfondly accustomed to it, he drew out his drug pipe and stuffed in his fey petal to smoke. It got her attention, and she could see that he took notice of that.

"It helps with the sleep," he said. "Do you wish to forget?"

Valaythea just stared in absolute repulsion at the beautiful man with whom she had formerly been infatuated. She had begged to return into his care and flee from the fate of the Thrench on the day of the murder in Lovers' Labyrinth, but her stomach still found a way to twist in knots every time she was forced to watch his unappealing addictions.

"It also helps when you are awake," he said to himself, looking despondently down at his pipe. "It helps then too."

"How do we make it go back to what it was?" Valaythea whispered with a cracked voice from severe dehydration. She hadn't cared to consume much water throughout the past couple of days, and the crying was not alleviating that issue.

Izayus brought his pipe and came to sit on both knees next to her bedroll. His voice was soothing, and he seemed in the mood to talk for the both of them.

"There are many pieces being moved around the realm right now, Val. This is a cycle foretold to be of many miracles and travesties. North, south, west, east, there are pieces, and all being manipulated by men more powerful than me. You will come to find that I am just another one of these pieces, as you are now, as you always have been, but that does not mean that we are disposable. We are intended to suffer the travesties before we can become the deliverers of the miracles." He seemed to believe this himself, as if these words had been preached to him by some lifelong mentor to become ingrained in his very being.

"I am numb. My heart," she murmured, gazing with glassy eyes straight through her sword at nothing in particular. "My heart is …" She fumbled again. "I will never be the same. I want you to leave me here to die, please. If you ever cared for me at all, leave me here to die, Izayus."

"We can start with that," Izayus said. "About my name. I should not be who I am."

Please, no … "Stop," she growled, defeated to her core. She lay down on her back and closed her eyes to accelerate sleep into taking her, but curiosity prevented her from having any peace of mind until she heard him say it. "I can bear no more."

"Few know the truth, but it is there, and it is real," he began. "Coldborn and his most trusted agents of the Oathemic Cabal were behind it thirty years ago. They hid him away in the north to be fostered in a haven that only Coldborn was aware of. I have only recently been enlightened of the contingencies to come."

Valaythea opened her eyes and looked up at him. "Hid who?"

"The one who is walking around that should be sitting on the imperial throne after the assassination of his father, King Kythaeus

Goldfyre. His name is Kyson Goldfyre, whom everyone thought had been murdered as a babe. It never occurred."

Valaythea impulsively sat up. Her life continued to spiral into a warped, bizarre reality, falling through a bottomless well that led toward her absurd destiny. Valaythea had no response to give. Even entertaining any of the events that had already occurred since the strange Cycle of Kingfall had begun seemed an act of insanity.

"I know the story." Valaythea was temporarily sidetracked from her overbearing woes in that moment. "All in Az'Dayne know the story of baby Kyson and that tragedy. What is your concern of him, and why are you telling me this?"

"Because I intend to do what I must to see the man whose life I stole welcomed back home, and brought out of the shadows. I am no longer the Prince of Az'Dayne. I never was," Izayus said bluntly. "The empire I am sole heir to is his."

Terminal depression slipped back through her veins. Intrigue and plotting had lost its flavor shortly after her blighted wedding. Izayus seemed to register that he was losing her interest.

"Better to show you when it is time rather than try to make you understand. But first, we must change our look. They will be looking for us."

"Change our look?" *How?* she started to additionally ask but never got the chance to when he finally lit his pipe to strike a signal that prompted the Silverback agents to enter the tent in an aggressive fashion. Two of them seized her while another man yanked back hard on her long red hair.

"Hold still. They have good intent." Izayus failed at consoling her. He remained knelt in submission to accept what was about to transpire.

Two Silverbacks held on to Izayus as well to keep him safely still, while the third on him produced a pair of barber's shears and began clipping away his wavy reddish-blond locks nearly down to his skin. She could feel the same happening to her. The man with the scissors against her formerly beautiful strands of hair was not remotely gentle at all.

The seventh Silverback agent was armed with a jagged knife and a thick glove. Its short blade radiated a hint of orange evidently from being plunged into some form of fire outside that she was unaware of. The man took the knife to the left side of the prince's face, just above his eye and cheek, planting it broadside until the skin seared and bubbled it into an instant blister, indubitably causing an untreatable scar. He then turned toward her as if chopping her hair away were not enough.

"No!" Valaythea screamed. She could see the green halo flash in her right eye, and her hand was already holding the deadly spellblade. She hadn't moved from her kneeling position. She didn't need to. Every Silverback in the room got the meaning and halted.

The one with the scissors tossed down a translucent flask of what looked like black oil and told her to die.

"Die?" She repeated back to him, honestly wanting him to oblige to put those sheers to her throat instead.

"No, dye," he corrected, "for your hair, my lady. Needs to be black come dawn."

The Silverbacks then retreated out of the tent to leave the two be.

Izayus was grunting and writhing in agony, rummaging through his pack for some ointment. He frantically rubbed it over his fresh burns. He then took three huge puffs from his pipe and dropped it to crawl over to his side of the tent and groan more.

"Remember what I told you when we first met?" He grimaced in severe pain with every trying word.

She recalled it all as if it were yesterday, and she swore she would sacrifice anything in her deities' divine names if they could just take it all back and make it as if none of it had ever happened.

"If you hoped this might turn into a love story," Izayus whispered, repeating his original warning to her on the first evening of their official imperial conjoining, as he began drifting away into a drug-induced slumber, "then you are reading the wrong book."

Valaythea grabbed the discarded pipe beside her bedroll and snapped it like a twig between her hands. It was an act of anger that she hoped would give her some remedy of satisfaction, but instead she only felt guilty after she did it.

I could have used that ... she mulled to herself. Not thinking twice on it, she was already rummaging through her husband's pockets for another avenue to accept his invitations to escape and forget. She found shavings of the dried up yewr root in his pouch and did not hesitate on choking down more than she intended.

She felt a turn in her stomach so strong, she had to escape the tent for fresh air. She didn't want to be around the prince or anyone else. It was just her and the celestial blanket of bright stars now, settled over the coming Sunder's night sky.

Valaythea caught a glimpse of a flash of violet light just over the hill, on the night's horizon. Her eyes shifted back to the fire of the Silverbacks' camp nearby, then back to where she had seen the strange radiance. It appeared again, a glowing violet ball moving toward her.

She shook her head, surprised at how fast the yewr root seemed to be inducing obvious hallucinations. The violet wisp-like spirit began rapidly moving toward her, and for some reason, she wasn't scared of it.

She hoped it wasn't an illusion from the drug. She prayed it did mean her harm. She moved toward the charging ball of violet light.

She heard a murmur in her mind from her sword trying to speak to her. It was Adyssaira's voice combined with the echo of another, which she somehow knew was that of her mother's murderer, Sheyelle. They both whispered the same name as the violet wisp drew nearer. *Carolelle ...*

Valaythea's wobbly legs failed her, and she collapsed into the grass outside her tent. Her dizzy gaze dug deeper into the mind-numbing mirage as the actual yewr root hallucinations hit her. It felt like she was slipping into the most vibrant lucid dream, a bridge into permanent sleep or the afterlife. Either would suffice.

ATHANIEL (V)

THE WRITS

"These are your key writs for the Sunder. May your promotion to Keeper of the Hive Order serve Az'Dayne well," Master Claydius concluded as he placed a bag of several writs in Athan's hand. Formerly, only Claydius or Coldborn himself had directed the Hive Order in their writs before the new rank of Keeper had been created for Athan's faction.

The Dawning mage director was already secure in his stone sarcophagus, naked and tucked comfortably upright against the plush body cushion within that formed around him. He was ready to embrace the long sleep for the next five months. It was the first furrow in the Cycle of Kingfall, the day between the end of the Dawning season and the start of the Sunder season. Every Dawning mage across Penthara would be turning in now for their necessitated magical rest period, known as Transbernation. The insuppressible slumber that came over them would last an entire season, and they would awaken on the furrow before the Reaping. This was a mage's handicap. It was this limiting impower alone, of forced hibernation, that made all mages weaker than normal men, in Athan's eyes.

But Master Claydius had been Athan's mentor since he had first been inducted into the Oathemic Cabal as a boy. The wise old spy-tactician had been more of a father to him than his actual father for the latter half of his life. Claydius was a perfectionist and an overly meticulous organizer of death-dealing and death-dealers. He was the head administrator of the central hub of the entire Cabal's infrastructure, which had been constructed underneath the Plaguefolk Villages. Claydius had lived a long and lucrative existence. And today was the day, against his knowledge, that he would die.

"May I, as Keeper of the Hive Order, serve the Oathemic Cabal well," Athan elegantly corrected his master.

There was indeed a mass change underway within the notorious assassins' guild. What had once been a Dominadom-endorsed assembly of legalized killers was secretly about to experience a violent divergency. The founding ideals established by Coldborn for the Oathemic Cabal were contradicting the evolution of Az'Dayne through the conspiracy of the Neveril involvement that had infiltrated the empire with shape-changing neverborne qindrid.

Coldborn had discovered that there were already several neverborne double agents within his assassin network, and his tolerance for it held no quarter. The first to turn to the Dominadom's antagonistic demands were Master Claydius and his Dawning mages in the Hunder Order. As of now, there was even a group of capable fighters being gathered from Frostdale, under the guise of training as paladin initiates to join the ranks of the Pentagogue. In reality, they would pledge themselves to the Oathemic Cabal with the true purpose of getting close enough to Coldborn to assassinate him personally.

Coldborn had a cold reply to give them all in a signature of spilled blood, carried out by Athan's hand.

Athan looked into his aged mentor's green eyes as he fondled the many kill contracts in his hands. He noticed that his own hands were not shaking. He was not sweating. There was not a single nerve in his body stirring with uncertainty. *Nothing. I feel nothing.* He was ready to carry out the deed.

Before Athan closed the lids on Claydius's sarcophagus, he opened the writs, one by one. These writs from Claydius were all sealed with the sigil of Az'Dayne. He doubted Coldborn had ever even seen them. Eight high-priority Dominadom-endorsed writs:

Target: Haelyn Rook, archon of the Silverlakes, leader of the Silverbacks
Last Location: Frostdale, Barredom

Target: Barturon lon'Chandoss, spellblade Silverback agent
Last Location: the northern Tairanheart

Faction: all Silverback agents and associates
Last Location: scattered abroad

Target: Zahnastaazjah, alias Scarless, Crime Queen of Goldgarden, leader of the Stormtrees
Last Location: Scarless Square, Goldgarden

Target: Xalo, spellblade bloodguard of Scarless
Last Location: Scarless Square, Goldgarden

Faction: Stormtrees inner circle
Last Location: Scarless Square, Goldgarden

Recovery: Prince Izayus Az'Ampion
Last Location: Castle Chandoss, Chandoshia, Az'Dayne

Target: Valaythea Az'Chandoss, spellblade fugitive
Last Location: Castle Chandoss, Chandoshia, Az'Dayne, believed to be with Prince Izayus

Athan's heart proved that it still felt something when he read the last name on the writs. He slipped the tiny scrolls into his belt pouch to decide how to delegate the writs to the assassins in the Hive Order. He immediately decided that no one other than himself would know about his sister's contract. That was for him alone to carry out, if he so chose.

He had another contract in mind to introduce to Daerlem—a forged one. Falsifying a seal was an ultimate infraction of their code, with the penalty of severe torture until death, followed by the extermination of one's entire family.

Target: Valdean lon'Chandoss, Count of Chandoshia
Last Location: Castle Chandoss, Chandoshia, Az'Dayne

Athan toyed with the counterfeit contract beside the others in his pouch, considering when to convince Daerlem with the lie that it had been necessitated by Coldborn to be their first writ to pursue. Athan knew the consequences, but he did not care. Fury fueled his ire more than logic calmed his predetermined will, which could not be deterred from its blood-destined course.

Athan took one last look at Claydius and gave a most subtle nod of former respect. He had intended to bow, but he simply could not command his body to betray his mentor, who held so much trust in him. He shut the modified sarcophagus lids, first the one to enclose the body from torso to feet, and then the smaller section that concealed the neck and head. He looked to his right to watch the rest of his Hive Order assassins doing the same, locking the Dawning mages down in their vertical stone compartments to go under for Transbernation.

Next, they locked the mages away for their own safety, in case they incidentally woke too early due to a bad dream, as was not unknown.

Stoneplay. Elixion. Athan noticed the two sarcophagi next to Master Claydius's. He remembered his last experiences not long ago with the two Dawners. He wished he were a different person in that moment so he could know what it was like to feel a pang of guilt for the actions that were about to follow. But he was not a different person.

He was Athan Chandoss, the pragmatically detached assassin, Keeper of the Hive Order of the Oathemic Cabal. Life as a silent killer made one more numb than even the most battle-hardened soldier. Ending all of their existences was a callous unquestioned duty. Nothing else.

Athan took out his two Cabal-endorsed writs, signified by their black dagger trinket and green string, which had been delivered directly from Coldborn. He opened them, held them high, and stuck the two kill contracts to Claydius's sarcophagus with a piece of adhesive clay he had readied.

Every assassin in the Transbernation Corridor's vicinity came to witness the words of Coldborn:

General: every Dawning mage alive
Last Location: anywhere on Penthara

Target: Master Claydius Orlaithe, Director of the Oathemic Cabal headquarters
Last Location: in front of you

Daerlem and the rest of Athan's assassins all moved into place behind the stone coffins. The slits between the lids that separated the mages' heads and bodies had been tampered with, sawed deeper in the stone and wider in access to allow penetration down to where their necks were vulnerable.

Athan held one dagger up above his head to prompt the men to ready their razor-wire garrotes. Eighteen men did as prepared behind all eighteen Dawning mages of the entire Oathemic Cabal. "For Coldborn," he said as he dropped the blade to the echoing tiles.

Before his dagger hit the stone, the garrotes all wrapped around each mage in his individual sarcophagus, and the Hive Order assassins pulled the wire strings against their helpless necks until the gurgling went silent and the blood poured heavily out of the cracks.

The Dawning mages of the Oathemic Cabal were dead. Athan had several more writs to go. It was going to be a busy Sunder.

ODYSSERAE (I)

TEARS OF VENGEANCE

"Come child, I know," Valdean pulled her in tightly to console the unbearable sorrow. The cold golden surface of the Medallion of House Chandoss pressed against her tear-soaked cheeks. He knew she could not hear so he grabbed her by the face and forced her to look into his dark red eyes as she read his lips. "Ssh, shh, I know … I know …"

Oddy hated that she needed his touch as an outlet for comfort. It disgusted her to no end, but she had always been weak to deny him. He was a giver and a taker, but above all, he was her master and he was in love with her. He had caught her at an early age, before she knew any better, and now she was in too deep to escape this tragic way of life she was cursed into.

Valdean wasn't even trying to hide his true qindrid form in front of her. They had no secrets between one another. His skin's current pigment was grey. To everyone else he maintained the appearance of what a great-granduncle would be expected to look like – pushing mid-seventies in age, yet with the vigor of a man in his prime.

But in truth, that form was always a lie. He had earned his right of Transcendence some fifty years ago, becoming one of the first neverborne to ever take the turn in Az'Dayne. Valdean's early pledge with the regional umbran had earned him swift promotion as the Count of Chandoshia, which only strengthened when he assassinated his own brother, Nikayle Chandoss the Firstnamed, High Bloodguard of the Crown.

Valdean's natural aesthetic was arguably handsome, ageless in his late twenties. His hair was not thin as it was in his shifted guise of his elderly version. It was thick and black, worn elegantly back.

Oddy was not the first family member he had manipulated to his will. Before her his puppet had been Delphine, her father's first wife, who he sired Emberalda with. But when Nikayle had failed Valdean as a double agent informant against the Oathemic Cabal, Valdean did not seem to hesitate to find a way to make Delphine's death appear as an accident when the plague struck her and only her. Evidently Valdean "loved" her as well, as he so often promised to Oddy, but love was a very low rung on the ladder of priorities in her great-granduncle's schemes for achieving his supreme legacy.

They were in Valdean's private chamber in the forbidden Echo Wing. No candles were lit today. There were only two oil lamps faintly illuminating the small room. One could hardly differ the color difference between the red and black pillows checkered into the walls and ceiling. The corner altars were empty, obscured by the darkness that enveloped them.

Valdean pulled away from hugging her, and made sure she was reading his carefully enunciated words again. "We are leaving. Just you, me, and Ise'andahr. Spellspire is a long way from here."

Oddy glanced at Ise'andahr standing next to her. She looked at him with his grey skin that matched Valdean's. His scarred scalp was hairless, making his pointed ears that extended outwards appear even dramatically longer. His colorless eyes were downtrodden as always, perpetually fixed in a submissive demeanor as if he was apologetic for even being alive. He was the product of two of the most sadistic villains that could have ever existed, the umbran who lorded over Chandoshia. Torture and servitude and death were all he had ever known.

The rogue-Neveril elvan was more like a brother to her than her own blood brother, Athaniel, was. Ise'andahr had been born cursed in his own way, which had always made Oddy feel a tinge of relatable sympathy for him. While her hearing impairment double hindered her faculty to verbally communicate, Ise'andahr was also inept in his speaking ability. Rogue-elven were not like normal elven. For some reason, being the progenies cocooned from their umbran parents, the rogue versions of elven rapidly lost their aptitude to talk the older they got. Studies said that by thirty or so years of age, they would almost succumb to being fully feral, more as animals in mind than anything resembling the intelligence of other elven.

Valdean hurriedly moved to a specific red pillow on the wall. She knew this one. When he pulled on it the plush leather thing opened like a mini doorway, showing access to the safe where

Valdean kept his most prized and secret belongings. He retracted an exquisite black leather satchel and slammed the safe back shut before turning to face her once more.

"What a mess that's been made." This time he gestured his audible words in Hands so she could better understand with the limited light. "What a mess your sister has made, and now I have to answer for it."

Which sister? Val? Addy? Ember? Sashka? You have turned me on all of them! Her eyes narrowed furiously, and her drying tears burned like fire. *"They made me kill Ember,"* she hammered out with her fingers, *"I murdered her. And it was your idea to have me do it!"*

"My Oddy," he went back in for an embrace, but she shooed his arms aside. "My poor Oddy," he persisted, but when she stepped back defensively, he relented.

"Your greatest weapon I have gifted to you is the wrath you contain within. It is I who has given you this, and you will unleash it in time. But not now. All that I do, I do for you. For us, my love."

She felt her nose crinkle and her mouth awkwardly open. Her jaw was debating whether to clinch or submit to more crying. *"You are evil! And I hate you!"*

She had never spoken to him this way; never even risked dreaming it into reality. The punishment was always too great before, but nothing could hurt her worse than what she had already suffered.

"There is no evil in this world. Only the aspirations of others for those that you choose not to understand," Valdean said while simultaneously translating in Hands. "I forgive you. I know you do not mean that."

He picked off an imaginary fragment from her shoulder as if there were some flawed chip on it. "I am simply shaving away your weaknesses, one at a time. Ember was a weakness to us all. A blight on the Chandoss legacy, which is all we have in the end. And we must appease the Neveril at all costs. I will spend all my days finding ways to have you forgive me."

Valdean stared off into the darkest corner of the room and pondered for a long moment as if transfixed in regret. "Adyssaira," he sighed with grief in his eyes, "that was not supposed to happen."

"Her body," Oddy gestured. *"We cannot just leave her there."*

"Ise'andahr. See it done. Quietly and quickly," Valdean agreed. "Bury her proper and meet me back in the tunnels before dusk."

"I go with him."

Valdean did not deny her that wish. He gently placed both of her hands in his and lifted them eye level to inspect. "You will not need to speak with these soon. We are off to Spellspire. You will take the Transcendence and become as I am. You will speak your own words and hear them."

He used Hands again to convey, but this time he did not say the words aloud. *"You can become whoever you wish to be."* Valdean's qindrid grey skin gradually shifted to a typical human pigment and his youth seemed to restore even younger.

"Say goodbye to home. We will not be returning for some time," he concluded.

* * * * *

The rain had come on strong throughout the burial, but it was down to a drizzle in the prime of twilight under the starless night sky. The full moon loomed above, watching and judging the deeds of the wicked below. Oddy was soaked to the bone, but the wet could not affect those that were already ice cold. Her veins were on fire with silent rage, frozen by choice until it was time to act. And that time was near.

Her eyes could not leave her sister's grave; a fitting place here in Lovers' Labyrinth next to the elaborate well, which was Adyssaira's favorite place to visit. Oddy laid a bouquet of drenched flowers down atop the mound that Ise'andahr had hastily dug and closed back up with her poor sister's corpse inside.

Oddy finally looked away from the mud. Her eyes drifted to the yellow Savatarm silk sash — Adyssaira's special blindfold — now tied around her right elbow. Whatever tears remained had since blended with the rain, leaving no evidence of sorrow. She felt a large part of her go hollow. Pieces she could never recover. She had lost each of her sisters in the blink of an eye, each in different ways.

Little Luna nestled up next to her leg and purred, bringing her attention to the black tiger. Luna was a gift from Sundorion to both her and Adyssaira, but Oddy had not put forth the effort into pampering the young beast as her sister had. Evidently, Luna must not have left Adyssaira's body after the tragedy befell her. Oddy discovered the tiger right where she last saw her, curled up in her sister's limp arms.

Luna was a loyal pet, and loyalty was not a virtue Oddy planned to ignore. She reached down to stroke her wet coat and inwardly vowed then and there, that wherever she went, Luna would join.

Oddy then palmed the two charms that hung from her neck, one in both hands. They were the water-watches of Sundorion and Timmurian, named *Old Patience* and *New Patience*. She knew they were instilled with arcane properties, but as to how to apply their magic, that was to be discovered.

They were intended as trophies, gifted to her by Zsa'vauge as a prize for playing her part in getting the two Zandaryn elven captured. But Oddy aimed to exploit them to her advantage as much more than simple trinkets.

Oddy forced Ise'andahr's attention on her when she grabbed the shovel from the mound and flipped it upside down, then handed it to him. The mute Neveril elvan glanced at her confused, likely wondering what else she was insinuating for him to dig.

"Will you still do what you promised me? Will you help me, now more than ever?" Oddy gestured in Hands to him. It was a language he understood well and the only way they had ever communicated.

Ise'andahr gave a single nod, but his eyes proved his unwavering determination. Still, she needed reassurance before it began.

"Show me. Show me the names of those we will kill when it is time. I need to know that you are my friend to the end. You promised me," she finished signaling, then tapped her foot on the shovel.

Ise'andahr began using the shaft of the tool to do as instructed in the mud mound over Adyssaira's grave. He spelled both names that she needed to see.

VALDEAN

ZSA'VAUGE

Oddy scowled at the sight of their names and felt a wave of life flow back through her. Their downfall was her entire reason for existing. She just needed to embrace the Qindrid Transcendence first. She would become neverborne and then allow them to die.

But there was just one more name to add to the list of retribution. A new name. She took the shovel from Ise'andahr, and made sure he saw it clearly when she was done etching the letters into the grave.

VALAYTHEA

APPENDIX

Human Elemental Descendancies

Tairancians: Tairan descendancy. West central Penthara.
- (Modern) Tan or fair skin, brown eyes, blond or brown hair.
- (Indigenous) Tan skin, brown eyes, dark brown hair.

Khalimishe: Fire descendancy. South central Penthara.
- (Modern) Brown skin, amber eyes, red or black hair. Southern look. (Indigenous) Brown skin, red eyes, red hair. Southern look.

Sho'Lonese: Sky descendancy. Eastern Penthara.
- (Modern) Pale skin, light blue eyes, blond hair. Eastern look.
- (Indigenous) Pale skin, grey eyes, blond hair. Eastern look.
- (Skyborne) Grey skin, light blue eyes, white hair. Eastern look.

Vhall: Shadow descendancy. Northern Penthara in recluse.
- Black skin, grey eyes, no hair. Endangered race. *(Eight feet tall)*

Thrench: Water descendancy. Western islands and eastern Penthara.
- Brown skin, blue eyes, black hair. Islander look.

Daynish: Tairan and fire descendancy. South central Penthara.
- Tan or fair skin, amber or brown eyes, blond, brown, or red hair.

Elothians: Tairan and sky descendancy. South central Penthara.
- Pale skin, light brown eyes, blond hair. Eastern look.

Aggeans: Tairan and shadow descendancy. Northern Penthara.
- (Barredish) Fair skin, brown eyes, blond, brown, or black hair.
- (Aggedonian Stoneborne) Grey skin, crystalline eyes, no hair.

Utamians: Tairan and water descendancy. West central Penthara.
- Any natural color skin, any natural color eyes, any natural color hair.

Tongans: Fire and sky descendancy. South eastern Penthara.
- Black skin, brown eyes, red hair. Islander look. *(Over six feet tall)*

Psages: Fire and shadow descendancy. West central Penthara.
- Brown skin, red eyes, no hair. *(Five feet tall)*

Behemons: Fire and water descendancy. Southern islands.
- Brown skin, brown or blue eyes, black hair. Southern look.

Caelduyans: Sky and shadow descendancy. North eastern Penthara.
- (Skyborne) – Grey skin, light blue eyes, white hair.

Oriyans: Sky and water descendancy. East and west Vist-based isle.
- Tan skin, blue eyes, black hair. Eastern look.

Vellyans: Shadow and water descendancy. North western Penthara.
- Brown skin, blue eyes, black hair. *(Seven feet tall average)*

The above height descriptions are for the average adult human male, five feet ten inches. On Penthara the average adult human female is six inches shorter than the males.

Elvan Elemental Descendancies

Sylvanil: Tairan descendancy. North western Penthara and all groves.
- Brown skin, luminous yellow eyes, gold hair. *(Eight feet tall)*

Ibyssai: Fire descendancy. Race extinct.
- Reddish skin, luminous red eyes, vibrant red hair. *(Five feet tall)*

Shirenar: Sky descendancy. Eastern Penthara.
- White skin, luminous silver eyes, silver hair. *(Over six feet tall)*

Dendrar: Shadow descendancy. Northern Penthara.
- Black skin, dark grey eyes, black shadowy hair. *(Four feet tall)*

Oceanil: Water descendancy. Western Penthara oceans underwater.
- Pale scaly skin, luminous blue eyes, blue hair. *(Seven feet tall)*

Zandaryn: Tairan and fire descendancy. South central Penthara.
- Tan skin, orange eyes, yellow or orange hair.

Terollar: Tairan and sky descendancy. Northern Penthara.
- Fair skin, green eyes, blond hair. *(Seven feet tall)*

Wyldenar: Tairan and shadow descendancy. Northern Penthara.
- Tan skin, controlled color eyes, controlled color hair.

Tortharan: Tairan and water descendancy. Race extinct.
- Brown skin, green eyes, green hair.

Solaril: Fire and sky descendancy. South eastern Penthara.
- Tan skin, pink eyes, females pink hair, men vibrant red hair.

Neveril: Fire and shadow descendancy. Subterranean Penthara.
- White skin, red eyes, no hair. *(Five feet tall)*

Forlore: Fire and water descendancy. Race extinct.
- Light-brown skin, purple eyes, purple hair.

Shiniryn: Sky and shadow descendancy. Eastern Penthara.
- Fair skin, silver eyes, intermixed silver and black hair.

Vistaryl: Sky and water descendancy. Vist in recluse.
- Pale skin, light-blue eyes, light-blue hair. Endangered race.

Lunaril: Shadow and water descendancy. North western isle.
- Black skin, dark-blue eyes, dark-blue hair. *(Over six feet tall)*

The above height descriptions are for the average adult elvan male, six feet. On Penthara the average adult elvan female is one foot shorter than the males.

Elvan Impowers

Zandaryn – *tairan and fire descendancy*
Passive Impowers: Polygamous procreation (can have an unlimited amount of lifemates). Rapid procreation (females can bear offspring once per cycle). Quasi flexibility (males can still pass seed on to their female Zandaryn elvan lifemates even if they become quasi). Their lifetrees only last around one hundred years.
Resistances: None.

Terollar – *tairan and sky descendancy*
Passive Impowers: Regeneration (in outside elements). Tirelessness. Blooding (progressive adrenaline rush, can cause heart attack). Hair continuously grows back to the longest state it can be.
Resistances: Electricity. Poison, drugs, alcohol (due to regeneration).

Wyldenar – *tairan and shadow descendancy*
Passive Impowers: Tairan-bending (tairan terrain bends in their favor in immediate vicinity). Shadow-bending (cold terrain and shadows bend in their favor in immediate vicinity). Can change hair and eye color at will. Animal affinity. Become deathly ill outside of nature.
Resistances: Poison. Cold. Disease.

Neveril – *fire and shadow descendancy*
Passive Impowers: Wall-walking (walk on walls and ceilings as if on level ground). Darkvision (light-blinded). Crystalyte communion (can communicate with anyone touching them through psionics). Silent movement.
Resistances: Cold. Disease. Fire. Heat. Smoke.

Shiniryn – *sky and shadow descendancy*
Passive Impowers: Enhanced running speed (twice that of humans). Enhanced endurance (twice that of humans). Wind-walking (glide on air as if walking on it). Wind affinity. Slow-fall. Sun-sickness.
Resistances: Cold. Disease.

Solaril – *fire and sky descendancy*
Passive Impowers: *to be discovered …*
Resistances: *to be discovered …*

Vistaryl – *sky and water descendancy*
Passive Impowers: *to be discovered …*
Resistances: *to be discovered …*

Lunaril – *shadow and water descendancy*
Passive Impowers: *to be discovered …*
Resistances: *to be discovered …*

Sylvanil – *tairan descendancy*
Passive Impowers: *to be discovered …*
Resistances: *to be discovered …*
Immunity: *to be discovered …*

Shirenar – *sky descendancy*
Passive Impowers: *to be discovered …*
Resistances: *to be discovered …*
Immunity: *to be discovered …*

Dendrar – *shadow descendancy*
Passive Impowers: *to be discovered …*
Resistances: *to be discovered …*
Immunity: *to be discovered …*

Oceanil – *water descendancy*
Passive Impowers: *to be discovered …*
Resistances: *to be discovered …*
Immunity: *to be discovered …*

Qindrid and Umbran Impowers

Stoneborne — *tairan and shadow*
Maker: Wyldenar umbran
Passive Impowers: Hardened skin. Enhanced strength. Cannot be harmed from falling. Sleeplessness. Cannot produce offspring. Agelessness. Darkvision.
Resistances: Cold. Poison. Acid. Drugs/herbal side effects.
Immunities: Disease.

Skyborne — *sky and shadow*
Maker: Shiniryn umbran
Passive Impowers: Enhanced speed. Slowfall. Throw voice in the wind. Wind affinity. Sleeplessness. Cannot produce offspring. Agelessness. Darkvision.
Resistances: Cold. Electricity.
Immunities: Disease.

Neverborne — *fire and shadow*
Maker: Neveril umbran
Passive Impowers: Shapeshifting. Wall-walking. Silent movement. Sleeplessness. Cannot produce offspring. Agelessness. Darkvision.
Resistances: Cold. Fire. Heat. Smoke.
Immunities: Disease.

Greyborne — *any shadow*
Maker: Qindrid with no umbran or born from other greyborne.
Passive Impowers: Sleeplessness. Darkvision.
Resistances: Cold.
Immunities: Disease.

Umbran — *shadow dominant, in addition to their elvan descendancy*
Elvan Subrace: Wyldenar (tairan), Shiniryn (sky), Neveril (fire).
Passive Impowers: Those of their elvan subrace. Cerebration. Node aura. Qindrid transcendence. Sleeplessness. Darkvision.
Resistances: Those of their elvan subrace.
Immunities: Disease. Cold.

Geography of Penthara

(WEST SIDE OF MAP)

Starfell - Lunaril homeland, Thrench-ruled.
Depyreoshlinyoq - Oceanil underwater homeland.
Vellyon - Vellyan Kingdom homeland.
Oriyen - Oriyan homeland, split by the Vist.
Tortharus Isles - Thrench-ruled, formerly Tortharan.
Vistyzus - Thrench-ruled, formerly Vistaryl.
Throng - Thrench Empire homeland.
The Sisters - pirate isles, formerly Daynish-ruled.
Forlornedian Isles - Thrench-ruled, formerly Forlore.
Behemon Isles - Behemon homeland, Thrench-ruled.
Artopia - Wyldenar-occupied, Sentinel Order capital.
The Dendrallthae - Dendrar secret homeland.
Aggedon - Aggedonian qindrid clan country.
Nrathe - former Vhall homeland, desolate ruins.
Glace Isles - Terollar battle outposts loyal to a khomo.
Barredom - Barredish Kingdom homeland.
Zsolindal - former Neveril northern sect, abandoned.
Undawned Lands - unclaimed barbarian territories.
Mageholme - sanctuary region for the hunder-touched.
The Insurmounts - Psage mountainous homeland.
Psage Coast - Psage Trade Union territory.
The Tairanheart - no-man's-land of many territory lords.
The Tenwoods - village colonies ruled by Psage seers.
The Sevenmoors - governed by seven witches.
Utamia - Utamian homeland, land of free states.
Goldgarden - Penthara's largest city, ruled by Seven Seats.
The Silverlakes - Free region lorded over by an archon.
Tairancia - Territories split between Az'Dayne and natives.
Az'Dayne - Daynish homeland, Dominadom capital.
Savatarm - neutral province trade hub for the west coast.
Khalimia - Khalimishe Queendom, Daynish-ruled.

Geography of Penthara

(EAST SIDE OF MAP)

Umbralle - Vhall retreat location after the fall of Nrathe.
Skystone Isles - raider isles and land of intelligent beasts.
Tundura - Wyldenar homeland of scattered tribes.
Teralloe - Terollar homeland of scattered tribes.
Caelduym - Caelduyan homeland, skyborne country.
Helderak - coalition of Terollar, Neveril, and Shiniryn.
Cabernus - Neveril surface army, access to Caldwuera.
Caldwuera - Neveril capital of eastern underrealm.
Blood Beach - disputed region of Terollar and Thrench.
Ghost Isles - Neveril underrealm highway.
Kol'Kolar - Shiniryn homeland of scattered tribes.
Julkunda - New Throng, Thrench-ruled, former elvan exiles.
Xai Lon - Sho'Lonese free states of greyborne majority.
Sho Kung - Sho'Lonese skyborne kingdom.
Sho Jan - Sho'Lonese human empire of the old ways.
The Westway - Sho'Lonese and Oriyan tradeway.
The Shirene - Shirenar homeland, Vistaryl refugees.
Brutonga - Brutongan homeland of scattered tribes.
Majamn - Brutongan kingdom of fanatics and mages.
The Sacreds - Brutongan ritual isles.
Arastarianar - Solaril homeland.
Solfeiel - Solaril exile and dungeon isle.
Old Elothia - ruins of a nation, destroyed by Neveril.
Az'Eloth - Elothian homeland and union, Daynish-ruled.
Zandabar - Zandaryn homeland, mostly Daynish-allied.
Wroth - Zandaryn extremists against human rule.
Sundorion Isles - unsettled beastlands, formerly Ibyssai.
Az'Elvenyah - Neveril underrealm beneath Az'Eloth.
The Netherall - underrealm formed by Dawning mages.

The Pentharam System

TIME

Day - Twenty-five hours.
Furrow - Intermittent day between seasons.
Pentday / Pent - Five days.
First-Day - First day of a pent.
Second-Day - Second day of a pent.
Third-Day - Third day of a pent.
Fourth-Day - Fourth day of a pent.
Fifth-Day - Fifth day of a pent.
Month - Five pents, or twenty-five days.
Season - Five months, or twenty-five pents, which is one hundred twenty-five days.
Year - Fifteen months, or three seasons and their following furrows, which is three hundred seventy-eight days.
Cycle - Five seasons and their following furrows, or six hundred thirty days, or one and two-thirds years.
Generation - Twenty-five years.

Dawning - First season, tairan element, gold as color.
(translation is most relative to Spring)
Sunder - Second season, fire element, red as color.
(translation is most relative to Summer)
Reaping - Third season, sky element, white as color.
(translation is most relative to Autumn)
Umbra - Fourth season, shadow element, black as color.
(translation is most relative to Winter)
Torrent - Fifth season, water element, blue as color.

Powers and Organizations

The Ashenwave - the infamous armada of the Thrench Empire, known for bringing the Tortharan, Forlore, and Ibyssai elvan races into absolute extinction, subjugating the Lunaril of Starfell, and conquering the Vistaryl elven to cross over the Vist from the west to the east to establish New Throng in Julkunda.

Avanthyl - a loose organization of Zandaryn reformists who support the Az'Dayne Dominadom and promote the Taboo of the Quasi and bringing Z'shun into the world.

Az'Dayne Dominadom - the largest land nation on Penthara, overseen by Dominarchs Vaximus Az'Ampion and Sriyah Hazhalah. It consists of many countries with former kings and lords under its vast rule: Az'Dayne, North Khalimia, Az'Eloth, Tairancia, Barredom, and former kingdoms of the Tairanheart.

Blue Blades - formerly the largest gang in Goldgarden, now a name for the original members of the Stormtrees.

Boarneck Cavaliers - the mercenary faction of horsemen in the Boarneck Company, captained by Tristostopher Boldandgold.

Boarneck Company - the mercenary company founded by Oldan Boldandgold. It owns most of the farms throughout Worestaschia and monopolizes the entry districts in Goldgarden through many ambitious enterprises. It also acts as the gatekeeper for the Dominadom's conspiracies to take political control of the city-nation.

Centron Guard - formerly the Centron Spears, a gang in Goldgarden now under control of the Stormtrees. It operates out of Centron Hills.

Cobra Collective - a branch of the Stormtrees guild that answers to Scarless, operated by a man named Threpetoe, with a primary focus of procuring critical information from the Az'Dayne Dominadom's revolving machinations.

Copper Jacks - a gang in Goldgarden now under control of the Stormtrees. It operates out of Copper's Side.

Dayne-Web - the behind-the-scenes faction of the Oathemic Cabal. It consists of stewards, defenders, and collectors.

Forwoken - an order of monks from the Qaegons, in Barredom, who swear an oath to remain silent and covered. In truth, they are all Terollar elven who have had their ears cut with a salve to prevent their regeneration. They act as a spy network for Khomo'Jhuvonus.

Glazjhendun - the war party of the Glace Isles, under the command of Khomo'Jhuvonus.

Goldguardian Watch - the city guard of Goldgarden.

Green Byway - a company of sellspell mages that specialize in the impower of Traversement to offer fast-traveling services to buyers who can afford them.

Greyfire Revolution – the crusade the Neveril Empire has staged to counteract the forces of the Thrench Ashenwave. It is set to begin in the Sunder season of the Cycle of Kingfall, involving many movements across the realm at once.

Hive Order – the assassins' faction of the Oathemic Cabal.

Hunder Order – the original faction of the Oathemic Cabal, consisting of individuals who are hunder-touched, mages, and spellblades.

Ironarms – a gang in Goldgarden now under control of the Stormtrees. It operates out of Turftown.

Kingdom of Barredom – northern kingdom under the sovereignty of the Az'Dayne Dominadom. It is ruled by two neverborne qindrid against the public's knowledge, both Queen Annison Roth and an imposter posing as King Aerik Roth.

Nectar Order – the espionage faction of the Oathemic Cabal. It consists of writ-runners, spies, and informants.

Neveril Empire – the largest power on all of Penthara, ruled by Zsinsinyrahn. It governs not only the Neveril elven but secretly also the Az'Dayne Dominadom, the Helderahki elven, and all individuals involved in the Umbran Pledge and Greyfire Revolution.

Night Street – a gang in Goldgarden now under control of the Stormtrees. It specializes in espionage, assassinations, and larceny.

Oathemic Cabal – the organization of assassins founded by Endrith "Coldborn" Goldfyre, not aligned with the Pentagogue or Dominadom. It mainly consists of absolved mages, spellblades, and stealth-trained killers who perform assassination contracts to protect the integrity of Az'Dayne and its people.

Pentagogue – the theocratic power that dictates all matters of the law for the Az'Dayne Dominadom. It consists of paladins as the enforcers and veritans as the magistrates.

the Quiver – a faction of the Cobra Collective, comprised of all women, that are used for information extraction or delicate assassinations, often utilizing the subterfuge of sexual methods for completing their assigned tasks.

Salt Lords – a gang in Goldgarden now under control of the Stormtrees. It operates out of the North Docks.

Seven Seats – the secret political council that rules over Goldgarden. Each seat has a different jurisdiction.

Silverbacks – a clandestine vigilante organization that opposes the Oathemic Cabal, the Pentagogue, and the machinations of the Az'Dayne Dominadom.

Sol-War – the movement of Sunder mages organized by Shypriss Sol-War of the Mage Ward, in Goldgarden. It plans to expose the neverborne pandemic on Penthara with an attack directly on the Pentagogue, in Everdawn.

Stormtrees - a guild of controlled gangs in Goldgarden, founded by Zahnastaazjah, "Scarless." The guild is sanctioned by the city to eliminate underground threats.

Sylvanil Sentinel Order - the timeless guardians of the regional groves for the majority of the elvan races across Penthara. It also acts as a faction of reserved but zealous wardens, who seek out capable opposition to defend against those who would disrupt the creed of the Balance.

Tolltakers - a gang in Goldgarden now under control of the Stormtrees. It operates out of Festival Row.

Thrench Empire - a sea nation ruled by Emperor Djediheth Emmonost. It is notorious for its history in conquering and annihilating territory occupied by the elvan races, and it consists of many territories in the west and now the east: Throng, Starfell, the Tortharus Isles, the Forlornedian Isles, the Behemon Isles, the Sundorion Isles, Vistyzus, Julkunda, and Blood Beach.

Umbran Pledge - an oathbound network of those in the Know of the Neveril Empire's presence and of the neverborne scheme to take over the human power nations.

Word Glossary

arcanic imprint - the proper technical term for a magemark.

archmage - a tier-five mage. There can only be one tier-five mage from each elemental linked season in the realm at a time: Dawning, Sunder, Reaping, Umbra, and Torrent. Only if one dies, a tier-four mage can potentially ascend by meeting magic prerequisites.

archon - a territorial leader that has been granted entitlement by the regional sovereign to rule over a state within a country.

the aging - a condition suffered by an elvan who has had their lifetree destroyed, causing them to age at an accelerated rate depending on how old they are.

animayan - elven who have chosen the path of the Taboo to have their wisp reincarnated in an eligible newborn animal aligning with their descendancy, keeping the majority of their intellect and memory.

aspirant - the title of a paladin or veritan knight in their initiate stage.

badwater - saltwater or impure water.

Balance - the universal elvan creed based upon the belief in absolute neutrality in all aspects of life and the elements.

Beyond - the afterlife for all hunder, acting as a symbiotic conglomeration of spiritual entities that exist on another plane of existence within the Vist.

blast salt - an explosive compound invented by alchemist Symbelle Goldfyre Sol-War. It consists of white granules that disintegrate most materials immediately in a bright red flame.

bloodguard - an individual assigned as lifelong personal protector, typically decreed by someone in higher regal power.

bloodlink - the term for a sibling used by the elvan race.

bloodrime - a poisonous parasite that tends to feed on lifetrees in its native region of Teralloe. It has been known to be carefully extracted and constructed into weaponry.

bogbile - a tarlike growth found in marshy regions that is extremely acidic to organic tissue.

bornday - an individual's birthday.

bugsthrone mushroom - a poisonous mushroom that when cooked produces an odorous gas that causes deep unconsciousness in low doses and death in high doses.

burnguard - a protective oil created by the alchemist Symbelle Goldfyre Sol-War. It is applied to materials to make them temporarily fireproof.

cerebration - an impower afforded to all umbran that allows them to see and hear through any qindrid they have turned as a vessel of surveillance, also discovering their precise location, but by invoking such the umbran is left vulnerable and immobile, allowing all of the qindrid they have turned and the progeny they have spawned to know of the umbran's location as well.

cinder oil - a protective body oil created by the alchemist Symbelle Goldfyre Sol-War. It can absorb a blast of heat from fire or withstand the initial wave of a fire.

Civil - the common language taught to and understood by almost every culture on Penthara.

cross-descendancy - elemental lineage of two elements

crystalyte - a mineral that is typically radiant red in color. It glows bright if put within an atmosphere of lethal conditions, due to poison or lack of air, or if any living being not of the Neveril race comes within close proximity.

decem - a unit used to measure ten of something.

descendancy - the specific elemental lineage of a human or elvan, which can define their race, eligibility for certain transcendences, and impowers at birth if they are elvan.

Dominadom - a vanity term for a nation considering themselves larger than an empire, such as with Az'Dayne, ruled by dominarchs.

dominarch - a ruler of a Dominadom above all others.

ebonice - a phenomenon of black ice that rarely occurs in the north during the Umbra season. It cannot melt.

ejahra - a Khalimishe performance style of blade dancing that incorporates visually elaborate martial arts with swords, reputed to be impractical for application in actual combat.

Entity - the tormenting sentient essence inside a hyperi, formed by an anomaly of the assimilation of wisp spawns conglomerated together. This sentience is always an extreme representation of the specific element from the archmage mother of a hyperi. Its counterpart is the Entropy, from the specific element of the archmage father of the hyperi.

fairwater - freshwater or pure water.

fey petal - a natural plant that is popularly smoked as a recreational psychoactive drug to produce a mental high, similar to marijuana.

Five and Five - the popular human religion that adheres to the worship of the five gods of the elements and the five goddesses of the seasons.

ghost - derogatory slang for a Neveril elvan.

Godslands - the concept of the levels of afterlife in the Five and Five religion, believed to exist in the deepest areas of the natural elements on Penthara that no mortal can reach.

goodcaps - a type of mushroom that produces an odor with certain recovery effects to the health of the mind; however, if imbibed instead of inhaled, they cause hallucinations

grove - a protected sanctuary of elvan lifetrees.

hunder - an elvan's soul, connected to their spiritroot.

hunder-touched - a human who had a genesis wisp interfused with them within the womb or during infancy.

hyperi - a human born from two archmages. A hyperi develops a special hypersight, with which they can see magic auras, impowers, hunder, wisps, spiritroot trails, and even the geonomalies in the Vist, but at the cost of having volatile states of mind, suffered by being assimilated with the symbiosis of the Entity and the Entropy (*read above*).

hypersight - the special sight hyperis are born with that allows them to see many aspects invisible to most: magic auras, impowers, hunder, wisps, spiritroot trails, and even the geonomalies in the Vist.

Imperiar - the imperial offspring of a dominarch from the Az'Dayne Dominadom.

impower - a special inborn or acquired supernatural power with some elemental influence.

the In-Between - a mirror plane of existence, only visible to the naked eye in the Vist, that entities such as hunder, wisps, and spiritroots exist in.

khomo - a Terollar elvan term for a Chosen of their race, recognized and honored by the Sylvanil Sentinel Order, often bestowed with the same respects as a king.

lifemate - an elvan's permanently bound partner through conjunction of each other's lifetree. An elvan can only reproduce with a lifemate and never again with another.

lifequest - a calling an individual considers as their life's destiny, whether chosen for it by others, or by coming upon the aspired quest by personal enlightenment.

lifetree - what an elvan is born from, hatched from a cocoon from their progenitors. The elvan is bound to their lifetree, which determines the length of their lifespan and elemental connection to their impowers.

mage - a hunder-touched human, bound to a single season and correlated element, who has been interfused with a catalyst wisp, acquiring the supernatural faculty to cast magic, gaining more impowers as they advance in tiers.

magemark - a specific glyph-like design on a mage's skin in a specific location on their body that represents an impower or spellpower that they can cast.

masque - a mask that symbolizes one's status or family in Az'Dayne.

matriarch - a female parent in elvan culture.

modernesque - a style of contemporary dance popular in Az'Dayne.

mortali - a revered elder in Terollar culture who acts as a shaman, a sage, and the specialized groomer for assigned hairstyles within their specific tribe.

mutt - a human who has been through enough interbreeding of elemental descendancies to no longer be considered of any descendancy.

overman - a form of supervisor rank within guilds and gangs on the western mainlands; regard as *lieutenant*.

paladin - the knighted male enforcers of the Pentagogue's law in the

Az'Dayne Dominadom.

patriarch - a male parent in elvan culture.

pentamony - a privileged matrimonial union that entitles a man to conjoin with five paramours to be bound to him for life, whom are to serve his needs in a consensus of wifehood between the five of them, while the man enters a loose contract of husbandry for provided means of wealth and protection, and sometimes absolute immunity and absolute atonement, for the paramours' families.

phoenix - an endangered, territorial orange bird native to the Sundorion Isles that has limited flight capability.

progeny - the term for son or daughter used by the elvan race.

progenitor - the term for a parent used by the elvan race.

qindrid - a human who has been turned by two umbran lifemates into an altered state of their former self with acquired elemental impowers, mentally linked to their creators with shared agelessness.

qindrid (greyborne) - a severed qindrid whose umbran creators are no longer alive, but they can reproduce with other greyborne. Offspring of such qindrid are also greyborne. Characteristics include grey skin, hair, eyes, and nails, immunity to disease, an inability to sleep, and resistance to cold.

qindrid (neverborne) - a qindrid turned by two Neveril umbran, with certain impowers of the fire element. Characteristics include grey skin, red hair, black eyes and nails, infertility, an inability to sleep, shapeshifting, silent movement, wall-walking, immunity to disease and burns, and resistance to cold and smoke.

qindrid (stoneborne) - a qindrid turned by two Wyldenar umbran, with certain additional impowers of the tairan element. Characteristics include grey skin, hairlessness, diamond-colored eyes and nails, infertility, an inability to sleep, armored skin, enhanced strength, immunity to disease, acid, and falls, and resistance to poison and cold.

qindrid (skyborne) - a qindrid turned by two Shiniryn umbran, with certain additional impowers of the sky element. Characteristics include grey skin, wind-affected white hair, light-blue eyes, white nails, infertility, an inability to sleep, the ability to throw their voice, slow-fall, enhanced speed, immunity to disease and wind, and resistance to cold and lightning.

quasi - elven who have chosen the path of the Taboo to forsake their connection to their lifetree, disallowing the conjoining with an elvan lifemate, to reproduce with humans instead.

sandling - derogatory slang for a Zandaryn elvan.

score - a unit used to measure twenty-five of something.

season (bound) - the season in which a mage has been first interfused, matching the descendancies of their genesis and catalyst wisp, which is the season their spellpower is intended to be cast within.

season (null) - one of the two seasons within which a mage cannot invoke spells or impowers without consequence of rapid aging and weakening; following their slumber season and ending before their primer season (tier-five mages treat null seasons as primer seasons).

season (primer) - the season before a mage's bound season in which they can cast a limited capacity of their spellpower from their genesis and catalyst wisps.

season (slumber) - the season following a mage's bound season in which they are forced to under Transbernation. Resisting or having interruptions to it will cause instant aging to the mage, and casting spells during it could be fatal (tier-five mages do not need to hibernate during their slumber season and treat casting spells within it similar to other mages' null seasons).

Severance - an ability all elven have that permits them to release their spiritroot's attachment to their lifetree and sever their hunder from their body to become a wisp, killing the elvan in its mortal form by suicide.

seersight - a temporary divining of the past or future granted by consuming a seerstone. The ability requires extreme training to properly navigate the visions without dying from consumption of the geode.

seerstone - a rare geode mined in the Dendrallthae or the Insurmounts that has special properties to allow the consumer clairvoyance into the past or future of individuals or items if one is trained in how to properly navigate the seersight, but it is lethal upon consumption under certain circumstances.

sellspell - a mercenary mage.

shablue - hides typically stripped from sharks or rays, tailored for nimble body armor, that are dyed dark blue.

shadow - the element that represents a combination of cold, disease, and darkness on Penthara.

skarpaka - a feathered bone spear of ceremonial utility gifted by tribal elders to female progeny that are expected to take the role of alphas or warriors within the Terollar culture.

skinny dust - a supplement created by the alchemist Symbelle Goldfyre Sol-War. In low doses, it suppresses appetites and aggression and boosts metabolism, but in high doses, it causes severe dehydration, muscle enervation, crippling of the mind, and fearful hallucinations.

Sojourn - the Thrench term for one's rite of passage and respect they must complete before they are considered a true Thrench soldier of strong bloodline; typically assigned at a young age by a mentor in rank within the imperial navy.

solesce - the artistic physical practice of using a variety of tools or weapons that are set on fire for enhancing performances.

sorcerer - a common reference for a tier-four mage.

spellblade - a sentient sword bound to specific individuals within a bloodline, crafted with an enchanted glass blade, gold hilt, and emerald pommel that has been magically forged to absorb spells from mages that are slain by it, and to allow the wielder to channel the martial abilities of the prior wielders through their captured essences.

spellblade - the chosen bound wielder of a spellblade sword.

spellforging - the uncompromising craft of breaking down wisps into components that can be interfused within items to imbue them with specific magical properties.

spiritroot - an elvan's invisible, ethereal umbilical cord between their hunder and their lifetree.

Starfell steel - a whitish-silver metal imbued with special properties that is mined on the island of Starfell by the Lunaril elven.

stormtree - a native Teralloe tree, immune to electricity, that acts as a conduit for lightning storms during the Reaping season and energizes the land around it.

Taboo - an irrevocable transformation elven of mixed elemental descendancy can take, depending on their race (examples include the Path of the Umbran, Quasi, and Animayan, among others to be discovered).

tairan - the element that represents *earth* on Penthara (wood, rock, soil, metal, gems, etc.), in both natural or manufactured forms.

tairan-form - to magically shape anything considered of the tairan element by channeled control.

Transbernation - the first impower, gained by a tier-one mage. It necessitates an elemental transformation for a five-month hibernation that the mage must succumb to following the season they are bound to. There are irreparable consequences of instant aging if a mage attempts to cast magic during their slumber season, and rapid aging if they do not remain in hibernation in their post-seasonal symbiotic form.

Transcendence - the process of one's transformed evolution from their natural aesthetics and capacities to acquire supernatural impowers, such as in the circumstance of becoming qindrid or a mage for humans, or umbran, quasi, or animayan for elven, to name a few.

Telecommunication - the second impower, gained by a tier-two mage. It allows a mage to communicate with their genesis wisp and catalyst wisp, or even surrender cognitive control to them. Furthermore, it allows the mage to leave messages within objects affiliated with their bound element for other mages to hear.

Transfusion - the third impower, gained by a tier-three mage. It allows a mage to draw on and dissect wisps in order to manifest them into spells or glyphs through spellforging for magic weapons.

Tranquility - the final impower, gained by a tier-five mage. It allows a mage to stop aging altogether for an entire cycle, as long as they relinquish their link to evoking any spellpower for the cycle, by a form of magic disconnection.

Traversement - the fourth impower, gained by a tier-three mage. It allows a mage the ability to fast-travel by entering an ethereal hovering state.

The mage can rapidly move over terrain affiliated with their bound season and can transport up to two travelers.
tribesvan/tribesven - elven members of a tribe.
troll - derogatory slang for a Terollar elvan.
undersight - a potion that grants infrared vision.
umbran - an elvan of cross-shadow descendancy (Wyldenar, Neveril, Shiniryn, Lunaril) who has chosen the path of the Taboo to transcend with the shadow element, undergoing great physical change and altered impowers.
veritan - the female magistrates of the law in the Az'Dayne Dominadom.
wisp - an elvan's soul that has left its mortal body and can roam much like a spirit. It is invisible, invulnerable, and incorporeal to most.
wisp (ancillary) - a wisp that interfuses with a mage after their catalyst wisp, granting access to another spell.
wisp (catalyst) - the second wisp that enters a hunder-touched human. It allows the hunder-touched to transcend into a tier-one mage and grants them access to spellpower. It also has as much influence on the mage advancing in tiers as the genesis wisp.
wisp (eldritch) - a wisp that cannot become interfused with a mage and is not free-roaming. It is bound to a genesis wisp to whom it had a close emotional connection in life, and it orbits in the immediate vicinity of its bound genesis wisp so long as it is activated. It is violet in color.
wisp (genesis) - the first wisp that interfuses with an eligible human infant, making them hunder-touched, granting them as a potential mage and their first spell after becoming interfused with a catalyst wisp.
wispbane - a poison created by the alchemist Symbelle Goldfyre Sol-War. It temporarily prevents a hunder or wisp from granting any impower or spellpower.
westwalker - slang for a Sho'Lonese or Oriyan human.
writ - an assassin's contract from the Oathemic Cabal, typically endorsed by both Az'Dayne and the guild.
water-watch - a magic watch made in Spellspire that can greatly slow down time from the perspective of the wearer.=
wyrkenido - an Elothian martial art focusing entirely on mastering ropes to be utilized in combat, with a variety of rope weapons and skills: the rope dart, lasso, and garotte, to name a few.
the Vist - the mystical prime meridian of Penthara. It has the appearance of a green mist and geonomalies with unified hunder throughout its vast ethereal composition.
yewr root - a natural fungus, purplish in color, shaped like a small mandrake root, which carries similar psychedelic effects upon ingestion to that of magic mushrooms.
Z'shun - the offspring of a quasi and a human, which makes them a hybrid half-elvan with minor impowers from their elvan parent. They can mate with humans, but not with elven.

ABOUT THE AUTHOR

Ezekiel was born in Southeast Texas, and now resides in Houston after the global pandemic brought him back home from his exploits living in Las Vegas where he first published Kingfall. He is happily married to his beautiful wife Stephanie, his biggest supporter and best friend. He has been an avid lover of the fantasy and science fiction genre since he was a child. Telling the saga of the Neverborne Series and sharing the world of Penthara are his greatest passions in life.

www.ingramcontent.com/pod-product-compliance
Lightning Source LLC
Chambersburg PA
CBHW020718310726
48979CB00004B/967